DANCING TO THE LYRICS

Finding an Inner Rhythm

Dwayne A Ratleff

Cover Art designed by
L&J Graphics
Leann E. Johnson

In a world of self-made men, I am not one. I was made by many. My every breath is a thank you to those who have helped me build the emotional infrastructure to thrive. Just as important, I would like to thank those who I often have mistakenly cursed, the ones who placed obstacles in my path and threw adversity in my face. They were the fire that transformed me into iron.

CONTENTS

CHAPTER 1 ALL THAT GLITTERS

Three inches of snow covered the ground. Although only four years old, I was allowed to play outside, alone but not unattended. My grandmother stood watch from the kitchen window overlooking the side yard, washing the morning dishes. A gentle tap on the window and her sternly pointed finger drew a square in the air, clearly marking the area in which I was allowed to play.

Icicles glittering and hanging tentatively from the roof caught my eye. I stood there transfixed by the frozen water garnishing an otherwise drab house. I hastily cobbled together a poorly formed snowball and tossed it, more than threw it, at what I desired. Of course, the snowball fell apart merely a foot into the air. Three or four more snowballs, each one more poorly made than the last, could not dislodge what I wanted. Perhaps it was the wind or the creaking of the old house, but through no effort of my own, one of the icicles fell from its upside-down perch, landing gently in the snow not far from the door to the coal bin.

Removing one of my mittens I quickly snatched up the prize with my bare hand, only looking at the icicle for a few seconds before placing it to my tongue. The taste held none of the appeal that the beauty of the icicle implied. It tasted of tar, roof and dirt with a hint of coal dust, but it still was beautiful enough to warrant keeping.

Since the icicle was not edible, I soon imagined it a magic wand and promised myself I would never let it go. I was thinking of all the good it could do and planned on hiding it under the bed, away from my two younger sisters. My youngest sister would eat the wand no matter the taste and had just recently grown enough teeth to do the job. I would have to hide it before they woke from their nap.

I looked up to the window to show my grandmother the ice wand, but she was momentarily away. Now that I was alone, this would be a good time to practice my imaginary magic. Except, I was not really alone. Most of the houses south of the Silas Moss Ditch could see me. There were no fences anywhere, and people on the West End of Bellefontaine, Ohio could not afford the timber to build separation, nor could they afford that kind of separation. Fences would only impede the backyard trade of mutual aid, communal babysitting and gossip. Addy, my grandmother, would hear about any transgression before the good Lord got the news. Therefore, it was best not to make any news.

Unfortunately, even standing still on a beautiful winter's day, holding the most beautiful thing I had ever seen could turn into unfortunate news. The pain went from unnoticed to causing tears in just moments. My hand was hurting from the inside out. The frost nip was taking hold of my bare hand, yet I could not associate the pain with the wand. Looking through my tears I could see my grandmother, now back at the window, tapping and gesturing for me to drop the wand.

It was as much the concerned expression on my grandmother's face as the increasing pain in my hand that caused me to finally drop the icicle, no longer a wand but something that just hurt. It lay in the snow. Its magic had already faded away. With the coming afternoon sun, the icicle would follow the magic when it melted. Next winter the icicles would be back, but for me the wand, along with its magic, would never return.

Attempting to escape the pain I ran for the front porch, holding my hand as far away from me as possible, hoping this gesture would somehow distance me from the pain. Trussed up in a brown snowsuit sealed tight around a light layer of winter fat made any distinguishing features indiscernible. I was brown and round, waddling through a white world seeking safety. My grandmother was already at the door with a whisk broom in hand. Tears or not, no uninvited dirt or water was permitted in the house.

Her tawny face held several different emotions simultaneously. Present were love and concern, but the tilt of her head down and to the left indicated that annoyance could easily win the battle of emotions for ascendancy.

"Grant! Why did you take off your mitten?" my grandmother asked, not really expecting an answer.

A few sniffles and syllables stifled by sobs and cries were all she got. My snowsuit was swiftly brushed off and removed, after which I was ushered upstairs to the bathroom sink to soak my hand in warm water. This brought on an even more intense bout of sobs and huffs of breath striving to become words. "It waaas," sniffle "so beautiful," I whimpered.

My grandmother did not lecture me about how holding something cold in an unprotected hand can hurt. The icicle had already given its lecture on the subject. Strangely, my grandmother spoke of dandelions from the previous summer. The memory of the summery flower somewhat distracted me from the pain of my hand. So abundant and dominant on our untended side lawn, yet so fragile once picked and placed in a used jelly jar. Drooping within an hour and fading away within a day. I had cried then as well.

At four I normally would not have put winter and summer together in the same memory and certainly not icicles and dandelions. My grandmother and events had led me here. The pain from this winter and the wilt from last summer still fresh in my mind, I was open to listening if not yet comprehending.

"You can't possess everything you see. Things have means of defending themselves against being possessed," she said with a serious smile, revealing her own acceptance of this fact. She elaborated: "They fight back with pain; they wither or grow callous from too much handling, becoming too undesirable for ownership... Worst of all, after a time they may even come to possess you."

Her words were beyond me at the time. I think she said them aloud as much a reminder for herself as a warning to me. Desire would be a lifelong partner for me, but on that day, caution, desire's more prudent companion, was born.

After a few minutes my right hand returned to life, so I promptly put my left hand in the sink to play with the water. My Grandma Addy took this as a sign of renewed vigor and tipped the soap into the basin and commanded me to wash my hands. I sighed. The thought momentarily crossed my mind to lift my hand and limp the wrist slightly to feign re-injury, so I did not have to wash my hands. Too late anyway, she had moved to the bedroom to wake my sisters.

By the time I had finished washing my hands, my sisters were already stumbling into the bathroom, displacing me immediately as the bathroom was too small for three small children and an adult. They had to wash their hands too, even after a nap. A stray finger may have gone to a nostril during their sleep and my grandmother would have none of that.

One hour of sleep had not disheveled my sisters' hair as much as a full night's sleep would have. They were spared the brutal hair brushing many a child had to endure before going out in public. Pretty brown faces with hair topped with red barrettes peeked out of the bathroom at me. Lotion had been generously applied to anything pointy and ashy, such as knees and elbows.

The older of my two younger sisters, Beatrice, who we called Peanut, was the only one who had to change her clothes. Gwen, the youngest, and I just received a thorough hand-brush down the front and back of our clothes, banishing any wrinkles or lint that might try to sneak out of the house with us and bring shame to the family. Oh, how I hated being presentable, even then!

We filed downstairs in the order of our birth: me, Peanut and Gwen. As young as we were, we knew the drill. My grandmother walked to her bedroom, which was at the foot of the stairs. We were to go to the living room, sit on the couch, hush and be still until my grandmother got herself ready.

The smell of soap from her early morning sponge bath had faded, now replaced by the smell of furniture polish and other cleaning products. Two spritzes of perfume bought from a long since extinct Five and Dime would banish those smells until tomorrow.

She emerged from the bedroom with her purse resting in the crook of her arm. Her arm and purse were locked in the shopping position. She gave us the look that said, "You better be on your best behavior or I will be on you." We put on our coats, were brushed again and readied for display.

A determined sun had already reduced the blanket of snow to small, scattered oases of white surrounded by the bleakness of winter. We stepped mostly on dry pavement and piled into our eight-year old black and cream two-tone 1956 Buick. Of course, it had no seat belts, car seats or air bags; two steel fenders and the mom arm across the chest at sudden stops were its only safety features. A sleekly designed airplane hood ornament suggested speed and distance it was unlikely to travel. Livelihood, family and commerce were all within a three-mile radius of our house.

We crossed the railroad tracks, leaving behind the West End where the citizens with an abundance of overtime were striving desperately to mimic, with some success, the prosperity of a then industrialized America. After all, we were driving a Buick worth more than our house. A right turn onto S. Main Street revealed a downtown that would bring a wave of nostalgia to any American, even to those not born during the era. It was clean, quiet and prosperous, with just a hint of history. We parked next to some of that history, at the corner of Court Street, the first cemented street in America, the pride of our town.

My grandmother exited the car, purse still on one arm and Gwen on the other. Gwen's little goose bumped brown legs dangled low enough for me to take hold of one of her shoes with my thawed hand while holding Peanut's hand with my other one. Our little daisy chain safely crossed the street and entered a store. It was an old brick building with polished floors that creaked. Even the smell of new clothes and shoes could not keep at bay the smell of a nineteenth century building. It was small but adequate, and the display windows were filled with mannequins wearing clothes for every age. Although I had met the owner on only four occasions, I still remembered him well.

The proprietor of the store had a kind face and a ruddy complexion with slight tendrils of gray fingering through his brown hair. Thirty more years and pounds and he could make extra money playing Santa Claus at Christmas. Despite all of this, he had the demeanor of someone who had fought in the war, and not on our side. In fact, he was among a handful of Ohio's 8,000 German and Italian prisoners of war who had returned to the land of their captivity to make it a land of opportunity. He greeted us in poor English with bad breath but offered good prices. Each of his words had a strange sound and smell, and his surname took so much breath and effort to pronounce that everyone just took to calling him Franz or Mister Franz. He was renowned for his ability to drink coffee and smoke cigarettes simultaneously, brim and filter on the lip at the same time. I guess some days you needed your nicotine and caffeine in the same minute. Nice as he was, you did not want to do much heavy breathing around him.

Mister Franz would make a fuss over you and force a piece of barrel shaped candy into your hand. He had lived in the Midwest long enough to know that no well-raised child could willingly accept or ask a stranger for candy. This was driven by pride, not fear based. Accepting charity in any form was not acceptable but being rude was worse. His forceful kindness didn't give the parents a chance to say no or give their children the look that said no.

I wisely put a reluctant look of acceptance on my face to appease my grandmother, but inside I jumped at the chance for some tooth decay. Candy was a rare commodity in our house, reserved for company, served on Jesus's birthday and when he rose from the dead. Add a few pieces of candy corn on Halloween and that was the extent of our exposure to candy. Truly grateful, we uttered in unison our well-rehearsed thank you.

Mister Franz gracefully switched his attention from my sisters and me to his impending sale. Shopping was a chore, not a leisure activity for my grandmother, especially with young children in tow. If she walked into a store, it was to buy something. It was like her to look at a store mannequin and buy everything it was wearing, and that is exactly what she did, at least in my case. If it was good enough to be on display in a window on Main Street, it was good enough for us to wear.

This was a transaction between my grandmother and Mister Franz; we were just there for sizing. No opinion was expected from us. In truth, I had no opinion about the style of clothes, but shoes were another matter. I really wanted a pair of soft, gray Hush Puppies, but a mannequin my size was not wearing them. It sported a pair of stiff Buster Brown penny loafers with two shiny pennies in them.

Mister Franz, reading my grandmother's mind, said, "They come with the pennies."

My grandmother replied, "With new shiny ones?" He nodded yes and my hopes were dashed. How could soft Hush Puppies, which I could not yet tie myself, compete with slip on shoes that came with their own currency? Peanut and Gwen were each getting a pair of black Mary Jane shoes.

Mister Franz had the shoe measuring tool, a Brannock device and the shoehorn handy, but these were more like props and were rarely used. With a brief finger pinch at the heel and toe of each foot, he had your shoe size. The former Army quartermaster knew his trade and was rarely wrong. In the event that he actually was wrong, as a child, you would not be believed; it was obviously your misguided feet that were wrong. Adults were never wrong in 1964.

The shoes actually fit, which meant they were slightly loose with room left for growth. My sisters' and my feet would fill the gap in the shoes within a couple of months. After that we would use the shoehorn to get into our seemingly shrinking shoes, only receiving a new pair just before our ever-expanding toes could break through the leather.

Our clothing was as predictable as the shoes. One by one each item displayed on the mannequins appeared at the register. Some came in boxes, others on hangers, including two short dresses with fitted bodices and wide skirts with crinoline; they were basically modified frocks that puffed at the sleeves and also from the hips down. Gwen's was navy blue and Peanut's a plain red.

Our grandmother also chose several pairs of white frilly ankle socks, under garments and a brown belt and socks for me. The pièce de résistance or rather, the piece to be resisted, was a sickly, yellow-colored short-sleeved button-up dress shirt. The color barely had the strength to pose as a pastel yellow. Its true identity was some-where between anemic and jaundiced, and looked in need of a doc-tor. Anyone spotted wearing this shirt by any medical personnel would surely end that day in a hospital ward next to the morgue.

Mister Franz actually had to climb into the window to remove the ill-favored shirt off the boy mannequin. As it was the only one he had ordered, he began dropping the price as he unbuttoned it. The more he unbuttoned, the lower the price got. He was a fair man and admitted the color was a mistake but believed my nutmeg col-ored skin could redeem the shirt. My grandmother, despite the price drop, grew hesitant. She didn't want any of her grandchildren wear-ing mistakes.

Hearing the word mistake kindled something in me. I suddenly felt a kindred spirit with the shirt no one wanted. Interceding on the shirt's behalf, I began begging and pleading for it. Defying my grandmother in public was one of the important, "Thou shall nots," of my family's many strictures. What stopped any swift reaction from her was the reason for my defiance. With the exception of shoes, you could put any item of clothing on me, backwards, wrong side out, it didn't matter. I would wear it without challenge or complaint. Clothes were just not that important to me. Not giving her time to recover, I further promised to give my sisters my barrel candy in exchange for the shirt. Her confusion shifted to shock. I never ever willingly shared candy with anyone, once going so far as biting my sister Peanut to protect my right to a piece of lint encrusted mint we both had been reaching for behind the couch, but I was learning to share. For the first time in my short life I anticipated my grandmother's thoughts. Remembering our earlier conversation about owning things, I actually had the presence of mind to counter her unspoken words. Pointing emphatically with one hand to my chest while simultaneously offering the candy with my other, I proudly announced, "Grandma, the shirt wants me!"

A fleeting nod from my grandmother unfroze Mister Franz, whose hand had paused on the last button of the shirt during my outburst. She opened her purse and I dropped in my promise. Kept promises were a rare and very dear thing to Addy. She kept hers and I was learning to keep mine. She gave me a broad smile and a quick you-done-well wink. I would never taste that candy, but I would be wearing the shirt when I did two things for the very first time. Thus, began my long love affair with neglected and unwanted things.

CHAPTER 2   HE IS A HIDDEN MIDDEN

We made one more, well behaved stop at the grocery store and then went home. The house was built as interim housing, meant only to last until more prosperous times made their infrequent appearance, at which time a better house would take its place. Prosperity, when it showed its face, lingered only long enough to add electricity, plumbing and wallpaper. She wore her outside paint like an old woman wore excessive makeup, too much to make her pretty, yet not enough to fill in the cracks and wrinkles. No one was fooled except the kind and the blind.

A sense of dread leaked from the house and the air felt different the moment we cracked the door. Normally, the only things we dreaded were naps and our Saturday morning dose of castor oil, but this felt different. I could feel the tension from Peanut through our joined hands. We both turned slightly to face each other, and both of our faces mirrored a hesitant look, an expression we had not yet learned to conceal, almost as hunted animals would look just before dipping their heads to drink at a watering hole. Only a gentle push from our grandmother forced us across the threshold.

Big boisterous laughter echoed throughout a house much too small for it; the house was better suited for whispers. The laughter was all bravado and no mirth. This somehow heightened our tension, and the abruptness with which the laughter halted marked it as false. Our mother was home, and she was not alone.

The only thing we could see from the hall was my grandfather sitting on the couch. His hair was nearly as gray as the overalls he still wore from work. He gave us a fleeting smile, half its normal strength and brightness. He waited for our grandmother, Addy, shrouded in a quiet that barely masked the fact that he had much to say. Our grandmother gestured to us to stay where we were and put Gwen down next to us. She maneuvered past us, then sat next to our grandfather, placing the bag of groceries she had been carrying at her feet. Neither went to finish the task of unloading the other bags from the car. Half-done tasks and a half smile were the final proof something was amiss.

They sat like silent protesters in their own home, refusing to bring us any closer to whatever it was that awaited us in the dining room. My sisters and I admirably stood our ground, neither fleeing nor advancing. I could not see him but could hear my Uncle Vincent say from the dining room, "Let me take a picture of the bride's proud parents."

The flash from the bulb of the Brownie camera etched the after-image of my grandparents stoically sitting on a doily-covered couch on my eyes for a few seconds but in my memory forever.

No matter how many times I would see that black and white photo of them on the couch, it was my view from the hall that was the vivid memory. Photos can often assist a fading memory. In this case it was my memory that assisted a faded, deceptive photo. The photo only caught a second of surprise, not the predominant emotion in the room, which was lightly veiled disapproval. The only fact the photo got right was the date, March 1964. This meant they were forty-three, yet my memories always make my grandparents older.

The sound of chairs pushing away from the table in the dining room and the realization that we had a new father arrived simultaneously. Our mother stepped into view wearing a dress she had modified from a McCall dress pattern. She loved clothes and would marvel at any of the fashion that occasionally and accidentally stumbled off the highway into town. She needn't have bothered. She was the marvel. Carol didn't need fashion. Fashion needed women like her. On her, sack cloth looked like silk. Even after three pregnancies she still wore her belts on the slimmest notches. Most women made do with compliments such as "You look good in that dress." Women such as my mother heard drawn out expletives such as "Wow!" or "Damn!" followed by, "You make that dress look good." Two very different compliments. One was store bought, and the other came from a fortuitous birth. Men would strain their vocabulary trying to make an impression on her. Every child thinks their mother is beautiful; ours really was.

Our mother came into the hall, stooped down, and with a slender graceful hand beckoned us forward. Hers was the first generation in our family whose hands had never touched a hoe or had their youth husked from their skin from tenant farming.

Her voice sounded as if it whispered from the cover of a fashion magazine. "Come children, I have someone I want you to meet." This was not her normal voice. She was shedding her small-town ways right before our eyes.

My grandparents' rising from the couch more than my mother's stooping, encouraged us forward. Even in a house with the ceiling blocking out the sun, my mother was still in my grandmother's shadow. Three pregnancies by the age of twenty did not yet make her a mother. Motherhood was at best an awkward and clumsy role for her. We loved our mother, but we depended on our grandmother.

Change was not more than twenty child size steps down the hall. Surrounded by family, in the safest place in the world, I still felt like an effigy of myself being dragged to its funeral pyre. I did not want to meet this man. Nor did I want him moving in with us. Things were fine the way they were. Can the living haunt a house? Yes, they can and already did.

As we reached the dining room, Grandpa Neil and Grandma Addy filed in behind us for support. In my state of mind, it felt more akin to a blockade, ending any chance of retreat. I walked into the dining room with my face down and turned to the side. My apprehension gave me little courage to do anything other than take a glimpse of the man. I heard the man speak but could not reply. My mother gently cupped her hand under my chin to lift my face.

"Mister Ketchum is speaking to you," she said. "You were raised better than that," she continued in an expectant voice.

My throat and emotions had mauled my first greeting so badly that its leap from my lips was more a suicide attempt than a response. It tumbled down my chin onto the floor and expired. No one heard its faint demise. I quickly followed this with a clipped, "Hello."

Before me, stood the opposite of my mother. Unlike her, his crisp Air Force uniform would be the only thing about him an honest person would give a compliment about. Yet at slightly over six feet tall, he had a presence that dwarfed his height. Power shined from his eyes. But if examined closely, fear of being weak was present as well. He was not unattractive, but not much effort had been expended on making his face. It looked as if it had been made on an assembly line, assembled ahead of schedule and under budget. His skin actually was a nice color, the color of a Brazil nut; unfortunately for him, it was also the same texture as the nut. Although clean-shaven, stubble-filled pock marks covered each cheek.

He bent eye level to us. My moral training had not yet advanced to the point that I felt guilty about focusing on his flaws while he gushed on about how cute we were. Children are honest, and instead of making eye to eye contact, they make eye contact with whatever flaw they see, be it pock marks or spinach in teeth. You want honesty, don't look in a mirror; talk at face level to a child and follow their eyes.

I gave him an insincere, obligatory sealed-lip smile. He was not yet worthy of a teeth-filled one. Nothing short of a team of draft animals could pull a smile from Peanut. Her glare bypassed all of his physical flaws and centered on his soul. She did not flinch or recoil from what she saw, but she did not trust it. Only when I followed Peanut's eyes and focused deeper did I see what she saw.

Mister Ketchum was a rigid man but was quite capable of bending others to his will and enjoyed doing so. He certainly was already commanding our mother, and through her would command us. Only the presence of our grandparents was deterring him thus far. Individually either of them was more than a match for Mister Ketchum. Paired as they were and in their own house, I dared hope that he would be no more than a spot in our house to avoid.

Perhaps if I had been a precocious child with minimum math skills, I would not have dared hope. There were three small bedrooms in the house. I slept with my uncle and the girls slept with our mother. Where would Mister Ketchum sleep?

In the middle of my false hope my mother put an exaggerated look of surprise on her face and spun her dress around creating a slight breeze simulating flight, "Guess what kids, we are going to fly on a real airplane!" Not thinking clearly, I began to spin excitedly, not creating much of a breeze. Realizing it would take a dress to create the appropriate wind, I took Gwen by the hand and gave her a twirl. I always forced Gwen to do feminine gestures I was not allowed to do, and Gwen gladly complied.

Peanut, who was not as easily distracted as Gwen and me, stood still and stone faced. Our grandfather's calloused hands clamped down on our little shoulders, stopping us in mid-whirl, bringing our little imaginary planes in for a hard landing. "Stop this nonsense," he clipped.

We swiftly joined Peanut in her stone-faced stance, more stunned than scared. Our grandfather never reprimanded us, ever, but the reprimand was not for us. It was for our mother.

Annoyed, he continued. "Stop playing with their feelings and tell them everything. Don't sugar coat it, tell them." He was not angry. He was insistent. The culture of our family was undiluted bad news was delivered first; good news, if any, always came second. No age restriction.

Mister Ketchum wisely used this momentary divide in our family to legitimately assert his authority over us. He both gracefully agreed with my grandfather and came to my mother's rescue in one sentence. "I think it would be best if I handle this," he said, out of pride more than concern.

From behind me I felt my grandparents' nod of acceptance more than saw it. Their nod was a subtle transfer of power. Pragmatism governed every aspect of their lives. They did not complicate reality with their fantasies or helpless emotions. At this age I was governed by nothing but fantasies and helpless emotion. I awoke from my fantasy realizing Mister Ketchum was not going to live with us. We were leaving, and not just down the street as had happened when my mother had married Gwen's father. Planes took you far away.

My voice became suddenly violent and defiant. "You are not my father and I don't have to listen to you," I hissed, more spitting the words than saying them.

Peanut joined me with a venomous, "Yeah," of her own.

Even in anger I knew I was not permitted to speak to an adult in this manner. At best I had hoped my grandparents would scold me for my poor behavior, but politely tell Mister Ketchum that I was right. They did neither. It had been a mistake; all adults of that time read from the same script and defiance was not tolerated.

I had given him a legitimate reason to drop his mask. Up until that point he had been nothing but polite. Now he was expected to deal with my defiance.

He harshly said, "Follow me."

In its own way it was a Pyrrhic victory for me. At least now his demeanor matched his soul. I no longer had to focus too deeply to see the real him, but I also no longer had the support of most of my family.

Peanut, because of her support of my defiance, had to follow me and Mister Ketchum down the hall to the stairs leading to the second floor. We both sat on the fifth step up, which gave us the illusion of privacy. We could not be seen, but if it was your nature to listen in on others, one would not have to strain too hard to hear the conversation. My mother and grandfather would strain. My grandmother and uncle would not.

Mister Ketchum had assumed the possibility of witnesses and cloaked his speech in a matter of fact tone, one we were well accustomed to. However, his tone was not meant for us but for the witnesses. His body language was for us. He had decided not to win us over but to intimidate us instead.

He put his left foot on the second step and leaned into us with a threatening, controlling, smug face, no more than a couple of inches from ours, "I married your mother. That makes me responsible for you. Yes, I will take good care of all of you. I am now your dad, and you will mind me." The crooked sneer he used to punctuate each sentence made it sound like we were now his property.

The fact that the tone did not match his face frightened me more than the words or the face itself. It sounded like a normal conversation, but from our vantage point it did not look like one. I would never forget the seemingly calm reasonable words emerging from a seething face. On some level I knew there were two people inside

Mister Ketchum, and one of them was mean. I was sure of that now. The other one I wish I could say was good, but it was more empirical and pragmatic, therefore preferable. Both were self-serving. My mother had unwittingly committed bigamy. She had married someone with one driver's license but was getting two different drivers.

Mister Ketchum paused in his speech and gave Peanut and me equal portions of his commanding glare. It was not just his stare. It was the cold emanating from him. At first, I thought it was just the draft coming from under the door behind him, but the tattered towel our grandmother used to keep the cold at bay was across the foot of the door. It was the type of cold not produced by weather or the setting sun. My whole body now shared the same fate as my hand earlier in the day. Peanut and I shivered in unison.

Satisfied, he continued, "I am taking your mother and all of you to Baltimore to live with my family. You can start calling me dad right now," he said, with a slight hat tip to fairness, "or you can start calling me dad when you get off the plane in Baltimore. Your choice."

Despite his words he clearly wanted to hear the word dad now. Seeing the inevitable and willing to say anything to end this ordeal, I croaked out an appeasing form of the word dad. It came out like a breached birth, misaligning teeth in its wake. Thankfully he had not demanded to be called daddy. Saying daddy would have left me toothless and soulless. The word dad would become a word we used from habit, one we always said but never felt. Peanut would wait for Baltimore.

We returned to the rest of the family in the living room, shoulders hunched from our wounded feelings and a little sour faced, but at least we were not alone with "The dad" anymore. He stood behind us while our mother greeted us. She tried to cheer us up with the very words that were partially the cause of our distress.

She said, "We are going to Baltimore to live with your new dad."

Her excited comment left our faces unmoved. She acknowledged our hurt feelings by mimicking but not mocking, our sour faces. She was happy and she wanted us to be too.

There were so many confusing emotions in the room. My mother was happy, we children sad and scared, our normally warm grandparents were noticeably colder, a smug new father and an eager uncle ready to blind us at any moment with another flash from his camera. The burden on the room lessened slightly after our mother and her new husband departed for Columbus for their honeymoon.

Witnessing an event and understanding it can occur decades apart. I remember the day vividly and understood much of it. Rather I should say I understood what was happening but not why it was happening. It was almost as if the Grant from that day swam up through the decades and took the present-day Grant by the hand and brought us both back, reuniting us with this moment, pleading for answers.

The answers were rather simple and common. Small-town girl desperately wants out. Air Force radar station full of men promising to get her out. Three children and broken promises later she is still there. Just before becoming resigned to her situation, a man with a wedding ring and a destination appears. Our mother was as much grateful as in love. The future me came with a question of his own, one that could only be answered by those long turned to dust. A question that had the courage to present itself only after it no longer could be answered. Why was no one from our family at the wedding? I could not answer as a boy, only when I became a man.

CHAPTER 3   THE UNSEEN CHILD

Easter can fall from as early as March 22nd to as late as April 29th, but regardless of what day it fell on my grandmother always took the preceding week off from her job at Westinghouse. Easter Sunday was considered the final battleground between winter and spring. In 1964, Easter fell on March 29th. Even if spring clearly had been bested in the battle, and snow or last year's dead grass still covered the ground, children were expected to look cute and reverent in their thin, pastel spring outfits. Jesus rose to the occasion and we were expected to do so as well. I could occasionally pull off cute, but reverent and I always tussled.

Fortunately, reverent and I did not often have to be in the same room. Due to some falling out with the minister, who apparently thought he was God's twin on earth, we were unaffiliated. We were what people back then called, "Stay at Home Baptists." Death and marriage were the only events that coaxed us into church. Our grandparents would not send us where they would not go themselves. That did not always mean we were pardoned from dressing up. In addition to being Easter weekend it was also my birthday, which fell on Good Friday that year. This ensured that I would have to spend the entire weekend entombed in pastel colors.

Normally my sisters and I did not keep track of our birthdays. The adults told each of us when it was our birthday. If there was extra money, we would be told of our birthdays in advance. If not, our birthdays would pass with a whisper and a small cake. As it was my fifth birthday, I had been told early and had some anticipation. Wedged as it was between my mother's wedding and Easter, my excitement had been dampened somewhat. In addition, we were leaving for Baltimore that Wednesday after Easter. My birthday celebration had been moved to Saturday and transformed into a birthday/bon voyage party. The early afternoon would be primarily for my birthday.

My Aunt Porch was the first guest to arrive. She had a sister in Baltimore and visited her often, and my mother wanted to know more about it. Although it was my birthday, she had also bought a game for Peanut and Gwen. No sooner had we opened our gifts than our mother took them upstairs to be packed later. My mother did not want us to get bored with them before we boarded the plane.

Aunt Porch was not my real aunt nor was her real name Porch. She was my grandmother's closest friend. Her real name was Emma Reeves, but everyone called her Porch because in the warmer months she practically lived on her front porch. No one came or went on Walker Street without her knowledge. Unlike most people who kept their phones in the living room or the kitchen, she kept hers on a table in the bedroom, which had a window that opened onto the porch. She could easily reach the phone through the window without leaving her chair. Just the sight of her sitting on her porch, craning her neck and reaching through the window for the phone kept most of the children of Walker Street righteous. She just looked like someone who would tell on you.

She didn't care what other people thought of her and believed if you truly cared so much for the thoughts of others, then your discretion should match your level of concern. Don't do things in the day that should be done in the dark. Day does not keep secrets as well as night and neither did Aunt Porch. Her favorite line to people was, "I don't want to see it, and you don't want me to see it, so don't do it in front of me." Odd thing about her, she never spread gossip she heard from other people, only information vetted by her own eyes was worthy of passing on.

Often, she would hold her tongue, but give Aunt Porch a reason, and she would tell you the unvarnished truth. She would pretend the truth had accidentally slipped out, but in truth she had given it a good hardy shove. Feigning discretion, Aunt Porch looked over both shoulders and in a low voice said to my grandmother, "You do know that this wedding was more like a welding?" She sighed, "Even Ray Charles can see this marriage will not last. There are just too many things going on besides love."

Aunt Porch searched my grandmother's face for signs of denial and finding none continued, "Lord have mercy! That is one crowded marriage, and that's without the kids."

My grandmother took one of Aunt Porch's hands into both of hers and reassuringly said, "You know I don't believe in casting judgments on the future from the present, but I am no one's fool either. Just get me some extra shift work at Westinghouse and I will take it from there."

My grandmother noticed me listening and diplomatically

offered Aunt Porch a piece of chicken, as much to be hospitable as to give her mouth some busy work and end the conversation.

Before taking a bite of the chicken Aunt Porch said, more with concern than criticism, "My criticism does not come from some lofty perch upon high but from my own gritty, dirty personal experience."

Her voice lowered further and flattened as one often does before speaking of an antique sadness. "You know I married wrong too!" The funeral for Mister Reeves was legendary, and I remember hearing this story one day while I was pretending to be asleep on the couch. Her narrative was so vivid I frequently have to remind myself that it was a story I overheard and not an actual memory.

Aunt Porch had been married to Quincy Reeves for eleven miserable years. He never laid a hand on her, ever, but his tongue was akin to the lashes of a bullwhip, wounding yet leaving no visible marks except for the welts on her soul. He would buy Emma beautiful dresses and a new car every two years, but he would berate her brutally. He was like an alcoholic without the alcohol. Verbal beatings were followed by extravagant gifts and soon to be broken promises of better behavior. The gifts got bigger but so did the berating. Their marriage had become more like mortar and pestle than husband and wife. Each day she was ground smaller and smaller until one day she hadn't the strength to open a gift or bear one more unrepentant apology. How had she become a person who lived in another's shadow instead of casting one herself?

On this day, she calmly walked to the kitchen and grabbed a butcher knife from a drawer. With the knife behind her back she called Mister Reeves into the kitchen. The kitchen had linoleum, which would clean easily. Even in a state of temporary insanity she was still a good housekeeper. She had decided that she would have a divorce or a funeral, her decision but his choice. If he would not let her go, she would kill him, or he would have to kill her. With a calmness that bordered on insanity, she told Quincy she wanted a divorce.

He said he would not divorce her. Even in my pretend sleep I stiffened waiting for Aunt Porch to finish her story. Her description of rubbing the thumb of her left hand across the thin width of the blade to test its sharpness sent a chill down my spine. She had decided she would stab him in the heart.

Just before she pulled the knife from her shadow, Quincy whispered, "I am dying."

Mister Reeves had prostate cancer and was not expected to live more than a year. Emma went to the doctor's office the next day to confirm that Quincy was not long for this world. Pending death did not bring out the best in Quincy. Most people want to make amends and clean up a messy life near the end. Not Quincy, he simply no longer had the strength to be mean. However, it did bring out the best in Emma. She took respectful, if not loving care of him for thirteen months. She no longer loved him. At times she outright hated him and herself for letting such a miserable life sneak up on them. After months of tending bedpans and holding a hand that withered with each day, her hate faded to pity, and pity flirted with forgiveness.

His death was anticlimactic and came simply as a relief for them both. She had been emotionally free of him months before he had died and only mourned the wasted time and a crumpled life. Emma went to her husband's funeral looking sexy and vibrant. A ruby red dress clung to her as if she had been wed to it. She wore a pair of red and cream two-tone high heels so pointy her stroll to the casket nearly shredded the carpet of the sanctuary. A chin-bob haircut framed a face that after a long absence had returned to its former ebony beauty. She wore two strands of pearls, one around her neck, the other a set of pearly white teeth that beamed from a broad smile. She was proudly and inappropriately dressed for a funeral from head to toe. The last person who would ever reign over her was dead. She was not attending a funeral so much as midwifing her own rebirth. She looked down into the casket as if she were reading the last page of a tragic book.

The old Emma would dip every word in sugar before she spoke but not the new Emma. What she was about to do was disrespectful to her husband's death, but she had lived and told her last lie. From that day forth lies would tremble before her. Emma knew from eleven years of personal experience the worst lies were the ones you told yourself. Unlike many of the lies told by others, you have the means to dispel yours.

She would always tell the young children and many an undeveloped adult, "Acknowledge when something is your fault, because if it's your fault you most likely will be able to do something about it, but if the fault lies with someone else you may not be able to do anything about that."

Emma hated hypocrisy, believing it to be a dark shadow that looms over most religions. Believers curse Darwinism as if it were the scriptures of Satan himself, yet practice survival of the fittest with a fervor with which their self-diluted faith could never compete. She was sure her glee and attire were offensive to Quincy's three sisters. She didn't care, because they had upheld their brother in every wrong, he had ever done. A fossilized faith, desiccated and lifeless, was at the center of each of their souls. The three stuffy, unwed crones for Christ sat smugly in the front pew judging and convicting her with their eyes. Eyes so full of stalactites and stalagmites, it was either a miracle or hypocrisy that they could see the specks in the eyes of their fellows. They claimed the moral high ground solely for the vistas it offered of the flaws of others, not for the sake of being better people. They didn't stand on moral ground so much as defile and trample it. Quiet as it's kept, the high moral ground is where the most egregious sins occur, not in the gutter.

Emma looked at all three sisters, any number of invectives swirling around inside her head, not knowing which one would come forth until it did.

"Jesus saves," she said, pointing a finger at the sisters and drawing an imaginary circle around them. "You judge and criticize. Even now I am fighting an urge to give all of you a Three Stooge's line slap across your blessed assured faces. Secretly each one of you evil heifers think you could have stayed on the cross longer than Jesus, but I am not going to let you ruin my chance for an afterlife. I'm going to leave you right where I found you."

She rolled her head and eyes from the sisters to Quincy's casket, nodding her head in a quick jerking motion as if she were metaphorically tossing them into the casket with him. She buried everything that needed burying that day, including the meek, "keep her head low" Emma. The meek shall inherit the earth for they shall be buried in it.

She walked toward the door, head held high, her pointy shoes and sharp tongue cutting a path out of church into an honest life. Aunt Porch detested preachers who used scripture to manipulate instead of guide.

She pivoted just before the door to chastise the minister as well: "Only God is fit to judge my complicated life," she affirmed, signaling she was abandoning the church but not God.

The last thing the assembled congregation heard from Emma was, "God lives on both sides of this church door. I don't need a hypocritical, morally lopsided preacher to supervise my prayers. I have to be careful who I'm seen praying with, so all my prayers will be from the street side of that door from now on."

The Reeves sisters would later start a rumor that Emma was an atheist. Emma made it perfectly clear she believed in God but didn't always believe in the people who said they spoke for God. She detested individuals who treated their relationship with God as if it were a ventriloquist act, sitting God on their lap and putting words into His mouth. She considered Christians who worshiped charismatic ministers more than God to be no better than idol worshipers. Men were not worthy of worship. They were modern day versions of graven images carved out of flesh, who preyed on those who prayed. From that day forth she was as free as a bird and saw religion as a cage. She would politely inform proselytizers that her soul was much too important a subject to discuss with anyone else but God.

She often said, "The high priests of men guard the gate of their heavens with coin boxes. The gullible will get what they pay for."

The church predictably divided along those lines. Half of West Bellefontaine thought she had defiled the church. The other half thought she had cleansed it, albeit with words the strength of lye, but she had not lied. The latter group in the months to come stopped worshipping the graven image of a minister and built their own house of worship, which Aunt Porch attended occasionally out of support more than to worship.

Aunt Porch had come to the party early at the request of my mother. Her only sister lived in Baltimore, so she had been there many times. Aunt Porch went upstairs to give her sister's phone number and address to my mother. In private I am sure they talked of more than the pinnacles and pitfalls of Baltimore. They both came downstairs fifteen minutes later, my mother undeterred. I never saw Aunt Porch's expression as she was detoured by a knock at the door.

CHAPTER 4   BREAKING TIES

A large family and lack of space would have normally required different invitation times, as not to overwhelm the house. Since we were leaving soon it did not matter. Everyone was invited at once. My grandmother's side of the family were very punctual. She had seven brothers and sisters. The Sanders came from different points on the compass, some lived in town, others lived just outside of it. They would arrive together and on time. One knock on the door announced them all.

My grandfather had nine brothers and sisters. Most of the Coles lived on our street or the next block over. They came from a single point on the compass but arrived at vastly different points on the clock. Often there'd be a knock with no one there. They had knocked then suddenly remembered they had forgotten something and rushed home, retrieved the item, come back a few minutes later and just walked right in. The exceptions were my great grandmother who lived just up the street and an aunt who lived across the street from us. They were on time.

Aunt Porch opened the door but tactfully delayed our guests while our mother assembled my sisters and me into a school room line, oldest to youngest. Being the oldest and the birthday boy, I would take the brunt of the heavily lipstick-laden kisses from our aunts.

Aunt Libby was the first person to walk through the door. She was a patchwork quilt of a person. A pleasant, delicate brown face sat atop a body that was more angles than curves. She could be pretty when she wanted to be but chose matronly for this occasion. Outwardly she appeared to be conservative but would be the first person to break with convention. Her every thought was on the tip of her tongue. She was a loving, burly personality in a petite frame.

She would hug you like a person twice her size. Her hugs made you feel protected and big at the same time. I lived for her hugs but endured her kisses. The only bad thing you could say about Aunt Libby was she used excessive lipstick. Her kisses were the wettest and messiest and made the loudest smacking sound upon impact. It seemed as if she used a tube on each lip and she never blotted the excess. Why bother when there were the foreheads and cheeks of young children to soak up the surplus.

I was prepared for her this time. I brought my hands to my cheeks feigning surprise to see her, but the gesture was really meant to leave my forehead as the only option for her to land a kiss. I wanted her kiss as far from my nose as possible, otherwise I would smell that waxy lipstick smell and saliva all day. She was not to be denied. She pried my hand from my left cheek. Her kiss made a loud wet landing, especially close to my left nostril, which was my biggest. Exposed to so much cosmetics, my left cheek instantly went into palsy. Then came the hug and the kiss was forgiven.

All my other aunts' kisses went on the right cheek by default. No one wanted to kiss anywhere near where Aunt Libby's lips had kissed. Small doll kisses adorned my right cheek while Aunt Libby's big kiss stood alone on my left cheek like a shunned child on a playground.

My mother's receiving line, which held some semblance of formality for my aunts, dissolved under the onslaught of my uncles. Big hands toughened from hard work lifted us off our feet and pulled us to rough faces and soft hearts.

My Uncle Lee was the biggest and the gentlest of all my great uncles. His smile was a collaborative effort of mouth, eyebrows, cheeks and joy. It never flashed across his face in a rush but lingered there inviting the smiles of others to come join in. He was the dark, rust color of a great antiquated industrial machine and was big enough and man enough to wear the color pink unchallenged. Today he wore it from head to ankle. Only his shoes were a different color. They were shiny and red. Pink on all that horsepower was truly awe-inspiring. It was hard to believe someone so sturdily built could be so delicate of touch. Watching him gracefully pick up Peanut was like watching a pink elephant pick up a tiny peanut. Their close resemblance to this image made me giggle.

I picked up Gwen and Uncle Lee picked us both up while still holding Peanut. He carried us to the kitchen making siren sounds like an ambulance, "Emergency! Emergency! Hungry kids coming through," meaning himself as much as us. He put us next to the table and all four of us stood like glutinous statues, eyes roaming over every dish.

Platters and pots of food had been pouring into the house as fast as people. I put a finger over my left nostril, blocking out the smell of waxy lipstick to better savor the aroma of the food. One of the few privileges we had as children was that we were served first. Uncle Lee ate first and twice, once with the children and later with the adults.

I cozied close to my Aunt Libby because I preferred her to fix my plate. She was as excessive with her food portions as she was with lipstick and her ladle would pull the least amount of vegetables from the pots. She was not feeding your body; she was feeding your soul. If there happened to be a vitamin in there somewhere, all the better but not the main point for her. A smile expressed while chewing was a balm for her soul. She savored your joy.

In the hope of making her excessive hand even more generous, I leaned against her leg as if it were the only thing keeping my rickets-ridden bones from collapsing into a famished heap on the floor. I was not a plump child, but my cheeks were fat enough to carry me unfed through a mild winter. Despite this, I gave her a look that said if I didn't eat soon, I wouldn't live to be six. It was a pitiful look that would have shamed even a hungry dog, but it always worked.

Her hand mercifully passed over the stewed tomatoes, organ meats and Aunt Vivian's macaroni and cheese brick. Everyone privately joked that Aunt Vivian's recipe was the secret to the Israelites making bricks without straw. Surely it had been dried in the sun or cooked in a kiln instead of an oven. Only the overly polite and strong would chisel a piece off the brick and eat it. The first teeth of young children were deemed insufficient for the task; therefore, her dish was considered a choking hazard.

My Uncle Lee winked at me and said, "Libby, give that boy some of that macaroni and cheese."

I quickly chimed in, "Yeah, I'm hungry," adding more credibility to the request by lifting my right arm and forming one of those cartoon muscles, the one that is firm at first then collapses into a wobbly mess that jiggles.

Aunt Libby's head swiveled to see that Aunt Vivian was not in hearing range. She kept her voice low and warned cautiously through clenched teeth, "I don't need to see your muscle, show me your teeth."

I complied with a smile and a "Why?"

"Oh, nothing baby," she said with a voice suited for singing the blues. "I just wanted to say goodbye to them."

With a deep vibrating chuckle and a dubious look directed at Uncle Lee, she dolloped some mac-and-mess onto my plate, taking care not to let any of it touch my other food. She knew the mac and cheese was really for my Uncle Lee. He didn't need to use me as a cloak to gain extra food. No one was going to say no to a six-foot, four-inch man in a pink suit. Big as he was, he didn't need anybody on his side, but he made you feel like he did and that was the bond.

If you were a child, Uncle Lee was always on your side. Often it was the wrong and losing side. It didn't matter to him if you were right or wrong or that your fate was already sealed: he was in your corner. He hated to see a child in distress. At the last family gathering, Peanut had spilled food on her favorite dress. She cried and wailed uncontrollably, and no promise or threat could calm her. The more attention heaped on her the worse the crying became. She was stained, ashamed and everyone was looking at her. Uncle Lee dipped his finger into the bowl of stewed tomatoes that seemed to show up unwanted at every family gathering and smeared it across the front of his shirt.

He reached down, grabbed Peanut's hand and proudly said, "See, we're the same."

Peanut probably stopped crying as much from shock as from having an ally. He loved clothes and food more than anything and he had just sacrificed both for her. If he never did another kind thing in his life, I would admire him the rest of my life for that reason alone.

So, when he winked for me to take the macaroni and cheese, I jumped at the chance to reciprocate. He was always creating little plots and conspiracies with the children of the family. There was a method to his madness. Children told Uncle Lee things no child wanted to tell a parent but were often things an adult needed to know. In fact, he was the first person my mother told when she found out she was pregnant with me.

We sat at a card table specifically set up for the children to eat. Uncle Lee was our monitor and etiquette coach. Instead of being the restraint, as usual he was leading the charge into abandonment. Food swapping took place swiftly and with order. A humble prayer of thanks, gnashing of teeth and some lip smacking and we were done. Oblivious to all the others who had not eaten yet we held up our empty plates as a sign we were ready for cake. My grandmother and aunts gave us the stink eye and circled the cake in a defensive position, much like musk ox do against wolves. We lost the staring contest and went outside, we to play and Uncle Lee to smoke.

My mother and her brother, my Uncle Vincent, were already sitting on the back porch, smoking. I saw my mother exhale some smoke and heard the tail end of their conversation.

She sneered, "I'm never coming back to this retched town ever again."

Her words mixed with the cigarette smoke in the air to form a cloud over my head. I was a child and did not know that it was hyperbole, frustration and a bit of sibling rivalry that made her speak the way she did.

Uncle Lee interrupted their conversation by saying "Girl, I know you're coming back to visit your Uncle Lee."

He was too tall, and his face was out of range of most kisses, so my mother grabbed and hugged him, with her face pressed hard against his chest. I heard a muffled, "You're the best thing about this town. Of course, I'll be back to visit you and you're always welcome to visit us."

Her assurances were mostly smothered by his enveloping arms and didn't rise high enough to dispel the cloud created by her previous statement.

She and my Uncle Vincent strolled back into the house to take their turn at the tables with the young adults and older children. Uncle Lee could see the distress in my face and promised he would come and visit us for sure. He wanted to reinforce my mother's assurance of at least coming back to visit but he would only make promises he would keep. He never spoke for someone else, not even to make you feel better.

Children for the most part stay in the moment. The past or future may stop by occasionally to pay a visit, but they swiftly move on. The past comes as a reminder but is too small to dwell on. Future comes as hope or worry yet is too vast to fully comprehend. Only the moment is manageable for a child.

Holding my index finger to my lips to shh my uncle, I set my plan into motion. He put his index finger to his lips signaling his compliance. It was a child's solution, feebly executed but grand in intent. On the porch was a piece of rope a good hundred feet long, not yet cut up to replace the three tattered clothes lines in our back yard. At first, I tried to tie Peanut to the column of the porch, a two by four wood beam holding up a tarpaper roof. She was having none of it. She strongly resisted, almost turning the table on me and tying me to the beam. Except neither of us could so much as tie our own shoes. My tying was more like wrapping that ended in a knot. I could tie a knot but not undo one. Peanut's tying was more like tangling without the knot.

Uncle Lee knew what I was trying to do and said in a voice that stated clearly, he would not aid us further, other than telling on us, "Who's going to tie up the last one?"

At least one of us would have to go to Baltimore while the other two would be safely tied to the beam, indefinitely facing the elements.

Until our uncle had spoken, Peanut had assumed I was trying to tie her to the beam to keep her from having cake, something I was not above doing. My child's logic still thought rope restraints were a good solution. Now one in purpose, Peanut and I focused on our grandparent's car, which sat on a patch of gravel and dead grass that sometimes served as our driveway. We tied the car up with the zeal of those who have no knowledge of the word futile. We wrapped and twisted the rope around the wheels and fenders. The Gordian knot was beyond the knowledge and capabilities of the children of a working-class American family. The entanglement ended with a simple knot around the airplane hood ornament. For good measure, I put a small lump of coal behind the back wheel to keep the car from backing up. I wiped the coal dust from my fingers on the dead grass and walked back to the house determined to blow out my birthday cake candle, knowing what my wish would be. A trussed-up car, a lump of coal wedged behind the back wheel and my birthday wish: we were not going anywhere.

Uncle Lee watched in silence the entire time but in the end, it was his inaction that had given us away. He would have normally been eating his second helping by now. This was unusual behavior, and nothing drew the attention of the authorities like unusual behavior.

Our grandmother came huffing through the back door, "Lee you've got to finish eating that macaroni and cheese." Her voice swiftly shifted to pleading, "I need to start soaking that pan in water now to give the soap a fighting chance." She paused as she caught sight of the car.

It had not occurred to me there would be consequences for my actions. The first expression on my grandmother's face jogged my memory. Consequences were always lurking about like a tax levied on every action, good or bad. Every action was subject to a stringent audit. No matter, it would be a small price to pay to stay. Before my grandmother could react,

Uncle Lee said flatly, "Addy, what are you really seeing? Look really close."

My grandmother's face changed instantly from one who dispenses consequences to one who had complete empathy. Regrettably the empathy was accompanied by helplessness. She could do nothing. Until that moment my verbal protest, admittedly muted and vague, had been ignored. It was as if I had been blowing a dog whistle in a room full of cats. Everyone kept purring and preening as if nothing was wrong. I felt unheard and unseen. My pictograph, car plus rope plus rock stated clearly what a five-year-old's vocabulary could not: I love you, I'm scared, and I don't want to go.

When children are scared, they close their eyes, pretending the pretend monster can't see them. As adults we often do the same only with our eyes wide open. We pretend not to see the monster, who unfortunately is no longer pretend, nor stays under or at the foot of the bed. Despite our best efforts it shadows us faintly by day but stalks us intensely at night. The monster has three heads: fear, worry and doubt, the three sirens of the night. I was growing up fast. I now had an adult monster yet only had a child's toys to fight it.

My efforts failed. The car was untied. I had failed to blow out one of my five birthday candles, nullifying my wish not to leave. Four days later I woke from an unsound sleep, the bags under my eyes packed with worry. Our car backed over the lump of coal behind the rear wheel, crushing it and most of my hopes into black dust. Not only was I leaving behind people I loved but good blueprints for becoming an adult. Our luggage was full of clothes I would soon outgrow but my memories were packed full of people whose shoes I hoped to fill one day. Could I wear an all pink suit with pride? Could I give a kiss that stood alone among kisses? And could I tell the truth, concerned only with what God or I thought? I fingered my jaundice yellow shirt from Mister Franz's store and dared to hope.

CHAPTER 5   ONE IF BY LAND, TWO IF BY SKY

The excitement of seeing the Columbus Airport had temporarily trumped most of my anxiety. Flying was a formal event in 1964, up there with weddings and funerals. You dressed as high as your means would permit. God forbid we should smudge or dirty the jet stream with unwashed bodies and rumpled clothing.

My mother and grandmother, who would normally argue with each other over the color of the sky, had joined forces against me. I was the errant child: no matter how nice the clothes, shirts, pants and shoes, clothing tended to view my body as a place of refuge. They relaxed, drooped, collected dust and wrinkles by the bushel and just did as they pleased.

My grandfather always joked, "A shirt could just look at you and it would begin to wrinkle."

So additional effort and starch had been expended on my behalf. Not the store-bought starch either, my grandmother made her own from cornstarch, water, alum and borax. Her formula would turn any ordinary dress shirt into a straitjacket.

I started that morning more resembling a refugee fleeing some natural disaster and awaiting an airlift than an airline passenger from the Midwest. Extra pomade had been applied to my short stiff hair to keep it steadfast. It was a bit overkill, much like taking a musket to a mouse; even if the plane had been a convertible and the captain intended to fly with the top down, my hair would not stir. It mysteriously only moved in my sleep and when it grew.

Two concessions were granted for my appearance. I was a toe walker, so every time I walked, the penny loafers had slipped off my feet or flipped back against my heels much like flip flops, except at three times the price. Aunt Porch had taken us back to the store to exchange the penny loafers for the gray Hush Puppies I had wanted in the first place. The Hush Puppies were also loose, but they at least spared my mother and sisters the indignity of watching me clippity-clop around the airport. The only reason I was allowed to wear the sickly colored shirt I had picked out myself was because my love for it put a little pride in my spine and walk.

Since we were going to live with Mister Ketchum's mother for a time, no precaution was deemed excessive. Our grandmother intended to send us clean, healthy, well dressed and well fed, with the subtle unsaid expectation that this standard would be maintained in Baltimore. My grandmother would not go to the airport. She stood on the porch, her posture somewhere between resolute and unhappy. As the Buick drove away, we waved and watched each other recede into our respective horizons. We did not break eye contact until the increasing distance forced us to.

The airport was hot, so I removed my coat. My mother immediately spotted an ashy elbow on her errant child, but there was no lotion available. Everything in her purse had a dual purpose. Without blinking an eye, she pulled out her tube of Chapstick and began erasing the dusty blemish as if it were a misspelled word. I was now fit to fly.

My mother's biggest concern was to not look like she was from Bellefontaine, Ohio. Although it was her first time flying, her facial expression did her bidding. She was able to hide her small-town excitement and act as if this were just an everyday common event. I always admired people who had control of their expression. My expressions were generally controlled by outside events or my internal feelings, rarely by force of will. I walked down the aisles every bit the small-town child I was. I looked like one of those rubber, squeeze toys, the kind when you squeezed the body the eyes bugged out.

The interior of the plane looked like Aunt Porch had described it. She had again been invited over the night before to give us pointers on how to behave. She was the only one we knew who had ever been on an airplane. Expensive as it was, Aunt Porch started flying in the early fifties primarily for the speed. She still had many relatives in the Deep South and air travel was one of the few forms of transportation that was not segregated. She hated paying to be inconvenienced, insulted and suffer the other indignities of segregated trains and buses. With the death of segregation Aunt Porch kept to the sky out of convenience. At least our journey would be free of that nonsense.

My mother sat in the aisle seat, Gwen sat in the middle, Peanut near the window and I sat in an aisle seat directly across from my mother. This seating arrangement kept all three of us within scolding distance of our mother. I realized I had been robbed because of the seating arrangement. I wanted the window seat. I was the oldest and felt it should be mine.

"Mom I want the window seat," I whined.

My mother gave me the look, and the hand puppet gesture of fingers and thumb clamping shut, signaling me to hush. Peanut copied my mother's hand gesture behind her back just to annoy me. To further annoy me, Peanut looked contemptuously out the window as if the site bored her and then pulled down the window shade and turned away. She acted as if this was all so familiar to her. Had she been of age she would have ordered a drink.

You would have thought the plane had decompressed the way I was struggling to take in air to form a verbal response. She didn't even want the seat. She just didn't want me to have it. This threw me into a hissy fit. My mother's hand puppet turned into snapping fingers pointing to my seat. With her other hand she fingered her seat belt in a threatening manner.

She leaned towards me and gurgled more than spoke, "All these belts on this plane and you want to show out in public."

I took a swift inventory of the number of seat belts on the plane and realized I had badly miscalculated. For some reason the flight was filled with uniformed military personnel, so no one was going to come to the aid of a poorly behaved child being disciplined.

A young, uniformed pinkish man with short straw-colored hair offered his window seat to me. Had I been older I would have described him as white with blond hair, but I was of the age where skin and hair color were merely descriptive, with no hint of the pejorative. Color and hair just described the outside of a person. I had no concept of other. If I had a view of humanity it was more like a garden of mixed wildflowers. Where we were going, man had turned the garden into a factory farm, plants separated by neatly weeded rows and each crop separated by a fence. On this plane we sat in the same row, and a kind man simply gave up his seat to an excited boy.

Once comfortably seated I noticed both of my shoes had come untied and all of a sudden, I wanted to sit next to my mother again. She was the maintenance department for my outfit, and I needed her to retie them. Unfortunately, my mother was busy getting Gwen and Peanut (the window thief) settled in. Instead of asking her to tie my shoe, I politely asked the pale, pleasant face, uniformed man sitting next to me, if he would. His whole presence was dominated by his hands. They were enormous and extremely hairy. What I could see of the veins looked more like the root system of a sturdy tree rather than the circulatory system of a human. The hairs on his knuckles were more numerous and longer than those on his head. The military surely had no regulation regarding hair length for knuckles or he would have been in violation. He quickly tied my left shoe, and just as swiftly untied it. He answered my confused look by instructing me to watch. He slowly retied it, giving me detailed instructions this time. Despite the clumsy, sluggish look of his hands he was so graceful, it was almost like he was knitting my shoelaces instead of tying them. We practiced over and over while waiting for the plane to take off. By the time I was ready to fly solo, so to speak, the plane was racing down the runway gaining speed and altitude.

I was so engrossed in my new lesson that I was oblivious to the take off. If I noticed it at all it was because the additional G force was making my newly acquired skill a little more difficult to manage. After untying and retying my shoes multiple times, I pointed my legs straight out to admire the lopsided bows of my laces. In retrospect I should have admired the fact that I had so much legroom. Rarely as an adult would I be granted as much legroom again, no matter the upgrade.

When I lowered my feet and looked out the window, I noticed the clouds below. Until that moment I had only seen them below my feet as murky reflections in puddles, ponds, or lakes. I had never truly viewed clouds from above but now had the privilege of peering down on their glorious towering crowns. Although hardly an angel myself, I now had the view of one. The clouds looked more as if they had fallen than as if I had risen above them. My mind had not quite yet grasped the concept of flight. Much like Chicken Little, I had a very terra-centric view of life.

I cried out, more excited than panicked, "Mommy, look the clouds fell down."

Everyone within earshot found it amusing. The man who had helped me tie my shoe took the time to explain why and how we were so high. He gave me altitudes and speeds in numbers too large for me to understand.

The world of a five-year old is full of ignorance, mysteries and seemingly chance encounters without comprehension. Slowly over time, ignorance diminishes while comprehension expands. Having flight explained to me and learning to tie my shoe were some of the first chips in the giant boulder that was my ignorance. Unfortunately, ignorance can keep pace with comprehension. You chip away at the boulder, yet it seems unfazed and undiminished. Not known to me at the time, my long term goal was to make my boulder small enough to throw as far from me as possible, much like a flat skipping stone thrown across some imaginary body of water, with me gleefully watching the last skip descend into a dive below the surface. For the moment the boulder was going nowhere.

My new knowledge of aviation did not contradict my high hopes of seeing angels, and I spent the rest of the flight with my nose pressed against the window searching the clouds for them. After all, was this not their realm? Surely, they would wonder what this strange object trespassing on their sky was and come to investigate. I strained my eyes but saw nothing. Perhaps like the children of earth they were not permitted to talk to strangers. No, angels talked to strangers all the time. Maybe the plane was snubbed because its cold hard steel wings were an affront to the warm soft-feathered wings of Gabriel and his kind. Whatever the reason, I never once glimpsed an angel. I could only hope they had seen me. Even if they would not acknowledge me, I could not fly through their sky without acknowledging them. I kept smiling and waving at the clouds and any hidden curious angels until the clouds became land and land became the terminal of Baltimore's Friendship International Airport.

Somewhere in my mother's house is an old sewing box at the bottom of a closet. In that box are old, sturdy buttons intended for mends never made and a tattered photograph of our arrival at the airport. It has the qualities of a lenticular image without actually being one. Tilt the photo this way it was one image, tilt another way it becomes another image. The differentiating factors are not the angle or position of the viewing, it is when and who is doing the viewing that changes the image. In that sense most photographs are lenticular images. Today nothing in that photograph exists or stands as it was. The airport was torn down, rebuilt and renamed. So too were we, the human inhabitants of the photograph.

Although the photograph was never valued enough to put in a photo album with its siblings, I always thought that it would have made a great album cover for a record. As we were destined to live only blocks away from the haunts of Billie Holiday, my mother would become "The Lady Sings the Blues" and we would be her backup singers. When women sing the blues, their children harmonize with every "Woe is me" verse. This was our first real day in the marriage. The needle had not yet touched the record, so not a scratch marred its surface.

In a time when luggage had no wheels, all except Gwen had to carry some type of baggage to the car. Peanut carried the little Colorforms puzzles Aunt Porch had given us to keep us entertained and my mother sane. We were still young enough that most of our toys had no gender. I played with whatever they played with. As the clouds had been my entertainment, my puzzle was still wrapped and pristine. Peanut's and Gwen's games were already missing some of the plastic pieces. A couple of Gwen's had bite marks in them, and one had been stretched out of shape in a tug of war for possession between the two.

I was not fully comfortable knowing a hand involved in a tug of war over toys was carrying one of mine.

My mother, seeing my apprehension, sweetly said, "Baby, if you trust your sister to carry your toy, mommy will trust you to carry her makeup case."

I wonder if my mother knew even then. My tiny little mandibles unhinged and dropped open with excitement. She gently reached down and lifted my lower jaw until she heard my teeth clink. Then she handed me the prize. It was robin's egg blue with gold metal trim around the edge and shaped like a small picnic basket. Not only did the case have her makeup, it held all her jewelry, nothing such as diamonds and pearls, mostly just plastic and glass, but I trembled as if I were holding precious stones and the workmanship of oysters.

The whole world of make believe rested in my hands. If it had not been 1964, and had we not been in public, I would certainly have wet my pants and come out of the closet right then and there.

Peanut and Gwen could bite and tug on my toy all they wanted, if only I would be granted an hour of unsupervised time with the makeup and my sisters. I pictured glamour and camera flashes. They would no longer want to play with plastic when they could be plastic. In reality, my heavy hand and my limited skills as a five-year-old would have had them looking like bejeweled raccoons or powdered donuts. Then there would be nothing to do but blame the clay, not the sculptor, for the flaws.

My stepfather thought my happiness was because my mother showed trust in me.

He chimed in, "Someday you will be big enough to carry luggage like these." I must admit he carried the two heavy pieces of luggage with ease.

"God, I hope not," I thought.

One day I would gain such strength, but my muscles would be primarily for ornamental purposes, not to be casually volunteered for menial labor, and my outer strength would never match my inner strength. Right now, my muscles suited me well enough. The heaviest thing in the makeup case was some lead-based lipstick.

We walked outside into a cold that caused a slight shiver before our bodies shrugged it off and acclimated. The same clouds we passed on the way to Baltimore now raced passed us overhead. They held no angels or rain. Their haste across the sky gave the impression that they were late for an appointment, perhaps to gather up the absent angels and rain.

We walked a short distance to the parking lot. Mister Ketchum did a presenting hand gesture towards a type of car I had never seen before. Everything about it said it was expensive, luxurious and not his.

My mother despite her poised posture, yelled, "A limousine!"

She excitedly advanced two steps toward the car, and from some remembered caution suddenly took one step back. Just then a man exited the driver's side of the limousine and my mother's one step back became a full-on apologetic retreat, her eyes searching the vicinity for her next clue on how to behave.

"Is this our car?" she asked, her voice equally laden with hope and doubt.

To his credit, Mister Ketchum didn't claim he owned it. He had procured the driver and the car through a complicated barter system often employed by people of lesser means to temporarily tap into the resources of the wealthy. He was not a friend of Mister Ketchum but merely someone who owed him a favor.

The driver began efficiently loading the luggage into the cavernous trunk. To this day I cannot recall the driver's name. It was something country and southern attempting to be Greek. You needed an extra tongue and lots of saliva if you hoped to get close to pronouncing it. His name was fancier than his rather nondescript appearance. That is until he reached for my mother's makeup case. Suddenly Mister Nondescript became a miscreant with meat hooks for fingers; his intentions were theft and mauling. I held on tight to my mother's case, wishing I had the muscles I had mocked earlier.

He was not entrusted with the case, I was. How dare he touch my mother's trove of smoke and mirrors. My eyes cursed at him in a manner a child's mouth could not. Unfortunately, I had eyes that were not always as mute as I would prefer. They were always tattling on my soul. Only a word from my mother would loosen my grip. To prevent the entire contents of the case from spilling onto the pavement my mother intervened. She made me turn it over to Mister Big Name and demanded my mouth apologize for the misdeeds of my eyes.

Mister Ketchum actually came to my defense. "Carol don't make that boy apologize. He did the right thing. This is Baltimore not Bellefontaine. You don't trust just anybody here."

His voice held the gentle authority of a teacher chastising a child who accidentally omitted a letter while reciting the alphabet.

We all piled into the car with room to spare and drove off. A landscape sailed by that was no different than the Ohio River Valley we had just left. It looked as if gray gravy covered everything. Winter had overstayed its welcome and at a time when you most wanted to see a hint of green, bleak trees were being stingy with their colors. Although the grass was less miserly, its color was not to be praised either. The sky was the most colorful thing the day had to offer.

With nothing scenic to distract me, and there being too many adults around to pester my sisters, I paid close attention to my new father. He looked at my mother with an expression I personally reserved only for the sighting of frosted cakes and shiny objects. Was this the look of love and desire, or was it just desire? I had not yet been properly introduced to all my emotions, so I was not familiar with how strangers became loved ones. My emotions tended to be random and came out as if picked from a grab bag. Is this how we picked our future husbands and wives? Was there a grab bag for that and more importantly can you put them back and choose another?

Most of the ride he spent making promises only a small-town girl or a child would believe. He used phrases that contained words such as plenty and eternal and added price tags as periods to the end of every sentence. Our mother wasn't buying it because she had already bought it. A plane and limousine ride out of Bellefontaine was all the promise she needed.

She kissed him and said, "I thank you in advance for all the wonderful promises you will keep."

Since this Mid-Atlantic state Santa Claus was handing out stuff, I had a few items I wanted.

"Dad," I said no longer choking on the word, "Can we go to the circus?"

My question caught him in the middle of preening himself, so his pride answered for him, "Yes, the next time it comes to town I will take you." I learned early, the best time to ask a man for something was when he was in the midst of bragging. My sisters squealed in a high-pitched tone, which started me squealing at an even higher pitch.

Mister Big Name chimed in, "I can probably help with that."

No doubt he was dating a clown or had clown relatives. Mister Big Name fumbled in his pocket while driving and actually handed my stepfather a business card. He took it as if he saw one every day. His fleeting facial expression said otherwise, either that, or he was surprised to get one from Mister Big Name.

My stepfather held up the business card, swept us all with his gaze and with a wink said, "I will treat you to a small sample of paradise."

The car seemed to slow from the weight of such a promise, but we were actually just making a slow turn into Baltimore.

CHAPTER 6   HOUSE OF SUFFERANCE

The scene outside the window called my stepfather a liar. The plane and limousine rides could be compared to dressing up to dine at a five-star restaurant, only to discover you were destined for a fast food restaurant where the neon lights intermittently flickered on and off, and the establishment was out of everything except rude service. If not for all the promises and buildup from my stepfather, and if you squinted just a bit, Baltimore could be considered almost beautiful. It had been the second largest port of entry for immigration after Ellis Island, so was a little worn for wear. She was not a ballroom beauty like her eastern sister Boston. Baltimore was the working-class girl who frequented dance halls, bought her own beer and asked men to dance. Most of the buildings were plain nineteenth century brick or stone and were stacked close together like canned goods in a supermarket. Concrete and asphalt everywhere ensured a tumble by any child ended with a skinned knee or elbow.

East Baltimore by developed world standards was poor. There were no dead cattle lying in the street or open ditches of raw sewage spawning periodic plagues to mark it as such, but it was. The brick and stone buildings drooped and sagged in a manner that gave the illusion the windows and doors were frowning. The front stoops of most houses were made of marble and were well tended with most of the dirt and trash confined to vacant houses and lots, which were tended by no one. Cleanliness was valued and not beyond the means of any of the poor. Yet tattered and worn were ubiquitous in a place where choices had to be made between bread and repairs. Stiff brushes and soap were not the equal of mortar and paint; they could only help but so much.

My mother peered out the window, muttered the street names of the intersection where we had just parked, "N. Eden and E. Eager."

Her face slipped into neutral before I could read it. The street names were a bit of an ironic slap in the face. Was Eden not synonymous with paradise? Across the street was a square patch of faded grayish green that could barely pose as a park and certainly was no Garden of Eden. The unworthiness of the park did not discourage me from a cursory yet unfruitful search of its barren trees for the proverbial apple from which to take a bite. My hope for expulsion from this paradise was swiftly dashed against the rough boughs of urban trees that never bore fruit. Nothing to do but exit the car.

Four houses east of Eden stood the tallest house on the 1400 block of E. Eager Street. From one of its windows a shadowed face more curious than welcoming peered out from behind faded, yellow, threadbare curtains. In a city with many abandoned houses the curtains were not for privacy so much as a notice of occupancy. For the briefest of seconds, I spotted three small figures with craning necks and eager faces before they were abruptly shooed away by the shadowed face.

After unloading the luggage, my mother's husband settled accounts with Mister Big Name using an elaborate handshake to discretely pass him a paper gratuity. In a time and place where coin tips or nothing at all were the norm, this was rather generous. With that done the only form of luxury any of us would see for quite some time slowly drove to the end of the block and made a right turn out of our lives.

The faces at the window had not been an accurate census of the occupants of the house. There were five additional people living in the house, for a total of eight. Our stepfather may have dreamed of life in the sky but had delivered us to a warren. Yet, he proudly ushered us into our new home. The wooden floors of the house would creak and groan in complaint as five more came to rest their heads on its weary bones. We were squeezing into a house with only one bathroom. No matter how welcoming the people, the house could never be.

No one greeted us at the door. We paused for a moment in a narrow hall adorned with wallpaper from two different eras. Paste eating silverfish and time had collaborated to expose patches of an earlier, deep red Victorian wallpaper beneath an Art Deco style celadon green and white flowered paper. The house felt and smelled like an old, rarely used library, minus the knowledge and the silence. We could hear the voices of our new family glide along the walls rather than echo off them. They, for convenience sake, had retreated to the largest room in the house, the dining room, which was at the center of the home.

Our stepfather used the pause to give our mother a kiss of encouragement. My sisters and I needed encouragement as well but were given nothing. I was not of gentle birth nor was I a shy or timid child. I could talk to a wall and get it to tell me its life story, yet this world we were entering was much coarser than what I was accustomed to. The pause was only sufficient for me to summon enough courage to withstand nothing more daunting than a light breeze. As we walked into the crowded dining room, children as human shields leading the way, my trepidation suddenly surged into full-blown fright. Peanut, who rarely cried, started wailing.

Everyone in the room was made nondescript by the presence of one person. Axel Ketchum was one of our stepfather's five younger brothers. He should have been the last person we noticed, as he stood at the end of the room in a dark corner made even darker by his brooding presence. Despite the poor lighting, I could see a face that was a combination of handsome and ruin. He glared from a metaphoric darkness deeper than any nature could forge. Long, thick, lush eyelashes framed eyes the color of a dark amber whiskey and gazing upon them could be just as intoxicating. They beckoned yet repelled with equal intensity, beautifully adorned gates that opened into a menacing place. Staring into them revealed only a few screws were in place and of these none had been fully tightened. He had ceased grasping at reality long ago. He was crazy, the kind of crazy that seeped into your skin.

Axel's chiseled features were marred by two knife scars, almost as if a sculptor's hand had slipped during his creation, or as if suddenly, midway through the work, the sculptor had decided to become an impressionist painter. One scar followed the right jawline. The other was a jagged keloid scar that ran from his left earlobe to the back of the same ear. At first glance the scars looked as if they could have been caused by a headfirst flight through a windshield during a car accident, but these scars had neither been created by sculptor nor by accident. They were from walking through the back alleys of Baltimore on a perpetual losing streak, accompanied by a bad attitude. He reminded me of a battered tomcat; no matter how many fights the cat lost, it always wanted back out into the alley. Surprisingly, the scars on his face distracted very little from his looks, although his face was probably only truly handsome when he slept. During his waking hours, all the demons that plagued him took possession and contorted his features. The scars were beauty marks by comparison.

A tight wiry body twitched beneath his rumpled clothing that had obviously been slept in. His physique had been formed by consuming cheap alcohol and foods found at the front counters of liquor stores, usually something pickled or packaged. His drug addiction had recently usurped his alcoholism to the point that food from a liquor store would be considered a bounty as now he rarely ate at all. He had climbed out of the bottle only to descend into the syringe. Heroin was not yet rampant, and he was the first heroin addict I had ever seen, patient zero of the coming epidemic. He was also the first person I dreamt of not being.

Apparently, he had arrived while our stepfather was fetching us from the airport. He had gotten into the house through stealth, creating a Trojan Horse constructed of pleas such as, "Please help me, forgive me mama," and "I want to change."

Hidden within these wooden words was an unrepentant addict. Selling lies was his livelihood. His mother had always been his best customer for some of his worst lies. How many mothers willingly sat through their child's poorly acted school plays, ready to hand even a child with a non-speaking role an Oscar for stage presence? He could have just as easily chosen to construct a Trojan Unicorn and gained entrance. The lie was believed before it was conceived and more charade than substance, transparent to all but a mother who thought she could love a child out of addiction.

Any objections to Axel's presence from our stepfather had been quashed by our arrival. Our new grandmother had opened her door to a stranger's three children. She certainly would not close the door in the face of one of her own. Locks to her house were mere formalities, there to make you pause to ask politely for permission to enter. It was almost always granted, with one stipulation; guests were not allowed to complain about other guests.

Axel came close to breaking this rule. He didn't complain about us, but he complained at us. Either he resented our presence, or we were a new audience for his pity party. Glaring in our direction he spit and hissed, something about the presence of an outhouse in the sky that hovered directly over his head, filled with celestial beings that had long digestive tracts whose bowels voided regularly and frequently, all of it landing directly upon him. I wanted to tell him I had just been in the sky and saw no such thing, but my confidence was waning under his vitriolic attack upon the heavens. Maybe I did not see the angels because they were all in the outhouse above this man's head.

Peanut stopped crying and giggled, "Angels go potty on man's head?"

No one had an answer for her, so her body now began to shake with full on laughter, head thrown back, mouth wide open showing every tooth, braying like a horse. Our mother gave Peanut a little pinch to stop her braying, but it only dulled it back down to a giggle.

She repeated her question again but now as a statement, "Angels go potty on man's head." Her laughter and disbelief had turned into concern.

We had recently seen a movie where a house fell out of the sky and landed on a witch, so to her, poop from the sky seemed possible.

Peanut with genuine concern said, "When I go to heaven, I promise I won't poop on your head." Her eyes gave me a side-glance excluding me from the promise.

She continued, "Mister, mommy has an umbrella you can use."

Axel dwelled in the gutter and disrespected himself constantly, but apparently, he had enough pride that it could be wounded by a child he perceived as mocking his delusions.

With the barest hint of shame cloaked in sarcasm he said, "Keep your mother's umbrella and buy three more because you are going to need them."

Alarm in our eyes and flight in our hearts, we gathered closer to our powerless mother, cringing and searching the ceiling and beyond for a most unpleasant rain.

The real power of the house interceded on our behalf. What many mistook for blindness was actually hope. Ruth Ketchum gave a disproportionate amount of love to her son, getting little back in return. What little shreds of love he had, had to be kept for himself. He was a deep hole that could never be filled. What love was thrown his way was used to plug the drain at the bottom of that hole, to prevent even the shallow pool of dregs that represented his soul from abandoning him. Ruth Ketchum knew what her son was. Only dreaming of what he could be kept her door and heart open to him. She gave him enough love to hang himself, which he usually did and was doing now.

"Hush, you can poison your veins all you want, but you will not poison my house. I am not having you curse heaven as a guest in my house."

Our new grandmother's stern stare held no give in it, nor did her demeanor leave room for bargaining, "Straighten up and fly right or else."

The undefined "or else" could be anything, but the tone of her voice weighted the expression with implied menace and consequences.

Axel withered as much from her harsh tone as from the beginning of his withdrawal from heroin. He tried to force a lame excuse disguised as an apology through pursed lips, but she trampled his malformed excuses and apologies before he could further stain the air with his insincerity.

Ruth turned to our stepfather, "Take Axel to the store and get some more milk and make him drink it."

Axel protested sourly, "Milk gives me cramps."

At that time, milk was believed to hasten the sobering up process, that is if you could get them to drink it. It didn't. In all likelihood the milk would simply amplify the cramping of a lactose intolerant heroin addict.

Ruth swiftly retorted, "Heroin gives you cramps too, but you can't seem to get enough of it." Her words were harsh more from being weary than angry.

Ruth, showing further signs that she was not fooled said, "The only reason you are here is because something or someone scared you off the street. Your fear is your chance to do better. Take that chance."

Weary as she was, she reaffirmed her love for him with a combination of soothing but firm words, "Baby you're always welcome in my house, but when you come back from the store wipe your feet and foul mouth on the door mat. I don't want you bringing any more of that street filth and talk back in here again."

My stepfather draped a supporting arm around his addicted brother. His fingers did a rhythmic, agitated tapping on Axel's shoulder. His arm was there to support and enforce the words of their mother and not for Axel's sake at all. My stepfather's finger tapping was like a ticking clock, slowly ticking down the time to a more forceful exit if Axel did not comply. Addicted but not foolish, he slowly strolled out of the room. Our stepfather did not bother waiting to retreat from earshot before giving him a lecture to go with his lactose intolerance. From the small bits I heard the lecture was sure to cramp his style if not his stomach.

With the passing of my stepfather and Axel through the front door, the air became enjoyable to breathe again. As one, everyone in the room exhaled the last of the miasma, a chorus of the relieved and reprieved. It would be decades before I would gain the verbal knowledge to form an appropriate metaphor for the experience. Science would call me a liar, but I had experienced a black hole on the Earth. Bending light and crushing things, yes it was indeed a black hole. Unlike the black holes of the cosmos, the human variety did not have an event horizon (the point at which there was no escaping its gravitational pull, a point of no return). You could escape their pull if you unbent the light and saw them for what they truly were. If not, the point of no return was within you.

One thing for sure, he had sucked the greeting out of the room. No introductions had been made the entire time we had been in the house, not until he left. We knew, or rather my mother knew, who some of the people were by earlier inference.

This fact was punctuated by Ruth's next sentence: "Hi, I am Ruth, welcome to my home."

The calm greeting after what had just transpired was similar to being awakened from a disturbing dream by the smell of coffee or pancakes as opposed to a rough shake or an alarm clock. Her statement held no sarcasm and could not be heard as "Welcome to my world." Nor was it apologetic. She knew no other world but the one she lived in and felt no need to apologize for its existence, nor did she apologize for the behavior of others. The implied and the inferred were in agreement, "Welcome to our home, we'll scooch over a bit and you squeeze in anywhere you can." Thus, commanded The Lord and Darwin, both in agreement in a home where the Bible was read but Darwinism was lived.

Of course, our mother graciously thanked Ruth for opening her door to us and said, "Children, this is your Grandma Ruth."

The introduction granted us permission to stare. The first thing I noticed about her was what was absent. She did not wear an apron at a time when this was the standard uniform for most housewives. I had never been in a house this close to suppertime where a woman did not wear one. Apparently, she had only cooked for her husband's pleasure and lost the apron the same year she lost her husband, or rather she had buried it and her cooking skills in the bottom of a drawer the same day she had buried her husband. Her cooking was purely utilitarian now. Also absent were wrinkles and worry lines from her face. Worry was for people who dreaded the coming of woes; for her woes were like phantom older siblings that had preceded her birth. They simply had always been there. Her face had grown inured to them.

Not absent but running late and not yet in its proper place, was her wig. Her head was completely exposed, covered in multiple tiny salt and pepper plaits. Her right hand was balled into a fist, which served as a temporary wig stand. She gracefully, without the aid of a mirror, placed the wig atop her head. With a twist and two tugs it was aligned properly.

The wig brought her features into focus. It was now easy to see her face was the darker, more feminine twin to her son Axel's. Indeed, her face looked even younger than his. Along with the slightly grey plaits, the only thing that betrayed her age was a small potbelly, which seemed precariously balanced on spindly legs, bowed from riding mules in rural North Carolina in her youth. Wearing a long dress and a girdle would have made her look in her late thirties. She was a forty-nine-year-old grandmother with two daughters, six sons and now with the addition of us, six grandchildren.

Of her eight children, three of them were still living with her for various reasons. All three of her biological grandchildren lived permanently with her as well. Oddly, none of the parents of the grandchildren lived in the house. Ruth's sister and niece had also moved in temporarily.

Crowded as it was, Gwen, Peanut and I should have been more grateful for our tenancy than we were. Our singsong "Thank you Mrs. Ruth," started out meaningless and went down from there.

Years later I would feel ashamed of my ungrateful thank you. As a child it was hard to thank someone who squeezed over to make room for you in an uncomfortable place. I had not yet learned that sometimes you just thank someone for the gesture.

Our mother gave us the look, which boosted our second attempt at thank you up to something a little more appreciative.

"Thank you, Grandma Ruth," we said with more feeling this time.

Somehow calling someone else grandma felt like betraying my grandmother back in Ohio. It had only been half a day since I had seen her, and I was already having wistful thoughts of her. Before those thoughts could turn into an ache, we were bombarded with more introductions.

Ruth took our mother's introduction of us away from her by accurately guessing who each of us were. Pointing a finger at each of us in turn, she said, "This must be Grant, Beatrice and Gwen."

Three little heads nodded in unison, acknowledging her accuracy. She rapidly sped through the introductions of the remaining people in the house, starting with the adults. There was Ruth's sister Big Betty and their brother's child Little Betty. Little Betty was actually bigger than Big Betty; the nickname designated order of birth, not size. The only person I liked immediately was my stepfather's other brother Reggie, who had nothing in common with Axel or my stepfather, other than shared parents and a love for alcohol. Finally came the children whose shadows I had seen earlier at the window. Darla was the oldest at seven, then came Keith who was my age, then Earnest who was the same age as Gwen.

The adults stood and watched the children, encouraging us with their silence and stares to interact with each other. Adults, contrary to all evidence, seemed to think children just automatically and spontaneously broke out into a shared camaraderie, simply because they had youth in common. We had to build bridges over awkwardness just as adults did, only with fewer tools.

Darla, Keith and Earnest were slightly better at bridging this awkwardness than we were because they had to be. It came from growing up around people other than their mothers. They had become emotionally agile because the ground was always moving beneath their feet. For my part, though the flight had not been long, it had made me tired. Moreover, my head was crammed with anxiety, insecurities and nostalgia for my very short life back in Ohio. There was very little room left to remember the names of all these new people, albeit people I would one day never forget. I only knew how to subtract and had no concept of addition. It felt as if one plus one was trying to equal one instead of two, with this new life attempting to bury my old one alive.

I was in such a defensive mode that any approach, be it curiosity or a simple invitation to play, would be viewed as an assault on my existence. So, when Keith touched my shirt, regardless of his intentions I pushed him. It was not as if I disliked him personally, although time would prove us to be completely different people. I was willing only to interact with my internal dialog and my past, not this unpleasant present.

A tiny, childlike tussle ensued which hurt feelings more than caused bodily harm. My mother was appalled and perplexed by my behavior. I never acted like this, but new conditions bring on new behavior. At five years old I did not have the skills to say, "I am feeling stressed. Give me a moment please, I need time to absorb all of this." Admittedly, even had I been able to form the words, I would have not been granted the time. Not in a house where necessities were often considered luxuries.

Grandma Ruth snapped her fingers at Keith and me, with the last snap ending in a gesture towards the hall.

"Both of you go sit on the steps in the hall and figure out how to use syllables instead of fists," she said turning away, assured we would do as we were told.

Anyone who could snap and flourish their fingers as she did was to be obeyed. It was one of the rules of childhood. She turned towards my mother and sisters to further the introductions into some type of relationship. Keith led me to the stairs with his index finger held to his lips, suggesting silence and a truce. We were comrades in punishment, thus in a way we were furthering our relationship as well.

By rights he should have been angry with me. I had started the fight and he was being punished for my actions. Anger was not a good option for a child in a house where you could never be alone with the emotion you wanted to have. There were always the emotions or situations of others ready to intrude, and adults' anger was always bigger than yours. Almost as swiftly as his anger had formed, it was replaced by fear. He did not seek to correct the injustice done to him, instead he remained small and quiet in the hope justice would not take note of him and mete out worse.

We sat there for several minutes with him periodically gesturing at me to be silent although I was not speaking at all. Finally, I grew tired of being hushed and spoke.

"Why are we being so quiet?" I whispered. He gave me a look meant to intimidate, but as a child he could not display intimidation very well on a face full of fear.

He leaned close to my ear and whispered, "I don't want to be sitting on these steps when Uncle Axel comes back. If we are really quiet, maybe we can go back into the dining room."

It now occurred to me that when Axel came back from the store, he and my stepfather would walk down the hall. Keith and I would be separated from everyone else and we'd be the ones closest to the volatility of an addict going through withdrawal.

The adults tended to act calm, as if everything were under control, but children are the honest pulse of a house. Keith was my closest peer, so his reaction was my gauge, thus his fear became my fear. Sadly, fear and not a toy was the first thing we shared.

We sat there trying to make our quiet, loud enough to be heard. Sometimes too much quiet brought adult attention swifter than a loud ruckus. Parental behavior can be as predictable as that of a child.

Sure enough, within a few minutes Grandma Ruth yelled from the dining room, "It's too quiet in there, what's going on?"

In unison, we both said, "Nothing."

"Well there better not be nothing going on in there," she retorted. Her voice lowered to a whisper, talking to someone else. It must have been my mother because I recognized her whispering back. My mother had not yet found her footing in this new home. Therefore, she was more of a witness or an advisor than an authority figure.

We were straining to hear any hint of clemency when Grandma Ruth's voice returned to full volume, startling us. "If you can give us ten more minutes of that nothing you claim is going on, you can come back in here."

The period at the end of her sentence cracked like the sound of a judge's gavel. Case closed. Ten minutes or ten hours, on a child's clock the second hand moves as slowly as the hour hand, tormenting us, lazily loitering on every second as it creeps around the dial. How long was ten minutes and how far away was the store? Keith's expression said, too long and not far enough. His face had the expression of a much older person, and he spoke as someone who had witnessed far too many inadequate apologies for an even larger amount of egregious wrongs. I could not yet make such a face.

My sense of torment was heightened by the fact that I could hear candy wrappers being opened in the other room. Little voices saying thank you confirmed that it was being passed out to the other children. Candy before dinner was a strange but welcomed concept, even if I could not partake of it now. Keith's expression hinted that the candy was just an advancement on an inadequate apology or no apology at all, a mere bandage offered to stanch the wound from a beheading. My emotions were now split between fear and want. Though I was sitting, and my emotions divided, their combined weight caused my legs to wobble.

Suddenly I heard a familiar voice say, "You can give it to them, but they can't eat it now."

I also heard a crunch as one of the children bit down on a hard piece of candy, scattering shards of flavor across their tongue. It was certainly my preferred method of dispatching candy. The determination of the crunching told me that it was Gwen. The sound was part of our punishment.

Reggie, one of my stepfather's younger brothers, stepped into the hall with a small bag of candy. I thought he was going to gives us the candy, then leave.

Instead, he sat down on the steps next to us and said, "I have never been in a plane before. What was it like?"

It had been less than two hours since we had landed, so I could go into detail and did, anything to keep him sitting on the steps with us. I was stalling for time and he was helping by asking detailed questions about everything. After the fourth question I realized he was staying until our time was up.

We were interrupted once when Grandma Ruth asked, "Why are you taking so long?"

To which he responded, "I am making sure they don't eat the candy."

He added a wink for our benefit. At that moment I knew our guard was our friend.

Reggie had a way of disregarding the wishes of parental figures at the right moment. He reminded me of my Uncle Lee in that way and the similarity buttressed my courage. I could live in a place where there was someone like him.

His kindness had elevated his stature. Had I described him before his intervention on our behalf, my description would have done him an injustice. A fleeting glance of him revealed nothing out of the ordinary. He was built like a blade of grass, thin and supple, tall and reaching for the sun on good days, low and hugging the ground while patiently waiting for the sun on windy and stormy ones. Atop that was a warm pleasant face that flirted with handsome without actually being so. You would only find beauty in his face if you lingered. Once noticed it was unforgettable; you wanted to live in it. It was as if his face had four walls and a roof. The colors of it were all earth tones, rich browns with pleasant angles that somehow had the gentleness of curves. Any future spouse would look upon it and call it home. Others would call it a sanctuary. His eyes reminded me of stained-glass windows or mosaics but not for their color. Although the shades of brown varied depending on the amount of light or emotion in them, he didn't have colorful eyes. It was that his eyes told sad stories in a beautiful way. Sometimes the story told was your own, reflected back with the sympathy of a kind narrator.

Keith asked, "Uncle Reggie, how long will the drawls be this time?"

Reggie answered, "The withdrawal will last about three to five days, depending what drugs he took."

He corrected a word I thought I knew with one I did not. Before I could ask its meaning, Keith, ignoring the correction, moaned, "Why does he have to do the drawls here?" Keith's tone sounded more annoyed than afraid.

Before Reggie could answer, Keith sighed, "He always does it here."

"Because he is family," Reggie said in a tone that people bearing a cross always use. Keith sucked his teeth but went silent after that. "Because he is family," meant the same in this house as it did in mine. It was the formal polite way to say, "Shut up."

I was grasping at anything familiar to make my transition to this life easier. Adults behaved poorly in my small town as well, but it was well cloaked. In Bellefontaine, adult life was almost a secret society. They only left it to tend to your needs, to play with you occasionally, or to discipline you. You were never invited into that society or allowed to see any of its proceedings until you became older. When I became an adult and accidentally cursed in front of my grandfather, he responded with a bout of swearing of his own and a sly chuckle. He could curse like a fleet of sailors. I was shocked, because growing up the harshest phrase I ever heard him say was, "Hell's Bells."

I remember him responding to my shocked expression by telling me, "I knew you would learn curse words eventually, but I wanted to be able to say you never learned those words in my house."

This was a tale of two houses. In this house no adult's bad behavior was shielded. You saw what you saw with no explanation given. The only consideration you were given as a child was that the adults did monitor their swearing if they thought you were within earshot, sometimes. This was not cruel. It was merely preparation for the world you would inherit.

"Because he's family" kept resonating in my head, but it wasn't my family yet, so the "Keep quiet" was not meant for me. I was emboldened by the fact that during the introduction everyone else was given a handle to pair with their name: uncle this, cousin that. Axel was just given a dressing down; no title or handle preceded his name.

"Uncle Reggie," I paused as much to see if I got his attention as to marvel at how natural it felt to call him uncle.

My next words did not feel so natural. I didn't know if I should use the word Keith used or the one Uncle Reggie used to correct Keith's. Maybe it was not a correction. Maybe it was a grown folk's word not to be used by a child. Any question asked using a grown folk's word would not be answered, so I chose a safe word within a bold question. "What is the drawls?"

Keith's failed guffaw quickly degraded to a giggle, a guffaw being a grown folk's word of sorts, its limited use enforced more by biology than stricture.

He said, "You don't know what the drawls are?" I responded by shaking my head. "It's not that bad," Keith said trying to sound brave at my expense.

"Hush, boy, stop pretending you're brave," Uncle Reggie clipped. He continued, "Keep it up and you can help Axel upstairs to the room."

There it was again, no handle or title to his name, just Axel. The threat instantly stripped Keith of his thin veneer of courage.

I barely heard "Yes sir," before it faded into silence.

With Keith no longer permitted to lord his knowledge over me, it seemed there would be no answer to my question. I mistook Uncle Reggie's long pause for an adult's prerogative not to answer any question. It did not occur to me that his pause was reflection. How do you tell a child what heroin withdrawal is? There were no first-grade primers for my new life. An inner-city basal reader or nursery rhyme would read quite differently from its national counterpart.

See Jack and Jill run up the hill. See Jack sneak away to buy heroin. Jill sees Jack passed out in an alley. See Jill lock Jack in a room. Hear Jack convulse for four days. Interesting read but not the norm, nor was there a basal reader for the life I wanted to lead. My Dick would have never let Jane be so plain. He would have applied better makeup and given her higher hair. "Oh Jane, what were you thinking?" There were only basal readers for the type of life I would not live nor want.

Uncle Reggie's dilemma was not softening his words, it was making them understood. He could easily have had me defer my question to my mother or more likely my stepfather, as my small-town mother no doubt knew little more than I did, or he could not answer it at all. To his credit, Reggie did answer my question. "Withdrawal is when your body has a temper tantrum because it doesn't get what it wants."

He smiled at my puzzled look and laughed when I asked, "Adults have temper tantrums?"

"Yes, we do," He said with resignation in his voice, "Adults and addicts have the worst temper tantrums of all," he shook his head, acknowledging a truth he did not condone.

His answer spawned twenty more questions but before I could ask what an addict was, he said, "Axel is going to get real mean for a couple of days, but he'll be too sick to be mean to anyone but himself."

Keith blurted out, "As long as you don't go upstairs." He covered his mouth with both hands, no longer trusting it to stay closed of its own accord.

Reggie did not contradict Keith, but in a low voice he did answer many of the questions showing on my face. A whisper sometimes can be more memorable than a shout; it lures you in and invites you to pay attention. We leaned closer and had to strain to hear him. The statement was not formed for a child's ears. He did not stoop down to bring the words to our level; we had to reach up and grasp the understanding on our own.

Nevertheless, I completely understood what he said. "Bad things come and go in life; there is no stopping this."

As he said this, he never lost eye contact with the front door, "What matters is how well you greet and bid them farewell. Don't get too familiar with them and don't let them stay. Keep them moving. If they won't move, then you do."

Before the words he had just spoken could cool to room temperature, the front door flew open and in walked Axel with my stepfather fast on his heels. The milk at the corners of Axel's mouth gave him the appearance of a rabid dog. Keith and I loosely translated Uncle Reggie's last statement as permission to move swiftly away from a bad thing and we fled to the dining room, leaving a clear path for Axel to retreat to his asylum on the third floor.

CHAPTER 7   SHIVERING ROSES

The adults, with the exception of Little Betty and Axel, had gone out to eat Chinese food, leaving Little Betty to mind Axel and feed six children. Apparently, none of us children had reached the age required to have Chinese food. Although Little Betty appeared to me to be an adult, she was only seventeen years old. She was not asked to take care of us, she had to, but to care for us well, she had been promised two carry out boxes of Yat Gaw Mein, also called yakamein. The fact that it was called ole sober by the drunks helped make it off limits for children.

What we had been served instead was not particularly unusual. Cereal for dinner was actually quite appealing, especially since it was one of the popularly advertised sweetened brands we rarely could afford back in Ohio. Back home, cereal came out of a boiling cauldron in three types: corn mush, wheat mush and oatmeal that was usually mushy. The witches from Macbeth would have been envious of my Grandmother's recipe. I hated warm cereals.

My eyes grew big at the site of the colorful, sugar coated, geometrically shaped cereal as it poured from the box and tinged into our bowls. Each of us snatched a piece between our fingers and thumbs, holding them up to the light, examining them as if they were precious gemstones. To us they were more precious. We each snatched a few more pieces and gulped them down before our hands were swatted away by Little Betty.

She admonished us, "This is dinner, not candy. You'll wait until I finish pouring the cereal and get the milk," as if pouring milk over that much sugar could make it a healthy meal.

Little Betty served supersized portions long before the term was in vogue. The box emptied out over Gwen's bowl. Little Betty then tilted the box over and circled around the table. Over each bowl she tapped the bottom of the box twice sending a light dusting of crumbs to garnish our meal. When she finished pouring, our bowls were heaping with color and sugar.

Little Betty liked to eat. Her figure had gone a little beyond buxom and was headed more towards plump. She had a nondescript face, but I distinctly remember her smell, which was not the cloying cheap perfume common for women of the time. She smelled like a bakery, or rather more like an open box of fresh donuts. She worked part time in a bakery, but the smell stayed with her full time. It was my glutinous dream come true, a plump person smelling like donuts pouring enough sweet cereal for two bowls into one.

Our colorful bowls stood in stark contrast to the drab kitchen. The walls were a color not found on any color wheel; only wear, tear and the smoke from cook fires could produce such a color. The kitchen, as with the rest of the house, was akin to living at an archeology site. There were several areas on the floor where you could see through several layers of linoleum down to the original wood floor. Each layer had a story it would not tell. You knew only that others had come and gone before you. The house was a permanent and lasting place, which stood as a silent witness to the nomadic life of those who had slept lightly within its walls. It endured the fate of being better than the places the nomads had fled but not good enough to be the final destination for any of them. They were grateful for a time, but they always moved on, saving their true love for another place.

I soon lost interest in my surroundings. When it came to food, I had tunnel vision. With the exception of Little Betty's hand opening the bottle of milk, which sat close to my bowl, I could see nothing but my food and utensils. My hearing failed me as well. In a house that creaked twice for every step taken, someone should have heard him coming. Perhaps without a soul, he lacked the weight to cause the floor to creak. His feet whispered across the floor towards us. A sweaty masculine hand snatched the clear bottle of milk from Little Betty's hand.

The adults had left Little Betty behind for a reason. She did not flinch or show any signs of fear. She stood with her hand on her hip, a gesture of power handed down from one generation to the next, with its use generally restricted to adult women. If anything, she relished the confrontation. It was kind of a rite of passage that she could use the gesture on a grown man.

She didn't attempt to wrestle the milk from Axel. Little Betty just stood and stared at him, daring him with her eyes to do something stupid or violent. Little Betty's name was a misnomer. There was nothing small about her. Axel was outmatched because of his weakened state. Besides, food and the kitchen were Little Betty's realm. She could not lose here. He had gotten the milk only because he was fast and needed it, but she would contest anything else.

Axel slouched over the table with the bottle of milk halfway to his mouth. He paused. His stomach was saying no to the milk, but folklore and its false claim of mitigating the symptoms of withdrawal was urging him on. His body couldn't keep up with the withdrawal; it was always one step behind. He was sweaty, yet shivering as if he was cold, and his lips were chapped from the constant heating and cooling of his body. The dead skin on his lips, now moist from the sweat, hung in ragged sheets. He rolled his lower lip a tiny bit into his mouth. Using his teeth, he clipped a piece of dead skin off and spat it toward the floor. Instead of landing on the floor its trajectory arched towards the table. No one saw where it landed but everyone assumed it landed in their bowl.

Our fear turned to revulsion. A casual meal had now turned into a game of Russian roulette. Whose bowl and which spoonful would contain the dead skin? We grimaced and pushed our cereal away. The more-hardy among us fingered the cereal aside looking to rid it of the unwanted flesh. No one wanted to bite into a piece of cereal that squished instead of crunched.

Perhaps if one of us had found the skin, the rest of us could have eaten their meal in peace, but before our search could begin in earnest Axel decided to chug the milk down. I assumed the time it would have taken to get a glass was too much for a body, which at this point, was all impulse. Just for a second he had the courage to down the milk into a stomach that was in full revolt, but he couldn't drink much milk in that time. He used most of that second just to tilt the bottle to his lips. By the time the milk hit his tongue, his courage had faded. His throat constricted, halting any foolishness on the part of his mouth. The milk hit the back of his throat but had nowhere to go but back up into the bottle. Watching the backwash bubble back into the bottle canceled any of our desire to eat. To make matters worse, after he pulled the milk away from his mouth there was less dead skin on his lips. Where did it go? Surely it had gone into the milk. If the milk was poured on our cereal now, it would have too much of Axel in it.

Little Betty snatched the bottle from his hand and rubbed her thumb around the rim in an attempt to clean it. The gesture was not lost on any of us. We were still expected to consume it, but to us it had become nothing but a bottle of poison, full of contagions that would turn us into junkies in a perpetual state of withdrawal. No punishment or threat could make us pour that milk over our cereal. Unfortunately for us it was the only milk in the house, so it was that or nothing. Hungry as I was, the thought of having nothing had more appeal than a bowl of tainted cereal.

Little Betty was highly annoyed. She had to watch six children, none of them hers. She had to babysit a sweaty addict, and her yaka-mein was running late because the adults had probably sat down to eat Chinese food instead ordering it to take out. Two boxes of yaka-mein were insufficient payment for the task at hand.

Little Betty's patience was waning. She cast her face up and mumbled a prayer. She had a worried look on her face that could be mistaken for fear by the imperceptive. If there was fear, it was the fear of what she might do to Axel. I was young but could interpret the situation. I strongly suspected her prayer was asking God to intervene on Axel's behalf. It was one of those prayers that also served as a warning. Most of it was in a low voice and unintelligible to all but her and God. The last words, the warning part of her prayer, confirmed my suspicion, and they were crystal clear. She lowered her eyes and stared into Axel's, now sure that she had his and God's attention.

Her words came forth through clenched teeth and pursed lips, not the usual form for a prayer, "God you know my nerves is bad, please keep me from killing this man in front of these children. Amen."

Axel flinched or twitched, either from the words or from a body that was betraying him. I could not tell. Neither could Little Betty, but she wanted to be sure it was the words. She paused for a few seconds to give a respectable distance between her prayer to God and her forthcoming secular threat to Axel. She no doubt also used the pause to compose a proper euphemism to shield our ears.

Little Betty soon ditched any attempt at euphemisms and went for the spelling, and I knew spelling meant swearing. An assured expression flushed across her face as her threat softened to a warning directed specifically toward Axel, "I am putting you on notice. Don't start no S. H. There won't be no I. T. What you start I will finish."

She put the milk down on the table to free both hands in case she needed to throttle Axel and drag him up two flights of stairs. Although she had on a short sleeve dress, for theatrics Little Betty made the gesture of rolling up nonexistent sleeves on formidable mahogany arms. She loosened the top button on her dress and removed her earrings. It was almost like watching a boxer doing a striptease.

She was ready. Her stance begged the question, "You think I'm playing?"

Axel could not fight on two fronts. With his body already at war with itself, he could not afford an additional confrontation with an outside force. The lines of communication from his brain to his feet must have been cut because he had trouble moving them. Little Betty sensed this and swiftly moved in close and crowded Axel's space to get him moving back upstairs. She didn't touch him. She just crowded his space and he'd give ground. She'd crowd his space some more and he'd give more ground. She kept on crowding his space until he was in a slow retreat to his bed on the third floor. Slow because between his sheets and beneath his pillows waited nothing but nightmares.

She guided Axel out of the kitchen and into the dining room, at which point she stopped crowding him. Little Betty stood in the door between the kitchen and dining room with most of her back toward us. Since Axel was out of sight, I could only guess his reactions by Little Betty's actions. Her body was angled such that we could see she had changed tactics and herded Axel by nodding and pointing with her chin. He must have hesitated near the foot of the stairs because she gave him three quick successive nods of the chin. When this didn't work, she walked into the dining room to light a fire under his feet.

My attention was snatched back to the kitchen. Darla, the oldest of among us at seven years old, picked up the bottle of milk and started pouring it down the kitchen sink.

The two years in age difference made her the only one tall enough to reach the high sink. She was also the boss when no adults were around. In this house, age and muscle determined who had seniority. Darla had both, at least over us.

Darla was an awkward looking girl with a great deal of potential. It was not that she was uncoordinated, she was not. It just seemed as if her limbs, head and even her hair could not reach a consensus and grow at the same rate. Each was taking its own sweet time and separate routes to adulthood.

Her hands and feet seemed too big for her arms and legs. She had the adult hands of a worrier; her nails were bitten well below her fingertips. Her feet were always one size ahead or behind what she was wearing. By the end of most summers, her baby toes had usually worn holes through the sides of her canvas tennis shoes.

Darla's brown oval face was too large to have such delicate features. She had beautiful, small, almost almond shaped eyes and a little, well-shaped nose, which were overwhelmed by too much forehead. Her scalp was rather stingy with the length of her hair, so she did not have enough to have bangs. There was barely enough to scrape together to make three small plaits, which had been greased flat to her head instead of adorned with colorful barrettes.

She was made to feel ugly when she was not, or rather I should say she was not ever made to feel cute. No adult ever used the word ugly, but they never used the word cute to describe her either. She noticed the omission and lived with it. She had no knowledge of her future beauty. It was far away, waiting for her on the other side of puberty, and boys and men would be the first to notice. The only hint of that future was her smile. She had such a big, beautiful smile, although very little to smile about, yet it was worth waiting for when it appeared.

Darla had that smile on her face as she began to spill the milk into the sink. Except this smile had a hint of mischievousness at its corners.

She answered the confused and frightened question on our faces and said, "You know they'll only give it to us tomorrow if we don't eat it tonight."

What she did not share with the rest of us was that by tomorrow morning we'd be hungry enough to eat the cereal with the milk. It was a given that we would be sent to bed without supper.

In that respect, this home was similar to my home back in Ohio; you did not waste food. It was practically an addendum to the Ten Commandments. Thou shall not waste food. Back there my grandmother used to make must-go soup. At the end of the month she would make a soup from all the ingredients in the refrigerator or pantry before they went bad, thus the name must-go. It must go before it was wasted. I soon found out how the homes were not similar.

"Why don't you pretend you dropped the milk on the floor?" I suggested.

Apparently, in this house, by accident and on purpose were not measured separately; they carried the same retribution. Darla shook her head and kept pouring the milk down the sink. She huffed and said, "Because I would have to clean up the mess and we'll still have to go to bed hungry." She stressed the word I.

She gave me a look that said, "You never had to work on an empty stomach?" I actually shook my head to the unspoken question, feeling bad that my poverty had not been as bad as hers.

"You flew here on a plane," her words were muffled by the last of the milk gurgling out of the bottle and down the drain.

She brought the empty bottle back to the table and finished chastising me. "So, you don't know nothing."

An hour ride in the sky was a luxury back then. In addition, seeing us pull up in a limousine made us seem rich and spoiled, two adjectives you would never use to describe most people from the West End of Bellefontaine. Although Darla was very mature for her age, she didn't pick up on the fact that our temporary luxury was mere boasting on the part of her uncle, our stepfather. We had made such a grand entry into such a bleak place. In any case, we had landed, and her poverty was now our poverty. In a curt way, she was letting us know she would be our tour guide through this experience.

We could still hear Little Betty coaxing Axel up the stairs. She was so focused on Axel she had forgotten about us. Darla pulled her cereal bowl back towards her and picked out one piece at a time. She'd hold it up to the dim light above the table, roll it between her fingers making sure there were no Axel additives present. Then she'd pop it into her mouth. Her pace quickened. We all followed suite. We had to search and eat as fast as we could before the sentence was carried out.

Little Betty came into the room and caught us after I had eaten about ten pieces. Darla confessed to the spilt milk. Whoever said, "Don't cry over spilt milk" must have been rich or had an abundance of cows. Our cries and pleas of germs, ick and yuck fell on deaf ears.

"So, you think y'all are going to sit here and eat that cereal like it's candy. Not on my watch," she snorted.

Little Betty, muttering something about ingrates, grabbed a handful of Peanut's cereal and tried to put it back into the box. She couldn't put the cereal back in because her hands were too big for the opening, so she stuffed the handful in her mouth. After chewing a bit, a puzzled look came across her face. She brought her finger and thumb to her mouth, using them like tweezers to remove the odd texture from her mouth. She shrugged and said, "Must be a hair," and flicked it down the sink. The older children grimaced, while the younger ones giggled. All of us at the table suspected that it was not hair.

Instead of pouring the cereal back into the box, Little Betty poured it into a very large glass jar with a lid on it to help keep the roaches out. There truly is a God because roach footprints and a piece of Axel's lip on my cereal would be too much seasoning for me ever to eat again.

On one hand, I was grateful, but on the other I was desperate. Ten pieces of cereal wouldn't hold me through the night. She hadn't actually said we had to go to bed without supper, but we all knew the penance for wasting food was a night of hunger. It was such a given that my question shocked everyone, even myself.

I exclaimed, "Can't we have some of the Chi-east food?" I could not pronounce Chinese.

Little Betty looked at me as if I had blasphemed. From the expression on her face, I thought that I would be chastised for questioning a writ that had been inscribed into our DNA, if not stone. It was madness to question such things. Her concerned expression shifted to mirth.

She chuckled and said, "You must have altitude sickness from flying so high. You ain't thinking right." She chuckled some more, sure that this must be the reason.

She didn't address my madness. She chose instead to address my ignorance. "Baby!" She said, "You aren't old enough to eat Chinese food. That's grown folk's food."

It was as if our kitchen had one of those signs you see at amusement park rides, the ones that say, "You must be at least this tall to get on this ride." Except ours would say, "You need to be this tall to eat this type of food." At the time I didn't know what Chinese food was, but having it put onto the list of grown folks' food made it suspect. Oysters and alcohol were on that list and I beseeched God nightly in my prayers to have liver and onions moved there as well.

Almost as if reading my mind, Little Betty said, "You wouldn't like Chinese food anyway." She didn't know how amusing her face looked, condemning a food she obviously lusted after. Her lips actually smacked with anticipation after she said the words "Chinese food," as if the words had soy sauce on them. She could practically taste them as they were being pronounced.

Little Betty continued speaking after smacking her lips one more time. "Stop stalling and go upstairs and go to bed. "Besides," she said with some sympathy in her voice, "You'll want to be lying down when you're hungry. It's better than standing and sitting. Trust me, I know."

Although her body revealed no signs of hunger, her face had the expression of someone who could sing "The Missing a Few Meals Blues." Hunger as a learning tool had been used on her as a child as well. Even as a young adult, she and Big Betty had skipped a few balanced meals to balance the budget.

Her expression also said she did not want to do this. She was adult enough to enforce the rules but too young to change them. I sensed that she would've rather swatted us on the behind, then taken us to the bakery where she worked and given us day old donuts.

My suspicions were confirmed when she said, "I will try to bring some donuts for y'all tomorrow. Fresh ones!" It was a kind act, but the anticipation would make our hunger greater and the night longer. Axel through the night, donuts in the morning.

She said with a smile, "Morning will come quick if you'll let it."

Darla was more patient. She could tell time, while the rest of us could only feel it. She was pleased and gradually built a smile from a frown. It started at the corners of her mouth. First one tooth would peek from behind her lips to scout ahead and make sure it was safe for the others to make an appearance. Once assured, her mouth suddenly unzipped, and a flash of white enamel dominated her face.

This was the first moment I remember witnessing a cautious smile. There had to be a reason for it, some rules governing its use, and there were. Baltimore would force me to adapt such a smile. There were always people who were eager to wipe a smile from your face, just for the pleasure of it, or because they couldn't make one themselves. Sometimes a smile could be an invitation to nefarious people, who sought out smiles like vultures circled carrion. There were so many unspoken rules, most of which were learned only by breaking them. I smiled primarily because Darla did, yet I had many questions imprisoned behind that smile. I also smiled because I knew a frown could cancel the promise of donuts, of anything. A frown was being ungrateful.

Little Betty led us upstairs. It was a typical Baltimore row house: the layout and rooms on the second floor were almost identical to that of the first floor. The hall upstairs had the same wallpaper as the downstairs hall. With the exception of the kitchen and bathroom, if stripped of furniture, you couldn't tell the difference or the functions of any of the rooms. The rooms were what the furniture told them to be.

At the back of the second floor was the large bathroom, which was directly above the kitchen. It, as well as most of the house, had the smell of a cheap cleaning product that poorly mimicked the scent of a pine forest, or rather I should say a pine forest after a fire. All the adults smoked. The smell of cigarette smoke could only be dampened, never extinguished.

The room facing the street was just above the living room and had a full bedroom set of furniture. Our luggage was in this room, which was normally Grandma Ruth's room. She would be sleeping on the couch in the living room because she had given it up to the newlyweds with three children. Except, my sisters and I would be sleeping with the other children.

Centered in the middle of the house above the dining room was the bedroom where all the children were to sleep. As with the other rooms, the only lighting was a high wattage bulb with no shade or ornamental fixture to soften the light, just a bare bulb not properly centered in a cracked ceiling. The light glared off the high glossed walls, painted a shade of green favored by 1950's hospitals and mental institutions. The room had all the mood lighting of said institutions. After the bathroom, it was the most sparsely furnished room in the house. I sensed more than saw a dark window that faced south onto an alley. On the west wall opposite the door from the hall was a single dresser. Above that was a lenticular picture of Jesus. Viewed one way he was being crucified, viewed another he was carrying a lamb.

There was only one bed. One bed for several people was not all that unusual to me. My sisters and I sometimes slept in one bed back in Ohio. However, this bed had no frame. A misshapen mattress, so flat it could easily be mistaken for a carpet, lay on the floor. From a child's point of view this proved quite practical for two reasons. No monsters could possibly hide under such a bed, and as there were six children sleeping on what I would guess was a queen-sized mattress, someone was guaranteed to be pushed off or fall off during the night. A one-inch fall would do no harm.

Further inspection revealed the mattress had not yet been covered with a sheet. It was slightly soiled with burn marks from cigarettes and a few small yellowish-brown rings of urine or worse. Tuffs of white material that resembled cotton bolls poked out of several holes. I feared there might be boll weevils even when I didn't know what boll weevils were. I remember them being mentioned as a scourge that plagued cotton by some older people from the south. Scourge didn't sound festive and weevil sounded too much like evil. The weevils replaced the monsters under the bed.

Little Betty and Darla hastily covered the bed with a material so thin that it looked more like gauze than a sheet, which made it seem as if they were dressing a wound rather than making a bed. Maybe the bed was wounded; burned, infested and stained with forensic evidence as it was. The sheet provided very little comfort and did little to protect the sleepers from the mattress. If any bed required you to wear pajamas before entering its questionable arms to slumber, it was this one.

My new cousins were already disrobing and preparing for bed. None of them had pajamas. They were just wearing their undergarments. Back home, we only did this in the summer. This was April. Until that moment I had not noticed that there was a slight chill in the air. It was only uncomfortable if you stood still or took off a layer of clothing. All the excitement and fear had been keeping me warm, or at the very least distracted from the chill. I really wanted to wear my pajamas, but I was slowly learning the unspoken rules, this one fortunately without breaking it. You didn't want the others to feel bad for what they did not have. I started to take off my clothes too.

As adults we forget how often as children we communicated nonverbally. Our vocabulary was small, yet our experiences defied its size. Peanut wanted her pajamas. I could see it in her eyes and the way her fist tightened like a padlock around the top button of her dress. She was halfway to defiance. Little Betty seemed reasonable, but defiance had a way of dispatching reasonable when any adult was confronted with it. I rushed to cover Peanut's mouth with my hand. She did not like being manhandled, but I gave her a look that said this was serious. Although we had found common cause with our new cousins at the dinner table, these people still were strangers.

Peanut rarely listened to any words from my mouth, and as my vocabulary grew, she would listen even less. Words can be manipulated in ways that have nothing to do with the truth. From her point of view, if my lips parted even slightly, I was lying. A flash of fear or warning across a face is older than any known human language and more reliable. It could be a false alarm, but it rarely lied. This unspoken warning is what convinced her.

Peanut was not happy about it. She roughly pushed my hand away from her mouth but undressed as slowly as possible. Her young, supple fingers trudged over each button, moving as if they were tired, gnarled, arthritic and in need of a medicinal ointment. The expression on her face held all the indignation of that of a sour faced repressed spinster, one forced to disrobe in front of an obstetrician to quell rumors about her potbelly. She was still undressing by the time I finished helping Gwen undress.

If the vaguely rectangular bed had not been so misshapen, we would have lain across it lengthwise, tucked in like sardines in a can. Foot and headboard barely had any meaning on a bed without a frame. Instead it was catch as catch can for all but the two youngest, for which a spot in the center of the bed had been saved. Darla lay down on the north end of the bed closest to the wall on the E. Eager Street side of the room. Keith chose to sleep on the south end. Unfortunately, I chose the east, drafty end of the bed closest to the hall door. Both Darla's and Keith's feet were facing my direction. After seeing Keith's jagged toenails, I thought it more prudent to lie with my head towards Darla's better-manicured feet, thus decreasing the likelihood of losing an eye. Since she had been dawdling, Peanut had to sleep on the west end of the bed under the moody picture of Jesus.

Little Betty watched us squirm, shift and settle into comfortable positions before she draped two blankets over us, not that this provided us with a double layer of protection from the chill. The blankets were meant for twin beds, so each blanket covered only half the queen size bed. Heads poked out from under the blanket where they could gulp a mouthful of air, then retreat back under to try to sleep. She wished us pleasant dreams and walked back downstairs.

Comfort eluded me. It just could not be found in such a cramped bed, so I settled for bearable. Bearable meant using Darla's ankle for my pillow, at least for as long as she permitted it. I had part of the blanket folded away from my face to get air, but this left me facing the lenticular rendition of Jesus. Except from this angle I could only see the crucified Jesus, not the one holding the lamb. If I stretched my neck a bit, I could see a blurred image of both but never just Jesus holding the lamb. Tonight, I needed the Jesus holding the lamb.

The longer I stared at the picture, the more I began to think it was not Jesus but one of the thieves or malefactors crucified with him. A picture of Jesus should not send a shiver down my spine. No, it was Jesus; there was the crown of thorns. Despite my fear, I wondered what plant the crown of thorns was made of. Guessing roses, I returned to my fear.

Few things at night scared me as a child as much as a portrait

68

hanging on a wall, particularly this one without a smile that stared and wouldn't break eye contact. Even when I closed my eyes, its eyes bored into me as if my eyelids were made of glass. Of course, my mind inferred all kinds of thoughts to go with such intense eyes. I felt as if I were being reproached for silently complaining of the cold draft at my back and shamed for not realizing comfort is a relative state. The draft at my back was preferable to splinters and lashes.

As penance, I felt a sharp pain on the top of my foot as if an iron nail were being driven into it. I whimpered out of fear more than pain, "Forgive me."

"For what?" I heard two confused childlike voices ask.

"Nothing," I replied sheepishly, realizing the nail driven into my foot was neither iron nor for penance. It was made of cartilage and was accidental. Keith's toenails would leave scratch marks but no stigmata.

There was no shout from downstairs telling us to be quiet. We were out of sight, so we were out of mind. Instead of the soft cooing sounds of sleeping children, there was only the rumbling and gurgling sounds of stomachs busy digesting nothing. My stomach was now pleading with my head for an explanation for its empty state. We gave up all pretense of sleep and began to talk. I was glad to be distracted from reading the mind of a portrait.

Darla's voice was more curious than envious. She asked, "What's it like to fly? Did you see any angels?"

I had assumed the question had been directed at me. Peanut chimed in before I could answer, saying she had seen angels on her side of the plane. She began to describe a celestial version of a playground, angels in swimming pools, on swings and seesaws. Her listeners had some doubt, but far more faith pushed aside the doubt. None questioned that winged beings could enjoy swimming, swinging and seesawing when they could fly.

Darla lifted her ankle from under my head and used her toes like knuckles to tap me on my forehead to get my attention. She said, "Did you see any angels playing?" Her question was asked in a manner that suggested she wanted an answer that deepened her conviction and not her doubts.

She wanted her beliefs vindicated and I wanted to save face and not be out narrated by Peanut. I said something along the lines that the angels on my side of the plane were playing hide and go seek, being angels, they were very good at hiding and I found not a one, but I knew they were there. I even convinced myself. Satisfied with my answer, Darla flexed her ankle two times to stretch the numbness out of it before offering it to me as a pillow again.

We continued to talk in low whispers. At first, we talked just to take the edge off of being strangers, but the conversation soon became informative. Darla told us that we were only going to live with them for two weeks.

At the age of five, I could only measure days and weeks by the habits and rhythms of the people around me. Back home, Sunday was the one day both my grandparents did not have to work. We always had supper together on that day. If my assumption was right, we would be moving in two suppers and two days. My few little interactions here thus far had made me leery of assumptions. This morning's flight had landed me on unstable ground. I didn't know what things I didn't know. Was Sunday the same here?

In all sincerity I asked Darla, "Do you have a day called Sunday in Baltimore?"

She didn't laugh at the absurdity of my question and answered it with a quizzical, "Yes." She followed up by repeating the days of the week, "Monday, Tuesday, Wednesday, Thursday, Friday, Saturday and Sunday."

After we confirmed our days were the same, we laughed. We should have known better, at least from a biblical point of view. God created the world in six days and rested on the seventh day. Man didn't create time, but he was always tinkering with it or trying to redefine it. Darla said she knew that there were different times in different parts of the world. That is why she took my question seriously. The rest of us knew there was a thing called daylight savings time. You went to bed one night in spring, only to wake up with an extra hour of daylight added.

Our voices rose and fell in volume according to our level of fear of detection. Darla told us in a normal voice, "I get to stay home from school tomorrow because y'all are here." She continued, "Then we all are going over to Mister Willie's."

Before I could ask, who Mister Willy was, Darla lowered her voice with no attempt at segue and said, "You know Uncle David is really mean?"

It took me a moment to catch-up and realize the Uncle David she was talking about was actually my new stepfather.

"How mean?" I dared to query.

I was hoping for specifics. Instead I got an exaggeration. Darla said, "You watch and see. He is so mean you will never see him and a roach in the same room at the same time. They leave when he comes in a room because they know better." Keith vetted her statement from under the blanket with a steady chorus of "mm hmm."

Seeking further clarification, I asked, "Is he mean like Axel?"

"No," said Darla, "Axel is crazy and mean. Uncle David is just plain mean."

I would later learn from experience what she was talking about and why she couldn't explain it better. His anger and meanness could come from a blank neutral face or a smiling one without warning, similar to a bolt of lightning flashing from a cloudless sky. My sisters and I would often flinch for no reason when in his presence. You could never know where you stood with him, at least not from his facial expressions.

Darla did elaborate further on Axel, "Axel is crazy, mean and on drugs."

By this statement she had ranked Axel as the number one concern. Whether this was how they were always ranked, or whether this was the rank for the evening, I couldn't tell.

Almost as if speaking his name had summoned him, Axel's door creaked open. I could hear the sound of his back and shoulders as they slumped against the wall for support. He slid along the wall down the stairs. "Oh my God," I thought, "He heard Darla called him crazy and mean." We were in for it now. As one we all went under the covers pretending to be asleep, hoping he was just going to the bathroom.

When I dared peeked one eye from under the blanket, I saw him staring at the mirror in the hall in front of our room. He shot a baleful stare at his own reflection, or was the stare for Jesus? Over his shoulders I could see the picture of Jesus reflected in the mirror. From this angle he was carrying the lamb. Axel began cursing into the mirror, blaming loudly. He was definitely cursing at the reflection of Jesus. Axel never took ownership of anything as heavy as self-respect and responsibility. When he blamed, he blamed big. A problem this big had to be God's fault. He talked to God as if He had fleas and his name was spelled backwards. I was horrified at the disrespect.

Axel summoned up enough courage to turn from the mirror and directly face the lenticular. He stepped closer, pointing a menacing finger towards the picture. One of Axel's feet landed two inches from my face. The other foot scraped my back and landed on the mattress. He stood straddled over me as he further disrespected our deity. I still faced the hall so I couldn't see his ranting and raving, but I could hear him moving his twisted slobbering mouth, his spittle suffixing every word, making them fouler.

Although the heel of Axel's foot painfully dug into my back, I didn't dare move. Neither did any of the other children. We were gripped with an atavistic fear, one that rivaled man's ancient fear of the dark and the things in it. I cobbled together portions of scripture I could remember. "Our father, hallowed be thy name," anything to ward off what I perceived as evil.

Actually, I feared two things; Axel turning his wrath on us and God striking him dead with lightning. His dirty hot ashes would fall all over me. Worst, maybe God would strike us all dead. God was known to do group punishment. God in the eyes of a five-year-old was not complex.

From behind me I heard Peanut, overcoming her fear scream, "You leave God alone."

I sensed him lunging toward Peanut. Then I heard Axel sneer, "Shut up you little bit—"

Before he could finish his sentence, I bit him, clamping down tight and locking my jaw onto his Achilles tendon. It felt like I was biting into a chicken leg and had hit bone. The taste of sweat sodden wool sock and unwashed body didn't set well on my empty stomach. I unclenched my teeth before I started to gag.

Axel bent down to swat at me. At five years old I had two defensive techniques, biting and running. I had bitten, now it was time to run. I bolted from under the blanket and ran into the front bedroom. Unfortunately, cleverness was not one of my defensive techniques. I had unintentionally trapped myself. There was only one way out. Axel had followed me and was now standing in the hall with no way around him. I took some satisfaction that he was favoring his right foot as he moved closer to me. My baby teeth had done their job.

I heard Peanut's squeaky voice yell, "Leave my brother alone!" She stood in the doorway of the bedroom I had just fled. She was angry and afraid.

Axel had two choices, attack the one who challenged him or the one who bit him. He paused, tossed a glance over his shoulder towards Peanut that said, "I'll deal with you later." Peanut moved back into the room. He decided on me and moved closer, blocking my view of the hall.

Fear turned my heart into a mad musician, frantically beating as if it were a drum. In turn the heart became a mallet striking my ribcage which had become a xylophone. Each rib sounded a different note, creating a rhythm that rattled my entire body. A thunderstorm of percussion instruments vibrated in my chest. Axel lunged to the floor and grabbed me by my ankle. He stood, one hand lifting me as if I weighed nothing. Hanging upside down caused all the terror in my heart to flow into my head. I imagined myself as the child in, "The Judgement of Solomon" but in my scenario, there was no wise Solomon to judge fairly, nor a mother to plead my case. Axel would surely cleave me in half. I started to cry. The tears ran between my eyebrows, down my forehead instead of my cheeks and onto my lips where I would have suffered the further indignity of tasting the fear and salt in my tears. Although heavy, they made no sound as they dripped to the floor.

Through upside-down tears I could see Axel leer at me as he said, "So you like to bite, do you?"

He continued, "So do I, and my teeth are bigger."

He used his left hand to help his right hand shift his grip to my calf, which was no thicker than my ankle. Still holding me upside down with his right hand, he rubbed the index finger of his left hand with mocking tenderness across my Achilles tendon.

"I am going to bite you where you bit me." He paused briefly as his stomach cramped. Shrugging it off he turned his menacing gaze toward me. "Except when I bite, I am going to cut your tendon and you won't ever walk right again."

He removed his left hand from my ankle and actually patted himself on the back. Looking down at me he sucked his teeth and said, "Look at me. I failed school but I am giving you your first biology lesson."

I twisted, squirmed and prayed for help. He smiled at my torment and elaborated on what he was going to do. "When I was in prison, I saw a friend of mine cut this man's tendon. We had a good laugh as we watched him hop away dragging his useless foot behind him." He chuckled briefly at the memory of it.

"Yeah, I haven't had a laugh like that in a long time." Then he said almost pleading, "Are you going to make me laugh, little boy?"

He lowered his mouth to my ankle and sadistically paused above it. My tears were now torrential, blurring my vision, which made him look even more sadistic. Instead of biting it he kissed it. I was so prepared for a bite that the kiss felt like a bite. At the touch of his lips to my ankle, I lost control of my bladder. A wet spot in my underwear grew and raced the length of my body to join my tears on the floor.

Axel giggled but he wanted a hardy laugh, so he slapped me as I hung upside down like a newborn, except with more force and in the face. He still could summon nothing more than a giggle.

Bored with his toy he tossed me into my mother's luggage. Except for the sting on my cheek I landed uninjured. My mother's jewelry case popped open. Plastic and glass masquerading as diamonds and pearls spilled onto the floor. I swiftly grasped a strand of plastic pearls from the floor, clutching them to my throat, mimicking the gesture of a distressed woman from a suspense movie. As afraid as I was, I refused to shed even a single, right side up tear for his enjoyment.

He looked right at me or rather into me. I wished the pearls had been a frock to hide behind. I felt naked before his stare. Ugly, cruel things made him laugh and something he'd seen in me brought it forth. It was a crippled laugh, somewhat hobbled by the waves of pain wracking his body, but it was still a laugh, a mocking laugh. Making it worse, he pointed an accusatory finger at me. He said, "I can see you have sugar in you. Lots and lots of sugar."

Reflecting back on it, I was surprised that someone with his coarse nature would choose a euphemism more befitting a church woman to refer to me being gay. He had openly cursed God; as a mere child I had less standing. Yet for some reason unbeknownst to me, he briefly blunted his cruelty. His restraint was not kindness. It lacked true compassion. Still, he could have done and said worse.

He stepped closer to me, making a sniffing gesture. His sniff ended with a sneer, "Oh yeah, you are going to have to fight all your life. You better learn how to make a fist without pearls in it."

He was the first person to know and verbalize what I was. Although bewildered by his words, I knew disdain when I felt it. Disdain was a new emotion for Axel, at least as the purveyor of it. He was quite familiar with it as its recipient. Axel rarely had the chance to step on others to uplift himself. He had seen something in me he could step on, as if in my chest secretly beat the heart of cockroach. My fear vanished and was replaced with anger.

I puffed out my small concave chest in defiance. If only the pearls I were holding had been brass knuckles, and I bigger and stronger. I wanted to assault him with my pearl wrapped fist. Alas they weren't even real pearls, and soaking wet from tears and urine, I might weigh forty pounds. I still envisioned beating him into silence. My fantasy wavered. First, I would beat full disclosure from him, because I had no idea what he was talking about. If what he said was really bad, then I would beat him back into silence.

Where I had hoped to inspire fear, I instead had inspired more contempt. Axel twisted his foot on the floor as if smothering a cigarette and wrung his hands as if touching me had somehow soiled him. He slowly backed away with his eyes focused on me. His blood-shot orbs roved over my skin like a paring knife, peeling away layer after layer until the peeling felt like carving.

Angry, vulnerable, confused and curious, I had never juggled so many conflicting emotions without dropping any. They were all on equal footing. Flee, hide, fight, or query, I had a choice to make but couldn't. Suddenly my mouth declared independence from my brain and spoke on my behalf. I spat out, "What are you looking at?"

A confused expression crossed Axel's sweaty face. I added pride to my juggling act. As he contemplated my question, his drug addled mind struggled with just the two emotions of cruelty and disdain. Although an expert at cruelty, he was a little awkward with disdain, thus his earlier exaggerated gestures of foot twisting and hand wringing. He was more familiar with and preferred callousness.

His voice started off a poor imitation of a doctor delivering a fatal diagnosis. "I am sorry to inform you but—" He swiftly switched voices to that of a mean boy, "You're nothing but a little baby faggot."

He paused briefly to see what damage his words had done. Seeing little or none, he continued. "God used inferior clay to make you. You are a birth defect. Every now and then He makes a mistake like you."

I was now stunned. All of my short life I had been told God never made mistakes. If He made a mistake it was sure to be a big one. The word faggot meant nothing to me. It was the first time I had ever heard the word, but a mistake of God definitely had meaning. I knew how people treated their mistakes. What did God do with His?

CHAPTER 8   THE DEATH OF SMILES

I've heard that men mortally wounded in battle use their last few precious breaths to call out to their mothers or God. My soul was not mortally wounded, but it had been roughly handled. I whimpered for my grandmother instead, not just for protection but for answers. I just discovered that I had been born in deep water yet couldn't swim. She was the only one I knew who could help me glide through these depths.

In theory, or if I had faith, God was closer at hand than my grandmother. I had faith in His existence, but I had doubts about His kind ear. Children are easily manipulated, especially in the face of violence. Axel had put words in God's mouth, laid his hands on me. I had been intimidated from praying.

My prayers usually were more like conversation than prayer. Sometimes I would just talk to God and not ask Him for a thing. I didn't want to be one of the faithful who only called God when they wanted something, hands clasped in prayer to disguise a hand, held out. Nor did I want to be one who only whined and blamed. After Axel's statement, I felt my prayer would be accusatory or at the very least not heard.

When I unfocused my eyes from the blank stare commonly used when thinking, I noticed Axel was still at the door, neither retreating nor advancing. He stood there smug and sweaty, my pain a temporary balm for his own. Misery was certainly enjoying his company, but for a split second I saw in his cold eyes the iceberg tip of fear.

Axel's hard exterior disguised a brittle interior. A softer one would have served him better; it would bruise from blows but wouldn't shatter. I could see he didn't want to be alone with his pain, yet he didn't know how to be around pleasant company. People such as Axel would burn your soul to the ground if they thought standing on the ashes would raise them a fraction of an inch. He had to make things unpleasant. Only then did he feel fit to join in. This was not the pain of withdrawal, which would usually make him isolate. This was another pain and went much deeper. It was a pain that needed a hug but would violently shun one if offered. A soft caress and a hammer's blow felt the same to him.

Out of ignorance and sympathy my face prepared to insult Axel. Pity from someone considered lower than oneself would not be welcomed, but that was what I was beginning to feel for him. God forbid I should show it.

Fortunately for me Little Betty crested the last step to the second floor. Her voice crashed into our standoff, mincing it into pieces small enough to blow away, "Who are you calling a mistake of God?"

Her voice had all the power of thunder. The electricity in it raised the tiny hairs on my arms. Paranoia operates at far greater speeds than real time does. There was no more than a two second pause between her first sentence and her next. In that time my mind had already composed an extensive list of reasons Little Betty might smite me from the earth.

Her next question was not directed at me but at Axel. It was a leading question meant to give him an out, which he did not take. She spoke almost as if she were using her teeth to sharpen her tongue for further battle if need be. "I hope you were calling yourself a mistake of God's and not one of these children?"

Axel failed to notice the sparks accompanying Little Betty's words and said, pointing his finger my way, "That little punk bit me."

Little Betty glanced my way and said to me, "Good for you. He no doubt deserved it." Her face also grimaced slightly at the thought of someone biting a sweaty addict.

"Why are you siding with somebody you don't even know?" Axel grumbled.

Little Betty replied, "Because I know that child didn't wake up and just decide to bite you for no good reason." She paused. "Besides Axel I know you. You manipulate, twist and tell half-truths just for the sport of it. If by chance the truth ever landed in your mouth you would probably have an allergic reaction and choke on it."

"Are you calling me a liar?" Axel challenged.

Little Betty looked at him as if he were a simpleton and answered back, "I am sorry if I was not clear. Let me stress the adjectives this time for you. You are a big, fat, bad, bald-faced liar. I wouldn't believe you if Jesus were standing in your corner nodding his head in agreement to every word you spoke."

She momentarily raised her head toward the ceiling and said, "Lord forgive me for using your name in vain."

She was now in the winter of her patience. What had once been lush green fields had withered to cold hard dark stubble. There was nothing left, not even for the most determined of gleaners or wintering birds.

Axel put salt on an already dead field with his next words, "Right or wrong we are family; we have to stick together."

Little Betty mimicked grabbing his words from midair, balling her hand around them and tossing them to the ground as if they were thrash. Her voice was weak from restraint and her words were almost a whispered growl. "I will stand with you before the gates of hell and have, but I will not cross that threshold with you. That is —"

Axel not listening, cut her off. "You always say we are family but when you have a chance to show it you fail. Don't lead with your mouth. Lead by example, show me!"

Little Betty closed her eyes and tried counting to ten. To her credit she made it to three. She had become too old to be easily manipulated. From the look on her face I thought she would lift Axel by his ankle and make him cry upside-down tears.

She raised her hand high in the air to back up her words. "You say one more word to me and I will slap the heroin out of you. You won't have to worry about withdrawal then."

She waited in silence for a moment and looked as if she half hoped Axel would choose door number one, the one with the slap option waiting behind it. Except for some low mumbles and face twitching he wisely chose the door marked shut up. A fleeting look of disappointment crossed Little Betty's face, showing she had had a preference. She had arrived, to the land of the sick and tired, where normally good people do bad things, tongues come untied and chains come undone.

She lowered her hand and replaced it with stern words. Her voice scolded him. "I cared until you crippled and maimed any sympathy I once had. You put dents and dings in every second chance ever given you. Why should I give you another?"

Axel accused her of abandoning him, but she would have none of it. She continued, "That's right, everyone abandoned you. Remember this! You curse people for doing to you what you have done to yourself. You were the first one to abandon you. Long before anyone else did, you gave up and walked away from yourself, hastily dumping the responsibility for your life onto anyone who showed the slightest signs of sympathy or didn't walk fast enough away from you."

Little Betty was fuming mad. Then in an instant the anger was gone. It was as if I had been watching a volcano rumble and quake, expecting to see lava spewing out but instead out popped soap bubbles.

Her voice suddenly softened and turned to self-condemnation, "How did I get myself into a position where someone who puts out no effort gets to judge my efforts? How does someone who is never nice get to tell me I am not nice? How? How? How?" Shaking her head in shame, she replied to her own question, "It's my fault."

Axel wouldn't recognizing an epiphany if it literally slapped him in the face. He mistook Little Betty's epiphany for guilt and saw it as an opportunity to get his hooks back into her. He nodded his head in agreement. "That's right it's your fault."

Not taking the bait this time, she agreed with his agreement. "It is my fault so it's mine to mend."

Little Betty, as so many, had been a camp follower of the army of the addicted, tending to their every need. By happenstance my sisters and I arrived on the day Little Betty had had enough. She was letting him go without letting bitterness in.

She stared at Axel and said sincerely, "Goodbye. I will miss you."

Unobserved I watched two people go through withdrawals, one from a drug and the other from an addict. She didn't move or reach for a hug. She stood still before a body that for all intents and purposes had become a grave. Her head was tilted down as if paying her last respects. Her last words, "I will miss you," were meant as a belated eulogy for someone still breathing but long since dead.

Little Betty's words were twisted by coincidence. At that moment we all saw the red flashing lights of police cars reflecting off the ceiling and walls. Because she had said "will miss you," Axel thought Little Betty had called the police on him.

Axel whined, "You called the police on me?"

The old Little Betty would have gotten defensive and claimed fidelity or tried to explain the coincidence. Instead she said to the stranger in Axel's body, "How do you know they are here for you? If they are, your behavior called them, not me. It's not like you have a job to pay for your drugs."

Little Betty's new tone and the slamming of the police car's door sent Axel into a panic. "Betty please go down and tell them I am not here." He must have been really afraid because he left the little off her name.

She responded, "Why don't you go down yourself and tell them you're not here. You changed so much they might believe you."

Her sarcasm was not meant to be mean or cruel. Little Betty was just furthering the point that she no longer served nor knew who this person was.

I was surprised at Axel's reaction. He sincerely looked hurt. It was the second sign of human I had seen in him. Then he became scared and ran back up to the third floor two steps at a time. This man should have been in full-blown withdrawal and in a weakened state, yet he had leapt up the stairs and lifted me, a forty-pound child, as if I weighed nothing.

Little Betty pushed past me and stood to the side of the front window. She didn't lean out the window. She stayed to its side and projected her voice out and down towards the police. "Sirs, please be careful. There are children in the house."

Having never seen the police come to our door for any reason back in Bellefontaine, I was curious and moved to look out the window. Little Betty held out her hand to stop me. She focused all the power of a glare into a quick glance my way. I knew that look. It said, "I am not angry at you, but I could be if you don't mind me."

From where I had been stopped, I could see nothing. The sound of police voices led me to believe that none of them had approached the front door yet. The clicks and beeps from the radios also told me there was more than one car.

One of the officer's voices rose above the others. He said, "We have a warrant for the arrest of —"

If he finished his sentence, I never heard it. A downpour of obscenities fell from the third-floor window upon the police. Axel was in a rage. Up until that time I had heard maybe six curse words my entire life, and half of those came from Axel earlier that day when we had first arrived. Tonight, I heard them all, in combinations only a crazed person could conceive. The word mother was forced together with words that brought a crimson color to my face. He threatened to go to the bathroom in places I thought impossible and bid the police to do things even a well-trained gymnast couldn't possibly do. At least I hoped they couldn't.

Finally, the obscene became incoherent, sounds boosted only by anger with no intelligent thoughts attached. The incoherence trickled down to silence, which hung there, patiently waiting to be filled. The police kept their distance. No knock came to our door.

The sound of a deep voice made tinny from speaking through a bullhorn broke the silence. "Come out with your hands up." Bullhorns were intended for clarity but often caused confusion, turning the human voice into pitches and squeaks that scratched like nails on a chalkboard. The next command from the bullhorn mostly scratched at the ears with only one clearly spoken noun, something about kids.

Little Betty must have understood or inferred what was said. She didn't take her eyes from the window but spoke in a concerned voice. "Grant go back to bed."

I backed up, but once out of her peripheral vision I slowed my backward pace. I could see nothing out the window but the lights flashing off the tips of the still dormant trees in the park across the street. The bullhorn spoke again using the same language as Axel. Nothing from it was coherent or intelligible this time.

Axel gained his voice again, but every word remained garbled and without meaning. The bullhorn and he were trying to speak over one another, same language but neither listening to the other. They both raised their volumes and muffed their ears. It was a race to see who would run out of words sooner. Axel eventually lost. His voice almost sounded like the "click, click" of an empty gun.

The shouting match was over. This time I heard clearly, "If you don't come out, we're coming in."

Axel may have run out of words, but he wasn't done communicating. If I had blinked even for a split second, I would have missed it. It was as if our house had become a modern-day fortress. In place of boiling oil poured down on those laying siege, Axel decided to hurl a TV set down at them. It still had three more easy payments left on it.

I could barely tell it was a TV as it rapidly dropped past the second story window. The only telltale sign was the tin foil encrusted rabbit ear antennas. They briefly sparkled red from the lights of the police car before crashing to the pavement.

I had never heard an explosion except for on TV, but the sound of the cathode ray tube as it imploded sounded just like one of those explosions. Being young and naive I thought the TV must have accidentally turned itself on when it crashed to the ground. There must be a war movie on, I thought. I didn't know TVs exploded when dropped three floors. It was the first real explosion I heard that was not on TV but still came from a TV.

I only realized the TV was broken when Little Betty muttered, "He broke my TV."

The next few minutes seemed as if an episode of some crime drama had escaped the broken TV set. It was now playing out in our lives without the benefit of commercial interruptions. The event unfolded so rapidly Little Betty didn't have time to scold me for not returning to bed when I had been told to.

She ushered me back into the bedroom to join the other children cowering beneath the two faces of Jesus. I wedged myself between a heel and a head. No sooner than I put my head down onto the mattress did I hear the crash from the police breaking down the front door.

At seventeen Little Betty was a seasoned urban dweller. She knew you didn't want to be the first person the police saw when they broke down your door. As soon as she heard the crash, Little Betty stepped out of the hall into our room, leaving a clear path from the first floor to the third floor.

Little Betty sounded like an informant when she poked her head out into the hall and yelled, "He is on the third floor." Her words were not traitorous. They were meant to shepherd all the possible coming violence toward Axel.

The thunderous noise of the police rapidly ascending the stairs was in sync with the lurid flashing red lights of the patrol cars. It was almost as if a thunderstorm were showing the severity of its anger through the use of red lightning instead of its usual white flashes. I was afraid of thunderstorms and now one was in the house.

I could have turned my back to the hall and closed my eyes, but I didn't. Fear wanted to restrict my vision while curiosity wanted me wide eyed. They compromised. I squinted. This only made the red lightning seem more frightening, and although the eyes have nothing to do with the ears, squinting somehow amplified the thunder.

The nearer the thunderous footfalls came, the louder and more frantic grew Little Betty's chant of, "He is on the third floor."

I fully opened my eyes just in time to see three pairs of shiny shoes pass the bedroom door, heading to the third floor. A fourth pair stopped in front of our door. The sound of the hard soles clapping down on the floor sounded like a close lightning strike. I could feel the rumble of it through the bed. The shoes had been burnished as if they were made of steel instead of leather. Reflected back at me from their round tips, were twin distorted images of my frightened face. It looked as if my eyes had been replaced with those of an insect, bulging and unblinking, full of fear of being stepped on.

I craned my neck to look up to the cop. My eyes traced a crease that went the length of his pants. It continued on past his paunch, up his arm and ended at a gun. Fear of being stepped on was replaced by fear of being shot. The gun was pointed at the picture of Jesus. Did the cop see the crucified Jesus or the Jesus with the lamb? I couldn't tell. He must have been Catholic because he tilted the gun away from the image of Christ and crossed himself before it. It was a strange dichotomy. His left hand held a gun while his right hand performed a spiritual ritual. For a world that made no sense to me, it was the perfect gesture.

I could feel the other children's and Little Betty's fear more than see it. My sisters and I were being introduced to a fear common to violent households. We neither felt safe within its walls nor felt protected from the things outside. We dwelled halfway between the fire and frying pan, hoping the indecision would make the heat bearable. Little Betty definitely had not called the cops.

From the third floor I could hear Axel receiving the wages he'd earned by throwing the TV down on the cops. He was resisting arrest by hurling his face at the fists of the cops. They would make him forget the bite I had given him.

The armed religious officer at the door of our bedroom holstered his gun and relaxed his back against the doorframe. He said pointing to the bed, "I hope they are too young to remember this."

Little Betty said matter-of-factly, as if describing an obvious blue sky, "Thank you. This memory will probably be replaced by another that is worse." She was not contradicting his kind words; in a coarse way she was returning his kindness.

Suddenly the officer snapped his finger and pointed at Little Betty, "Aren't you the girl who serves me my coffee and donuts every morning. Betty, right!"

The dimly lit room and seeing someone out of context had delayed them recognizing each other.

Little Betty replied, "Yes I am, and you're coffee black, two jelly donuts. I'm sorry, I didn't mean to call you by your usual order." They both laughed. "You're Stevens," she said. "Don't you usually work during the day?"

"Yes, but I took an extra shift for financial reasons," he said.

It seemed so strange that such small talk could take place on such a violent night. Small talk is much ridiculed and thought to be for small minds, forgetting it often serves as the pause to build up courage for big talk. Officer Stevens and Little Betty viewed it as if a length of thread had been dangled from a bridge and offered as the only hope for one drowning in a deep river. They both grabbed it as if it were the thickest of ropes.

They were not friends. Both happened to have jobs that sometimes required them to wear name tags. Little Betty and Stevens were decent enough that they had actually taken the time to read the name tags. The fact they were acquaintances helped evaporate the last bit of fear out of the room.

I couldn't see his face clearly; the low lighting and red flashing lights lent the room a sepia tone. I could tell Officer Stevens was one of the pinkish, white people, only from his voice.

He said to Little Betty, "Am I that predictable? Do I order the same thing every time I come in? A man in my line of work should not be that predictable."

Little Betty gave Officer Stevens a teasing laugh. "It's a good thing you are predictable."

Puzzled, he asked, "Why?"

Little Betty answered, "Because by the time you get to the shop in the morning the jelly donuts have sold out. I always put two aside for you."

He said, pleased but confused, "Thank you." Even I could hear the unspoken "Why?" in his words.

Little Betty replied between giggles, "Well it's not a bribe and I don't have a crush on you."

They both laughed at the obvious reasons it could not be a crush. Neither took offense. There were too many barriers between them. The twentieth century was a little past middle age. It was 1964 and I was five years old. The obvious could be well hidden in plain sight from a five-year-old. Things were just not discussed. If they were discussed at all, adults would say you didn't see what you thought you saw, as if everyday life was a mirage.

Little Betty turned serious and said, "When I am having a bad day, sometimes I just pick a face out of a crowd and do something nice if I can. I picked yours one day."

Little Betty paused, then giggled and apologized. "I am not laughing at you, truly I'm not, but that day, the look on your face when you saw the empty tray of jelly donuts, Lord have mercy, you'd have thought you were five years old and had been told on Christmas Eve that Christmas had been canceled."

Stevens looked surprised, "I remember that day."

Little Betty continued, "Well I like jelly donuts too, so I gave you two I had been saving for myself. No use in everyone having a bad day. Ever since, I've always put two to the side if you are running late."

A little voice came out of Stevens that did not match his uniformed, armed status. "That was a bad day for me too. I remember those donuts well." He didn't elaborate about the bad day but said, "Is it silly to say that those donuts gave me a ray of hope?"

Little Betty retorted, "Maybe to a skinny person." They both laughed.

"Wow!" Stevens said. "You gave me your last two donuts."

Before Stevens could improperly thank her, Little Betty confessed, "Your usual order is two, mine is three. I still had one left. As I said, I was having a bad day too." They both laughed at her greediness and kindness.

Stevens tossed a glance up to the ceiling and said, "I'm sorry for what's happening upstairs, but once he threw down the TV, I had no choice." It was hard to believe that Stevens' voice was the one on the bullhorn; one frightened me the other made me have sympathy. Two loud thuds from upstairs confirmed his words.

Little Betty was adept at sifting the kind from the cruel and replied, "He's just bringing in the sheaves for that which he hath sown." She mixed scripture with hymnals. Seeing the confused look on Stevens' face, she corrected her statement. "He is reaping what he sowed. Besides, that was my unpaid for TV he threw out the window. I am just glad no one was hurt or worse."

Neither Little Betty nor Stevens was apologizing for the behavior of the others. They were apologizing for the fact they could do nothing about it. The police and the residents of East Baltimore operated on the same code. They both protected their own, right or wrong, because at the end of the day that's who they went home with and saw every day.

It was no longer a moral dilemma for many but, for individuals like Little Betty and Stevens it always would be. They were brave enough to resist conforming to the code personally when possible but not enough to confront it directly. Their bravery appeared to be cowardice to the uninformed observer, observers who are often very brave outside the circumstance or after the fact. My grandmother called it couch courage.

Little Betty and Stevens were two kindred souls who could not be friends or physically hug. Instead they had hugged each other with carefully chosen words. They reminded me of two children on opposite sides of a fence, who weren't allowed to play with each other because their parents didn't get along. They awkwardly tried to play with each other through the slats of that fence, ever mindful of the disagreeing parents.

The thuds upstairs became voices as the cops began bringing Axel downstairs. Hearing the others, Little Betty and Stevens both guiltily straightened their clothes almost as if they had been caught having out-of-wedlock sex. They smiled at each other quickly one more time before burying their expressions deep inside. What a shame, for a smile's proper place is on the face.

As one, the other children who had been feigning sleep rose to their knees and peered through the door, hoping to see Axel. He was using the two cops at his sides as crutches. The third cop had a handful of the back of Axel's shirt, to support or shove as needed. His chin was slumped into his chest. His hands were behind his back and he was wearing two steel bracelets connected by a steel chain.

Peanut stood and walked to the door as if to pass through it. Without looking down, Little Betty raised her leg to block Peanut. Steve followed suite. Together they made a fence of their own. The hall was no place for a child.

The cops holding Axel paused in front of the bedroom door to talk to Stevens. Both Axel and the cops holding him were a little unsteady. They swayed back and forth. Peanut waited patiently. When one of the sways brought them close to the door, she swatted at Axel. She missed. Frustrated, she stretched her arm across the leg fence, swatting rapidly, missing every time. She reminded me of a predatory cat, disparately sticking its paw between the legs of a fence, to catch a bird. "You were mean to God and my brother," she hissed.

Darla grabbed Peanut by the shoulders and whispered something to calm her down. Keith took Peanut's place. He sucked his teeth and pointed his finger at Axel. "Because of him we won't get to watch cartoons anymore."

I half expected Officer Stevens to take out a pen to write these new crimes down. Little Betty told us to, "Shush" in the strongest of terms.

Stevens turned to Little Betty. His voice was now officious. "I don't think you will be allowed to post bail for him."

Little Betty didn't appear that disappointed. She said, "With a busted TV laying in the street and a broken-down door to replace, it wasn't going to happen anyway." She gave the cops holding Axel the underhand wave to shoo him away.

Stevens nodded his head toward the other cop, confirming Little Betty's shooing gesture.

It's easier viewing others through a microscope rather than viewing oneself in a mirror. Axel blamed us for his plight. He lifted his chin from his chest and gave us a vicious parting smile, one that was better suited for a growling, rabid wolf, so venomous and hateful that it left bite marks on our souls. Then he was hauled away.

Officer Stevens turned to everyone on the bed. I could see his face clearly now. He had a pinkish, pleasant face. I think he was happy to see our relief at Axel being arrested. We could have been crying and begging him not to take Axel away instead. The emotion so dominated his face that it suppressed further description of any individual feature such as hair or eye color. He easily could have been the model for the smiley face, which had been created the year before in 1963. The smiley face also has no discernible hair or eye color, yet it one day would be easily recognized by most people. I could recognize Stevens just from his smile.

His smile eased up a bit as he said, "I am sorry for disturbing your sleep. You shouldn't have to see things like this, but it looks like he was causing problems for you too."

Little Betty nodded her head in agreement with Stevens. So did Darla, followed by Keith. I reached up and touched my forehead, still moist from upside-down tears and added mine to the chorus of silent nods.

Many pretend goodwill toward men for personal gain, but Stevens' words were a sincere gesture that, with time, would become startling for its rarity. My first interaction with the police, all things considered, was not bad. Usually everyone in the house was viewed with as much suspicion as the suspect and treated as such. Best case scenario you would be rudely ignored. Yet Stevens had talked to us like the frightened children we were.

He turned to Little Betty and said, "I will see you on Thursday morning. I will try to order something different to be novel."

Little Betty laughed and said, "I will keep at least one jelly donut aside just in case being novel turns out to be a disappointment." She followed Stevens down the stairs.

First Keith, then all but Earnest and Gwen got up and ran to the front bedroom window. We jockeyed for the best position to see Axel being put in the back seat of the police cruiser. The window seats held not a jury of his peers but one of his prey, his victims. A guilty verdict would be a forgone conclusion if in fact we had been a true jury. We watched from the window to make sure he was truly leaving, or we would not be able to sleep. Each child was lost in their own private thoughts.

I actually didn't feel as if I were thinking my own thoughts. The child of then couldn't interpret all I had seen and experienced. It felt as if my mind were merely making a recording to place in a time capsule to be examined at a later date by an older me. I remember the day as it actually happened, but I see it differently now.

The day had started with such possibilities and it had not disappointed. It was only that morning that the car had backed over a lump of coal, a pretend barrier to this new life. I had flown for the first time, learned to tie my shoe, searched an empty sky for angels, rode in my first limousine and gained a new family, all before dinner.

Then the day turned on me. I met my first drug addict, was punished for a fight I started, almost had cereal for dinner but went to bed hungry instead. I bit a drug addict, cried while being held upside down, was outed while clutching pearls. I don't quite remember the first day I knew I was gay, but I do remember the first day that someone else knew I was. The memory had so many companions, how could I ever forget it? In addition, I witnessed that TVs can't fly, and cops really do like donuts.

The adult also remembered something the child did not. That day was April Fools' Day. Both grandmothers held the same belief that there is enough foolishness in the world to bother with celebrating a day dedicated to it. So, I was ignorant of the holiday. I would learn what April Fools' Day was in school. Had I known about the day back then I would have foolishly waited for someone, anyone, to say, "April Fool!" and dismiss the day's events as a grand prank.

I had a child's explanation that would never permit me to tell the story purely from an adult perspective. I remember looking down onto the street. The commotion had drawn quite a few gawkers, but my mind mostly blocked them out. I was focused on the broken TV which was on the sidewalk surrounded by its broken parts, death by defenestration, a fifteenth century execution for a twentieth century device. The two little balls at the end of the antennas reminded me of beady eyes. They stared up at me. I stared back hoping it would do something.

There was a part of me that expected the cop cars to turn into smoke, reenter the TV and return to their regularly scheduled time slot. Not just the cars, the whole day seemed to belong in a venue where sponsors could benefit from the entertainment value of it. The TV just laid there; no attempt was made by the broken vacuum tube to suck back in this made-for-TV life. I imagined its last dying breath saying to me, "This is your life now."

The flashing red lights abruptly cut off and brought me back to the real world. As the last bits of Axel disappeared into the cruiser we heard, "Darla come downstairs. I need your help."

Before I could ask, Darla said, "I have to help block the door." She ushered us back to bed before going downstairs.

It was a question you only wondered about after being supplied the answer. "What happens after the cops break down your door and leave it wide open in a crime-ridden neighborhood?" The cops don't post guards. Although it was not later than eight o'clock, no locksmith would come here after dark. Darla and Little Betty had to use a combination of door stoppers and a chair of suitable height to wedge under the doorknob. You had to post your own guards.

My mother and the rest of the adults had not yet returned. They wouldn't be able to get in unless someone was manning the gate.

Unbeknownst to us, not more than seven blocks away, Little Betty's box of yakamein shared the same fate as her TV. The takeout box laid on a sidewalk. It had broken open, its contents bled out onto the street, a victim of a robbery. My mother and the others had been robbed under bright streetlights by three inexperienced juveniles, two of whom had guns. Their inexperience made them dangerous; juveniles always have something to prove. It also made them careless. The robbers took all the cash but didn't steal my mother's and stepfather's wedding rings. Instead one of them smelled the yakamein and snatched it from my stepfather's hand only to drop it on the sidewalk.

Almost simultaneously, but blocks apart, the cops and robbers faded into a still waxing night. East Baltimore's version of the welcome wagon had officially greeted its new citizens from the Midwest.

CHAPTER 9 MAKING BRICKS WITHOUT STRAW

Bits and pieces of light from the sun filtered into the room from a window facing south onto an alley. The window had three large cracks. Each crack had a makeshift ribbon of yellowed tape covering it. It was too early for sunbeams. We only got secondhand light from a sun that seemed weakened from its battle to push back the dark of last night. Its light was too frail to have awakened us. Hunger is what woke us.

Even the smell of mush would have been welcome. I couldn't smell cold cereal from the second floor, but I remembered it from last night. I was so hungry. Despite my hunger I kept still. None of my new cousins moved so neither did I. In a bed with six children, it was a mass awakening. When one awoke, we all did. Our growling stomachs were going off like six little alarm clocks. As I said, I could not tell time yet. There was no such thing as five o'clock or seven o'clock to me. There was wake o'clock and eat o'clock and right now it was both.

I heard Grandma Ruth coming up the stairs. Little Betty had gone to work already, so the task of preparing breakfast had fallen to Grandma Ruth. Serving breakfast had been her goal at first, until she saw and smelled me. Both my white underwear and undershirt had yellowish stains on them that matched the yellowish tape on the window. I slept that way the entire night. Now I was glad I had not worn my pajamas.

She didn't single me out specifically, that would have brought up too many questions from last night. She didn't have to know everything that happened. The broken door and smashed TV said enough.

Grandma Ruth looked at me and said, "Everyone needs to take a bath. Darla you get the tub up here ready for the girls. Boys you follow me." From the looks on Keith's and Earnest's faces this wasn't going to be pleasant.

Before taking us downstairs she tapped on the front bedroom door. I heard my mother's voice say, "Come in."

Grandma Ruth, leaned into the room and asked, "Carol could you pull some clothes from the suitcase for your children? I'm going to get them cleaned up."

I could barely see into the room before she closed the door. I was glad. I really didn't want to remember what happened in there. Of course, I would always remember it, but the hunger in my belly kept the memories at bay for now.

When we reached the first floor, I could see the barricaded front door. We didn't tarry. At the speed with which we moved, it felt as if we were driving a fast car through the house. The scenery seemed to pass by, blurry and indescribable. We walked through the kitchen into an enclosed back porch.

The porch floor noticeably leaned south toward a small yard. Everything in here was a tribute to Grandma Ruth's past rural southern roots. Baskets, rusted tools, terra cotta pots filled with dry dirt and dead plants were strewn everywhere. Even the decor said North Carolina. The door to the yard and the ceiling were painted blue. It was believed that ghosts would not cross over water. The blue paint represented water. It had chipped and faded over the years. This suggested she had once believed in such things, but her fear of ghosts had faded along with the paint. Real life was far scarier in Baltimore.

I didn't notice the large zinc wash tub until she took it down from the wall. It was then that I also noticed the chill in the air. I clearly remembered thinking, "It's not summer yet." A zinc tub was as close as we got to having a swimming pool back in Ohio. In summer, my sisters and I took turns pretending to swim in one. Then I realized we were going to be bathed in it. Things already small on me grew even smaller from the thought of the cold. I could have easily bathed with the girls, my gender now undetectable.

Grandma Ruth filled a stockpot three times with hot water from the kitchen sink and dumped it into the zinc tub. The water was not very deep and was rapidly cooling. She then grabbed a scrub board and put it in the tub. I feared she would grab me and rub me across the ridges of the board. Instead she grabbed a bar of soap from a shelf and roughed it up on the board to make the water soapy.

"Out of those clothes," she ordered me and Keith. She was already helping Earnest take off his clothes. We soon stood naked in a rudimentary line in front of the tub. It wasn't just me now, we all looked like sexless dolls, rendered genderless by the cold air. How small could these things really get?

I was bathed first, maybe because I was the guest or the filthiest.

At least I was warm up to my mid calves. The water steamed not so much because it was hot but because the room was so cold. Even cool water would've steamed. Earnest and Keith looked as if they wanted to cut up some carrots and potatoes, toss them in the water with me and put the tub on the stove. They were annoyed with me. My wetting myself had caused all this.

Fortunately, before my bath was finished, my mother showed up with clothes for me. While my sisters bathed comfortably in a tub made of enamel, Darla had chosen some clothes for Keith and Earnest and arrived steps behind my mother. Darla left the clothes on the kitchen table and swiftly returned to tend to my sisters.

My mother stayed to help with the boys. She and Grandma Ruth talked with more ease and less formality than they had yesterday. A shared experience such as being robbed at gunpoint tends to form bonds between people. They fell into a natural rhythm. Grandma Ruth washed. My mother dried. The boys mostly shivered and squealed.

Keith and I could dress ourselves mostly from the waist down. We needed help with our shirts. Concentrating on dressing myself, I really wasn't paying attention until I heard Grandma Ruth say, "It really isn't fair for the boys to have to bathe on this porch. This ain't North Carolina weather."

It was nice to hear our discomfort acknowledged. Keith, Earnest and I would always get the leavings. As boys, everything we did was considered training to become men. This included enduring shortages and discomfort in silence.

Grandma Ruth said, "After last night, we will have to make bricks without straw." The robbery was spoken of in the adult code of euphemisms and spelling. I would not find out about it until later.

I didn't know what a euphemism was and couldn't spell. I kept my secrets by closing my mouth. Half of last night's secrets were kept by the adults, the other half by the children. I never told anyone about what Axel said and did to me that night. The story stayed in the closet as long as I did. It hung from a hook in the darkest corner, untainted by constant retelling. If my sisters and cousins heard or remembered anything, they never spoke of it either.

Axel had his secrets as well. No one seemed to know why he had been arrested. Nor did anyone question his guilt or give it too much thought. The general mood in the air was, "This is a new day and much work needs to be done to erase the old day." Bad days were like plague-riddled corpses. They had to be buried promptly for health reasons.

Grandma Ruth continued, "The house you will be moving to is a nice place to start out. And it is not far from here." She continued with a smile, "It's half the rent of this house and the one on Barnes

Street that fell through. You can stay here an extra week and move into the new place slowly."

The look on my mother's face told me she had no idea the cost of rents in Baltimore. Nor would she ask. It would be rude and show her ignorance on the subject. She hated showing her ignorance, but she knew half of a vague price was still a deal, so she hurried a thankful smile onto her face.

Grandma Ruth pulled a shirt over Earnest's head and said, "Besides it will only be for a couple of weeks. I can give you more details if you want, but as soon as Reggie and David finish washing up, we will walk over there anyway."

We originally were prepared to stay on E. Eager Street for one month, until a house around the corner on Barnes Street became available to rent. We had to give that house up but fortunately for us, Grandma Ruth's brother Ike had found a new place. He had gotten the deposit back from the old place to put down on the new one. We could move in right away, but still planned on waiting two weeks to move in, until we could buy some beds.

My mother said, "I don't need details. I can wait." She was just about to go upstairs to help the girls get ready when they entered the kitchen. They looked well put together except for a few braids, which needed to be redone. She continued upstairs to get herself ready instead.

Grandma Ruth opened the back door of the porch and spilled the dirty water from the zinc tub into the yard. She didn't have to tell us to sit at the table for breakfast. Our empty stomachs gave that order.

She hung the tub back on a peg on the wall and went to fetch the cereal from the top shelf of a cupboard and put it on the table. From a lower shelf, she pulled out six bowls. Not one was a twin to another; they were all different shapes and colors. She pulled six spoons from a drawer. With the exception of two that differed, the rest were all mates. One had a bent handle, which she straightened with ease before placing it next to a bowl. The settings were as mismatched as the children.

The fact that she did not go to the refrigerator, told me Little Betty had given her some details about last night. She knew there was no milk in the refrigerator. I thought we would have to eat the cereal dry. Instead she went to another cupboard mumbling to herself, "Where did I put the powdered milk?"

I thought to myself that unless it was still in the cow, milk had to be refrigerated. She found it.

The unrefrigerated milk came in a cardboard container. Perhaps it came from mechanical cows? The box featured pink and white flowers, which suggested a bucolic life. I had never seen powdered milk before.

She reached into the cupboard again to retrieve a clean milk bottle and poured the milk powder into it. It looked as if she had placed the bottle under an old wizened cow with arid utters and instead of milking it, just let the dry milk spill into the bottle as if it were sand from an hourglass. She then added some Baltimore tap water, and with her hand as the cap she shook it well and presented it to us as milk. A little less water and it easily could have been used as paste in art projects. A little more and it could have been used to whitewash a fence. It tasted of something in between the two.

After eating all the cereal, I left a puddle of milk at the bottom of my bowl despite my hunger. I hated that milk. The adults ate nothing at all.

The household was penniless. This was an era when a penny still had worth and could buy you something. It was not yet the inconvenience at cash registers it would become later in the century. The older person at the cash register, counting pennies one at a time as they gingerly place them on the counter, came from this era. The annoyance directed at them comes from the present era.

My mother had carried her money with her because she didn't know better. My stepfather, as a native of East Baltimore, should have known better than to carry all that cash. Some of it had been him showing off to his new wife. The main reason was practicality. Although he had a checking account, cash still was king in 1964. Only one out of ten Americans had a credit card and women could not get a credit card without their husband's permission. David Ketchum was planning to pay cash for the furniture for our new home. The infrastructure for writing checks to pay for goods was not fully in place yet either. Banks were still giving away toasters to anyone who would open a checking account. They had to bribe the parents and children of the depression to pull their money out from under the mattress and put it in a central vault. Later the banks would charge you to use your own money. You would have to make a bill to pay your bills.

It was different for my stepfather. With a drug addict in the house, putting money under a mattress was as good as handing it over to a drug dealer. Axel would have been beaten within an inch of his life for stealing it, but he would have done it anyway. My stepfather had only enough money left in the checking account to keep it active. Grandma Ruth and Big Betty had little money to begin with. Reggie always had a job, but none of his clients had paid him yet. When the guns were pulled on him, he could pull nothing out of his pocket but lint.

It was time to thresh money from any friends and relatives who could spare it. My mother went first. She was supposed to call back home today anyway to let everyone know we were all right. I didn't know my mother as well back then as I know her now. This was a hard phone call for her. It would hurt her pride to tell them she had left Ohio only to be thrown into the middle of a crime wave.

Grandma Ruth led my mother, sisters and me to the living room at the front of the house to make the collect call. Collect calls were very expensive in 1964. As a general rule, my grandmother back in Ohio would rarely accept one.

She used to always say, "It's almost always someone calling to borrow money, and I will be charged to give them the privilege of asking. The fact that they are calling collect is already telling me they're broke." She used to shake her head and mumble, "Charging me money to ask for money I don't have. What a racket."

She was partially right in this case. The call was more about saving face than asking for money. My grandmother accepted the charges because the collect call had been agreed to beforehand.

My mother's first words were a lie, "We're fine." My grandmother must have asked how we were doing. She also must have asked to speak to us. My mother cupped the phone with her hand and gave us our lines. "This call is very expensive so only say, hi, I love you and I miss you." She didn't let us hold the phone. She held it next to our ears just in case one of us tried to ad-lib and tell the truth. Gwen went last but couldn't do her lines very well, so my mother pulled the phone away from her.

"Oh yeah, Baltimore is a very nice city," my mother exaggerated into the phone. "It's more expensive than I thought, and we've run into some extra expenses." I guess armed robbery can be classified as an extra expense in East Baltimore, listed under miscellaneous. My mother continued without directly lying, "I don't want to be a burden on these kind people so could you telegram us some extra money?"

My grandmother was not very image conscious about most things, but she was very mindful of how her grandchildren were perceived. The thought of us being a burden to strangers was the right button to push to open the cash register. The call ended with my grandmother already walking out the door to go to the Western Union office. By coincidence my stepfather was to start his new job at Western Union tomorrow, too late to get the family discount.

It was now time to hit up his family for money. We would kill two birds with one stone. We were going to visit our new house, and on the way, we would stop by our stepfather's uncle to borrow some money.

A few minutes later our stepfather and Uncle Reggie came downstairs. We bundled up because the weather was only just above freezing, unusual for Baltimore this time of year. My mother, step-father, Uncle Reggie, Darla, Peanut, Gwen and I walked out the back door through a small yard into the alley that ran into N. Eden. It was a roundabout way to get back to E. Eager because the front door still was barricaded. It was just easier than un-barricading and barricading the door repeatedly. Keith, Earnest and Grandma Ruth decided not to go at the last minute.

We walked west on E. Eager Street. There were people on the streets, but it was not crowded. I guessed it was a little after nine o'clock. Everyone who had a job or went to school was already there. My mother carried Gwen. Our group could only move at the pace of our slowest member, which was now Peanut. The cold made me want to move faster but my curiosity wanted time to take everything in. I could see my breath in the cold air and in between breaths I saw lots of brick buildings.

I had never seen so many brick buildings. Brick buildings were abundant in Bellefontaine, but its homes were mostly made of wood. It wasn't the abundance of brick homes in Baltimore but the lack of wooden structures of any kind that fascinated me.

It was as if all the homes had been built in preparation for the arrival of the big bad wolf. Despite the story I felt safer in a house made of wood than in one made of brick. Grandma Ruth had said our new home was half the rent of hers. She also said we were going to make bricks without straw. Was this because the straw was needed to build cheaper homes in another part of town, one in which we were to live? Can a straw house have electricity? The insecurity of last night led my imagination to reference the straw in *The Three Little Pigs* rather than the straw in Exodus, the book of The Bible. My fears were unfounded. The landscape of brick and stone went as far as my eyes could see.

We passed Saint James the Less Roman Catholic Church and Rectory, which took up the whole 1200 block of E. Eager Street. It was a mix of styles: Victorian, Gothic and Romanesque. It was beautiful in a manner a child couldn't quite appreciate, yet it intimidated in ways that were familiar. At 256 feet, it was the tallest brick building I had ever seen. The tip of the spire pointed directly into the sun when it was noon. It was the queen of the East Baltimore skyline. The sheer height of the church inspired me to believe there might be a back door into heaven, for people who sinned only a little bit. If so, it had to be through the doors of Saint James the Less.

In contrast to the church, across Aisquith Street stood Latrobe Homes public housing. If Saint James the Less was the back door to heaven, Latrobe Homes was the back door to hell. There were hundreds of apartments within a three by four block area. They were well built if nothing else and still clean. The buildings reminded me of boxes of saltine crackers, only made of red bricks and windowed.

We walked two more blocks on the outside perimeter of the

housing project until we came upon another church. Saint John the Evangelist Roman Catholic Church was a sand colored, stucco, Italianate building at the corner of Valley and E. Eager Street. Unlike Saint James the Less, which stood on the edge of the projects, Saint John the Evangelist was surrounded on three sides by it. It was an island of Catholicism, built in 1856, surrounded by a sea of Southern Baptist.

We turned left into the projects at Valley Street, then right onto Abbott Court. There were a few sturdy, older women busy sweeping stoops. Shoulders hunched against the cold, their sweeps were short, hurried and efficient. The elderly had a curfew, enforced by common sense. The restriction extended from sunset to sunrise. Shade swiftly became shadows this time of the year. It was wise to avoid any portions of the day where the sun cast long shadows: early morning but especially late afternoon. Long shadows could swiftly become night if you lost track of time.

Although violence primarily stalked the place by night, the middle of the day was vulnerable as well. When the old women with brooms finally passed away, there would be no discernible difference between night and day. Even now the air was so thick with menace and danger, you could cut it with a knife, dulling the blade in the process. Most people were upgrading to guns instead.

The center of the court was filled with clotheslines, empty except for one, lone forgotten sock. It hung on the line, starched stiff from the cold. Its toe pointed towards the door my stepfather began knocking on.

A woman on the older side of pretty answered the door. She didn't give us her name. She gestured us in and promptly walked upstairs, letting us know she minded her own business. As she ascended the stairs, even I noticed the curves that caused men to act foolish. Those who could, gladly thinned their fat wallets to be in her presence.

This woman didn't belong at Latrobe Homes. There were moving boxes all over the place. Except for one, lone table with four chairs in the kitchen, furniture was either draped or packed. The kitchen table had been left unpacked because it had to host one more meal for my stepfather's Uncle Ike.

Ike Carter's size made the table look cheap and rickety. He was in his late thirties, crowding forty. He was not quite as big as my Uncle Lee, but they were the exact same color, rusty reddish brown. He was almost handsome. I could imagine Ike had once been a frog and a princess had merely blown a kiss his way instead of actually giving him one. He hadn't quite changed into a handsome prince. Most of his features were a mix of plain and pleasing, all but the eyes, which still bugged slightly. I was almost surprised to see bacon and grits

96

on his plate instead of flies and gnats.

At the time I saw many people who I considered almost handsome or almost pretty. Of course, now I know that these people would be considered sexy. Although I was a child and not sexual yet, I still could see it. I just didn't know what it was, so I called these people almost handsome or almost pretty.

Ike was extremely masculine. Although desirable, his type of masculinity was beyond my reach. I had only learned to stand properly at a urinal yesterday morning at the airport. My masculinity was pretty much tapped out after that feat.

Unlike many men who were that masculine, he had his masculinity completely under control. His testosterone didn't lead him around by the nose. He didn't get tangled in needless conflicts. Despite his size, his intellect was the real brawn of his being. It was what elevated him to head much of the organized crime in East Baltimore. I didn't know it that day. I learned this over time. The understanding of him was similar to building a puzzle. I had to add a piece at a time to build the whole picture.

The first pieces of the puzzle lay on the table next to his plate. There was a Colt 45 pistol sitting where the soup spoon normally should rest. A can of Colt 45 malt liquor sat in the place reserved for a white wine glass. On the ring finger of his left hand, he wore a horseshoe shaped ring. The diamonds were set on a blue background to match the colors of his favorite football team, the Baltimore Colts. He loved his colts: the gun, the beer and the football team.

In his younger years, because of his reddish-brown skin, he was nicknamed Redbone. As he grew into his vices, people took to calling him Red Colt. Over time, mispronunciation turned it into Red Coat, which had nothing to do with his attire or the British attack on Fort McHenry.

Ike said, "How are two of my favorite nephews?" He spoke with a Southern accent and had a deep voice you could feel as well as hear. His bass tone reverberated in your chest as if it were a second heart. It simultaneously commanded and calmed.

He didn't wait for Uncle Reggie or my stepfather to respond before he stood and took my mother's hand. His hands were massive, even for a man his size. The hands of the largest women would appear dainty when held by his. My mother's hand looked fragile by comparison.

He turned to my stepfather and said, "Looks like somebody married up." His words were fluffy and lightly battered in charm, telling the truth without marring the conversation.

I liked him for that, if for no other reason. He had said in a polite jovial way what I felt in earnest. "Why is she with him?" I didn't realize my mother had three strikes against her: Grant, Beatrice and Gwen. Our mother had squandered many of her assets before she knew she had them. With three children in tow she was always playing catchup. Unwed mothers were common at Latrobe Homes and not a problem for Ike Carter. In truth he had supplied the world his fair share of unwed mothers.

Most women who loved him knew they were renting, not buying. He belonged to no one. The woman who had answered the door was the love interest du jour. He paid the bills and stayed here but didn't live here. Not much caring for the place, he was moving her to a more suitable one. After moving her up, he would soon move on. Ike never left a woman in worse shape than he found her, at least monetarily. He always gave more than a court of law would grant for a separation.

He was charming my mother without words. Ike was a rare man for his time. He liked smart women. My mother may have been in a vulnerable and weak position, but she was not stupid. Although Ike still held her hand, she waited for my stepfather to introduce her. Ike was the person David Ketchum wanted to impress the most with his new bride. Ike also would be the one to most appreciate her.

My stepfather stepped closer to my mother beaming as if he had won best in show. With a puffed-up chest, he said, "This is my new wife, Carol."

Peanut's, Gwen's and my introductions were to be separate. We had to wait so that Ike could heap praise on our stepfather's excellent choice in women. He purposely left a pause in the introduction for Ike to fill in as he pleased.

Ike said, "Pleased to meet you. I am Ike Carter."

Our mother interrupted Ike and said, "I've heard so much about you Mister Carter."

Ike had a suspicious look on his face. He turned to both his nephews and demanded, "What have you been telling this young woman about me?"

Lumps appeared in the throats of both of his nephews. After all, his line of business required silence. Before Reggie and David Ketchum could choke on their indiscretion, Ike laughed to let them know he was joking. He turned to our mother and displayed a mischievous smile that would have shamed the Cheshire Cat. He jokingly pleaded, "Please, please, please never call me Mister Carter. Oh, I can't bear such a pretty thing as you, calling me mister. All these young people rushing me off to an early grave with all their 'misters'."

Ike hated any honorifics that denoted age, such as sir or mister. At a time when young children were taught to put a handle to every adult's name, this caused a social dilemma. Adults were always addressed with Mister, Mrs. or Miss in front of their first names, such as Mister Ike or Miss Ruth. Children added Miss to the first names of married or unmarried women as well, reserving Mrs. only for when using their full or last names. Most children took to calling him Uncle Ike when they remembered. Enough misters slipped in would cause him to grind his teeth.

"Miss Carol," Ike said, being a hypocrite to emphasize his point. "Most people call me Red Coat, but you may call me Ike or Dwight."

This was an honor. Only his sisters and legal documents called him Dwight.

Ike blanketed our mother in a huge paternal hug and said, "Welcome to the family." Over his shoulder he gave his nephew a "you done good" wink. He pulled away from his new niece, looked her in the eye and said, "By the way Carol, how old are you?"

She was at an age most women would gladly respond to that question. "I will be twenty-one years old this Saturday."

Ike leaned into the kitchen to pull a glass from the cupboard. He filled the short water glass about a third of the way full, from the can of Colt 45. Then handed the glass to her. She queried, "Is this legal?"

Ike responded, "You're an accessory to at least four or five crimes just for being in this apartment with me." She laughed, but Ike was not joking.

Before she would drink, our mother turned to introduce us to Ike. He walked toward us, paused to kiss his great niece Darla on the top of her head and listened to our mother call out our names. Then he bent down in front of us and kissed the hands of my sisters and shook mine and said, "You can call me Uncle Ike."

He returned to our mother so they could finish their drinks. The small-town Midwest girl in our mother didn't want us to witness her break any law. She twirled her index finger in midair and said, "Turn and face the window until I tell you to turn back around."

Ike told Darla to turn and face the window as well. Annoyed, she turned and directed her resentment toward the window. She rolled her eyes and mouthed the words she was not brave enough to give sound to. She should have known better. Reflective windows are notorious tattletales and one of the panes told all of Darla's business.

Ike said, "Girl, you have something you want to say to me?"

Darla stiffened from the sound of his voice. She dared not speak but shook her head no instead.

The adults returned to their business. They should have known better as well. If they could see us reflected in the window, some of us could see them. Thank goodness Peanut was too short to see most of the reflection. She would have waved out of spite and probably gotten us sent out into the cold.

From my vantage point the reflections were not as clear as they were for Darla. Their images were dark, much like watching a shadow puppet show. I saw Uncle Ike's shadow getting two more glasses and handing them to shadows of his nephews. If I had been older, I would have seen the shadow of hypocrisy as well. Although our mother didn't want us to see her drink, from that day on she formed the habit of also going to great lengths to hide our stepfather's drinking from us. He was not the type of drinker who suffered brief respites of sobriety between long stretches of drunkenness. He was a moderate drinker; therefore, it was easy for her to hide the act of drinking, but he was a savage drunk. That she could not hide. We would rarely witness him with drink in hand. He wouldn't sit at our table and slowly build his way, drink by drink, to his drunken rage. He would come home already drunk and catch us unprepared but not today. Today he was only going to take a sip.

Uncle Reggie asked for water instead. He preferred cheap wine to beer, but Ike said it was bad luck to toast with water. Toasting someone with water was akin to wishing them dead.

Ike poured beer into each of his nephew's glasses, then held his can high. "Carol, may Baltimore be as good to you and your children as it has been to us."

Three shadows of glasses touched the shadow of the beer can, making a thud instead of a clinking sound, heralding in a future to match the sound. The toast was made to our backs. In some culture somewhere, it surely must be bad luck to make a toast to someone's back. If I had known, I would have defied the adults, stared the toast down and gotten another future.

Darla sent a coded message by tapping her impatient foot. It said, "We know you drank the beer so can we turn around and be ignored to our faces?" Reading the code or her mind Ike said, "Ok you can turn around now." Darla's last tap turned into a pivot toward the adults.

The adults continued to ignore us. It was to be a short visit because none of us of took off our coats. However, Ike did offer our mother a seat across from him while he continued eating his breakfast. He said, "Eating in the presence of a beautiful woman helps with my digestion."

Some beautiful women would have bristled at being compared to an antacid. Our mother didn't react as these women would have. She generally didn't rummage through compliments looking for hidden insults. She accepted Ike remarks gracefully and took the seat across from him. Her husband took the standing sentinel position at her back.

Uncle Reggie broke away from the adults to distract us and himself from a conversation he had no interest in. He began telling us an age appropriate story about a prince and princess. I would later prefer the fairytales he told when he was inebriated. Stories with titles such as "The Pole Vaulter and the Pole Dancer" could raise a crimson color to even the darkest faces. These stories had a different kind of happy ending, which at the time I didn't understand. I loved them because I knew listening to them was scandalous.

I was not interested in his sober narration but pretended to listen to his story while eavesdropping on another. I had been distracted long enough to miss my mother's first statement but did hear her say, "They took everything that we had."

Ike reached his hand out to hers to reassure her and said, "They didn't kill you, so they didn't take everything." He was not making light of the situation but acclimating her to her new world.

He addressed his newlywed nephew. "Where did they rob you?"

"Robbed?" I thought. No longer in the eaves, I all but pulled a chair up to the table, forgetting to pretend to listen at all to Uncle Reggie's story. The key was to stay unnoticed. They would start spelling if they knew I was listening.

My stepfather answered, "Near the corner of N. Gay and Aisquith Streets. We were coming home from Take Take." That wasn't the real name of the restaurant. I never knew the real name. It was called that because their yakamein was considered better than most places but cost twenty-five cents more. The name was meant as an insult and a compliment: an insult when you couldn't afford it, a compliment when you could. It was a poor man's "impress your girlfriend" type of place.

He continued, "Three kids with two guns stopped us on the corner. To tell you the truth, I wasn't expecting it. The street was not really busy but there still were plenty of people out and about. It was bold and brazen even with the guns."

Ike responded, "No it wasn't. Teenagers with guns can thin and silence a crowd mighty fast.

He scooped up some grits from his plate and paused with the fork in front of his mouth. He asked, "Did you see which way they ran?" He punctuated his question by pushing the fork of grits into his mouth. When he pulled the fork out, it looked as if it had been washed clean.

My stepfather waited for his uncle to swallow before answering, "They ran south on Aisquith Street toward Jonestown. They were probably heading toward the Lafayette Court projects where we will never find them."

Resigned, Ike shrugged and said, "If you ever find out who did it, let me know. I can't have people openly robbing my sister at gun point, nor my new niece."

He changed the subject by pointing his fork at his nephew and said, "I heard about Axel too. His girlfriend came home from work and took a brief inventory of her apartment. Axel and some of her possessions had gone missing at the same time. She came here looking for him. I gave her some advice. I told her breaking up by cop was the best way to go. She figured out where he was and must have made an embellished phone call to the police. Actually, I didn't think she had the nerve to do it."

Since my stepfather had his back to me, I could feel his distaste for his brother rather than see it. He said, "You're not going to bail him out, are you? Don't let my mother talk you into it."

"You know I won't say no to my sister, but it doesn't matter. I think the same girlfriend who called the police on him will post bail for him in a couple of days. She has a good job, a large trust fund and a lonely heart. Axel will convince her that his selfishness and theft were a misguided attempt to protect her from his depraved behavior. His pretense of pushing her away will surely draw her in deeper."

Ike paused and lifted a piece of brittle bacon to his mouth. The crunching sound and residual bacon bits falling back to his plate went straight to my salivary glands; my teeth were swimming.

My stepfather filled the pause. "He won't be given bail. He'll be considered a flight risk."

Ike snorted a derisive laugh and said, "A tick don't ever run far from its dog. Throwing a TV down on the police is the more likely reason he won't get bail. Sometimes I think that boy has nothing more in his head than a cathode ray tube, nothing but a vacuum up there. One of these days he is going to mess with the wrong person, and someone is going to put a bullet in that empty head of his." Ike sort of petted his gun while saying this. The gesture hinted that he would kill any person who harmed his nephew. Deep down inside he knew he could only avenge Axel, not protect him.

When he looked up from the gun, he made eye contact with me. I had been caught listening. Instead of changing the subject he interrupted Uncle Reggie's story. "Bring them children over here. It's too hard for them to pretend to listen to your boring fairytales and try to overhear our conversation at the same time. I have something I want to say to them."

Uncle Reggie hurriedly said, "And everybody lived happily ever after," then herded us over to stand in front of Ike.

Often being invited into a conversation is not as interesting as overhearing it. The invitation made me lose interest fast, that is, until I heard Ike say, "Axel won't be given bail, so he isn't coming home for a while."

This was the third time I heard the word bail. I remember thinking bail must be what people in Baltimore called the key to the jailhouse and was thankful to whoever was being stingy with it. Ike spoke to all of us but made eye contact specifically with Darla.

Axel was only important to Darla because he was important to her grandmother. Her real feelings for him ranged from indifference to fear. In the presence of her grandmother she would've feigned sadness but now, free to express her own emotions, she simply shrugged her shoulders in a manner that said, "Good riddance."

When her shoulders fell back into place, I let out an emotional, "Good!"

Out of context my exclamation sounded rude. My mother was horrified, "Grant!"

Darla came to my defense, "Miss — I mean Aunt Carol, Axel was really scary last night. Didn't you see the busted down door? We didn't know what he was going to do next."

Darla didn't elaborate further on the previous evening's events, for which I was thankful. She was the oldest of all the children and would spend equal portions of her time as our defender and tormentor. She still was of an age when children tried on cruelty and kindness as if they were clothing, figuring out which emotions suited which occasion.

Once assured that I was not alone in my feelings and no one was offended, my mother backed down.

Ike shifted his eyes toward me but was addressing my sisters as well. "I know it was really scary last night, but this doesn't happen all the time."

Darla sighed and begged to differ: "Uncle Ike, it does happen all the time."

Her words were trampling his reassurance into the dust. A single event can be so overwhelming it bleeds across time and we remember it as if it happened more frequently than it actually did. Ike patiently reminded his great niece that the police only broke the door down two other times. One time was for Axel and the other time was a mistake; the police had the wrong house. No matter what Ike said, Darla would remember it as happening all the time.

Losing a battle to a seven-year-old girl's perception, Ike switched to an apology, which was quite genuine. "I am truly sorry any of you have to see things like this." It was almost exactly what Officer Stevens had said last night. The other adults may have shared this sentiment, but it was the cop and the criminal who actually expressed it to us.

Ike didn't linger on our apology because he wanted to make a bigger one on behalf of the great city of Baltimore. Ike turned to his new niece and said, "It's a shame that you were robbed on your first day here. Unfortunately, that does happen all the time." Ike started laughing and said, "I was robbed not even one hour after stepping off the train from North Carolina. It's almost like Baltimore can't stand the smell of the country on you so she puts her own scent on you. She's like a mother with calloused hands and chapped lips; her hugs and kisses are rough, but you grow to love her none the less."

Ike reached for his wallet and pulled out the real apology, green portraits of former presidents. He handed the money to my mother and said, "Baltimore wants to make it up to you."

By handing my mother the money, Ike was saying it was a gift. Had he put the money on the table, and had she taken it, it would have been a loan. This was his peculiar way of doing business. No matter where he was, if the money was a loan, he would place it some place where you had to pick it up and take it. If outside, he would put it on the hood of a car, or on the steps to a building, any place that had a flat surface. Taking it was akin to signing a simple contract that said, "Pay it back or I will take it back in a way of my choosing." Interest and late payment fees varied, ranging from a visit to the hospital to a trip to the county morgue.

My mother hesitated. Ike waved his hand around the money as if doing a magic trick and said, "Carol, there are no strings attached. You have that guarded look of someone who is both relieved and scared that they left their small town. This money is to help you get past the scared part." Ike paused. "Or do you want to go back to your town where the most exciting thing for young women to do is watch the laundry dry?"

My mother looked confused. Her eyes actually did a motion that had they been her lips would have been considered stammering. They didn't bat, wink, or twitch. Her eyes traced a subtle, rapid, repetitive pattern. They tilted up to her head, searching for an elusive response, then back down into a blank stare. Up down, up down. The last tilt up to her head must have found the answer and brought it to her lips. She said, "The laundry dries quickly in Bellefontaine and then there's nothing to do. Thank you, Dwight."

Ike said, "You are more than welcome. I just wanted you to keep the robbery in perspective."

When I saw her put the money in her coat pocket, I realized she didn't have her purse. I loved that purse. Secretly it was my favorite toy, but now it laid empty and defiled in some alley in Jonestown. I was so angry I wanted to grab the gun from the table and search for the purse myself. Once it was found, I imagined the spectacle of me flouncing through the streets of Baltimore accessorized with a purse and a pistol. People might notice. I chose an alternative and said, "Mommy I think you should buy a new purse."

"Don't worry, I will baby," she said, probably thinking I missed the sticks of gum she sometimes kept there. Whenever she caught me playing with her purse I always lied and said I was looking for gum.

She confirmed this by saying, "I will buy you some gum as soon as we leave."

Ike drew her back into the conversation by saying, "When you get a new purse don't carry all your money in it. Especially at night! As a matter of fact, I'm going with you. I have to see Mister Willy anyway, to count his money for him."

He yelled to the woman upstairs, "Cora I am going by Mister Willy's to take care of some business."

Cora yelled back, "Ok Red, take your time. I still have some packing to do. You'd only be in my way. Bye."

Ike grabbed his coat from the back of a chair. He put it on and stuffed the gun into an inside pocket. He took two quick bites of bacon but left three pieces on his plate. He must be rich. I never knew anyone to leave bacon on their plate before. My stomach always ran a deficit of want and missing a meal last night didn't help. There were three pieces of bacon and four kids. I could do food math: none of us would be offered a piece. Ike also seemed to be in a hurry.

CHAPTER 10   LIFE TURNED TO STONE

If I were left to believe only what my eyes told me, I would have thought the 800 block of Forrest Street looked to be a fun place. The first thing I noticed was what appeared to be a castle. Not a castle for princesses but one for warriors. Battered and worn, it was made of dark grey angry stones and had a sharp pitched, stained roof that peaked into a cupola. Four stunted towers, tipped with small cupolas, formed a square around the roofline. A parapet wall ran the length of the western side of Forrest Street.

The walls were built strong to keep any enemy out, but it wasn't a castle. It was meant to keep people in. Darla asked Ike, "Is this where Axel is going to be sent?"

Ike answered her question while staring at the cold, stone wall. "I don't know, but jail will be better for him than the streets. Though he might not be sent to this one."

What I had taken to be a castle was actually the Maryland State Penitentiary, one of the oldest in the country. It had held onto its old ways for as long as possible. Only within the last ten years had it ceased using gallows as a form of execution. The gas chamber was somewhere within its walls. Last time it had been used was less than three years ago.

My mother didn't flinch at the revelation of this being a prison. Carol had escaped hers. She barely glanced at the walls of this one. To each their own.

We were moving to the slums of the ghetto, a very key distinction; one described the state of the buildings, the other the type of people. East Eager Street was almost a nice suburb in comparison. Most people here did not make enough money to keep decay at bay. All they had was effort, and that was not enough.

She stepped farther into Forrest Street to get a better view of the houses on the east side of the street. I shadowed her. What we saw was unusual for Baltimore. Before us stood a row of red brick houses. Instead of steps made of marble or concrete, these were made of wood. In fact, this was the most wood I had seen so far. The houses were built into a hillock, exposing the front halves of the basements to Forrest Street, thus putting the first floor of each house a full story above ground level. A flight of wooden steps was cheaper than marble.

There were eight houses on the block. Two adjacent houses stood out from the rest. One was boarded up and the other should have been. I knew the one not boarded up was ours. My mother knew it too. We both walked and stood in front of it as if we had been given the address.

Ike and both his nephews asked, "How did you know it was this house?"

My mother and I just shrugged.

Of the two neglected houses, ours looked as if a little loving care could perhaps revive it. None of the other houses had real curtains. Sheets, old newspapers, old towels, even a layer of dirt were the only options for privacy on most of the homes. In our house, spider seamstresses had spun matching cobweb curtains that clung to the inside corners of every window. A sufficient amount of dust had settled onto the gossamer curtains, enabling them to cast slight shadows when the sun peeked through the western windows.

We had claimed the house just in time. Nature had started to claim squatters' rights. Dormant vines from the previous summer had started twining their way up the first three steps. Their advance, temporarily halted by winter, would continue with the coming of spring. There were remnants of a bird's nest in the rusted rain gutter. In some parts of the rain gutter, weeds had started to encroach and then died.

Despite the broken gutters, the roof must have been in good repair. When Uncle Ike opened the front door, the house smelled of dust and wood rather than musty, dank floors. All the floors were wood. Even the kitchen floor was untouched and unloved by linoleum. The interior walls were covered in a highly water resistant and durable lead-based paint. There were no cracks anywhere on the walls.

The house was built to function in another time and had begrudgingly made room for the conveniences of a modern day that was now a couple of decades in the past. From the state of the gas stove and refrigerator, they must have come into the house about the same time that the gas and electricity were installed. The appliances looked out of place. The stove still worked but the refrigerator did not. The refrigerator was unplugged and pulled away from the wall as if awaiting its pallbearers to take it to its final resting place.

In the northeast corner of the kitchen sat the home's original and only source of heat, a black potbelly stove surrounded by a wooden crib.

Sitting on a three-legged milking stool next to the potbelly stove, stoking a fire, was our new neighbor, Mister Willy. He, the house, the milking stool and potbelly stove were contemporaries. Even with his back to us I could tell he was old, yet not feeble. He turned to his right to grab a small log, which he placed into the maw of the stove. There was no shoving, banging or cursing of inanimate objects that would not do his bidding. His ancient muscles had long ago discovered the most fluid and efficient manner to perform any task. His hands showed all the patience of many years of use. Each movement was measured and graceful.

He spoke with his back still turned to us. "I thought you would like a nice warm house to come into."

Ike spoke up and said, "Thank you, Mister Willy, but you didn't have to do that."

Mister Willy said, "And you didn't have to add all those words after you said thank you. People always add too much to their thank you these days. My name ain't on every task in the world but anything needs doing within range of my hands gets done."

What most people considered was hard work, Mister Willy viewed as leisure. He good-naturedly groused on about the evils of labor-saving devices.

Ike stayed quiet and listened deferentially to Mister Willy. It was not just the respect a younger person generally gives to an older person for being born first. There was that, of course, but there was an undertone of awe and love as well. Only great deeds garnered this type of respect. Ike stood silent and slightly hunched, as if any sign of disapproval from Mister Willy could mortally wound him.

Mister Willy stood and turned to face us. He was not a tall man and the aging process was further eroding his height. His bearing was that of a king without a country, one in exile with nothing left but a birthright and a quiet pride.

White stubble on his chin, cheeks and atop his head resembled a porcelain cup, which ringed a round face the color of dark roasted coffee with a drop of milk added. It was just as welcoming as the morning brew. The essence of life steamed off his face, reviving those in need of a stimulant. Despite the sunglasses he wore, he had a broad, brilliant smile that served as the window to his soul, a smile that could never reach his eyes, because Mister Willy was blind.

I knew it was going to happen moments before it did. Peanut has always been one of those people who whispers in a normal tone of voice. She thinks she's whispering when in fact she is simply disguising her voice by making it gravelly. Being young, she must have thought blindness and deafness came as a pair. She whispered loudly, "Grant, I think he is blind."

Our mother was appalled at Peanut for no doubt voicing what she thought.

"Young lady you are correct. I am indeed blind," Mister Willy said with a smile.

He swiftly left the subject of his blindness in the dust and began telling us about the virtues of living across from the Maryland State Penitentiary.

Mister Willy was a simple man and had no sarcasm in his voice when he said, "In addition to our block being one of the safest in East Baltimore..." He paused for effect and flourished his hands as if he were a game show host. He stood in front of a kitchen door that opened onto a back yard. His gestures hinted that behind this door was the grand prize. He opened the door and continued, "we have this."

My sisters, mother and I crowded into the doorframe for a better view. Before us lay scattered, tattered patches of grass that had been beaten brown and flat by things worse than winter. The yards were communal much like back home; no fences marked the property lines. Into half the yards, including ours, overflowed the refuge from a junkyard. Two blocks beyond the junkyard was the Latrobe Homes projects. My shrill of glee drowned out the disappointed hush of my mother and sisters.

A junkyard was a little boy's dream and a mother's nightmare. Whereas I saw a poor man's toy box, my mother no doubt saw a series of tetanus shots and emergency room visits.

Uncle Ike interrupted the grand presentation. "Mister Willy, only you and young boys would think a junkyard is a selling point."

Mister Willy retorted, "Isn't it?"

Uncle Ike ignored the question and continued, "Looks like you have a new recruit."

Mister Willy had a standing order with all the children on the block who played in the junkyard. If you brought him something useful, he would pay you in candy. Payment varied. Serving utensils or a single intact plate got you a piece of candy, usually a Now and Later. A matching set of anything got you the entire pack. Wooden furniture got you a whole candy bar.

Mister Willy would repair or clean them and give or sell them to people in need. He was the middleman for poor people who were too proud to be seen taking things from a junkyard. It was easier to say you were buying stuff to help a blind man than that you actually needed the goods he salvaged from a junkyard. He was a buffer for people who did not want to admit they were poor.

Mister Willy only kept two things retrieved from the junkyard for himself. The first were any unbroken blue bottles, which were the only things he would give us money for, usually a penny a bottle. But they had to be blue. At the time it struck me as strange that someone blind would be so insistent on a color. He would always touch the bottles to verify the color and all the young children believed he could feel color. It did not occur to us that nearly all the blue bottles were old milk of magnesia bottles, which had raised lettering molded on the bottom, easy enough for him to feel.

He needed them for his bottle tree, which was little more than a wooden post with wooden sticks protruding out from it. Onto each stick he would jab the neck of a bottle to keep it in place. Although the tradition did not make it en masse to Baltimore from the South, some of the older people still believed the bottles would trap any evil spirits trying to enter the house, holding them until the morning sun could destroy them. Mister Willy swore the tree had to be on the east or south side of the house. He feared that the sun may not reach the bottles to the west or the north in time, possibly giving the spirits time to trick their way out of the bottle. I heard several versions of this superstition, but I always liked his version the best.

I once would have the honor of finding the other item he would keep. It was a cast iron skillet that had not been out long enough to rust. Mister Willy had suspected it of being cursed. In his mind there could be no other explanation for throwing out such a perfectly good skillet. To rid the iron of its evil, he placed a metal cross on the bottom of the skillet, then filled it only halfway with cornbread batter and placed it in the oven. The cross and heat were meant to drive the evil into the bread, thus it was not meant for human consumption. When done, he retrieved the cross from the cornbread and placed it back on his neck. Then he walked back outside into the yard, crumbled the rest of the cornbread into large pieces and scattered them on the ground. This was done to tempt crows to dine as opposed to pigeons. With a junkyard as a back yard, there was no shortage of crows. Once the bread was devoured the crows would fly away, scattering the evil spirit to the four winds. For the evil spirit this was the avian equivalent of being drawn and quartered, using their favored black birds against them.

This process was much more complicated than going to the store and buying a skillet. Mister Willy gave me a nickel and two candy bars for my find. Later that day from that dark black skillet he served me the best cornbread I have ever tasted. I remember it well, as food tastes best and is more memorable when seasoned with a story.

Before I was to experience this, I had to be seasoned much as the skillet had. Today my sisters and I were to encounter the first of some of the local beliefs and superstitions. Had we not rented the house next to Mister Willy, we still would have met him. Despite being fairly well educated, Uncle Ike, as was the case with many members of organized crime, was a superstitious man. He had insisted that we be presented to our new neighbor, who would perform what most people would call a blessing, but Mister Willy called a strengthening.

I would only hear Mister Willy claimed to be a root doctor once but, having two parents who had been root doctors, he could never deny it either. The story of their deeds outlived them and journeyed up North during the Great Migration. Some said they were merely good herb doctors while others whispered that they dabbled in magic. Whispered, twisted, bent words carried the day at the expense of clear, audible, enunciated ones. Most people believed one of his parents had worked root to serve evil while the other had done so to serve good. Depending on who you talked to, some whispered it had been the mother who served evil, others claimed it had been the father. At the time I doubted the story, because I could not imagine good being wed to evil. I have since been to many such weddings.

In voices lower than whispers, another story was told, one in which one of his parents had worked root on him while he still was in the womb. Some believed it was the reason Mister Willy's father had died eight months into his wife's pregnancy. His death was not unusual, but his funeral was. Mister Willy's mother's water broke while she was grieving at the foot of her husband's open grave. Tendrils of life-sustaining amniotic fluid flowed to the lip of the grave and a few drops tumbled in, as if life were reaching out to death. Mister Willy was born not far from the foot of his father's grave and swaddled in his mother's black mourning shawl and veil. Worn for death, they had been used to swaddle a new life. The story outlived all those present at the funeral and birth.

Thus, Mister Willy had been born into this world whole of body except for his eyes. Many people believed his sight had been condemned to stay in the spirit world to set watch and warn his mother of coming events, and he was only blind in this world. No one bothered to ask why he was blind. It was considered impolite. The preference was to spin fanciful stories rather than breach decorum in pursuit of the truth. Born blind at the foot of his father's grave and swaddled in mourning clothes, people were ready to believe anything about him. At one point I did ask him if he knew the cause of his blindness. He told me it was from untreated or untreatable congenital cataracts. He was not clear as to whether there had been no cure or no money for the cure for his type of blindness.

Mister Willy's life was like an onion; the more I peeled away the layers the more I cried but not from pity. How people treated him seemed to leave no marks on him. I cried because everyday people unknowingly tried to steal pieces of his dignity, not knowing or caring that he had the fortitude to weather their cruel acts of kindness. It bothered me that people heaped pity where it was not wanted, swift to offer it instead of patience. He always suffered these people with such grace and poise, the ones who forced help on him because they could not bear to witness someone slower and seemly less efficient perform daily tasks. Mister Willy was very patient with people who pretended to be patient. In a metaphorical sense, more often than not, it was Mister Willy who helped many of them cross the busy, perilous streets in their lives.

It was this outlook on life that he tried to pass on when performing a shielding. There was no pretense that his shielding would protect you from the adversities of life. It certainly hadn't protected him, nor did he perform it for just anyone who asked. I remember him telling our mother, "Closing the door to pain also closes the door to pleasure, for they come through the same door." He needed to have you in his presence to determine that you had an inner strength. If so, he reinforced that strength with a ceremony. I remember one phrase: "May the things that damage your body and break your heart only strengthen your soul."

As an unwanted touch was considered intrusive, he would not touch us. We had to touch him. Out of curiosity, Peanut and I were more decisive in doing so. We had never seen or touched a blind person before, so we readily jumped at the chance. Gwen was cranky for some reason and wasn't having it. Mister Willy didn't interpret Gwen's fussiness as a sign of her being unworthy. He patiently waited for her to touch him. Speed was not essential.

Uncle Ike flippantly said, "I remember Axel was this hesitant and refused to touch you."

Uncle Reggie replied, "And we all know how that turned out."

Suggestion of the possible similarity of Gwen to Axel caused my heart to pound against my ribcage. I didn't want Gwen to grow up to throw TVs out the window, or worse. Mister Willy couldn't leave Gwen out of the ceremony, he just couldn't. I had to act.

"Hey Gwen, let's play tag," I encouraged. I touched her shoulder and continued, "And you're it." I knew she would frantically run around touching everyone in the room. She had some internal chronological clock, which led her to tag others starting from the youngest then working her way up to the oldest. She had her own rules. She wouldn't give up the power of being it until she touched everyone in the room. The last person would become it and that person would be Mister Willy.

She ran around and touched everyone, then stopped in front of Mister Willy, paused, then ran around again touching everyone for a second time. On the second round she finally touched Mister Willy's hand and said, "You're it."

He briefly held her hand and tapped her on the shoulder and said, "I am too old to run around, would you be it for me?"

She responded by swiftly whirling around the room tapping everyone again. It occurred to me then, the reason she chose the oldest person last was for this reason. They would often let her be it on their behalf and she could be in charge that much longer. She made three more rounds and stopped in front of Mister Willy again, a little winded and tired this time. He took her hand, held it for about three seconds and said, "I will do it."

I didn't realize until he spoke that my mouth had been frozen in a frown. Hearing him agree to do a shielding, my mouth instantly reversed direction into a smile. I still didn't know what a shielding was, but I knew Axel hadn't had it done. I didn't know what I wanted to be, but I knew what I didn't want to be and that was a start. Had my mother known this fear she could have used it to her advantage. "Axel didn't eat his peas," she could have said and watched me wolf down my portion as well as my sisters'. "Axel didn't take baths," and watched as I stayed in the tub until my skin wrinkled and blued.

I took off my coat, expecting the ritual to be grueling. Mister Willy heard me and said, "Keep your coat on young man, we are going outside."

Going out the front door I had a perfect view of the prison wall. The crest of the wall was topped in places with barbed wire and perched crows. Had I known at the time about the crows and cornbread I would have been concerned but only slightly. Mister Willy could have had me drawn and quartered by the crows as well, and I would have consented. Anything was preferable to ending up like Axel. To this day, I journey down a memory lane lined with cold grey granite, barbed wires and crows, or ravens. Edgar Allen Poe's grave was only a mile southeast of the prison as the crow flies, so maybe they were ravens come to pay their respects to Baltimore's dark, adopted son.

On the way down the steps he explained adamantly that we each had to have our own stone from the wall but didn't explain why yet. We crossed the street with very little concern for traffic, as this was not a busy street. It was quiet enough that it would be a good alternative to playing in the junkyard. When we came close to the wall, Mister Willy touched a stone about the height of a child. He told us all the stones south of his hand had been claimed by other children, many of them now adults. I looked north along the wall and saw there were still many stones left for future generations. Far too many for Mister Willy to have children touch them all. He only performed this ritual on children below the age of thirteen. As with most institutions of the time, superstitions were also sexist. While I was allowed to choose my own large stone, Mister Willy chose marginally smaller ones from the wall for Peanut and Gwen.

He made us remember our stones, then he told us the story of the stonecutter who is content with his life until he sees a king pass by along the road. He becomes envious and wishes he were king. Suddenly his wish is granted. As king, the fate of every man is in his hands, and all is well until one day his attendants forget his umbrella on a hot day. The power of the sun scorches him into becoming envious of it. His envy is indulged once again and he now becomes the sun, beaming down excessive amounts of heat, turning every bit of green to cinder and evaporating oceans into clouds. The clouds soon usurp his power, denying him access to, or influence over, the Earth. His envy is now a fever hotter than any sun. To cool his envy, he becomes the cold dark cloud, raining down far too much water for the world to stand. All were washed away, except for a stone mountain too old and strong to be bothered by the rain from a measly cloud. His soul becomes heavy with envy and falls from the sky to become the stone mountain. He reigns supreme, bending before nothing until he feels an insignificant man making him smaller, slowly but surely, by chipping away at his base. It was a stonecutter. His envy of others eventually brought him back to himself.

The king ruled the men.
The sun wilted the king.
The cloud impeded the sun.
The stone resisted the rain.
The man broke the stone.

I remember this story because of the manner of its telling. It was very tactile. I literally had been touching stone cut by a stonecutter at the time, and somehow the stone from the story and the prison wall reinforced the foundation of myself, which had been so badly shaken by Axel the night before. The stone had become a counterintuitive life preserver, which I would cling to in times of doubt, buoying my spirit instead of dragging me to the depths of despair.

The story, although it impacted me greatly, had been merely a prelude to the shielding. He explained to my mother that the shielding was not meant to protect her children from the adversities of life. It would be done in the hope that any adversities encountered would build character instead of diminishing it. This was not something to be protected against. It was much like food and water; you couldn't live or grow without it. You didn't want to become obese from it either.

Mister Willy brought his attention back to us and said, "Put your hands back on your stone." I had never released mine. He touched my right shoulder and moved his hand down the length of my arm until his hand was touching my hand, pressing it gently but firmly against the stone. His hand was as hard and rough as the stone, yet warm.

He instructed our mother and stepfather to do the same to Peanut and Gwen. Peanut got our mother and Gwen got our stepfather. He then told us, "Do not take your hand from the stone until I say amen." I had no intentions of letting go.

He began the ritual with a prayer to God. Most of what he said went over my head and was intended more for the adults. "May God protect you from the things your parents cannot," was one of the few sentences I remember from that portion of the ritual. He also asked God to give us the strength of the stone and the warmth of the sun all our days. Then I heard a soft thankful amen and my hand was pulled from the wall.

His voice raised, full of anger and authority. It clashed so heavily with his soft amen, it startled me. At the far end of the parapet one of the prison guards yawned and looked at his watch, unconcerned with what was happening at the foot of his fortress. The crows flew over our heads in the direction of the junkyard. My first thought was that something had gone wrong and we would not receive the strength of the stones or the protection of God. Surely, Mister Willy was cursing the stones for defying his pleas and the request of God.

He slapped the wall above our stones. His voice was more strong than loud. His metaphors were confusing. The stones, individually, were worthy of praise and beseeching, while the wall deserved nothing but contempt. Realization finally dawned on me. He was cursing the prison walls, which I would gather many years later were the proxy for the justice system. His tone of voice scared the memory of his words into me.

Mister Willy turned and touched each of us on the top of our heads and proclaimed, "You, wall of poor judgement, may not have these children. They will never pass through your gates. This day is the only day you will ever touch their lives. Their handprints on your wall is all that you may ever have of them. Remember them well. They will bounce balls off you when at play but only from the outside. You will shade them in summer, but you will never overshadow them, and one day you will watch them walk away from you forever. Feel what you may, sad or glad, for they were never yours."

Mister Willy spoke to us and advised, "Show contempt for the wall." He quickly corrected himself and said, "Do something to show the wall you don't like it."

This was strange to me; adults were big protectors of property rights. You could not handle most things without permission and never roughly. We had been given permission to do both. We look toward our mother for confirmation. She nodded. Peanut went first; she kicked the wall. I made a face at it and Gwen turn her back on it.

Reassuring us that we had captured the strength of the stone without being trapped by the walls of which they were a part, Mister Willy continued, "Good, now none of you will ever go to prison." We returned to our house with the knowledge that we were protected against incarceration.

CHAPTER 11   PRETENDING TO BE INFINITE

At the insistence of Uncle Ike, inspection day developed into move in day. He responded to my mother's and stepfather's reluctance: "Look, you will take another two weeks to save up enough money to minimally furnish this place, right?"

His nephew gave up a grudging nod.

Ike continued, "I assume you want your mother to continue to like your new wife, so don't tax your welcome by staying too long."

A look of concern flashed across my mother's face. Ike nodded towards my mother, so his nephew didn't miss his wife's concern. My stepfather moved to caress his bride's hand and reassured her. "Don't worry, my mother will be fine, and everything will be alright."

Ike interrupted the conversation he had manipulated into being. "Of course, everything is going to be alright because you are going to make it so," he said to his nephew.

Ike then turned to apologize to my mother. "I only made you feel guilty to manipulate your husband into doing the right thing. You have to be careful with men. They will make their family suffer to save their pride if you don't interrupt their foolishness with some common sense. My sister would probably not begrudge you a month stay at her house, but why strain kinship if you don't have to?"

My stepfather tucked his lower lip under his teeth in guilt. He was wavering. The conventions he chose to obey, he strictly adhered to. One of these was no borrowing of money.

Ike was already ahead of him and took a humorous, haughty tone with him, "You know in some cultures it is customary to receive gifts after a wedding. Last I checked you belonged to one of those cultures."

Ike was not good at hidden manipulation, or maybe he was but never favored it. Obvious was always his weapon of choice. He was a sin seller and knew human nature extremely well, manipulating you to your face. His trademark line was, "You know what I am selling you; not only will it destroy your life but the people you love too." Most still bought. He didn't have to lie, he just presented the goods and watched people overestimate their strength, underestimate their weakness and be dishonest with themselves. The very first person every human lies to is themselves. Once he learned that, Ike would never be poor again.

His family was a different story. People he loved he manipulated to their gain. As contradictory as it may sound, he used their desires against them for them. Ike used my mother again. He turned to his nephew. "Me offering you money as a gift shows your wife how in high esteem, I hold you. You can take it, or you can refuse it and show your wife how your pride comes before everything."

Ike was giving his nephew no room to maneuver. He continued, "A self-made man is very often a self-serving-man." In addition to the money he had given to our mother earlier, Ike pushed a moderate sum of money towards his nephew and asked, "Can you tell the difference or are self-made and self-serving the same to you? I suggest you take this money now because I am going away for a few months and you will not be able to get ahold of me."

A nod and a smile from his new wife pushed him into accepting the additional money. Well, almost. Suddenly, he withdrew his hand from the money and spoke to his uncle. "Did this money come from your cleaners or from the street?"

Ike put the money back in his wallet and said. "This money came from the street. Let's go to my cleaners and I will get you some clean money."

Ike had started a legitimate, dry cleaning business on E. Biddle Street before he turned to crime. From whispers, bits of cutoff sentences and careless adults who did not notice children were present, I learned Ike had gotten into crime because three amateur thugs, the type that could only intimidate shop clerks, tried to extort protection money from his business. One day he purposely waited for them to come to collect their money. Ike had a surprise for them. Waiting and hidden among the racks of clothes were true thugs, the kind that scared shop clerks and cops alike. Of his four thuggish friends, only Ike knew how to properly operate the pressing machine, which could get out the toughest wrinkles. It could also get out the deepest truth when used properly. One scorched hand later Ike and his cohorts had the nucleus of a new business. The three amateurs were given the choice of a bullet in the head or a bus ticket out of town.

Ike didn't want to keep the extortion part of the business. His partners in crime, however, did. Ike had to convince them it was more trouble than it was worth. He told them there was big money to be made from people making poor choices. He was proven right. People lined up and threw money at them for the pleasure of making bad choices.

He initially kept the cleaning business as a backup. It was an honest business and made money, not as much as making things dirty but a respectable amount. It also came in handy to aid his sisters, Ruth and Big Betty. They didn't like his new choice in business but would look the other way because he was their younger brother. Ruth and Big Betty didn't judge him but wouldn't take money from him no matter how badly they needed it...that is until he promised them that any money, he gave them, came only from the cash register from his cleaners. For some it may have been a distinction without much of a difference, but it was enough of one for his sisters.

He admired his sisters for their stance. There are many who curse the butcher yet eat the meat, in their hypocrisy often demanding the finest cuts as well. Ruth and Big Betty were not saints nor were they hypocrites. Sometimes his promise meant making an extra trip to the cleaners, but he never told them dirty money was clean.

Ike also promised not to sell drugs to their children, a promise which he kept. He couldn't promise they wouldn't do drugs. Axel went to West Baltimore to buy his drugs where there was no prohibition on sales to him.

Although Axel wasn't coming back to E. Eager Street, his drug withdrawal and encounter with the police left his presence, haunting the place while still alive. Our mother didn't know the half of it, but what she did know had made her uncomfortable. That conversation between her and my stepfather went unheard by me. We never went back to finish our two-week stay on E. Eager Street. A gradual move in had become a sudden one.

Ike said to his nephew, "David, you know you are just the middleman for this money because your wife is the one who is going spend it. She can furnish this place better than you can. So, let's take her shopping." Money came in waves in places such as East Baltimore. You rode them when you could, buying new furniture one day, missing meals the next.

Although generous, the money Ike was giving the newlyweds was just enough to keep us from sleeping and eating on the floor, maybe enough for a couple of beds, a refrigerator and a kitchen table. We would see what my mother could do. She kissed us on our foreheads, told us to behave and walked out the door with her new husband and Ike.

We were left in the care of Mister Willy, Uncle Reggie and, to a lesser extent, Darla. Not only was I not uncomfortable being left with strangers, I relished it. They were unguarded and fluid. Although I didn't know it yet, these were my favorite type of people. Mister Willy and Uncle Reggie were different sides of the same coin. Both were entertaining and informative. Mister Willy tended to tell scary stories while Uncle Reggie favored bawdy ones. One would think the natural outcome for a child listening to such stories would be for that child to become a pervert afraid of his own shadow. Most children block out the stories that don't interest them and the ones they don't understand. I remember every single one of them.

Uncle Reggie would tell stories that would not make me flinch at the time of their telling, yet I would gasp and blush many years later when I remembered them and finally understood their meaning. Mister Willy's scary stories scared you at the time of their telling and at bedtime but generally did not haunt you into adulthood. Their stories were far more than scary and bawdy. They told fables and facts of life stories, full of contradictions that somehow complemented each other. Both having great insight, Mister Willy's stories were for those who couldn't suffer the consequences of their actions and Uncle Reggie's stories were for those who could. Cautionary tales pitted against tales of caution thrown to the wind, the extremes of choices.

When I heard the door opening and saw our mother, I thought she had forgotten something, but there was nothing to forget. We hadn't moved in yet. Mister Willy and Uncle Reggie had just made the hours pass as if it were only ten minutes. They were better than anything on sixties TV, which was a good thing because at the time we didn't have a TV.

Mister Willy smelled it first. "Oh, someone has been to Corned Beef Row, and it smells like it's from Altman's." Mister Willy was pulling our leg. If Ike went to Corned Beef Row, he always went to Altman's. Corned Beef Row was the section of E. Lombard Street in Jonestown where many of the best delicatessens in the city were located, cheek to jowl. Uncle Reggie preferred Weiss Deli but was wringing his hands in anticipation. It was possible to have a preference without ever being disappointed; on Corned Beef Row second and third choice were still pretty good.

We spread out on the floor, using the waxed white paper wrapping of the sandwiches as our tablecloth. My first urban picnic and first taste of ethnic food was exciting. Baltimore had eleven public markets, some of them among the oldest in the country, but Belair Public Market near Gay Street was the only one we would shop at. It was the Noah's Ark of food. The length of a football field, it was filled with stalls selling everything from blue crab to pit beef to skinned muskrat. I would see foods with names I couldn't pronounce. Often the names sounded better than they tasted.

The food we ate in Bellefontaine may be considered ethnic food somewhere by somebody, but no ethnic group claimed it as their own. It was plain and simple fare, one in which mustard, pepper and sweet relish were considered daring condiments. We ate everything on the pig except the oink, but we ate it blandly. Our dinner table resembled a dissection table. Years later I almost failed biology class because I knew the culinary names of the organs but not their biological ones. Writing hog maws on a biology test instead of stomach would get me a red X and a raised eyebrow from my teacher. For now, I thoroughly enjoyed my breast of cow sandwiches from Altman's Deli.

Uncle Ike had connections. By the end of our meal, a rickety old truck, which must have detoured through the dust bowl en route had trundled across our neighbors' back yards to parked in front of our back door. The clean cardboard and plastic covered refrigerator and furniture looked misplaced among the dust and rust of the bed of the truck. Two burly men in crumpled clothing exited the truck. I recognized one of the men. He looked like Mister Big Name, the man who picked us up from the airport. This version of him had the honesty of a hard day's work about him, someone you could have in your house unattended without having to take inventory upon his leaving just to confirm nothing was stolen. This was not Mister Big Name. It was his older brother, Sam. The brothers owned a livery service together. The business consisted of a limousine, a truck and two horse-drawn wagons. Each task finds its master. Sam handled the sweaty, dirty, gritty end of the business, including the money. Mister Big Name was the smile of the business. He told stories and drove the limousine.

I never ever saw Mister Big Name again, but I saw Sam all the time. Sam was most familiar to me sitting in his brightly colored horse-drawn wagon. In Victorian London they were called Costermongers. It was sixty years past the Victorian era, yet Baltimore still had hundreds of these street peddlers selling wares from the back of horse-drawn wagons, and here they were called arabbers. It was not quite a year-round business. Sam mostly drove his wagons during the warm months. Summer was for selling produce. During portions of winter they could be seen hauling anything from appliances to coffins. A few weeks before Christmas, one of his wagons could be seen piled high with toys and festooned with bright ornaments.

Although not on a person, the first time I actually saw drag was when one of Sam's horses was made up to look like a reindeer. She even had a drag name: Queen Pinky. She had glitter covered cardboard antlers attached to her head, which looked more akin to a cheap tiara than antlers. The antlers drooped slightly from the weight of too much glue and glitter. Although young reindeer do not have them, white spots had been painted on her haunches to give the illusion of youth. When fed carrots she ate with such gusto she frothed at the mouth, raising concerns that there was a rabid reindeer among us. She had a form of vitiligo. On horses it is called Arabian Fading. It left her nose and the right side of her face pink. Unlike Rudolf's nose, Queen Pinky's nose could only guide Sam's wagon until dusk, no night driving for this makeshift urban Santa Claus. It was bad drag at its best, a bit cheap and bedraggled, yet somehow festive. In addition to her pink nose, under her bright shiny coat, she was three shades of crimson from embarrassment, because no amount of makeup can turn a nag into a young mare. But if you squinted until your eyes were almost shut and you had a vivid imagination, you could almost see her as a reindeer. She was the lead reindeer because she was the only one. Alas, Queen Pinky would never grace a Christmas card, nor would any of the other reindeer be seen with her in public while sober, but she would be my first reindeer sighting.

It was just past Easter and far from Christmas, yet Sam was the first person to give us a present. Instead of shredding the box the refrigerator came in, he carefully scored the bottom of it and slid it off the refrigerator. He tipped his greasy hat with greasy fingers and tossed the box to us to play with. It was alternately a castle, a boat, a tank, a house and when we got bored of it, a punching bag. Sam didn't shred the box because he knew how much fun we would have shredding it. When finished, the pieces were tossed mere feet into the waiting junkyard, almost like putting our toys away. We moved to the junkyard to continue our play. Refuge made the best toys and it opened our eyes to the possibilities of the junkyard.

We were wedged between two places full of broken things, a prison to our front and junkyard to our back. It was the beginning of a childhood of learning to appreciate broken things without becoming one of them. My sisters and I played house with chipped teacups and dirty, orphaned, amputee dolls. We pretended to mine gold by shifting dirt through old window screens and played hide-and-go-seek among the coiled, rusty, skeletal remains of mattress frames. We played ball with the castoff baseballs of the inmates, either hit over the wall by them or thrown down to us by the guards. What are crumbs to some is bounty to others. The first playground I would go to seemed meager and impoverished by comparison.

We would generally play in the junkyard until the setting sun or our mother's rising voice called us to dinner. With the number of adults present and the sparsity of furniture, moving in and assembling only took an hour. Thus, my first day's catch from the junkyard was only a blue bottle for trade with Mister Willy and a little fire truck with three wheels.

I was about to bundle up my new treasures to take into the house when Darla stopped me and said, "You're not going to take those into the house are you?"

"Why not?" I responded.

A seven-year-old city girl is a seasoned sage compared to a five-year-old country boy. With contempt and pity she explained, "Your father is not going to let you bring something dirty into his nice, new, clean house." She paused. "Everything is a show for him. It has to look right and respectable even if it really isn't."

Seeing the confused expression on my face, she elaborated. "It's like if you smile when you really want to cry, or like playing hide-and-go-seek when you were real little and you covered your eyes and thought no one else could see you because you couldn't see them. Everyone knows, they just pretend with you. Your father will demand that you pretend with him."

Unbeknownst to me at the time, Darla had just given me crib notes on the rest of my childhood. In sympathy she suggested that I hide the truck. "Peanut, take Gwen into the house and tell the grownups we will be there soon," she commanded.

Darla hastily built a toy garage from some of the broken bricks that had collapsed into the junkyard from an adjacent abandoned house. It was simple, built much like a house of cards, but instead of cards she used six bricks. Our little makeshift firehouse stood out too much. We scurried around the heaps of refuse seeking a tarp or blanket to cover it. Almost giving up, at the last second Darla turned over a coffee can that had spent the winter turned upside down. In it was a faded, crumpled newspaper, still legible for those who could read. I could not and Darla barely could. The picture was clear enough to recognize as Jackie Kennedy in a black veil on the front page mourning her husband.

I had a vague memory of seeing a similar image on TV not quite five months earlier. Recollection is fickle; the paper that jogged my memory became my memory. Well into adulthood my image of Jackie Kennedy would be that faded, crumpled newspaper draped over a makeshift firehouse built of broken bricks that housed a three-wheeled fire truck.

Ignorance was the sovereign over my life. The only way to learn was to show my ignorance. I confidently said, "Wasn't her husband the president of Ohio?"

Darla laughed and replied, "Silly, he was the president of the world."

"Then I was right, that makes him president of Ohio too," I answered defiantly.

My first instinct was to defend my ignorance, then never bring it up again. Geopolitics was way beyond me. I had a city state view of the world, a concept that grew only as I did. I remember holding onto my chair for dear life when I first found out in school the world was round and spinning and trying to throw me off.

Darla waved her hand in the air, dismissing my ignorance as if it were a pesky fly, she would let nowhere near her. She continued onto to something more important. "You can bring the toy into the house after the first time he gets drunk. If you pretend he wasn't drunk the night before, he will pretend the fire truck is new and came from the store. Just make sure you do it after the hangover."

My mind was racing behind a blank face. I knew drunk happened when you drank too much beer, but I had never actually seen anyone drunk. What was a hangover? It didn't sound good.

Darla read my blank face for what it was, confusion. She dispensed her knowledge as if it were alms to a beggar, charitable but with pity attached. My mind was a greedy open palm waiting for more, pity or not.

Darla said, "Hangovers are like withdraws but not as bad. Just be really quiet and don't turn on lights and you should be fine."

It appeared the only way to get luxuries under my new circumstance was to be brutalized; afterwards you were given a guilt gift. It would have been nice to know the going rate: three hits got you cake; being thrown against the wall got you a Saturday matinee; being dangled upside down and called "faggot" got you a corned beef sandwich. It was all so random.

My desire to play with my fire truck and my fear of more violence were fighting for ascendancy in my head. Fear had the edge. At the rate I would be biting drunks and drug addicts, I would be toothless and malnourished in no time.

I trudged towards the house dragging my fear behind me as if it were a cape. It trailed me into our new house, biding its time until it would transform into a hangman's hood. The real me would be muted, blinded, unheard and unseen. Holes for my eyes and mouth occasionally would be cut in the hood by my stepfather so that I could witness the birth of his lies and speak them to the world. Usually the lie was just a nod of my head and shameful look away from inquisitive eyes. I could never quite say my mother was clumsy and fell down the stairs. Within his lie I would tell my own. To get my passive aggressive dig in, sometimes I would say, "No she didn't fall down the stairs," pausing long enough to cause concern in my stepfather. I could not say the lie he said. I would say she tripped going up the stairs. Few would question how the stairs and floor could have left marks in the shape of handprints.

If doubt lingered too long in someone's eye a sickeningly nice voice with undertones of menace from my stepfather would force a smile to my face. Just as his tongue was stuck on a lie so was my smile stuck on fake. It took as much effort to put on my face as if it had been carved from stone or ice. I had to be careful never to let the thin line across my face become a frown.

Our mother would usually take up the lie and push my sisters and me aside to spare us any more violence in case we flubbed our lines. She would laugh clumsily about her clumsiness. Even when there was no one to lie to, we sat at the dinner table as if in a hurricane, huddled in the eye of the lie, waiting for more and rehearsing each line. Our home would become a prison, trapped between a prison and a junkyard. Mister Willy had had us put our hands on the wrong prison.

CHAPTER 12 JUNKYARD TOY BOX

Although we had played in the yard the first day, the next couple of days we were not permitted to go outside and play, especially in the junkyard. Our mother needed an adjustment period. Everywhere she looked she saw tetanus. She was particularly concerned because one of her great uncles had died from lockjaw. He died long before she was born, but the fear of lockjaw would be handed down from generation to generation almost as if it had been a genetic trait.

My inability to grasp medical knowledge led my mother to give me a simple but brutal explanation of the disease. You get a dirty cut, your jaws lock shut, and you starve to death. Old Greedy Guts, a nickname my sisters would give me in a few years, was traumatized by the thought of not eating. My mother's story ensured that I came running to her with any cut or abrasion so she could apply the stinging reddish brown liquid to it; better to sting than to starve. She always had at least two bottles of Mercurochrome in her purse.

Fear of the disease led me to have lockjaw practice. I would cut my meat as small as possible or take a bean and push it between my clenched teeth and pudgy cheeks, using my finger to slide it down the side of my teeth until I found the space where my wisdom tooth would one day be. The space was large enough to let the meat or bean tumble the rest of the way down my throat. I did not want to starve to death. Instead I almost choked to death. I found out the hard way you need your teeth for a reason.

Frankly, I was fine being in the house the first couple of days. Our mother spent most of those days trying to make the house pretty. Most boys would be a hindrance trapped in a house with girls and a woman making decisions on frilly things. I loved frilly things, because I was a frilly thing. Even at such a young age, poorly designed homes disturbed me.

The biggest challenge in the house was the bedroom I would

share with my sisters. The room was garish and brutal. Its bright colors stabbed at the eyes repeatedly. Long after turning off the lights or leaving the room you still could see the striped wallpaper. It was as if a dust mite had blown into your eyes; blinking several times or rubbing them briskly was the only way to cleanse them. Except it wasn't really wallpaper. The previous tenant could not afford wallpaper, so they had painted yellow and purple stripes to deceive the eye.

It reminded me of a cheap French bistro in Paris I would one day dine in because I didn't know better. It was the type of place that would have pictures of the food it served in the window; it had a menu in twenty languages and served your food in English. If the food didn't give you indigestion, looking at the walls surely would. Painting the walls with Mercurochrome would have been an improvement and a good choice, for the walls had been wounded.

Our mother decided to paint the walls white. To keep us busy while she painted, she gave us a box full of worn-down crayons and one of the garish walls to draw on. Peanut drew such a good drawing of a palm tree that we protested greatly when our mother went to paint over it. We squealed and squawked until she relented. She painted a square around it to make it look like a framed picture. It would have looked eclectic had it not been two feet off the floor. Instead it looked like what it was, a mother giving in to the whims of her children.

Saturday finally came. This was the day we were released into the yard. April 4th was a cool day made cold by the wind. It was also our mother's birthday. She was now considered an adult by law. Three children and now a husband had made her a de facto adult long before this day. Her birthday was our birthday. We enjoyed it more than her because she did all the work and we had all the fun.

Our stepfather was new at Western Union, so he had to work Saturdays. She straightened his tie and sent him on his way. She turned her attention to us and said, "You have been playing by that smutty stove when I told you not to."

Our silence was as good as a confession. We only used the cast iron stove at night to heat the house. By the morning it was cool enough to use as our base to play hide and go seek.

She had already moved past jury on to judgement and the sentencing. "Y'all don't want to listen. Well now you are going to have to have two baths, now and one tonight. I am not letting you play in that junkyard looking like trash."

The number of tears we cried was a bath unto itself. Our tears were witnesses for the prosecution. Their tracks exposed lines of clean skin down our faces. We looked like overly made up ladies bleeding our mascara over the dearly departed.

She wiped the grey teardrops from our faces. "Mommy would like a little cooperation today for her birthday."

Peanut's stance and eyes said, "Well you ain't getting it, so ask for something else."

At this age, Peanut hated bathing more than anything. My mother would have had more success getting a cat into a tub full to the brim with water and dogs than getting Peanut to take two baths in one day. Gwen and I would cry but eventually acquiesce. We could bathe together and more or less sat in the hot water as if we were two old stewing hens. Half the time Peanut had to be bathed by herself to prevent a bath from becoming an accidental drowning. She would become a pinwheel of flailing arms and legs. The calm surface of the bath water would froth and churn as if a fierce hurricane had decided to take a swim beneath the sea, transmitting all its anger through the water.

Our mother had no time to give four baths, so she dropped the tempest into the tub. Before doing so she said, "If you don't settle down, I'm going to give your brother and sister your piece of cake."

Gwen and I instantly pulled away from Peanut to give her plenty of room to act the fool and hang herself. She could see in our eyes that we were already dividing up her portion. Gwen would get the cake, I the frosting. Peanut and I were close but not that close when it came to cake.

Greed and gloating combined, I taunted Peanut with her real name, "Since Beatrice is not having cake can me and Gwen have bigger slices too?" My two-faced smile was meant to tempt my mother into generosity and goad Peanut into losing more of her portion.

My mother grew impatient with negotiating away pieces of her own birthday cake because of one stubborn and one greedy child.

She said, "This is how it is going to go. You get a quick bath now and go outside and play all you want. Then have dinner and a big piece of cake and the usual Saturday night bath later. Or I will let you out of this tub right now. You can sit in the house all day, no going outside and no cake and you still get the usual bath later. Your choice."

Our mother was the queen of Hobson's choice.

I turned to Peanut and said, barely hiding my gluttony behind disingenuous concern for her comfort, "It's kind of cold out, maybe you want to stay inside."

My mother splashed water in my face. "Hush boy!"

Peanut said, "Ok wash me first."

I chimed in, "Me second!"

As our mother dried Gwen last, she said, "Look how dirty that water is. That's why I told you not to play near that stove."

The tub water was the color of black tea that had steeped too

128

long. I could feel shame and guilt struggling to be born but it was a stillbirth. I knew I was supposed to feel these emotions but didn't really care how black the water was. I lowered my head and cast down my eyes to appease her. After all it was her birthday and if she wanted me to feel shame and guilt, I could at least pretend to feel them for her.

We still were not allowed outside. The wisdom of the time said you had to wait an hour before going outside after a bath or you would catch your death of something. As I waited for my pores to close, I began to feel guilty for not feeling guilty and faking it. A shame-and guilt-ridden child was considered a sign of being well-raised. Instill guilt so that it could be used against them by their elders and later by manipulating strangers. If nothing else, I did want to please her. I just didn't see the need, even at that age, to feel bad about it.

There was a big junkyard out back; I was sure I could find something for her there. Although my grandmother's birthday was in early October, I could always scrape together some flowers that defied the coming winter by displaying one last burst of color. I did the same for my sisters whose birthdays were in summer, but in early spring there was nothing to offer my mother but dirty snow. My Grandma Addy went out of her way to make those cursed with winter or early spring birthdays feel special. She made brightly colored cakes that made your birthday feel as if daylight savings time had come early.

Our mother's birthday would be the first celebrated away from Bellefontaine. I wanted to help put extra light into her day just as my grandmother had. I would scour the junkyard for something pretty for her. People threw pretty things away all the time.

Right now, the best thing we could do for her was get out of the house. All her threats of keeping Peanut in the house had been a bluff. She didn't want us running around the house and possibly making her cake fall.

Wrapped in our coats to ward off the wind and tetanus, we were finally turned loose in our yard, which we ignored. We gravitated toward the towers of trash. The first item we found was a mattress that had a giant hole burned in its center. We tried to use the unburnt edge as a trampoline. Either the fire had taken the bounce out of it or, more than likely, no one in this neighborhood could afford a bed with bounce in it. We bored of it quickly.

I said, "Let's look and see if we can find a present for mommy for her birthday."

Surprisingly my sisters were just as excited about it as I was. Other than an occasional glance from the kitchen window from our mother, we weren't supervised, not even by a seven-year-old Darla like last time. We reverted to a feral state, foraging deep into the heap and bringing out broken gifts: a plastic tulip with a missing petal, a waffle iron with no cord. Heat from the waffle iron would have been greatly appreciated, as the wind was making it cold. Curiosity makes its own heat. We only shivered when we paused from searching. The broken tulip almost made us stop the search. It was the first spring flower we had seen in Baltimore and the first ever found on my mother's birthday. Although we found it in the dirt, it did not spring from it.

Our search was proving unfruitful, until I saw it, half buried in the dirt. It was a small, Delft plate with a blue windmill design on it. I pulled it out of the dirt, hoping it was a full moon plate. Most of the plates we would find here would be half-moon plates, broken in half with no way to repair them, or the other half was missing altogether. This one was perfect except for one chip near the edge. The windmill looked so realistic I held the plate up to the wind almost expecting its vanes to turn in the breeze.

The vanes didn't turn a bit, but the wind did blow a newspaper into my face; it was the one Darla and I had used to cover the three-wheeled fire truck. I had forgotten about the toy until the wind and paper reminded me of it. Retrieving the truck, I put it next to the pile of stuff we had already salvaged, which had grown to include an old pressure cooker and a hot comb with no handle.

We stood over our pile and came to an easy consensus that the windmill plate would be our mother's gift. We took turns using our spit and fingers to rub the plate clean. Suddenly a shadow loomed over us from behind. Fresh from a small town we made the fledgling mistake of having our backs turned in the same directions. Playing in circles or facing one another was the prudent practice of most children in neighborhoods such as ours. The term "I got your back," no doubt was coined from this practice.

The shadow alerted us but didn't startle us. A sweet although somewhat gravelly voice calmed us before we took sight of her. The shadow spoke with the voice of an angel who had taken up a two pack a day smoking habit, "Those things are so pretty," the shadow said.

As we turned, standing over us was what appeared to be a female mummy. Thank God for that voice, for had I turned around and seen her standing there in silence I would have run as fast as I could in a screaming panic in search of a safe place to faint. She truly looked as if someone had put a skirt on a mummy. Wrapped in strips of rags from head to toe stood Penny Pile, our local rag lady. Her rags were spotlessly clean, and she was fighting her colors, putting a box of crayons to shame. The first time I would see a gay pride flag my memories would take me right back to my first sighting of Miss

Penny Pile. She looked like an expanded version of the pride flag, with more colors and just as much pride. My memories would also correct her age. At the time I pictured her as being older. Some of her rags were older than she was, so she was no older than perhaps early thirties. She even had a raggedy, multicolored scarf that covered her head, wrapped in such a way as to expose just her face.

She was an average looking sealskin brown woman. If dressed differently, you would not be able to single her out in a crowd. To do any justice to her I must describe how her face made me feel rather than how it looked. It was as if Santa Claus and an ambulance had fortuitously showed up at the worst moment in your life. Miss Penny Pile's face was the antonym to Medusa's. It could turn a stony, stressed expression into one that was calm and relaxed, but only if you looked past the rags.

Few misread her face. It had seen more than its fair share of sadness to be sure, but it said, "Whatever my past circumstances, I am happy now." This raised a question among the young and those born in Baltimore. What place or previous life could be so bad that made her present situation a better choice? Maturation would teach those that lived long enough that a fall down can sometimes be a step up. She had an "Everything is going to be alright" kind of face.

Despite the rags, her posture brought dignity to the dump, a beacon to all and proof that one could bring dignity to all stations of life. Pity was misplaced if heaped upon her. Her rags invited it, but her expression pushed it right back at you, marked "Return to sender, address unknown." You need your pity more than she does. If you looked too long into that face, you began to question even some of your better choices in life. She, for the most part, was happy. Were you?

She repeated herself, "Those things are so pretty."

This time I picked up the nuance of want. I said, "You can have everything except the blue plate. Today is our mother's birthday and we are going to give it to her for a present."

She gave us a big smile that warmed the air slightly as she picked up the broken waffle iron and plastic tulip to place into a sack she had made from sewn rags. Miss Penny Pile warmed to us because we were young and naive enough not to see shame in giving our mother something from a junkyard for her birthday. Thank goodness she didn't want the toy fire truck because I had inadvertently left it on the list of things she could have.

"Hi y'all, my name is Miss Penny Pile. What're your names?"

I said, "I'm Grant and this here is Peanut and Gwen, my sisters."

Peanut huffed into the conversation. "My real name is Beatrice, but I don't like it."

Miss Penny Pile laughed and said, "My real name is Hazel, but I didn't like the life that came with that name, so I changed it. Penny Pile was the name some people called me behind my back, so I took to calling myself that to spite them. It took a lot of time and courage for them to call me that to my face, but I insisted on it. So never call me Miss Hazel. Well you can, but I won't answer you."

Muttering about how most people couldn't distinguish the difference between a treasure trove and a trough, she pulled out a clean rag from her sack and burnished the blue plate, adding a sheen to an already beautiful gift.

Focusing on my sisters she said, "I like y'all so I will share my scrapyard with you. Y'all appreciate beautiful things." She continued, "Grant, you are an interesting little fellow so you can play in my scrapyard too. I usually don't allow boys in here because they break things just for the fun of it."

I hastily replied, "Mam I'm sorry, we didn't know this was your yard."

"Actually, it ain't mine, but I make my livelihood from it so it's mine from need."

I had no clue what livelihood was. It sounded close enough to ownership for me, so I left it at that.

She eyed me appraisingly before she spoke again. "Grant, you are a different kind of boy. Most people only see beauty where they're told to see it or where it is supposed to be. You see it where it is and can coax it out of hiding when it's not visible to others."

She pointed out a rose bush next to a refrigerator that would flower in summer and a broken pot of crocuses that were one or two warm days away from sprouting. "Wait until you see those bloom," she said. Miss Penny Pile beamed with pride when she added, "This is one of the prettiest scrapyards in East Baltimore."

I nodded enthusiastically in agreement, as if I were an authority on the junkyards of East Baltimore. My sisters parroted my nodding head.

Mister Willy must have heard her gravelly voice. He peeked his head out of his door and invited her in for tea and trade. They would laugh and negotiate over what Miss Penny Pile harvested from her scrapyards, which she tended as if they were her personal gardens. Nothing in East Baltimore was broken or useless until Miss Penny Pile said it was.

I didn't want to miss out on the interaction. Despite being raised not to intrude, I did anyway, "Miss Penny Pile, can we come with you to Mister Willy's? It's cold and we can't go in the house yet because our mother doesn't want her cake to fall down."

She answered me by taking my hand and escorting me to Mister Willy's back door. "Willy, do you want some young company in your house?"

He responded, "We would love some company but y'all have to let your mother know."

There was no need. Our mother had come out to check on us after seeing her child holding this strange rag woman's hand. Any concerns she had about Miss Penny Pile were dispelled by the fact that Mister Willy had invited her into his house. He introduced them both and they had the usual small talk that accompanied most introductions. After being assured we were safe, she wanted to make sure we were not a nuisance.

Mister Willy could smell the cooking cake and addressed the issue. "You can be polite and formal and let them ruin that cake and run you ragged, or you can be neighborly and let them use all that energy up in here." He paused, using his sunglasses as if they were eyes to make eye contact with our mother. "Besides, if I save your cake, you will bring me a piece later, won't you?"

She agreed readily. The only thing that came out of her kitchen that she could be proud of was her baking. She was an amazing baker but a bad cook. The two are very different. Her stews were the worst. She'd toss all the ingredients into a pot and it would become survival of the fittest, with no clear winners. It would start off as a colorful dish and boil down to a gray or brown putty. Looking into her pot felt as if you were attending an open casket funeral that should have been closed. You felt nothing but sadness for the sudden death of the flora and fauna of our local grocery store. We said grace when a eulogy would have been more appropriate, the kind of eulogy given by someone who did not know the departed well, for often you could not tell when the ingredients had been alive, whether they had had legs or roots. Usually teeth-touching-bone was the determining factor. So many things had died to make nothing. Mister Willy would soon learn to ask only for cakes and biscuits.

Rushing back to her cake to keep her promise to Mister Willy, she tossed a glance over her shoulder at us that said, "Behave and don't embarrass me."

Mister Willy said to us, "Well come on in."

CHAPTER 13   TEA AND GOSSIP

We entered a kitchen that was the mirror to our own. Utilitarian was much too extravagant a word to describe it. Pilgrims meeting poverty and trading their candles in for light bulbs and a TV, was an apt comparison. A bare light bulb hung from the ceiling, which was primarily for guests and also served as a beacon to guide flies toward a no pest strip. The strip of flies, long dead, dusty and desiccated, hung like a chandelier of pestilence about a foot from the light bulb.

On the kitchen table sat a TV, which Mister Willy was using as a radio. The screen was solid black with not even snow or vertical lines displayed on it. Emanating from behind the black glass curtain was the voice of the stuttering cartoon pig, speaking to a blind man and three children who had recently lost their TV in a tragic accident. Even so, the pig spoke better English than my sisters and me. Two big knobs on the TV gave the illusion that you had a choice of channels ranging from two to eighty-three. In fact, most places in America at the time only had four channels. Miss Penny used the little knobs to adjust the screen so we could watch Porky go through his antics on a wavy, snowy screen. She picked up a pair of pliers to turn a nub that was missing a dial and lowered the volume.

Mister Willy asked us if we wanted some sugar water to go with our cartoons. Of course, we agreed. The beverage was near the bottom of the hospitality drinks on offer in the poorer homes of the neighborhood, just above plain water and nothing. Except for tea, it was the best he had. Miss Penny offered to prepare it for us while Mister Willy went to the stove to make some tea for the adults. He approached a stove so old I would not have been surprised if he had pulled out two pieces of flint from a fur pouch to strike together to start the fire.

The kitchen was the only modern room in the house. The twentieth century was full of time-saving appliances, but they had to be bought on the layaway plan. You had to work more hours to buy the machines that saved you time, so that you could spend more time with other machines. Mister Willy thought saving time was a waste of time. It meant you were bored with now and in a hurry to get to later, unaware that later may not be as pleasant as now.

Besides being poor, this was the main reason he didn't have a phone. Information and gossip had to be very important for you to take the time to walk it over to his house to give it to him in person. Mister Willy would always say, "My hearing is very precious to me, and I don't appreciate people using my ears as trash cans, dumping all kinds of gossip into them or trying to sell me something I don't need and can't afford." He didn't consider talking on the phone to be real talking. Real conversation was such a tactile experience for him. You couldn't offer someone a warm beverage or a warm hand to hold over the phone. He would good naturedly chuckle about people holding that trashcan to their ears and clucking into it all day. He would walk to a neighbor's or a phone booth if he needed to make an important but terse phone call. Mister Willy was an antique in his own time.

His living room reflected his antique spirit more than the kitchen. The room looked as if he had tamed a tornado. There were overturned crates, which were used as tables. Most had dried plants or herbs laying on them. Along the walls that had no windows were shelves of mason jars filled with everything from bones to marbles. Little footpaths ran through his collection, indicating he accessed it regularly and was not a hoarder. Hoarding was an illness of the sighted. Perhaps the strangest things of all were two pews from an old church that sat under the window facing the prison. A great view for making penance, but Mister Willy made it perfectly clear that no one was to sit in them. Upon his death they were to be made into a coffin for his funeral. He often joked that he was going to Trojan Horse his way into heaven. No one ever sat on them, not on coffin wood in a root doctor's house; no one dared.

I was so enthralled with the room that I barely noticed the glass Miss Penny had placed in my hand. The room was such a tactile place, yet I knew not to touch anything. Mister Willy was at an advantage here. His sense of touch was so much greater than mine. He used his hands as eyes, but in his world, I had to use my eyes as hands. At the time I didn't dare touch anything, not even when he was not around. I truly believed he would be able to feel my residual fingerprints on any of the objects I might have touched. He would tell my mother and then I would have her fingerprints on my behind, for touching something that didn't belong to me. We were of a place and time that if a blind man had said he felt your fingerprints on something, he would have been believed.

I held this belief for many years despite the fact Miss Penny was already sitting at the kitchen table sorting and folding Mister Willy's money by denominations and putting it back in his wallet. He only trusted her, Uncle Ike and Uncle Reggie to fold his money for him. Many found it odd that he trusted a criminal, a wino and a rag lady to handle his money. He trusted them because they had already exposed their true selves. People craving vice threw money at Uncle Ike, Uncle Reggie only took from bartenders, and Miss Penny Pile took things that had been thrown away by others. They had already declared to the world from whom they took.

My sister's giggles brought my attention back to the TV. Peanut and Gwen shared a single chair at one end of the table. They sat peacefully, sipping their sugar water and watching cartoons the TV was distorting into images that looked as if they had been created by Picasso or Dali rather than animation artist. In addition, it must have been speech impediment Saturday, for I could now hear a cartoon duck lisping an argument to another intellectually and letter R-deprived cartoon character. I lost interest and slid my sugar water over to the adult end of the table, watching Miss Penny folding the final bills and placing them in Mister Willy's wallet.

Watching him talk to Miss Penny, I could see why he hated talking on the phone. His laugh was too big, and his mouth opened wide enough to accidentally swallow the receiver of a phone. He didn't have a full set of thirty-two teeth, but they numbered in the high twenties. His canine teeth had been ground flat, which made his smile more that of a well-fed herbivore than that of a hungry predator.

Miss Penny Pile was more frugal with her laughs and smiles. Her smile scurried across her face as if it were a skittish Cheshire cat, but her smile went well with the black tea she was sipping. It was not quite *Alice in Wonderland*. She had her own title to the story; *Penny in a Pile*.

"What is the rumor de jour?" Mister Willy teased.

Miss Penny Pile eyed him suspiciously over the top of the teacup that had paused briefly before her lips and said, "Take care fish, don't mind the sky, tend to the sea. Your water is a mite dirty." The corners of her elusive smile peeking around the edges of the teacup said it was just a friendly reminder to mind his own business.

Mister Willy heard the smile in her voice and pressed. "What rumors are the young people making up about you today?" Most of the adults knew her story but stayed silent on the matter.

"Now I am a deflowered nun searching the junk lots of Baltimore for my virtue," she retorted.

"As if our virtue could be hidden in such a lofty place as a junkyard," Mister Willy responded. They both laughed. He held his teacup in midair and she clinked her teacup to his to signal agreement.

He continued, "Reggie said your new outfit makes you look like a mummified nun. What did you expect?"

"It doesn't matter what I wear, people will talk. Besides, I rather like this rumor. So, feel free to spread this one."

There were all kinds of strange rumors about Miss Penny. She preferred the rumors to the truth. The gossipmongers' thoughts were not dark enough to rival the truth. The lies they spun kept them entertained and away from the real truth. Individuals who tried to be fair were the ones she feared most. They cared what the truth was and kept searching and prying. She always had to remember to hold her head low to make them think they had accidentally stumbled on the truth, occasionally confessing to a rumor to keep the false talk going. Some days she was lucky and could forget the truth and believe the rumors herself. She was always honest about the now, but about her past she was either mute or evasive.

Mister Willy had more rumors about him than did Miss Penny Pile, but his inspired fear and respect, whereas hers inspired judgement and pity. I heard her called Pitiful Penny Pile more than a few times. Over the years, as drugs and violence would become more prevalent, she clung to this mantle even more. Her low status protected her somewhat from much of the crime. When the addicts and alcoholics woke from their stupors they could see where the bottom was. They needed her alive to have someone to look down on. "At least I am not as low as Pitiful Penny Pile," they could tell themselves.

On more than one occasion, she and the crows would find a lifeless body in a junk lot, used up and thrown away. People found out the hard way Miss Penny Pile was not the bottom. She merely had blocked their view of it, the point where gravity and poor behavior can pull you no lower than an undignified death. They would lie there, veins so full of toxic drugs, the crows, although drawn to their lifeless bodies, would not partake of their flesh. For some, crows and Pitiful Penny Pile would be the only funeral attendees they would have, the disappointed caw of the crows and a call to the coroner their only requiem.

Mister Willy and Miss Penny had a way of turning hateful words, meant to be daggers in their hearts, into annoying gnats easily brushed aside with a wave of a hand. They were so nonchalant about it and actually made it look fun. I asked, "Can you make a rumor about me?"

Mister Willy cocked an ear and she an eye my way. He gestured a hand toward Miss Penny, giving her the podium. She twirled her finger in the air making an imaginary circle that happily included me with her and Mister Willy and said, "People like us are talked about all the time. We are too busy living our lives to use our tongues to paint unflattering portraits of others."

Mister Willy interrupted. "I think the boy wants to know why we don't care what others say about us."

Recognition dawned on Miss Penny's face and she told me, "Don't worry, people will make up lots of rumors about you. You have a lot of sugar in your blood so . . ."

I mistook her awkward pause as a sign I was being impolite and drinking too much sugar water, so I pushed the drink away. "Sugar in his blood" was a polite euphemism for being a homosexual which I heard for the first time when Axel used it. The term took the sex out of homosexuality in order to make it fit for polite company.

The pause went on long enough that I thought they were looking for a way to change the subject. In fact, they were looking for a way to garnish it and present it to a young child.

To them and many others of that time and place, children were adults in training. A happy childhood was kind of left up to the child. Adults would throw happiness in when they could, but their main goal was to raise a well-adjusted functioning, adult.

Mister Willy and Miss Penny were very familiar with adults of my kind, and I realize now they knew gay people, but this was before Stonewall, which was only five years away. Those who came out of the closet back then came out wearing everything in it. Many were show people. For the rest, the closet was like a vampire's coffin; they only came out of it at night. The light of day was deadly to them.

Miss Penny was not Axel. She tried to steer me away from shame. She tussled with how to present the concept. She paraphrased a Billy Holiday song, something about a child having his own stuff. Miss Holiday had grown up, or rather had been beaten down, not more than two miles from here.

The blank look on my face caused her to move from blues verse to Bible verse. She corrupted John chapter fifteen verse two: "Sometimes people will use criticism to cut off every branch in you that bears fruit."

Mister Willy interrupted her. "Lord have mercy, Penny, I can hear the boredom in the child's face from here. Let a blind man help you cross this street."

He turned towards me. As I could not see his eyes behind his sunglasses, it seemed as if his chin was staring at me. Searching for the right words, he paused a long time before finally speaking. "Grant, don't ever explain yourself, just be yourself. No use in going through life justifying everything you do to people who don't really matter. Don't worry about appearances, 'clothes make the man' is a lie. Man makes the man. People have to learn how to wear themselves well, first and foremost. 'Woe is me' doesn't look good on anyone."

As if on cue the TV stabilized for a few seconds, long enough to see a cartoon rabbit stuff his ears under a wig and his big rabbit feet into 1940's style pumps, to become a much bigger character. The cartoon helped me understand the gist of Mister Willy's words. Under all the drag was a whole lot of confidence. I wanted to have the self-confidence of that rabbit. "Please God, draw me the courage to be comfortable in my own skin," I thought to myself.

I could do simple math, and I knew it was easier to please one person, yourself, than it was to please everybody else. Harsh and unjust criticism is a form of censorship. If you let it, it could cause you to mind your words and actions to avoid the critiques of others, until even sitting silently in a corner could be criticized. Mister Willy and Miss Penny did not sit quietly in corners. I hoped I wouldn't either. They threw hints at me and it was my task to build confidence from those hints. They had noticed and appreciated what Axel had tried to stomp on. This had given me hope that when I grew out of these shoes and this skin, I might be comfortable in the next ones.

Changing the subject, Miss Penny turned her kind heart to a task she could complete now. Pointing to the door, she said, "Grant, go get your toy truck and we will fix it for you."

By the time I returned, Miss Penny had dumped a jar of old buttons on the table. My sisters were lured away from the TV and began searching through the pile for the right size button to be a tire for my fire truck. Peanut found a black button with a ribbed edge, which sort of looked as if it would match the other three tires.

Before she could ask him if he had any glue, Mister Willy was already handing her another jar with three or four black tar balls in them.

With a frown on her face that also reached her voice, she said, "Willy, nobody uses pine pitch glue anymore. How old is this stuff? And did you make it yourself?"

"No, I didn't make it. Although I do know the recipe, I have never made it myself," he retorted. "I got it from old Miss Ida over on E. Chase Street. She occasionally makes it, but I don't know how she collects the pine resin at her age and in the city. Besides it's all I have."

There still was a lively trade of "do it yourself" goods among the older people of East Baltimore. Younger people were distancing themselves from these skill sets, deeming them too country and backwoods to complement their urban style. Pine glue and polyester clothing didn't marry well.

Despite her complaints, in no time Miss Penny heated the ball of pine glue, applied it to the toy axel and popped on the repurposed button. She didn't spill a drop on her raggedy outfit.

She told me the button wheel was for show and not to put too much pressure on it when I played. Demonstrating, she tilted the fire truck as she ran it along the table; only the wheels on the right side of the fire truck touched the surface. Somehow the motion of the wheels caused the red light on the fire truck to light up. I didn't know it could do that. Sitting there in her multicolored rags, with her sunny smile, she was my earthbound rainbow.

Mister Willy interrupted our repairs with his hosting. "After all that hard work, your tea has grown cold Miss Penny. Would you like me to warm it up for you?" Mister Willy held up a bottle of amber liquor and began waving it in the air as if it were a piece of yarn taunting a cat.

"Oh Willy, it is much too early in the day to have a drink yet," she said, without much determination.

Mister Willy's lips were pursed in indecision, whether to frown or smile. When he finally spoke again the words came out of a patronizing smile. "Why do folks put a clock on a bottle of alcohol? Holding out until five o'clock just to prove to the world they are not alcoholics. If they drank when they needed it, when the desire was only a twinge, maybe folks wouldn't overindulge after five o'clock trying, to make up for perceived lost time."

Miss Penny's mouth still was arguing but her hand was lifting the teacup into the air, already meeting the bottle of rum halfway. Just to be ornery she confronted his statement. "There is a clock on life itself. Why wouldn't there be one on everything in it?"

Mister Willy sat the bottle of rum down on the kitchen table and said, "If you quit your arguing, the tic toc of that clock could be the clink clink of our cups." With that statement Miss Penny's teacup retreated back to the table to join the bottle of rum. Mister Willy poured and she sipped.

Her argument soon became a compliment. "Although you make a fine plain tea, your rum tea is superb." The heat of the stove didn't stand a chance against the warmth of the rum.

After only two sips, her words already smelled of alcohol. With a puzzled look on her face she asked, "Willy, why do you so fervently defend the pleasures of drinking while you rarely have more than few drinks yourself?"

"That is the small part of what I am saying; in general, I am coming to the defense of the here and now. Your next breath is not promised. So, you are right Miss Penny, there is a clock on life itself."

"Today is a rare day indeed. I get a drink and agreement from you. Hold your cup still Willy, so I can give you that clink clink you mentioned." Their cups clunked more than clinked.

He continued, "The basic answer is that one or two drinks makes me feel good. Any more than that I start to feel bad. Also, I don't like to drink in public with strangers. That always seemed strange and dangerous to me. Bunch of folks who don't know each other well, washing away their inhibitions as fast as the bartender can pour. Next thing you know you are sitting next to a strange stranger who is getting stranger by the glass. No, I prefer to drink at home with people I know."

Miss Penny laughed. They clunked cups again.

Mister Willy continued, "When I first moved here, I went out to a bar with an acquaintance. His name was Broken Dice. You don't forget a name like that. We get to the bar. The man starts drinking as if prohibition were coming back tomorrow or Jesus had reversed himself and was now turning wine back into water. Running from sober like it was a demon, he was drunk within half an hour. Two hours later he was out of money, so he decides it is time to leave. Why do drunk people try to be helpful the more helpless they become? He then insisted that he help me home. At this point the man couldn't speak five words without stumbling over at least three of them. Yet he kept insisting on helping me home. You know the kind of help I am talking about, where you do all the sweating and someone else takes all the credit and propriety demands that you thank them for it. It was more like I was his cane."

"Lord have mercy I hate help like that," Miss Penny agreed.

"He was a big man too. Drunk as he was, I could not resist him. I would have fared better if he had passed out on top of me in the bar. Somehow, we made it outside, and unfortunately the fresh air revived his strength but not his senses. Instead of leading the way across busy streets, he forcefully but not harshly pushed me ahead of him. He was using my blindness to steal the right of way from oncoming traffic with no regard for lights or our safety. At the top of his voice he yelled, 'Blind man coming through!' The cars yelled back with horns and screeching tires. One car came to a stop, and the fender, despite the sound of screeching tires, gently touched my leg."

Undeterred by the cautionary tale, Miss Penny took a big gulp of rum tea and said, "Oh my, Willy."

He continued, "The car almost hitting me sent him into a rage. He snatched my cane from my hand and crashed it down on the hood of the car, scaring out what little bit of alcohol I had remaining in my system. Instead of pushing me he now led me through the traffic, swinging my cane like it was a machete clearing a path through moving traffic. If there ever was a time, I needed a drink, it was in the middle of that street. The cane would hum in the air, then crash on another car. Hum crash, hum crash until we made it to the other side, with I don't know how many more streets to go. It was scary because I didn't know the streets that well back then, so I couldn't ditch him if I wanted to. So, I was pulled the rest of the way home through a gauntlet of blaring horns, angry shouts, threats of violence and the scent of brakes applied too hard and too fast."

Mister Willy set his drink down on the table and pushed it away in remembrance of the incident. "Yes, I am very careful who I drink with. Very careful indeed."

My grandmother back in Ohio was the same way. She would warn anyone who would listen, about the evils of general admission. Frequenting places where the only screening process was how much funding you had in your wallet seemed odd to her, especially when it came to drinking alcohol. She practiced a limited form of prohibition in her own home, yet she considered herself a good host by her own standards. At parties she would circulate the house with a bottle of scotch in one hand and a pitcher of water in the other. She served scotch to the well-behaved and water to those known to have misbehaved in public. Her decision was based on what she heard about their behavior at our local bar, The Pink House. It was amusing watching the futility of the more determined, hardier drinkers following her around the house with an empty glass that would never be filled. Sometimes they would mingle their glass in with a crowd of glasses, hoping for a case of mistaken identity, but she always gracefully and tactfully kept track of which hand was connected to which glass. Often, I wondered if she had a bad experience with alcohol as well.

The worst thing about a bad experience was not learning anything from it. Learning from your mistakes and staying true to yourself often alienated peers. Mister Willy and my grandmother did not succumb to peer pressure because they had few peers. Unlike most people, they didn't care what others thought of them. I asked both of them the same question several years apart: "Why don't you care what other people think of you?" Almost verbatim they gave the same answer: "Most people don't think all that much. So why should I care about so little?" In general, both of them could not be bothered with what others thought of them until those people tried to turn their little thoughts into actions.

There are some experiences you do not learn from so much as you have to learn to live with. This was the case for Miss Penny. She segued into her story by finishing the rum tea Mister Willy had pushed aside. Picking up his drink was akin to picking up his mood. She sat in silence for a few moments, long enough for the alcohol to bring out the maudlin.

Her mouth wavered between a smile and a frown, smiling because of a good memory, frowning because it was only that, a memory. Her private thoughts were planning their escape into the world. Miss Penny had a faraway look in her eyes, almost as if she and her story could not be in the room at the same time.

She brought the empty glass of rum tea to her mouth to distract it, to no avail. She mumbled into the glass instead, which muffled and echoed her words simultaneously. The weight of the glass pulled her arm back to the table, but she didn't release it. She worried the glass as if it were a strand of worry beads. The smell of alcohol on her breath would have tainted her story if it had been on someone else. It had a life of its own. I pictured the story as a small man inside her mouth. He placed his feet on her bottom teeth, and with raised palms pushing against her upper teeth, he pried her mouth open and escaped.

Miss Penny more sighed her woes than spoke them. "My head is a haunted place, full of memories of long-gone loved ones. Sometimes I see them in places where they once were: restaurants, street corners, phone booths, pews and, worst of all, cribs. How is it that I can miss a place where I still live? I am homesick in my own home, where the loudest laughs and broadest smiles are those of phantoms. They mock and belittle the laughs and smiles of the living. The past is more potent than the present. I never moved away from home. Home moved away from me. I am homesick for 1957. Sometimes I think of leaving, but who would tend the memories?"

Miss Penny only hints about the house fire that turned her parents and siblings into smoky memories. It was a story I heard but don't remember who told it to me, mainly because over time I heard bits and pieces of her story from many different people. She was not so much unhappy with the memories as she was weary of maintaining them alone. Miss Penny kept their memories alive and the memories, in return, kept her alive. From the manner in which she told the story, I knew this was not the life she ran from. These memories were between that horrible place and now, the time after she was called Hazel and the time before she was called Miss Penny. If the other memories haunted her, she never said. However, tragically her good life ended, the fact that she had had it at all is what sustained her. Out of necessity Miss Penny could travel farther through life on fumes than most people could on a full tank.

These were not the stories parents would tell their children. For a moment we were not children; we were safe ears to speak into. Mothers and fathers tend to wrestle a great deal with the appropriate age to discuss certain subjects with their children. In this regard parents are often the laggards to their children, who have great coping skills and generally dismiss things they don't understand until they need to understand them. Mister Willy and Miss Penny were not parents. But listening to individuals such as them would be the only private school I would ever attend. They were a school with no books or blackboards, yet their personal histories were spilled on the floor as if they were toy blocks which could be used as building blocks. "Take what you want but, more importantly, take what you need," was the unspoken motto. I would learn to read people long before I learned to read books.

Subconsciously, I stored the inappropriate away until it became appropriate. There would be huge portions of my life where I did not think about Miss Penny. I never forgot her, but she dwelled in the attic of my mind. Then the AIDS crisis struck, stripping my life of friends and familiar faces. Suddenly I knew how it felt to be home-sick in your own home. I didn't have to conjure up the words to describe those feelings. They had been given to me when I was five years old. Her words pushed past decades of memories to stand by my side when I needed them the most.

When I remember Miss Penny, I also remember Mister Willy. He ended the conversation that day by saying, "It is an obvious and strange revelation when we realize the things people touch can out-last them. We either love these things or resent them for outliving our friends."

I understood Miss Penny in my thirties in a way I could not at five. She prowled the junkyards and lots of East Baltimore, for they were filled with items. Things, that if only they could put pen to page, would be able to write great novels. Possessions could become treasures simply for being touched by someone that was loved and respected. I thought of her, Mister Willy and their words when I paid the rent an extra month for a close friend after he had died, simply because I was not ready to part with anything he had touched. I re-membered them every time I sat in a lonely room full of furniture that had been made sacred by death. These memories, separated by many years, are now one in my mind. One thought brings the other. They did not start out together, but the mind can give birth to twins separated by many years. If not twins, then they are close friends, holding hands everywhere they went.

These memories also have darker companions. Searching my early past is akin to sailing a sea of sameness and forgetfulness in search of islands of clear memories. Most are islets clustered in an archipelago that are only connected below the waterline. I don't remember anything below the waterline. The islets are eventful, ei-ther happy or sad and sometimes both. My first day in Baltimore and my mother's birthday were the big islands of memories.

CHAPTER 14   CAN'T BREATHE

Mister Willy shooed us back outside with an invitation to come back any time. Miss Penny escorted us to the junkyard. Before going about her business, she handed me the toy fire truck and the Delft windmill plate. Her hand now free, she waved goodbye to us. I waved goodbye with the hand holding the plate. After Miss Penny disappeared, I ran to place the plate and the truck on the back stoop of our house and returned to my sisters.

We scanned the junkyard, looking for mischief. There was a refrigerator lying on its back that I imagined a boat. I just needed my sisters' help to open the door. "Let's be pirates looking for treasure. This will be our ship," I said in an authoritative voice that carried little authority.

Being the oldest, I always invented games where I was the boss. Seeing the mutiny in Peanut's eyes, I said, "Peanut you can be the second captain and help make the crew behave."

I only had authority if I gave Peanut some as well. The only mutiny Gwen could muster was a frown. A ship with two captains and one crew was not going far, but we did cooperate long enough to push open the door and lean it against a brick wall. Whoever discarded the refrigerator had coiled its electrical cord and wedged it between the base of the door and the frame to keep it from locking. Otherwise we would not have been coordinated enough to pull the handle and push the door up at the same time.

There was a pile of records not far from our rectangle ship. As captain I took a larger seventy-eight album to use as a steering wheel. Peanut readily accepted the smaller forty-five and sat at the rear, signaling there were going to be two helms on this ship. I had imagined us sitting side by side. Apparently even in the world of make believe, Peanut didn't trust my driving. Gwen, wise beyond her years on some things, threw the electrical cord over the side of

145

our ship and made a plopping noise with her mouth to signal we had just anchored. This game was going nowhere fast.

Sometimes our games turned into battles, which in turn were games unto themselves. We practiced conflict resolution the hard way. Left to our own devices, bruising and tiring our bodies until they had no fight left in them, was how we generally resolved conflicts. We would apologize when supervised, but the words had to be hand fed to us by adults. Outside threats were the surest ways to force us to swiftly resolve conflict among ourselves. Wordlessly standing together shoulder to shoulder was our strongest and sincerest apology.

Our game of pirates turned into a game of Underground Railroad. We ducked before we even saw the threat. Much as a real ship would announce its presence by its prow cutting through calm waters, we felt him slightly before we saw him, except he didn't move with the grace and ease of a sailing ship. He walked as if his body and soul had not been properly introduced. There was a strange confidence to his steps, but it was the confidence of someone with nothing to lose, and he wore losing as if it were a badge of courage. My mind accused my eyes of lying, until the chill running down my spine corroborated their story. The impossible passed not more than fifty feet away, but he did not see us. Axel was out of jail.

Having survived withdrawal and incarceration, consequences seemed to slide off him like water off a duck's back. How was he here? He stole from his girlfriend and for God's sake threw a TV down on the police. People were incarcerated for years for lesser offenses. Axel was an illegal miracle. Fortune fell on him in his darkest moments so he could continue doing bad things.

The hand of fate had spun the wheel of misfortune and the arrow now pointed at us. Actually, it was more the hand of Axel's girlfriend pulling strings. She must have been well connected in addition to having money. Simply dropping the charges would not have been enough. Her money must have found a technicality or loophole as well. She had freed her lover and my hater. Uncle Ike's and my stepfather's nickname for her was Keys. Now I knew why they called her that.

She saw something in him no one else did. Poor woman was trying to get honey from a hornet's nest, only to find cone-shaped paper filled with nothing but undeveloped larvae. She was repeatedly and savagely stung with no sweetness to compensate her for her effort and so were the rest of us.

Axel bravely strolled not more than a hundred yards from the prison, ignoring the fact that he was destined to return to it. The only sign of caution he showed was when he cut across Mister Willy's yard. Stooping low and creeping by a blind man's house certainly spelled nefarious. Had this been a movie, his footsteps would have had their own eerie soundtrack.

Once past Mister Willy's window, his boldness returned. He stepped up onto our back stoop. His left foot, the one I had bitten, sought revenge on the Delftware plate I had placed there for my mother. When he stepped on it, instead of pulling his foot away as one would have if it were an accident, he twisted and ground it into the plate, turning a portion of it into a blue and white powder.

He raised his right foot to crash down on my fire truck, but my mother opened the door, interrupting his act of retribution. His shift back to a calm, reasonable person was swift, but he couldn't quite hide Mister Hyde completely. An expression of caution warred with one of hospitality on my mother's face. She threw a side eye towards Mister Willy's house. Thinking we still were there, she reluctantly invited him in.

The common wisdom of the neighborhood was that we were safer than other neighborhoods because of our proximity to the prison. Who would commit crime so close to a prison, with guards walking its parapet practically at our doorsteps? We certainly never had break-ins, and I would only see one incident of violence on our street. A man, obviously drunk, had pushed his girlfriend against the wall of the prison, threatening her with a knife. One of the guards pointed his shotgun down from the wall at the man, telling him he would blow his head off if he didn't stop. The guard held the man at gunpoint for ten minutes, sending the woman on her way. All the guard could do was give the woman a head start. To this day I wondered if she used her ten minutes well.

It defied all logic to perpetrate a crime at the gate of a prison. In time, I would learn logic was often impeded by one's emotional state and substance abuse. The statement, "They wouldn't do that because it isn't logical," isn't a logical statement. Logic never considers the illogic to be its equal, when in reality illogic often bests it. As a child, if logic entered into my life at all, it had stumbled in by accident or had been artificially imposed by adults. Unfortunately, there are plenty of adults who act like a five-year old in the world. My mother could be in danger.

Acting without much thought, which is the purview of a true five-year old, I pushed my sisters farther down into the refrigerator and slammed the door shut. The loud noise brought no one's attention. No one knew they were there, so I thought they were safe. If I had a plan at all, it was to bite Axel again, giving my mother and I time to run back to the refrigerator and hide. If he found us, together we could hold the door closed. It didn't occur to me that back then, refrigerators locked from the outside. Axel could get in, but we couldn't get out. The part about him not getting in dominated my thoughts. Us getting out was not the concern it should have been.

Strong emotions pushed me toward our back door. The peach fuzz on my back and arms was bristling with aggression and fear, rubbing against the flannel shirt under my coat, sending a tickle and a chill down my spine. Despite the cold air, my face was hot. It was as if my skin couldn't decide if it belonged to a warm-blooded mammal or cold-blooded reptile.

I paused momentarily on our stoop. Without walking in I pushed the door open hard, causing it to say, "Ah ha!" in my stead. There was nothing to ah ha. Axel calmly sat at our kitchen table as if it were the first day of creation and he didn't have a sordid past. His face said otherwise. The cold air had caused the skin on his face to appear ashen everywhere except the knife scars and a bruise near his right eye. I pulled off one of my gloves with my teeth, reminding Axel I was armed.

Although my mother was displaying her Midwestern girl hospitality face, she stood and kept herself strategically placed between the butcher knife on the edge of the sink and Axel. Aunt Porch had taught her well.

Assuming her daughters were still over at Mister Willy's house, she said, "Grant go back next door until I come for you." Her voice held a hint of annoyance meant to hide her real feeling of concern. She knew he was violent but didn't know all that he had said and done that night.

Before I could decide to defy her, Axel interrupted. "Carol, let him stay."

I didn't like that he had just touched my mother's name with his dirty mouth, but I was in agreement with him because I wanted to stay.

He continued, "Actually I owe him an apology. My girlfriend convinced me that my behavior the other night might have been a little off putting."

I didn't want his apology. Coming from his mouth it would be nothing but filth and lies. If he spoke the truth it would not be much better. He might repeat every vile thing he had said that night so that my mother could hear, which I didn't want. I now wanted to silence him by biting him on the lips to swell them shut. In hindsight this would have only confirmed what he had said about me. Fortunately, he gave the truncated version fed to him by his girlfriend. He never made eye contact with me. His eyes kept tilting up to the cue cards placed in his memory by his girlfriend. When he strayed away from her script the apology turned into a bunch of excuses that almost begged an apology from us for his wretched life. The insincere apology suited his character and my needs. His mouth probably tasted worse than his socks anyway.

My response was a cold silence. Words just would not come to me. I looked to the walls to my right and left as if I could borrow or rent words from them. I stared at the floor between my feet but there were no crib notes there either. My silence lasted so long my mother nudged my shoulder and said, "What do you say?"

It seemed such a small apology for something so terrible. I wanted to say, "I am sorry you are such a wretched person." But my mother's birthday cake sitting on the counter was blackmailing me. Rude behavior meant no cake tonight. I had hoped that I could have gotten away with saying nothing, but she stood there giving me the Ten Commandments stare. I truly did not know what to say, so I shrugged my shoulders for help.

Finally, my mother had to put the words in my mouth. "Thank you, Uncle Axel. I appreciate you taking time out of your busy day to come by and apologize," she suggested.

I practiced with her in front of Axel, repeating the words back to her several times before finally repeating them to him, thus taking all the sincerity out of my acceptance. It was similar to learning the alphabet by rote through song. I didn't know what the letters meant outside of the song, nor did Axel. "Now, I know my ABCs. Next time, won't you stay away from me?" For God's sake I hoped there would not be a next time.

Axel's whining apology caused my mother to let down the rest of her guard. She said, "Grant go next door and get your sisters."

Normally I would not have corrected my mother's assumptions, but despite Axel's apologies I wanted him to know how much I didn't trust him.

"Mommy they're not at Mister Willy's," I said, my chest puffed up like a champion for thinking of hiding my sisters.

"What do you mean they're not over Mister Willy's. Where are they?" Her voice was annoyed and concerned.

"I wanted to protect them from —" my eyes finished the sentence as I glanced at Axel. "They're in the refrigerator out back."

She looked at me with a face I felt should have been reserved for Axel. It was one of complete terror. It unnerved me to see that expression directed at me. I started crying, praying and apologizing for every woe in the world.

She shouted, "Please God, not my babies!" My crying, apologizing and praying became more specific. It had something to do with not enough air. Too late, I remembered hearing stories about children dying in refrigerators when the door locked behind them.

The Refrigerator Safety Act banned the production of lock latched refrigerators in 1956. Despite the law, children would still die decades after its passage. In some states it was a felony to abandon a lock latch refrigerator where a child could find it. In East

Baltimore this unintentional felony had to get in a long line of intentional ones.

My mother ran outside. Her cotton apron and house shoes were no match for the inclement weather. However, her determination sent the wind and cold scurrying and yelping to other climes. She arrived at the refrigerator hot and sweaty. I arrived by her side holding my breath, hoping that for every breath I didn't take God would donate one to my sisters inside the refrigerator. I had nothing else to offer. I didn't want to believe that my sisters could die because of my fear of Axel and his lengthy, lame apology. All I wanted to do was protect them.

My mother frantically pulled on the handle four or five times in as many seconds. Each time her fingers slipped off the handle before she could lift the door. I exhaled for I now needed air to fuel my sobs and cries. They were the most guilt-ridden breaths I have ever taken. I had been holding my breath by choice and when I wanted air it was there, not so for my sisters. My mother also took in a deep breath to take the edge off her panic. It helped. She wiped her greasy hands on her apron and pulled the handle a sixth time while I pushed.

We pushed and pulled so hard that when the door gave, I slipped and fell on the door frame, half my body in the refrigerator and half dangling out. The door hit the brick wall hard with sufficient force to send shrapnel of red-fired clay flying everywhere. In addition, the door bounced off the wall, threatening to close again and guillotining me at the waist. With one hand, my mother blocked the door's descent; with the other she yanked me from the doorframe. In that split second I had a glimpse of my sisters curled up in the fetal position.

At the sight of her daughters she called out their names, her voice a crescendo from a roar of Gwen's name into a piercing screech of Peanut's, which nearly shattered me into pieces of glass. Not old enough to deal with life-threatening situations, I borrowed whole cloth from my mother's emotional state. Unable to tailor the emotion down to my size, the wobbly knees of my soul began to buckle from the weight of it. I began to wish that she had let the refrigerator door fall on me.

Time, the gatekeeper of the empirical world, abandoned its post in favor of the surreal. The seconds alternatively crawled and raced forward. My mother's hand appeared to be one with time, almost as if her hand was that of a conductor setting time's pace and rhythm. Inching forward slowly and then speeding forward, her hand reflected her inner struggle. When she reached down to touch her daughters, would she find life or death? She wanted to know, and she didn't want to know. If death, there would always be a part of her that could never move from this moment. Time would obey her hand until she bid it go backwards. Then it would startle awake from this dream, for time's biggest nightmare was the act of flowing backward, devouring everything it was and had created. It would be cannibalism on a cosmic scale. Time swore allegiance only to the present and the future.

Only because I had played dead with my sisters, multiple times, did I notice Peanut's left eye was squinting. She was never good at playing dead, and to play dead you had to be alive. From behind a thick curtain of eyelashes, I could see Peanut's pupil scanning her new world for signs of safety. The emotions I had borrowed from my mother lifted from my soul. My mood had gone from dread to relief and ventured a little towards playful. I yelled, "Olly olly oxen free."

Although not a rule generally applied in playing dead or pirates, Peanut and Gwen rose reluctantly from their fetal positions. Peanut made eye contact with me instead of our mother because we had the same fear. She whispered, "Is he gone?"

I smiled which Peanut took to mean yes. My smile was not meant to deceive. For all our short little lives, we had never ever been separated for longer than an hour. We were each other's shadows. I vaguely remember Gwen coming home from the hospital a few days after she was born, but Peanut was just always there. I knew real death was some type of separation that lasted longer than an hour. Sometimes we needed an hour away from each other, but I couldn't bear more than that. Despite the fact they were both on their hands and knees in a grubby refrigerator, my happiness dressed them up as fairy princesses. They both never looked so good to me. Peanut peered up at me from the vegetable section of the refrigerator, while Gwen, dressed in Peanut's hand-me-downs, aptly sat in the leftover section, staring up at our mother.

Our mother pulled away the hand with which she had been reaching for her daughters. Joining her other hand, she ran both of them down her face to wipe away tears of anguish and make room for new tears of joy. Then she bent to pick them both up, one in each arm. She smothered them both in kisses as if she were a five-year-old girl holding her two favorite dolls. The scene reminded me of the story she told us about herself as a little girl. She had tied two of her favorite dolls together with a string so she would never be tempted to choose her favorite. Her arms, encircling her daughters, were now that string. If she squeezed them any harder my sisters would have become one.

By rights they should both be dead. They had been trapped in that refrigerator for over fifteen minutes. Unlike the citizens of other cities who went around removing the doors of any abandoned refrigerator that presented itself as a hazard, the Good Samaritans of East Baltimore had their own unique solutions. Our mother was too busy being thankful to notice the reason her daughters had not suffocated. Someone had purposefully and strategically shot three bullet holes into the refrigerator, one through the door and two through the sides. I didn't know they were bullet holes at the time; I was just grateful for the air holes, regardless of the source.

I thanked God and then I asked him to thank on my behalf the unknown person who had made the holes. My grandmother had taught me that being grateful was a thick, rich stew, to be shared generously, not a thin soup to be greedily hoarded.

Meanwhile my mother's gratefulness was wearing off. She turned her eyes toward me, staring, weighing the hypocrisy of throttling one child after thanking God for saving her other two from the death grip of a locked refrigerator.

Fortunately, Peanut intervened on my behalf by saying, "Grant saved us from the bad man."

Our mother pivoted her head in search of the unseen threat to her children and asked me, "Which way did he go?"

In unison Gwen, Peanut and I pointed to the back door of our house. Realization dawned on our mother that the man we feared was Axel. She looked around again, confused as to why he was not here. I heard her mumble, "Why didn't he come and help?" She couldn't chastise us for our suspicion when her own, which had been dormant after Axel's insincere apology, suddenly awakened. Fortunately, her anger entirely skirted me for locking my sisters in the refrigerator and was now building towards Axel for his callousness. Strolling back towards the house I realized that her anger, no matter how great, was no match for Axel's cruelty and in hindsight neither was mine.

My mother was carrying Gwen and towing Peanut, so I beat her to the back door. Before entering the house, I picked up the toy fire truck Axel had almost stomped on. With childlike hope I spun its wheels, which caused the red light to flash. I held my toy turned talisman up to the window of our door. Perhaps Axel would see the flashing light and have a Pavlovian response and flee the scene. Moments later my mother caught up to me and told me to stop my foolishness. She pushed past me into our kitchen.

The talisman seemed to have worked, for Axel was nowhere to be seen. My mother yelled, "Yoo-hoo!" to confirm he was truly gone. Little things tell on a person; the fact that she yelled, "Yoo-hoo" in her own house told volumes. No one yells yoo-hoo in their own house or one where they at least feel comfortable being. She was not completely comfortable here yet and not just because of Axel. Nonetheless, she released a barely perceptible sigh of relief when she got no answer.

Her sigh was a little premature and should have been exhaled in regret instead of relief. Peanut, because of her height, noticed it first. Our mother's overturned purse was on a chair under the kitchen table with some of its contents spilled on the seat. Peanut somehow noticed it was theft before anyone else did. She whined that the bad man had taken the gum in our mother's purse. Except Axel had no use for gum. He had taken all our mother's folding money.

It was a kindness of sorts that he had made his theft obvious. Matters would have been worse had she found out tomorrow while she was at the checkout line at the grocery store, reverse shopping as she ran the cart back through the aisles restocking the necessaries, she had just discovered she could not afford. She was a small-town Midwestern girl. As embarrassing as it would have been, she would not have walked away and left the items on the counter for someone else to deal with.

Our mother turned the purse right side up and rummaged through it to discover Axel had indeed taken everything except some small change. Drug dealers hated getting paid in pennies. She put her hands in front of her face to hide her emotions until she gathered her strength to show her children the face we needed to see, the confident mother in control. Sometimes worse news turns bad news into good. She smiled and looked at her still breathing daughters to buffer the fact that she had been robbed twice in less than a week, once at gun point, the other under the guise of an apology.

Until that day I never knew you could regret accepting someone's apology. I had no idea that people could say they are sorry and promise never to do it again for the sole purpose of deceiving you into actually letting them do it again. They manipulate your forgiveness and put you on a subscription plan for their apologies, apologizing weekly and daily with no intention of ever changing. Taking liberties with being weak and flawed themselves, they never reciprocate when you reach a breaking point and finally ask them for forgiveness for not being strong enough to accept one more of their numerous apologies.

After years of listening to other people's versions of the definition of forgiveness I would eventually develop one of my own. I had a right to have a breaking point. Forgive and trust are not synonymous. My forgiveness can provide you an opportunity to build trust again, and sometimes forgiving is simply a pleasant way to say goodbye. I have no right to condemn you, but you have no right to be in my life.

As a child, I was defined by adults because I had no definitions of my own. It was not as if my mother could ever say to me, "I am sorry

I made you accept Axel's false apology instead of teaching you to be discerning."

Instead she tried to sugar coat it, literally. She brought over the bowl with the leftover icing from her birthday cake and three spoons. It was to be a temporary distraction from the whole ordeal. Unfortunately, Axel took even that from us. Peanut said, "Mommy, you didn't finish icing the cake."

Our mother responded, "Of course I did honey."

Peanut raised the spoon our mother had just given her, pointed it at the cake and said, "See, you missed a spot."

Apparently on the way out Axel decided that he needed a little dessert to go with his theft. He had left a finger-sized gouge in the side of the cake. The remainder of the icing had to be used to spackle that gouge. Despite the repair the cake had a noticeable dent in it. That left only enough icing in the bowl for each of us to run our finger once around the bowl. I was content with the dab of icing on my finger because I was already plotting to get the icing rich dented piece of the cake when it was cut.

Our mother retreated into routine to banish the events of the day. She cleaned places she had already cleaned and made her grocery list for tomorrow's shopping even though we had no money. She absentmindedly searched her purse two more times.

Finally, she made us a late lunch of grilled cheese and tomato soup from the last of the cheese and bread. With the exception of a can of baking powder, the can of tomato soup had been the last can of anything in the cupboard. For the most part everything that was left to eat in the house was on the counter ready to be prepared for the evening meal. We had done just enough shopping on Thursday at an expensive local store to carry us through to Sunday.

After serving us, she went back to the kitchen counter to prep our dinner. As the hands of the clock sped toward five o'clock, a look of confidence gradually returned to her face. The man who got her out of Bellefontaine would be home soon. He could do anything.

CHAPTER 15 NOT ALL THE WOUNDED RECEIVE A PURPLE HEART

The turn of the back doorknob was tentative, almost as if my step-father wasn't sure he wanted to come home. As time wore on, I learned to gauge his mood simply from the turn of the key or how roughly the doorknob was handled. In homes where we had two doors, if the doorknob signaled malice when he came in one door, if I was able, I fled out the other. Today there was sadness in the turn.

My mother rushed to him to unburden her bad news. She could not read doorknobs yet. She only paused because of his expression. His face was a blank slate waiting for her voice to write an emotion on it. The doorknob had displayed more emotion.

"What's the matter?" she asked, true concern in her voice.

What I had mistaken for a blank face was really a shade pulled down over his emotions. He was vying for time to compose himself so that he could display the emotions he wanted the world to see instead of the ones he was truly feeling. Men tend to turn their vulnerable emotions into something else. Frustration, discomfort, annoyance and anger become the masks for fear, grief, sadness and depression. My mother wisely chose to stifle her bad news.

Nibbling her lip from worry, my mother pressed him further, "Is everything all right?"

He chose frustration and discomfort to pose for us today. That was as vulnerable as he was willing to get. Pulling at his tie to loosen it brought him no comfort. He took a seat directly across from Peanut's chair. He uncoiled his tie and tossed it on the table as if it had been a vice around his throat stopping him from speaking. He started a sentence three times but each time it died on his lips.

Finally, he slapped the table hard and barked out, "I will tell you later, after dinner." His anger was not directed at us, but anger desires a target and vicinity is often the determining factor rather than justification.

After a few moments of awkward silence, Gwen, Peanut and I returned to our chatter, which seemed to outwardly calm him. Wanting to be anywhere but inside his head, conversations headed back towards somewhat normal. He reverted to his military training, mostly giving us orders. "Wash your hands, don't put your elbows on the table, clean your plates." Finally, at the end of our meal, his frown struggled to become a smile. He got up and reached into the pocket of the coat he had hung from the doorknob. He retrieved a small, gift-wrapped box.

The gift he was giving had invisible strings attached, invisible even to him. It probably was not his intention when he bought it, but now he had pinned his hope on the ability of our mother's gratitude to pull him out of the remainder of his mood. Him standing there presenting his gift was almost as if we were watching a tow truck pulling a wrecked, stranded car from a fast-moving treacherous river. Then the cable snapped, or rather was inadvertently cut by my words.

Envious, I said, "We had a gift for mommy too." I paused to avoid the honorific of Uncle and continued, "But your brother Axel broke it."

My words were well-meaning although they were tinged with a little jealousy. He was giving our mother a gift and I had nothing to give her; we had nothing to give her. We had never before given our mother a substantial birthday present, because we simply never had the means, or someone did it on our behalf. We now lived near a junkyard, a place where, "It's the thought that counts," could be turned into something tangible. Bits of the gift I had intended to give our mother, the Delft plate with the windmill that wouldn't turn, still lay on the back stoop and on the ground. The parts ground into powder under Axel's heel had been whisked away by the wind.

He gave me a confused look and said, "Did your grandparents pack a gift for your mother? Did Axel damage it the night he was arrested?"

From his questions my mother knew he didn't know his brother had been released from jail. She tried to clean up my bad timing and salvage the situation with a question of her own, "You didn't know he's out of jail either?"

He shook his head.

Our mother tried to make light of the situation with Axel. Then she began prying and querying her husband into disclosing the events of his day. She wanted to escape so badly into something that wasn't her fault. Try as she might to distract him from talking about Axel, she couldn't. He wanted to escape his day as well. Each was running from their own burning building into the others. As they passed one another they both yelled to the other, "Don't go in there."

Finally, he asked, "Did he hurt you or the kids?" By default, they were back in her burning building.

She shook her head to say no.

Being ashamed was her first mistake. She was crawling and begging with her words, taking the blame for events beyond her control. In her world you didn't shut the door in the face of family, in-laws included. In any case she couldn't have locked the door with Axel and her children on one side of the door and herself on the other side. Although she thought we were over at Mister Willy's house, we could have come home any time and found the wolf at the door.

She ended her confession with, "If it hadn't been for the bullet holes in the refrigerator, my daughters would've suffocated."

He just stood there and said nothing. All of a sudden, he grabbed my mother's birthday cake and hurled it against the wall. Before the cake completed its slide down the wall to hit the floor, he was out the door, slamming it on his parting words, "What kind of mother are you?"

She had been abandoned by a husband that she had hoped would catch and wipe away her tears; instead he had been the cause of them. Her tears were too heavy for us to catch and too high for us to wipe away. My sisters and I stood stunned. We had never seen our mother cry. She cried and lied, pretending that everything was going to be all right. I felt bad on so many levels. She had always humored me in my games of pretend. If I looked at the sky and said a cloud was a bunny, she would see it too. Last year for Mother's Day I had saved a plastic ring from my box of Cracker Jack and wrapped it up in some leftover Christmas paper to give to her. She pretended it was Christmas and that I had bejeweled her with the Star of India. Yet I couldn't reciprocate. No matter how hard I tried, looking at a smashed cake on the floor, I just couldn't see things were alright. All I could do for her was hold back my own tears so she could tend her own. Fortunately, my sisters did the same.

Once the cake was cleaned off the floor and wall, my mother's words became believable again. It was as if the smashed cake had been calling her every word into question. She stopped crying as well, which helped. She finally said something we could believe, promising us she would make another cake and we could have as big a piece as we liked. A big slice of cake in exchange for a small life, the promise made us all feel a little better. Anything else would have been a lie.

The rest of the evening was one of distractions. Our mother took us upstairs early for our baths. We begged and pleaded not to have to take a second bath. She relented and instead gave us sponge baths.

I didn't mind sponge baths because she only washed the parts that showed. She wet the washcloth and moved it over our arms and faces, just enough to push the dirt around. It was more like being dusted than washed. Her heart just wasn't in it. Her touch was so slight the wet cloth left a light streak of mud across Gwen's forehead, which matched her hair color. For a moment it looked like Gwen had sweeping bangs. A second swipe of the washcloth erased them.

The bathroom was at the back of the house. It was the only room unto itself. There were no halls. All the other rooms ran into each other. We air dried then our mother led us through her bedroom into ours, which was in the front, overlooking the penitentiary. We went to bed early, but we didn't go to sleep. Our mother went downstairs and brought up some paper, scissors, crayons and my fire truck.

She joined us on the bed in our nest of cotton sheets and woolen blankets. She cut paper dolls for us while we colored them. I used every crayon in the box. My doll had a pink polka-dot dress which clashed with all the other colors I had used to make her a plaid and paisley fireman's coat. Despite her attire and mode of transportation, she was still a lady. I folded her at the waist and knees so she could sit side-saddle as I got out of the bed and gave her a ride around the room on my fire truck. The room filled with the sounds of giggles and my high-pitched siren sound as my pangender paper doll and I circled the room.

A few crayons, paper, attention from our mother and a little peek into my closet helped to temporarily banish the events of the day. Our mother allowed us to be silly a little past our bedtime. Then the giggles gradually turned into yawns, and yawns turned to sleep. My sisters fell asleep gently clutching their paper dolls. I followed suit shortly with my pangender doll nestled against my cheek and my left arm draped over my fire truck. I had choices to make.

I woke to the sound of whispers. It wasn't the buzzing insect sound of a whisper that was spoken close and into the ear. It was more the sound of distant moving water, flowing along the ceiling from my parents' room, much as errant raindrops flow along the ceiling from a leaking roof. The whispers hung there momentarily, growing ever heavier with emotion before losing their perch and falling into my ear. "Shush, David don't wake the kids," I heard my mother say.

My stepfather yelled, his voice bouncing off the walls with such force I imagined his words leaving dents in them.

"Don't shush me in my own house. I'll say whatever I want as loud as I want." All his *s*'s hissed from the scotch he'd been drinking.

Our mother whispered a retort that was swiftly stomped into

the ground by my stepfather's bellicose voice. He yelled and she whispered. The battle was already uneven.

For a brief moment I was on his side as he said, "I have to go to work and worry about you letting money fly out the door because you let my brother into the house when I am not here. I don't ever want him in my house when I am not here."

I didn't want Axel in our house under any circumstances. Then he called my mother a bad name, and I was back on her side again. At the same time, I heard him angrily punch the wall near their bed, accidentally knocking the lamp on the nightstand onto the floor. The light cast long menacing shadows of his lower legs and the legs of the bed onto the walls and ceiling of our bedroom. I heard my mother grunt. As one, Peanut and I jumped out of bed to run into our parents' room. I saw our mother slumped over the edge of the bed. Before I could form an emotion, she lifted her torso back onto the bed, bringing the lamp onto the nightstand minus the lampshade.

Our stepfather yelled at us, "Go back to your room. This is between your mother and me."

Fear froze us in place. Our legs quivered beneath us, but we would not budge except to circle nervously in place. Unconsciously we hoped to be a distraction, an interruption to the fighting. We played the reverse role of baby birds pretending to have broken wings to lure the fox away from the mother bird.

Not to have her role as mother usurped, she stopped our bird dance. She said in a firm, commanding voice, "This is grown folks' business. Now go to your room and stay there."

We still didn't move.

Seeing our hesitation, she switched to a voice that was more a plea. "Please go get under your covers." Not go back to bed but get under your covers. Don't go to sleep but hide.

We went back to bed, dragging our useless gesture of defiance behind us. Defeated and deflated. I didn't have to pretend to have broken wings. They were not fully formed yet and they were already broken.

That night I learned how nestlings must feel as they listen to their mother being devoured by a predator while they were hidden in tall reeds, a sacrifice made so one day they might fly.

Peanut and I crawled into bed to join Gwen. We tucked the edges of the blanket under our bodies to form a protective dome of wool around us and we slowly worried our hips into the mattress. For the moment my world had shrunk down to this pitch-black cocoon filled with stifled sobs and heavy breathing. The dark was not comforting for long. Its gentle hug slowly began to constrict. The metal object that I had unconsciously picked up before running into my parents' room turned out to be my fire truck. I now nervously played with its wheels as if they were worry beads. The little red light came on and cast a glow, which illuminated my sisters' faces. The toy emergency light distorted their faces into papier-mâché masks of fear.

Gwen laid between Peanut and me. Instinctively we had put the youngest in the middle. Peanut had her arm draped over Gwen. Both were clutching their paper dolls for comfort, their frail little hands acting as flesh and bone corsets, cinching their dolls at the waist. Their squeezing did not produce the mechanical sound of a real doll's cry. Their dolls could only crinkle. I heard my paper doll crinkle under my shoulder. I reached for it, letting the fire truck's light die. I didn't want to see the papier-mâché children crushing their little paper dolls. Similar to our dolls our souls were being crushed like paper.

Our fearful fingers continued to tighten the already thin waists of our dolls past the point of anorexia. When our hands could crush the dolls no further the crinkling sound stopped. Then our stepfather's voice seized the night.

Drunk as he was, he purposely and carefully chose each word to disarm our mother. He had everything over her, strength, dependence and the home court advantage. All her friends and family were hundreds of miles away. This was still not enough for him. He needed more vulnerability. He wanted no resistance from her at all. Had he not laid a hand on her the damage still would have been done.

He also was a master at disguising his cruelty as kindness. With a voice so sincere, his tongue almost wept as he said, "I am starting to love your children and you almost took them away from me with your carelessness and foolishness. How would I have explained to your parents if our children died on my watch?" With those words he had taken possession of my sisters and me as well as disarmed his wife.

Worse than disarming her, he had enlisted her as an ally in her own destruction. I could almost hear the internal silent beating she was giving herself, matching him blow for blow. Young as I was, I knew she was doing it because I was beating myself up inside as well. It was I who locked my sisters in the refrigerator, causing this. I was afraid but didn't want our stepfather to come looking for me only to grab the wrong person from under the blanket. Our judge did not have discriminating hands. I lifted the covers to join my mother in her punishment.

Peanut dropped her doll and grabbed my wrist. Her grip was insistent that I not leave the bed. Her sharp nails digging into my flesh and the pulse running through her fingers was like having a living shackle attached to my wrist. It tightened the more I struggled. I would have to sprain her fingers and shred my wrist in order to break free.

Instead I kissed Peanut's hand and said, "Watch Gwen."

She instantly released my wrist. Even a dry kiss on the hand from her brother was too wet for her. At first, I thought she withdrew her hand to wipe away my affection. Instead she placed her arm back over Gwen in a protective arch.

I grabbed my fire truck for comfort. The floor creaked as I stepped from the bed. Although my stepfather was rapidly shoveling coal onto my mother's guilt, she was aware enough to take notice and said, "Grant, stay in your room."

My stepfather turned my immature chivalry against my mother, saying, "Look how willing he is to protect you, but you couldn't do the same for them."

I stayed in the room but did not go back to bed. I wanted to yell and say it was my fault, not hers. Before I could say anything, he got her to confess it was her fault. Although I could not see into the room from where I stood, I could see their distorted shadows cast on our bedroom floor from the light my stepfather had knocked the shade off of. Their shadows looked like elongated praying mantises with human heads. Although shadowed and distorted, I still could recognize the defeat in my mother's nod of guilt.

He was now emboldened to strike her. The shadow of my mother's cheek tilted slightly up toward the shadow of his open hand as though anticipating the blow. As the shadow of his hand came down, it balled into a fist. The slap sound I had been expecting became a thud and a crunch as the bones of his fist, covered thinly with flesh, connected with her cheekbone.

Her shadow disappeared from our bedroom floor as the blow knocked her into the bedding. His shadow loomed over the shadow of some pillows and a silhouette of the top of her now disheveled hair. He paused as if he was sunning himself under the sixty-watt light bulb on the nightstand, basking in his power over her. Small people have small suns. The shadow of his head pivoted expectantly almost as if he was seeking applause from an audience. He heard the beginnings of Peanut's, Gwen's and my cries. That was applause enough.

I looked down at our bed. The outline of my sisters under the blanket grew smaller as they held each other, both trying to hide inside the other. Their cries were muffled but audible. My body shook and shuddered from crying myself. I was breathing fast and taking in huge volumes of air, yet I felt as if I were suffocating. My crying was stealing almost all my air, leaving me only enough air to stand paralyzed, able only to watch the shadow puppet show on our bedroom floor. Had I been able to, I would have lifted my free right hand into the air to grab invisible hunks of oxygen to shove into my deprived lungs. My mouth and nose simply were not taking in enough to feed my crying.

I watched my mother slowly lean back up from the bed, not even raising her hand to salve the blow on her cheek. Why bother? More were coming or maybe she was too busy tending the wounds inside to be bothered with surface ones.

The shadow of his head turned toward the crying coming from our room. Our crying only brought us further into the fight. It called attention to us and he used us as a weapon. He yelled so loud I could actually see the shadow of his mouth opening and closing. It was as if I were watching a shadow poorly lip-syncing to its own songs and verses. The lips on the floor seemed to elongate and exaggerate every word. Yet they were out of sync with the words crashing on my ears from their bedroom. It seemed almost as if his shadow was drunk instead of him.

However, his next words were crystal clear: "You never really wanted your kids, did you?"

She shook her head in agreement, not knowing I could see her affirmation on the wooden slats of our floor. She lifted her head and said, "But—." He swiped his hand in front of the space between them, seemingly snatching the word out of midair as if it had not been spoken. His hand ended raised above his head in a backhand striking position, ready to silence any forthcoming words that would contradict his narrative.

It was true we were not wanted, but it was truth stripped of all its grey areas to make it uglier than it really was. We were her children, but we were also three broken promises, consequences of acts of desperation. We were not born to a loving mother and not loved at first. More like suitors than children, we had to court our own mother, building her love for us brick by brick, touch by touch and kiss by kiss. But in the months leading up to our leaving Bellefontaine she had grown to love us. We were an obligation that grew into love. But this love did not have a long history on her part. He was going out of his way to make sure we knew it. He had balled up our ill-conceived births into a fist and verbally punched us all in the center of our souls with it.

My mother defied his threatening raised hand and said, "I do love my children."

My stepfather's shadow feigned pity. He lowered his hand to a neutral position and said, "I didn't say you didn't love them, I said you didn't want them."

She turned her face away from his harsh words. The shadow of her profile now became a shadow of just her head. He wouldn't let her escape, not even into herself. He was turning her internal refuge into a place where the gavel of self-judgment clapped like thunder and her own nails raked across her soul. He was making the beating her fault.

He yelled, "Look at me when I am talking to you." He punctuated his sentence with a slap across her face that spun her profile back to facing him.

She didn't yell out, keeping her expressions in chains so as not to antagonize him further. With him even a blank face could be considered back talking. Her shadowed profile implied nothing. He inferred anything he wanted to.

His voice suddenly held sympathy. "I understand you wanting to get out of your town. Damn, there are more letters in its name than there are people on its streets." He continued, "I really get that."

He gently cupped her chin in his hand and said, "Some might say you were a whore for having three children by three different men. I would not marry a whore. I used the military to change my situation and you used the men in the military to change yours. In my mind that makes us the same."

The sympathy in his voice and his hand on her chin had been a mirage, something you wanted to see but wasn't really there. He loved to be in control of your emotions. He'd make you feel one way one moment and jerk you the opposite way just to see the expression on your face. He enjoyed watching the hope in your eyes as you searched his face for any signs the violence would soon end. Then he would watch it die and attend its funeral as you realized that he was just beginning.

The hand that had been caressing her chin swiftly moved to her throat. He growled, "But it wasn't your plan that got you out of that town. It was mine. All of those other men broke their promises. I kept mine."

He had her throat in his hand, tilting her head side to side, examining her, contemplating which emotions he wanted her to feel next. Meanwhile my own emotions swirled around inside me. I was desperately trying to coax them into forming a queue so I could deal with them one at a time. Finally fear subdued the other emotions, and I backed away from the shadows on the floor. I was not afraid of my own shadow. I was afraid of other people's shadows.

He slapped my mother a third time, followed up by a question. "What is it that you think I expect of you?"

I don't know if she didn't answer his question or if I didn't hear it.

His left hand came down hard on her face, spraying blood in the air and across the bed. I saw the blood as a faint shadow arching across the floor. Some of it landed on the hot light bulb next to the bed. Within moments the faint smell of burning blood was added to the sights and sounds of violence. I continued to back up until my retreat was halted by the sill of the window overlooking the prison. Their shadows merged, fell onto the bed, and I heard my mother scream. I heard the rip of clothing. The violence intensified and became more intimate.

I turned away from the merged shadows and looked out the window. The cold emanating off the glass window felt like the warmth of a fireplace compared to the chills coming from the other room. The panes were covered in raindrops. It was as if the house was weeping on our behalf. I watched more raindrops appear on the window. They landed as quietly as tears.

Reflected in the panes of the window I saw an old face on a young boy. The expression on the face made me feel as if I were the reflection. I touched the glass with my hand. It was cold and wet, and I was real. Yet I envied my reflection because it was on the other side of the glass. There was a crash from the other room that startled my reflection and me. Then I realized he was not safe on his side either.

I did my best to block out the world behind me, her whimpering and his angry moans of pleasure. Although the sound from the bed sounded similar to the ones made when my sisters and I jumped up and down on our bed pretending it was a trampoline, I knew better. The pace was too rapid and violent.

There was no physical place for me to go. My mind grew feet so it could retreat further into the window. The reflection of tears on my cheeks and the spatters of rain formed a collage of wet, cold and glass. I bonded with the rain. It was as much my twin as my reflection, a physical confirmation of how I was feeling. It did as I did. I saw tears run down my cheeks. Enough rain had finally accumulated on the windowpane for the drops to run like tears down its glass cheek.

The windowsill on the inside was flat. My tears and condensation pooled there. I looked at the little boy in the window. I saw he had a fire truck in his hand, which meant I had one in my hand. It was a rickety thought born of desperation. I hoped to use the red light of my fire truck to signal the guards in the prison to come to our rescue. I ran the truck through the puddle on the sill. The wet kept the wheels from creating friction, which kept the little red light from coming on. I wiped the sill with the sleeve of my pajamas and ran the truck over the sill again. The light came on and started flashing, which it had never done before. My hope grew a little only to die moments later. It was only a little red light in the dark, in a rainstorm. No one saw and no one came.

For sanity's sake I continued to push the truck long after my hope had died. I pretended the truck had sound and that the wails and cries of my mother were its siren. I pushed so hard the wheel Mister Willy had fixed broke off. The exposed metal started gouging the windowsill. My arms grew tired. I still pushed. The truck gouged deeper into the wood. I pushed harder. The light died. I still pushed. If I stopped pushing, those sounds would belong to my mother. No child can hear such sounds emanating from their mother and remain an innocent child.

The child that I buried that day would sometimes be exhumed at the strangest moments. Years later I was among friends who lightheartedly discussed how mortified they were when they had accidentally caught their parents making love. They laughed an embarrassed laugh while I cried behind a fake smile and kept silent about the first time my stepfather raped my mother. It was only shadows and sounds, but I had witnessed rape.

It is physically impossible for children to witness the consummation of their parents' marriage as the act predates them. But the groom was not our father, and this was consummation by violence; that night the obey part of their marriage vows was enforced. The bloody sheets were not from being deflowered but from being disempowered and were not proudly displayed as confirmation to a proud village. They were secretly washed by the victim, hurried back onto the bed and covered up with blankets and lies.

CHAPTER 16   CHAIN ME NOT TO HIM

I woke to my sisters standing over me staring down at me. I had fallen asleep under the windowsill. My pajama sleeve was still damp from wiping the windowsill to clear a path for the fire truck. The fire truck sat on the sill looking as weary as I felt. Had I pushed it all night? Peanut and Gwen stood in silence. Their pupils had motes in the shape of question marks in them. "What do we do now?" their eyes asked.

I always forget how much of our communication was nonverbal at that age. Without speaking we came to the consensus to go downstairs where we could hear our mother in the kitchen. Loud snoring coming from the bed in the next room blocked our path. We clung so tightly together that had anyone witnessed our passage through our parent's bedroom, they would have sworn that it was a six-legged animal in transit instead of three, frightened children.

We scurried past our sleeping stepfather as if we were whistling past a graveyard. Unfortunately, my eyes briefly landed on the light bulb with my mother's dried blood on it. My metaphoric whistle turned into a pucker with no sound.

Seeing the blood on the light bulb frightened me. I was torn between running to our mother and fearful of seeing her. Gwen set the pace of our descent down the stairs. She was of the age where she scooted down the stairs on her butt instead of walking down them. I was both grateful and angry with her for slowing us down. I went last, but before descending the stairs I caught a glimpse of something white and bloody on the bathroom sink. It was the day after our mother's twenty-first birthday; she was now the legal age to drink alcohol. Instead of imbibing from a shot glass, she took her alcohol on a cotton ball applied to a split lip.

Before we had reached the bottom step our mother told us to sit at the table. Her voice held no command. It was faint and weak. We

166

obeyed out of habit and went to our chairs, our heads bent towards the table as if saying grace. None of us dared to look at our mother yet. Our eyes darted back and forth among us, daring each other to look first. I don't know if Peanut lost her patience or summoned her courage, but she looked first. Gwen and I swiftly followed suit.

Our mother's back was turned to us. Her shoulders were hunched, her head bent so low her chin must have been touching her chest. She was also afraid to look up at us. Making eye contact had been beaten out of her.

She was intentionally keeping her back to us. Normally she brought our bowls of farina to the table. Instead she summoned us to retrieve them from the counter near the stove. Peanut and I grabbed our bowls. The counter was too high for Gwen, so after getting my bowl I returned to grab hers. I tried to peek at our mother's face, but she avoided me by opening the refrigerator door, pretending to search for nothing in its vast emptiness.

If I had been paying attention, I would have noticed our farina was at half portions. We would be eating farina for a while, and then the only thing we would have for dinner would be sleep. Her bowl held even less than ours, compliments of Axel, a beating and hunger.

For the most part she kept silent. When she did speak, it was from behind her hunched shoulders with her back turned towards us. It was mostly small talk that did not match the situation. I knew Peanut would lose patience first. She didn't have words to express her frustration. Instead she reached over to Gwen and pinched her arm as hard as she could. Gwen squealed on cue. Our mother reacted instinctively and turned to face us. Gwen's crying was cut off in mid wail by the sight of our mother's face.

We all stared into each other's wrecked faces, hers from a beating and ours from horror and shock. What she saw earlier in the mirror in private was nothing compared to looking into the mirrors that were her children. Glass mirrors only showed what she looked like. The mirrors that were her children showed the damage beyond her face. If pressed, she could call the glass mirror a liar but not us.

If our mother had looked into a magic mirror, she would have seen only half of her former self. Normal mirrors were literal and only reflected light. A magic mirror would have shown her image with a crack down the middle. The half that still was her was barely recognizable. The other half was a stranger, having been destroyed and replaced by the narrative her husband had chosen for her. He tried to make her into something he wanted without knowing exactly what it was he really wanted. It would change with every beating. He had no form himself. It was as if she was molding clay. He just liked slapping and pounding the clay. He knew how to get what he didn't really want. He liked the power of taking. Once obtained, he disdained it and crushed it before the giver's eyes.

My only point of reference for violence up until that time had been TV. I had only seen black and white cartoons beaten as badly she had been. She stood before us, her bruises in full color. Unlike cartoons, who healed by the next scene, measured in mere seconds, our mother's next healthy scene was days or weeks away.

Things also ached inside of her that had no name or discernible location. There was so much sadness and shame in her, the emotions somehow dwarfed the bruises and abrasions on her face. It was no longer a face fit for smiles. For our sake she tried to smile, but her lips could raise no higher than a wan sneer. Smiles are heavy when you try to lift one to a face that doesn't really want it. I thought of her makeup case, the one I had guarded all the way from the airport, makeup instead of bandages, but her ruined face could not support even a painted-on smile. I was desperately searching for my mother hidden under the bruises and shame.

The night's violence had separated us and sent us scurrying for shelter deep inside ourselves. We were timidly reemerging from ourselves to gather together. We stared at each other, trying to get used to each other again, or rather the new us. None of us were the same anymore. We ate in silence.

We heard the toilet upstairs flush. Shortly thereafter he descended the stairs. With the exception of our mother, we each struck a pose that we deemed suitable for appeasement. Our faces were like chameleons, twisting and distorting to accommodate his mood. Sometimes our compliant faces were insufficient and there was no accommodating him. I dreamed a chameleon's dream of changing color to match the garish wallpaper or the plaid couch. Even in despair, I never wanted to blend into something as bland or simple as a plain wall. Try as we might, the best we could come up with was sullen.

He entered the kitchen stretching and yawning as if it was just another morning. When he lowered his hands, I noticed that the knuckles on one of them had cuts and was swollen. I got a pitiful form of satisfaction from that, until I looked from my stepfather's hand to my mother's face.

Unlike us, he didn't have to go searching for the damage he had done to her. She had not turned her face away from him. The look she gave him was not quite defiant. She was too injured for that. She tried to salvage her dignity by making wavering eye contact with her husband. I got a brief glimpse of the strangle marks on her neck before her chin retreated back to her chest. No matter how much my stomach protested, the half portion of farina proved too much to force down past the sympathetic lump in my own throat.

He showed no reaction to seeing his wife's face. It was as if his own face was made of stone, making it nearly impossible to quarry any expression from it. When he went to kiss our mother, she turned away from him. Her mannerism said, I am not ready for your kiss yet and even if I were, there is no pain-free space on my face to place one.

Her rejection of him made chisel marks of concern at the corners of his mouth. He said, "About last night, maybe I was a little hard on you." His apology sounded like he was merely apologizing for being five minutes late instead of beating and raping her.

The silence emanated from us, the judge and jury, over his insincere apologies. It was not as if my mother, sisters and I had suddenly retrieved our courage. We simply had no place else to run. We individually had retreated into ourselves only to find no solace. Our backs were against the wall. He had all the room to move. We had none.

He gave us a withering look that commanded we forgive him. He had the nerve to demand from us something by rights he should have begged for. We remained unmoved. I never had to forgive someone on such a deep level. Most transgressions against me had been small things that I didn't even have to forgive so much as I would simply forget about them.

He offered her another excuse disguised as an apology. The first one died of hypothermia from the cold shoulder she was giving him. Still failing, he began to spin an explanation that would make her the bad guy for not forgiving him. Sliding over a chair from the other side of the table, he wedged himself between us. Peanut and I sat to the left of him and Gwen sat to his right. He was using us against her again. He took turns leaning his liquored-up breath into our faces. Sleep had further distilled the alcohol on his breath into an equally distasteful morning breath. His halitosis was the only honest thing about him.

As bad as the beating was, the manipulation was worse. He would manipulate her into thinking that tending to her personal needs was an extreme act of selfishness; only breathing and serving his needs were considered appropriate. She was trapped in a relationship of selfless service to an unworthy cause. He often manipulated her through us.

He turned his back towards Gwen and our mother and looked into Peanut's and my eyes as if he were a politician speaking to a camera. He was not really speaking to us. He was speaking to a broader audience, our mother. The expressions on our faces and in our eyes were his invisible cue cards. He read them expertly.

Pretending to seek absolution, he reached his hand toward us, the one puffy from striking our mother's face. Peanut held her hands in her lap, with a now guarded expression on her face, depriving him of one of his cue cards. As my hand was flat on the table, he beckoned it to reach out to his. My hand had reservations. It pretended to be a mouse, sniffing at the hand of truce as if it were a well-baited trap. I tentatively met it halfway, hopeful that as long as he was talking, he was not hitting. I felt as if I were a survivor from the Titanic, desperately seeking safety by swimming towards the very iceberg that had caused the situation. There were no more lifeboats; freeze or drown. His puffy hand pounced on mine, stealing the heat from my hand without warming his own.

Whether I liked it or not I was to be his confessional, to receive his pittance of penitence without the protection of a screen, lattice, curtain, or sneeze guard. The cold expectant look in his eyes begged for a Bloody Mary over a Hail Mary. I was a child, not a bartender or priest, but I was a male child, possibly entitled to some future respect. It turned out not to be a confession. It was manipulation.

The way he framed the conversation was meant to discourage any dissension. I was a young male who didn't understand yet but one day, according to him, I would. Women couldn't possibly understand, ever. It was the way men who thought themselves superior to women could talk behind women's backs to their faces. You wouldn't send a dog out of the room to talk about it. You assumed it didn't understand and even if it could understand, you didn't care; you were the master. Except he did care in a selfish way. He wasn't quite the master yet. He still had to be careful. He had beat her too early into the relationship and wasn't sure she was in deep enough not to run.

He said, "Last night I did not set a good example of what a man should be, and you are a boy without a father. You need a male example."

The hidden message to my mother was, "You may be able to raise your daughters to womanhood without a man but not your son."

I was already learning by negative example. I did not know what type of man I wanted to be, but I was learning what type of man I didn't want to be. One such sat across from me. That day I crossed misogynistic rapist off my list. I was destined to become a man as much through the process of elimination as by examples.

He continued, "I let anger get the best of me and you should never do that, but I was pushed."

His apologies were always clipped and short while the excuses were long and accusatory. "I did it, but you made me do it." It was the template for all the abuse and apologies to come. Just change the time and place and insert a lie. Except this was the first and last time that I almost believed him.

He continued, "If Axel hadn't been let into the house, we would still have money and you wouldn't have almost killed your sisters. How do you think it feels to come home from a hard day's work only to find all your money has been stolen and you have two funerals to pay for?"

I would have felt some guilt for my action had I not lived in fear of two potential funerals becoming four real ones. Deep down inside I knew this man could kill us. Calm was what he presented, but volatility lurked behind his every word. It was as if he were presenting a twenty-pound turkey as garnish for a sprig of parsley instead of the other way around. Carve the parsley up, put gravy on it and pass it off as the main course. No one will know the difference.

I wanted to ask, "Why didn't you go find Axel and beat him like you beat my mother?" but the invisible hand of common sense pulled my tongue back from my lips. I swallowed my words and washed them down with a spoonful of farina. I had to keep my mouth occupied with something other than speaking the truth.

It was my job to listen, not to speak. He was clever. Although his back was turned towards my mother, he was able to gauge her facial expression from my own. After each comment or question I unconsciously glanced towards my mother and transferred her expression to my face. It was easier than creating my own.

Encouraged, he said, "Yesterday I found out a good friend of mine was killed in Vietnam." He never told us the friend's name.

Along with most of America I had no clue we were at war. I had only heard of two wars up until that time, the Civil War and World War Two. My grandfather and most of his brothers had fought in the latter. I knew wars were dangerous and destructive but had no concept of geopolitics. I thought the world was flat. When I heard a term such as around the world, I pictured drawing circles on a flat surface more than circling the equator. Vietnam could be anywhere between here, the North Pole and Candy Land. Visions of shell-shattered peppermint houses and smoke rising from igloos flashed across my mind.

I didn't look for cues from my mother this time. The look on my face was my own and it asked a question without words: Would Bellefontaine and Baltimore be next?

Using my expression to his advantage, he said, "Vietnam is far away. The only people from here who will die are those who fly or sail there. My friend was one of those people. War will not come here, but my friend will not be coming home to his family."

My facial expressions could not keep up with the conversation. My face had stalled on relief that here in Baltimore we were safe from foreign wars. Our danger was homegrown. Before my face could register concern for his loss, he pivoted his chair toward my mother. I was no longer needed. He didn't look directly at her. His head was bent low, not to hide his feigned pain and shame but to hide his darting, calculating eyes. He sat, pretending to stare into his hands, which were resting in his lap, palms up as if ready to receive alms. In truth it was an imaginary book from which he read his script.

I know now my mother was waiting to hear any story that said it was not a mistake to leave her family to come live with this man. One beating was not too high a price to pay for her exodus.

He tailored his story to her need. "My friend is not coming home to his family and I felt guilty for coming home to mine. You were a victim of a victim. I wish I could have stopped the pain at just me instead of passing it on to you. I was unconsciously trying to destroy my family and drive you away. I understand if you want to leave and go back to Ohio. Maybe I don't deserve this family."

My mother was crying tears of guilt. They ran down her cheeks, salting the wounds on her face. Wounds she now believed were self-inflicted. She bent down to hug him with the parts of her body that didn't hurt. Her forgiving him swiftly transformed into apologizing profusely for her insensitivity. We were a few years past the dance craze "The Twist" but no one could do the twist like my stepfather.

I watched him avoid the hurt parts of her body as they hugged, kissed and made up. He gently caressed an arm until he reached a bruised elbow. He skipped over the bruised elbow down to her hand, but he could only touch her thumb because her fingers were swollen from her failed attempts to block his blows. He cupped his hand on her lower back and gave her right side an old chump hug. Her left side winced even against the touch of her clothing. He kissed the right side of her lip, leaving the ruined left side unattended.

He handled the death of a friend by beating his wife. I would rarely know what would set him off. Prying often would make it worse, because listening to his excuse that was not reasonable would only add to the suffering. Listening to a drunken mind playing make-believe at your expense was a beating within a beating. To make it all stop you would promise to never again do what you never really did in the first place. My mother, sisters and I would become the stunt doubles for the images he had of us in his head. The family in his head transgressed against him, but we paid the price.

He would use the death of a friend in Vietnam as an excuse one more time to rain down destruction on our house. It was after the battle of La Drang Valley in November of 1965. Although the war would be over before I reached the eligible draft age, 1965 was the year I had reached the eligible age to get beaten along with my mother. I was part of the legion of boys who tried to stand up for their mothers, only to be backhanded into cheap plastered walls. The war abroad and the one in our home would not go well or away.

I rarely paid attention to the news. But for several weeks after the Battle of La Drang Valley, I paid attention to the casualty reports on the nightly news, because he had used a death in Vietnam as an excuse to fuel his violence against us. The Vietnam War was for most Americans a TV war that could be watched while eating TV dinners on trays. A knock on the door could suddenly make a TV war very personal. The practice of sending death notifications by cab drivers or Western Union would change to a personal notification system shortly after the Battle of La Drang Valley. Similar to many families from past wars, we had received unfortunate news of the war from a man from Western Union, our stepfather. Although after 1965 he never brought news of death through our doors again, a high casualty report on the news and fumbling keys at our door late at night would still cause my teeth to chatter. When not chattering I would use them to whittle my fingernails to nubs. Many lived in fear of a visit from the man from Western Union, but the man from Western Union had keys to our house.

He hadn't delivered bad news so much as he was bad news. He was a walking, living telegram that read, "ACCUSE ACCUSE ACCUSE STOP EXCUSE EXCUSE EXCUSE STOP LIE LIE LIE STOP." The form of the message was always the same: only the types of accusations, excuses and lies changed. Keeping track of the lies and excuses was pointless. I would do it anyway in the hope of heading off his temper. I thought I could appease and please my way out of violence by chasing his whims. He was always a step ahead while I was always a fear behind. If it wasn't bad news, then it could be dirty dishes. He would find dirty spots on a dish that a team of forensic scientists couldn't. I would scrub so hard that I would rub the lily of the valley pattern off the plates. Then he changed excuses. As time went on the excuses grew smaller and pettier.

He would become creative with his cruelty. Sometimes he would catch my sisters and me doing something wrong or fabricate a wrong for us. Then he would pretend it was nothing and he really wasn't angry with us. He would make a joke about how clever and funny we were. Sometimes he would tell several jokes, extending the charade for several minutes, taking us far from our initial fear, relaxing us with laughter. Then out of nowhere he would slap or punch us. With a grin on his face that mocked our mirth, he would ask us what the hell was so funny. It could end there or get worse depending on his mood. Although the slap hurt, it was not nearly as jarring as switching between opposite emotions so suddenly or the knowledge that you lived with someone who prompted a laugh or smile from you for the sole purpose of destroying it.

It wouldn't be until I was around the age of thirteen before I would get over my apprehension of adults telling jokes. I would always hesitate at the punch line, leading many to believe I was slow and didn't get the joke. In actuality, I was afraid to laugh because in our house the punch line often was an actual punch. I also grew to dislike the somewhat common tradition of mock spankings of the birthday recipient, a smack on the bottom for every year of life. According to this standard of measurement and from the events of last night my mother was decades older than she appeared.

Watching my mother and stepfather make up was a relief but it seemed false. Children pretend, adults fake it but not that day. The adults pretended everything was all right and it would be prudent for me to fake a smile to protect their pretending. People who pretend often hope you reciprocate with faking it. Over the years I learned pretending is when you deceive yourself. Faking it is deceiving others, often with their consent. Something deep inside me that had no name and no formal language told me I had to fake it. I didn't know about instinct at the time, but fortunately it knew about me. It is not wise to suddenly wake someone from a nightmare, and very dangerous to wake someone from their pretending. I mimicked one of my toys, Mister Potato Head. I fumbled around in my box of emotions, found a plastic smile and pasted it on my face.

Later that night I found out that faking it required words too. The man from Western Union came to visit us at our bedside when it was time for our nightly prayers. What little I knew about his job at Western Union made me nervous. All I knew was that he sent and received messages. I didn't know how he did it. There was a part of me that thought he was there to keep our messages from going out to God or that we were only to send the messages he wanted us to. It turned out to be the latter.

He stood there instructing us to insert different people into our prayers. Not particularly unusual, we added his friend, the one with no name. We had to say, "Daddy's friend," and leave it at that. Then he inserted himself into our prayers. The part where he made us add, "God bless daddy," turned the saliva in my mouth into glue. I could barely move my jaw. He frowned at my hesitation. Finally, I mumbled the coerced portion of my prayer as swiftly as possible. The regurgitated words tasted like liver fried in castor oil. I wanted my mouth washed out with soap. I briefly thought of randomly yelling out a curse word in the middle of the prayer, loud enough for my mother to hear. She surely would come and wash my mouth out with soap. Hell was the only bad word I knew at that age. Although I was in it, I never uttered the word out loud until the age of nine.

Peanut was a harder nut to crack. She did not cave as swiftly as I had. Gwen accidentally mangled her portion of the prayer by saying, "Daddy bless God," instead of "God bless daddy." Gwen's mistake was Peanut's escape. Peanut repeated the mangled portion of the prayer as if she also didn't know any better, anything to thwart him. We collectively left off the amen portion of the prayer. If not said, maybe God wouldn't get the message. In modern terms, we wrote a text message but didn't press send. Our stepfather didn't question our omission.

I didn't want a repeat of a dictator standing over me intimidating and censoring my prayer, turning it into a lie and making it a sin. The following night I told my mother I was a big boy now and wanted to say my prayers in silence from now on. In silence I could tell God what I really thought of my stepfather. It wasn't "God bless daddy."

CHAPTER 17   WE DON'T OWN A CAT

In a world of clocks and measurements, a night can never be longer than a week. Yet in my world it was. I would not learn to tell time until the first grade. Until that day adults had always interpreted the clock for me. School would teach me that time was measured by the world spinning on its axis while circling the sun. Unlike the world of clocks and measurements where planets stayed in their proper orbits, on the nights of violence my emotions spun and crashed into one another, distorting my perception of time. More than the hands on a clock I would learn to watch the way the doorknob turned when my stepfather came home in the evenings. It warned me of his emotional state. On the nights of violence, he turned the doorknob counterclockwise. It seemed almost as if the doorknob had the power to unwind the clock, thus slowing down time.

Nights of violence bled into the days that followed. It usually took me a week to recover from the turmoil. On the second day I spent the last minutes of my daylight playtime sitting on our front steps. I looked longingly at the prison walls, wishing I could make a coat of its stone and wrap it around me for protection. I daydreamed about being some place new and different. Mostly I dreamed of an old familiar place. Bellefontaine was somewhere west of the prison walls. It sat at the base of Campbell Hill, the highest point in all of Ohio. Family legend has it that we settled there because we could spot slave catchers coming miles before they got there. I dreamed of returning to my family, of them keeping watch for my slave catcher.

Dreaming was my only escape. I would sit so long my daydreams would turn into dusk dreams, belonging to neither the day nor the night. When you sit and dream near dusk, the suddenness of the approaching night startles you. It is as if you and the sky are sharing a book together. The sky, in its impatience and unconcerned for your pace, has suddenly turned the page to a night scene. You desire to turn back the page to the sunset you had unintentionally missed, but the book is in the sky's lap and you never really had any say in the matter. You are not the page turner. You long for the day when you can wet the tip of your index finger and turn you own pages.

The days crept by. I was not old enough to create ways to escape my mood, but I did know how to seize a moment when it presented itself. A cheerful event or an appropriate distraction usually helped me bury the violent night in a shallow grave. It was easily exhumed the next time my stepfather took a drink, but I kept burying it as many times as it took. It had no right to be in my life.

A series of events helped tow me out of my muddy mood. Until I heard the knock at the door, I had not realized that we had only spoken to one person in the last six days since my mother's birthday. My mother had briefly taken us over to Mister Willy's to tell him her cake had fallen while baking. She promised to bake him his own cake after her husband's next pay day. Mister Willy couldn't see the marks on my mother's face. There was an abandoned house between us and him, so maybe he hadn't heard anything either.

My mother opened our windowless front door without saying, "Who is it?" My new uncle, Reggie, stood at the door with an envelope in hand. He briefly but kindly chastised her for not having the door locked and opening it without confirming who was there.

Until moving to Baltimore I had thought doors were for merely keeping the cold, rain and snow out of the house. One did not deadbolt doors against the elements or family and friends. In Bellefontaine we rarely locked our doors. This was a mistake in Baltimore. My mother had forgotten.

Despite her haste to drop her small-town ways, they clung to her like lint to a cotton dress. It was not the only thing she had forgotten. She had politely invited Uncle Reggie into a house where we had nothing to serve a guest. This morning she had emptied the box of farina and I hadn't seen a new one come in the house. Even the salt and pepper shakers were heading toward empty. Back in Bellefontaine this would have never happened. At the very least you could offer a guest some must-go soup. Thankfully he was in a hurry and did not accept a potentially embarrassing invitation.

Not crossing the threshold, he handed my mother the letter and said, "This was delivered yesterday. I think it is from your parents."

His eyes lingered for a moment on a bruise on her face that had faded from purple to a yellowish green. He said nothing. Experience would teach me that people who didn't question her injuries suspected what happened. They just didn't ask intrusive questions that rubbed salt into the wound. She would only lie, and they would have to pretend to believe the lie. Too much talking would transform their suspicions into certainty. The worst ones were the salt rubbers. These people administered the psychological beating after the physical beating. They would ask detailed intrusive questions with no intentions of helping, relishing her lies and encouraging her to tell more. There were a few kind individuals. They would hint that they would help with what they could when she was ready. Professional help was not available anywhere in the country. This was 1964. There were no battered women's shelters. The first one would not open until 1973, in Saint Paul, Minnesota.

Uncle Reggie would later evolve into a hinter but today he was a pretender. Before leaving, he extended an invitation from his mother to join them for Sunday dinner. My growling stomach was already RSVPing.

My spirit was lifted by the first part of my mother's response but had crashed by the end of her sentence, "We would love to attend, but we have plans for that day."

He shrugged his shoulders and said, "I hope there is good news in that letter."

He waved goodbye. Halfway through the wave his hand gesture turned into a twisting motion, a reminder to lock the door behind him. She closed the door. Eyes focused on the letter she had already forgotten to lock it. I could hear through the door that Uncle Reggie had paused on the steps. Peanut pointed to the lock as another reminder. Our mother caught the gesture out of the corner of her eye and locked the door without taking her eyes from the envelope. The sound of the bolt engaging sent Uncle Reggie on his way.

She stared at the face of the letter as if she was reading a novel, taking far too long to read just names and addresses. Small things come to prominence when you are far from home. The new five-digit ZIP code system had only been in effect for nine months. Other than that, the address was the same one she had lived at almost all her life. Her eyes lingered on the top left-hand corner of the letter, the return address, numbers and names that once meant home. Yet it was a return address she could never return to. She was homeless with a roof over her head, no place to retreat to and heading forward not looking too promising.

I remember mail coming to our home but rarely letters. Letters were like avatars, representing people who could not personally be there themselves. My grandmother and grandfather were in these words.

My mother strolled to the kitchen to retrieve a paring knife to open the letter. She sat at the table to read it. Although we were too young to read, Gwen took the plum spot in our mother's lap, with the best view of the letter. Peanut and I pressed against our mother's side, vying for second and third best viewing.

The miracle of writing was that it transformed the spoken word from something for the ears into something for the eyes. Gwen, Peanut and I could not take part in this miracle, as we could not read yet. I remember thinking how pretty print and cursive looked on paper even without knowing the meaning of the words. At that age I saw words and letters as patterns similar to plaid or paisley. The written word was art to me, worthy of being hung on a wall in a wooden frame or as wallpaper. I thought if I could collect enough letters, they would make a great wallpaper for the bedroom. As I came late to reading, I held this view for some time. When form became meaning, the shapes of letters and words lost their beauty to utility. I would not get that feeling for form again until I saw written Chinese and Arabic. I could not read these languages. I could only enjoy their forms, but these languages would remind me that I once viewed written English the same way.

I took exception to one letter in the alphabet at the time. I could recite the whole alphabet and write every letter in it except the capital letter Q. It was the letter O made ugly by the little line added at its lower right-hand corner. Round things should not have corners. For the purpose of symmetry, I always wanted to put the line at the bottom center. The rules be damned. I wanted the letter Q to look like a short stick lollipop, not a short handle magnifying glass. I would come to hate words that began with this letter such as quiet, which people were always telling me to be and queer, which I was told not to be.

The letter w redeemed the letter q. It reminded me of waves or the pattern a strong beating heart makes on a machine in a hospital. Words that started questions had w, as their first letter. Who, what, when, why, which and where, were the words I employed most often to ask adults questions. Also, w was the biggest letter in our alphabet cereal and soup. I was petty and hungry enough that such matters counted.

Our mother gave us a few moments to touch and look at the letter. Writing seemed as complex a technology as a phone, actually more so. It was more amazing to me that words came off a sheet of paper than that a voice came out of a machine. I could answer a phone but not a letter. Unfortunately, the letter was handwritten in cursive so I could not find the w's I liked. Cursive was beautiful as a whole, but finding individual letters was beyond me.

Our attention span and our mother's patience ran out at the same moment. She started reading the letter. The words entered my ears as my mother's voice but registered in my head as my grandmother's. It was almost as if the letter had my grandmother's vocal cords. In later years, before letter writing would go extinct, I would read letters and hear the voice of the person who actually wrote the letter.

I heard her voice say how much she missed us. She talked about the seeds she had just bought for this year's planting in her garden. In my mind I could see the seed packages lying on her kitchen table: string beans, carrots and fast-growing radishes for impatient young gardeners such as my sisters and myself. I briefly wondered if we could grow a jigsaw puzzle of a garden between the broken glass and broken bricks in the hard, packed dirt between our house and the junkyard. Unfortunately, these plants would receive more footprints than sunshine and never mature.

The letter was two pages long, front and back. Our grandmother talked mostly about familiar routines that despite our absence seemed to continue on. There were two births coming due. A great-great aunt was celebrating her one-hundredth birthday. There was a part where she told us our grandfather missed us too, but I didn't hear his voice. There was a promise of Aunt Porch visiting us sometime this summer.

When our mother turned the last page over, she slowed her pace, drawing it out. It was not slow enough. Suddenly my grandmother's voice in my head stopped. I could see that there was more to the letter. Although I could not read, I could tell our mother had skipped over the last part of the letter. She was getting ready to finish up by reading the postscript.

I asked, "Mommy why didn't you read the last part of the letter?"

I already knew the things adults left unsaid were sometimes the most important. In addition to not being able to read, I was unable to understand the adults' secret language of omission. I often would know something was missing, I just didn't always know what.

She looked at me and said, "It was not very important."

All the round features on my face, eyes, mouth and nostrils dilated into an expression of stunned surprise. I could have easily been the model for the surprised emoji that wouldn't be seen for another thirty-five years. I said, "What do you mean it's not important? Everything she says is important."

My sisters nodded their heads repeatedly and rapidly in agreement. Their features rounded in surprise much as mine had. They looked like bobblehead emojis.

Our mother said, "It is just a recipe for grandma's chili."

I guess we knew more about the adult language of omission than I realized. My sisters' heads stopped nodding. It was as if their stone faces had made their heads too heavy to bobble. My expression joined theirs. Our mouths said nothing, but our combined stony expressions said we would further unravel her frayed nerves if we were not given every word our grandmother had written.

Our mother read the list of ingredients and the cooking instructions as if it were of the utmost importance. I could almost smell the preparation. The letter's list of ingredients also reminded me that at the moment food was fiction in our house. Unfortunately, not one of the ingredients listed in the letter was present in the house. All my senses anticipated something that was not coming anytime soon. We had to wait for our stepfather to cash his paycheck when he got off of work. Then they would go shopping.

The last instruction in the letter was for our mother to give us each a kiss and a hug on behalf of our grandmother, which she did. After she kissed and hugged us, she went to fold the letter to put it back in the envelope. We squealed and squawked for more. She had to read the letter two more times before she could put it peacefully and quietly back in the envelope.

Reading the letter three times still left us in late morning and a long way from eating. There would be times as an adult when I would go without eating far longer than my present situation. It was the first time I felt food insecurity, and I felt I had no control over when it would end.

The other day Mister Willy had offered us some biscuits and cracklin. Our automatic polite refusal was barely audible over our growling stomachs. Even after our refusal, our stomachs continued rumbling, contradicting every word we had just said. My mother was so embarrassed that she chimed in with, "Thank you Mister Willy but I don't want to ruin their dinner."

I didn't understand. We had been having breakfast for dinner for days now. Dinner was already ruined. I wanted Mister Willy to ruin our farina dinner with his real one. Pride taken to the extreme was the cause of our hunger. My stepfather was part of the legion of fathers who thought their children couldn't have anything if they didn't personally provide it for them. On occasions when there was want, we had to either pretend that he would eventually provide it for us or pretend we didn't really want it.

I needed food to keep up these types of airs. Pretension and politeness were being starved to death. After my mother put the letter away, I asked to go over to Mister Willy's house to listen to TV. It was the last place I had been offered real food. If he offered me anything, this time I was taking it.

My mother said, "No."

She knew there was no guarantee that I would not beg for food while over there. I wouldn't have outright begged, but I would have strongly hinted that I was hungry. Except, I didn't know how to drop hints for a blind man. I couldn't lick my lips, rub my stomach, or give him my starving dog stare. I guess I would have had to wait for him to hear my stomach growling, crowding his personal space to make sure he did. Perhaps going so far as putting his head against my stomach so he could hear the hunger kick. Hints could get ridiculous after a while. I already hated hints, all that circling and dancing around what you really wanted to say, but I was born into a world that loved them. My hints always sounded as if I was trying to play "Silent Night" on the piano with a metal mallet.

Why couldn't I go over to Mister Willy's and just say: "These adults still need training wheels. They messed up and fell off their life cycle and hit the pavement, taking us with them. We stand in need. Could you spare us a pork chop?"

Instead I had to put on a face that didn't match my mood. Lord knows you couldn't wear polka-dots with plaid together, but it was perfectly acceptable to mismatch a smile with pain. My mother would not let me go over to Mister Willy's house dressed in an inappropriate emotion. I did not know how to match a smile with pain. Had Mister Willy had no food to spare, he at the very least would have dispensed good cheer and smiles as if they were refreshments at a lavish party.

Our mother did her best and spent the rest of the day entertaining us and distracting us from our hunger. An hour before our stepfather came home, we begged her to read the letter one more time. Despite aggravating my hunger, it put me in a good mood. Not just a letter, it represented standards. It reminded me there was a place where there was always food, and people didn't hit each other because they felt like it.

Putting the letter away a second time, our mother continued the theme by talking about our family. She even shared a few stories about her childhood, something she never had done until now. Some stories needed distance before they can be told. She was hundreds of miles away and had three of her own children standing between her and her childhood.

They were not appropriate stories for our situation. She told us how much she hated rice pudding and refused to eat it when she was a child. I wanted that bowl of rice pudding right now. The first time she had no choice but to choke it down. Then she wised up. Since rice pudding was a dessert, thereafter she claimed that she was too full, from supper to eat any. Her parents grew up during the Depression. Once the food was on your plate you had to eat it. You could refuse dessert but not food items deemed good for you, such as liver, soup and a weekly dose of castor oil. The rice pudding sounded tasty, but the thought of liver, soup and castor oil briefly anesthetized the pain in my stomach. My mother strongly believed that people who went through the Depression had no taste buds. They would eat anything.

I worried for a moment that if I didn't get food soon my taste buds would fade or die, and that I wouldn't be able to tell the difference between spinach and candy. Then I remembered that only our

Uncle Lee would eat Aunt Vivian's macaroni and cheese and that my mother's strong belief was merely a perception. All my great uncles and aunts had grown up during the Depression and they all avoided the macaroni and cheese. When good times came back, apparently so did discerning taste. Maybe the Depression affected some people differently.

Our mother probably told us the story to pass the time, with no other intent or meaning. I don't think she meant for me to take it as kind of a badge of honor that we were going through a Depression just like our grandparents. I had no idea that their Depression lasted over a decade, twice as long as I had lived. My grandparents would have chuckled at my comparison of our few days of Depression to their years of it.

My mother's story had planted the seed of a thought. Maybe not being able to tell the difference between spinach and candy was a good thing. Better yet, maybe spinach started tasting like candy if you went hungry long enough. My grandmother used to say hunger is the best seasoning for food. Anything tasted good if you went hungry long enough. This belief settled near the surface of my childlike mind. It would still be fresh when I would soon retrieve the thought, misinterpret it and inappropriately apply it to my situation.

Just as my mother ran out of stories, I heard the sound of fumbling keys at the back door. I could hear the turn of the doorknob, which also served as a dimmer switch that set the mood lighting for the whole house. How it turned set the mood for the remainder of the day. No one else was permitted to set the mood. The unspoken rule was he could sour our mood, but we could never sour his. Thankfully the knob turned the mood to light, cheery and celebratory.

He came through the door with a handful of money, waving it like a fan with a promise to soon extinguish our hunger. Scabbed over knuckles reminded me it was the hand that had struck my mother. It was as if we were part of a sparsely populated audience in the cheap part of town watching a low budget, poorly acted one-man disaster movie. Most of the true acting was done by the audience, who out of politeness or anxiety suspended belief and feigned interest. His entrance was like watching the fire scene. We had to pretend the fireman who just came through the door to save the heroine was not the same person in the last scene, who had set the fire in the first place. Even as he smelled of smoke and still held the book of matches in his hand, you were supposed to see a fireman and not an arsonist. If you knew what was good for you, you had to pretend bad liars were good liars. I just wanted the popcorn and soda.

He wanted the hero's hug without performing any acts of heroism. Our mother went to hug him first. Then she stepped aside and shepherded each of us in turn into his embrace. I reluctantly hugged the breadwinner part of my stepfather. I didn't care too much for the rest of him. I was really hugging the money. No, I wasn't hugging the money. I was hugging a bag of groceries. I pretended he was the bag with the eggs, marshmallows and bread in it. I didn't squeeze too hard, hoping my reluctance would be interpreted as gentleness. I pushed from his embrace almost as soon as I entered it.

I paid the troll his toll. The hug gave me permission to ask, "When do we eat?"

He answered me indirectly by telling my mother to grab her coat because we were going shopping at one of the grocery stores on Gay Street. It was the closest shopping district to us. She went to the living room closet to retrieve her coat and ours, but he told her to put our coats back because we were not going. He felt it would take too long to get us ready and the reasonably priced stores were closing soon. She gave him a dubious look, not sure she wanted to leave her children alone. He pushed that thought out of her head by hurrying her. He always rushed her when he didn't want her to think. One of his constant refrains was, "Everything is going to be alright. Just hurry up." It wasn't alright, because my mother was going shopping on Gay Street without her gay son. Such a pity.

It was the first time my sisters and I had ever been left alone but not the last. We would rarely have someone babysit us. Usually our babysitters were each other, a set of instructions and a piece of paper with a phone number of a nearby neighbor, family member, or the place where our parents would be. This was a time when people always answered their phones. The instructions were generally simple. Don't burn down the house and don't answer the door. Then they would hand me the phone number, as I was the oldest. The number always seem to contain an abundance of zeros, nines, eights and sevens. These higher numbers were particularly hard for little fingers to drag all the way around to the finger stop, especially if the last two digits were the higher numbers. Inevitably your fingers would slip on the last numbers. Then you would have to hang up and start all over again. I thought it would be far easier to set the house on fire and use the smoke to send signals to my parents, but they had instructed us not to burn down the house. We presently didn't have a phone, so all we got was the instructions.

We sat at the kitchen table, bored to death two seconds after the door closed behind our parents. We spent the first couple of minutes searching the surface of the table for any stray splashes of farina. Unfortunately, our mother was a good housekeeper. Not a morsel marred its surface.

Bored and hungry, it wasn't long before we started antagonizing one another by making faces. Peanut was the mockingbird of facial expressions. Although quite original in creating her own, she excelled at mocking you by mimicking your expressions back at you. Losing the war of making faces to Peanut, I challenged Gwen instead. I lost this one as well. Not because she was good but because she was bad. Try as she might Gwen's expressions all looked the same, cross-eyed hungry, sticking-her-tongue-out hungry and finally drool-on-her-chin hungry. Looking at Gwen only made me hungrier.

I started thinking about the rice pudding my mother wouldn't eat as a child. Maybe my mother was too picky. She hadn't gone through the Depression like my grandparents, sisters and me. She had been hungry along with us, but somehow, she hadn't experienced our mini Depression in the same way. There were things she still wouldn't eat. It had not been long enough for her. Einstein could have done the theory of relativity based on food. Hunger that occurs at the same time for one observer could occur at a different rate of time for another.

It was pride and prejudice that was keeping us hungry, our stepfather's pride and our mother's prejudice. There had to be food in the house. I didn't think she was holding out on us. She just wouldn't feed us anything she wouldn't eat herself. At the moment my standards were far lower than hers.

I took my first foray past my mother's limitations. Sure enough, as I searched the lower cabinets, I found a box of dry cat food. The cover of the box had a picture of a happy, dignified cat prancing toward the bowl of food. Its tail was raised high in the air, which I knew was how cats smiled. I deluded myself into believing it was really a box of cat cereal. A little bit of milk and a lot of imagination and we would soon be eating Kitty Crunch Puffs. Unfortunately, there was no milk, which left my imagination a little high and dry. We didn't have a cat, so the box had been left over, from the previous tenants. My mother had kept it to feed a stray cat from the junkyard. We could feed it, but we couldn't ever pet it. Therefore, we never named it. Cats can be that way.

I grabbed the box. It was half full because the cat had passed on its evening meal from last night. For some reason the crows would not eat it either. There still was dry cat food on our back stoop, so the cat had not eaten this morning or afternoon either. No doubt the cat had found better fare in the junkyard. The dry food was merely its backup meal. Now it was ours.

Our cereal bowls were out of reach in the upper cabinets. Preparing to dine communal style on food that had been rejected by an alley cat and crows, I poured a pile onto the bare table. The pile looked better than the leftover cat food on the stoop but not as good as the picture on the box.

Peanut and Gwen were dead set against communal eating. They knew the most food went to the fastest eater. Unsupervised, that was me. They demanded that I dole out the triangular kibbles one by one. I handed the first pieces to Peanut and Gwen, ladies went first because this gentleman ate fast.

Gwen took advantage of her head start by eating each piece as I handed them to her. It sounded as if she was cracking walnuts with her teeth. She didn't chew. She just bit down once to break it into pieces and swallowed. Her lips puckered as if she was eating lemons. Ooh, I liked lemons. This was a good sign.

Peanut collected hers in a pile and used her left arm as a wall between me and her kibbles. Her other hand met me at the arm wall to take each piece from my hand. I was not to cross the wall, not even to add to her pile. She was leery that my deposits could become withdrawals. When her pile grew to a decent size, she reached for the pepper shaker and seasoned her kibbles liberally. Then she put the pieces into her mouth one at a time, sucked the pepper off and swallowed them whole.

I grew bored with being the provider and put the box down on the table. It was time to eat my little pile. I put a small handful into my mouth and started to chew faster than my tastes buds could react. I had already reduced the kibbles to a gritty paste before the taste registered.

I had deluded myself into thinking hunger would make cat food taste like candy. At first it had the light taste of chicken, almost as if someone had made teabags out of an old stewing hen and dipped them into hot water for a few seconds. It was like having weak chicken tea. Then flavors came to the forefront, which had been allowed to steep far longer than the chicken had. Bland and stale overpowered the weak chicken flavor. There was an underlying taste of metal or rust, as if the kibbles had been stored in cans instead of cardboard. It tasted similar to what I imagined old age must feel like. I had a sneaking feeling that the box of cat food had always been there and the house, old as it was, had been built around it.

Perhaps it didn't taste as bad when you did as Gwen had, biting each piece into smaller pieces and swiftly swallowing them, or as Peanut had, overwhelming her taste buds with pepper so that bland, stale and rust glided over a spiced tongue. Mine was the worst possible stratagem. The gritty paste was now trapped between my teeth and coated my tongue. What was barely tolerable now became disgusting the longer it lingered in my mouth. My tongue felt as if I had licked a nuclear power plant. Heaven only knows the half-life of cat food.

Peanut, seeing my plight, offered me one of her peppered kibbles. It was at that very moment that the back door opened. In walked our parents to a scene no parent wants to see, their children eating lower on the food chain than an alley cat, all because of their negligence. I must have looked a fright to them. Grayish brown cat food drooled down my chin while Peanut was stuffing another kibble into my mouth as if I was a patient in a convalescence home. Gwen had the look of a contented cow, chewing cud, except she was crunching kibbles.

The kibble that Peanut was pushing against my pursed lips bounced off them, landing on the table. She promptly picked it up and placed it in her own mouth. She crunched her kibble in sync with Gwen. Peanut now had an expression of distaste scrawled across her face. It was not directed at the feline feast before us, or the taste in her mouth. Her face said loud and crunchy, look what you made us do. She picked up another kibble and crunched it out of spite, or rather as if to add an exclamation point to our plight.

She had noticed something I at first had not, the look of horror and shame written on our parents' face, especially our mother's. Our mother's emotions came from concern for us, not so for our stepfather. Shame was such a rare emotion for him that he had almost forgotten how to wear it. The emotion had been in the back of his closet far too long. He wore shame as if it were a cheap suit from two or three seasons passed. It was flimsily made and ill-fitting. What made the emotion appear cheap was the absence of concern for us. It was as if he was wearing a suit with a clip-on tie and without shoes. His face was wearing only what he could afford.

We had hurt his pride by providing for ourselves. He was ashamed for not meeting the expectation he had set for himself as a provider. I would become aware many years later that he, along with many men, took this role seriously. At its extreme it gave such men power over their families and permission to do as they pleased to them. If you took provisions from these men, you had to take anything else they dished out as well. You became the target of their every emotion. Unbeknownst to me at the time we had put a dent in his justification.

The first thing he said was, "Don't you ever tell anyone you ate cat food. You hear me?"

For the moment, I forgot the stale taste in my own mouth and relished the small taste of shame he had received. It was a chink in his armor. There were many positive acts I employed to salvage my childhood, but in fairness to the totality of my experience, I must pay homage to the negative acts as well. I needed to see a weakness in him even if I was too young and scared to exploit it. As much as I hate to say it, sometimes negative thoughts gave me hope. Brought down to its essence, I generally employed negative acts to survive and positive ones to thrive.

I responded to his demand with a nod and gave him a big cat food stained smile. My smile grew wider as I fantasized about meeting new people and saying, "Hello, my name is Grant and I eat cat food, and this is Peanut. She eats cat food with pepper on it. Oh, and this is Gwen, she eats cat food like a cow." I was now more ready to meet new people than I was ready to eat. I could hardly wait to tell God in my prayers tonight.

Disgusted by my smile he continued, "Go upstairs and brush your teeth."

An older, wiser, braver me would have loved to respond with, "Dad, why don't you come upstairs with us? While we are brushing out the taste of stale cat food from our mouths, you can brush out the taste of failure and shame from yours."

CHAPTER 18 HOME COMES HOME

I remember photographs were taken of my first day of school, but they were not developed until I was ten years old. Then they were lost in a fire when I was twenty-one. Even without the photos, I vividly remember that day and the anticipation and excitement of the week before. The feelings I had was similar to the ones I had leading up to Christmas. More than any other event, starting school first established my position as the oldest child. Normally, with the exception of our individual birthdays, we received our presents together and in equal amounts. Not this time; my sisters each got a token stay at home dress, but I got going-to-school clothes, two shirts and two pairs of pants. Peanut would join me the following year and Gwen the year after that, but this event was all mine. Along with the clothes I received, I also got new shoes and, for some strange reason, a big rubber eraser but no pencil, the ability to correct mistakes and no means to make them.

After receiving two letters promising a visit from my grandmother's best friend, Aunt Porch, she finally came a few days before I was to start school. She had flown to Baltimore to visit her sister who lived on Ashland Avenue a few blocks from Saint Wenceslaus Church, which was about eight blocks from our new grandmother Ruth's house and a mile from ours.

Aunt Porch had landed too late to pay us a visit, so she had gone straight to her sister's house. We were preparing to visit her early the next day. She had flown hundreds of miles, so it was common courtesy that we would travel just a mile to see her. She was more than Aunt Porch. She was an ambassador from my entire family, a little piece of Bellefontaine right here in Baltimore.

I was also very excited because we were going to take the bus. I had never taken a bus before. Despite the fact we would live in Baltimore for years, this would be one of only a few times my sisters and

I would ever ride the bus. In the future, we would most often walk, occasionally have someone drive us, and rarely take a cab. Except for being taken to the Baltimore Zoo and Fort McHenry, my sisters and I rarely were taken more than a mile from our house. Adults knew what neighborhoods to go to and when. We didn't. During the day we lived in Baltimore but at night we lived in Balkin-more, a city with many, very clear boundaries. For the most part, people lived in relative peace until someone shot an archduke or the son of a former sharecropper.

Unfortunately, this was the day I noticed race for the first time. I had noticed different colors before but not race as a separating factor. There was nothing cruel or traumatic about the event. It was several little observations brought together and into focus by one bus ride.

Our walk to the bus stop seemed to take as long as the bus ride itself. My mother's ignorance of the system was in evidence as she held up a dime pinched between her finger and thumb to hail the bus driver. Her gesture was part hitchhiking and part hailing a cab. She knew enough to push us onto the bus first. Then she paid her fare. Children rode for free. The roar of the engine and billowing smoke from the exhaust pipe implied great speed the bus never obtained. It no sooner pulled away from one stop than it appeared to pull over to another. It was as if the bus was a giant taxicab, which took lots of people close to their destinations but very few directly to where they were going.

Not long after crossing Broadway, I noticed something I had not seen since we had arrived in Baltimore almost five months ago. I saw a few pale pink children playing on the sidewalk. I had not noticed their absence until their brief reappearance. I occasionally saw white adults but not children. Over the last several months pale pink people were slowly becoming white people. Their color still was an adjective, a descriptive and not a noun yet, but it was changing. Limited contact was the main force behind the change. I only saw them manning the stone walls of the prison with guns, behind sales counters in stores and behind the windshield of official vehicles. They all wore uniforms or aprons. Once we crossed Broadway the reverse was true. The few brown people I saw all wore uniforms. I wondered why we needed uniforms to visit each other's neighborhoods. Was that the rule here? I pulled at my plaid summer shirt, wondering for the first time in my life if I was dressed appropriately. It was unspoken, but your entry visa was your clothes, preferably with a name tag attached.

Unbeknownst to me at the time, we had just entered the neighborhood known as Little Bohemia. The inhabitants were not the impoverished and marginalized artist types. These Bohemians were an ethnic group from Czechoslovakia. We had to walk another three blocks once we left the bus. I noticed that a few of the windows and doors in this neighborhood had lovely paintings hanging in them. I thought it was nice they had put their art in the windows for everyone to see instead of hanging them on their walls inside where only they could see them.

The paintings were not on canvases but on window and door screens. Most of the paintings were rusty and faded. The art form had been introduced to Baltimore by William Oktave, an immigrant from the former Austrian-Hungarian Empire. Screen painting was well in decline by the mid-sixties, a good decade past its peak. This neighborhood had been the epicenter of the art form. For many it was a reminder of lands they had fled from but still beckoned. Little squares of wire mesh painted to look like distant pastoral villages or other rural scenes fought against the close quarters of the brick and stone row houses. Urban dwellers walked past little squares of country life that few under a certain age had ever seen. They were also Baltimore's polite peep holes. They were painted in such a manner that pedestrians from the street could not peer into the homes while the people inside could see out. Standing behind a screen painting was as if you were part of the painting looking out. You could be nosy without being noticed.

Aunt Porch's sister had inherited a house from a woman she had been taking care of for years. She was the first of a wave to come. As more native-born Americans of African descent pushed into the former immigrant neighborhoods, times changed. Most of the Bohemians were older now, their children rapidly fleeing to the suburbs. The children I saw playing in the street were probably visiting their grandparents. Over time, the music coming from behind the rusted, faded paintings of Eastern European bucolic scenes would reflect the change more than anything else. Foreign born music such as Polkas, Waltzes and Grand Marches were slowly being supplanted by the native-born music of Blues, Jazz and Soul. Eventually Soul Train would come and completely push The Lawrence Welk Show out of the neighborhood. A little over ten years later, the neighborhood would change its name to Middle East. This was how time flowed in the land of many lands.

As we walked down Ashland Avenue, my mother didn't have to figure out the address. Aunt Porch had urbanized her nosiness. Instead of sitting on a wooden porch, she sat on the marble stoop in front of her sister's house. Her eyes scanned east and west on Ashland Avenue as if they were surveillance cameras. Behind her on the screen door was a privacy screen painting, which she had no intentions of hiding behind. Aunt Porch could act as dignified and regal as a queen or as common as a milkmaid. She traveled up and down her full emotional range without a passport or a care for what others thought. Once she saw us, she did not urbanize her greeting. She screamed our names as if we were in a far-off pasture in the country. She danced and squawked on the stoop as if she were a chicken on a hot stove getting ready to lay an egg in a skillet.

Once she stopped flapping her limbs, Aunt Porch opened her arms into a u-shaped corral, inviting us into her love. My mother was at the right height to receive the full brunt of the hug as Aunt Porch pulled her in close toward her bosom. Peanut and I each hugged a thigh and Gwen hugged the lower leg. Ironically, we had each gotten our favorite part of the chicken, our mother the breast, Peanut and I a thigh and Gwen the leg.

My mother started to cry. They were tears of happiness, not tears of intention to return. I did not know you could miss a place you never wanted to return to.

Almost as if acknowledging my mother's state of mind Aunt Porch said, "You don't have to visit home. Home has come home to visit you."

Aunt Porch was our ambassador from Bellefontaine. The main purpose of the visit was to see her sister. As ambassador, her secondary duty was to check on our wellbeing and report back to my grandparents.

Not one to hide behind the obvious, Aunt Porch outright said to my mother, "I am not someone who can ignore the elephant in the room nor am I someone to hide behind it. I am letting you know, anything I hear or see goes straight back to your mother as soon as I can get to the nearest phone. I came to love you through your mother. Despite the fact that after all these years we have a separate relationship, my loyalty is to her first."

My mother laughed and said, "Aunt Porch you are the elephant in the room!" It was half joke and half compliment but all truth.

Aunt Porch shrugged, then invited us into her sister's house.

The home smelled of old people's medicine. My nose caught hints of greasy vapor rub and, liniment, two ingredients used to embalm the living. The aroma was more of an invitation for death to visit than a deterrent. Something about the house said an old person had recently died. Slowly the house was coming back to life after serving as a convalescent home for one.

Aunt Porch's sister was not present, but from the decor and smell of the home I pictured someone who wore white hosiery and sensible white shoes. It was one of the few times I would accurately picture the way someone looked before actually meeting them. As I was finalizing my image of her sister, my eyes landed on a photo of a woman in all white. Presumably she was a nurse or a nurse's aide. Her sister was next to a pale woman and looked exactly as I had pictured her, a worse for wear version of Aunt Porch.

All observation of the house stopped when Aunt Porch said, "I have something for all of you."

She went upstairs and brought down a small suitcase. It was Aunt Porch's suitcase, but it had been packed by my grandmother. In it were three more shirts, three pairs of pants and a pair of shoes for me. Added to the clothing and shoes my mother had purchased for me earlier, I could now go to school for five days straight without repeating an outfit. These would be the most school clothes I would ever receive, and never again would I own more than one pair of dress shoes in a school year. The long distance had made it difficult for my grandparents and mother to coordinate their efforts. In the future when I would receive new pants and shirts, I would learn to mix and match the tight clothing from last year's school clothes with the new oversized clothes of the current year. I often would go to school looking fat one day and slim the next, or like I was a year behind or a year ahead of my actual grade, depending on what I chose to wear.

There was already a noticeable difference in the size of the clothing brought by Aunt Porch. Although wearable, it was on the rather large side. In addition, there was a light but noticeable smell of smoke, which meant my grandmother must have shopped at Mister Franz's store. Sure enough, I looked into one of the shoes and found three pieces of barrel candy along with a belt. My grandmother's love of economy tended to make her choose room to grow over form fitting. Now she had been regulated to someone who had to guess the size of her grandchildren from photos of us sent by mail or phone calls to our mother. Her personal observation of my size when we lived with her was downright snug compared to the large sizes brought to me by Aunt Porch.

At the bottom of the suitcase were two coloring books and crayons destined for my sisters, which annoyed me, not because I did not get one but because they could not color between the lines, while I could. Metaphorically speaking, Peanut would never learn to color between the lines because lines were too much like rules for her.

While I tried on clothes and Peanut and Gwen colored the dresses of the princesses in their coloring books the wrong colors, Aunt Porch slipped my mother a white envelope. I couldn't care less about my own clothing, but princesses should not be wearing pastel colors this close to autumn. Princesses' clothes were like leaves. They needed to change with the seasons. If I had been let loose, I would have grabbed a black crayon and colored the next princess's dress black. She should be in mourning for the fashion choices made by my sisters for the other two princesses.

My mother kept turning my head away from my sisters and correcting my posture. Good posture encouraged growth. Nonetheless the legs of my pants draped and pooled at my ankles.

Aunt Porch mentioned the clothes needed a little tailoring. Raising the hemline was not an option. Although my mother could sew well, the sewing machine she used was back in Ohio. I would have to cuff my pants or lengthen my legs. Cuffing and rapid growth were the only tailoring these clothes would ever receive.

My mother shrugged and decided the better fitting clothes she had bought would be what I would wear the on first couple days of school. A first impression was important.

Although I could undress myself, I was swiftly shucked out of my new clothes because I was not yet trusted to fold them properly. Aunt Porch folded them and placed them back in the suitcase. Then she asked, "Who wants pancakes?"

We had already had breakfast, but the mere mention of pancakes made me hungry again. If my mother said no, Aunt Porch would circumvent her by cooking a stack of pancakes way too high for one person to eat. Then she would ask us to help keep her from wasting food. I of course would be chivalrous and save the fair damsel from the choice of overeating or being wasteful. Any pretense of my chivalry was laid to rest the moment the plate was placed before me. She made blueberry pancakes and served them on plates with blueberry motifs printed on them. Several times I stabbed my fork at painted blueberries instead of real ones. Aunt Porch laughed as I tried to eat the pattern off the plate.

Finally, Aunt Porch made one last small pancake for herself. She made two cups of tea for my mother and herself and joined us at the table. I was not allowed to interrupt adult conversation unless it was important. I generally didn't interrupt because not only would I be rebuffed for doing so, I would usually be told to leave the room. Then I would have to strain my ears to hear conversations that bounced off walls and crept down halls. In particular, I didn't interrupt Aunt Porch because given ample time she gave every detail, leaving nothing out.

She sipped her tea and painted a scene of life in Bellefontaine that had not changed all that much. Her words created an image of a warm home with a cold draft blowing in from an open door. I hadn't really closed that door when we left. I had left it open in the hope of returning. Friends and family went about their routines, minus us. We were definitely missed, but life hiccupped and went on. I didn't expect life to stop because we were gone but I thought at least it would limp along slowly until we returned. I thought I could just jump back into that life. All my grandmother had to do was brush off the dust from the place I had once occupied in their lives. Then life could pick up as it was.

The expression on my mother's face was joyous but resolute. She had closed the door when she left. The finality in her expression now closed my door. I now had something in common with the Bohemians; I was not going home either. This was home now. I wanted to take my memories and the painted words of Aunt Porch and put them on the screens of our new house as a reminder. Hanging a portrait of your old home on your new home was a nice custom indeed.

Both my mother and Aunt Porch took sips of their tea. When the cups touched the table, my mother began to speak. She started telling Aunt Porch about our lives. I immediately lost interest because I already knew what here was like. I went over to my sister, picked up some crayons and pushed my way into coloring a page in Gwen's coloring book. I still half listened. The story my mother told Aunt Porch closely resembled the books we were coloring in. She outlined our lives in black lines that showed a simple version of our lives in Baltimore. There were plenty of blank white spaces in my mother's version. To come anywhere near the truth, my sisters and I would have had to use crayons to fill in the outlined spaces of my mother's coloring book. It needed bright, vibrant colors for the happy days and somber black and grey for the sad days. I would have had to leave some pages devoid of color. Although I had lived the events, I had no idea what color to give them.

My mother spoke at length. A picture is worth a thousand words. Aunt Porch patiently listened to those thousand words. Now she wanted to see the picture. Nothing my mother said had made her suspicious. In many ways it was an injustice to call Aunt Porch a nosy person. She was curious and inquisitive to be sure, but she didn't generally meddle. The few times I would be alone with her, she didn't question me about my mother and stepfather behind their backs.

If she had seen my mother's face the day after her beating, she would have intervened to the best of her abilities. She may not have been able to do much, but she would not have ignored it. She detested people who blatantly and brazenly behaved poorly in plain sight, expecting everyone to turn a blind eye. She felt it was not her job to keep your secrets, especially after you dumped them in the street for everyone to see. Aunt Porch bullied these people because they tried to bully everyone else into silence. Then I remembered this was a woman who was willing to stab her abusive husband to death before she found out he had cancer. Snitches get stitches but snitches can give stitches as well. The Aunt Porch I knew was not one to be bullied.

We took a cab back to Forrest Street. About three blocks from home my mother started apologizing for the state of our house and neighborhood.

Aunt Porch waved the apology away and said, "Let's be frank, the houses here are nicer than the houses in West Bellefontaine." She paused and continued,

"I just hope life is treating you well here." Life in this case was a euphemism for my stepfather.

My mother didn't bat an eye. "He treats me and the kids well and besides, I have to make this work."

My mother had been walking a thin line. Three kids by the time she was eighteen. My grandparents loved their grandchildren unconditionally, but we were also three examples of my mother's poor choices. They weren't judging her past, but they did use it as a gauge of her credibility. Being leery and weary of a behavior is not necessarily passing judgement. She had escaped their judgement but, as parents often do, they showed hope to their child's face while privately harboring doubts. A better future leaves a better past, but you had to be given a chance to make a better future, and the number of chances given is often based on your past. It was strange that something so linear as time could become such a vicious circle. One way to break the circle was to start over someplace else.

Aunt Porch replied nonchalantly, "Well Carol, make it work. Don't turn a new place into the same old place."

Aunt Porch ended the brief conversation by reaching into her purse to pay the cab driver. She nodded her head approvingly of our house but shrugged at the sight of the prison walls. She entered our house, which was sparsely furnished but had been well decorated with elbow grease and cleanliness. Floors were waxed, curtains and linens starched. Our windows had been so thoroughly cleaned the glass looked as if it were made of thin air. Cleanliness pardoned the poverty. It was perfectly acceptable to be poor, but not to be dirty.

We had just gotten a TV about three weeks ago. At the time, in my mind you couldn't be poor if you had a TV. When you ate cat food and had no TV, that was poverty. Now we had a TV and ate fried bologna sandwiches once a week. One needs comparisons to feel poor. We were poor the first two weeks we were in Baltimore, but now we lived like everyone else. Ironically, TV, one of the symbols of modern prosperity for most Americans, would eventually wear away at that sense of prosperity by bringing comparisons and dissatisfaction into their homes.

My mother had cleaned the house yesterday wearing a rag over her head and old, worn clothing. She had dusted a TV set that broadcasted she should be cleaning the house wearing stylish clothes and pushing a vacuum cleaner while wearing three-inch high heels. The commercials made mops and brooms seem almost as if they were dance partners that moved gracefully across dirty floors, rather than tools of drudgery. Over their stylish clothes these women wore tiny aprons the size of a merit badge, suggesting the ease of being a housewife, if only you used their advertised products.

Aunt Porch looked around and praised my mother's housekeeping. She heaped extra praise for doing so with three children below school age.

Together they put away the school clothes and coloring books. They sat at the kitchen table to continue catching up. My mother slipped back into her midwestern accent as she offered Aunt Porch a pop instead of a soda. She opened a refrigerator that had a respectable amount of food in it. Nonetheless, Aunt Porch suggested we go shopping after she finished her pop.

She forestalled my mother's protest by saying, "I certainly will be having more than a few meals here, and you know your Aunt Porch has her preferences and likes her portions large. I couldn't possibly impose my standards on you."

Of course, that is exactly what she was doing. She would only eat a fraction of what she bought and, truth be told, her preferences were all over the place. She could serve chitterlings and caviar at the same dinner without batting an eye. We were really going shopping for us, while pretending we were shopping for her. Aunt Porch was exploiting our hospitality for our benefit. She always made her charity seem as if you were really helping her by taking it.

She finished her pop and said to my mother, "You have lived here almost five months now and I have visited here many times. Let's combine our knowledge. I am sure you know where to shop by now, and I know how to shop."

My mother started to make a grocery list, but Aunt Porch interrupted." We aren't doing that type of shopping. This is going to be strictly impulse shopping. Lists are for needs. This is all about want."

She graciously and politely thanked Aunt Porch but sternly told us not to be rude and ask for anything.

Aunt Porch said, "Why don't we skip over the part where you tell them they can't have anything? You know they and I are going to win. So, let's not have guarded, whispered disagreements in public. It just makes your defeat look worse. Besides, it is leverage, to get the kids to behave. I am only buying it. You get to dole it out."

Aunt Porch told us that, within reason, we could have one thing to play with and one thing to eat, but we couldn't pick anything out until the end. She didn't want us changing our minds and exchanging things every ten feet. This was a change of pace for me. Normally I would beg for lots of random items in the hopes that my mother would cave on one of them. Sometimes I stared at a particular food item as if it were a stray puppy that needed a home. If my hungry stares had been given a monetary value, I would have been rich. Keeping an account of my impulses and choosing them from a lineup later kept me from pestering my mother and Aunt Porch. Instead of nagging them, I would nag myself. Aunt Porch also made it clear that any whining and pleading to get more would get us less. Be thankful, don't be greedy. Begging for another one got you none.

Aunt Porch wanted to walk the four or five blocks down to the Gay Street shopping district. The Belair Public Market was an indoor market that ran the length of a football field. There were dozens of stalls inside and lots of little mom and pop stores nearby.

Before going shopping, my mother wanted to stop by Mister Willy's to ask if he needed something. She had learned several months ago that Mister Willy was strict about who he let help him. He didn't mind people lessening his burden as long as they didn't insist on being a burden by ramming their charity down his throat. Like anyone else he appreciated a favor but didn't want people to live his life for him. He also wanted to reciprocate. He had been politely blunt with my mother when he said, "If you help me, I need to able to return the favor. If I offer help, it is something I want to do and am capable of. The polite refusals of my help by well-meaning people would isolate me from my community and send me to an early grave."

To her credit, my mother didn't stumble over an awkward apology. Instead she said, "You are absolutely right." She continued in a jovial tone, "Mister Willy, I don't mean to be rude, but aren't you already a few decades too late for an early grave? How long are you planning on living?"

Mister Willy got a good chuckle out of that and responded, "Not long enough."

From that point on they got along well. We lived in a community where a clock hanging on the wall was more decorative than useful, time being more a suggestion than a statement. Although very different people, their commonality was a great respect for efficiency and punctuality. My mother already knew what Mister Willy would want from the store. By this time of the week he had usually run out of buttermilk, eggs and bacon. She was using this as an excuse to force a meeting between Mister Willy and Aunt Porch.

The thought of going to the store with permission to buy two things was like a mini-Christmas. Having two of my favorite people meet would be like waking up and finding an Easter basket under the Christmas tree and witnessing Santa and the Easter Bunny shaking hands. I desperately wanted someone from my old home to love someone from my new home.

Initially Aunt Porch showed no interest in a meeting of any kind. She sat at the kitchen table fussing with items in her purse, waiting for my mother to return with the list from Mister Willy. To attract her attention my mother used her real name. "Mrs. Reeves, I really want you to meet this man."

Aunt Porch had sworn off men for a while after her experience with Mister Reeves. Also, the fact that my mother had referred to him as Mister Willy, implied he was an older man. Still, old habits die hard. The words "meet" and "man" in the same sentence had sent Aunt Porch on a search to the bottom of her purse for her reddest lipstick. She had painted her lower lip before my mother interrupted her and said with a mock scolding tone, "He is not that type of man, but go ahead and put on the rest of your lipstick and you can practice your sex appeal on Mister Willy."

My mother put a finger to her lips and made a shh gesture to keep me from warning Aunt Porch that Mister Willy was blind. We walked out the back door. Aunt Porch's high heels only added minimally to her stature. The remainder came from within. She appeared tall without being so. Her movements were graceful and alluring. Her walk beckoned but also cautioned men to keep their distance. It always amazed me the way her hips swayed from side to side, supported by nothing but two spindly little heels. It was as if each body part had its own motor. When Aunt Porch walked down the street men stopped, giving her the right of way. She smiled at them but never lingered. Since being widowed and emancipated, no man had ever stopped her in her tracks, until Mister Willy.

Mister Willy must have heard us coming because he opened the door as we approached it. Before my mother could say anything, Mister Willy proclaimed, "I smell a pretty lady."

My mother knew the greeting wasn't for her. She bathed with the same soap every day, and when she wore perfume it came from the same store, two aisles over from the soap. Without hesitation my mother tried to introduce Mister Willy to Aunt Porch, but Aunt Porch had stopped about ten feet from his back stoop and stared in silence at Mister Willy to the point that it became awkward. When she finally gained control of her eyes and tongue, she apologized for staring so long.

Mister Willy laughed and said, "I didn't notice you staring. I noticed your silence. I thought you were mute. I'm sure someone clever could make a joke in poor taste about such a meeting."

Aunt Porch put a chuckle in her smile for Mister Willy's benefit and elaborated further on her behavior. "It's just that you look so much like my grandfather who I loved very much. Your face took me to a very happy place."

Mister Willy spoke with a sly grin, "My face has been called many things but has never been referred to as a mode of transportation."

Aunt Porch's family had been too poor to take a photo. The only image she had of her grandfather was a piece of wood six by six inches into which her grandfather had carved a raised relief of his face and given it to her just before he died. I remember seeing it in Aunt Porch's house many times. It held a place of honor in a glass case next to a few pieces of Wedgwood China. The walnut wood captured his image in a way sepia on paper could not. Unlike a photo you could touch it and feel the wrinkles in the wooden face. Indeed, Mister Willy, minus his sunglasses, did look like her grandfather. I wondered if Mister Willy had been able to touch the carving, would he have been able feel the resemblance?

This not only explained her awkward stare and silence, it explained the startling change in her body language. She had gone from appearing sexy and alluring to resembling a little girl in awe. It was almost as if her high heels had shrunk down to a pair of Mary Jane shoes and her round hips had flattened out into straight lines. The light, husky command in her voice became soft and deferential. She stood before him almost as if she were the one who was blind. Mister Willy held out his hand for her to shake. She unconsciously reached past his proffered hand to touch his face, her fingers seeking flesh instead of wood for the first time in years. She caught herself just before touching his face and lowered her soft hand into his callused one.

Aunt Porch said to herself more than to Mister Willy, "Even your hands feel like his."

She was predisposed to like him from the physical resemblance alone. Similar to her grandfather who had carved hard wood, Mister Willy's hands were rough from carving a living from a hard life. For her sake he held the handshake a little longer than he usually preferred. He didn't want people to infer that a long handshake was a hint for them to lead him somewhere. For the moment both of them were where they wanted to be.

She said, "I am sorry for using you to connect with an old memory." Despite her apology she didn't disengage from the handshake.

Mister Willy said, "Go ahead and use me." It was not a lecherous comment. He had aged from a mother's touch, through a lover's touch and now to a daughter's touch. Though Aunt Porch was not his daughter or granddaughter, the distinction was there. From my point of view Aunt Porch's hand looked perfectly safe and comforted.

Aunt Porch pulled her hand away from his only after Mister Willy invited her and my mother over for rum and tea later in the week. She accepted and replied, "I like putting tea in my rum. It makes lowering one's inhibitions look respectable."

When she said her goodbyes and walked away from him, the little girl that stood before Mister Willy instantly inflated back into a full-grown, voluptuous woman.

My mother teased Aunt Porch by saying, "What happened to your practicing?"

Aunt Porch ignored the friendly gibe, grabbed my mother in a big hug, and said that meeting Mister Willy had paid for her trip many times over. Tears ran down her cheeks to the corners of a broad smile, reminding me of a summer day when rain seems to fall from a sunny sky.

Aunt Porch half-danced and half-walked the rest of way to Gay Street in a gay mood, insisting that she pay for Mister Willy's groceries. My mother was the intermediary for Mister Willy's no. She said no because her no would be politer than Mister Willy's. Spiking tea with rum and breaking bread with him was usually all he required from people he liked.

My sisters and I would have been the recipient of all Aunt Porch's pent up generosity had my mother not insisted that we were to adhere to the original agreement of each of us receiving one toy and something to eat and nothing more.

We occasionally shopped in several stores on Gay Street itself, but we mainly shopped at the Belair Public Market, which had been in the same spot for two centuries and had dozens of stalls. The choices would be difficult because of the sheer variety of the wares and foodstuff on display at a child's eye level. Beyond eye level seemed infinite and thus in the realm of adults.

The only disturbing thing at eye level was the glass case at Marty's Meat Mortuary. I don't believe that was the actual name of the place, but that is what I remember hearing everyone secretly calling that particular butcher's stall. All the meat looked as if it were lying in state without the trappings of a coffin. Even the choice cuts were more suited for a grave than a skillet. I would not have been surprised if some of the more reverent shoppers didn't cross themselves as they passed the glass case of this butcher's stall. Only people who came up short financially at the end of the week or month shopped there. No worries, the piece of meat you saw last week would still be waiting for you next week when you got paid. Although my mother husbanded every dime and every penny when called upon, we tended to buy our meats from another butcher stall owned by a pale man named Bishop. He had been at the Belair Market thirty of the market's 200 years. We had shopped there often enough to get a nod of a greeting as we passed his stall.

There were mostly food items in view and not as many toys but still plenty to choose from. I thought my choices would be difficult, but after ten minutes in the market I already knew what I wanted. Now I had to wait for my sisters to make up their minds, which they changed every time we passed a new stall. My aunt slowed the process further by deciding she wanted to have Chinese food for lunch at a new restaurant on Orleans Street called The Emperor's Chow.

I didn't want lunch to ruin my snack. Therefore, I changed my food choice from a pickled onion to a bag of packaged sweets, which I could eat later when I was hungry again. I was not very good at delayed gratification. It was something generally forced on me, but it was better than no gratification. This was the first time I remember anticipating a full stomach and altering my behavior accordingly. Despite being pickled, a pickled onion needed to be eaten promptly to be fully enjoyed.

I thought I would have to change my choice again when my mother said, "Do you think the kids are too young to eat Chinese food?"

Aunt Porch responded to my mother's question by dropping a bit of the obvious into her lap: "They have children in China and, if I am not mistaken, they eat Chinese food."

As we entered the restaurant, Aunt Porch told us we could make our two choices after we ate lunch. The door opened onto a scene from a movie. I couldn't remember its name. There were individual booths with roofs that had upturned flying eaves, a defining Chinese architectural feature. Little bamboo fences separated the booths from each other. It looked like a small Asian village inside of a western style brick building. I noticed the wait staff looked slightly different than any other people I had seen before. The concept of foreign was foreign to me. I certainly noticed differences, but I didn't yet have a value judgement to add to those differences. My response to different was more likely a curious wow than a frightened eek.

I would have fixated on the difference and asked embarrassing questions had it not been for a large gong hanging behind the cash register. It reminded me of another movie in which the gong was struck, and all kinds of good things were summoned, or a genie would appear. I wanted to summon an Arab genie with a Chinese gong. Geography was not my best subject.

We had a fairly good view of the kitchen from our booth. I had never seen a wok before. Watching the cook toss food into the air and catch it was very entertaining. I was young and foolish enough to believe the air was a special type of seasoning. The thought of food that had been juggled instead of simmered was appealing to me. Unlike southern food, which could take longer to cook than it did to grow, Chinese food was fast. Some older Southern folks wouldn't eat Chinese food because they were afraid of food that fast.

My attention was equally focused on the gong behind the cash register and the man juggling the food in the kitchen. When the waiter asked us what we wanted, I spoke over my mother and Aunt

Porch. "I want whatever the man in the kitchen is throwing into the air. And could I have extra air on mine?"

My mother, thinking I was mocking the man, scolded me with a soft voice through clenched teeth. "Mind your manners or else."

In response, I gave her the mother appeasing face and posture, back straight in my chair, hands folded politely in front of me, an expression full of remorse hiding a heart that had none. I truly thought the cook was tossing the food into the air to season it.

Aunt Porch, ever the rule breaker, ordered for us. At the end of the order she asked with a straight face, "Could we please have extra air in the broccoli beef?"

Without skipping a beat, the waiter scooped up the menus and repeated the order back to us, including the request for extra air. I was happy until I realized we were getting broccoli. I was not a fan of eating a plant that resembled the tops of trees. Peanut moaned in agreement, "Not trees for lunch!"

When the meal was brought to our table, one of the few things that was recognizable was the broccoli. I recognized a piece of food here, a piece of food there, but for the most part it was all new to me. It was not a deterrent. I held my plate up to be served. A plate left flat on the table was too passive for me and generally received mere dollops, while one held up to an adult's face tended to be heaped with food. When Aunt Porch went to serve the broccoli, I laid my plate flat on the table. There was barely any room left on the plate. Therefore, I received a small portion of the broccoli beef.

I carefully ate everything around the broccoli beef, but I especially enjoyed the egg rolls, as much for the fact that I was permitted to use my fingers to eat them as for the flavor. I also really enjoyed the yakamein, which was a separate bowl and had no polite way for children to eat it. Inspired by Aunt Porch using the wooden fingers provided by the waiter to gingerly dispatch her food, I took out the straw from my soft drink. I used it to search the beef broth for noodles and sucked them up through the straw. My mother was too busy cleaning up Gwen to notice my ill use of utensils. If Aunt Porch could use sticks to eat with, I could use a straw. Aunt Porch didn't bat an eye. The only instruction I received from her was to clean off my straw before I placed it back in my soft drink. I took a sip to ready my courage for the broccoli beef.

Now only the broccoli beef remained before me and it proved to be more daunting than the other dishes. I sucked the beef sauce off the now cold broccoli and dipped the trees in the Chinese ketchup, which I learned later was plum sauce. The plum sauce dampened down my facial expression from a mortified gag to a subtle grimace. Fortunately, the fortune cookie cleansed my palate and left me with a very good impression of Chinese food.

I didn't know it at the time, but exposure would be the best gift I would ever receive from anyone, then and now. It was as if someone had presented me with a giant gift-wrapped box. Upon opening it I found dozens of little presents inside, each one needing to be unwrapped and discovered. The unwrapping and discovery are the real joy. Aunt Porch let me experience it my way. I would not sit in another Chinese restaurant for almost thirteen years, but I remember the experience well. Every now and again when I dine in a Chinese restaurant, I have to fight down the urge to pick up my straw to suck up noodles. One day I will lose the fight and be five years old again in a public place.

Aunt Porch paid the bill and we backtracked to make our choices. Gwen chose a doll and a cherry pocket pie. Peanut, although too young for it, chose a paint-by-numbers set. She could only count to nine so any numbers after nine would remain blank white unless an adult helped. Fittingly, she chose for her treat a can of peanut brittle. I chose a big bag of Safe-T-Pops, the lollipops with the looped paper stems that resembled a pacifier when you sucked on them. Such a large bag begged to be shared. There was no way or reason for me to keep my sisters' grubby paws and maws off my lollipops. I lingered and dawdled, not from indecision but trying to summon up the courage to ask for what I really wanted. Aunt Porch showed no sign of losing her patience. It was I who was losing my patience. Despite dragging the time out, I was losing my courage as well.

My choice looked desperate and hurried although I knew from the first offer what I wanted. I selected a large box of tea bags. Aunt Porch thought I had made a mistake and corrected me by saying, "Grant, you can have something to eat and something to play with. Tea is not a toy."

One of the big rules in my grandparents' house was you didn't play with food. At first, I thought I had blundered and worried that Aunt Porch was of the same school. Nonetheless I could sense from her sympathy and a strong spine to be defiant. She was open to the unconventional. So, I said, "Some of the tea I will give to Mister Willy so he can make rum tea. The others I will need for my tea parties."

Aunt Porch, sensing a back door to give something to Mister Willy, jumped on my purchase and trampled all over my mother's no, saying, "A promise is a promise. If that's what he wants that's what he will get."

She fumbled with her purse and politely asked, "Can I come to your tea party?"

I said, "Yes and no. The imaginary you can come but the real you cannot. I don't want the real you to ruin your lines." My bluntness made her laugh, and I got my tea.

I enjoyed having tea parties with the broken dishes I found in the junkyard. I thought real tea bags steeped in cups that had caught rainwater from afternoon showers would be a nice touch for my guests. Unlike little girls, who had tea parties and invited dolls or imaginary characters, my guests were imaginary versions of family and friends, whom I placed in imaginary settings. The people I loved and admired didn't intersect in real life as closely as I would have liked. The most important people in my life often never met each other. Mister Willy and my grandparents would never meet, but at my tea parties they sipped tea together from chipped cups and rested them on mismatched, cracked saucers. They talked about big important things while I, normally a magpie of a child, sat and just listened.

One day my stepfather came home early from work, crashed my party and stomped on my junkyard tea set, chastising me that boys don't have tea parties. After that I moved the parties deeper into my head where only invited guests could come and the tea settings, beverages and food were now imaginary. I never really grew out of this. Later in life, my guests included the dead, sipping, dining and talking with the living. The only hall where they could ever dine together was in my head. My mind would always be full of parties for people who should have met but never did or couldn't possibly have met. These parties laughed at time and death. They were a place where guests would wear era appropriate clothing. Older family members wearing church clothes sat next to friends wearing wildly patterned disco shirts, while gospel and disco music played in the background. Despite my imaginary parties, my greatest wish is that some of my favorite people would have met each other through me instead of within of me. I was five and I had yet to meet most of them.

CHAPTER 19   OVERDRESSED FOR THE OCCASION

Rub a dub scrub, three kids in a tub. Who do you think they be, the younger, the faker, the scandal maker and all trying not to pee? We resembled sexless dolls as we sat in water hot enough to wrinkle the skin on real plastic dolls. Not only was the dirt scrubbed off, but the layer of skin that came into direct contact with the dirt had to be scrubbed away as well. The water was left brown from dirt and melanin. We got a new layer of skin every week.

That Saturday night bath was my last communal bath with my sisters. Despite bathing with them on Saturday, I was bathed again separately on Tuesday night in preparation for school. The tub was only a third full, which was my portion of the usual Saturday night suds and water. I missed the extra two thirds of water and my sisters.

Our gender roles were starting to be enforced. Despite being bossy toward my sisters, I had no leadership abilities. I was being pushed out ahead to lead the way for them. The public-school system, similar to the last of the ten plagues of Egypt, came for the first born. I could count to ten, occasionally skipping over five and seven. So, it was a shaky ten count. Peanut technically was one number ahead of me because her count was true. She could count to nine without skipping a number. More than anything else she wanted to go to school and I really didn't. My sisters and I would spend our entire childhood playing leapfrog. One would be more developed and advanced one day, the next day it could be one of the others. As girls they were expected to diminish their abilities, whereas as a boy I was expected to exaggerate mine. My sisters were not very good at their roles, nor was I. We took turns being the younger, the faker and the scandal maker. Today I was the faker.

There were two cameras in the room. My mother had an old Brownie with a bulb so bright when it flashed it faded my clothing with every shot. Ten photos from that camera and I would be going to school wearing all white. I gave all my chin-over-the-shoulder poses to my Aunt Porch's new red camera. I enjoyed having my photos taken, but in the photos, it appeared as if I was more enthusiastic about going to school than I was. I would have been happy if they had just taken photos of me in my new school clothes and sent them to my grandparents and the truancy officer as evidence I had gone to school, then let me stay home with my sisters.

My sisters chose their best outfits of their own accord. They wanted to look nice as they walked me to the bottom of the stairs of our front door. A part of them and, to be honest, a part of me as well thought at the last minute they would be allowed to go to school with me. We rarely were away from each other and never for more than an hour. If we were all going somewhere together and one of us behaved poorly, instead of that individual being singled out and left behind, it was more likely none of us could go.

Peanut politely asked if they could visit me in school. Maybe she and I could have our late morning fight on the playground. We usually fought around ten o'clock and were hugging each other and saying we were sorry by ten thirty. My hopes hung on the answer but were dashed by my stepfather's no.

I did my best Shirley Temple impression: I stomped my foot on the floor, pouted my lips, crossed my arms in defiance and cried, "I won't go to school if they can't come with me." Perhaps I would have looked more defiant if I had stomped a foot shod in patent leather and crossed my arms over a pink frock. Shirley received an Academy Award for her performance. I got yanked upstairs.

My stepfather was actually sympathetic, and he gave me the first of his many, "This is a Man's World," pep talks. Essentially it put men in the protective role over women and children, similar to a sheep-dog protecting its flock. He omitted the part where every now and again the sheepdog sneaks off to have a few drinks and comes back to the flock as the wolf. He would take me to school; then, when it was my sisters' turn to go to school, I would play his role and take them to school.

Despite his many faults he sincerely believed in his world and was an excellent instructor on the ways of that world, one I wanted no part of. I had to pretend to learn it, then parrot it back to him. I repeated the master's words as if I had feathers. I never felt any of the things he talked about. Polly simply wanted to fly away or stay home with his sisters. He slapped two handfuls of cheap aftershave on my hairless cheeks to bolster my courage. The aftershave was the only mask I had to hide behind. Its primary ingredients being alcohol and a small portion of an advertised manly scent, most of the mask evaporated before I left through the front door.

He was full of nothing but encouragement and praise as I began my journey to school. When one of the prison guards gestured for me to cross the street and stand under the wall, my stepfather was all smiles and thumbs up.

I crossed the street. The guard tossed a baseball down to me. Instead of joy, my facial expression was that of a child who had witnessed the shooting of the partridge in a pear tree. I shied away from the thing that could drop but not fly. Next Christmas, The Twelve Days of Christmas would be down to eleven. For many of the boys in the neighborhood, stationing themselves below the wall during the inmates' recreation time was better than Christmas. The inmates had access to baseballs, the boys did not. Baseballs came over the wall all summer, either hit over by the inmates or tossed down by the guards. The other boys would scramble to catch them. None of the boys had mitts, but a few with some ingenuity used last winter's gloves to catch the balls. I always lingered at the back of the crowd, pretending to be lethargic instead of disinterested. Occasionally I held my hand up in the air to catch the ball, but my gesture looked more as if I was stretching my arm and yawning then a sincere attempt to catch it.

Apparently, this guard had noticed I had not gotten a ball all summer. He was being kind and was dropping the ball to me without any competition except the pavement. Even so, the street almost took possession as the ball rolled down the gutter towards the sewer. My stepfather's foot blocked its eventual path to the Chesapeake Bay. He came to my side with the baseball and nudged my shoulder as a reminder to express gratitude. A weak thank you parted my lips and climbed the prison walls in search of the guard's ears. The guard tipped his hat and wished me good luck on my first day of school. The only time I ever played with that ball was when I tried, without success to push pieces from my Mister Potato head through its leather skin.

Johnston Elementary School was four blocks from my house. Right, left, right and we were there. It took me three days to learn the three turns, at which point I was expected to walk to school by myself. The journey to school was one of the few times I almost bonded with my stepfather.

The school was a nondescript, L-shaped brick building with classrooms that opened onto the schoolyard. We entered my kindergarten class from that yard. My stepfather lingered to talk to the teacher for a moment. I clung to a man I was lukewarm to at the best of times, my first experience with the concept of the devil you know. It was one of the few days in my life I can ever remember being shy. He gently pushed me toward a group of children whose intense focus on some blocks I mistook as a snub. It was not as if they were purposely trying to shut me out. They didn't notice me because most of the children came from the Latrobe Projects and, as was the case with myself, had never seen so many toys outside of a toy store. I was losing the battle to be noticed to donated toys, worn down crayons and picture books.

I turned to ask my stepfather to take me home, but in the brief moment I had taken to assess the situation he decided to make his exit. I turned to hear the door slam shut with him on the other side. He was walking away, waving goodbye through the glass window and carrying the baseball I didn't really want. My shriek turned into wails as I ran along the inside window, the glass muting my pleas for him to take me home. The windows ended at a cinder block wall. Then he was out of sight. I pushed against the wall and raked my nails down its porous surface. That day I had no shame in chasing after the very person I would later most want to get away from. Tears streamed down my cheeks, washing away what little remained of the aftershave and its advertised manly scent.

Mrs. Johnson was my kindergarten teacher. I remember her as if it was yesterday. Imagine a linebacker from any major football team. Now put that person in a dress, sensible shoes, with a helmet hairstyle, some perfume dashed on, with a pay cut and in a room full of five-year old children. This was my kindergarten teacher. The only thing soft about her was her voice. It contrasted dramatically with her starting lineup body. She had a harsh beauty that often is never given its due. She sternly stopped my wailing but kindly and patiently let me sob in a corner until I was ready to join the other children. Her last name being similar to the name of the school, Johnston Elementary, I thought it was her school and was particularly obedient to her.

She was doing roll call and instructions when I took the last remaining seat near the edge of the group. All the other children sat in their chairs hunched toward her as if she was a warm fire on a cold day. Mrs. Johnson was a great segue into the public-school system. I remember she wore a cheap perfume that women would stop wearing by the late seventies. It was cheap in price but rich in memories. Some of my favorite women wore that perfume. Although my chair was the farthest away, I could still feel her warmth and smell her five and dime store scent.

Despite her valiant effort to make us a group, I never fit in. Even at five years old my classmates could smell the rural Midwest on me. I was never singled out, but I was never added in either. Additionally, I was one of the better-dressed children, not from my own sense of style but thanks to Aunt Porch and my grandparents. Most of the children came from large families. It might have been the first day of school for that particular child, but it was not the first day of school for the clothes they were wearing. Hand-me-down clothes stayed back and repeated grades often in large families.

Neat and clean was the fashion standard for Mrs. Johnson. Your cleanliness was your clothing. All our clothes were neatly pressed and starched; in some cases, the starch was the only thing holding the fabric together. Teachers would turn a blind eye toward poverty but not dirt. Some teachers kept scrub brushes in their desks. We had to present our nails to the teacher, and dirty nails were sent to the janitor's closet to be scrubbed clean in the mop sink. Although in different schools, my second-grade teacher and fourth-grade teacher would become the strictest enforcers of this rule. Because I had scratched the walls in panic when my stepfather left suddenly, I was one of four children who had to scrub the dirt from their fingernails. Fortunately, this particular classroom had a sink. I was overly scrubbed and dressed for the education I would receive.

I would attend this school for two years. The classes were overcrowded, so anyone who wanted to avoid an education could. Teachers short on time only paid attention to the most eager and the brightest. I was neither. Every day teachers took attendance. They called your name and you answered, "Present." I was truant in plain sight of the teacher, physically in attendance but mentally elsewhere.

I remember clearly two events, my first day of school and in the first grade being punished for not kissing a girl. My first-grade teacher, Mrs. Fords, had decided to put on a classroom play about Sleeping Beauty. It was the first time I remember a group of boys ganging up on me. They lay in wait, not with fists but with compliments instead, not the usual urban gang scene. They scoured my entire being and told me I had manly eyebrows. Therefore, I should be the prince. It was the only manly thing they could find on me, so they worked with it. I batted, my girly eyelashes beneath my manly eyebrows, eating up the compliment.

When Mrs. Ford asked for a volunteer to be the prince all the boys kept their hands down, leaving the air above our heads free for my lone, raised hand. The princess had been chosen the day before. Her name was Linda. I didn't really know the story at all. Mrs. Ford gave me instructions and I hammed it up. The highlight was me wielding a yardstick pretending it was a sword, which I swung as if it were a sparkled baton. I could almost hear my stepfather saying, "Put some starch in that limp wrist." After twirling my sword through imaginary thorns, I found Sleeping Beauty slumbering peacefully on a foam mat. Mrs. Ford instructed me to wake her. So, I shook her by her shoulder.

"No," Mrs. Ford said, "You have to kiss her."

All the boys except for me knew there was a kissing scene and were of the age that they giggled and tittered at the thought of it. They had made me their sacrificial lips. Their reluctance was a phase. The boys laughed at what later they would seek most. In another ten or fifteen years some of the boys would be filling baby carriages as fast as they could make them. My reluctance would become a way of life. I didn't want to hurt the girl's feelings, but I didn't want to kiss her either, not even on the cheeks. Maybe on some deep level I was rebelling against the early, subtle socialization of becoming a man. I had kissed many girls and women on the cheeks, but they had all been family members. It was not entirely about kissing girls. It was about kissing a stranger. I really didn't want to kiss a stranger. I pursed my lips to make them as small as possible and covered them with my hand, unconsciously seeking to keep them chaste. No matter what Mrs. Ford said I just kept shaking my head no.

She finally lost her patience with me and sent me into the coat closet to reflect upon my defiant ways. It was the punishment for misbehaving students. The term, "In the closet," is a metaphoric one for most people. Mine actually had a physical location and dimensions. It was in an elementary school in East Baltimore, was ten feet by five feet and was full of late autumn outerwear. I only spent thirty minutes in there, but fifteen years later it was that very closet I pictured coming out of when I told people I was gay.

Our school had lots of little rituals, such as saying the Pledge of Allegiance, but I remember them in clumps, not individually. I remember a few other small events from my first two years in school, but they were not tethered to a particular day. They move in my head like a pinball, bouncing off more fixed flashy memories. I remember Mrs. Johnson giving some of the children pieces of chalk worn down too small for her to use any longer. These were used mostly to draw the patterns for hopscotch and foursquare on the pavement. In first grade I learned to tell time. I remember learning to write my name. The letters were big, awkward, squiggly characters that on paper claimed to be me. Everything was still new to me, and I was still new to myself.

The obvious was a mystery to me. As I would progress through higher grades, teaching would become more specialized. I would have teachers who taught only English, history, or math. There were no teachers who solely taught the obvious. No one ever told me you had to learn it. Every adult around me must have thought that learning the obvious was too obvious to discuss.

I suppose I was born with some innate knowledge of the obvious, but most of it I had to learn. Perhaps that is one of the reasons I also remember my first day of school. At some point we all had to learn the world is round. Most of us assume we always knew it, but

I happen to remember that first day in kindergarten when I learned this fact. I had heard references to the world being round. When people said the term, "around the world" I thought it was like circling the rim of a flat plate or pouring round syrup rings on a flat pancake. I thought the world was flat and round, not round like a ball.

My lesson was not supposed to be part of the curriculum of kindergarten. Someone had accidentally left a globe in the corner of the room that belonged in another class. Two boys were spinning it as fast as they could. Left to their own devices the two would shortly rip the world from its axis and try to bounce it. Mrs. Johnson intervened before that happened.

A voice rose from a five-year old. "Is that really how the world looks?"

Another child said, "Why did they put all the land and water on a ball?"

I was not the only child who assumed the world was flat. None of us came from homes where the conversation was, "We have a little extra money this week, let's buy a globe for the study." None of us knew what a study was either.

Mrs. Johnson brought the globe over to the center of the room for all to see. She gestured towards the paper sphere and said, "How many of you think the world is flat?"

Half the class proudly raised their hands in the air. I was not as committed to my ignorance as the others. I started to join them but thought better of it. My hand hovered timidly under my chin. I nervously balled it into a fist to create a pedestal for my chin so I could do some thinking. With my other hand, I held onto the bottom of my chair just in case Mrs. Johnson was right, as I was starting to suspect. Just as toy dolls represented real live people, the paper ball represented the world. Now that I thought about it, my grandmother's favorite soap opera, As the World Turns had a turning world in the opening credits. TV blurred the line between fact and fiction, so I still had my doubts.

I ventured a question, "If the world turns and is round, why don't we fall off of it?"

Mrs. Johnson paused for a moment to gather her words. Then she gave me the best answer a five-year-old could handle: "There is this invisible glue called gravity that keeps us from falling off."

The prankster in me wanted to go to the store and ask if they sold gravity glue. I planned on using it on my sisters to keep them still so I could steal spoons full of cereal from their bowls. Of course, I also would have had to use the glue on their mouths to keep them from sounding the alarm. Before I got too comfortable with that thought, Mrs. Johnson elaborated, "Gravity allows us to move without completely freezing us in place," making it useless against my sisters.

After answering a few more questions, Mrs. Johnson asked for a show of hands for those who thought the world was round. It was a shaky unanimous. We all thought or pretended to think the world was round. She brought the lesson down two or three grades and started to read to us the story of The Three Little Pigs. A visible expression of relief crossed the faces of many of the children. Talking pigs were so much more believable than a spinning, round world.

Throughout the day we were introduced to singsong lyrics that at first some of us had trouble learning. Later in life these lyrics would accompany many of us into senility, remembered when all else was forgotten. Mrs. Johnson taught me the only dance I would ever do well, "The Hokey Pokey." Shortly after the dance of putting our various body parts into and out of a circle we were let out of school.

I walked the sixty feet to the corner of Valley and E. Chase Street, where I was to meet my mother so she could walk me home. To my surprise, instead of my mother I saw my Aunt Porch leaning against a light pole talking to a cop. It was the only school that I would attend that had a police officer stationed near it at the beginning and ending of the school day. Someone put the notion into my head that it was because we were so close to the prison. Later someone else dispelled this notion, stating that most of the recently released inmates would get as far away from the prison as their release agreement would permit them. Those released on parole generally had to stay in the area. The ones who served their full sentences could go as far as their gate money would take them. All of them had their dress out clothing on, so I never saw released inmates that I recognized as such. I would never feel unsafe walking to and from school past the prison.

Aunt Porch continued to talk to the officer but held her hand out for me to come join her.

Forestalling my question, she said, "Your mother and I decided I would come to pick you up."

She ended the private conversation with the cop, by introducing us. "Officer, this is my nephew Grant. I know you have to keep an eye on all these children, but could you especially keep an eye on him?" She said it in a manner that implied I was a little bucolic behind the ears, more than that I was a menace. The cop stared at my face for a few seconds to put it to memory, then nodded his head to acknowledge my aunt's request. She thanked him and gave him a beautiful, broad, sincere smile that would brighten a couple of his days, then walked away.

Aunt Porch didn't ask me how my day was, which I thought was strange. She normally would ask you how your day was even at nine o'clock in the morning when not enough had happened to determine what type of day it was yet. She told me to be quiet until she gave me permission to speak. It was not a rebuke for I knew I had done nothing wrong. The tone was more one of "I have a surprise for you."

We waited our turn on the corner to get the signal to cross the street. I was doing my holding my pee dance, not because I had to go but because I had to tell. Instead of my hands over my groin I had them over my mouth. I was busting at the seams to tell her about the new dance I learned and that the world was round and spinning. Her only response to my dance was to ask me if I had to go to the bathroom. I shook my head no.

We crossed Valley Street and then E. Chase Street and entered the phone booth on the opposite corner from the school. Touch-tone dialing had been introduced by the phone company less than a year ago, but nearly everyone still dialed on dials. Very few had the square buttons arranged in the shape of a rectangular box on their phones yet.

Aunt Porch pulled out a large change purse pregnant with coins and sat it atop the pay phone.

"Grant baby," she said, "I am going to call your grandparents and will let you talk to them for ten whole minutes." She paused, then continued, "It's not that I didn't want to hear about your first day in school. I just think it's best your grandparents hear about it first."

I was so excited. As much as the confines of the phone booth would permit, I did a combination of the Hokey Pokey and my holding my pee dance.

I had spoken to my grandparents a few times long distance before, but our talks had been more like proof of life confirmation from a kidnap victim than an actual conversation. "Hello, I love you, bye-bye," and hand the phone back to my mother. Many of my modern-day text messages would be longer than these calls.

Long distance phone calls were very expensive, especially calls during the week before six o'clock. Some years later I heard the phone company at the time charged a fifth the price of a train ticket from the city you were calling from to the city you were calling to. In any event, the call, depending on duration, could easily be half a day's pay or more for a minimum wage earner.

Aunt Porch dialed the operator and got the price of the ten-minute call. She must have spent a minute just feeding the phone money. Once one of my grandparents picked up the phone she spoke for a few seconds, then handed the phone to me. One of them must have summoned the other to the phone. They had the phone cradled between their faces for I heard both my grandparents' voices at once. The first ten seconds of conversation was a battle for turns, everyone speaking at once.

My grandparents, ever gracious, let me go first. Words dripped down from my brain onto my tongue and I spat them out with no rhyme or reason. Instead of telling them about my first day of school I asked how the dandelions in our back yard were doing. My grandmother laughed and answered, "Turned from disk of yellow to balls of white and blown away." This was the last verse to a folk song I have long since forgotten. I think it was a song about growing up and moving away. I could hear the smile in her voice as she recited it. "And how are my dandelion seeds doing in Baltimore?"

I paused as I comprehended that my sisters and I were the dandelion seeds. An older wiser me would have replied, "Not bad for landing on concrete and asphalt between a penitentiary and a junkyard." The bad feelings I had been harboring about our situation had been diminished by my stepfather's good behavior the last several months and the arrival of Aunt Porch. Had this conversation taken place five months earlier it would have been ten minutes of sobbing. Given enough time to heal, the positive always took the foreground with me. So, when I spoke to my grandparents, the prison became a castle, the junkyard a large toy box and the asphalt a giant chalkboard.

What I had meant to speak of first I spoke of next to last, which was my first day of school. Aunt Porch let me recite one verse of the Hokey Pokey song and let me put one body part into the circle and shake it around before ushering me on to the next subject. Her generosity ended at paying an hour's salary for me to recite the Hokey Pokey in its entirety long distance.

Still thinking of the Hokey Pokey song, I asked, "Grandma, Grandpa, did you know the world turns around?"

I could hear the confusion in their silence. I elaborated further. "Grandma, Grandpa, the world is round, and it spins."

My grandmother, humoring me, responded, "I think that is why they call my favorite soap opera, *As the World Turns*."

If I had thought further about it, I suppose the spinning world would also explain the title of another of her soap operas, *The Edge of Night*.

Answering the unspoken question, I thought they should ask, I said, "There is this invisible glue called gravity that keeps us from falling off." I heard bass and alto chuckles coming through the phone at my teacher's explanation of the world.

Not disputing my teacher, my grandfather said, "And no, you are not getting any of that gravity so you can glue your sisters to something."

My mouth hung open wide enough to swallow the mouthpiece of the phone. How did he know that was my first thought for the use of gravity glue? Of course, I didn't know adults couldn't read minds, but they could definitely read patterns. A five-year-old was fairly predictable.

I spent the last minute or so of the conversation telling them about Peanut and Gwen. Aunt Porch pointed to her watch and said, "The call is almost over so say goodbye and I love you."

She was by no means cheap. She simply didn't want the operator to taint the moment by chiming in on our loving goodbyes, demanding more money. I complied and said, "Goodbye, I love you," but didn't know how to hang up the phone for I had never had a phone call all to myself. In the past, either I passed the receiver to my sisters for their turn to talk or handed it to my mother for her to say her goodbyes before she hung it up. I tried to pass the phone to Aunt Porch, but she pointed to the phone cradle and told me to do it. Standing on the tips of my toes I was just barely able to do it. Just before I cradled the phone, I heard a faint plea from the operator asking for more money for additional time.

Aunt Porch had no need to talk to my grandparents; she would see them in three more weeks. I was so thankful she had allowed me to have my grandparents all to myself. The rest of the journey home I happily sang the Hokey Pokey, untucked my shirt and spun as I thought the world did. Although, *The Sound of Music* would not premiere for another six months, my spinning more resembled that of Julie Andrews in a meadow south of Salzburg than it did the world on its axis. My shirttails billowed and puffed as I spun on the streets of Baltimore just east of the Maryland State Penitentiary. I did a combination of the Hokey Pokey dance and the Julie Andrews spin all the way home. No matter the music or dance style, from disco to hip hop, from that day forward all my dance moves would have a hint of the Hokey Pokey and Julie Andrews' spin to them.

I ascended the stairs to our house and spun one more time on the threshold before entering. The first day of kindergarten had only been a half-day, so I had arrived in time for lunch. Screams of joy from my sisters and the smell of tomato soup and bologna sandwiches greeted me as I walked toward the kitchen. While waiting for our soup and sandwiches to be served, I taught my sisters the tabletop version of the Hokey Pokey. As we were confined to our chairs, we could only put our upper body parts into the circle, and we wiggled more than we turned ourselves around. Our mother served the food but put a stop to the dance when we stuck our hands holding the bologna sandwiches into the circle and shook them all around. A piece of bologna fell out of my sandwich into my soup.

Forestalling my mother's annoyance Aunt Porch said to her, "Maybe you should have packed the bologna tighter into the sandwich."

My mother responded, "The sandwich was only going from the table to his mouth, generally a short and swift journey. Besides, they know better."

Two snaps of our mother's fingers and my sisters and I returned to our polite table manners. We dispatched our soup as fast as little fingers could use big spoons. We left our manners behind once again as we swirled the last of our bologna sandwiches in the bottom of the soup bowls to sop up the remains.

We retired to the living room. The TV was off, but I was on. I had my sisters' full attention as I recounted my day. They pouted when I told them I had talked to our grandparents. Aunt Porch, in a rush to stop their whining, did not choose her words with care. Instead of telling them they would get to do the same as I did when they got older, she said they would when they grew up some more. When you say grow up to a child, they think physical not cerebral, height not bright. My sisters spent the rest of my narration sitting on the floor facing each other, tugging on each other's legs to induce growth. They both wanted their own phone call after only a few minutes of pulling on each other's legs.

Our mother rescued Aunt Porch with a distraction. She pulled out paper cups of frozen powdered drink from the freezer. We ate our frozen red dye and sugar while I told my sisters the world was round. Peanut acted as if she already knew to spite me, and Gwen could care less because her world was now her frozen treat.

Later that night in private, with no adults around, Peanut pestered me about the world being round. Her pestering me went on for two more nights. On Friday night she showed me two dirty spoons she had smuggled into the house from the junkyard. Tomorrow was Saturday and she convinced me that we should dig down to see the other side of the world.

CHAPTER 20 JUNKYARD DOG

Saturday morning came. Gender inequality reared its ugly head; because I wore pants and Peanut was too young to have cleavage, we hid our spoons in my socks, under my pants. We finished our breakfast and headed toward the back door without watching our cartoons. Our mother thought it odd and questioned us. "What are you up to?"

We replied, "Nothing." Our denial was practically a confession.

Our mother, a step ahead of us said, "Since you are doing nothing, three can do as much nothing as two. Take Gwen with you."

We were a little reluctant to take Gwen because, as of late, she had become a tattletale. She was, for the most part, only speaking in two and three-word sentences, but let her catch us doing something wrong. Then she spoke with the diction of a news anchor. Before the good Lord got the news, she would be reporting back to our mother about our wrongdoing. She was also an anchor in the sense that she slowed us down. Gwen was as reluctant to leave the TV as we were to have her come along, but our mother gave us no choice.

We could feel our mother's eyes on our backs as we walked into the junkyard. Our attempts to act nonchalant were pitiful as we stiffly pretended to play tag. The ringing of the telephone distracted our mother. Freed from her gaze, we had enough sense to start our digging at the lowest point in the junkyard, which happened to be thirty feet behind Mister Willy's back door. The spot had the added advantage that if our mother returned to the back door, she could only see our backs as we were digging but not the spoons. She would have taken the spoons from us, assuming them to be hers and added them to our mismatched set.

Gwen didn't ask questions. She found an old car antenna and started digging beside us.

We heard a voice say, "What are you looking for?"

Without looking up we knew it was Miss Penny Pile. Peanut replied, "We are looking for the sky."

Perplexed, Miss Penny continued, "Y'all can't reach the sky by clawing in the dirt. Looks like you're digging to China."

Without lifting my head from the hole, I sincerely responded, "Isn't there a sky over China?"

Miss Penny, just as sincere, said, "I see. You're taking the long way. You sure do have high expectations. Don't let anybody tell you Grant can't."

Peanut, incensed, made it clear that digging in dirt and looking for sky was her idea. Her anger was quickly replaced by excitement. She whispered to me, "We are going to China."

I thought if we were really fortunate, we would end up coming out in another restaurant similar to The Emperor's Chow. In reality, had we been able to dig past the core of the Earth, the antipode or the opposite side of the earth would have put us in the Indian Ocean, with the closest town being Augusta in Western Australia. Had we been successful, the blue we would have found would have been wet. Yet we dug. Our excitement grew as we saw bits of blue peering through the dirt. It was only imitation Delftware, but it inspired us to continue.

Miss Penny bid us farewell. She went to Mister Willy's and let us have at it. In a few more minutes our eager digging had left the hole too deep for our spoons to be useful. Gwen kept digging because her antenna was still long enough, and she liked egg rolls. She wanted to get to China as soon as possible.

Peanut and I went further into the junkyard to find longer items to dig with. Peanut found an old broken mop handle. I saw a weathered bamboo fishing pole next to the old refrigerator my sisters had been locked in. The pole must have been put there to keep the newspapers under it from blowing away. As I lifted the pole, a light breeze blew the page of the newspaper off what it had been covering. Lying under the paper was a man on his back. His eyes were wide open as if contemplating the sky, but there was no comprehension in them. He rested among the refuge, not with the stillness of sleep but of death.

On some level Peanut and I knew the man was dead, yet we had to confirm our suspicion. Peanut used the end of the broken mop handle to nudge the man's shoulder as we called out, "Hello. Mister, hello, mister please get up."

We called him mister, but he was no older than eighteen. His dead eyes looked strange on such a sweet face. They reminded me of the unblinking fisheyes on display at Belair Market. The face of death should have wrinkles framed by grey hair. Yet the young man's skin, although an odd color, was as smooth as velvet, and he had just had a fresh haircut. Just beneath his heart his shirt had stains that looked as if he had spilled chocolate on himself. For a moment my young mind kept at bay that it was dried blood. If denial was pushed to its limits, the young man looked as if he had merely laid down in bed to read the newspaper while eating chocolate.

Peanut tugged on my elbow and directed my eyes to the hole we had been digging. Her eyes asked, "Do you think we should bury him there?"

The hole to China had seemed a small undertaking until I saw it as a potential grave. Death had given birth to perspective. We had started our morning looking for the sky on the other side of the world by digging in the dirt. It was a journey of thousands of miles, but we could only travel the depth of an old mop handle. As a grave we had dug only deep enough to bury the young man's shoes. Reality dawned. Our hole would not take us to China, nor would it house this man's body. The stain on the young man's shirt was not chocolate but dried blood. My head was spinning. I caught a glimpse of the bullet holes in the refrigerator that had saved my sisters' lives. Then I saw the bullet hole in the young man's shirt that had ended his life.

Removing the newspaper from the man's face had attracted the first crow. Its wingspan momentarily eclipsed the sun before it landed and perched on an old potbelly stove as black as itself. It flapped its wings towards us, as if birds had now taken to shooing away humans. Its black eyes and pointy beak said, "There is no need for the hole, I am here." It flapped its wings once more in our direction, this time as if conducting a choir to begin singing. It suddenly cawed to summon its fellows. We in turn cried out to call our mother. Stumbling upon death was one thing. Finding murder was another. Although unknown to me at the time and a very archaic term for a group of its kind, a murder of crows, finding a murder victim would later in life be remembered as a very dark, poetic coincidence.

Three more of the crow's feathered fellows arrived. Our aproned mother ran toward our cries. Seeing the gathering crows, she flapped her apron at them to shoo them away. The apron had a repeating pattern of red robins with cherries in their beaks. It was probably the only time robins bested crows in a fight.

Although our mother thought she had rescued us from the crows, knowing our propensity for mischief she still sided with them. Having not seen the body, she turned and gave us an angry look that said, "Why are you starting fights with crows?"

Pointing my finger toward the body I said, "The crows came for the dead man." The crows had actually come to the junkyard looking for other scraps, but the body would do. Peanut punctuated my sentence by going up to the body and pushing the shoulder once again with her old mop handle. The resistance of the shoulder made the man seem as if he was giving us a begrudging shrug that said, "I don't know, I'm dead."

Finally seeing the body, our mother stepped in front of Peanut to push her away. Clutching the area of her neck where pearls should hang, our mother was grasping for composure instead. She stood just as still as the man at her feet. Fear and indecision played tug-of-war with her facial expression. The crows returned in greater numbers but kept their distance. Their presence tugged her expression toward defiance. She ran toward the crows screaming and yelling, driving them away and giving her time to call the police.

She turned from shooing crows to shooing her children toward the house. As I moved toward our house, I saw over my shoulder that our mother was placing her apron over the young man's face and upper body. He was now covered in robins instead of crows, small favors for the dead. I never saw that apron again.

Hearing all the commotion, Miss Penny came out of Mister Willy's house. Mister Willy stood at his back door, waiting for an explanation. Miss Penny strolled up to my mother. From the back steps of our house I could no longer see the body. Miss Penny looked down but had no visible reaction. She told my mother to explain to Mister Willy what happened and to call the police.

While my mother explained the event to Mister Willy, Miss Penny stood over the body with her head bent toward the ground in prayer. She looked as if she were a scarecrow acting as a supplicant for the dead. She raised her head and finished her prayer looking up toward the sky. For a brief irreverent moment, I wondered if heaven was round just like Earth. It seemed to me Miss Penny was praying in both directions just in case, to the sky on the other side of the world and the one directly above us. It also made me think heaven was vast while hell was finite. In his creation of the universe, God had high hopes of filling the heavens with us. Limited space in hell was a sign of a forgiving God. My thoughts were buttressed by the sight of a praying scarecrow standing in a field of junk, keeping the crows away.

After a brief explanation to Mister Willy, our mother herded us into the house to call the police. The phone call would have been much easier if our mother had sent us out of the room. Finding a murder victim practically in our back yard had made her leery of letting us out of her sight. For our sake our mother tried to use polite euphemisms for death. This must have started a flurry of questions on the other end of the phone. We heard her answer, "There is no need to send an ambulance." She probably sounded evasive to the police, but she was trying to find the right words for the police and her children. She finally found the compromise she was searching for as she said, "There is a deceased person in my back yard." Continuing, she explained she believed it was a homicide. From context I was able to guess the meaning of deceased and homicide. Finding a body in a junkyard had moved us beyond the need to hear polite euphemisms for death. Words can't pretty-up death once you have seen it, especially murder.

Shortly after hanging up we heard the first sirens. Not wanting to answer any questions from the police, Miss Penny took flight along with the crows. All the questions fell to my mother.

This was not the last body we would find. Over a year later, Peanut and I were walking to school. We noticed a man sitting at the curb in the process of changing a tire. A tire iron was in his lap and the new tire was propped against the car. I knew nothing about changing tires, but Peanut and I knew about death. A break from work didn't look like this. His arms were propped behind his back, resting on the pavement as if he was getting ready to push himself up from the sitting position. The weight of his body had locked his elbows into position.

Although we were not supposed to speak to strangers, as was the case with the first body we said hello to see if the man would stir. The man was a stranger, yet death was not; it was very familiar to us. What should you say to the suspected dead? Peanut and I formed our own etiquette. We said hello but didn't introduce ourselves. As before, our hello went unanswered.

As we moved closer to the man, we could see a bullet hole in his forehead and a trail of blood running down his cheek, taking the path normally traveled by tears. His head lolled onto his chest and his eyes were closed. He couldn't have been dead more than a few minutes. Confirmation came from an old woman looking out the second-floor window of her house. Her face was contorted and animated with the intensity of someone about to yell, but she only let out panicky whispers. "The killer is still here," she uttered. Pointing to the man with bloody tears, she elaborated, "The killer is still in Mister Cain's house robbing it. Run!" The sound of ransacking emanated from the house next to the woman. It was the house of the man just introduced to us, postmortem, as Mister Cain.

Fortunately for us, the sounds of burglary were moving from the front of the house toward the back of the house, away from us. We probably would have run back home instead of running toward the school if it hadn't been for the cop who was also the crossing guard. He appeared out of nowhere and motioned for us to duck walk toward the school. I was Jesse Owens duck as I sped toward the cross walk. Peanut was lawless duck as she took advantage of the distracted crossing guard and duck jaywalked between parked cars. We arrived just as the bell rang. We switched from running for our lives to playing with blocks and choosing which color crayons to use that day.

My sisters and I found bodies but never received explanations. I always remembered the victim in the junkyard as the young man with the fresh haircut. The victim changing the tire with bloody tears was Mister Cain. We never knew anything else about them. Who they were, who killed them? Were their killers ever caught or did their murders remain a mystery? The unwillingness of the adults around us to answer our questions ensured that the bodies stayed bodies, not people. Yet I remember their faces more clearly than the faces of any of the children from Johnston Elementary School.

Finding the last body was crossing the Rubicon from rural to urban. Rural continued to be a part of me, but it had grown faint and was now background me, not forefront me. Urban innocence had a definite taint to it. Despite finding bodies, eating cat food, hearing my mother raped and having the police break down my door, I was still a child. I believed in Santa Claus, the Easter Bunny and the Tooth Fairy, except I feared Santa Claus would come down the chimney on a Christmas Eve when my stepfather had been drinking and be beaten along with my mother. I feared the Easter Bunny would accidentally hop on a heroin needle, get high and forget to make his deliveries. I hoped no one would rob the Tooth Fairy of her dimes and nickels before exchanging them for my teeth.

After the age of seven I no longer would have even these rickety, wobbly beliefs. Not always, but often, Christmas was the time of the year when my stepfather would decorate my mother's face with cuts and bruises. Easter was not generally a beating or drinking holiday, so for the most part I continued to enjoy it. Besides, you received better candy on Easter. As for the Tooth Fairy, my last two baby teeth were knocked out by my stepfather when he slapped me. I dumped them in the trash without receiving compensation.

At seven years of age I received my first responsibility. It became my job to go to the store to buy my stepfather cigarettes when he was too hung over or busy to go himself. Cigarettes were his weakness, and I learned to exploit it. He would come home so drunk that he'd forget where his cigarettes were. I would hide his pack of cigarettes from him and watch as his nicotine addiction drove him to frantically search the house pell-mell for his Pall Malls. He would look under the couch. Then he'd look under the kitchen table. He thought if he retraced last night's drunken steps as a sober person, he would find them, but I had erased all his steps.

One of my favorite tricks was to put the pack in his back pants pocket, one of the last places he would look. Before placing them there, I would crush the pack first, thus ruining the cigarettes and leading him to believe he had sat on them. When he found them, I would act as if I was the most helpful concierge in the most expensive hotel in the world, gladly feeding him helpful suggestions. I would say irritating, helpful things such as, "Maybe you can wrap tape around them and still smoke them. Or maybe you could put all the cigarettes in the ashtray and set them on fire and breath it in like incense."

The hardest thing was to keep a straight face and appear sincerely concerned. I was slowly learning the art of the timed release, screw you. It was the medicine of the powerless, a way of being defiant without being defeated. My mind would record every moment so I could savor it in private, laughing into the air like a crazy person when he wasn't around. Until then I bent my stifled laughter into a sincere looking smile.

If for some reason I could not get his cigarettes from him, I would empty all the books of matches in the house or flush them down the toilet. Unfortunately, he would light the cigarettes on the gas stove. Once I had blown out the pilot light to get my satisfaction, endangering us all.

Another time Miss Penny Pile found a pack I had hidden by our back stoop. She was sitting on an overturned bucket, coolly blowing smoke rings into the air. I said, "Miss Penny, I think those cigarettes are my father's."

She said, "Could be, I found them by your back steps. He must have lost them when he came home drunk last night."

He didn't deny coming home drunk because he wanted his cigarettes back. She took her finder's fee of four cigarettes from the pack, stuffed them in her pouch and handed the rest of the pack back to him. My stepfather did not contest her made up rule. Either that or he would have had to ask to borrow one of his own cigarettes.

She blew another smoke ring into the air and said, "If it wasn't for drunk people and wasteful people, I would have no bread on my table. We live in a world where everything lives off something else." It was not a justification or judgmental statement. It was one of gratitude, almost as if ravens could talk, and they were thanking God for death so they could eat.

A few months later I took her lesson to heart. Occasionally I would find a whole, unopened pack of cigarettes and hide them from him. Trapped between a bad hangover and a nicotine fit, he didn't bother with a search. Instead he would send me to the store with a note and money to buy a new pack, which cost thirty-one cents at the time. I bought that amount in candy, hid it and gave my stepfather the pack I had hidden from him. His nicotine addiction fueled my sugar addiction.

At the age of seven I had my first experience with eminent domain. The vote to expand the prison had taken place a few years ago. Since then there had been whispers of paper notices forthcoming in the mail. Then the whispers became an official notice from the city and county of Baltimore. I was not going to prison; it seemed as if prison was coming for me. We had until the autumn of 1966 to leave. By the end of first grade there were only three occupied houses on our block: ours, Mister Willy's and an older woman, her only identifying feature that I can remember was a floral-patterned apron she wore into a yard full of feral cats.

The families on our block had left first. With their departure had also gone the pressure for me to scramble to retrieve baseballs hit over the wall by the inmates or dropped down by the guards. Our block became a ghost town in the middle of a crowded city. Some of the boys from the projects came by occasionally to pick up the baseballs I ignored from our street. Yet it didn't sadden me that no one came to play with the boy who was indifferent to baseballs. I had my sisters and we would be the last children to play and giggle beneath the walls of the prison. An expanding prison system chased us from our homes.

Eventually bulldozers and excavators came and deepened the hole we had started digging to China. Juvenile Hall would be built where the junkyard and our house stood. I took nothing physically from the junkyard, but I had learned one of the most important lessons of my life from it. I learned how to make do. Even better, I learned how to find beauty where no one else saw it, to repurpose and repair. From Johnston Elementary School I learned to do the Hokey Pokey, that the world was round and to write my name. School showed me what my name looked like on paper. The junkyard showed me what I looked like on the inside and who I could be: not garbage, never garbage. There are always people who can use you for better purpose, even after you've been discarded. If that person can be you, all the better. I learned how to refurbish and repurpose a discarded me. I played with broken things, but I would not become one.

CHAPTER 21   RUST COVERED IN DUST

The summer of 1966 was more a ghost to me than it was a season, my hopes more real than actual memories. Do ghosts see ghosts? People certainly don't always see other people. My obsession that everybody I loved should one day meet was at its height. I spent a portion of that summer hoping people would accidentally bump into each other.

Aunt Porch came early that summer to help with our move. Instead of flying she had driven her car. When she returned to Ohio, she would drive us back to visit our family. The heavily built steel cars of the era would barely notice the additional weight of three children. On the return trip our Uncle Lee would drive us back. He was going to visit some army buddies at Fort Meade, just south of Baltimore. Aunt Porch's and Uncle Lee's cars were like time machines. Aunt Porch's car drove us backwards and Uncle Lee's would drive us forward. For ten days Baltimore and Bellefontaine would overlap each other, but they did not join.

No matter how much I hoped and prayed or stared at doors, Aunt Porch and Miss Penny never met. Although clean, Miss Penny's rags kept her from ever crossing our stepfather's threshold. I always interacted with her outside, per our stepfather's unspoken wishes, something I never noticed until my summer of watching doors. The closest Aunt Porch came to meeting Miss Penny was over at Mister Willy's. They missed each other by a few minutes. Aunt Porch had to leave in a hurry for some reason and left without finishing her rum tea. Miss Penny arrived shortly after and saw the half-full glass of rum tea sitting on the table. No respecter of sanitary etiquette, she finished off the rum tea left behind by Aunt Porch. Their lips graced the rim of the same glass but they never so much as shook hands.

Spurred on by that near encounter, that afternoon I had my last imaginary tea party in the junkyard. This was the tea party my stepfather stomped on and then forbade me to ever have one again. There were so many guests present that there were not enough chipped teacups to go around. I had to use old jelly jars and tin cans to serve the imaginary tea. Why my imagination didn't conjure up fine china for such fine people remains a mystery. Perhaps the chipped teacups, jelly jars and tin cans tethered me to reality. If so, barely. I felt as if I were an order of broccoli beef tossed into the air at The Emperor's Chow, with no assurance that I would be caught by the same chef.

What awaited me in Ohio? After two years away my memories were no longer shiny. Would I dust off old memories only to find rusty ones? With the exception of the one call, my Aunt Porch allowed me, all my conversations with my grandparents had been clipped, monitored and timed. When speaking with them the hands on the clock spun as if they were the blades of a fan. They had a cooling effect on our conversations. I learned more from eavesdropping on my mother's conversations with them than I did from talking directly to them. There was talk of my grandparents moving away because the railroads were laying people off. The rust belt was being pulled through its first loop.

Our visit to Ohio felt like the intermission in a two-act play. While we were away, stagehands in Baltimore wearing dark clothing were moving the sets around while I went to the bathroom or sat in my seat pretending not to notice. We would not return to Forrest Street, nor would I ever see it again. The stage lights would come up on Barnes Street. The house we were originally supposed to move into had become available. There was a junk lot across the street from it, but it was smaller and mostly covered in pieces of broken brick and glass from broken bottles. It didn't have the class of our old junkyard, and I feared it was not worthy of a visit from Miss Penny.

My sisters and I spent part of the early evening over at Mister Willy's house. It was more to keep us from under foot while our mother packed than to allow us a long sentimental visit. Miss Penny was there as well. It was fifteen minutes past dark before she turned on a light too dim to be worthy of the name. Their laughter flickered like fireflies in that dark. I wanted to capture the moment in a jar so I could listen to them anytime I wanted but realized that anything captured in a jar died of suffocation. My sisters and I laughed at things not meant for children to understand. We laughed at their laughs, not always getting the joke but always getting the laugh.

So much of my childhood was up in the air that I remember the times I had solid ground under my feet. That night I could hear myself walk. I was well on my way to becoming a toe walker, due to walking on my tiptoes around other people's moods. My heels touched the ground in Mister Willy's house. At the end of the evening they bid us farewell in a manner that said we would see each other again, but their smiles and waves of goodbye held no guarantees of how often.

The next morning Aunt Porch pulled up in her convertible dressed like a stylized aviator, looking more suited to take to the sky than to the road. A sheer scarf covered her hair and she wore rhinestone sunglasses. Road trips were affairs you dressed up for. It was church on wheels. As a matter of fact, we were wearing our Easter clothes from a few months ago for this journey. The only allowance for comfort was granted to the driver. Aunt Porch's high heels sat between the driver's and the passenger's seat. She planned on driving the whole way barefoot.

My stepfather and Uncle Reggie loaded the luggage into the trunk.

As Aunt Porch's toes pushed us away from Forrest Street, my last glimpse of the house was similar to my first glimpse. Our mother had been focused on packing, so the spider seamstresses had returned and made curtains on the outside corners of the windows. Little beads of dew had gathered and clung to the webbing. My grandmother used to call these spider's pearls. The spiders built the strings and the cool morning air put pearls on them. I remember the first time I had seen some. I wanted to gift the web necklace to my mother, thinking the spider's pearls would look better on her than in a window frame. Without asking the spider's permission I had grabbed two ends of the web. My touch caused it to collapse and shed its clear water pearls. I feared for the spiders who were still there when the wrecking ball came.

Aunt Porch kept the top of the convertible down as we drove through the streets of Baltimore. Peanut had recently taken to watching old movies where people who drove convertibles had long, billowing hair trailing behind them as if the wind was running its fingers through it.

Peanut asked, "How fast do you have to drive before our hair starts blowing in the wind?"

Aunt Porch looked in the rearview mirror and saw my sisters' hair, which had been plaited and secured with butterfly shaped barrettes. Ironically, wing-shaped plastic creatures had been used to keep their hair from taking flight. Aunt Porch lifted her sunglasses, gave my sisters a sympathetic look and said, "Babies, this car does not go that fast."

The look on Peanut's face was more confused than disappointed. It also had a tinge of hope. "Maybe if you had a better car and drove directly into the wind it could happen."

I absentmindedly reached up to touch my quarter inch length of dense hair to make sure it was still in place. I was relieved. Other than being brushed or combed, my hair only moved when it grew or was cut and fell to the floor.

Aunt Porch eyed me in the rearview mirror, seeing the worried look on my face. She said, "Grant baby, there is no car that goes fast enough to move your hair."

Peanut gave my hair a pitying look that said hers could, but mine never would move in the wind. Wind didn't dare go through my hair. It went around it. I liked it that way.

I didn't listen to those old, lying movies that turned an inconvenience into something glamorous. Years later when riding in another convertible, I had a friend who looked as if she had not been a passenger in the car but had ridden the whole journey as a hood ornament. Her hair was a fright. Wind-tossed hair was not the same as hair that had a tussle with the wind. Only the fact that there were no smashed bugs on her forehead told me she had been behind the windshield.

Aunt Porch pulled over to the side of the street, lifted the top and rolled up the window for our mother's sake. As we went beyond the city limits the view out the window changed from bricks to bark and leaves. By comparison, the city parks looked as if they were mere planter boxes for trees. A vast forest stretched from the outskirts of Baltimore and beyond, interrupted only by the occasional town, pasture, or billboard. I had been in Baltimore for two years and this was the first time I had been to the countryside. The trees and the smells put me in a blissful trance. Not once did I utter, "Are we there yet?" After stopping at a rest stop to eat, the trance turned to sleep. The glass window became my pillow and the sound of rubber on road became my lullaby. I awoke to the sound of, "We're here."

We drove down Walker Street unnoticed because Aunt Porch, the one who noticed everything, was behind the wheel instead of on her porch or on the phone. The car snuck into a parking place directly across the street from our grandparents' house.

Our greeting awaited us inside. This gave me ample time to observe. Although not as old as the brick house in Baltimore, the timber framed house before me looked elderly and frail by comparison. Its bones had osteoporosis. The roofline was swaybacked, and it leaned west toward the setting sun and its final days. You could clearly see where new pieces of wood had been cut to fit and nailed into place to patch over holes. The patches looked like wood versions of flesh colored band aids put on the wrong color flesh. It had not changed one bit since we left.

What struck me as odd was that our front lawn, which was always more dandelions than grass, had been mown. After the last frost we generally ate our lawn. Dandelions were the first fresh greens we ate after a long winter. My grandmother and aunts used the direct translation for dandelion from French and called their dishes lion's tooth greens. There was no way my grandparents would use an herbicide to poison or mow down a potential food source. It was late June and the lions should be displaying their manes of fluffy white seeds. In anticipation of our visit our grandfather had mown our dandelion lawn and beheaded their puffy white tops. The blades of the mower had replaced our lips and blown the seeds violently into the ground and air. There were a few dandelions near the corners of the house that the lawn mower had missed. Although the blades had missed them, the wind created by the blades had not. Their proud manes had mange, more bald patches than fluff.

Great effort had been put into making the outside presentable. The inside was always presentable. My grandparents only did the outside for important guests. We were the important guests. Guests got the very best our house had to offer. I should have been happy at the honor, but the honor seemed as if it was a downgrade. Being a guest came with so many perks; the one disadvantage was you had to leave. I would now be a guest in a place I once called home, a guest in my own bedroom, at the dinner table, even in the bathroom. I was now an important guest when I would have rather been an unimportant denizen. It was a light sadness, the sadness of realization. The walls of the house and I were now estranged.

Then the door opened, and my grandmother hugged me in a manner she would never have hugged a guest. She and I were not estranged. I smelled on her the same cheap perfume my kindergarten teacher Mrs. Johnson wore. The scent acted as a second set of arms that enveloped you. I could never smell that perfume without thinking of my grandmother's hugs. Years later the company discontinued a memory when it decided to discontinue that perfume. That smell also meant safety. I felt safe for the first time in a while. There was a part of me that knew Peanut and Gwen needed the warm embrace as much as I did. The gentlemanly thing to do was to step from my grandmother's embrace and allow my sisters to each have their own private hug and a taste of safety. I simply wanted to linger there. My phone conversations with my grandmother had always been rushed and timed. I was not going to allow her hug to be. I begrudgingly made room for my sisters, but I did not leave our grandmother's embrace.

Our grandmother indulged our lengthy hugs as much for her own sake as ours. It was also a delaying tactic. She had to figure out how to hug her daughter. How do you hug someone who needed it badly but didn't want it? You hugged them only to have them grow cold and stiff within your embrace. My mother gestured for my Aunt Porch to go next. Their hug was brief but had all the affection of old friends who had not seen each other for several weeks. Then Aunt Porch stepped away.

There was genuine warmth in my mother's voice as she stepped toward her mother and said, "Mom, I'm so happy to see you."

My grandmother gave my mother a hug I would have melted from. All my mother could do was receive it. She made a feeble attempt at hugging her mother back, but her arms only raised halfway from her sides and made a semicircle a few inches from my grandmother's hips. My mother could not close the circle to complete the hug. Comparison can bring clarity. At that moment I realized that shortly after the first or second episode of domestic violence our mother had stopped hugging us. We hugged her but she did not hug us back. She would encircle us in her arms, but it was not a hug. Onlookers would see a woman embracing her children, but it did not feel like a hug. Seeing her not hugging my grandmother made me realize my mother's lack was not personal. It was nothing we did, but there was nothing we could do about it. You cannot hug a hug out of someone, squeeze them until they squeeze back. I had just witnessed the best hugger in the world attempt it and fail. My grandmother and mother loved each other very much, but they didn't know how to like each other.

Our grandfather stepped past his wife. Instead of a hug we got a brief merry-go-round ride as he picked us up individually and whirled us in the air. Our Uncle Vincent patted us on the head and went to the car to retrieve our luggage. He brought it into a house that was in the process of packing itself.

The house looked almost the same, but I noticed things were missing. I could feel their absences but could not quite pinpoint what they were. Then I noticed a slightly off-color rectangle on the wall of the dining room. A picture had once hung there. I didn't remember what the picture looked like, but I remembered it had been there. All the pictures in the house were gone. I suddenly remembered the one in the living room above the couch. It was a picture of a well-tended garden, much like the one in the back yard.

I ran to the back door to see the garden. There were things missing there as well. It was easier to tell what was absent by comparing our garden to the neighbors'. My grandparents had planted cool season vegetables such as kale, peas and spinach, but warm season vegetables such as corn and tomatoes had not been planted. The space where the corn and tomatoes should be was nothing but turned earth. Weeds had started taking advantage of the absence of the corn and tomatoes. If I had been old enough to put two and two together, I would have realized that the decision to move had been made around the time of the last frost, and it had been a hasty one.

My grandmother came to the back door to survey the garden with me. I point blank asked her, "Are you moving?"

It was not a secret. Most information in our former house was based on need to know. My sisters and I were rarely on that list and when we were, we were the last to know. News was usually old and common knowledge by the time we received it.

She said, "We are moving a week after you leave to a place called Litchfield, Connecticut."

I was both relieved and saddened that she had not said Baltimore, Maryland. The two parts of me had a brief conversation with each other. One wanted the additional support of more family members. The other worried for my grandparents' wellbeing if they moved to Baltimore. I had lots of questions but a short attention span.

As much as I wanted to stay inside with our grandparents, spending eight hours in a car left my sisters and me with plenty of pent-up energy to burn. As I ran around the yard, muscle memory reminded me where my old play boundaries were: no farther north than Silas Moss Ditch, no farther south than the apple tree near the Wilsons, not west of where the corn was supposed to be and not east of where the front lawn turned to pavement. Gwen had no memory of the boundaries. The look of horror upon Peanut's and my faces when Gwen crossed the boundaries drove her back instantly. Although we now lived in Baltimore and walked to school by ourselves in one of the most dangerous neighborhoods in America, these boundaries still marked the edge of our old world. The boundaries were not restrictive but comforting.

After a good night's sleep, we went to see family who lived close by first. Our mother decided to sleep in. When we were escorted around the neighborhood by our grandmother, there were a few things missing there as well. Much of the area was still family but a few had moved away. The picture I had in my head of Bellefontaine was the same, but someone had changed the frame it was in. As we walked down to Jay Street, I started toward the walkway to my great grandparents' house. My grandmother pulled me up short just as a dog with its ribcage visibly peeking through its fur lunged toward me. A shirtless boy around my age pulled on the dog's rope. I could also see his ribcage under dirty pink skin. He was the first Appalachian person I ever remember seeing.

Some people said they kept their dogs hungry to keep them mean and make better guard dogs of them. The only thing the dogs guarded was their owner's pride, for pride was their God. They sacrificed everything to Him and got nothing in return. Even in East Baltimore, I had rarely seen people this poor. Sympathy to them was akin to a slap in the face. Not knowing the boundaries of Appalachia, I assumed my stepfather was one of them. At the very least they worshipped the same God. The boy and I were similar. We had both dined on another man's pride and found it neither appetizing nor filling. In my case I had merely snacked on another man's pride. This boy dined on it regularly.

The present and my memory of my great grandparents' house clashed violently. When they lived there the yard and house had smelled of abundance. Seasonal pies, fried chicken, clove studded hams and biscuits kept at bay the diesel smoke from the nearby passing trains. All those smells seemed to have left on the last train out of town. Even from thirty feet away the house now smelled of unwashed bodies, alcohol, cigarettes, hunger and despair. The Appalachians must have come by bus or car. A town that was once a major railway hub and had a railway named after it, Bellefontaine Railway, no longer had trains. They came but they rarely stopped. Ironically, every train that did not stop took a little piece of the town away. At several of the town's road crossings the trains acknowledged the town's existence. Two longs, a short and a long blast of the whistle said hello but more emphatically said goodbye.

My memory had holes in it. People were not where I had last left them. In addition to my great grandparents leaving, three uncles had left to join the military, Mister Franz had moved his store to Columbus, and our neighbor Mister Wilson had died. I remember him because he had given me as many apples from his tree as I would ask for but would not allow me to pick one without permission. He would report me to my grandmother if I so much as sneaked an apple off the ground but ask and he would give all that he could spare. The boy from Appalachia was going hungry surrounded by very generous people.

My grandmother, sisters and I continued on Jay Street over to Lawrence Street. Whereas Walker Street was half family, Lawrence Street was nearly all family. It was like Halloween in June. We walked up and down the street, visiting house after house dressed up as kin. Large amounts of food were dispensed at each house. As the day progressed, the portions grew larger as our appetites diminished. "I am full," was not an acceptable excuse. Homemade storage containers were filled and placed in bags for later. While feeding us, the adults gushed on about how they used to change our diapers. What do you say to someone who saw you naked and messy? I gave them an embarrassed little giggle and thanked them for the food and the diaper changes.

The first home we visited was Aunt Libby's. She had already called first dibs on us via a long-distance phone call to our mother the week before. We walked up to the house of the most generous kisser in all of Bellefontaine. As we strolled up the walkway, I caught a glimpse of Aunt Libby in the window slathering her lips with ruby red lipstick. We entered her home prepared to receive two-year's worth of kisses in the span of two minutes. Normally I would have dodged them, but what once I had dreaded was now comforting. It was familiar. I stood there and let her place her kisses anywhere she wanted. I expected her to reload her lips with more ruby red before moving on to kiss Beatrice and Gwen, but she simply blotted the remainder of her lipstick on their cheeks.

In every home we entered that week it would be the same, greetings and farewells, welcome home to the returning children from Baltimore but goodbye to the emigrants to Connecticut. The goodbyes were stronger, and by the end of the week we had to say goodbye as well.

Our visit had been long enough to repopulate my memories with familiar faces. The task was made easier because of a strong family resemblance on both my grandparents' sides of the family. In addition, my mother kept the memories alive with stories from her unchanging years of living there.

I had reacquainted myself with our old house and loved the inside of it. I knew I would never return to it, so I committed everything to memory. With the exception of the missing pictures, I can still decorate that house as it was in 1966. The couch, TV, drapes, kitchen table and my grandparents' bedroom set were low-end, cheap midcentury modern. The rest was either handmade or hand-me-downs.

I thought of my town and family as an unchanging artifact that could be preserved in the museum of my mind. When I was not around, they broke free of their glass cases, grew and became something new. Later and further downstream our grandparents would reenter our lives, but the family in Bellefontaine, the ones I wanted to grow up with, would be relegated to our yearly family reunions, holidays, weddings and funerals. Hurry up and become a Cole again, then leave after two weeks.

Over the years I made the best of it. I witnessed change in others and wanted it for myself, but I rarely saw any in me. I had a childhood to hurry through. It felt as if I was playing the game "Mother May I?" The mother of growth was rather stingy. I wanted giant steps forward, but she doled out mostly baby steps. When I received a giant step, I was so pleased. One of those giant steps would become a great leap forward.

Until I reached the age of five, Silas Moss Ditch, my northernmost boundary, appeared impossibly wide. Once, against my grandmother's wishes, I had leapt across it, my heels barely clearing its dirty water. Since then I had only crossed it using Walker Street, which ran over it. Its impossible width, hidden by weeds and young trees, became a fixture in my memory until the age of eleven. When I returned, I saw that my grandparents' house had become an abandoned lot, an unofficial playground for the children in the neighborhood. One of my younger cousins threw a ball across the ditch. I walked into the weeds and trees prepared to leap across its width and found that I could merely step across it to retrieve the ball.

A leap had become a step. I was growing out of old things into new ones. My stepfather seemed impossibly wide during that time period. I hoped the man would become the ditch. Maybe someday I would be able to step across him as I had Silas Moss Ditch. Things that seemed big when you were small become small when you are big. That revelation was four years into the future. We were returning to the man in Baltimore in a couple more days.

The visit to Bellefontaine had seemed like a brief intermission in a long stage production. While I was eating food, sipping beverages and chatting with family in the lobby, my stepfather, along with his brothers and friends, were rearranging the stage back in Baltimore. The curtain would rise on a new house, neighborhood and school but the same old situation. In the span of less than two weeks I closed the door on two homes I could never enter again. I felt as if a bulldozer was following me through life tearing down the structures of my past. Fortunately, I had a good memory, because it was the only place I could visit my first two homes.

CHAPTER 22   OTHER ROOMS AND STREETS

Uncle Lee's storytelling and fast driving made the trip back to Baltimore seem as if it took no time at all. As he drove down Barnes Street the sheer size of his car turned it into a one-way street. There was no parking allowed on Barnes Street, but there were several large American cars parked in empty lots across the street from our nineteenth century row house. Most of the cars were driven by older, single men. Having come from unincorporated and unpaved areas of the south, several men were old enough that in their youth they had ridden mules and horses. They had given up God's creation for one of Detroit's. The cars were man-made secondary sexual characteristics meant to attract women. More often than not they attracted extended family members with children who needed a ride somewhere.

These men had not completely given up reins for steering wheels. One of several arabber's stables scattered across the city was located on N. Spring Street, which was half a block down from our new home. It had eight stalls for ponies and horses. A few of the men drove horses and cars. Many eastern cities had once had arabbers selling goods from horse drawn wagons. Baltimore was the last holdout city for this profession. I hadn't seen any horses yet, but there were some wagons parked in the empty lot at the corner of Barnes and N. Spring Street. N. Spring Street ended at Barnes Street, forming a T. Our new home was at the top center of the T. Facing down N. Spring Street, the wagons were parked in the empty lot on the right side and mid-century automobiles were parked in the lot on the left. In later years I would come to think of it as the corner of the nineteenth and twentieth centuries.

We had traded in our prison and junkyard for a stable and an empty lot used for parking. It was too late in the day to explore my new neighborhood, plus I didn't know my new boundaries. Every place I lived had a version of Silas Moss Ditch I was not permitted to cross. I hoped the stable would be on my side of the ditch.

Uncle Lee carried our heavy luggage into the new house as if he was carrying a small coin purse sparsely populated with change. Our mother had gotten the keys before going to Ohio. She unlocked the door for us. Uncle Lee deposited the luggage just inside the front door because he was not staying. It would take another thirty minutes to drive to Fort Meade, and he wanted to be there before dark.

Hearing us come in, our stepfather came downstairs to greet us. Our mother walked toward the open arms of her husband and they hugged each other. Gwen, Peanut and I waited just inside the front door. We didn't run toward his hugs. I could sometimes fake the hug but never the joyfully running toward him. He came to us to dispense his hugs, but we rarely gave them back willingly. Uncle Lee reached across my sisters' and my heads to shake the very hand that had strangled and punched our mother. My stepfather's hand acted as if it was completely innocent and lied as much as his words and smiles did. Every part of his body was a co-conspirator. He couldn't just tell a lie, he had to be it.

Uncle Lee promised to stop by for a longer visit on the way back to Bellefontaine and went on his way.

Our stepfather was in bragging mood, so we were safe for now. I relaxed enough to enjoy the tour of our new home. It was larger and in better shape than the house on Forrest Street. It was three stories high and had four bedrooms. This would be the first house where I would have my own bed. Though there were enough bedrooms for us each to have our own room, my sisters and I would continue to sleep in the same room, because we had only one bureau. Peanut and Gwen still had to share a bed.

The only new piece of furniture in the house was a new bed for Peanut and Gwen. Our stepfather had merely taken the furniture from our old four room house and scattered it around an eight-room house. The furniture reminded me of myself when I was dressed in clothes too big for my size. There was not enough furniture for the house. Our mother called it roomy. We would never have enough money to make it cramped.

Our new house was a shotgun house. Rooms ran into rooms with no intervening hallways. There was a living room, dining room and kitchen on the first floor. On the second floor were two bedrooms, a room to wash clothes and a bathroom. Finally, on the third floor were two more bedrooms and a door that led out onto a flat roof, which had rain gutters as its only guardrails. All the rooms, with the exception of the kitchen and bathroom, had different types of wallpaper. The patterns were better suited for pajamas or aprons than for walls. Both the bathroom and kitchen were painted in a high-gloss, nondescript color.

The shiny walls acted almost as mirrors. One's image was reflected back as in an impressionist painting. The image looked more like a colorful shadow than a reflection. Viewing my image in the high-gloss walls started an odd habit of mine. My image was vague, almost like clay. With a little imagination I would sometimes mold the image on the wall into a new me. I eventually transferred this habit from our high-gloss walls to actual mirrors. In every new house I entered I looked into the mirror, hoping each would show a different me. It wasn't a vanity thing. I wanted to grow so I could just leave. Each time I looked in a mirror I saw a cocoon instead of a butterfly. I would have settled for moth, anything that could fly.

Mirrors were my escape hatch and my playground. I mostly did adult male drag. The closest I ever came to putting makeup on was using my mother's eyebrow pencil to draw a thin mustache on my face. I wanted to be a man that had a good job and lived by himself. In the mirror I was not rich, but I had enough money to buy a plane ticket to anywhere I wanted to go. Sometimes I had enough money to take my sisters and mother too. The only plane I had been on thus far had brought me here. I thought the only way to leave for good was by air. Cars driven by adult family members always brought me back to Baltimore.

My journey that night took me to the kitchen table for a bologna sandwich, to the bathtub and finally to my old bed. Gwen spent most of the night traveling between the two beds. She had always slept between Peanut and me. Regardless of which bed she chose, one of her flanks would be exposed. Her loyalties were divided, and the purchase of a new bed was similar to going through a bad divorce for her. She couldn't choose. It was summer, so body temperature made the decision for her. Peanut's body temperature ran cold, whereas mine ran hot. Three really hot days in a row and Peanut got full custody of Gwen.

Hot days also meant the end of hot cereals. No more mushy, lumpy nutrition. Instead we woke to find three bowls of sugar disguised as cereal. Regardless of which type of cereal we ate, the boxes were adorned with various cartoon characters that had more substance than the actual food they were advertising.

While we were eating our breakfast, I could smell a rainstorm coming. In Ohio I loved this smell. In Baltimore I dreaded it, for it meant we could not go outside and play. When it rained on school days I was sent to school with the refrain of, "You're not made of sugar. You won't melt." Apparently when it rained on weekends and summers days I *was* made of sugar, because my sisters and I were not permitted to go outside. This was not the case in Bellefontaine.

There we could play on the porch in the rain. During storms not accompanied by thunder and lightning our grandmother sometimes gave us leftover slivers of soap to use to take showers in the rain. We got wet in the rain and ran under the eaves of the house or onto the porch to soap up. Then we ran, stood under our broken rainspout and rinsed. We repeated this until the soap was gone or the clouds moved on. Sky showers were the closest thing we had to a swimming pool. They were better, as you didn't have to know how to swim.

Our present house was in better repair than the one in Ohio. There were no broken rainspouts to rinse under. Most of the homes had flat roofs and had no eaves or porches to soap up under. Nor did we have any leftover slivers of soap. We could only watch from dirt streaked windows as the filth from the buildings and street washed down the gutters. It was a taunting rain, stopping long enough to raise our hopes but dashing them when it returned as soon as we opened the door to go outside. We had to play indoors while our mother cleaned the house. In the near future she would relent and at least let us shower in the rain.

Our game of choice on rainy days was hide-and-go-seek. It should have been particularly fun because we were in a new house. Unfortunately, we had never played this game in a house that had such squeaky floors. I faced the kitchen sink, closed my eyes and counted to thirty. The floors immediately tattled on my sisters. I could hear Gwen as she walked through the dining room into the living room. Peanut ascended the noisy stairs. I could hear the peal of our clawfoot bathtub as she clumsily climbed into its enamel basin. I finished my count and immediately walked to the living room to find Gwen hiding near the couch. Then, I proceeded directly to the bathroom to find Peanut. Ours ears acted as eyes in the back of our heads. We eventually had to modify the game. In addition to closing our eyes, we had to put our fingers in our ears to make it fair. Gwen could only count to ten, so when she reached ten, she would start over two more times to give us our thirty seconds. By the end of the game our eight rooms now seemed small. Our giggles and footsteps had christened every room. It was now home.

Dark clouds blocked the sun for two more days. On the fourth day we were set free. The mad dash out the door resembled the first day Noah opened the door to let the remnants of life back out to roam free again. We made animal noises, mostly the sounds of fowl and swine, as we clucked and squealed our way toward our concrete pasture.

It was a strange coincidence that the first person we saw after the deluge was Miss Penny Pile, clad in her rainbow rags. Admittedly, she resembled a rainbow that had fallen on hard times. Nonetheless she was a welcome sight after the storm. Fortune had come our way in that the stables were within our boundaries. The only reason Miss Penny came to this block was to feed the horses wrinkled apples and wilted carrots. Before we could ask if we could go feed the horses our mother was shooing us toward her.

Our mother switched to a closely approximated version of Miss Penny's dialect as she said, "After three days of rain with three kids, my nerves is bad. Y'all have a good time."

Miss Penny laughed in sympathy and herded us towards the stables.

We passed between two paddocks of broken bricks and glass. Halfway down N. Spring Street the asphalt turned to cobblestone and the smell of hay, manure and leather displaced the urban smells of tar, exhaust and starched cotton. I could hear the arabbers practicing their songs of the day. Rather than call out the names of the produce for sale, they chanted and sang about the sweetness of their goods. The songs echoed off the bricks and cobblestones of the narrow confines of N. Spring Street, making the men sound like a choir. Today's song was about the sweetness of cantaloupe. My ears made my mouth water.

Soon the choir of produce sellers would disperse and spread their songs across East Baltimore. Some of the horses were already hooked to wagons.

Miss Penny led us toward two stalls that had horses in them. Many arabbers didn't allow people to feed their horses. Apparently these two owners didn't mind. I peeked through the slats of the first stall and caught a glimpse of Queen Pinky, the drag queen horse, except she was out of drag. She was still pretty to me, and I was so happy we were now neighbors. It was almost as if I had a celebrity as a neighbor. There was a show on TV with a horse that could talk, and I thought Queen Pinky would make a great wife for him. Alas, two more loved ones that would never meet. Now there were animals at the imaginary tea parties I gave in my head.

Sam, Queen Pinky's owner, came to fetch her for work. Sam said hello and gave my sisters and me each a peach. I fed Queen Pinky the last carrot from one hand and ate my peach with the other.

Miss Penny said, "I have to take y'all back to your mother before I go and see Mister Willy."

That was a big mistake on her part. We had not seen Mister Willy in almost two weeks. There was no way she was going to get rid of us now. She shifted the decision to our mother. "If your mother says you can go, I will take y'all to see him, but she has to come and pick y'all up. I am not coming back this way for a couple of days."

Within my glee was a little lump of sadness. I had grown accustomed to seeing Mister Willy nearly every day and Miss Penny several times a week. Miss Penny only came to the stables twice a week, and now I had to be escorted by an adult to see Mister Willy. Although he was only two and a half blocks away, he was on the other side of N. Caroline Street, across the street from my new school. My world was three blocks long and one block wide, bordered by N. Caroline Street to the east, N. Eden to the west, E. Biddle to the north and Ashland Avenue to the south.

Our mother said Miss Penny could take us to see Mister Willy and she'd come pick us up in an hour. It was midmorning and was already hot. We walked up the east side of N. Caroline Street, as it had just recently emerged from morning shade and the pavement was still rather cool. The homes on this street were a little more prosperous. They were three windows wide instead of two, like the homes on the south side of Madison Square Park. These houses didn't look like some place Mister Willy would live, that is until we got to the corner of E. Biddle and N. Caroline Street. There was a funeral home on the corner and one stoop down from there sat Mister Willy.

Having been born near the foot of his father's grave on the day of the funeral, Mister Willy was comfortable living next to a funeral home. People's superstitions had made a grand house rather inexpensive for him. Very few people wanted death as their neighbor. He used to laugh at that fear, knowing death is our neighbor no matter where we live. Mister Willy was going to give his neighbors something to stare at, a good and well-lived life. He was taking his morning sun before it became too hot. As we approached him, I could hear him mumbling to himself, mostly gossiping with the sun and the sky. He often talked with the inanimate, finding life even there. Hearing our approach, he finished his conversation and greeted us.

Hearing Mister Willy's voice momentarily smoothed out the kinks and wrinkles in the fabric of life. The transition from Forrest Street to Barnes Street was not as bad as the one from Bellefontaine to Baltimore. I was able to see Mister Willy and Miss Penny, not as often as I would have preferred but often enough. Two doors down from a funeral home the scene of one of my favorite memories would take place. My favorite part of the memory was only a few minutes long. I rarely took note of dates or days of the week, but I know with certainty this memory took place on Tuesday, August 2, 1966.

I wish I could say the memory was earth shattering. If anything, it was the opposite. In a world of confusion and chaos, banal and tranquil moments become the memorable ones. For a few minutes I stood on solid bedrock.

Shortly after our arrival, Uncle Reggie arrived at Mister Willy's stoop to have his morning drink of fortified wine without any judgement. He joined Mister Willy and Miss Penny in small talk. At first their conversation waxed and waned between light and heavy. They were talking about a sniper in a tower in Texas who yesterday had shot and killed a bunch of people. It was the first mass shooting I remember hearing about. At this point my mother and Uncle Lee arrived. Mister Willy folded all the different personalities into the conversation as if he was making a seven-layer cake.

There was no room on the stoop, so Uncle Lee leaned against the building. His body language said he was in no hurry to leave. Other than them talking about the shooting in Texas, I don't particularly remember the conversations. All I remember was that the people I loved being with enjoyed being with each other. Personal space was down to the bare minimum, eye contact was intense and joyful. It was turning into one of my imaginary tea parties.

The party grew larger. In the middle of the conversation I could hear the song about cantaloupe drifting our way from E. Biddle Street. Around the corner came Sam and Queen Pinky. Sam's territory was mostly west of here. He only came down N Caroline Street to sell to Mister Willy specifically before heading back west on E. Biddle Street. There was more talking than selling. On a hot day such as today Sam's cantaloupes would sell out by midafternoon. He was in no hurry.

I was so busy enjoying the gathering that I didn't notice the arrival of Little Betty. She had come to give Uncle Reggie a grocery list from his mother. Not long after we had moved to Forrest Street, she and Big Betty, had moved out as well. She visited Grandma Ruth fairly regularly, but our paths rarely crossed. I had not seen her more than a couple of times since the night she intervened on my behalf when Axel terrorized me. Often there were signs she had visited, as in a box of day-old donuts left behind. By the time we visited Grandma Ruth, the day-old donuts were usually half a day older and the only ones left were the old fashions. For a couple of years, I actually thought stale was a flavor of donut.

Once I spent the night at Grandma Ruth's and was there when Little Betty brought a big box of donuts. There had been so many obstacles to me saying thank you to Little Betty that I had not said it. My gratitude would bring up a bad memory for both of us, so I had withheld it. The need to say it was growing stronger. So, on that day I used the donuts as my proxy for saying thank you. My eyes were filled with tears as I said how much the donuts meant to me. It was much too much gratitude for a box of day-old donuts but not enough for someone who stood up for me. Little Betty misunderstood my gratitude for hunger. She opened the box and gave me two old glazed donuts. My teeth cracked the day-old glaze. The shards of sugar slashed my tongue and appeased it at the same time. I ate my donuts, confused about why I had to disguise my gratitude. It was the closest I ever came to, thanking her for that night.

Little Betty acknowledged us by pulling out some candy and handing some to my sisters and me. Then she moved on to buy some cantaloupe from Sam. She picked out two and told Uncle Reggie to cross those off the grocery list as she handed them to him. Apparently, she was not going back to his mother's house. She went back to talking with Sam, then a police car pulled up. Stevens, the officer who arrested Axel, stuck his head out the window to say hello to Betty. With the exception of my mother and Uncle Lee, we all relaxed when we saw it was Stevens. My mother and Uncle Lee shortly relaxed only because everyone else had.

Everyone briefly talked about the shooting in Austin, Texas. Mass shootings were a rare event in America at the time. What I perceived from the conversation was that everyone was horrified by the fact that the shooting was mostly random and not personal. Murder was common in Baltimore, but it was nearly always personal or for personal gain. It put a crack in the notion that if you were careful, didn't offend someone, or publicly display something coveted by others, you would be reasonably safe.

The conversation soon broke into little pieces. Little Betty talked with Stevens. Miss Penny negotiated with Sam about the price of his produce. Uncle Reggie and Uncle Lee took a liking to each other and planned a night out on the town together. Mister Willy and our mother talked about her getting a job when Gwen started school next month.

Behind the impersonal face of the big city were hidden hundreds of little villages. For a brief moment this was my own personal village. Everyone in it had, at some point, been kind to me. I had a warm glow in my soul that was pleasant despite the oppressive summer heat surrounding my body.

Then a call came over the police radio. Stevens abruptly ended the conversation with Little Betty. He turned to his partner, whom I hadn't noticed until that moment and said, "Make a U-turn and don't turn on the sirens until we get to Eager. I don't want to startle the horse."

Horses and sirens were a minor problem in Baltimore. The horses were generally accustomed to sirens as normal background noise of a city, but they could startle if the sirens were suddenly turned on right next to them. This was just another reason why most individuals who interacted with Officer Stevens thought of him as a considerate person with a gun and badge, rather than a cop.

His car sped south down N. Caroline Street. Little Betty bid us farewell and headed up N. Caroline Street. Goodbyes begat more goodbyes as one by one Miss Penny, Sam and Uncle Reggie left to tend to their days. Finally, it was our turn to say goodbye to Mister Willy.

Before we left, Mister Willy negotiated to have his house and that side of N. Caroline Street all the way down to Barnes Street included in our boundaries. Even with this addition my world was a rectangular box, one block wide by three blocks long. My box contained one corner store, a butcher, a pool hall, two barbershops, a park, a bar, two churches, a school, a horse stable, one funeral home and a mulberry tree.

I only left my box unescorted by an adult maybe a half a dozen times, all without permission and most directly from school. On all but one of my excursions I used my lunch money to buy a bag of day-old donuts from a shop two blocks west of my school. On my last and farthest journey, I would visit the grave of an assassin.

CHAPTER 23 BRING YOUR OWN CRAYONS

The last two years we lived on Forrest Street we only saw our cousins every other weekend. Now they were a daily feature in our lives. Darla had been volunteered by Grandma Ruth to escort us to school on our first day. She came to our house with Earnest in tow. As with Gwen, it was his first day in kindergarten.

Keith was already in school. He attended a Catholic school that had once been Saint Anthony's Orphanage. It was five doors up from us and across N. Eden Street, and it started slightly earlier than the public schools.

Geographically it was the closest school to us, but it was rather far financially. Keith's mother had a good job with long hours in Philadelphia, thus she could afford the tuition. Her money visited him more often than she could.

Darla's tap on our door was more a whisper than a knock. She hated coming over to our house when our stepfather was there. When we first arrived in Baltimore our cousins were the experts on the fear of our stepfather. Now we were and they followed our lead. If we looked at the ground hoping to hide in place, or if our lips curtained our teeth to guard our smiles from his uncertain mood, so did they. Fortunately, she missed him by a few minutes. He had gone to work early that day.

Darla may have been timid around our stepfather, but she was one of the toughest girls in school. It would be advantageous for us that the other students saw we were related to her. She already had established a reputation, so we didn't have to.

In addition to Darla, a girl name Willa who lived three doors away from us joined our convoy as we walked past her house. She was flimsily built. Her frame looked as if it could barely carry the plain cotton dress she was wearing. Any addition to the dress such as a print or color would burden her frame to the point of buckling her knees. Heavy winter clothing would make her look like a sickly pack animal, burdened beyond its strength and unable to finish the journey. Something about the way she walked reminded me of a newborn colt trying to take its first steps. She had three speeds: start, stumble and stop.

Despite Willa's carriage, she was a powerful addition to our convoy. She had the uncanny ability of being in the right place at the right time for her but the wrong time for others. If a student did or said anything wrong, it was guaranteed Willa would be in the vicinity to catch them in the act. Not that she had any authority herself, but she would tell the nearest person who did. Right after God, she was the last person anyone wanted to witness them doing something wrong. Unlike God, she took bribes. She might take your last piece of gum or ask you to save her a place in the lunch line in exchange for her silence. Everyone seemed to owe her a favor. In high school she would have been beaten up for telling; in elementary school children paid up. Behind her back everyone called her 'I'm a tell'. Some of the younger children thought she personally had Santa Claus's ear and was the one who actually put their names on his naughty list.

I personally made sure if I did something wrong, 'I'm a tell' had her fingerprints on it too. 'I'm a tell' didn't tell on herself. Despite my precautions, Willa and I grew to become friends. On the few occasions she did catch me doing something wrong, she politely let me know she had seen me but informed me that her silence was gratis. On several occasions she used her clout to get me out of situations.

Our convoy sailed the concrete streets of Baltimore on our way to school. I don't know when Madison Square Elementary School was built, but it looked like a brand-new palace of learning, mostly made of brick and glass. It looked out of place. The school's mid-century design mocked the nineteenth century row houses it sat among. It had a presence that said to the row houses, "My kind are the future and your eventual replacement."

The row houses laughed back saying, "We watched you being built. We were old bricks when you were merely wet clay yet to be fired in a kiln."

We entered through the western gate onto the playground. There were hundreds of children running about. Because it was first day of school, none of us ran with the abandonment we would have preferred. It was the only day the children of East Baltimore could be called dainty. Hundreds of children in their individual homes heard the same speech that morning: "Don't mess up or tear your clothes on the first day, because you aren't getting new ones anytime soon." Usually this meant not until Christmas. The additional incentive was if you took care of your clothes and didn't grow too fast you received more toys at Christmas. Few children at that age wanted necessities for Christmas. For most children receiving clothes for Christmas was like getting a gift-wrapped box of oatmeal.

We didn't linger on the playground long. Darla personally escorted us each to our classrooms. Madison Square Elementary School's inside matched its outside and was state of the art. It had an intercom system, an auditorium and a cafeteria. Most of the teachers were caring and dedicated but unprepared for the waves of ignorance that flooded their halls every autumn. For many students there was nothing elementary about their elementary school. Late bloomers, although not killed by an early frost, had to live in the cold shade of those rapidly rising to the sun. The student body was divided by future potential. In elementary school, nothing represented this more than one's choice of writing utensil. The talented tenth chose pens, for they rarely made mistakes. Pencils were for those destined for lower middle class. Their mistakes were erasable. Crayons were for future janitors and inmates, and we were the mistakes. As long as we colored between the lines we were advanced to the next grade. I was scared to death of pens.

This division was represented even in school plays. Late bloomers were given non-speaking parts in the Christmas play. We were to be silent snowflakes dancing in the sky, slowly descending to the stage floor where we were to lie still, nothing more than stage props. The cast of snowflakes was instructed to wear white T-shirts, sneakers and gym shorts to lend to the illusion that we were snowflakes. This still left brown legs and arms protruding from our white outfits. To my surprise, all the snowflakes agreed to my suggestion that for the day of the play we wouldn't put on lotion before we walked to school. On a cold day we were all sure to be ashy and a muted white for our snowstorm on stage.

When the storm on stage began the other children resembled snowflakes. I was just a flake, or rather an ice pinball that bounced off the graceful snowflakes, turning our snow flurry into a blizzard. I had forgotten our little dance moves. My heavy feet landed in the wrong spots, injuring some of the other snowflakes. They limped to the ground as best they could. The uninjured ones settled to the ground as fast as possible to avoid injury, leaving the sky solely to me. I fluttered around the stage so long a teacher had to come onto the stage and yank me to the ground. The other children with speaking parts could not come onto the stage until all the snowflakes had settled. As I laid on the floor my hand did one last graceless flourish before joining the blanket of snow on the stage floor. I had colored outside the lines. In the next play Mrs. Betts decided my body had too many unpredictable movable parts. I was assigned the part of a telephone and was given the triangle to play. With a metal rod I circled three times inside the triangle to simulate the phone ringing and was escorted off stage. A girl with a pencil answered the phone.

The first two weeks were the culling period. There were no special classes for those of us who were not where we were supposed to be academically. With only so many minutes in a day, teachers could only do so much. The students with pens and pencils were assigned to help those of us with stubby crayons. Actually, there was no one in my class who had a pen. Pens were handed out in the third grade. I was in the second grade. Even the talented tenth was somewhat anemic. Many of them had been drained away to Catholic schools. Parents who had enough money hunted down a good education wherever they could find it, even if it meant their children attended Catholic school during the week and Baptist or Methodist services on Sunday.

Two weeks into the school year, the Catholic school up the street from my house had some more openings and four students from my class went, leaving our class still overcrowded and shorthanded. One of the students assigned to me was among those that left. There now were four students with crayons who had no one assigned to them. The teacher paired us off with each other so we would not be alone in our ignorance.

We could have been behavioral problems, but teachers and parents were in lockstep back then, and teachers' words were considered the gospel. Also, we kept a low profile because we dreaded going to the blackboard. Pens and pencils were scary, but chalk was downright frightening. You could not cup your hand to hide your writing from prying eyes on a blackboard. The whole class could witness your ignorance. Walking toward it was akin to being sent into a dark basement where the string to turn on the light was at the bottom of the stairs.

My little group of four spent most of our time hiding our ignorance and very little time addressing it. We had the blood of the lamb on our foreheads and we were passed over, then were passed on to the next grade. We did have a burst of accelerated learning in early January when the school was hit with an influenza outbreak. During that time up to a third of the class was absent. None of us four got sick. If nothing else, we were hardy. By default, more resources went to us. That was the week I learned the proper usage of the words to, too and two, all because of the flu. By the end of the week we got a substitute teacher who repeatedly read nothing but Dr. Seuss's books to us.

I memorized *Green Eggs and Ham* and *Cat in the Hat*. In the second grade we were not expected to be great readers, but I was definitely lagging behind most of the other students, and the standards were not high. Despite the satisfactory marks on my report cards, my stepfather was becoming suspicious. Oddly, it was he who was more concerned with our education than our mother. I didn't want any more unwanted attention from him. The teacher let me borrow the two books to take home. I pretended to read the books to my stepfather. I looked at the pages, but I was not really reading. I remembered the pace of the sentences and had even memorized when to turn the pages. My eyes kept pace and it appeared that I was reading, but all I was doing was parroting what the teacher had read to me multiple times.

I was not stupid. I just was not yet interested in school and wanted to be left alone until I became interested. This was not so much a thought as it was a strong, intuitive feeling. Most of my effort went into defending my ignorance. I felt as if I were a town under siege. The walls always had to be strong. To further strengthen the walls, I stripped the masonry from the homes the walls were meant to protect and added it to the wall. Eventually the homes were reduced to nothing worthy of protecting. The walls would hold until the fourth grade, at which point I was found out.

Inadvertently my stepfather helped me hide my illiteracy for another couple of years. Because of my stunt with the Dr. Seuss's books, he decided I was advanced enough to learn to play chess. Within two weeks I was beating him regularly. It was a risk beating him on the board. He could have taken his defeat and turned it into a real life beating for me. Men who beat do not like to be beaten. To his credit, he merely took credit for exposing my talent and bragged about my ability all the time. My newfound talent threw my stepfather off the scent of my ignorance. He still monitored my spoken word and insisted we speak standard English. Twangs, drawls and swallowed words were hunted down and exterminated like vermin. As long as I enunciated my words correctly to his face and kept beating all the adults at chess, I was free to stay as ignorant as I wanted to be.

Hands-on learning and the real world interested me more than school did. At the time I didn't know what to call it, but I was very much a student of human nature. I was particularly drawn to different behaviors, ideas and concepts. Many people view different as shocking. To this day I am always shocked at what people find shocking.

Mister Willy had the best explanation for this. New ideas or things are like ghosts that suddenly appear out of nowhere. Some people are startled by sudden appearances. They treat new concepts and ideas as if they are ghosts instead of newborns. I learned this from a man who had very little schooling.

Around the same time that some students left for Catholic

school, I saw one of these ghosts. A new girl showed up at our school. Her name was Jane Lewis. She had thick eyelashes and dark, unblemished skin. Her face was a natural habitat for her perfect smile. I gathered she had been kicked out of Catholic school. In contrast to her beautiful face, she wore a plaid parochial school dress with a boy's T-shirt underneath it. Her shoes were a pair of hightop Converse sneakers with no socks, but the most shocking thing about her was that she had an Afro. No child in 1966 had an Afro.

Much of the early sixties was merely the fifties spilling over into the future, attempting to claim more of the twentieth century than it was rightfully entitled to. Most Americans were content to continue the decade until the end of the century.

There were radical changes going on across the nation, but the movement was mostly confined to college campuses and TV. The first intrusion into the homes of America was long hair. White men hadn't had the wind blow through their hair in decades because of pomades, oil, tonics and restrictions on length. The prison sentence for black hair was longer and more restrictive. In my neighborhood many women had been straightening their hair for so long that they could not grow an Afro, nor did they know how to take care of one. When the Emancipation Proclamation declared us free, it forgot to tell us our hair was free as well. It had been restrained in every manner imaginable: covered, braided, plaited, shaved, greased, pressed and prematurely greyed from the stress of it all. Female dancers and jazz singers in the late fifties started wearing Afros, but it was the extreme of norms. It was the opposite of the straight, slick, conk hair worn by men. Most of these men were entertainers, ministers and criminals. Before the late fifties you only saw Afros in the circus, such as P. T. Barnum's "Living Curiosities" the "Circassian beauties".

Teachers and students were caustically polite about suggesting solutions for Jane's hair problem. Speculation ran that she had no female relatives to tend to her hair, that her family was extremely poor, or that they had recently returned from missionary work in Africa. There was no shortage of women and girls who volunteered to transfer their afflicted hairstyle onto Jane. She dismissed their charity with a shrug and patiently waited for them to catch up to her in the late sixties and early seventies, when most of them would sport Afros.

Jane was my first crush. Crushes don't have sexual orientation. Just being near her or catching a glimpse of her could put extra sunbeams in my day. She was a year ahead of me, so I only saw her on the playground or in the cafeteria. I knew several adults who played the starring role in their own life, neither chasing applause nor running from boos, but she was the first child I met who didn't care what others thought about her.

We played on the playground quite a bit. She laughed back at the people who laughed at her, making normalcy seem foolish and boring. I was already getting a sense that people who cared too much about what others thought did not have lives of their own. Deep down inside I didn't care what most people thought of me either. To be sure, I feared others turning their thoughts into harmful actions and cared what certain people thought, but mostly I saw others caring, so I thought I should as well. Jane coaxed me out of my first closet with these simple words: "I hate worrying about what other people think I should worry about." To be honest, my hand was already on the doorknob when she yanked it open.

I would have one encounter with peer pressure later that month that would put me off of peer pressure for a while. As I grew older, I didn't succumb to it because I didn't have peers. My peers were in hiding. Jane and I didn't have our sexual orientation yet. We were homos without the sexual. She and I were going to grow up to be 'We don't serve your kind here' type of people.

She was also the first child I knew who celebrated the ridiculous. I had plenty of adult examples such as my Uncle Lee, Aunt Porch and Miss Penny who did as well. Once I heard someone say to my Uncle Lee, "You don't have a sense of the ridiculous."

He replied, "I have a sense of the ridiculous, but I am not afraid of it like most people are."

Jane and I were still children, so we had to be mindful of authority. Rules applied to our bodies, but our minds were feral. We came up with elaborate scenarios to escape our gender roles. I would play the prince defending her honor until I was injured in battle. Instead of becoming the nurse to tend to my wounds, she would pick up the sword and keep my adversaries at bay until another girl pretending to be a nurse showed up. When she was the princess being chased by villains up the monkey bars, she called me in as her stunt double. I claimed to be the new princess for moral reasons. The boys could not be trusted not to look up the princess's dress as she climbed higher up the bars. When I became the princess half the boys stopped playing immediately, but for a few moments my heroine's scream shrilled from the highest point on the playground.

Jane and I were beyond ridiculous. I personally was fond of the practical but madly in love with the ridiculous and strove for it every day. Ridiculous is the prophetess of the future, laughed at, yet she is never sad. She reaches high for the fruits from the crowns of the tallest trees, leaving the low hanging fruit for her sister Practical. She does not resent the many suitors who are smitten with her at first, then forsake her and wed Practical. Ridiculous was once the mistress to flight, footprints on the moon and women wearing pants. I am a proud groom of Ridiculous. Practical was the bridesmaid at our wedding.

I was glad to have someone to be ridiculous with for a few moments each day. Besides, she was one of the strongest personalities on the playground.

CHAPTER 24   SCHOOL ON THE ASPHALT BLACKBOARD

I did learn some things in class, but overall school had not made a very good first impression. In the classroom the teacher did most of the talking; on the playground everyone talked. It was there that I learned to socialize.

Adults said so many things in a day that I didn't pay attention to half of it. Mostly because I didn't understand the words or the concepts. That day I learned that, as tempting and natural as it may be, it was not wise to enclose other people within your paradigm. An individual's personal history can determine how they hear your words, leading them to infer when nothing was implied. My mouth and other people's ears not properly aligning would be a primary source for future conflicts. I would become angry because I felt they were soiling my words almost before they were spoken, and they would resent having me use their ears as a trash can. I have been at both ends of this conflict, the offending mouth and the offended ear.

Grandma Ruth called this Miss Speaking and Miss Listening. She always said, "The first things you must do in any new relationship are to learn that person's personal etiquette and teach them yours."

Her advice was both prudent and polite. At the age of seven I was still learning polite and didn't understand the concept of prudent. This led me to unintentionally antagonize a boy named Robert Clement Russell III.

There really was no Robert Clement Russel the first and there were two contenders as to who his father was, so the second was questionable. Speculation ran that his mother must have thought it sounded better and had named him high to keep him from going low. Perhaps she hoped he would reach the height of his name. Unfortunately, he wasn't doing fine even with a suffix attached to his name. In a school that rarely failed students, Robert was repeating the third grade a second time, and repeating it a third time was likely.

Everyone called him Number Three behind his back. If no one intervened Robert would never leave school. He would grow up in place and eventually become Robert Clement Russell III, school custodian. I innocently asked him why everyone called him Number Three. In Robert's experience no one ever asked him innocent questions; they were always veiled put-downs.

In truth he didn't really know why people called him Number Three. He had his suspicions, but he mostly just reacted violently to those bold enough to call him that to his face. He didn't want to know why, he just wanted them to stop. I asked him the question in a low voice and at a safe distance from the ears of other students, believing they weren't paying attention. I was wrong. The fact that I was bold enough to ask the question emboldened the prying ears. My question made Robert momentarily vulnerable. He remained silent because he had no answer. The other children answered for him in a most cruel and mocking manner.

The mocking was contradictory; half the children joined in accusing him of thinking he was royalty. After all, few of us had generational designating suffixes at the end of our names. There were a couple of boys who had Junior at the end of their names. Anything after Junior was considered getting above yourself. The other half thought themselves above Robert because he was repeating the third grade. Both groups finally joined together to form a consensus and started calling him "Robert the Third, King of the Third Grade." With the exception of some of the bigger children, none of them would have been bold enough to taunt him to his face by themselves.

I came to Robert's defense and yelled at the kids taunting him. The mob didn't turn on me: Robert did. He couldn't fight the whole group, even with my help, but he could fight me. In the hierarchy of hurt, you hurt who you could, not who you should. Robert wanted to stop hurting. He accused me of starting the whole thing and wanted to fight me. There was not enough time left in recess to pummel me the way he wanted to. He challenged me to a fight after school. The chant of the taunting students, "Fight, fight, fight!" brought the attention of one of the teachers. My second-grade teacher Mrs. Betts put an end to the taunting.

Left to my own devices I would have pretended the whole thing didn't happen. Robert perhaps would have done the same if given enough time. Emotional wounds stung much longer than physical ones, still Robert was not one to hold a grudge beyond a day. When he stopped hurting, he no longer wanted to hurt others. Of course, the instigators would not let it be. I went back to my class with my flock of instigators and Robert went with his.

My classmates almost had me convinced that I could beat Robert in a fight. Some of the girls went so far as to feel my arm. They oohed and aahed over the raised lump of skin that pretended to be a bicep. These false compliments and my own denial fueled my confidence. I have since learned that if one enters a fray while in denial, the battle is lost before it is joined.

Mister Willy use to say, "Just because you're fooling yourself doesn't mean you're fooling anyone else." Then the last bell of the day rang and all of a sudden, I wasn't even fooling myself any longer.

As I walked down the hall, I had thoughts of sneaking out the rarely used door on the west side of the school. Unfortunately, most of my second-grade class was at my back cutting off that route. I saw Robert up ahead walking toward the eastern entrance, followed by the third graders from his class. He was already a head taller than everyone else around him, but in my imagination, it seemed as if he had gone through puberty since this morning and had grown even more. I could practically smell the scent of burning hairs as he dragged his hairy knuckles across the hall floor.

An unruly crowd could do simple geometry such as forming a circle. When I exited the door, Robert was already standing on the street with a semicircle of children behind him. Before I knew it, my semicircle of children had joined his to form a ring around us. Perhaps it is instinctual for humans to form rings around their sporting events. As I grew older, I would favor venues such as theaters and amphitheaters over arenas and colosseums. The bloodshed in the former is paint and in the latter it is real.

Robert stood on his side of the human ring with a look on his face that said, "Let's get this over so I can go home and watch cartoons." He was not as angry as he had been earlier and was probably only going to give me a show beating. I was not one to let him just beat me. I would fight back, but his victory was a foregone conclusion.

Robert and I moved closer to engage, but before we made contact my cousin Darla came out of the crowd from behind and said, "You're a fool if you think you can beat this boy."

Over my shoulder she gave Robert a withering glare, which significantly chastised and cowed him. He was certainly afraid of her. We were of the age when dimorphic characteristics such as larger size for boys and curvier figures for girls were not yet displaying themselves. Darla was almost as big as Robert, and she was tougher. Aside from that he had a crush on her. Darla had been very kind to him when very few others had. He was not going to jeopardize that for any reason. Hurting me would be hurting her. He had forgotten she was my cousin. The urge to fight drained from him.

I was emboldened to become the type of person I intensely disliked. Before that day I could honestly say I never understood why some people, to gain status, would rather burn others to the ground and stand on the few inches of remaining ashes when they could have enlisted the person's help and taken turns standing on each other's shoulders. By the end of the day I understood why, and I was ashamed. This shame would plague me two more times before the age of ten, at which point I learned I didn't want to walk in high heels made from the ashes of others.

Unfortunately, I saw a chance to be viewed as stronger, but I had to make Robert look weaker, and I really hadn't thought out the consequences. Instead of letting Darla pull me away, I postured and put on a front that I really wanted to fight. I got mouthy and pushy and said, "Let me at him." Darla grabbed my arm, pulled me away and said, "Boy don't be stupid, let's go home."

Seeing Robert's slumped shoulders should have inspired sympathy. Instead I moved a little closer to Robert, repeating, "Let me at him. Let me at him." I did this about five times. Each time Darla would grab my arm and pull me away. I should have stopped there.

The sixth time I made a fool of myself and found another reason to hate arenas over theater. In front of me the crowd got my tough guy act. My face and words were belligerent, but behind me I was already reaching my arm back to make it easier for Darla to grab it to pull me away. This time she didn't pull me away. My right arm waved desperately behind me in search of salvation. The only greeting my arm got was the laughter of the students behind me. My mouth had not yet received the hint that Darla had grown tired of my show. I kept on saying, "Let me at him. Let me at him." The tone was slowly turning into more of a question than a statement. The confusion my arm was experiencing finally reached my face but not before I got out one more "Let me at him."

Finally, Darla interceded but not on my behalf. She ignored my now frantic arm, grabbed me by the shoulders and pushed me face to face with Robert. She said, "You want at him, well here he is." She stood to the side with her impatient arms now crossed, taking a stance that said she would not interfere. I don't know if the sound of me yelping actually left my mouth or stayed internal. From the sound of laughter around me I must have yelped out loud. What everyone found more laughable was that my right arm still remained suspended in midair behind me, searching for a rescue that was not coming. It felt safe and comfortable back there, and my arm knew I could now only save pieces of myself. It planned on being one of those pieces. I had to force a message down my arm to call off the search, for it was now needed in front for defense. As pathetic as it looked behind me, in front of me it was beyond pitiful. My stance made me look as if I was expecting a kiss on the hand from a gentleman caller rather than preparing to throw a punch.

Robert proved to be a gentleman. He magnanimously dismissed me by saying, "If we fight, we are both going to miss the first few minutes of cartoons. I can't beat you up and run home in time." He left me standing in a puddle of my own humiliation and sauntered off to watch his cartoons. He was kind enough not to reschedule the fight.

The children laughing around me made me feel slightly embarrassed, but the laughter was a lenient punishment for my act of cowardice. I can laugh at how ridiculous my posturing was and I often do, but that was not my act of cowardice. What I tried to do to Robert was my real act of cowardice. I could never laugh at that.

I tried, in an inept way, to put Robert down in the manner that Axel had put me down. The scent of Axel was all over me. I wanted a bath, but only an apology could cleanse how dirty I felt. Many adults don't know how to make their apologies as big as their mistakes. They knock the person to the ground with their transgressions but won't stoop down to retrieve the friendship. Robert and I were not friends, but the human in him was worth retrieving regardless of the relationship. Besides, the ground was much cleaner than what I had done, and I was retrieving myself as much as him.

Robert and I were on the playground twice a day, once in the morning before school and during recess. I could have avoided him, but the next day I interacted with him as much as possible and treated him with deference.

Finally, he said, "Look, I am not going to beat you up." My whole body shook from being sorry, not from fear.

I said, "I know but I am still really sorry." I had more to say but he cut me off and accepted my apology by choosing me first to be on his dodgeball team.

It was one of the most uncluttered and sincere apologies I ever offered someone. I can't say we became friends, but we formed an unspoken secret alliance from that apology. On some level we knew we were kindred spirits. We both had a blatant honesty to ourselves. We didn't bother other people, but we overreacted when others bothered us. He and I would never go out of our way to hurt anyone; we hurt only when we were hurt. If anyone bothered me on the playground, he would appear by my side with no need to hear the other side of the story. In his eyes the other person was always wrong. Once he kind of taught me to fight, I did the same for him, but usually I was emotional support and he was brute force.

Robert was more blatantly honest than I was, at times to the point of being inappropriate. Although I would learn later in life that being appropriate often required you to lie at best or, at worst, be untrue to yourself. "Yes, Aunt Vivian, your macaroni and cheese is delicious," I would say through chipped teeth.

Sometimes inappropriate behavior could be appealing or appalling. In the case with Robert, it could be both. A year later, shortly after the 1968 riots, a well-meaning patron decided to bring the ballet to our school. Music calms the savage beast. Black America was angry and white America was afraid. Not to disparage her efforts, but she was playing the music to the wrong savage beasts. Nonetheless I appreciated the exposure in more ways than one.

Our teachers instructed us to wear our best clothes the day of the performance. It was after Easter and despite the fact that most stores had been burned in the riots, nearly all of us stepped it up. Robert was the exception. I noticed him on the playground where none of the students were roughhousing. We had to be on our best behavior. Robert's clothes were nice but growing fast and always a grade or two behind, they were a little tight on him. In addition, his best clothes were from Christmas. His mother had not made it to the stores before they had been burned down.

After lunch we filed into the auditorium by grade, except the kindergarteners, who went home after lunch. The first and second graders were in the front rows. Robert did finally make it to the fourth grade and was just behind me to my right. At the end of my row stood the woman who sponsored the event. She looked as if she had stepped out of a TV commercial. I saw mostly pearls and furs. Wealth dripped off of her. For a moment I thought she was going to try to sell us something that we could not afford even if we all pooled our lunch money. She didn't go on stage but stood near her seat to receive her accolades from the principal and faculty. Gracefully taking her seat, she waited for the curtain to rise.

The lights only dimmed slightly, as many of the first and second graders were afraid of the dark. Half the students continued watching the woman in pearls and furs when the curtain went up. As this was my first ballet, I watched her as well, seeking guidance on how to behave. She pulled a pair of broken glasses from her purse. One of the earpieces was missing and the other one was bent down. She held the broken glasses to her eyes. Of course, the glasses were not broken. The bejeweled frames attested to that. I had never seen a lorgnette before. Realizing that I did not have the accoutrements to mimic her behavior, I turned my impoverished eyes toward the stage.

On a stage where I once played a buffoonish snowflake stood real dancers. The women in their white tights and tutus resembled real snowflakes that had fallen onto a pristine pasture, whereas our dance had resembled snow that had fallen on gritty, urban concrete. Their attire was not interrupted by happy brown faces; they were white from head to toe. The stage accurately mimicked our real lives.

It took me longer to notice the men, as they wore only tights. Despite their wonderful physiques, most of my attention was focused on the women. It was as if God had taught snowflakes to dance and had no intention of ever letting them melt. Instead of lying on the stage floor as we had, these snowflakes were caught in swirls of wind that moved them across the stage in ways that defied the stiffness of ice and bone. As I watched, enthralled, I made plans in my head of using toilet paper to festoon the waists of my sisters to mimic tutus. I dreamed of lifting them into to the air with the grace I had witnessed on stage. In real life my mother wouldn't permit me to use that much toilet paper. Nor would my spindly arms have the strength to lift my sisters.

Our patron must have had children of her own, for she timed the length of the performance to suit the needs of fidgeting children. Two short dance performances, then a bathroom break and two more performances took all the attention span we had. Students had different reactions to the show. Some were enthralled, others were bored, while some of the girls were more enamored with the lorgnette our patron had used to watch the performances. A few of the girls came to school the day next day with their glasses broken and bent the earpieces as much as possible to create a low-income version of lorgnettes. This fad faded within two days.

The reaction that was the most memorable was that of Robert. Near the end of the second dance I heard giggling behind me but blocked it out because I was enjoying the performance. As the light came to full brightness, the giggling grew louder. Fortunately, before the lights came fully up our patron used the brief intermission to go backstage and talk with the dancers. Mrs. Kidman, my third-grade teacher stopped applauding and immediately went to the rows where this fine performance was being disrespected.

With her hand resting aggressively on her hip, Mrs. Kidman asked, "What is so funny that you thought it more appropriate to laugh than to applaud?"

I saw the reason before Mrs. Kidman did. Robert was sitting in his seat with his erect penis pulled out of his pants. He was nonchalantly pulling pieces of underwear lint off his male member and dropping them on the auditorium floor. He was not playing with his penis. He was grooming it. I refused to join the other kids in giggling at Robert.

When she saw what Robert had in hand, Mrs. Kidman asked, "What the heck do you think you are doing?"

Most of the giggles turned into oohs. Many of the children heard worse at home or on the street but never in school. Authority figures didn't swear. Ministers of course could use hell because they had to tell you where you were going if you were bad. Heck wasn't Hell but hearing it from a schoolteacher, it may as well have been.

Robert's response was, "I can't help it, they's clothes is so tight."

I didn't realize he was referring to the ballerinas. I thought he had misspoken and meant his clothes were so tight. After all, he was wearing this past Christmas's outfit, so of course there wasn't room for expanding private parts. But actually, it was both; his clothes were too tight and so were those of the dancers.

One of the older boys in fifth or sixth grade behind Robert yelled a helpful hint: "When they come back on stage again, close your eyes and let it cool down."

All the bright lights and attention were already having a cooling effect, but Mrs. Kidman had no intention of letting Robert rise to the occasion a second time. Robert managed to get it back in his pants but couldn't zip up. There was further cooling needed. Mrs. Kidman gestured for Robert to come with her. As he reached the end of the aisle, she absentmindedly reached for his hand to escort him to the principal's office but thought better of it at the last moment.

What was mildly amusing at the time has grown funny over time and with more understanding. Today, remembering the look on Mrs. Kidman's face and her reaction to the situation makes me laugh. I try to imagine what was running through her head. The thought of the rich patron turning her lorgnette toward Robert's exposed male member would have been a scandal. The Baltimore Sun front page would have read, "Ballet Dancers Arouse Youth" and no more cultural events for us.

Further exposure in life made me realize that below the surface something much bigger was happening. No doubt Mrs. Kidman was uncomfortable with the early budding of Robert's sexuality, but she also knew what I was yet to learn. Black boys and men did not get the benefit of the doubt for being innocent, mistaken, fumbling, awkward, lost, or accidentally inappropriate. The penalty could be incarceration or death.

CHAPTER 25   NO MORAL TO THE STORY

During the beginning and at the end of the school year I would walk down N. Caroline Street. If Mister Willy was sitting on his stoop, I would cross the street to sit and listen to his stories. I preferred him to afternoon cartoons. On cold winter days I would walk down N. Eden, for I knew he wouldn't be sitting on his stoop in winter. I rarely saw him during this time. Being two blocks away as opposed to two doors away made a difference. None of the homes on Forrest Street had fences, so before we moved, I had seen him on his back stoop every day, even in winter. His house on N. Caroline Street had a tidy fenced in yard that had no connection to a community. I only went in his back yard a couple of times.

As far as creature comforts went, Mister Willy had moved several decades into the future. The new house had a furnace instead of a potbelly stove. He still preferred stoking a fire to adjusting a thermostat, but he adapted. The house was much bigger, so the paths between his possessions were wider and longer. He finally acquiesced and had a phone installed. If you wanted to talk to him by phone you had to ring once, hang up, then call again. This let him know it was somebody he knew. He didn't want to waste his time answering calls from strangers. Dialing twice also meant the news was important enough to be worthy of his time.

Most of the calls he received were invitations from Uncle Reggie to join him in drink and conversation in Grandma Ruth's yard. It was there on summer afternoons and late Sunday mornings that I spent extended time with Mister Willy, Uncle Reggie and occasionally Miss Penny. It was not as much time as I had spent with them on Forrest Street, but I remember more of it because I was older. I would always find little amusements in the yard to keep me on the edge of their conversations. I was an uninvited guest that was welcomed but rarely joined in the conversation and asked few questions.

I paid my first visit to one of their backyard sermons the second Sunday after I had started my new school. To reach the yard, I had to bypass a bar and a storefront church that stood opposite each other on the corner at the end of my block. It was not an uncommon sight in East Baltimore. The flashing neon martini glasses of bars often competed with the steady neon crosses of storefront churches for patrons and attendees. Bar stools versus pews, cash registers versus collection plates and jukeboxes versus choirs. Many people needed both, shot glasses and prayer. No one could blur the difference between Saturday night and Sunday morning like the people of East Baltimore.

The middle of September was still summer, and the days varied between warm and hot. When I arrived, I found Mister Willy and Uncle Reggie under a mulberry tree that would offer no shade until midday. Mister Willy was lounging in a tattered lawn chair under which he had parked his shoes and socks. His ten wrinkled toes reminded me of crawdad's tails. They curled into the earth, announcing his intention to stay awhile.

Uncle Reggie was connecting his portable record player to a train of extension cords that ran back into the house. Then he opened an umbrella and sat it next to the record player to keep the sun from warping the records. In early summer it also would serve to keep the falling mulberries from hitting the record, preventing it from skipping.

A portable radio would have been far easier, except there was only one in the house and Grandma Ruth was already listening to her gospel program. At two o'clock she would bring it out to listen to the baseball game. Out would come my cousins as well. I don't remember if we would listen to the radio out of deference to Mister Willy or because there was no working TV in the house. The Orioles were playing the Chicago White Sox that day. A few weeks later the Orioles would sweep the World Series in four games, shutting out the Los Angeles Dodgers to win their first championship. I would listen, not out of interest but because you were a social invalid if you could not talk about the Orioles that autumn.

Had there not been a game that day Uncle Reggie would have still opted for the record player. Radio stations tired of older music sooner than he preferred. Much of his taste was years behind what was current. He enjoyed the newer music, but his heart was with singers such as Dinah Washington and LaVern Baker. I think he enjoyed the way they looked as much as the way they sang.

Uncle Reggie preferred buxom women. He often said, "Baby, I won't waste your waist."

He would have married LaVern Baker if she would have had him.

He liked a woman who could eat plenty and still be pleasing to the eyes no matter her weight.

Uncle Reggie always joked he didn't believe in mixed marriages. He was not referring to race. He felt that if you should marry, you should marry someone with similar morals or similar vices, preferably both.

If Mister Willy had a preference, he kept it to himself. He showed his age by referring to LaVern Baker by her old moniker, Little Miss Sharecropper.

On the Sundays that he brought out the record player, Uncle Reggie always played LaVern Baker's version of Bessie Smith's "On Revival Day". He found LaVern Baker singing about attending church more appealing than actually going. That particular Sunday LaVern's unintentional backup singer was Mahalia Jackson, who was singing a different song, "The Upper Room." It drifted out of the back porch at a low volume from the radio in the kitchen. It was more mournful and had more stamina. It outlasted "On Revival Day". When LaVern's voice faded, I suddenly heard the muffled sounds of the choir and tinny piano from the storefront church a hundred feet away on Barnes Street. Two blocks farther, Saint John the Lesser called to a congregation that had moved to the suburbs, far out of range of the peal of its bells. But God's ears are truly infinite.

The ears of the earthly listeners are not infinite; each heard only their own song and had their own version of heaven. Uncle Reggie had his version of heaven too. He could envision a heaven without alcohol but not one without the happy effects of it, and Earth would be unbearable without it.

He was fond of saying, "If God is truly kind and loving he will give me the heaven I want. Of course, I'll be grateful for any heaven as long as it doesn't smell like a church full of old Bibles and cheap perfume. Lord knows I couldn't bear an eternity of that."

Don't judge a person by the books they carry. With a bottle in hand, Uncle Reggie was far kinder than many people who carried a Bible in theirs. Liquor loosened his tongue, and what usually came out of his mouth was his leery love for humanity. If he said an unkind word about someone it was outweighed by the truth of the matter.

He and Mister Willy were of the same mind. They never volunteered unpleasant truths, but if you asked them for their honest opinion, they gave it to you unvarnished. Usually the individuals asking the questions were the ones who were dishonest. Either they were not honest with themselves about their ability to process the truth, or they asked leading questions to elicit compliments.

Neither went over well. Many would have their feelings hurt.

The only salve they received for their injured feelings was a warning: "Don't go fishing for compliments in the Dead Sea." I hated when Uncle Reggie or Mister Willy referred to themselves as the Dead Sea. They were some of the most alive people I would ever know, and compliments, when given, were sincere. Over time, only the hardy would ask them for their honest opinion.

Ministers were not spared either. Both found their souls much too important a subject to discuss with other people. "Don't make the mistake of thinking your religion gives you permission to mind my business. My soul is my business, mind your own," was their stance.

Uncle Reggie went further and strongly stressed, "I will tolerate your religion as long as it carries out its threats solely in the afterlife and not in this one. If you decide to dispense celestial punishment on Earth on behalf of God, we are going to have problems."

Occasionally Mister Willy would put pushy ministers in their place by responding, "I am not a sheep, and if I were one, I surely would not be led by another sheep."

Uncle Reggie would back him up with a retort of his own, "Why buy from the grocer when you can go straight to the farm?"

Both considered most religions to be too small-minded and wondered why members tried to convert others if there was no room for everyone.

Mister Willy occasionally went to church for fellowship but would not be led. He hated the hierarchy of organized religion.

I often heard him say exactly the same thing Aunt Porch believed, "Hypocrisy is the dark shadow that looms over most religions. Believers curse Darwinism as if it were the scripture of Satan himself, yet practice survival of the fittest with a fervor they never bring to their faith."

Uncle Reggie only went to church when no one else was there and prayed alone quietly. God was very personal for him. He had a slightly different take than Mister Willy and felt churches were full of people who thought they could curry favor with God by being angry and insulted on his behalf. He bore those individuals no ill and was not critical of their criticism, but he didn't want to interact with them. Judgment belongs to God but making judgement calls belongs to man.

Many never learn the distinction between being judgmental and making a judgement call. Uncle Reggie knew the difference between offensive and harmful. He had a high tolerance for the former but very little for the latter. People who hurt themselves could hurt you.

He knew he didn't have the stomach for a lot of emotional pain and often said, "I can't help you and watch my back at the same time or be your friend if you are your own worst enemy."

Uncle Reggie would be the first person to help others in a bad situation, but if you fought his help, he'd leave you be. The world is full of people who need to be rescued from someone they are trying to rescue. He had figured out that not everyone belonged in his life. Choices had to be made, but he didn't employ character assassination to do so. Every person has their own difficulties and problems. Adding to or critiquing another's problem was anathema to him.

I heard him say many times, "Thank God for my problems, because I couldn't deal with other people's problems. I'm used to mine and rarely take them to bed with me."

Coming from Uncle Reggie's mouth it was a comparative gratitude and was not meant to put others down. Thrive for better but be grateful for what you have yet to acknowledge there are worse situations and fates than your own. Similar to looking both ways before you cross the street, good and bad travel in both lanes.

Occasionally when he and Mister Willy disagreed on matters of faith, Mister Willy would amusedly chide him, "What can I expect from a man whose favorite miracle in the Bible is Jesus turning water into wine?"

Uncle Reggie drank wine that didn't have a vintage. It had been aged for weeks or months rather than years. Mister Willy drank very little and adapted his conversation to all forms of sobriety or non-sobriety. He would sometimes taunt Uncle Reggie by claiming that upon Jesus's return he would turn all wine back into water. Uncle Reggie would shudder in disbelief. If he happened to have a glass or bottle in hand at the time, he would take a reassuring sip, smacking his lips in satisfaction that the reverse miracle was not happening today.

Once I interrupted their banter and asked Mister Willy what was his favorite miracle. I suspected it would be Jesus restoring sight to a blind man. Reading my mind, he said, "I never had sight, and at my age I think sight would confuse me." He continued, "Jesus raising Lazarus from the dead shortly before his own resurrection is my favorite."

I rarely asked two questions in a row but continued, "Whatever happened to Lazarus?"

Mister Willy answered my questions in a manner that stated he enjoyed telling the story more than he actually believed it. If I didn't know better, I would have sworn that he winked behind his sunglasses.

He whispered the tale so that I had to lean in close to hear. "The story goes that Lazarus had four children after his resurrection. Since they came from his loins after his death, it is said they had great powers as healers. They could not stop death, but they could extend life. His children had many children themselves and traveled the world practicing their art of healing. Some believe that all the great healers and doctors of the world are Lazarus's descendants. Because we were root doctors, many people believe my parents and I are descendants of one of Lazarus's children."

I was enthralled with the story to be sure, but I also remember it because it was the only time I ever heard him refer to himself as a root doctor. Others mentioned it all the time, but I had never heard it from his mouth until that day.

Stories like this kept me coming to their Sunday sermons as often as weather and time permitted. They were men who generally talked freely about their personal experiences but could be tight lipped about some subjects around certain people. I learned from them a dog who will bring a bone will carry a bone. Meaning a person who will bring you someone else's business will carry your business to others. When they got quiet in front of certain people, so did I.

Mister Willy and Uncle Reggie appeared to speak freely around me. I am sure anything they didn't want known they kept to themselves. Sometimes Grandma Ruth would join in the conversation but spoke less freely. She had a mother's tongue and ear. She was much more aware that I was listening and lowered her voice or sent me away when the conversation got interesting.

Conversations were sweet and sour. I learned that Mister Willy had nightmares about getting lost but dreamed of swimming. Uncle Reggie feared six sober days in a row yet was in demand as a house painter for the five days he worked. He had a waiting list.

Although he seemed older, Uncle Reggie was only twenty-two years old. He was closer in age to me than to his mother or Mister Willy. Despite my age difference, having moved to Baltimore from a small country town made me feel closer to Mister Willy and Grandma Ruth. They laughed when I hinted at the similarities and politely referred to me as a North Star Negro. I had not the slightest clue the term referenced me being born up North to descendants of runaway slaves and freemen, nor did I understand what all that entailed.

Yet, when they and other older people spoke of the shock of moving to the big city, I felt I could relate on some level. They spoke fondly of Pennsylvania Avenue in West Baltimore. From the thirties until the late fifties, this was where people brought newly arrived relatives from the South to awe the country out of them. There were more freedoms and things to do on that one street than there were in whole towns in the rural South. That is how I felt when I was taken to Gay Street and Belair Public Market. From there our experiences diverged; mine was nothing like theirs.

Many of the older people were guarded about why they left the

South. Most agreed that in the North, if you got a job that made you sweat, you received dollars instead of pennies. The first dollar some spent was on a bragging phone call or letter back home. For Grandma Ruth the good life was being able to wear a slip and lipstick. It was not a grand dream, but it was what she claimed made her leave the farm. She spoke of going to the Royal Theater to see the greatest entertainer of the day. She frequented the restaurants and dance clubs of Pennsylvania Avenue as often as she could afford.

Despite her present figure, she used to be quite the dancer. Her nickname was Jump Up, because every time she heard a dance song she wouldn't wait to be asked to dance. She would grab any partner, jump up and start dancing. One day she jumped up and danced with her future husband. They eventually settled down and had eight children. From then on, she only jumped up to change diapers in the middle of the night. She didn't complain. It was just a different dance.

Somehow in the midst of all the poverty and crying children they maintained a strong love. They could go through anything as long as they had each other. After sixteen years together death suddenly took him, leaving her with eight children ranging in age from two to fourteen. People spoke of his death, but no one ever talked about how he had died. There was an invisible wall around the subject. Not even the consumption of alcohol could breach this wall. Occasionally Grandma Ruth would over imbibe but would sober immediately if conversation strayed too close to the wall.

I never found out how he died. Of all people, it was from my stepfather that I heard how much his mother loved his father. I clearly remembered him telling my mother, my sisters and me about the day of his father's funeral. It was the day he felt he became a man. He had escorted his mother up to the closed casket. What his mother said stayed with him for years, and through him it would stay with me.

She leaned in close to the casket and said out loud what many mourners feel but can't put into words. "On the day I need you most you can't be here, because the day I need you most is the day of your funeral."

I would feel the weight of these exact same words and repeat them twenty-seven years later. The words felt selfish because I was still alive, but it was one of the most honest sentiments I would ever express. I hadn't thought of Grandma Ruth for a while at the time, but I would remember her and her words that day. I would take a moment from my grief to thank her. Fortunately, I did not have children.

After her husband's death, she fell into as much grief as having eight children would allow. It was quite considerable. She saw her children only out of the corners of her eyes. It took two parents to keep the street out of her house and away from her children. Jump Up had become Iron Ruth, and people made of iron don't dance. When next she focused on her children, Axel, who had been a sweet but troubled child, was now nothing but troubled. His sweetness had died with his father. A child who had normally seen dawn on the horizon now only saw dusk and the ever-looming night instead. It was hard for me to envision a sweet Axel.

I was learning that we see individuals after they have arrived at their destination, but rarely do we see the road they have traveled. A hard journey and battles with adversity don't always leave one with a better character. It certainly had left Axel with nothing. I feared such a road as his, hardship that left you nothing.

Many of the people I loved and admired had traveled such roads with different outcomes. They were flawed individuals to be sure but had developed strength of character.

In his humble way Mister Willy laughed at himself, saying, "It is hard to believe that I can get this much flawed human being into a pair of shoes every morning. Sometimes I feel like going barefoot."

I wanted Mister Willy's shoe size. Listening to these conversations I wondered what my road would be like. Later in life, after earning my strength of character, I would joke that I would have preferred to receive my character sitting on a sofa knitting rather than through trauma. I would later learn a privileged life can damage you as much as a life of misfortune. The life you lead is not as important as the character you develop. A petal that has known only the touch of the sun and rain will wither at the barest hint of frost. As is the case with all currencies, you get what you pay for.

I was vaguely aware of the fact that I was an adult in training. Several adults made that plainly clear, but the outcomes and rewards were too far into the future to give it my full attention. Presently I could envision nothing farther on my road beyond this coming Christmas.

CHAPTER 26 THERE GOES SANTA CLAUS

Gwen, Peanut and I had been perusing the toy sections of the three major mail-order catalogs since August. Getting the proper toys from Santa was a complicated process. It involved bribing him with good behavior, picking your toys from your head, or looking through catalogs, then relaying it all through your parents or making a wish directly to him. In Baltimore, or at least in my neighborhood, we had an additional method. At the end of summer, we would cup our hands around a dandelion flower gone to seed and whisper what we wanted, then blow on it in the hopes the wind would carry our wishes to Santa Claus.

I complicated the process further by trying to manipulate Gwen's wish list. Somehow, I knew it was inappropriate to ask for girl toys for myself. Looking over Gwen's shoulder when she was looking through catalogs, I would suggest to her how great she would look in the Pocahontas Indian Princess dress on page sixty-one of the Spiegel catalog, not the one on page sixty-two. That dress would make us both look like dumpy duchesses. I was somewhat appalled that neither dress came with a slip, but I had to assume toy dresses didn't come with them.

Either way, Gwen was going to look dumpy. In order for me to fit into the dress, she would have to wish for a larger size. I gushed about how beautiful she would look in that dress. I told her that once she became an Indian Princess, we would have to listen to whatever she said. That convinced her.

The hard part was convincing her to order the larger size. I told her Santa would only give her the dress one time, so she had to wish for it in a larger size so she could wear it for several years. When this proved not to be convincing, I contradicted my first lie with a second one. At the moment Gwen was obsessed with growing taller. I told her if she got the larger dress her growing would speed up to catch up to the dress. She would soon be tall, beautiful and the boss. Lies don't have to be convincing when the person really wants to believe them.

Peanut would have been more difficult to convince had we not both wanted the same things. She wanted the Big Bertha Tank a little more than I did, and I wanted the toy oven much more than she did. We wished on each other's behalf. The rest was in Santa's hands and, for a brief moment, perhaps Gwen's.

Gwen woke from a normal sleep in early December and told us she had a dream and saw all our presents. Unfortunately, she didn't have her glasses on in the dream, so everything was blurry, including a dress that could have been a frock or a princess dress. Her vague descriptions were raising and dashing our hopes all at once.

The next night I cleaned Gwen's glasses really well in order for her to see her dreams clearer, and Peanut put them on her before we fell asleep. Our hopes were dashed again as Gwen had only nightmares that night. Matters were made worse for her twisted dreams had twisted her glasses into double-handled lorgnettes. We were growing up during the age of mend and repair, so we were fortunate that the glasses were easy to repair at a reasonable price. Our mother had gotten them repaired before our stepfather came home from work.

We gave up on Gwen's dreams. There was nothing to do but wait for Christmas Day and the shredding of the packages.

Christmas of 1966 would be my last with the man in the red suit. The holiday would come and go for many years to come but without Santa. He disappeared from real life and was relegated to cards, gift-wrapping paper, ornaments and a few TV specials. He suffered his demise in an accident on the third floor of our house and, by association, so went the Easter Bunny and the Tooth Fairy. Unfortunately, the Tooth Fairy would later resurrect as the dentist who would take both teeth and money.

One evening, a week before Christmas, my stepfather asked me to help him bring down the Christmas decorations from the front bedroom on the third floor. After sunset neither I nor my sisters dared to walk up to the third floor. The stairs and floors up there creaked more than anywhere else in the house. Despite the holiday cheer stored in its closets, the third floor was scary at night.

We walked through the first bedroom, which eventually would become Gwen's, Peanut's and my winter bedroom. He opened the door to the front bedroom. My eyes adjusted to the dark before his did. When his finally adjusted it was already too late. I had seen some of our presents lying on the floor. For sure I saw the boxes with the Big Bertha Tank and the toy oven. Before I saw anything else, he grabbed my hand and whisked me away from the scene, telling me it would be more fun for me to be with sisters making Christmas cookies. That was my argument in the first place before he dragged me up the stairs to Santa's funeral.

I ran a few scenarios through my head before I finally pulled the plug on him. Briefly I thought Santa didn't want to come to the house of a drunkard. Rather than having us passed over because of his drunken behavior, our stepfather assumed the role of Santa and would pretend he came anyway. Then all the stories I'd been hearing from the older children about Santa being fake, which I had been pushing away as false, came crashing down as true. There were so many lies I had to pretend were true, so I didn't confront him on this immediately.

I walked down the stairs, pretending it had been too dark to see anything. Adding to my rouse, acting as if I had lost interest in the third floor, I asked if I could have a cookie when I got to the kitchen. He agreed too readily, which was final confirmation that there was no Santa Claus.

Upon descending the last step, I immediately walked to the cooling tray of cookies on top of the stove. This batch of cookies was all cut outs of Santa. While I had been upstairs my mother had been burning him in effigy in the oven. His edges were slightly burnt, and he was naked without his red frosting suit.

My stepfather was already explaining to my mother it was ok for me to get grabby. As Santa was no longer real, I bit off his arms with no remorse. In the past I avoided eating Santa-shaped cookies, because in a strange way I viewed them as voodoo dolls. I didn't want to hobble him before Christmas Eve. My sisters knew something was up, because they were very aware of my superstition. It was a self-imposed restriction that was to their advantage. They were allowed a cookie each before my mother sent my stepfather to the store to buy red dye to clothe the remaining Santa cookies.

With the guardian of our words gone, it didn't take long for Peanut to start enquiring. Our mother was reading a recipe from a cookbook, so she was not paying attention.

Peanut pinched her face into an expression of suspicion and asked, "Why are you eating our Santa cookies?"

With a smug smirk I replied, "Because there's no such thing as Santa Claus."

A concerned expression crossed both of my sisters' faces. If true they would be losing two types of Santa, cookies and gift giver. The cookie crumbs at the corners of my mouth had already started to crumble their belief.

With less confidence Peanut said, "Prove it."

Peanut and I verbally tussled for a few more sentences, while Gwen's eyes acted as pendulums following our every word. Before

Gwen could break the deadlock by whining for our mother, I said, "I can take you to the third floor and show you our toys. Mom and dad already bought them."

Gwen was still confused. Peanut was starting to grasp the concept of no middleman. A light went on in her eyes. Without Santa watching us, we only had to be nice to our parent's face. In addition, we could now directly lobby them for what we wanted. Maybe over time we could whittle a no into a maybe and eventually a maybe into a yes. No more blaming Santa for undesirable gifts. From now on our parent's bad taste or lack of funds would be at fault.

For a brief moment Peanut's face held a wake for Santa. Then her expression moved on to the joys of being on the receiving end of the mercantile experience.

Gwen was a bit more reticent. Peanut remedied that by reminding her about her experience with sitting on Santa's lap last year. Gwen would not have anything to do with that Santa. She screamed and hollered incoherently, as if she was afraid Santa wanted to give her a bath, but Gwen wanted Santa to take a bath. He smelled of old carpet and cheap liquor. His beard was nicotine stained near the mouth. His cheeks and nose were red from rosacea. The coloring was more from broken capillaries than from a blush.

I had settled her by letting her use me as a lap mat. I sat on Santa's lap and Gwen sat on my lap. If he hadn't had a stack of toys to hand out to children, I would have avoided him as well. I feigned a smile, received Gwen's and my toys and got off his lap as fast as possible. Something had told me he wasn't the real Santa.

Peanut said, "At least we don't have to sit on any more stinky Santa Claus's laps to get what we want."

Our mother had not heard one word of our conversation, but the moment my right foot hit the first creaking step to go upstairs, she said, "Where do you think you're going?"

I can't believe how brazen I was. I answered her, "If you won't lie, I won't lie." I cut her off before she could deny it and continued, "Now that we know there is no such thing as Santa Claus, we are going to the third floor to look at our presents."

She stared at three faces with doubt cast in stone. Only the chisel of truth could alter our expression.

With a sheepish smile she admitted there was no such thing as Santa Claus. She said, "I was hoping you would believe a little longer. I love the innocent looks on your faces on Christmas."

After two years in Baltimore our innocent expressions had waned considerably. It seemed strange that parents would lie to their children to extend an innocent expression. Perhaps her lies were justified, as our souls were prematurely graying. When lies are the guardian of the innocent, the guards eventually destroy the very thing they protect.

As lies went this one was not soul crushing. The delivery system had been changed, but we would continue to get our toys. That evening we left our innocence behind to become consumers.

Peanut said outright, "Let's go get our presents now."

Our mother lost her apologetic, sheepish demeanor and returned to parenting. "There may not be a Santa Claus, but December 25th is still real, and it's two weeks away. So, you are going to have to wait."

Apparently, all the anxiety and impatience of waiting for Christmas Day would remain in place. Our parents wrapped the presents that night and placed them under the tree. We started the day believers and ended it as schemers. The next morning, we sized up the shapes of the presents and made uneducated guesses as to content. Too many packages looked as if they might be clothing. I held out hope that at least one of them had to be a Pocahontas Indian Princess dress. When no one was watching I shook some of the presents, my ears searching desperately for the sound of bead-tipped fringe buckskin rubbing against cardboard. One of the presents was the right shape and big enough to be the dress. On Christmas Day when Gwen opened the present the only thing big was my disappointment.

The tension was worse for Peanut. Curiosity was killing her inner cat. About a week before Christmas our cat, Ibo, was playing with some tinsel hanging from the tree and accidentally scratched one of our mother's presents open. Boring cat was no help at all. The box contained a plaid scarf from our stepfather and did nothing to relieve or curiosity. Our mother cursed the cat and rewrapped her own present. She would pretend to be surprised on Christmas Day.

Gwen and I brought the cat near the tree, hoping for a repeat performance with our presents. The cat sat there, merely licking its paws with its nails sheath. We gave up after two or three tries. Peanut was not to be deterred.

The next day was a school day. When we got home, from four o'clock to five o'clock we were not well supervised. Our stepfather was at work and our mother was usually busy in the kitchen. Gwen and I occupied ourselves with assembling a puzzle we had received last year. We played with this puzzle all the time. When completed there were two or three pieces missing. We simply imagined the missing pieces to be in place. As our toys from last Christmas depleted from wear and tear, our imaginations expanded to fill the gap.

Peanut's imagination could become reality in a resource rich environment. Our family was in much better financial condition on Barnes Street than we had been on Forrest Street. We had cat food and a cat now, and only the cat ate her food. Peanut was determined to turn a house cat into a draft animal.

She came downstairs with the cat in her arms and moved toward the Christmas tree. I raised one eye from the puzzle to admire her determination. Why was she bothering? The cat had lost interest in the tree. I ignored her futility and had placed two more pieces on the puzzle when I heard the soft sound of tearing paper.

My first thought was, "How did she entice the cat? Did she rub cat food on the presents?" Gwen and I abandoned our puzzle in the hopes of having an early Christmas after all. Whatever Peanut had done, we were going to be there to reap the benefits. Maybe she had a bit of food leftover so Gwen and I could rub some on our presents.

What I saw upon entering the room was not what I had expected. Peanut had taken it further than I would have. Since Ibo had accidentally scratched open only a single present of our mother's Peanut was not leaving anything to chance. She was resting on her knees on the floor with the cat gently bundled in her dress. She was methodically searching for the presents that had her name. None of us could read, but we did know what our names looked like on presents. Once she found one of her presents, she squeezed the pad of the cat's paws to force it to unsheathe its claws. Then she raked the claws across her present.

When she took notice of us, with all guilt purged from her face she said, "You saw it, the cat did it."

Most people want insulation between themselves and their lies. Ibo served as both oven mitt and crude letter opener. By nodding our heads in agreement to her statement, Gwen and I had tethered ourselves to Peanut's lie.

Regrettably, we forgot to tether the cat to the lie, or rather Ibo was too tethered to it. While Peanut was using the cat's paw to open another present, Ibo startled and leaped from Peanut's lap. The poor thing fled from the living room trailing strands of wrapping paper hooked to her claws. We were so invested in our lie we had no fear a cat could rat us out. Parental forensics would only find claw marks.

Confirmation came from the kitchen, "Ibo, don't tell me you did it again?"

We were definitely having an early Christmas. The creation of the high five was ten years in the future. Instead we gave each other congratulatory smirks. We had a scapegoat and planned on using her to open more presents.

Our innocence looked a little too staged. We sat on the couch as if it was a pew, our hands folded in our laps holding imaginary hymnals. Our mother came into the living with Ibo at her heels. Parental forensics were more advanced than I had imagined. What we thought of as pews, our mother thought of as theater seats.

Her tone was accusatory as she asked, "So you three just sat there and watched Ibo tear open the presents?"

At that moment Ibo jumped up on the arm of the couch. She began licking her offended paw, staring at us accusingly. For a number of years after the incident I would classify cats as a type of rodent. They most certainly can rat you out. Our mother investigated further and noticed the open presents were all Peanut's and had been pulled two feet away from the tree.

She turned towards Peanut and asked, "Did Ibo open all of these?"

Peanut, not one to cut her losses, nodded her head and went deeper into the lie. She was in that stage when the only way to extract the truth or an apology from her was to give her the Heimlich maneuver.

Our mother countered, "So you want me to believe that Ibo has learned to read and has been going to the gym?"

Peanut's nod was a little less self-assured now, but still she said, "What that cat does with her free time is none of my business."

Our mother conjectured, "It seems strange that Ibo opened only your presents and hefted them to the side of the tree."

The way Ibo was licking her paw up and down, it seemed as if the cat was nodding its head in agreement with all our mother's accusations. Peanut's nods turned to darting eyes. Gwen and I instantly pulled away from Peanut, giving her two thirds of the couch, which was now a witness chair. Not finding a way out of her lie, Peanut became aggressively honest and said, pointing to one of the presents, "I just knew I was going to get an ugly sweater for Christmas. When Santa went away, I wish he could have taken this sweater with him."

I took note of the green, ornate Christmas sweater peeking out of the box. Peanut was not fond of ornate clothing. I could already envision her putting the sweater on the ironing board and using Ibo's claws to iron it. She was not done with the cat yet.

Our mother had to prioritize. Starting with Ibo's safety and dignity, she decreed, "Any more presents supposedly opened by Ibo will be returned to the store and not replaced. So, I suggest you keep an eye on her."

Ibo jumped off the couch and rubbed against mom's ankles, purring in gratitude.

Peanut couldn't let it go and said, "Well you can take that sweater back. I don't want it."

Our mother was losing her patience and unbeknownst to us all, also burning dinner. She said, "Listen young lady. I am going to rewrap these presents and when you open them a second time, you are going to act like it's the first time and pretend to be surprised or disappointed as the case may be. Now go upstairs and get me the wrapping paper."

Peanut acquiesced and gave our mother a parting pout. Before she left the room, our mother took pity on her and said, "It's a Christmas sweater from Grandma Ruth. You only have to wear it once or twice before New Year's, then I wash it in hot water, and it goes to Gwen."

Decorum first, then hot water and re-gifting. Peanut left the room full of the spirit of Christmas, or capitalism. I would always mix the two up.

Trying to placate one child had incited another. Gwen started crying because she didn't want to be the recipient of an unwanted gift.

I came to Gwen's defense and said, "Don't worry, I will just put it on and stretch it back out for Peanut to wear next Christmas."

I had a brief fantasy of me kneeling in front of the toy oven making apple pie while wearing Peanut's Christmas sweater atop Gwen's Pocahontas dress. I would have my own cooking show in no time, *Cussing in the Kitchen.*

Cussing in the Kitchen would prove to be appropriate title for my experience with the toy oven. Christmas came with no more assault on the presents. They all had been opened. There was no Pocahontas dress, but as expected there was the toy oven. I was a little disappointed that it was harvest gold instead of avocado green, but little boys in closets can't be choosy.

Christmas was the ultimate enforcer of gender roles. I was too young to rebel against the rigidity of societal norms. I was old enough to sense we were all prisoners, but it seemed as if everyone loved their chains but me.

Before me was my Big Bertha Tank. Generally, I enjoyed playing with boys' toys, but the draw of the forbidden fruit of girls' toys was very enticing. I played with my tank, making war on the living room furniture.

Anyone who had a little extra money in our neighborhood embalmed their furniture by encasing it in plastic. We could only afford to encase an armchair. Turquoise colored polyester under polyurethane, and it was our stepfather's unofficial throne. I hated it. The chair was fairly new, therefore there were only one or two burn marks from his cigarettes. In the future I would witness my drunk stepfather stub out or rest cigarettes on the plastic, thinking the arm of the chair was an ashtray.

Mainly because I had a keen sense of smell, my unofficial job was fire marshal. I could smell melting plastic before it became a fire. A new fire truck would have been more appropriate than a Big Bertha Tank. My official job was to clean the chair every Saturday morning using glass cleaner. Imagine cleaning upholstered furniture with glass cleaner! My still developing gay sensibility was appalled.

I launched my first missile at the abomination. The sound of plastic hitting plastic, however ghastly, was not the sound of war. I added sound effects of explosions, pretending to be the war itself as much as a boy. The joy of assaulting the armchair soon faded. "Make pie not war," sang in my head. Much like the Vietnam War on TV, I was not fully committed. Half my mind was on another plot. I wanted that toy oven and its miniature rolling pin so desperately I ached.

A phone call from Grandma Ruth drew our stepfather away from our house for what he said would be no more than an hour. The best parts of my childhood were crowded into the moments when he was absent. It was timed happiness. Therefore, we made the most of it.

No sooner had he walked out the door than I brought my war to a crescendo. My explosions were louder as I doubled my attack on the armchair. I claimed a great victory, though a great victory would have been the missiles shredding the plastic on the armchair to the point that it had to be removed.

In spite of my stepfather's absence, I still had to play a role to get what I wanted. My role could be more elastic in the presence of my mother and even more so when alone with my sisters. I had to skirt convention by being creative. I explained to my mother how war was hard work and my sisters needed to feed the troops.

My mother did not look up from reading the instructions for the oven. She said, "Have an orange from your stocking."

I sighed, testing my mother's ignorance with my own. My voice had a pitying tone as I said, "Mom, I don't think an orange is what the army cooks fed grandpa when he won World War Two."

Still not giving me eye contact she said, "And the armchair is not fascism."

Not understanding what fascism was and misunderstanding her, I heard, "And the armchair is not fashion."

Had she read my mind? Did she find the plastic ugly as well? I was momentarily distracted. Would she turn a blind eye if I used Ibo's claws against the offensive plastic? I had to push thoughts of the armchair out of my mind and focus on the oven.

I had lost all patience and abandoned all subterfuge. I said to my mother, "I want to play with the oven too."

I gained ground with my frustrated honesty. My mother responded with, "If you want to help you can take the light bulb out of the lamp on the end table and bring it here."

The oven required two one hundred-watt light bulbs to cook. My mother had already used our last spare bulb and needed one more. There was nothing higher than sixty watts in our house. I retrieved the bulb from the lamp and kneeled less than a foot away from the tiny rolling pin and pie tins.

Thankfully, neither my sisters nor my mother could manage the tiny rolling pin. I was the last choice but the best choice. In no time I had the piecrust rolled out to its proper size.

Not to be bested, Peanut abandoned the oven and started playing with my tank. She moved it to point blank range and fired some missiles at the armchair. She actually put a couple of small dents in the plastic. We both had our specialties.

I returned my attention to the pie. It was downhill from crust on. Our mother opened the package of dried apples and out poured what appeared to be wood chips. I offered to donate one of the apples from my stocking to make a better filling. Gwen and our mother wanted to follow the instructions to the letter. Adding water and stirring turned the wood chips into a lumpy apple oatmeal. Gwen poured the concoction into a tin plate that had barely enough of a raised lip to be called a pie pan. The pie would be very thin.

There was not enough dough to cover the pie. I reached for another package of dough mix to roll out the topping. My mother stayed my hand. Since we were cooking with light bulbs, we had to leave the topping off. I sighed inwardly. Basically, we were now making apple pizza, but at least I was making something. My diminished hopes were buttressed by curiosity. I was now more interested in how well light bulbs could cook compared to gas flames.

The light bulb that had easily browned our cheap white lampshade struggled to turn the pale crust to a light shade of beige. In addition, one of the light bulbs burned out halfway into the cooking process. Rather than have me retrieve another light bulb my mother extended the cooking time.

After the additional time had passed, the tray door slid open and our mother pulled out a pie that looked dead, pale and literally pasty. She may as well have opened a vault door at the morgue and asked Gwen and me to identify a loved one. I loved pie, and this wasn't it. I wanted the pie advertised on TV, not its stunt double.

We still ate it. The taste was not unpleasant, but the texture was off-putting. We bit past the dry edges into the moist apple filling and gooey dough. The sensation that someone else had already eaten the pie and spit it back into the pan became overwhelming. It was hard to eat food that may have already been chewed by someone else. Eating cat food when we lived on Forrest Street had somewhat prepared us for eating food partially cooked under light bulbs. We grimaced, kept on eating and retrieved treats from our Christmas stockings to cleanse our palates. When we ran out of the ingredients that came with the oven, we made pretend food, which was more appealing.

Materially, this Christmas was abundant. It was show and tell for our stepfather. At the end of the day, and especially when company was coming over, we had to put all of our toys back under the tree to be displayed. This was done until New Year's Day, at which point we took the tree down.

New Year's Eve was the one time of the year our stepfather was guaranteed to come home drunk. The year before he had gone on a rampage, damaged half our toys and knocked the tree to the floor. He replaced the broken ornaments but not the toys. The cover story was that we were ungrateful children who were reckless with our toys. In our house blame had wheels. He blamed us for his violent behavior, and we blamed our cat for our espionage. Taking responsibility is usually the first thing to flee most crime scenes.

We adapted to the mixed message, give then destroy. As soon as our parents went out for New Year's Eve, we played reverse Santa Claus. Hoping to prevent a repeat of last year's destruction, we took our favorite presents to their original hiding place on the third floor. It had become our habit to put our toys away every evening to prevent them from being casualties of drunken rage.

Happily, the next morning we found him passed out in the plastic armchair. There were two additional cigarette burns in the plastic, but it had not caught on fire. We snuck our still intact toys back under the tree. When he woke up, we took down the tree and counted ourselves fortunate. This had been a good Christmas.

CHAPTER 27   POWDERED ICE CREAM

We lived in Baltimore between the time of the great blizzards. With the exception of the nor'easter of Christmas Eve 1966, snow clouds tended to veer north of us, or drop their cargo before crossing the Appalachian Mountains. I can clearly remember snow falling, but it rarely landed on the ground and didn't stay long when it did. Dark skies promised more snow than actually fell. The gray and wet of winter kept us inside more than the cold or the snow did.

Our toys took a beating during the winter. We never brought our Christmas presents out on the street to play. There was no rule against it; we just didn't do it. Toys were indoor things that I did with my sisters. Not that I didn't play with my sisters at other times of the year, but during winter our company was forced upon each other. By spring we had wearied of each other and our toys.

The cold left first, then went the wet. By the end of May girls started wearing culottes, and I wore Bermuda shorts that I pretended were culottes. Sometimes we would return to our toys during summer rains. But we preferred gazing out the window with bored expressions on our faces, searching for a break in the clouds.

If the rain fell on a Saturday and our mother was feeling charitable, she would let us have a bar of soap. We would put on our swimsuits and shower in the rain. In truth these were the only showers I ever took until around the age of thirteen, at which point we moved into a house that had a shower. We would soap up in the covered alley near our house and rinse in the rain or under the rainspout above the alley that had recently broken off at head height. If we felt the rain begin to slack off, we crowded under the rainspout together and rinsed as one.

Some of the neighborhood women with pressed hair looked on in horror or envy at that much water pouring down on my sisters' untamed hair. Adulthood had taken that freedom from them.

We tried to use our first outdoor shower as a way of evading our Saturday night baths. We wanted to bring out our toothbrushes to preclude the need for any indoor bathing at all. Our mother drew the line at us brushing our teeth in the rain. Apparently, summer showers didn't meet our mother's stringent standard for cleanliness. We'd come in from the rain and dried ourselves off just enough to walk through the house, go upstairs and be dumped into the bathtub. Mom's bath didn't miss the ears and in between the toes. However, rainspout showers were more fun than indoor baths.

Outside was more appealing than inside, despite its lack of toys. By summer, dust started to gather on our toys. I held out a little longer than my sisters and traded a pack of gum for full ownership of the toy oven. Peanut had long since bored of it. Her eagerness to part with it told me I had paid too much. Once the deal was done, I went to our mother and told her Peanut had a pack of gum she wasn't sharing. Gwen and I got a stick and a half of gum back.

Eventually I also bored of the oven and gave it to Miss Penny. She was the poor man's Santa, and their children's Christmas was in July, which was about the time most of the better-off children truly bored of their toys. She knew who all the unfortunate children were in the neighborhood. If it was broken and she could fix it, she would leave it on the doorstep for the intended child to find. Finding was more palatable than charity. Everyone knew who was leaving the toys on the steps. For many people it was awkward to thank someone considered less fortunate than themselves.

Miss Penny looked the part, but she was anything but unfortunate. She lived life against the grain and rubbed fur the wrong way. I always thought she was rich because she had so many things, even though she usually owned them for only a short time before passing them on. To me that was a type of wealth. That was the year I decided to give her the fire truck I had found in the junkyard on Forrest Street, so she could give it to someone else.

This was also the year I was allowed to go to the park across the street from Grandma Ruth's house without an adult. I walked by or through the park five times a week during the school year but was not allowed to go any other time without an adult until a few months before I turned eight. One of the conditions was that I had to take my sisters with me if they wanted to go.

The newfound freedom came from necessity more than from maturity. Shortly after the Christmas of 1966 my mother began seeking employment. A friend of a friend of Grandma Ruth said she could get my mother a job at Crownsville Hospital, which was the hospital for the Negro insane of Maryland. The patient population had been integrated the year before we moved to Baltimore, yet the hospital continued to wear its former moniker.

Crownsville Hospital was located in Anne Arundel County. The county was not served by public transportation, or at least not served well. My mother was not guaranteed a shift at the same time as the woman who had a car. The job fell through. Fortunately for my mother, the woman pulled some strings and got her a job at Spring Grove State Hospital, which was located in Catonsville in Baltimore County and was served by public transportation. Spring Grove was the second oldest psychiatric hospital in the country. The pay was the same, but working conditions were better at Spring Grove State.

She started working the night shift at the end of January. It was a festive evening as we watched our mother prepare to go to her first real job. I was particularly enthralled, as if she were dressing to attend a ball instead of tending bedpans. At the suggestion of Grandma Ruth, our mother had bought a wig. I don't know if the suggestion came from her personal fear or personal experience. She claimed that until you knew which ward you were going to working in, it was prudent to wear a wig or hairpin your hair close to your scalp. Better that a volatile patient grabs a handful of a wig instead of a fistful of hair. She would stop wearing the wig after a month.

We went to bed shortly before she left the house and woke to her serving us hot cereal in the morning. After she received her first paycheck she traded in the hot cereal for cold, boxed cereal and an extra forty-five minutes of sleep. We, along with our stepfather, began pouring our own breakfast and getting ourselves ready for school or work. When she came home, she would kiss us goodbye and we would kiss her goodnight. Sometimes her kisses would turn into yawns mid-kiss. By summer we knew how to start our days quietly so as not to disturb her. Our newfound freedom was dependent on our silence.

Despite having more access to the park, I stuck with the urban games that could be played on concrete and asphalt. We played four square, Duck, Duck, Goose and hot peas and butter. Sometimes when Uncle Reggie was drunk, he would bring his portable record player out on the stoop on E. Eager Street and have us bring out chairs from the kitchen to line up on the sidewalk. We would play musical chairs to songs by James Brown and Dinah Washington.

My chances of being the last one seated when Dinah Washington played were almost none. Her songs were enjoyable, but the dances to them were dated. The children paid more attention to Dinah's songs, so when the music stopped, they were swift to take a seat. Since the dances around the chairs to James Brown's songs were current, the children found it harder to disrupt their rhythm and take a seat when the music stopped. As I could rarely find the rhythm, my dance around the chairs was more of a march. The split second it took the other children to break their rhythm gave me an edge.

The poverty of the children of East Baltimore had a richness to it. Trash could be toys. We used old bottle caps, filled with used gum or melted wax from old crayons to weigh them down, to play skully. The game was a cross between bocce ball and billiards, played on a scruffy, hand-drawn board, best played on asphalt instead of concrete. It involved strategically flicking the bottle caps onto the board. To me personally, making the skully caps was more fun than playing the game itself.

When we found discarded soda or beer cans, we would stomp our shoes on the middle part of the cans. The bottom and top of the cans would collapse inward, locking onto our shoes. Then we would run along the sidewalk pretending we were wearing horse-shoes. When the arabbers drove down the street with their wagons, we would race on the sidewalk alongside their horses. Our tin can feet tapping the concrete of the sidewalk sounded tinny and im-poverished compared to the noble clip-clops of the horses' iron-clad hooves striking asphalt.

Unlike most of the other horses, Queen Pinky didn't wear blinders. She occasionally would catch glimpses of young, urban children poorly imitating her stride. Her response was to proudly prance down the street, lift her tail to swat at flies, or drop a road apple to show us her contempt. None of us could proudly prance and poop at the same time. We knew who our betters were, so we turned tail and pranced in the opposite direction.

One day we found an old hand-crank ice cream maker on our stoop. It was certainly a gift from Miss Penny. Normally our stepfather would have thrown it in the trash. With both parents working I was doubly sure he would have tossed it out. Our perch on the lower ledge of middle class was growing less tenuous with each paycheck my mother brought home. We certainly were now the most prosperous family on the block. Christmas had always been disproportionate to the rest of the year. Our daily lives slowly began to align with Christmas.

Shortages no longer devolved into stretching what was on hand but instead became substitutions. Nothing represented this more than milk. The beginning of the month we would have real milk. Then our stepfather would mix in powdered milk with the real milk to make it last. Next was powdered milk alone. Finally, we would open a can of evaporated milk and drip it into a bowl of water until it turned an anemic white. Then we added the cereal. Cow in a can was not appealing. I hated evaporated milk, but I had to eat it. Ever since we had eaten the cat food on Forrest Street, we were never allowed to miss a meal, but some of the substitutions made me long for our former feline feast.

With one more paycheck coming in we finally had more than enough. Plenty entered our vocabulary and stayed awhile.

The ice cream maker was a rite of passage. I believed that is why my stepfather kept it and used it. We still had some packets of powdered milk. Newfound prosperity did not mean waste. He decided we would use the last of the powdered milk to make ice cream and proclaimed we would never have to drink powdered milk again.

If we didn't like powdered milk, what made him think we were going to like ice cream made from it? What made matters worse was that we didn't really know what we were doing. It was the toy oven all over again, using a low wattage bulb that burned out. In this case we used table salt instead of rock salt and used a packet of powdered strawberry drink mix and sugar as flavoring. We had high hopes for such lowly ingredients. No matter how much we turned the crank the concoction never completely solidified. We were finally able to whirl the solution into the consistency of a melted milkshake and call it a success. The finished product looked very similar to the pink liquid medicine our mother gave us for stomachaches. She poured five equal portions into glasses. We still didn't have matching dishware. The fortunate among us received our portions in a plastic glass and didn't have to suffer the visual of sipping from a glass that seemed never to empty. We drank familiar ingredients, yet the taste was illegible to the tongue. There are hundreds of thousands of words in the English language, yet none of them sufficed to describe how it tasted.

After a few more sips, our stepfather rose from the table without a word and poured the contents of his glass down the sink. He returned to the table, and in quick succession he poured each of our drinks down the drain as well. That was his last word on the subject. He never threw food away. It was the first time I consciously remembered seeing him throw food away. Milk didn't turn, food didn't go bad, and if mold couldn't grow on an empty plate it didn't grow at all. Middle class meant opening the refrigerator and seeing mold on food.

We had been playing tag with middle class since shortly after arriving in Baltimore. One minute, tag we were it; the next minute, tag we weren't. Middle class was a state of mind as well as an income level. Disposable income meant that more of the things you bought literally became disposable. You weren't really middle class until you threw away something your parents or grandparents would never have thrown away. Pouring pink powdered milk down the drain was our rite of passage.

CHAPTER 28   URBAN CHILD

In our home, the summer of 1967 was bracketed by violence in late spring and early autumn. That spring I was not party to the lies my mother told the people at her job, but I was perplexed that people didn't wonder why a woman rode a bus to work at night wearing sunglasses. She could only be blind or beaten. People minded their own business. When the bus stopped, they got off and went to their own lives and worries. In autumn her bruising was so bad she had to call in sick. Overhearing the conversation was painful. Although her ribs hurt, she held the pain in check long enough to cough convincingly into the phone to pretend a beating was a cold.

Until that summer my emotions and intellect lagged behind my circumstances, and I had no explanation for most of the events happening around me. At times I was faint of heart, yet I didn't have the luxury to completely shut my eyes against some of the disturbing things around me. I had to be ever vigilant. Attempts to close my eyes would turn into a slow blink, as they would soon pop back open. I still tried to keep them closed. When they couldn't be trusted to stay closed, I placed my hands over them, only to peek through split fingers a few moments later. As much as my circumstances pleaded with me to shut down and close off, the world countered with good experiences and stimulated my curiosity. Our house remained violence-free the entire summer. It was hot, and no chill from fear ran down my spine to interrupt its heat, nor did I have to try to close my eyes once. It would be the summer I replenished and expanded my humanity.

Much of that expansion would come from my parents trying to keep us cool. We kept cool at night by putting a bowl of ice in front of a fan or placing a wet washcloth over it. Our stepfather worked in an air-conditioned office during the day. To cool off while he was at work our mother would take us to the Washington Monument.

It was America's first major monument to George Washington and was located in the Mount Vernon neighborhood of Baltimore. It was just a fifteen-minute walk from our house on Barnes Street. Designed by the same architect as the one in Washington D.C., it predated the more famous version by thirty-seven years.

There was a museum at the base of the 178-foot tall tower. The thick marble kept the building much cooler than the outside. Our mother would linger as long as possible and read all the information on George Washington, as much to stay cool as to inform us. It was my first history lesson, one that I ignored. My mother lost me when she claimed he was the father of our country. I was having difficulty dealing with the father of our house and wasn't interested in having another one.

The first time we went, we climbed the 227 stairs and had great views of Baltimore. Unfortunately, our view of the Chesapeake Bay, Baltimore's doormat to the Atlantic Ocean, was blocked by the office buildings of downtown. Viewing it would have had an additional cooling effect. Although we were only a mile away from the harbor when we lived on Forrest Street, my sisters and I had never been. It wasn't until we moved to Barnes Street that we had our first glimpse of the bay. The dark, murky harbor was ringed with piers with no place to even dip our feet.

Seeing the longing in our eyes and the sweat on our brows, our mother would take us to swim at the Chick Webb Recreation Center. Located only a few blocks from our house, it was the crown jewel of activity for the youth of East Baltimore. During its glory days, Ella Fitzgerald, a former protégé of Chick Webb, would perform there at Christmas. It was here that my sisters and I learned to swim. I also learned that the hair of boys, mine in particular, was not worthy of being protected by a bathing cap. The only girl to enter the pool without a bathing cap was Jane, the girl from my school who sported an Afro, and she rarely swam there.

Public venues were the only places to keep cool, and movie theaters were both of my parents' prime choice. At the time, Baltimore had over fifty movie theaters. It was the sixties, and the Hayes Code still governed what could be shown in American theaters. The code didn't govern who could view the movies. The voluntary MPAA film rating system would not take effect until November of 1968. Except for the occasional cartoon shown at the beginning of a movie, my sisters and I never saw children's films. I would not see my first animated children's film in a theater until I was an adult; as a child I watched only adult films.

Mostly we watched rereleased films of Hitchcock and Betty Davis. Because of the adult nature of the films we were often the only children in the theater. Therefore, we had to be quiet and hold in any questions until after the movies. With newsreels or cartoons plus two movies and intermission, we could be in the theater for up to five hours. The cigarette smoke was so thick that the light from the projector arrived on the movie screen stripped of much of its color. When I went to the restroom, I could find my way back to my seat by counting the rows of lit cigarettes. Each row, at a minimum, had two cigarettes lit at any given moment.

After five hours in the movie theater I had ten hours of questions. Why was Tippy Hedron wearing high heels on the beach in *The Birds*? I outright laughed at this scene in the movie and received a pinch from my mother for my mirth. *What Ever Happened to Baby Jane*, why was an old woman such as Betty Davis wearing so much makeup and dressed as a girl? She looked as if she were a senior killer clown trying to be a juvenile killer clown.

My mother's response, "Betty Davis was playing a character who was insane." She added, "She reminds me of one of my patients at work."

Her answer caused me to have fitful sleep for the next week. Despite its benign name, Spring Grove was more commonly called an insane asylum. In the movie Betty Davis kills the help, and my mother was the help. That entire week my mother would come home to find me sitting in our plastic covered armchair with our cat Ibo in my lap. At the sound of the key in the door, Ibo and I instantly relaxed. She purred and I cooed in relief. Cat and bird forgot their differences for the moment and greeted their mother.

Ibo lived for my mother but treated the rest of us as most cats do. We were merely part of the furniture until she needed something. When we called her name, she acted as if the walls were named Ibo instead of her. Not the case with my mother. If she called, Ibo arrived in seconds. There was rarely a need for my mother to call Ibo, as she lived under my mother's feet or in her lap.

She was mostly an indoor cat and had been trained to use a makeshift litter box in the basement. The litter box was a plastic tray with a raised lip, which we filled with old shredded newspapers and was used by Ibo during inclement weather or if there was a bullying cat outside. Shredding the newspapers was Peanut's and my job. At first it was fun turning today's news into tomorrow's cat litter. Then it became tedious, a chore we dreaded.

The litter box was also part of Ibo's birth control plan. It enabled us to keep her in the house when she came into season and was our alternative to spaying. Using closed windows and doors as the rhythm method for a cat was destined to fail. It worked the first couple of times until an unseasonably hot day in late spring left us no choice but to open the windows. Out the window went the cat and the method.

Five weeks later my mother noticed Ibo was pregnant. By this time in my life I had seen several pregnant women. My experience thus far had been that women's bellies grew large, then they went to the hospital and came back with a baby. I had never seen a pregnant animal. If I thought about it at all I just assumed pregnant animals went to the hospital too. We didn't have a car, so I thought when it was time for Ibo to have her baby, we would take her by taxi or walk the seven or eight blocks to Johns Hopkins Hospital.

Baltimore was the first place I saw death and the first place I saw birth. Ibo began the birthing process by yowling. Unlike most cats, who sought a private place to have their kittens, she stayed close to my mother until the time of birth. Then she jumped on my mother's lap, deciding this was the safest place to have her kittens. My mother carefully picked up Ibo and wrapped her gently in her arms. Instead of going to the hospital as I had thought, my mother told my stepfather to grab some old towels from the bathroom. She made a nest of towels on the linoleum floor in the kitchen.

Within twenty minutes Ibo gave birth to her first kitten. At first it looked as if Ibo was blowing a grey bubble from her hindquarters instead of her mouth, which couldn't be true, because cats didn't chew gum. I honestly expected the bubble to contain air until she started licking and tearing at the grey mass to reveal a kitten inside.

My eyes were more dilated than Ibo's birthing canal. I had no idea that cats laid eggs. Our mother informed me that it was not an egg. She explained to us that, unlike humans, each kitten came out in its own amniotic sac. I clung to the portion of the statement where she said, "Unlike humans." Despite the evidence before me, I didn't believe this was how my sisters and I came into the world. A woman went to the hospital, the doctors pressed the woman's belly button, and somehow the baby came out. I didn't press my mother for more details. I wanted to hold onto my sanitized, ignorant version of human birth just a little bit longer.

By the time Ibo had eaten the placenta and cleaned the first kitten up, another one was coming. I was still confused but fascinated. She gave birth to two more kittens. The first one was a smaller version of its mother, but the last two looked totally different. Many years later I would learn that cats can continue to conceive after becoming pregnant. One litter could have been fathered by multiple males.

After the kittens were weaned my mother worked hard to find homes for them. Two of the kittens found homes in the western suburbs of Baltimore. My mother snuck them on the bus to work. She had arranged to hand them over in the parking lot to two nurses who would be going off shift when she arrived.

Shortly after that, my mother paid the money to have Ibo

spayed, because she didn't want to keep trafficking kittens to the suburbs. I don't know if it was harder to convince people in our neighborhood to take kittens because of superstitions or financial reasons, but we kept the last kitten three weeks longer than the others. He was finally taken in by Miss Frances, a woman who lived four doors from us. Her son had been drafted and sent to Vietnam. She planned on sitting out the war with the cat as company. Her hopes were reflected in her choice for a name. She named him 'Come Home'. It was a pleasant, persistent way to voice her sentiment several times a day without consciously thinking about it. She knitted, wrote letters, petted the cat and waited for her son to come home.

There were so many ways to be a mother, but matronly, heart-of-the-hearth, kisser-of-wounds and keeper-of-the-future was the standard bearer, and it bullied women into compliance. At the time, only a little over a third of women worked outside the home, and most of these jobs were second incomes, not careers. Women had part time jobs and men had part time families. Much of this repressed female power, aspirations and frustration with these inequalities had to vent itself somewhere. The release valve was often their children. Men also vented their dashed aspirations through their children but for different reasons.

Children have to adapt and sustain themselves on the love that is available. Sometimes it's a feast, while other times a mere morsel. Similar to Oliver Twist, many children stand before their parents with an empty bowl in hand pleading for more. Although I had not yet read Dickens, I was very familiar with the desire of his character. It was not until that summer that I met Oliver's polar opposite. Strangely enough her name was Olivia, and she stood before her mother with an overflowing bowl pleading for less.

I became acquainted with Olivia early that summer when the breeze from the Chesapeake Bay could still challenge Baltimore's blistering heat. She and her mother were visiting Olivia's aunt, who lived behind us across an alley. The alley had no name, was a block long, and ran between Barnes and E. Eager Streets. It always seemed to have a rivulet running down its middle that was more filth than water. All the homes on the E. Eager Street side of the alley had fenced-in yards. Our house, along with all the houses on the Barnes Street side, had only the alley for a yard and no fences.

I was in Grandma Ruth's back yard that Sunday morning when Uncle Reggie's and Mister Willy's conversation had grown too adult for my ears, and she sent me home. I took the shortcut through the alley.

My first sight of Olivia was of her sitting on a blanket in her aunt's concrete yard. She was surrounded by dolls arranged in the sitting position, pretending to sip tea from a toy tea set. Unlike my mismatched broken teacups from the junkyard, there was no tea in hers, but in the center of the blanket was a plate full of animal crackers. Olivia would give her dolls pretend nibbles of her cookies, then she would take a nibble herself that was barely bigger than the pretend nibbles of her dolls.

Unperceptive eyes would look at the yard full of dolls and cookies and not see want. Although my eyes bulged from looking at her plenty, I could tell she was lonely. She nibbled because all her siblings and friends were made of plastic. Olivia was a pristine, slightly darker version of her dolls, playing in a yard off a dirty alley that within a year would be unsafe to play or walk in.

Her mother intentionally kept her away from other children. I knew nothing of her mother's childhood, but I was already gathering experiences that I would later match up with concepts. Whatever was lacking in that childhood, Olivia's mother wanted her daughter to have the childhood she hadn't had. If the situation remained unexamined, Olivia, in turn, would one day give her child the childhood she never had, thus the pendulum of childrearing would continue to swing wildly from extreme to extreme for generations.

Olivia was an inmate of her mother's well-intentioned dreams. Her only crime was being born to a mother whose childhood had been stunted in some way. For this reason, Olivia was sentenced to fulfill someone else's fantasy, to bow and be grateful for things she didn't want. As is the case with many children, pleasing her parent was her admission price into the world. Such children are constantly told what is good for them, until the little voice inside grows louder than the ones outside, and they have to hurt other's feelings to become themselves.

She looked as if she was someone I couldn't understand, but I did. When Olivia noticed me watching her, she abandoned her dolls and ran toward human contact. We exchanged names, and intuitively I began talking about the one thing we had in common, our tea sets. Mine had long since been destroyed by my stepfather, but the memory of it was still intact. Olivia was enthralled that I was allowed to rummage through a junkyard and get dirty to collect my teacups and had used real tea bags. I was enthralled that she had a plate of animal crackers all to herself.

As I had sensed her want, she had sensed mine and offered me some animal crackers. I had no teabags to offer her. Regardless, her mother would not have allowed her daughter near anything that could spill and stain. I, along with the tea, was something that could spill and stain, but her mother was not home. Her aunt kept an eye on us from the kitchen window but tolerated my presence.

Olivia wanted to feed me as she had fed her dolls, except my nibbles were real and would be gulps. Instead, I suggested we play rescue the animals. Being a captive herself on some level, the game was appealing to her. She hid the animal crackers in her cupped hands, snuck them to the fence and daintily pushed them through. We pretended that they were escaping the zoo, and I pretended my mouth was the wild. We had to choose a bigger chink in the fence when it was time to set the giraffe free. The only opening big enough was near the bottom of the fence. Eventually all the animals were set free.

Her aunt finally called her inside but before parting she asked, "Will you come back tomorrow with some more of your imagination?"

I acknowledged my intent to return with a nod. My imagination had spilled and stained Olivia. She enjoyed being sneaky and feeding cookies to someone that could actually eat them. We both left the fence full but for different reasons.

The next day around the same time I waited in the alley. This time her aunt escorted Olivia to the fence. With some sympathy she explained to both of us that we could continue to play as long as Olivia didn't get dirty. She emphasized that the rule was Olivia's mother's, not hers, but she would enforce it.

Olivia challenged my imagination. She carried a large dodge ball and wanted to play. There was no door in the fence so we each had to stay on our side of it. The only physical contact we could have was touching fingers through the links. I had not yet been introduced to net games such as volleyball or badminton. In any case our net was made of metal, therefore, we could do no more than toss the ball back and forth. Her side of the fence was pristine, whereas my side was a filthy alley. The moment I missed the ball it would land in filth, and that moment would come sooner rather than later. My next toss would bring that filth across the fence and end our playtime.

Her aunt, not quite trusting us yet, sat on the back stairs to referee our first few moments together. I asked them to wait a minute, ran into my house to retrieve something and swiftly returned. Olivia's first toss didn't make it over the fence. Her next attempt went over but was erratic. I had to chase it and catch it before it landed on the ground. I tossed it back, but Olivia was more uncoordinated than I was. She had to let the ball bounce before she could catch it. All her throws were erratic and on the fourth throw I dropped the ball. I saw the disappointment take control of Olivia's eyes. Her aunt would call an end to our game due to the dirty ball. I pulled out the handkerchief I had retrieved from my house. Before Olivia could begin to cry, I dabbed the handkerchief, not at the corner of her eyes but instead searched the ball for the dirty spots and wiped them away. I tossed the ball back over the fence minus the dirt from my side. Her aunt was appeased and left us alone.

Our good behavior allowed us a chance to play another day. Before we parted, she again asked me to please come tomorrow and bring more imagination. To keep that promise I stayed home the next day while my cousin Darla took my sisters swimming at Chick Webb's pool.

Each of my sisters had their own set of jacks. While they were off swimming, I borrowed both sets, took them to the fence and waited for Olivia to come out. Instead of taking turns with the jacks, I lent Olivia her own set. She kneeled on a blanket, tossed the jacks on her side of the fence and retrieved her onesie as best she could. I did the same on my side of the fence.

The next day was a partly cloudy day. We decided that some of the animal crackers we had set free a few days ago must have died and gone to heaven. With eyes turned upward we searched the sky for cloud shapes that bore a striking resemblance to those animals. Our observations revealed that the camel, lion, elephant and giraffe had gone to heaven.

Each day we had met the challenges of coming from separate worlds and slowly reduced the fence from a barrier to a minor nuisance. Although I had not yet met her mother, I was very much aquatinted with her rules. Though her mother's standards were stringent, Olivia and I managed to play together without her getting dirty. She and I took great pride in our success. We spent one of our days dreaming that the reward for our good behavior would be that the fence would come down.

We were too young to realize that had the fence come down we would still be in cages. Hers was gilded, mine was bigger but still cages. At our age, only our dreams could slip through the bars and roam the world as they pleased.

I told her I wanted to take her to the stables to feed the horses and meet Miss Penny. I think I unconsciously chose Miss Penny because she represented a type of freedom Olivia had never seen. She didn't question my choices and told me she wanted to drive me to Disneyland and wanted me to meet Lassie, the famous TV rescue dog. Perhaps her dreams were bigger than mine because her cage was smaller. That day our dreams mingled and created larger ones, dreams we couldn't have created alone and so big no one could put a fence around them.

When we parted, she asked me to come back tomorrow and bring more dreams. The next day it rained. Rain was not dirt, so I hoped that Olivia's mother had no rule against playing in it. I borrowed my mother's umbrella but snuck out a bar of soap and wore my swimming trunks under my pants to show Olivia how to shower in the rain.

I stood in the alley until my mother needed her umbrella and called me back into the house. Olivia was not the type of girl whose name you yelled in an alley to come out and play. To continue my surveillance, I retreated to the only place in our house that had a view of the alley and her yard, the window above our bathtub. I grew irritated every time my sisters wanted to use the bathroom. They had no interest in the boring girl behind the fence, whose mother sent her out to play but didn't let her play. Nor had they any sympathy for my interest.

The rain continued long past the time Olivia would have been permitted to come out. That night I went to bed, retiring that day's dreams as too stale to present to a beautiful bird born in captivity. If tomorrow's sky would cooperate, I had a better dream for her.

Tomorrow came and the sky more than cooperated. The clouds were a menagerie of animal shapes of every type and size. I wanted to tell her that when I grew up, I would take her on a plane so she could get a closer view of the animals in the sky. I would let her have the window seat and convince the pilots to roll down the windows, so she could pet the fluffy cotton skin of any animal she wanted.

I went to the alley and brought the dream as Olivia had requested. Every time the sun peaked out from a cloud, I thought it would be the perfect intro for Olivia to come into the yard. Finally, I heard footsteps descending the stairs, too heavy to be that of a child. It was her aunt, and her steps were heavy for a reason.

She strolled over to the fence and said, "I saw you standing in the rain yesterday and should have told you then, but I didn't want to rain on you on an already rainy day."

I was confused but concerned. Before she continued, she told me her name was Miss Nellie, as if the bearer of bad news should have a name. She continued and said with great sadness, "I'm sorry, but she's gone."

The words were said with such finality I did a brief scan of the sky to see if there were any Olivia-shaped clouds up there.

Miss Nellie accurately interpreted my glance towards the sky and amended her statement. "She and my sister took the train to New York to start a new life."

It was a great kindness that she left out the part, "And you will never see her again."

There was no need; deep down inside I knew I would never see Olivia again. As the day progressed, the sadness deep down inside spread to my entire body. I retreated to the third floor where my parents had hidden our Christmas presents, and I unwrapped my sorrows there. The room was empty, with the exception of an unused, festive roll of wrapping paper standing in a corner, clashing with my mood. Whimpers echoed back to me as wails. Tears clouded my eyes, but I did not wipe them away. My hands were occupied. In an attempt to drive one pain away with another, I dug the nails of my right hand into the palm of my left. No matter how hard I dug into my hand, my emotional distress claimed all of my tears. I cried myself to sleep in the middle of an empty room in the middle of an empty day.

I had just experienced what some years later my grandfather would describe as a funeral for the living. It is held for the dearly departed who still walk the earth. Events can take the living away from us forever without taking their lives. There are two types of funerals for the living; one is held for those we have to banish from our life in order to maintain a healthy mental state, and the other is for those ripped from it.

Olivia hadn't known her mother was taking her away that day or she wouldn't have asked me to bring more dreams. She had expected to see me too. Years later when my grandfather first described the funeral for the living to me, the first person I thought of was Olivia. It was only then I realized that she no doubt had had her own funeral for the living, for me. She attended mine and I attended hers; such is the oddity of the funeral for the living.

I haunted the alley for three days. On the third day, Miss Nellie came to the fence and handed me a box of animal crackers. With a lump in her throat, she profusely thanked me for the four or five days I had made her niece very happy.

Her gratitude set me free to move on but not without Olivia. I now had a number. During a time when I couldn't make a difference in my own life, for four or five days I had made a difference in someone else's life. There were times when I expended Herculean effort to help someone to no avail, and I have been the recipient of such effort, also to no avail. This was not the case with Olivia and me. We had helped each other by merely being ourselves, just existing and breathing next to each other. Help that simply said, "I am here and you're here. I see you and you see me." It was the type of encouragement that inspires you to take another spin on the globe for one more day, then another and another until you've lived a full life.

We spent just four or five days with each other over fifty years ago, yet I remember her as well as individuals I have spent years with. I have thought about her many times over the years. Sometimes my memory keeps her a little girl, while other times my mind makes allowances for age progression. I imagine that she has escaped her mother's prison of perfection. She has a lock of grey hair out of place and a smudge of dirt on her chin as proof. She retains some of her mother's sensibilities. I have her wearing bell bottoms in the seventies, but my imagination doesn't give her a mullet or a Jheri curl in the eighties. She doesn't have wrinkles, because her mother drilled into her the practice of moisturizing, and Olivia uses oil of delay, daily. Her smooth face lies about her age. I would not recognize her as being my age if I encountered her on the street.

Sometimes I imagine striking up a casual conversation with a female stranger at a party or an airport. A superficial, "Where are you from?" turns into "I'm from Baltimore." Inquiry by inquiry we retrace our steps back in time and discover we were those little children ripped away from each other years ago. She is happily married, and I am happy for her, because the love I have for her would not block that happiness. Olivia has a daughter whom she has raised well, and she hasn't overcompensated because of her own childhood. She shows me a photo of the daughter, who looks as if she has been seen and heard by her mother. I have no photos of children to show her; I didn't overcompensate for my childhood either. Instead I didn't bother, and Olivia lets it be. We both thank each other with no need to explain. I never experienced any of this, but it is what I want to believe, because the little girl in a sundress sequestered behind a fence had to have escaped her cage as I had escaped mine.

Gradually that summer soured into a temperamental autumn and winter. Most days started with varying shades of gray. The good days progressed into a vibrant, colorful world with each color mated to a pleasant sound and fragrance. The bad days resembled a black and white photograph of a rainbow, just a shadow of what it should be, the color of leaden pewter dueling with noise and fume. Both versions were two opposing ruts running through the road that was my life.

As a child, each day has the potential to be the one that changes everything forever. Yesterday is the ancestor of today. Tomorrow will be the child of today. Most days have a strong family resemblance, changing very little over time, until one of your days has an affair with another reality. New Year's Eve, 1967, was my unfaithful Eve. She gave birth to the turbulent days of 1968, and none of the children resembled Adam.

CHAPTER 29   MADE FROM ADAM'S BACKBONE

An added bonus of our mother working was that we now spoke with our grandparents more often by phone, and the conversations were not so rushed. Not long after we had last visited them, they had moved to Connecticut, along with my uncle. I could not imagine them in another place. When we talked by phone, I continued to ask about relatives back in Bellefontaine, whom they had not seen any more recently than we had.

My family had lived in Bellefontaine for over 130 years. People grew old with the same individuals who would eventually be their pallbearers. It was a time when kith and kin were always your kind. The hamlets and villages of America could no longer ignore the existence of planes, trains and highways. For those who chose to leave their past behind, their departure could take them farther and faster than ever before. American minds were not always as fast as their transportation. Regardless, kith and kin soon would not always mean just your kind.

We were supposed to go to Connecticut for Thanksgiving to meet our uncle's new wife. We had spoken to her briefly over the phone once. Her accent was not unfamiliar. I had heard it on TV, but it was odd that it came from the phone. I had only spoken on the phone with people who spoke as I did, primarily because neither I, nor my sisters, were allowed to answer the phone unless requested by an adult to do so, and all the calls were family or local people.

I assumed my Uncle Vincent had married an actress. Since nearly all actors were white, I correctly assumed his wife was white. That summer the Supreme Court had invalidated all anti-miscegenation laws, the laws that had banned interracial marriage in many states. Connecticut never had laws banning interracial marriage, but Maryland had just repealed its laws shortly before the Supreme Court made its ruling. My uncle and his wife would no longer be breaking the law, nor could they be sentenced to prison or banished from the state, but they were breaking with custom. I had no idea such restrictions existed.

White people, when I thought of them as different at all, I saw as uniformed personnel, actors, or foreigners. As a child, any prejudice I had was directed toward stewed tomatoes and liver. The coming year, 1968, was the year I learned that some white people viewed me as I viewed stewed tomatoes and liver.

Our mother had saved enough money for us to take the train to Connecticut. This was too much independence for our stepfather to tolerate. Despite the fact that men could call down the power of church and state upon women anytime they chose to, our step-father physically and ruthlessly asserted his authority over us and suppressed his wife's fledgling independence. His attempt to rule over us, despite our pain, was truly pathetic. His kingdom consisted of crying children and a bruised wife. Was it a contradiction that the powerful could be pathetic? I was starting to have my suspicions that it was actually the norm.

Make believe was something I was very good at and did for my-self constantly, but fake believe was done for others, and I had no enthusiasm for it. It was becoming harder for me to fake that I be-lieved any more drunken lies or excuses. Directly confronting a lie would have been hazardous to my health. The best I could do was stay silent on the matter. Gwen, Peanut and I refused to talk with my grandparents on the phone. We left all the lying to my mother. My stepfather didn't completely get his way either and the lies to my grandmother didn't go as planned. She wouldn't get off the phone with my mother until she had an invitation to come visit us at Christmastime. This gave my mother's face another month to heal back into something my grandparents would recognize.

In anticipation of the visit, my mother had put the money for the train tickets toward buying two new beds for her parents to sleep in when they came to town. After they left, the new beds on the third floor were intended for my sisters to have their own beds in a shared room. Our parents finally had achieved the financial means to provide us separate beds, but we were not emotionally ready to sleep apart. Gwen, Peanut and I had been weaned from sleeping in the same bed but not the same room. After the visit we would continue to sleep in the same room together. Our mother would make the new beds two nights before Christmas.

The holiday and the visit of our grandparents doubled our ex-pectation, and time slowed to the point that it felt as if it was taking a nap rather than progressing. In retrospect, it seems as if the last month of 1967 was purposely dragging its heels to avoid 1968.

Christmas fell on a Monday that year. For reasons unbeknownst to me, our grandparents, along with our uncle and his new wife, would not arrive until Friday, December 28th. The drive from Connecticut was about six hours. Though we were not the ones traveling, our house took on the characteristics of a car full of children taking a road trip. Instead of, "Are we there yet?" we chimed every few minutes, "Are they here yet? When will they get here?" The only benefit of waiting for someone instead of traveling was we didn't have to wait for bathroom breaks that were always over the next horizon and often seemed to be just as far away as the actual destination.

We received a call from our grandmother saying they had checked our uncle and aunt into a hotel ten minutes from our house and they all would be over shortly. Although our ears had been straining for hours to hear a knock at the door, we barely heard it when it finally came.

Our grandparents were young enough that we could leap full force into their arms. Kisses and robust hugs initially stifled the awkward conversation that sometimes accompanies a long absence. The outburst of love my sisters and I had for our family blocked the entrance to our house, preventing them from crossing the threshold. Our greeting resembled a disturbance of the peace more than a family reunion. Squeals and squawks slowly shifted back into syntax.

Desires clashed, I had so much to say and hear and wanted to talk and listen at the same time. Although a magpie by nature, I chose to listen to the songs of others. My ears were happy, for praise had returned to our house. Rarely did our parents praise us. They spoke highly of us to others but not to us. We were more likely to hear about their praise from a third party. Encouragement was offered to some extent, but our accomplishments were more a reflection of our parents. It was more bragging than praise. To be honest, I had not noticed the absence of praise, but I certainly noticed its return. Our grandparents applauded our very existence.

As a child you are at a distinct disadvantage in acknowledging the growth of loved ones. Children are always the recipients of statements such as, "You've grown so much!" or "I barely recognize you." This is flattering to youth who are eager to grow up fast. Thinking as a child I wanted to reciprocate, but my grandparents looked exactly the same. I had no clue that my silence on the matter of their aging was a form of flattery. I wouldn't notice my grandparents getting older until I was in my late twenties. When I did start to notice, similar to a mother who laments the loss of her child's innocence, I mourned the loss of their vigor. My mind took a photo that day. The age they were when they first walked through our door in Baltimore would be how I would remember them for many years.

After letting nearly all the heat out the door, my sisters and I made room for our grandparents to enter the house. At this point we noticed our Uncle Vincent and his new wife. Peanut and Gwen ran toward him for their hugs, but I stayed back. He had to come to me if he wanted one. My uncle was someone I thought I had to love because everyone else in my family loved him. The words, I love you, always felt foreign on my lips. There was no animosity between us, nor did I dislike him. I sincerely felt nothing for him. He was someone I merely tolerated.

Sometimes, marriage can be the back door through which someone unpleasant can come into your life, a person you would not normally associate with. Before my uncle could finish introducing his wife as our Aunt Janet, I was already hugging her, putting a crack in the illusion of whom you had to love and who you really did. I liked her immediately and would grow to love her, something that would never happen with my uncle. Though she was white, I would often pretend it was my uncle who had married into the family.

Aunt Janet was pale and had dark hair styled in a flip. She had on cat glasses and wore dark clothing, which made her look as if she was a librarian attending a funeral. Strangely enough she was not yet the Aunt Janet I would love. She was in transition. Any fears or anxieties that showed on her face were tremors and aftershocks from a past experience and had nothing to do with us. Considering that she came from a nearly all white, small town in Connecticut she was doing well, open but nervous. East Baltimore being nearly all black was not a problem for her but it being a big city was.

If I had contemplated more on the subject, I would have realized that Aunt Janet was the first white person to enter our house peacefully and invited. Previously, the only white people who came into our house had been uninvited police officers who broke down the door to arrest Axel. Unfortunately, this was how most white people entered the homes of black people in Baltimore. We entered their houses to work, and they entered our houses to arrest, which was in essence a form of work. I had only mere months left in my color-blind world where I didn't have to think like this.

Even in the worst of times, her being my aunt would always trump race. Similar to my grandmother, Aunt Porch, Uncle Reggie, Mister Willy and Miss Penny, she didn't decorate the truth beyond recognition to accommodate others. I would rather have friends or family hurt my feelings with the truth than strangers or people who don't have my best interest at heart do so. Some friends and family withhold the truth under the guise of being kind, letting far more ruthless people bear the message. Because of their age, Aunt Janet and Uncle Reggie could be clumsy with their delivery, but they were never ruthless with it. People who had your best interest at heart could come in any color.

Aunt Janet paid as much attention to my sisters and me as our grandparents did. She divided her attention equally between the adults and children. Our parents and uncle were more focused on the coming New Year's Eve party at Uncle Ike's house.

As if speaking his name had summoned him, Uncle Ike knocked on the door. It was not uncommon for him to show up at our house when he was in town. What was unusual was that my Aunt Porch was with him. I had no clue she was in town. Apparently neither did my mother, for she had a surprised look on her face as well. A bottle of something adult was opened up. The men stayed in the living room and the women retreated to the kitchen. I was young enough that I was still grouped with the women when conversation broke down along gender lines, but as soon as Uncle Ike came into the kitchen to pour a second drink for all the women except my grandmother, we were whisked off to bed.

Fortunately, because of all the anticipation and excitement, my sisters practically fell asleep while putting on their pajamas. I pretended to be asleep because I wanted to sneak to the top of the stairs to eavesdrop on the women's conversation. The added weight of my sisters at the top of the landing would have given away our position. By myself, I was just light enough not to make the floor creak when I stepped on it. My mother was in such a hurry to return to the conversation she forgot the old adage, "All shut eyes ain't asleep." I gave her no more than twenty seconds to return to the conversation. Forgoing slumber for gossip, I skulked over to the top of the stairs, pleased with myself for cleaning my ears the night before.

Without preamble my mother asked, "How long have you been dating Ike?"

Though the question was directed toward Aunt Porch, my grandmother answered, "Since last Easter."

Aunt Porch had been visiting Baltimore lately a little more than usual; now I knew why.

From the long pause before my mother responded, I could tell she was caught off guard. I knew my mother's facial expression from her voice. Her next words showed she was annoyed but had acquiesced to the fact that she was not the first to be privy to all their secrets.

She finally said, "If you had told me you were dating him, I could have given you some vital information. I like him a lot, but he is not husband material."

Both my grandmother and Aunt Porch laughed at my mother's statement. Their laughter was a polite reminder that despite having three children from three different men, or maybe because of it, she didn't know as much about men as she thought. Aunt Porch's laugh was cut off by taking another sip of her drink. From the noise, it sounded as if Aunt Porch had slid the kitchen chair closer to my mother. She hadn't had too much to drink yet but had forgotten that she should whisper to keep the men from overhearing. I was in little danger of not hearing. Just in case, I moved to the third step down, the one that didn't creak.

The first words she spoke were still wet from the liquor on her palate but were clear. "I know who I am dating."

To quell any doubts before my mother could raise them, Aunt Porch continued, "I know he has ties to organized crime and is a ladies' man. The fact that he is in organized crime bothers me more than the fact that he is a ladies' man. I know he doesn't have the stamina for the long term. He has said as much. To be brutally frank, that is the appeal of him. I don't have to pretend this is going anywhere. I was a naive young girl once, so I empathize with them, but when you date a man like Ike, you better be aware that you are leasing, not buying."

My mother tried to interrupt, but Aunt Porch had a strong personality made stronger by having a few drinks in her. She said, "What? You're going to tell me how many women he has hurt?"

There was a long thinking silence before my mother responded with, "It's not that he hurts them, he just leaves them wanting more."

Speaking from personal experience, Aunt Porch said, "I would rather that than having so much of someone that you feel trapped. There is a happy medium to be sure, but until then I am going to enjoy myself."

Although my grandmother was very traditional when it came to marriage, she and Aunt Porch had been friends long enough not to bother with disapproval. They were there to support the weak joints in each other's frames, not to add the additional stress of judgement. Their attitude towards each other was, "If you like it, I love it."

My grandmother spoke next. "In a way, I see the appeal of a man like Ike. He absolves himself of responsibility for your feelings by being honest from the beginning. I personally would run away from a man like him, but I respect him for giving women the options right up front. If he is taking advantage at all, it is of women who are not honest with themselves. Love does not conquer all, and it's not a weapon. In fact, I have seen it overwhelmed many times. Some people think they can change any behavior with their love. It doesn't work, because hidden behind the love is a scheme. These people are trapped, always trying to catch the fish that got away."

Aunt Porch chimed in, "That's not the animal analogy I would use. It's too messy and slippery. I know who I am dealing with, and I quite enjoy the sex and short-term but intense intimacy. The difference between me and some of the other women he's dated is that I believe what he says. He is what he is. You mate with a wildcat in the wild. Don't bring him home and try to domesticate him. He'll just scratch up your furniture and pee in the corner."

The sound of a drink being spit out and a choked guffaw was what I heard next. My Aunt Janet had not yet learned the etiquette of not drinking while some members of our family were speaking. It was not so much etiquette as prudent. She was left apologizing and laughing at the same time. That my grandmother and Aunt Porch had spoken so freely in front of her was their way of giving her a chance. Spitting her drink out in their presence was preferable to staring with grim-faced judgment. It was a rite of passage of sorts, and she had passed.

From that point on I heard my Aunt Janet's voice as much as the other women. Mostly she answered questions about Connecticut and what it was like to grow up there. She said it was mostly a place of green valleys and mill towns. Either she was being modest, or she was describing her version of Connecticut, because at the time, it was the wealthiest state in the country.

My grandmother mentioned that well-paying jobs were plentiful and hinted that we should move there. Of course, her daughter dismissed the suggestion out of hand, claiming she was a city girl now. Aunt Porch reminded her that she was a mother long before she was a city girl.

I could hear my mother trying to move onto another subject, but her mother and Aunt Porch were not having it. Her out-of-hand dismissal had landed her into a web where two spiders waited. Both women politely confronted her with the option that life could be better someplace else for her and her family. If she had said no after some consideration, that would have been the end of it. My mother had to retrace her steps, retrieve her words and fend off her mother and Aunt Porch by saying she would revisit their suggestions next year.

I wanted to be near my grandparents, but my hopes were not high. My mother was simply stalling to fend off big personalities. If we would not move, I was content to have so many big personalities visiting. They pushed my stepfather into the background. When I did notice him, his nicer edges were on display, and his cutting edges were sheathed until later.

CHAPTER 30   NEW ERA'S EVE

Ever since I had found out that my parents were Santa Claus, I had formed the theory that New Year's Eve was adults' version of Christmas. They needed a reprieve from all the whining, shopping and wrapping. It being an adult day, I had expected to stay home alone with my sisters or, if she was available, a girl named Cassy, who lived on Ashland Avenue, would watch us. I was caught off guard when our mother announced that we were going to the New Year's Eve party. I had never been to one before. Apparently, no one was available to babysit us and, because our grandparents were in town and also going to the party, we were not going to be left alone.

I had rarely seen midnight and didn't understand why the beginning of the next day started in the middle of the night. Nor did I understand why the New Year started in the middle of winter. I wasn't going to argue with the whole world, but new days should begin at dawn, and the new year should begin in spring. I kept that to myself.

Shortly before our bedtime, my sisters and I were changing, not into our pajamas but into our nice school clothes. We never wore our school clothes past nine o'clock. My fingers knew the correct time, and it felt odd buttoning into them instead of unbuttoning out of them. Hair suffered the most. It was ready to resume its natural pattern once my head touched the sheets but instead had to endure another combing.

Worst of all we had to put on a happy face over our sleepy faces. Attempts to smile ended as yawns. Once Aunt Janet and our uncle showed up, we perked up a bit. There were too many of us to go in one car. Half would go by taxi, the others in our grandparents' car. Arguing revived my sisters and me far more than late night grooming had. We all wanted to ride in our grandparents' car.

Our grandmother wouldn't tolerate us arguing at any time but particularly not on New Year's Eve. Although not superstitious, she did think it was bad form to not give the old year a peaceful burial. Some folks thought it just as important how you laid to rest the old year as how you welcomed in the new one.

To ensure the old year would have its peace, my sisters and I, along with our stepfather, rode in our grandparents' car. Our mother, her brother and her sister-in-law took the taxi.

Uncle Ike lived in West Baltimore on W. Lafayette Avenue several blocks up from Pennsylvania Avenue. I only remember the street, because at the time the Royal Theater was still standing near the corner of both avenues. It was one of four sister theaters to the Apollo Theater in Harlem. Their wooden stage floors were the bedrock of modern American music. My stepfather had proudly pointed it out to my grandparents; otherwise I would not have noticed it. I craned my neck to look merely because they had. Had I been aware of its past I would have absorbed more of the memory of it. It was the only time I ever saw the theater at night. Its neon lights seem to fear the night. Lighting from the marquee was feeble, and only one out of three lines of neon tubes retained any glow at all. Their slow, lethargic flickering advertised its decline and lack of maintenance rather than the arrival of new exciting shows. Within three years the Royal Theater was gone, demolished along with much of Pennsylvania Avenue. Most people in West Baltimore had enough money for today and maybe tomorrow, but there were no funds left over to preserve yesterday.

Uncle Ike's house was on the edge of Sugar Hill. The neighborhood was no longer as sweet as it had been. Once one of the wealthiest black neighborhoods in America, it was now twenty years past its heyday. For years, much of the educated and wealthy class had been sneaking through the cracks in segregation. The slow leak eventually drained all the wealth away. Members of the old class would never have rented or sold a home to someone of Uncle Ike's standing. He could only have their leftovers after they had been sitting on the table for twenty years.

We pulled up to an Italianate style row house. Most of the ornamentations followed the roofline, doors and arched windows. Other than that, from the outside his house resembled ours.

Uncle Ike answered the door before we could knock. I had not been to any place he lived since we first met. Generally, he visited us, or the adults would visit him without us. He moved around a lot but had been at this house about a year.

On the inside his home was very different from ours. It was not a shotgun house; the halls connected every room and the ceilings were higher, the rooms were larger. The stairs had an ornate banister, but it was minus a few balusters. Despite having a few missing

304

teeth, it resembled a crooked smile that ran the length of the stairs. Once a grand house, she now was in a humbled state and forced to endure having her interior decorated with poor examples of mid-century furniture.

Entering the main living room, I beheld for the first time a stereo, radio and TV console. Of course, the first thing I wanted to do was play a record, watch TV and listen to the radio all at the same time. As a child that was the point. Although I admired the console, it clashed with the mid-century furniture and the Italianate interior. America's taste could not keep pace with its technology. The electronics were encased in a heavy, dark wood, fashioned into a style that hinted at Elizabethan, Tudor and Victorian but did justice to none of them.

Heavy had its advantages. Our portable record player was only good for listening to music. It was not suitable for dancing, as any dance that contained a jump or stomp would disturb our rickety floors and cause the record to skip. This was the main reason Uncle Reggie had us play musical chairs on the street. We danced in our house only to music that played on a radio. When Uncle Ike put on a record to play, a heavy console and sturdy floor ensured that no one missed a beat. As it was New Year's Eve, you couldn't just dance to the music, you had to dress to it, and I was overdressed for any of my dances.

Aunt Porch came from the kitchen. She moved through the dancing crowd to greet us and over the loud music she began introductions. Her ease and familiarity with Uncle Ike's friends suggested her visits to Baltimore were more frequent and longer than my mother had suspected. When she introduced our stepfather to people, even he didn't know, it confirmed she had been staying here instead of with her sister.

Finally, my mother, Uncle Vincent and Aunt Janet arrived. Someone else had let them in, but Aunt Porch's responsibility as hostess was to smooth them in. Everyone I had come to the party with except for Gwen followed Aunt Porch to the front door.

Gwen and I remained with Uncle Ike, who looked at the door as if it had reminded him to do something. He excused himself but walked no more than six feet away from us and beckoned one of his flunkies.

A rail thin man complied to the summons immediately, almost as if that was the sole purpose of his existence. Fashion for men at the time was trending more towards form fitting, but he was wearing a bulky suit at least a decade out of style and two sizes too large. The man's intimates would have had to hug a lot of fabric before they actually made body contact. For some people clothes are masks for the body, and they often reveal the very thing they are designed to hide. His announced to the world that he felt uncomfortable with himself. From his obsequious demeanor, he either owed Uncle Ike a large sum of money or his life.

Uncle Ike was a warden of a modern-day debtor's prison. Borrowers willingly turned dreams into cages. Their downfall was consensual. They paid their debts back with high interest, by performing risky favors or by forfeiting their lives. The rate of exchange was a pound of pain for a pittance of pleasure. Debtors had no right of refusal. This man would do as he was told.

I could get the gist of the conversation from where I stood but moving two feet closer got me full details.

It immediately became clear that Uncle Ike was talking about my Aunt Janet. Pointing to the door he said to the man, "You see that white woman over there? You are dark enough to be her shadow, and that's what you are going to be. If I see her out the corner of my eye, I better see you too."

Misunderstanding, I almost interrupted the conversation to inform Uncle Ike that he didn't have to worry about my Aunt Janet stealing. She wasn't a heroin addict. The heroin epidemic was getting worse. Many people no longer allowed strung out friends and relatives to have free range of their homes. Hospitality was strained, as some didn't even invite individuals into their homes if they thought they had to take inventory before and after the visits.

This was not his worry. Although my Aunt Janet was probably the safest person at the party, he wanted to be doubly sure no mishaps came her way. He was not speaking of intentional but accidental. With the exception of my sisters, myself and our Aunt Janet, everyone at the party knew the hierarchy of life within the justice system. Some drank to forget they lived in such an America, but it was not advisable to forget too much. Uncle Ike's illegal affairs could withstand most things but not an injured white woman in his house.

He jokingly said to his flunky, "On the off chance there is gunfire, you better be quick and change from her shadow to her shield."

The man didn't laugh but I did. I had grown familiar enough with violence to find minor humor in my uncle's suggestion. His statement was childish even to a child. Had there been gunfire and had the man jumped to shield my aunt, there was not enough of him for the task. Bullets would have whizzed through empty fabric by wide margins on either side of his center mass. I felt more at ease; Uncle Ike would have summoned a more substantially built lackey had the threat been truly serious.

My laugh brought attention to my eavesdropping, but it didn't matter. The conversation was over. Uncle Ike sent the man on his way without an introduction, which was fine with me, as I had reached my limit for placing names with new faces.

Peanut and our mother worked their way back through the crowd to join Gwen and me. She was seeking a strategic place to sit us where she could keep an eye on us and enjoy herself at the same time. Fortunately, another couple came with three children of their own. The party was getting more crowded; therefore, we were taken upstairs to mind ourselves. Occasionally, various adults came in to check on us.

We all fell asleep before eleven o'clock, but we were awakened just before midnight by my Aunt Porch and the other children's mother, ostensibly to welcome in the New Year. In reality anyone who had a gun at the party, and there were more than a few who did, would go into the back yard and shoot them into the air at midnight. People and especially drunks, tended to give wood and plaster more credit for stopping bullets than warranted. There certainly were enough high caliber weapons present that could pierce walls. A drunken celebrant might try to bring in the New Year by bringing down the plaster of the ceiling. We were taken below the line of fire.

I took a seat in the kitchen on a high stool from which I had a view of the yard. Roughly half the celebrants gathered on the back porch and in the yard. It was the night of the new moon. Already invisible, she wore a veil of clouds before her face. The sky was adorned with nothing. Fortunately, all the gun owners were sober enough to know pitch black was up. Most of the wobblers had gathered in the kitchen and pointed their champagne bottles toward the ceiling. A few with unsteady postures aimed their bottles whichever way their bodies swayed. One lone man in the corner by the stove had his bottle of Thunderbird, a cheap fortified wine, pointed toward the ceiling. He would greet the New Year with a twist of a cap.

Thin Man herded my Aunt Janet back into the kitchen, where if he had to jump in front of her at least his body stood some chance of stopping an errant cork. Two or three of him was not as durable as wood and plaster, which would make his effort pointless if he had to act as a shield for bullets. Uncle Ike truly had meant for him to be a chaperone after all.

At the stroke of midnight, I saw the man with the bottle of thunderbird twist its cap, then I heard pops and bangs. Champagne corks dented the ceiling while outside lead and steel pierced the night sky above Baltimore. It appeared as if its citizens had declared war on the sky. In response the sky soon retaliated with a light rain. Baltimoreans ran out of ammunition long before the sky did. The last of the lead and steel bullets plummeted back to earth mingled with the rain. Drop by drop, the rain united into a thin film that covered everything and then it froze.

The noise and excitement had stimulated us children to the point that we could not fall back asleep. A few minutes past midnight the party thinned, then filled up again as revelers from other parties started arriving. My mother and grandparents took a taxi to the party of a coworker of hers. We were to meet them back at home later.

I remained on the stool in the kitchen and enjoyed the view. Adults at play fascinated me. Most were in varying stages of inebriation. Many were now singing, as well as dancing to the music. There was a couple in the corner playing mommy and daddy without a marriage license. If Uncle Ike hadn't pulled them apart, I would've soon found out how babies were made. Other than that, most people were enjoying themselves and behaving well.

Some adults needed to drink to release their happiness. I often wondered who or what had imprisoned their happiness and why alcohol unlocked the door. Different people had different emotions under lock and key. Sadness, anger and disappointment could also be inmates. Alcohol was not so much the key as it was permission and excuse.

My stepfather had a smile on his face along with everyone else, but it looked as if a five-year-old child had drawn it on with a crayon. It was waxy, crooked and unnatural. Alcohol had opened the door, but what was within could not come out. The beast was free, but it could not roam. He was in his uncle's house. My uncle and our grandparents were staying with us. There was no way for him to be alone with the people he normally preferred to hurt.

His waxy smile melted a couple times from the smoldering heat within, but he put it back in place before any adult could notice. Every time he repaired his smile it took its toll. Each attempt to repair was less successful than the last one. The fake smile was slowly turning into a sneer. He had to leave the party before his act collapsed. Suddenly he became the concerned father who had to get his children home.

Coats were retrieved, and our stepfather supervised every goodbye to ensure they were abrupt. Because of his haste, I had forgotten my winter hat. He separated Aunt Janet from Thin Man by personally escorting her out the front door. Her shadow did not follow her into the night.

My Uncle Vincent came out of the party last with car keys in hand. Since he and Aunt Janet had come by taxi he deferred to my stepfather as to where the car was parked.

He snatched the keys from my uncle's hands and said, "You don't know the streets as well as I do, and I don't trust anyone who's been drinking to drive me home, except for me."

Some people stumble when they get drunk. Not my stepfather;

he was sure-footed as he walked the wrong direction in search of the car. Peanut and I knew where he parked the car, but we stayed silent until the cold finally forced us to talk. Our Aunt Janet got in the back seat with my sisters and me.

No sooner had we gotten into the car than he showed his anger through his driving. He angrily moved the stick shift through every gear two or three times before settling on drive. Then we bolted into the street. I didn't know West Baltimore at all, but I knew we were headed the wrong way when he turned right on Pennsylvania Avenue instead of left. There was a considerable amount of traffic on Pennsylvania Avenue, which was restraining the remainder of his anger, so he turned onto an empty side street.

He started to reach speeds that called into question his concern for the safety of his kids. After the second stop sign that he ignored, my uncle told him he needed to slow down. My stepfather reluctantly complied and reduced his speed from insane to unreasonable.

I hadn't realized I had been holding Peanut's and my Aunt Janet's hands so tight. Just as I loosened my grip the car flipped upside down. Suddenly the view out the window changed from passing buildings into an upside-down view of the gutter but only briefly before a wall of glass hit the side of my face. Although I closed my eyes, I could still feel the car continue to slide a number of feet on its roof before coming to a stop.

When I opened my eyes, the first thing I saw was my Aunt Janet's glasses speckled with what looked like blood. She seemed dazed but fine. Gwen was crying, but it was her scared cry, so I knew she was all right. Peanut was fine because she was already pushing me to get out of the car.

What was once a back window was now a door with remnants of glass in the corners. I was preparing to exit through the window when a man managed to get the passenger door opened on my Aunt Janet's side. We crawled over broken glass and emerged directly under a streetlight, which confirmed the specks on my aunt's glasses were blood. She started crying, not because the blood was hers, but because it was mine.

I felt fine and had no signs of pain except the inside of my right ear itched badly. Unaware that there was glass in my ear, I proceeded to scratch it, only to accidentally grind the glass deeper into the cut. I also had a gash above my hairline that continued to my temple and behind my ear. My hand came away from the side of my face wet and red. For some strange reason it reminded me of the first time I had done finger painting, except the canvas was my face and the paint was my blood. Then the pain began in earnest.

I began to cry, more from fear than from the pain, because I had never bled so much before. Wiping away the tears with my bloody hand spread the claret stain to my eyes and cheeks. Then I cried some more, which left streaks on my bloody cheeks.

Despite the blood and tears in my eye and the shock of the accident, everything started to come into focus. I also began to feel how cold it was. My uncle emerged from the car and immediately joined his wife. I could see their breath in the cold and watched as their steamy breaths disappeared into a kiss.

I turned to reconfirm that my sisters were alright and gave them the first sight of my face. They were my flesh and blood mirrors. Their faces told me the state of my face. Both were still too young to be able to hide their expressions to spare my feelings. Peanut's expression was more telling than Gwen's. Peanut was not shocked by the trivial. The fact that her eyes and mouth had rounded into big o's showed she was bothered by what she saw.

Gwen pointed at me and began to cry, which drew the attention of our uncle. He left his wife's side, grabbed me by the forehead and twisted the bloody side of my head toward the streetlight. After a swift examination, he announced that I had three minor cuts and that head wounds bled more than other wounds. It looked worse than it was. I probably wouldn't need stitches, which was a good thing, because at several dollars a stitch, I wasn't going to get any, needed or not. My crying diminished slowly and became a sniffle here and there.

The man who had helped my aunt out of the car had gotten the door of the driver's side opened. All four wheels of the tires pointed toward the sky. I noticed my stepfather resting his head on the portion of the tire that normally should be touching pavement. He was mumbling to himself. I heard someone beyond the edge of the streetlight ask what he was saying.

A car accident was a new experience, but everything else was the same. I knew the excuses would come faster than an ambulance could have, had there been a need for one. He blamed the ice on the road rather than the ice in his gin. Yes, there was some ice on the road, but there had been more gin than ice in his drinks. The crowd at the edge of the light believed his excuse but the man who could smell my stepfather's breath probably did not. He lost some of the believers at the edge of the light when he blamed the cuts on the side of my head on the fact that I had forgotten my winter hat. It was my fault for not dressing appropriately for an accident.

Normally a slap across the face would have reinforced the blame. Without flinching or thinking I turned my other cheek, not in the biblical sense but because the other one was already bloody. I braced myself. Only the eyes of the crowd stayed his hand. At the last second, the intended blow turned into a rough swipe of blood from my face. He looked at the blood on his fingers and amplified his excuses.

The man who had helped us get out of the car now coaxed my stepfather and the rest of us toward his sister's house, which was a few steps from the accident. Appropriate calls had to be made but none would be to the police. Before going into the house some of the men from the crowd, along with my stepfather and uncle, tipped the car right side up and pushed it to the side of the road.

My stepfather and uncle were led to the kitchen to use the phone. Aunt Janet went upstairs to use the bathroom. Within seconds the man returned with a vinyl-covered chair and escorted my sisters and me into the living room. He placed the chair in front of a Christmas tree and gestured for me to take a seat.

Sitting on a couch in front of a window opposite the tree were four children around our ages. No introductions were made. The man gestured for them to make room for my sisters, then went back to the kitchen. Vinyl chairs were washable, cloth couches were not.

As I sat in the chair, I noticed the side of my coat was also stained, but I could not determine whether the blood was frozen or dry. After I finished examining myself, I lifted my head to find that I was also being examined. Six or seven pairs of eyes, my sisters included, were focused on me. Occasionally a pair of eyes would stray and gaze upon the Christmas tree behind me. It was the Christmas tree's last night standing, and it was being upstaged by a bloody child. Brief glances at the tree soon returned to my face as silent stares.

The room was so quiet I could almost hear their eyelids blinking and the lights of the tree flashing. To escape their stares, my eyes roamed the room in search of a place to distract my vision. It did not occur to me to close my eyes or cover them with my hands. Instead I tried to summon tears to blur my vision, but they would not come. Finally, my eyes settled on a place worse than their stares. Above the other children's head, I caught a faint blurry reflection of myself in the window. The glass looked as if an impressionist artist had painted a macabre painting of a child dressed in a grisly Halloween costume sitting before a Christmas tree. Time also seemed to be in costume. Seconds masqueraded as minutes and minutes pretended to be hours. I don't know how long I stared at the disturbing child in the painting. If I did not move, the image remained a painting, but if I so much as flinched the movement would confirm the image was me.

The children's mother, returning home from a party herself, restored time to its proper pace. She didn't seem shocked to see a bleeding child sitting in her living room. Perhaps the wrecked car parked outside of her house or a nosy neighbor had already informed her of what she was going to find. Either way she summoned the men from the kitchen and chastised them for not cleaning me up. At that moment my Aunt Janet came down the stairs with a wet warm washcloth. Pausing briefly to take notice of the white woman in her house, the woman took the washcloth from my aunt's hand and sent her upstairs to fetch another one.

She gingerly wiped the blood from my face. Her harsh tone drastically clashed with her gentle touch. She had the fingers of Doctor Jekyll but the mouth of Mister Hyde. The men had been making calls instead of tending to a child. She berated them for their insensitivity and priorities, then banished them from her sight with a wave of her hand.

My aunt returned with another washcloth, and the woman cleaned the rest of my face. The last swipe of the cloth across my face was over my lips. It left a smile in its wake, because I felt better.

Despite my smile I wondered about the superstition that how you spent the first day of the year would be how the rest of the year would follow. I didn't know how far into the New Year I had tread, but so far, I had bled and cried. A bleeding child does not determine the fate of a nation, but in my case, it was a predictor. The rest of 1968 would follow in the path of my first day, for me personally and for the nation as a whole. Blood and tears would become the hallmark of the coming year.

CHAPTER 31 THE HOURGLASS BLED

Memories from the rest of the evening are buried in an unmarked grave in the misty portion of my mind. The mist appears to be penetrable, but it's actually an aggregate that solidifies into an impenetrable wall when I try to pierce it with a thought. My stepfather had been the one drinking, but it was I who blacked out. I don't remember how we got home, how the rest of the family reacted to my minor injuries, or the damaged car. I awoke to a house where everyone was cordial and there was no hint of tension.

During the night, my grandmother had leveraged the accident and made a deal with my stepfather. My stepfather didn't have to pay for the damaged car, but in return we were to visit them in Connecticut in the summer. She said she would even pay for the train tickets. I was just as excited at the prospect of taking a train as I was about visiting my grandparents. Make do repairs were made to the car and the next day my grandparents, aunt and uncle returned to the Nutmeg State, the land of steady habits.

When summer approached, we would be the odd man out. Nearly all the people who had extra money sent their children back down South to strengthen family ties that had been weakened by distance. When my third-grade teacher, Mrs. Kidman, asked the class what we were planning on doing that summer, I told her my family was going to Connecticut.

Her response was too big for a child and reflected her weariness of the crime and poverty around us. "I've been to Connecticut. You will love it. In Baltimore news happens to you. In Connecticut news is something you watch on TV. I loved being in a place where you can change the channel if you don't like what you see."

Her statement was mostly true, but 1968 would be the exception. That year, more than any other, Americans had to share their games shows, soap operas and sitcoms with graphic images of their sons killing and being killed in Vietnam. There was no changing the channel.

All three major networks had started broadcasting nearly all their prime-time programming in color by the fall of 1966. Many American homes would see the carnage in color. My stepfather felt we were falling behind the times. I don't know how he managed it, but by late January we joined the ranks of the twenty-five percent of American households that had a color TV.

The novelty of having a color TV would not wear off for several weeks. I spent every waking moment watching any show on TV. Normally, when the news came on, that was my cue to do something else, but I even watched that. I vaguely remember the capture of the USS Pueblo by North Korea. That event was soon pushed into the background by the Tet Offensive in Vietnam and the Winter Olympics in France.

What little I knew of the world was different from how I felt. I guess I thought of nations more as neighborhoods. In my head, countries such as Vietnam and France were similar to neighborhoods like Mount Vernon or Fells Point, just farther away. Later in life, all my bus, train and plane trips would enable me to wrap my head around the term miles per hour, and I finally would grasp how big the country and world were.

Color TV brought the war into our dining room. Initially the war remained remote to me. Not that I was inured to the violence, but the poor-quality analog images on the screen, though horrible, could not compete with the bodies I had stumbled upon while playing in a junkyard and going to school. If I turned off the TV, I could find almost as bad in my own back yard, but the numbers on TV were astounding. Every night, the body count for the war was announced on the evening news. Many evenings the numbers were higher than I could count. Being a child, one evening I actually tried to count up to the number that had been announced on the news but grew weary before I reached my goal.

That night, the scale of the war became real to me, for I realized that each number was a name. American soldiers received roundtrip tickets to Vietnam, dead or alive. Not all returned alive. Mothers remembered burping babies they soon would have to bury. Fathers remembered tossing sons their first baseballs, but now used those same hands to toss dirt on their sons' caskets. The body count for the Vietnamese was even higher. Whereas we buried sons and some daughters, they were burying whole villages and families.

At least the corpses I had stumbled upon in Baltimore had no facial expressions. They had taken their anguish to the grave. What I found more disturbing than the dead bodies, was the anguish emanating from the wounded on the news, night after night. Doses of morphine administered to the American wounded took some of the pain from their faces, but even a child could sense anguish behind the drug-induced stupors. Wailing Vietnamese mothers received no morphine for their pain.

In February, I would see something on the news one evening that even living in Baltimore could not have prepared me for. February 2nd started as a disappointment because the groundhog had seen its shadow that morning. By that evening, America would see its own shadow.

None of the participants were Americans, but it didn't matter. We and our allies were supposed to be the good guys, but what transpired didn't make us appear so. Peanut brought my attention to the screen by pointing out that a barefoot, handcuffed man was wearing the same exact green and white plaid shirt I had on. Within moments, I, along with millions of Americans, witnessed a South Vietnamese soldier summarily execute the handcuffed Viet Cong on our TVs. The soldier pointed his gun at the temple of the man in plaid and pulled the trigger. Just as his blood began to pool on the street, the camera moved away, and my mother turned off the TV.

The image was so overwhelming that the particulars didn't matter. Allegedly, the Viet Cong had killed an entire family, but we had not witnessed his crime. We witnessed a crime against his crime. That evening I learned the phrase "Two wrongs don't make a right."

February was a month of massacres. A week after the summary execution, the Orangeburg Massacre occurred. Three civil rights protesters were killed by the South Carolina Highway Patrol and twenty-seven were wounded. Four days later came the Phong Nhi and Phong Nhat Massacre, where close to eighty civilians were killed, mostly women, children and the elderly. Two weeks later the Ha My Massacre left 135 dead. Both massacres in Vietnam were allegedly carried out by American allies, the South Korean Marines. It appeared as if the world, which had not yet fully formed in my head, was coming apart.

Smack dab in the middle of the carnage was the Winter Olympics, in Grenoble, France, which was the first to be broadcasted entirely in color and to extensively use satellites. Many of the events were seen live or on the same day. The American team was making a comeback after the entire U.S. figure skating team had been killed in a plane crash in 1961. Peggy Fleming, wearing a chartreuse form-fitting skating dress trimmed in white, would win the only gold medal for the U.S. team during the games. Her grace and style stood out in a clumsy world.

Two images from TV would remain with me from that winter. In fact, I can't think of one without remembering the other. Both wore green and white. One was shot in the head and lay in a street in South East Asia. The other stood on a podium at the foot of the Alps wearing a gold medal. Both were on opposite sides of the world. Although someday I wanted to wear a chartreuse dress and stand on a podium, it was more likely that I would end up dead on the streets of Baltimore. I already had the plaid shirt.

By the end of February, I returned to my regularly scheduled programming. I had grown used to color TV and no longer paid much attention to the news. In March, world events did not intrude into my life. The world hinted that it was out there, and I hinted back that I was not interested. Occasionally I paid attention to the body count, in case my stepfather used it as an excuse to perpetrate violence against us. I need not have worried. All his excuses were now domestic.

Much of the news returned to the domestic front as well. Lyndon B. Johnson won the New Hampshire primary. Richard Nixon easily won New Hampshire in the Republican primaries. Four days later, Bobby Kennedy announced he was running for president. America was in the process of choosing a new president. I had no clue what that meant. The president lived about an hour's drive from our house. I lived closer to him than ninety five percent of Americans, yet he was remote to me. He had no visible influence on my day-to-day life. My world was small and ruled by my stepfather.

Despite the sporadic violence around us, I usually only felt unsafe at home and occasionally on the walk to school. Soon I would feel unsafe everywhere. There were forces more powerful and violent than my stepfather, and they were poised to make their presence known.

Events were happening in the world that I was unaware of. In the case of the My Lai massacre, which happened the same day Bobby Kennedy announced his bid to become president, just a handful of people knew of the incident. The American public would not become aware of the massacre until over a year and a half after the event. This time it was not our allies doing the massacring but our soldiers. Between 300 and 500 unarmed South Vietnamese civilians were killed, and America's self-righteousness was severely wounded.

Ripples from the Tet Offensive were starting to reach the shores of the United States. The objective of the offensive was to cause a popular rebellion in South Vietnam and overthrow its government. It missed its objective by thousands of miles, for the government it helped overthrow would be the presidency of Lyndon B. Johnson. On March 31st he announced on national TV that he would not seek re-election.

Amongst all of this I had a ninth birthday. I would never forget my ninth year. That year encompassed most of 1968, which was one of the most turbulent in U. S. history. I remember nothing of the actual birthday. Did I have cake and blow out candles? I couldn't tell you, but I distinctly remember my mother blowing out her birthday candles the evening of April 4, 1968.

CHAPTER 32   NOT MY COUNTRY TIS OF THEE

April 4, 1968 was a special day. My mother had taken the day off from work because it was her birthday. We were also celebrating that she had recently received a ten percent pay increase. She was now making $1.75 an hour. Since she had had a good night's sleep, she made pancakes for breakfast instead of serving us cold cereal. The pancakes were a partial salve on my disappointment about sleeping through the launching of Apollo Six that morning.

Apollo Six was brought to my attention by our third-grade teacher, Mrs. Kidman. It was the last, unmanned launch in the Apollo program. Mrs. Kidman said we would land men on the moon within a year or two. The day before the launch we talked of nothing else. She gave us a drawing assignment. We had to draw a picture of what it would be like for people to live on the moon. Many of the children were better artists than I was. Most drew pictures of domes and outbuildings with men in space suits in the foreground doing moon things. I went for an interior scene and drew an elegant woman with a bouffant hairstyle sitting under a dome, decorated by a twenty-first century gay designer who also happened to be her hairdresser. She sipped chocolate milk from a martini glass and made dinner with the push of a button. It was not a very good drawing, but it was unique, and I won.

I was given the honor of being the flag bearer the next day, which was the launch date for Apollo Six. Each day one boy, always one of the taller ones, would be chosen to hold the flag in front of the class. He was accompanied by two shorter boys, who acted as color guards, one on each side of the standard bearer. Then we would put our hands over our hearts and recite the Pledge of Allegiance. I had the honor of being a color guard several times but never the standard bearer. Mrs. Kidman was a stickler for standards and symmetry. The standard bearer had to be taller than the color guards, and girls were not allowed to be either. There were only two boys shorter than me in my class, so they became color guards by default.

That morning my mother sacrificed a few minutes of her birthday to put shoe polish on my scuffed-up shoes and brushed them until they shined. They shined enough for me to see a reflection of the flag if I chose to look down. But I would not be looking down. I would be holding my head high, for I had the honor of holding the flag. My excitement stemmed not from patriotic zeal but from prestige. Holding the flag was being special. Every morning we practiced patriotism for a country I had no concept of. Flags are pretty, but I loved people, and America was all those around me.

Before leaving the house for my special day, I got to see democracy in action. Although it was our mother's birthday, she asked us what kind of cake we wanted. I voted for lemon cake. Peanut and Gwen voted for chocolate. In a two-cake race, chocolate always won in our house.

At school I took my place in front of the class. My imagination had taken me places my stature could not. I was the tall one holding the flag for a grand total of twenty seconds. Anticipation was greater than the moment. Until I personally held the flag, I never realized the one holding the flag could not put their hand over their heart. I enjoyed having my hand over my heart. It was an unconscious reminder that there was so much within me.

At the time, no one was aware that I would be the last one in our class to be the standard bearer for the flag. The next day we would not say the Pledge of Allegiance. We had been pledging allegiance to a country that did not pledge back. When we finally resumed the pledge, we did so to a flag that stood limp on a pole in the corner, with no bearer or color guards. Doubt clung to it, as well as to the nation.

Mrs. Kidman allowed me to stay after class so I could make my mother a birthday card using school supplies. I knew enough lettering to write Happy Birthday in cursive with glue on red art paper. Then I scattered glitter on the glue. I was almost literate when I wrote in glue and glitter. To make up for the time lost from crafting the birthday card, I ran home as fast as I could.

Peanut and Gwen were already sitting at our dining room table watching TV. At the time, there were only three primary channels for two hundred million people. Therefore, TV was segmented by age and gender. It conformed to social norms, as well as reinforced them. It was an unofficial clock that regulated our lives. During the week, early morning belonged to children. Late morning to early afternoon programming was geared toward women. Children were allotted another hour or so in the late afternoon. News was shown after men got home from work, in case the women folk and children needed calming after seeing something tragic on the news. Prime time was for everyone. From nine o'clock until the national anthem played was for adults. There was nothing on TV for insomniacs until six o'clock in the morning.

Early April had borrowed some warmth from late May. The weather was too nice to watch TV. Shortly after giving my mother her birthday card, I abandoned my one hour of TV to play outside. I was not joined by my sisters and other children until the afternoon cartoons were over. Normally we played outside until five thirty, which was our normal dinner time. But dinner was going to be an hour late today; therefore, Gwen, Peanut and I stayed out to play with the children who ate dinner after six o'clock or ate no dinner at all.

Finally, our mother summoned us to a Sunday dinner served on a Thursday. During the week, most of our dinners came from the top of the stove. On weekends, much of it came from the oven: biscuits, cakes and roasts. If we had salad it would usually be on a Sunday. The salad bowl sitting on the table clashed with a school day. They rarely crossed paths during the week. Fortunately, there were no disagreeable vegetables on the table. Tonight, there was nothing we would have to be bribed to eat. Some nights we had dessert only if we ate what we hated: stewed tomatoes or liver for me, overcooked canned spinach for Gwen and Peanut. Tonight, was a celebration; we each would get a piece of cake without a standoff.

The news was on at my insistence. I wanted to see news footage of the Apollo Six launch from that morning. Between bites of ham and mashed potatoes I watched the clip of a pillar of fire pushing a metal needle into space. Though awe inspiring, I wondered when America's technology was going to catch up to the space shows on TV. But the overriding question soon would be, when would America catch up to its constitution?

After watching the launch, the news faded into the background, and we enjoyed a leisurely dinner. When we finished, my sisters and I helped clear the dishes from the table, more to hasten the eating of cake than to ease our mother's burden. Although it was her twenty fifth birthday, there were only twelve candles on her cake. We only had a box of twelve and had to imagine the other thirteen. Our stepfather lit the candles and turned off the lights. Fire and icing adorned the center of our table. Lights from the TV briefly bickered with those from the candles. We sang happy birthday and my mother blew out the candles. Before he could turn on the lights again, something on the TV caught my stepfather's attention. Instead of turning on the lights again he turned up the volume. We sat in the dark, with the scent of burnt candles and chocolate cake teasing our noses as we listened to Walter Cronkite announce the assassination of Martin Luther King Jr. At seven o'clock in the morning, America had sent a rocket into space higher than ever before. By seven o'clock that evening, America had assassinated the youngest person to ever receive a Nobel Peace prize.

We listened to the entire announcement sitting in the dark. After hearing that a light had gone out in the world, my stepfather turned the lights back on, but it did nothing to brighten the room. Both of my parents had sad, concerned expressions on their faces. My mother's expression had a tinge of guilt as well, almost as if she had blown out a life when she blew out her candles. Years later she mentioned that, although fleeting, the thought did indeed cross her mind. But I was more concerned with the reaction of my stepfather. At first, I thought this would be another reason to beat us, but his expression was wrong, and I was sure he didn't know Martin Luther King Jr. He alleviated my fears by hugging all of us and telling our mother to give us extra cake.

Eating birthday cake on a death day somehow felt wrong, but the confection was a distraction. Our stepfather wanted to make some phone calls he probably didn't want us privy to. Although the phone was in the living room, it was no more than twelve feet from the dining room table. We could hear anything we wanted to. Normally we either were given distractions as earplugs or told to go outside or upstairs. Just as he touched the phone to make his calls it rang.

As soon as he hung up another phone call came in. When the rings paused long enough, he would dial someone else. My cake lasted through two calls. Then my sisters and I paid attention whether we wanted to or not. The conversations were worried, sad and a bit angry. One of the calls came from my mother's coworker. She ended the call by consoling the woman on the other end of the line, then angrily slammed the phone down.

My stepfather visibly flinched from the uncharacteristic display of anger and asked her, "What is wrong?"

She hissed, "Maxine said that some of the white people at work outright cheered at the news of the assassination, and a few are walking around with barely hidden smiles. I am so glad I am not going to work tonight. I just don't have it in me to fake a smile for white people tonight."

I was caught off guard by two things, the venom in her voice directed toward white people and the fact that they would laugh or smile because someone had been killed. She had never said anything derogatory about white people before. My few interactions with them had been pleasant or neutral. Like many mothers, she hid from us the overt forms of racism as long as she could. She was always polite to white people, but the overriding reaction was that they were a nuisance to be avoided whenever possible. The fact that some had laughed or smiled at an assassination implied they were far more than a nuisance.

At the time, Martin Luther King Jr. was not a member of the pantheon of great Americans. Mostly revered today, he was anything but prior to his death. The vast majority of heedless white Americans either disapproved of him or outright hated him. Though still widely respected among his own people, younger black people thought of him as well-meaning but antiquated. He knocked politely at the door for civil rights, while they wanted to kick the door down.

Younger folks had grown tired of listening to white men on national TV debasing their own humanity by debating ours. Politicians prattled on about how great our country was for being able to debate the equality of human beings. Those being debated about felt it was a disgrace that it was a question at all. Some Southern senators told their constituency that someday the Negro would be equal to the likes of them but not today. All of those old enough to have an opinion felt that being the equals to such men would have been a downgrade for most of us.

Slowly over the last hundred years the descendants of slaves were replacing the cotton bales on their shoulders with pride, dignity and self-respect. Most white Americans would interpret it as a chip on our shoulders. Their barbaric behavior toward us was a figment of our imagination. Heavier than any bale of cotton, they projected the worst of their behavior onto our shoulders. We were the uncivilized ones, not they. Not pleased with their reflection, they brutally beat the mirror. Eventually it broke and the shards cut their fists, and they hated the mirror more, but now they feared it as well. This was the dilemma of black people in America; our very existence reminded white Americans they are not who they say they are.

I had only been nine years old for a week and knew next to nothing about geography or politics and vaguely remember when I had thought JFK was president of Ohio. I thought I knew who Martin Luther King Jr. was and believed back then that he was the president of black America, but we were still called Negroes or worse at the time. Four days before the assassination, the white president, Lyndon B. Johnson, had announced that he would not run for president again. Naively I thought maybe we could elect a president together and unite. Even at nine years old it was clear to me that we were two separate nations. The borders were unclear on paper, but in the collective mind they were well defined. In the coming days, I was shocked to learn that we were supposedly one nation under God, because we sure didn't act like it.

CHAPTER 33   NO FLESH COLORED BANDAGES FOR US

East Baltimore was shrouded in a collective blues. The heaviness of our souls pressed our feet deeper into our shoes. People who normally swayed and swaggered now slumped and staggered. Not that I really knew what was going on, but my feet mourned for those who did know, and I knew it was not a day for skipping. I traveled to school by myself, but my walk was more a slide. My feet only left the ground to step down or over curbs.

Instead of entering a playground full of children running around, releasing energy before they had to sit all day, I found clumps of children whispering. This was the first time the news had so deeply penetrated our playground. Immediately I sought out Jane. Intellectually she was way ahead of the rest us. Frightened, I listened as she said white people were already preparing to send troops into our cities. I wondered why they would do that. We were helping them fight another people in Vietnam. One of our neighbor's sons was there fighting now.

As foolish as it may seem, I knew color was country. I knew our people were tiring of the war. I didn't have to pay close attention to realize nearly everyone I knew was against the war. Martin Luther King Jr. was highly critical of it, and Muhammad Ali, the heavy weight champion of the world, refused to fight in it. With war raging, did white people have enough soldiers to send some here too?

I had been around large groups of white people maybe a dozen times and interacted personally with only four or five. The interactions mostly had been positive or neutral. But most of the other children had far less exposure to them than I had. One of the younger children doubted Jane's assertion by saying he didn't think that many white people would leave TV to come here. Jane was the only one who laughed. For most of the other children, that was where white people dwelled.

Jane said they would come from suburbia, and that suburbia completely surrounded us. With no context to accompany it, the name suburbia sounded menacing. My family had driven through it several times, but I didn't know that was what it was called. In many ways, most of us on the playground had experienced so much of the world. But in other ways, we knew so little of it. Our silly assumptions about a divided America were no more ridiculous than the reality. We were trying to digest a world that was trying to digest us.

The bell rang and we went to our respective classrooms. Mrs. Kidman's lack of a mood was a mood in itself. It was as if someone had taken a blackboard eraser and swiped it across her face. But her attempt to hide her emotions made them all the more apparent. We couldn't see them, but we could feel them, not just from her but all the adults. No one could give us an explanation because they were still searching for one themselves.

I briefly wondered who would be the flag bearer today? But Mrs. Kidman didn't acknowledge the flag at all. Instead of saying the Pledge of Allegiance, she led us in prayer for the welfare of Mrs. King and her four fatherless children. She spoke their full names in prayer. At its end, instead of saying God Bless America, we said God Save America and amen.

During recess, the story was much the same from the other students. Other than saying a prayer for the nation, teachers were not forthcoming. We were given busy work: their mood told us to keep our heads down and ask no questions. Even the most mischievous children kept a low profile. None of us wanted to have the mood of the teachers focused on us. The only child to have any information was Willa. True to her nickname, 'I'm a tell', she told us that she heard two of the teachers talking and one of them was crying. Before they closed the door to the teacher's lounge, she heard the one crying say, "Reverend King was our best effort, and they killed him."

An overheard statement from an unknown teacher succinctly expressed the feelings of millions of people. White America had killed our best effort. Along with our best effort, they had killed what little respect and fear some still felt for them. The assassination had been the last straw and had radicalized a patient people. Black Americans had grown tired of making white people feel good about the wrongs they did to us.

When I grew older, I realized the relationship between black and white Americans was similar to my parents' relationship. They were unevenly yoked in marriage. Just as my stepfather had, America crowed to the world about how wonderful our way of life was but, behind closed doors, both my stepfather and my country badly mistreated their wives and minority children. Our place was to stay in the background, beaten until black and blue, singing the blues. Within a year, other minorities grew tired too. Caesar Chavez had already been on a hunger strike. Native Americans would take over Alcatraz, and gay people would fight back at Stonewall.

White America's opinions of its minorities were bigger than its facts. It knew almost nothing about any of us but told the same story to the world my stepfather did when he beat my mother: "It was their fault. They are clumsy and fall down the stairs and walk into doors all the time. I never laid a hand on them."

The power to beat was one thing; the power to change the narrative was worse. When confronted by the truth, some white Americans wanted to do better, but most just doubled down on the national lies and status quo. My country, and the majority of its people, would rather lie than change.

Before the bell rang to release us to our parents, Mrs. Kidman adamantly stressed that we were to go straight home, no detours. It felt as if she were directly looking at me when she made the statement. I had planned on going across the street to Mister Willy's to find out what he thought but went straight home instead.

The atmosphere was no different at home than it had been at school. While other cities were already burning, Baltimore was seething but still calm. Spontaneous violence was so widespread that many white Americans believed the events were coordinated by extremists and communist agitators and were fearful that blacks were turning red. Predictably, they had the opinion of someone who was sitting on a soft cushion a comfortable distance from the problem. There was no real problem; black people were just ungrateful.

The assassination was the spark, but the kindling and fuel for the pyre had been accumulating for 350 years. Local conditions in each city either agitated or mitigated the situation.

In New York City, home to the largest black population in the country, there was very little violence. This was because of a bold move by Mayor John Lindsay. Lindsay had been deputy chairman on the Kerner Commission, which a month earlier had predicted the coming strife. He knew the root of the problem and against the advice of the police, drove to Harlem, where virtually alone he stopped a crowd of thousands of people just by acknowledging their plight and pain.

In Boston, a white man named White and a black man named Brown helped stem the tide of violence. Mayor Kevin White and the Godfather of Soul, James Brown, came to an agreement that his concert at the Boston Gardens would also be televised on WGBH, Boston's public radio station. The concert kept thousands of people off the streets and allowed James Brown to address their anger.

Oakland, hometown of the Black Panther Party, was spared

mass violence, but on April 6th the Panthers ambushed the Oakland police. During the ensuing shootout, the Panther's first member, Bobby Hutton, was allegedly killed trying to surrender unarmed. Through the swift action of the Oakland clergy, no further violence stemmed from this incident. Years later, I would hear one of those clergy members relating how hard it was for him to talk people down from violence when deep down inside he felt like throwing a brick, too.

Some cities, such as Chicago, were doomed because of poor leadership. Mayor Richard Daly made his infamous statement, "Shoot to kill. Shoot to maim." He said it several days after calm had returned to the city, but it brought to the forefront an unspoken sentiment. We were to be dealt with, not talked to. The National Guard and police were there to protect white property.

Baltimore's mood was similar to hot embers in a fireplace deceptively covered in ash. Bellows would not blow on the embers until around dinnertime that Saturday evening. Initially, to try to defuse the situation, people were handing out pamphlets to the white businesses along Gay Street, requesting them to close out of respect for Martin Luther King Jr. Many of the black businesses had closed, planned on closing, or put up black wreaths or black crepe in their windows. Apparently, the white business community refused, because many were already operating on low profit margins. But they also were selling to a community they didn't understand, nor care about.

Later, I was happy to hear that the store of a nice white woman who had sold us food on credit when we lived on Forrest Street had been spared. She had put a black wreath and photos of Martin Luther King Jr. and Jesus in her window. Few would throw a rock at a window guarded by such sentinels. Perhaps her understanding of the situation saved her business more than the sentinels at her window. For the other businesses the olive branch of pamphlets became thrown bricks and fire.

Initially our ears barely noticed the increase in the number of sirens wailing in the night. But around seven thirty their wailing overpowered the night and compelled my stepfather to walk to the corner of our block to investigate.

My mother was preparing to leave early for work, because on weekends the bus for Catonsville took longer. He was gone longer than expected. My mother couldn't wait any longer for him and went to leave just as he burst through the door. She leaned into his cheek to kiss him goodbye, but he blocked her from leaving.

She gently tried to push past him, but he said, "Baby, I don't think you are going to work tonight."

My mother looked concerned. We needed every penny to make

it look as if we were more middle class than we actually were. Our color TV still had 900 more easy payments on it. He answered her inquisitive expression by leading her and us to the roof of our house.

Scattered among the twinkling lights of the city were glowing balls of flames, most of them to the southwest of us in our shopping district on Gay Street. Before long, more fires started to the southeast of us. Only Johns Hopkins Hospital separated them. As we watched the fires to the south, smoke from the northeast tapped us on our shoulders. We turned that direction and witnessed columns of smoke blackening an already dark sky. Our city was ablaze.

My mother's bus route to Catonsville ran too close to the fires. She didn't call in sick, she called in under siege. By eleven o'clock that night the city was under curfew. No one could enter or leave the city until six o'clock Sunday morning.

Sirens and phone calls kept my sisters and me up past midnight. We had not stayed up this late since New Year's Eve. Domestic violence was the alarm clock that usually woke us in the middle of the night, but tonight an entire city was being beaten.

Around eleven thirty a white man with great hair and a pleasant face came on TV pleading for calm, but much of Baltimore was beyond hearing. Years later, I would realize the mayor of Baltimore, Thomas D'Alesandro III, was the older brother of Nancy Pelosi, who would become the first female Speaker of the House of Representatives and would be my congresswomen for over thirty years. He would only be my mayor for months. Sirens from outside drowned out much of what he said.

Ostensibly to prevent smoke and teargas from entering the house, my sisters and I helped our mother wet and twist some towels to place at the sills of some of our drafty windows and the threshold of our front door. Tear gas would be used no closer than a mile to us, but fire eventually would burn only a few blocks away.

The last thing I heard before going to sleep was the muffled yell of Mrs. Frances, our neighbor who had taken one of Ibo's kittens. Between a break in the sirens her screaming came through the wet towels at the windowsill. I heard her yell, "Burn it down, burn it all down!"

CHAPTER 34   ASH SUNDAY

The first thing I wanted to do after eating breakfast was to see what happened. I moved the towel away from the door and went outside. My sisters tagged along as we walked our three-block rectangle world to see how much had changed. There were six businesses in our small world, and all had been spared.

Everything seemed normal until we reached the corner of our southeast border on Ashland Ave, N. Gay Street and N. Caroline. Our world wasn't really a rectangle. Back then, before urban renewal would remove five blocks from its middle, N. Gay Street ran uninterrupted from southwest to northeast, cutting a corner off the southeast portion of our rectangle. Across N. Caroline near Gay Street we saw our first burned-out building.

As Baltimore was a city of row houses, the skeletal remains of the building had not collapsed. It was propped up by its fellows to either side. The image reminded me of two sober friends supporting a drunken one between them, except few of the burned-out buildings would ever sober up and become their former selves.

Suddenly a shape in the rubble that I had mistaken for a heap of refuse lifted itself up. It was Miss Penny. The store had been a jewelry store, so at first, I thought she was rummaging through the store for unburned diamonds. But all she had on her fingers was cold ash from the fire. She took the ash and made the sign of the cross on her forehead. As it was actually Palm Sunday, I thought it was an odd gesture. Ash Wednesday had been weeks ago.

In retrospect, it made some sort of sense. Almost no one I saw going to church carried any palms. Jesus may not have entered Baltimore City on Palm Sunday, but thousands of troops had. Though I couldn't see them from my vantage point, there were far more individuals carrying bayonets and bricks than palms. As the ashes for next year's Ash Wednesday came from the burning and blessing of palms from this Palm Sunday, there would be no locally produced ash for next year. But there would be plenty of ash from burned buildings. Miss Penny was making up her own ceremony.

We had not seen Miss Penny in a couple of weeks and tried to get her attention by gently waving at her. Something about the day restrained our voices; instead of yelling when she didn't notice us, we waved our hands louder, trying to make them yell for us. We heard gunfire in the distance behind us. Only then did she turn to notice us.

She gestured for us to cross the street, but we shook our heads. We had reached the end of our invisible tether and couldn't cross N. Caroline Street. I thought she would walk away, but instead she crossed the street to join us. I noticed as she was crossing that she pulled a small axe from her ragbag and was now carrying it in her right hand. Seeing a woman carrying an axe and displaying the sign of the cross on her forehead made of ash from a burnt-out building on Palm Sunday, should have raised our concerns. But it was Miss Penny; I only paused at the sign of the cross on her forehead. Then to make up for the pause I gave her a clipped greeting before Peanut and I, in unison, asked her, "What is going on?"

Not fully understanding our question and probably thinking her axe needed more explaining than a burning city, she tossed it in the air, caught it by the handle and said, "This is to set the horses free in case there's a fire."

Before she elaborated further, she said, to herself more than to us, "Let me put this axe away before I get bayoneted by some over-zealous white soldiers."

She apologized to us after seeing the horrified expressions on our faces by saying, "Don't worry, all the soldiers are busy protecting the white stores downtown. There're none around here."

She didn't say they wouldn't bayonet her if they saw her. She simply said they weren't going to see her. To emphasize her words, she walked us up a sometimes-busy N. Caroline Street toward the far less busy Barnes Street. Once on our street, she pulled out the axe again and walked us down N. Spring Street toward the stables.

She continued her explanation. "There are going to be more fires tonight, and with all the straw and hay in the stable I am afraid a spark could easily start a fire. Horses can't open doors, can they now?"

Not knowing it was a rhetorical question we nodded our heads in agreement.

She tested the rustiest and thinnest part of the chain and decided it would take no more than two or three hard hits to break the chain from the lock. Satisfied with that, we helped her find a place to sleep during the night. There were three empty produce wagons parked on the empty lot on the corner of N. Spring and Barnes Street. I mistakenly thought she would sleep in one of the wagons. But she planned on sleeping under one of them. She used her boot to test the dirt under each of the wagons to see which one had the least amount of broken glass and shards of brick and chose the tallest wagon, closest to the stables. It was a good place for a fire watch.

We were not wearing our Sunday best since Palm Sunday had become Ash Sunday. My sisters and I crawled under the wagon with Miss Penny and helped her remove some of the bigger bits of bricks from her makeshift berth.

Under the shade of a produce wagon I rephrased my earlier question, "Why is everyone so angry?"

Instead of tossing a particularly sharp piece of brick to the side, she scribbled in the dirt with it. I almost said there wasn't enough dirt under the wagon to tell the story, and besides my sisters and I couldn't read. But she was simply gathering her thoughts.

When she tossed the bit of brick to the side she said, "In this world crazy is the norm and sane is the veneer."

She pointed to the cross on her forehead and said, "This is not really a cross. It is a scratch in my veneer. I, along with many people, am angry because once again white Southerners are trying to stop progress with a bullet."

I thought to myself, "Just like my stepfather with his slaps."

She talked over my thought. "Everyone is not angry, or at least not at the same time. We are taking turns being angry. We Negroes are divided on this, not just amongst ourselves, but each individual is divided internally. One minute you find yourself angry, the next minute you're calming down someone else who has the same anger."

In the coming hours and days, I would experience and witness exactly what she spoke of. Ask someone a question about how they felt, then ask the same question five minutes later of the same person and receive a completely contradictory answer. Several days later, Mrs. Frances, the woman who had yelled, "Burn it down, burn it all down," was out on the street with her broom, cleaning the street trying to make it presentable for her son, who had been wounded in Vietnam. He was leaving one war zone but returning to another one.

The expression of anger was generational. Many of the older adults were using most of their emotional strength to restrain themselves from retaliating, yet they still tried to talk the young adults out of violence. Most of the righteous but misguided anger came from the young. Although older adults had seen far worst discrimination than their children and grandchildren, relative to the new generation, their expectations and hopes were lower. The hopes of the young had fallen from a much higher elevation, and the impact had shattered all patience and reason. Before the rebellion hit the streets, it happened first at home. Young adults who were normally extremely reverent and obedient defied their parents' threats and boldly walked out the front door or snuck out windows.

Although they broke the rules at home, they at least respected them. They only defied those rules to go outside and break the rules they hated. White Americans had made vile, immoral laws and hid behind the shield of law and order, a fake morality that gave permission for evil to thrive. Our lowly position was the law of the land, and questioning it was breaking that law. For 350 years, wide smiles on dark faces hid a justifiable rage. When the rage exploded, rightly or wrongly, it was directed at the symbols of white power in our neighborhood, white property and police. They bore the brunt of the anger.

Nearly all the looters were young. There were exceptions; I heard a rumor about an older woman who was too feeble to throw a brick herself, so she handed it to a younger person to throw on her behalf.

The most shocking thing of all was that white America was actually shocked. Their disbelief was what was unbelievable. Supposedly, at the time Lyndon B. Johnson was heard to say, "I don't know why we're so surprised. When you put your foot on a man's neck and hold him down for three hundred years, and then you let him up, what's he going to do? He's going to knock your block off."

Miss Penny expressed a more tempered view. "There is not one informed Negro in America who doesn't think white folks had this and worse coming to them. But many of us are of the mind that just because they had it coming, doesn't mean we should serve it to them. If you are capable of justifiable violence, you are capable of unjustified violence. There is a thin line between the two. Mass payback always has too many innocent victims. Besides, paying someone back empties your moral bank account."

She always talked to us as if we were ten years older than we were. I only understood half of what she said, but the knowledge I didn't understand, I put into a savings account and withdrew it many years later with interest and understanding.

Two wrongs don't make a right, but at times it takes a wrong to stop a wrong. But when a wrong benefits people, they often pretend it's right. Self-interest clashes with self-reflection, defeats it and a lie is born. Sometimes the obvious has to be exhumed because it has been buried under so many lies.

Miss Penny sniffed the air. Another fire had started nearby. She said, "The good news is, we are equal to white people. The bad news is, we are equal to white people, and I don't want to be that kind of equal."

I had not grown up on a diet of second-class citizenship and had not yet had the concept of inferiority beaten into me. Similar to wearing plaid and polka dots together, inferiority is a mismatched garment I don't look good in. One day I would actually wear to school a pair of red, white and blue bellbottoms with a green and white polka dots shirt, but I have yet to try on inferiority. From an early age I knew that being in an inferior position was not the same as being inferior. Yet for much of my life people would try dressing me in plaid and polka dots.

I could be easily hurt or intimidated by physical violence but not verbal assaults. I was swiftly learning not to be damaged by words; they were too easily and cheaply produced. In my teens the words nigger and faggot were just normal background radiation. What others said about me may or may not have been true, but it most definitely said a lot about the speaker. My identity did not come from the mouths of others and never would. But what always bothered me and still does, is the attempt to hurt. Not the words themselves but the attempt. I resented that people tried to hurt me for no good reason. As I grew older, I could only defend myself physically against some of the attempts, but verbally I was rarely outmatched.

Along with millions of others, I was America's boogeyman. People's reactions to me were comical, yet sad and sometimes dangerous. Sometimes the only advantage they had over me was state sanctioned skin color and mating rights. It was comical to watch some individuals fail miserably as they thought their skin color was a high IQ and tried to use it to step above me, sad because sometimes it worked and dangerous for me if I challenged it.

At the time white Americans were the most powerful people on the planet. TV portrayed them as fearless, yet deep down inside many of them were deeply afraid. They fearlessly parachuted from planes but wouldn't sit next to a black maid on a bus. Young white children in the South were breastfed by black nannies, then grew up to drink from "Whites Only" fountains. They boasted about their great knowledge yet had suppressed ours by enacting anti-literacy laws. White fear of blackness bordered on insanity.

White institutions were ridiculous and dangerous beyond belief. Their ridiculousness, although dangerous, sometimes made us laugh. Worse, it often made us feel better than them. I would often pray I was not their equal. But as Miss Penny said, "The good news is you are, and the bad news is you are, if not in deeds in potential."

Miss Penny's words, spoken to us as we sat in the dirt under a wagon, would help keep me from a false sense of self. The point of moral high ground was to help others reach it as well. It was not a vista point to look down upon others.

I had only crawled under the wagon to help her prepare a place to act as fire warden and watch over the horses, in particular Queen Pinky. But Miss Penny had given me a valuable perspective on life. I had no intentions of replacing white injustice with black injustice.

Just as it is ridiculous to be hated for your skin color, it is ridiculous to hate someone for their skin color. But there was not a moral equivalency; white people hated a skin color and black people hated a behavior. White skin was merely a warning sign for potential bad behavior. I never disliked white people who disavowed the poor behavior of the past or their fellows, yet so many of them trivialized or denied our experience to get past their discomfort with it.

Our fight for freedom is one of the two greatest struggles in our nation's history. When we were brought from Africa, the only physical thing we were permitted to bring was the dirt under our fingernails. We arrived naked, yet we would develop into some of the boldest, most colorful patterns in the fabric of the nation. But we were not permitted to celebrate our achievement because white people were the villains in that struggle, and they don't like to be the villains. Native peoples also were not permitted to celebrate overcoming their struggles. Genocide was a popular TV genre at the time. We called them Westerns. The slaughter of Native Americans was considered entertainment. They were the bad guys because they fought back. It would become popular to wear t-shirts that said, "I beat cancer," but it would be considered whining to wear a t-shirt that said, "I beat institutional racism" or "I have survived America's genocide"

We were a stolen people brought to a stolen land. If we weren't willing to be property we didn't belong here, but now we had too much American dirt under our fingernails. When we sang "We Shall Overcome," we sang about overcoming white Americans. But they needed to overcome themselves as well. There was a dishonesty to their worldview that if left unaddressed would someday consume them as well as us.

CHAPTER 35   RÉUNIFICATION

A government curfew had been put over my parent's curfew. No one, including adults, was allowed on the streets after four o'clock in the afternoon. Whether to keep us safe or to maintain adult prerogative, another hour was added to my sisters' and my curfew. As well as most of the children on our block, we were off the street by three o'clock. Inside our cat yowled and paced in front of the window facing the alley. She wanted out, but even cats had a curfew. It was almost as if a whole city had been grounded for bad behavior.

Since we could not be on the street my sisters and I went to the roof and spent the final hour before the government curfew there. As the edges had no walls or railings our play was restricted to low movement games. My sisters drew a hopscotch board on the rough tar surface. Gwen used a penny for her marker. Peanut ripped a button off of a sweater she hated to use as hers. They spent more time arguing about the rules than playing the game.

I played with plastic toy soldiers while real flesh and blood soldiers patrolled the streets below. I pretended to have one of the plastic soldiers toss his hand grenade off the roof, and I imagined the massive cloud of smoke to the west had been caused by the toy grenade. The smoke resembled a murky grey river flowing skyward; it had no banks and its flow was at the whim of the wind. Finally, the river blew our way and enforced its own curfew. Defused light from the sun mingled with the smoke, and for a brief moment before the smoke drove us inside, the sun actually did smell as if it was on fire. Shortly thereafter we would eat supper and watch *Walt Disney's Wonderful World of Color*. The world displayed on TV was vastly different from the one I lived in.

Between dinner and Disney, our grandparents called us from the relative safety of a valley in the Berkshires. This was their second call that day. They had checked on our safety that morning. But the news they were watching must have raised their concerns again. I remembered earlier that year my teacher saying, "Baltimore is a place news happened to you, and Connecticut is a place you watch news on TV." This was not completely true but true in relative terms at the time. I didn't have to watch the news on TV. All I had to do was go on the roof or to the end of my street to witness the day's events.

My mother turned the call around on them and asked how they were. Gwen, Peanut and I crowded as close to the earpiece as our mother would allow. I heard my grandmother say they were fine, but white people up there were really afraid.

It was my mother's turn to be concerned. She said, "There is nothing more violent in the world than scared white folks. So, mom, please be careful when you are on the street."

At the time I knew nothing of our nation's history, but my grandparents lived in abolitionist country. They lived in the town where John Brown was born, and my grandfather worked as a domestic a block from the childhood home of Harriet Beecher Stowe. They were concerned, but they did not live in the Deep South. Our grandmother felt safe enough to once again suggest that we consider moving to Connecticut. When our mother said she would think about it, it almost sounded sincere this time.

Once again, our mother missed work. There were rumors of sniper fire, which proved to be true, and the number of snipers intensified in the coming days. The next morning, our mother walked all of us to school. I had not been escorted by a parent to school in four years. Sniper fire did eventually come within a block of our school, but most of the shootings happened at night.

Jane was not the first person I saw on the playground, but she was the first person I noticed. She gave me a nod that said, "I told you so." Some of the children who lived west and north of the school were talking about seeing troops with bayonets marching down their streets. A few had seen armored personnel carriers, which they mistook for tanks. I lived closer to Gay Street than most of the other children, and although it had been heavily hit by destruction, I personally had not seen any soldiers yet. From the roof of our house I had heard them march down N. Eden Street, but hearing was not seeing. None had crossed my personal borders.

Bells summoned us to our classrooms. Children walked to class chatting in rumors. Most of us still didn't know what was going on. The best storytellers and rumors held court. Once in class, Mrs. Kidman, normally very strict about classroom decorum, did not issue one shush. A few of the more studious children tried to issue counterfeit shushes on her behalf, but we only recognized Mrs. Kidman's, so we kept on talking. Occasionally, others and I would take note of her sitting at her desk deep in thought. After about fifteen minutes, even the most loquacious of us noticed the absence of adult enforced restraint. The chatter wore itself out, and we all patiently waited for Mrs. Kidman to address our class.

We were already fifteen minutes past our normal time for saying the Pledge of Allegiance. Finally, she rose, faced the flag and put her hand on her chest. But the gesture, rather than an oath, seemed more as if she was checking to see if her heart was still in it. Her first few words of the pledge came out as a sigh. We followed suit, but our pledge sounded more like a dirge. For those who knew the truth, the final words, "With liberty and justice for all," had the taste of bile and burned the throat.

President Johnson had ordered flags to fly at half-mast until the interment of Martin Luther King Jr. Men had died in battle trying to keep the flag from touching the ground. One of our earlier flags actually had a rattlesnake on it with the caption, "Don't tread on me." But metaphorically speaking, white Americans without a care or self-reflection treaded on the flag every single day. We were not one nation under God.

I don't remember how Mrs. Kidman addressed the class after that point, for within five minutes of taking our seats the principal came on the PA system to announce that school had been canceled. Many of the kids were not happy. They depended on school lunches for a good portion of their daily meals and many of the grocery stores had been looted and burned. Larders were empty, with no way to replenish them.

Those of us who rejoiced at the news didn't immediately rush for the door. We still waited for Mrs. Kidman to dismiss us. When she finally did, I briefly scanned the halls for my sisters. We usually came to school together but rarely walked home together; more than likely they would walk with our cousin Darla or by themselves. We only lived two blocks from school. Not seeing them, I walked toward the exit on N. Caroline Street, and there I saw my first soldier. He was talking to the principal. Rumors had already started that the soldiers were going to use the gymnasium to house prisoners. He must have been an officer, because he had a sidearm strapped to his hip, but he didn't look particularly menacing.

As I walked toward the park, I could see dozens of soldiers with fixed bayonets occupying it, and they did look menacing. Those of us who lived south of our school had no choice but to walk by them. The group of frightened students at the corner reminded me of penguins crowding the edge of the ice to see which would fall into the ocean first to appease the hungry leopard seal below. Except we crowded the edge of the curb to see who would fall into the sea of soldiers first.

Initially, I was just as afraid as the other students. But something about seeing soldiers lounging on our grass transformed my fear into anger. The only other time I had interacted with white soldiers had been on the plane we had taken from Columbus to Baltimore. One had taught me how to tie my shoe. Unfortunately, the large group of soldiers in the park temporarily dwarfed my memory of the helpful soldier on the plane. This was the largest gathering of white people I had ever seen in my neighborhood, and they were all armed. My neighborhood was America, and it had been invaded by foreigners. We had to do something about it.

I was truly American, because I swiftly transformed patriotic spirit into an entrepreneurial one. Since school had been canceled before lunch, most of the students still had their lunch money. I promised the crowd that if they could come up with twenty-five cents among them, I would confront the soldiers and tell them to leave. Not that they would listen to me, but here was an opportunity to tell the soldiers what I thought of them and earn money as well.

Our transaction had turned some of the students' fear into curiosity. We crossed the street en masse and moved deeper into the park, but I soon broke away from the group to challenge the soldiers. Most of the students still kept a safe distance, but I was followed by a boy named Runny. His name was a misnomer, for he walked with a permanent limp and was slightly developmentally delayed. Ever since his older sister, Cassy, had started junior high school, he tagged along with a different person every day. Someone always escorted him home. Today was my day. He limped by my side as we approached the soldiers. A slow child and a gay child were all that stood between our fictitious nation of East Baltimore and the hordes from white suburbia. I had learned from Jane that was where they came from.

I took my stand in front of the largest cluster of soldiers, numbering perhaps twenty and all of them white. I yelled, "Why are you here?"

Some of the soldiers looked at me with an expression that said they wondered the same thing. Unlike other wars, only a few National Guard units were deployed to combat duty in Vietnam. Rightly or wrongly, the perception was that many men had joined the Guard to avoid killing or being killed in a war they did not believe in. Instead they now faced their own hostile citizens. But the black inner city was just as foreign to them as a Southeast Asian jungle. For some my words struck deeper than I realized, but other than facial expressions I got no response.

I escalated. I spat at the ground at my feet and yelled at them to go back to suburbia where they belonged. My mispronunciation made suburbia sound like an Eastern European country instead of the ring around Baltimore. Runny, who was standing next to me and had even less experience with white people than I did, started yelling at them to go back on TV. They were totally unreal to him. Most of the soldiers laughed, but some expressed their chagrin by pulling nervously at the grass.

Once the soldiers had laughed, any reservoir of fear evaporated, and the other children felt free to cross the park. Since it fell to me to walk Runny home that day, I walked through the center of the park. I saw two men who appeared to be the commanders. One of them had a map, presumably of Baltimore, draped over our water fountain. I overheard them talking about where they were going to deploy the troops. The ignorant, illiterate, partisan fighter in me thought this could not be good. I politely asked if he could move the map so I could take a drink. He barely got out of my way and held the map a few inches from the bowl of the fountain. The spray from the fountain was over calibrated. When I turned on the fountain the water overshot the bowl as it always did and got the map wet. I gave him an insincere apology and walked Runny home, smiling the whole way.

In retrospect I realize the military was much more civil than the police force would have been. The commander didn't seem particularly annoyed that I had drenched his map. As the hours, days and years progressed I would have more sympathy and respect for the National Guards. The National Guards had appeared out of nowhere and out of context, armed with bayonets. They didn't initially make a good first impression.

Later that day my impression started to change. My mother was making dinner, and she was missing some minor ingredients. The riots had prevented her from shopping. Our food supply was low but not exhausted. Making dinner had pushed the current events at our door out of her mind. She forgot there was a curfew. She put on her coat and told me to come to the store with her. I knew there was a curfew, but I depended on her to tell me when it was. My step-father was upstairs fixing something; otherwise he would have reminded her not to go out.

We walked to the end of our block to go to a store that was certainly not open. But we didn't get that far. As we turned the corner to go down N. Eden Street a soldier ordered us to halt. We were held at bayonet point. Current events returned to the forefront. We were in violation of curfew. He seemed just as shocked to see a woman with a child as we were to see a bayonet in our faces.

Seeing his young face as a child, I saw a grown man. Remembering his face over fifty years later, I saw a boy with a bayonet. He looked out of place in his uniform. With his rosy cheeks, it was almost as if one of Santa's elves had enlisted in the military. The young soldier probably hadn't shaved his face yet. He merely plucked a few hairs and splashed on some aftershave, the alcohol only stinging a few open pores. Furthermore, he didn't appear old enough to even drink alcohol. Nor was he old enough to vote. Men were dying in Vietnam who could not vote or drink. A few years later the Twenty Sixth Amendment would change that, but the amendment could not deliver maturity before it was due. The man was a boy, but he still had the gun.

After he told us to halt, he didn't really know what to do with a woman and a child. My mother pressed her advantage and assaulted him with the truth. She told him how she was not able to shop because of the rioting and that we were running out of food. The need to feed her family had caused her to momentarily forget there was a curfew. Rumor had it that if you were arrested after curfew your personal jewelry or watches were confiscated and dumped into a barrel, presumed to be looted items. Seconds into her story the bayonet dropped from our faces.

An unexpected maturity crossed his face as he said, "My uniform orders me to do one thing, my conscience another. I joined the Guard, so I didn't have to kill anyone. I really don't want to be here either."

He had no intention of arresting us. We went from being curfew breakers to a confessional for a soldier from suburbia.

He continued, "I just want you to know I don't believe all the lies that pass for our history. You have every right to be angry at us, and I have no right to tell you how to be angry. Just know that not all of us white people support this. Those of us who don't are not yet numerous enough to stop it."

My mother nodded and said, "I know that, but I can count on one hand the number of white people who have said what you just did and still have fingers left over. It's nice to finally meet another one in person, even if it was at gunpoint."

His gun suddenly became an embarrassment to him. The rose on his cheeks spread across his entire face. If he could have hid his gun behind his back, he would have. Not knowing what else to say, he bid us farewell by informing us that tonight the Department of Agriculture would be trucking in food and setting up three or four food distribution centers. One of the centers would be not more than fifty yards from where we stood, at the corner of N. Eden and E. Eager Streets. He told us to get there early, before they ran out of food.

That night we were reduced to eating cornbread and baked beans, which was not a hardship as I thoroughly enjoyed both. If we eventually had to eat cat food, this time it would at least be our cat's food, not some stranger's.

I wasn't going to tell my parents what I had done in the park, but the encounter with the boy soldier had emboldened me. I told them what I had done for our country by standing up to the invading soldiers from suburbia. Initially I stared into incredulous faces as I told my story. Then, without warning, they burst into laughter. I think they could not believe I had confronted armed white men. I really was in no danger, but they laughed at why I did it and my worldview. Then I embarrassed them by asking them why I didn't know what they thought I should know, if they didn't tell me.

Yes, the news on TV told me we were one country. History lessons would tell the same story, but I was not taught history yet. That would not happen until the sixth grade. Little everyday things hinted that we were one country, but the everyday big things yelled that we were not. I was a child; I listened to the big things. Talk was of unity, but the nation's actions were divisive. One nation under God was really one nation ignoring God.

Though I had been living in one my entire short life, a segregated nation was difficult to fathom. But beyond belief was the fact that some people wanted to take this poison to the afterlife. There were white people who thought they would still able to use the word nigger in heaven and believed it would be segregated. Or if not, at the very least black people would be their servants there as well. I was leery of a heaven where one man's reward was the servitude of another, or the promised servitude of virgins or any of the other bigotries that plagued the Earth. I was very leery of people who wanted to continue their hate in the afterlife.

My parents gave us their version of the State of the Union Address. They used a lot of big words I didn't understand and left out a lot. But after two more helpings of cornbread and baked beans the image of the nation I lived in became clearer. How much of that information Peanut and Gwen understood I don't know? I myself don't remember some of the particulars, but all the big things that screamed we were two countries made sense. I was not wrong. The emperor was not wearing any clothes. I was relieved that my perception was right, but I was also sad that it was. We were two nations pretending to be one. I was a child; I understood pretending. Also, what I learned that night frightened and angered me.

Many people made up alternate realities to justify their deeds. I had listened to my parents accurately describe the gossamer lies that white people told themselves every day. I would find no flaws in what my parents said that night, exception to be sure but no flaws. More white people have since confirmed my parent's assessment than not. But it wasn't just white people. They just happened to be the most powerful people lying to themselves. What was glaringly absent from my parent's narrative was a proper assessment of the alternate reality they had created to cover my stepfather's poor behavior. They also were lying to themselves. Over the years I would learn that someone could dissect with great precision the flawed alternative realities of others while remaining completely unaware of their own.

I didn't know who I wanted to be or where I was going. But I now knew where the obstacles were. Before becoming an adult, I would first have to confront an oblivious, cruel stepfather and an equally oblivious and cruel nation. Soon I would learn how cruel both could be.

CHAPTER 36   ADDICTED TO SUPREMACY

Baltimore's schools were opened the next day, but from what I heard later, only the children who had no food at home went to school that day. As most of the stores had been burned or looted, schools that had cafeterias were the only sources of food in many neighborhoods. Neither I, nor my sisters went to school that day. Per the soldier's instructions from last night, my sisters, mother and I got up early and were among the first twenty people in line at the food distribution center. Initially the line was not too long, because someone had started a rumor that the food was old and had come from fallout shelters. We received one grocery bag with bags of noodles and rice, some cans of stew, one tin can of grape jelly and one jar of peanut butter. I had never seen jelly or peanut butter in a can. Bread was the only perishable item handed out, and we were among the few who received a loaf before they ran out. Then all the food ran out.

After returning home and putting the food away, our mother instructed us to change out of our play clothes and into our school clothes. We had been kept out of school because Tuesday April 9, 1968 was the day of Martin Luther King Jr.'s funeral. Oddly enough, he was being buried on the same day that General Lee had surrendered to General Grant at Appomattox over a hundred years earlier. The death of Martin Luther King Jr. was a reminder that the Civil War was still raging.

My sisters and I had found two bodies in the street but had never been to an actual funeral. Although the event was only televised, our parents insisted we had to wear our best clothes. After seeing us in our school clothes our mother decided they were not good enough. We had to change again, this time into our Easter clothes. Our dining room chairs acted as our pews as we sat reverently in front of the TV. I was young enough that funerals were still boring, fidgeting events that I had no emotional attachment to, and I had no concept of the importance of the event.

Sad to say but my most prominent thought during the funeral was, "When will this be over so I can go outside to play?" No matter how deeply I dig through my memories, I can recover nothing but snippets of the event. For some reason I distinctly remember Wilt Chamberlain and Jackie Kennedy entering the church. When a veiled Coretta Scott King entered the church Peanut starting crying. Perhaps I was witnessing the birth of her empathy. Peanut cried not for Mrs. King's loss, but for the fact that she had to walk through a crowd of people who were all staring at her sympathetically. Sympathy is certainly welcomed at times such as this, but to endure so much of it in such a short amount of time can overwhelm a person. Perhaps the mask Mrs. King wore under her veil offered her a hidden sanctuary away from the peering eyes of the crowd.

Two months later I added a false memory to the funeral. False, in the sense that I did not view the funeral this way at the time. Future events compelled me to add an addendum to the memory of the funeral. The memory is false, but the addendum proved to be true. I would view the event as "The Funeral of the Three Widows" for in attendance were Jackie Kennedy, Coretta Scott King and Ethel Kennedy. Widow of the past, widow of the present and widow of the near future. The addendum became the stronger memory.

Others had their own view. A coincidence can be so compelling it takes on a life of its own. Shortly after the death of Robert Kennedy, rumors ran that the clan was sending their followers a secret message through murder, because the first initial of the three slain men's last names spelled out KKK. So much promise had been murdered in the sixties that any far-fetched rumor seemed possible.

Nearly fifty years later I would sit in the pews of Ebenezer Baptist Church, which by then had become a National Historic Park and cry delayed tears. I had witnessed events that needed to be mourned but lacked the maturity to do so at the time. After the death toll from the AIDS epidemic and the ravages of time took their toll among my friends and family, I was able to cry at the place where I witnessed my first funeral. I was thankful I had grown past my stepfather and men such as him and could cry in peace without them telling me to wipe that nonsense out of my eyes.

On Wednesday, we returned to school. The few soldiers we saw had guns, but none had fixed bayonets. Many businesses also opened, including the city's seven public markets. As the police had set up a command post in Belair Market, which was our public market, it was not looted or damaged at all.

A food store was not the first store I set foot in. There were only four days until Easter. We were not churchgoers but had to dress the part, because that is what you did on Easter in East Baltimore. After getting out of school a trip to the barber was in order, and the shop was filled to capacity. Most men were there to shoot the breeze, which was a more masculine name for men gossiping.

Despite the crowd, I immediately noticed Mister Willy seated comfortably next to my barber. He looked as if he had already had his hair cut. He wasn't staying so much to shoot the breeze as to chuckle at it. Mister Willy found it amusing that men sat around talking about solving the world's problems when many of them had yet to solve any of their own. His silence was his credentials. He rarely spoke, so when he did his words were deemed extremely important.

Occasionally some foolish man would try to sway the unbiased Mister Willy to their cause in an argument, but he generally stayed in his own camp. He didn't argue with people, especially about politics, because they often initially baited their trap with civil discourse, only to spring the trap of ignorance and aggression moments later. Experience would teach me that the world is full of strong personalities who defend weak positions. Mister Willy already knew this and didn't want the responsibility or the headache of trying to change other's opinions. He claimed that most people's opinions were bigger than their facts, and his trading facts for their opinions, pearls for pennies was not a fair exchange rate. Closed minds generally have already decided what their ears and eyes will hear and see.

When I started paying attention to the conversation, it was mostly talk of the troops leaving. Few of those present wanted to return to business as usual. Certainly, the return of commerce would be welcomed, but gone were the days of waiting for white America to stingily grant us our civil rights in small stipends over centuries. No longer would we beg for permission to breathe; no more explaining ourselves because good behavior does not have to explain itself to bad behavior. Patience was no longer a virtue. It had become a vice that kept us in place.

Many of the older men had done the most radical thing they could, which was to move North, but now there was nowhere else to go. The younger generation had no choice but to move a nation. One of the younger men had gone too far and insinuated the radical moves of the past were not that daring. He belittled the past and questioned how moving up North had been an improvement.

The older men grew silent and in unison turned toward Mister Willy. Of those present, he was the senior veteran of the sorrow wars of the South. After an uncomfortable pause the owner of the barbershop asked, "Mister Willy, why did you move North?"

He had never told me why he had come to Baltimore, but current events would flesh out his story. I hoped it wasn't my turn to get my hair cut during the telling. Mister Willy had my undivided attention, and I didn't want the barber turning the chair or my head away from him. A clipped ear or a jagged haircut would be worth the price.

For a moment, Mister Willy's rough hands began rubbing and sanding the smooth arms of his wooden chair. In his home he was a rather communicative person, but in the barbershop, he was mostly a listener. He was stalling, searching for the shortest possible answer.

When he finally spoke, he didn't give a detailed answer. "I left the fire for the frying pan, because the pan was a tad cooler."

Most of the men who had left the South nodded in agreement. They all had stories they could tell, but one would suffice, and that was Mister Willy's.

The owner pressed Mister Willy and said, "This young man's barely new to the world and still wet from the journey; he needs a slap on the behind to let him know what world he's in."

Mister Willy laughed and replied, "I am not much of a midwife."

But the fact that he used the term midwife announced that he was already journeying back in time. Although Mister Willy had never lost his Southern accent, it deepened as his memory returned him to the South. His speech was slow and deliberate. Each word did several slow laps around his tongue before being released into the world.

He continued, "Can't say it seems like yesterday since I first came up North but more like yesterday's great grandfather. It was a piece of time ago at any rate."

His words grabbed our ears and pulled us down South, especially those of us who had never been. Details of exactly when and where have faded from my memory, but it was somewhere in North Carolina just before World War Two.

One of the local white women, who years ago had been driven out of town by cold shoulders and gossip, had returned to attend her mother's funeral. Apparently, the cold shoulders and gossip had driven her into the arms of a man from Philadelphia who had managed to retain and expand his wealth through the Great Depression.

He worshipped his wife with money. If her husband even thought, she wanted it, she would have three types of it before sunset. The rumor mill had it he was going to buy the only mill in town for her, which employed nearly everyone in town, then close it out of spite. According to Mister Willy, the only spiteful intention she had was to toss the shoes on her feet and the tires on her car into the trash upon returning to Philadelphia. They had tread on the soil of her past, and she had no intentions of bringing that dirt back to her future.

She remembered Mister Willy because he had known her mother but mostly because he had been the only one to tell her she would do well just before she took the train North. He had not meant it to be a prophecy, but it was obvious to him that just leaving would be the improvement. Nevertheless, his words were a good omen, which she held onto until she made it come true.

As he always said, "I don't love everyone, but I do mean everyone well."

In a sea of discouragement, she never forgot his island of encouragement. She remembered everything about him. If he had not attended the wake, she surely would have sent for him. When he appeared at the back door to pay his respects to her mother, against custom she invited Mister Willy into the kitchen, abandoned the other mourners in the parlor and served him tea with her own hands.

She profusely thanked him for seeing a future she could not. At the end of the conversation, against custom she gave Mister Willy a long, thankful hug.

Before leaving the kitchen and returning to attend to the mourners, he heard her whisper sweetly but firmly to her husband, "You do something really nice for him."

Mister Willy was very leery of anything free, because often free could swiftly become very expensive. Graciously receiving a burdensome gift often makes the recipient the charitable one. But there was no gracious way to decline a gift from a man who could buy an entire mill. His refusal would be an affront to the man's wife. Mister Willy liked the man and realized he had nothing but good intentions and would allow him to shine in front of his wife. But when he suggested that Mister Willy get a seeing-eye dog, inwardly he balked at the idea. After all these years he really didn't need one. It would be just one more mouth to feed in a house where he ate all the table scraps himself and picked a bone cleaner than any dog could. The man cut off that argument by offering him a small monthly stipend to help feed the dog. Small being a relative term, so much money was left over from the stipend that Mister Willy had to change banks. Instead of keeping his savings in a rolled-up sock, he moved it to an old cigar box.

Not really needing a seeing-eye dog, he admitted initially accepting her for all the wrong reasons, helping a powerful man save face and for personal financial gain. But after spending a couple weeks training with the dog in New Jersey, which at the time had the only guide dog schools in the country, he grew extremely attached to her. Although the German Shepherd was a female, he changed her name to Moses, finding that name to be better suited for a dog trained to guide him through life. It was not advisable to change the name of the dog, but she really was more of a companion.

Mister Willy's and Moses's return was like the circus coming to town. Everyone wanted to see the root doctor who had taught a dog to see for him. This foolish rumor only added to his credentials. Despite his celebrity status, Southern hospitality and hostility still applied. Though the Americans with Disabilities Act was fifty years in the future, most businesses in town that served coloreds allowed Moses to enter as well. In fact, if unaccompanied Moses probably could have entered some businesses that Mister Willy could not. Mister Willy unconsciously taught Moses the rules of segregation. Neither he nor she could read the "Whites Only" signs, but both could feel them.

He didn't need Moses, but he grew to want her. She barked instead of talked, which in his book made her company preferable to that of most humans. Because of the monthly stipend he journeyed into town more often. He lived over a mile outside of town and half of that mile was unpaved. Until the arrival of Moses, all of it was lonely. Mister Willy didn't know if Moses made the journey faster or if her company made it seem so. Stipend day was their big shopping day. Moses would get butcher scraps and canned dog food. Mister Willy bought taffy and an ice cream cone for himself. Even after paying to have the groceries delivered and buying himself and Moses a few luxuries, he still had extra money.

It wasn't long before Mister Willy and Moses became a common sight on the road. Occasionally, a passerby would offer him a ride. With the exception of being caught in a sudden cloud burst, he generally refused their offers. He loved his time on the road with Moses. So, when the truck behind him paced him, he already had his polite refusal in his mouth. But no hail came from the truck. The truck was stalking him.

He had been careful not to tell anyone about the money. But he had not been silent in all the ways he needed to be. His extra trips into town had spelled it out for anyone paying attention. He had extra money. Sensing what was coming, he pulled the money from his pocket. He had been robbed before and didn't want to suffer the additional indignity of having his person searched. Fortunately, Moses had been trained not to react. She was not a guard dog, but just in case, he wanted to make it appear as if this was a normal transaction. Maybe in her canine mind she would wonder why he was giving money to someone and getting nothing in return. But it would be best for them both if this went as swiftly as possible.

The sport in their voices told him otherwise. They were going to toy with him. These were the type of men who had sold their soul to the lowest bidders, fear and hate. Being born in a "Whites Only" hospital was all they had going for them. They clung tenuously to the lowest rung of white society and needed their daily dose of "I'm better than somebody." It was Mister Willy's turn today.

Pulling in front of him to block his path, two men got out of the truck while the driver remained inside and goaded them on. Mister Willy handed one of them the money, but the man tossed it into the air. He could hear the money carried off by the wind. They didn't want his money. They just didn't want him to have it. In their minds, Mister Willy had inadvertently risen above them. White men in the South could turn very violent when what was once their floor suddenly became their ceiling. In the land of opportunity, black people were killed every day for doing better. For us, advancement was a crime. The men taunted him with every invective and pejorative America's caste system had to offer.

Similar to Moses, Mister Willy had been trained not to react. He would stay still and look down until the men spent their anger or moved on to their next insecurity. This was one of the first rules black people learned in obedience school.

He waited in his own personal darkness, anticipating when and where the blows would land. The man with the most venom in his voice stripped him of his sunglasses and crushed them with his foot, claiming Mister Willy was looking him in the eye. Then he snatched the white cane and tossed it a few feet behind Mister Willy. He laughed, claiming the nigger tried to hit him with it. Knowing full well the laws of the state would uphold every evil deed perpetrated against a black man, their taunts were as ridiculous as they could make them.

These men were manipulating the justice system, testing white supremacy to see the lengths it would go to uphold the rights of the lowliest white person. From their point of view, this was the beauty of Jim Crow. Not only did they get to keep black people in their place, but they could drag the white elite down into their filth as well. The system encouraged the ignorant and cruel to be bold and allowed uneducated men to manipulate educated men into pretending a blind black man looked a white man in the eye, or that he threatened one with a flimsy white cane.

The man harassing Mister Willy was a true disciple of the gospel that no black person should have better than a white person. Mister Willy tensed up when the man questioned why he had a seeing-eye dog when no white, blind person in the county had one. He wanted to explain complexities of the relation between a guide dog and its companion. They had to be taught how to work together. Without this training, Moses would be of no use to her new owner. He tightened his grip on her harness, determined that no matter how bad he was beaten, he would not let them steal her.

He mistakenly had attributed too much humanity to these men. As with the money, they didn't want to give Moses to a blind, white person. They just didn't want him to have her. Out of nowhere he heard a loud boom. Moses yelped, collapsed and pulled Mister Willy to the ground with her. The nothing of a man laughed and returned to the truck. They sped off, tires kicking dust onto Mister Willy and a dying Moses.

One moment she was a guide dog, doing her job. Then suddenly she was a victim of Jim Crow. Mister Willy remained on the ground with her, knowing full well that only he would be rising from it. She was whimpering and wheezing while large amounts of blood spilled from her, turning the dirt around her into mud. All he could do was make sure she would not be alone when she died. Moses said her final goodbye the only way a dog could. Before fading away she licked Mister Willy's hand, and with her last breath took in his scent. She was not parting this world without it. Then she was gone.

Tears built up behind his closed eyelids. Eventually trauma and sorrow pried his lids open. Crying was insufficient to release all the emotions he felt. He roared and pounded his fist into the bloody mud and wished he had the throat of each man in his hands so that he could snuff the life out of them. Mister Willy claimed he never before nor since has hated anyone as much as he hated those men.

He had to leave Moses's body unattended as he crawled on all fours searching the side of the road for his cane. Once he found it, although he was closer to his house than to town, he chose to go to town. There were people there who would help him bury Moses. She deserved more than to be left as carrion beside a road.

Bringing charges against these men in court could expose him to more violence. But that was not what concerned him. When white jurors walked into a courtroom in the South at that time, they wiped their feet on the doormat, leaving all truth and fact outside the courtroom. White men could convince a white jury that a seeing eye dog tried to viciously attack them and that she needed to be put down. He didn't have the strength to listen to these men slander her good nature.

As was the case with the Moses of the Old Testament, the Moses of the Jim Crow South didn't make it to the Promised Land. The next day he took the remainder of the stipend and caught a train to Philadelphia, but when the train stopped in Baltimore, he decided to get off there instead.

When he finished telling the story, I was emotionally still in the field with him holding Moses. Somehow, I thought I could go back in time to rescue a dog that had been killed almost thirty years ago. I was no stranger to the cruel ways of men, but this was so disturbing. I wondered how people got that way. Was it a disease? Could I catch it? Was there a cure?

When I came back to the conversation, I noticed the older men were all just shaking their heads in shame. They had witnessed so much that over time their expression of sadness had evolved into a simple headshake. What else could they do but shake their heads and move on, and that is what millions did. They left the South for opportunity as well, but the main reason was the oppressive caste system.

The urban centers of the North may have been crime-ridden, but there you suffered at the hands of criminals or insane people. In the South you could become the victim of insecure, law abiding citizens. Any white person who was having a bad day could take it out on any random black person and get away with it. Jim Crow gave them permission to do immoral things while still obeying the law.

I was years away from seeing my first real Confederate flag. But every time I would see one, I would envision Mister Willy kneeling in mud made from blood. The flag is a proud symbol of denial or an honest statement of "We don't care."

"I wish I was in the land of Cotton, Old times there are not forgotten; Look away! Look away! Look away! Dixie Land," and they continued to look away from all their dirty deeds.

For me, Mister Willy's experience epitomized the evils of racism. The young man who had instigated Mister Willy into telling the story had been humbled. He took a much more deferential stance to the deeds of the migrants. He politely thanked them for leaving the South, so he and others didn't have to, in essence freeing the younger generation to perform other deeds. Migrating up North had been a temporary reprieve. A less obvious and virulent form of racism awaited them in the North. It was a slap instead of a punch, but it was still an assault.

At the time, all but one of the heavily populated black cities of the North were governed by white mayors. The Promised Land had become our prisons, the mayors our wardens and the suburbs around us the guard towers. There were sprinklings of black people in the suburbs, but for the most part we were trapped in cities. If passed, the Fair Housing Act would disarm the prison guards surrounding us.

I have heard the riots of 1968 called everything but what they really were. It was black America breaking out of prison. Had it not been for the riots, the 1968 Civil Rights Act would possibly have been defeated or heavily diluted. Most of the bill dealt with Native American civil rights. But the fair housing portion was the anchor keeping it from going forward. There was floundering support for that portion of the bill from both parties. It was teetering on the morning of April 4th. Most of white America cherished their right to discriminate and was comfortable with the status quo. There was no reaching their conscience.

Congress didn't find its conscience. They found their fear. Some say President Johnson leveraged that fear to get the bill passed. Members of the Senate and Congress could literally see the smoke of black discontent rising all around them, as the capital was on fire. Not since the British had burned the capital during the War of 1812 had Washington seen so much destruction. Troops were posted around the White House, a machine gun nest was posted on the steps of the capital building, and an increasingly unpopular war was going badly in Vietnam. Something had to be done. The last portion of the bill, Title X, later known as the Anti-Riot Act, helped make a bitter pill merely tart. Both houses swallowed, passed the bill, and Johnson signed it April 11, 1968.

In a one-week period roughly spanning Holy Week, I began my lesson on what it was like to be black in America. My eyes were starting to open, but I had to learn to trust them. I would grow up in a nation that would constantly tell me I didn't see what I saw. One of us was a liar, and it wasn't me.

Over time I would discover glaring omissions and start to question the vision of others. I was a student in a nearly all white elementary school when I first opened a history book. Very few black people were mentioned by name, and only four or five paragraphs mentioned us at all. I would come to realize that much of what personally influenced my life was on the missing pages from American history. White historians had written our portion of our common history in their books with an eraser. But we were not to be written out, written over, or written off. Something stronger than paper would be needed to bear our story. We wrote our story on the soul of America. America was not America without us.

CHAPTER 37   LITTLE FEET IN BIG SHOES

One of the young men waiting his turn to receive his hair cut asked Mister Willy, "Whatever happened to the men who killed Moses?" Doubtful expressions on all the older men's faces claimed it was a ridiculous question. The answer was nothing of course. Mister Willy disagreed. Though he never returned to that town, he still had ears there, and knew no white man laid a hand on them. But none of them returned from World War Two. All three had died at the hands of Imperial Japanese soldiers.

Our barbershop was an informal classroom. Talk soon changed to the current war in Asia. Very little news of the racial tension going on in Vietnam reached the media at the time. But it was coming home to us in letters and occasional phone calls from our soldiers. As was the case in America, some white soldiers in Vietnam cheered the assassination of Dr. King. Others stooped to writing graffiti on walls that read, "I'd rather kill a Spook than a Gook." Some Southerners had taken cross burning from the Southeastern United States to Southeast Asia.

America had already brought with them the seeds of its defeat to Vietnam. During World War Two, black Americans supported the Double V campaign, which started from a letter to the Pittsburgh Courier from James G. Thompson, "Should I Sacrifice to Live 'Half American'?" The Double V campaign stood for victory over fascism abroad and racism at home. Victory over Japan Day, better known as V-J Day, brought an end to the foreign conflict, while the domestic war raged on.

A growing number of black soldiers in Vietnam couldn't care less about a double victory; the real enemies of democracy were their fellow soldiers and citizens back home in America. Only the victory at home mattered. America brought its domestic problems to its foreign wars. There would be no V-V Day, Victory in Vietnam

Day. The war in Vietnam was a lost cause for greater reasons than racial tension, but it was a factor. If unchecked, it could become a problem in future conflicts.

Race riots on bases and on ships indeed did become a problem. Additionally, black enlisted personnel would become a larger percentage of the military over the next decade. They would not tolerate poor treatment, and they had guns. Intentional friendly fire could become a problem. Something had to be done. Over the next couple of decades America's military surged ahead of its civilian population. It certainly did not eradicate racism within its ranks, but it at least had more incentive to address the issue.

Conversation at the barbershop was a great source of information, but it left holes in my education, and one subject rarely talked about was slavery. It was referred to or referenced in storytelling for sure. But barbershop talk generally referred to personal experience. There were plenty of men who could crow on about Jim Crow, but rarely a peep could be heard about slavery. Those who had personal experience with the institution were long gone, but most of us were familiar with its legacy.

It would be Mrs. Kidman who taught me and my classmates about slavery in America. The next day was a week after Martin Luther King Jr. had been assassinated and three days before the anniversary of the assassination of Abraham Lincoln. Before the lying history books got a hold of us, she had given us a sample of the truth. By the time I opened a history book three years later, I already knew what was missing.

If I thought about slavery at all, it was biblical and remote, slave owning pharaohs, not slave owning presidents. She made it close and personal. Slavery was only three generations back for me. Someone I knew and loved had actually spoken to a slave. My grandmother's father was one, and I knew his name.

Mrs. Kidman didn't go into the beatings and torture; that would have been too much for third graders. Nor did she talk about the lack of freedom as we knew it, because as children we were under our parent's thumbs and had very little freedom ourselves. She explained that slavery took away all but a few choices: slave on, run off, or fight and die. Even under my parents I lived in a choice-rich world. There would be times in life when I had a barrel full of good choices but would dig all the way to the bottom for a bad one. But I could not imagine a world in which all the choices were bad.

Worse was separation of family members who had been traded for paper or shiny metal. The great separator, death, claimed family members more often than the auction block, but death took them to oblivion or a better life. The auction block left no doubt: downriver was never better. Individuals were gouged from their families, which left deep canyons in everyone's souls.

As much as my sisters got on my nerves at times, I couldn't imagine coming home and not finding them there or being taken for a ride from which I would not return. This really upset me and made slavery personal. But I also wondered what type of people could do that. America eventually evolved to the point where her missing children would appear on milk cartons with a reward for their return instead of on advertisements with a price for their sale.

On some level it amazed me that people could hold dear that which was most destructive to them. This behavior reminded me of when I held the icicle in my bare hands, pretending it was a magic wand. Despite the pain, I would not let go of its beauty and pretend power. But I was a young child. Far too often when reason compels adults to release something painful, instead they hold on tighter. Slave owners would not let go of their power over the people they had reduced to chattel. Lincoln ended slavery with the help of two millions troops, over a third of whom were foreign-born or black. Hundreds of thousands died, and a third of the nation was in ruins.

Years later, some would pick Lincoln's bones clean of any meat of morality, claiming he really wasn't all that anti-slavery. I could never join this camp. He had his flaws and certainly had the racial views of his day, but I judged not his words but his deeds. Nor did I put much credence into what someone a hundred years later thought he thought. His Emancipation Proclamation may have been a military move as much as a moral one and only freed some slaves, but his avid support of the Thirteenth Amendment freed them all.

Mrs. Kidman taught us that the great men and women of the past would appear backward or ordinary by today's standards. She presented us with an example. The first person to harness fire was a hero of their day. Today we just strike a match or flip a switch if we want light. Light was a dear thing in Lincoln's time, dim by today's standards but still light. Dim as it may have been, someone felt they had to put it out.

It was becoming clear that anyone who advanced the cause of black freedom could be killed. Both leaders had been killed by men who were angry at an ever-changing world. They hurled words and shot bullets at a future they could not stop. King's assassin was still at large. But Lincoln's assassin was safely buried a few blocks away at Green Mount Cemetery.

One of my classmates raised her hand for permission to speak and said she had been to the grave of John Wilkes Booth to place a penny on his grave. Mrs. Kidman explained that it was the custom in some cultures to leave a stone on a grave. There were varying reasons for this custom, honoring the dead, keeping evil spirits from the grave, or keeping the spirit of the deceased from rising and roaming the Earth. In East Baltimore, the custom had evolved into placing only pennies on Booth's grave. What better sentinel above a grave than a copper portrait of the person murdered by the one interred?

Mrs. Kidman's lesson stayed with me until lunchtime. But there was only one thing I could take action on. My overactive imagination ran wild, and I was convinced that Booth's spirit had escaped his grave to become the assassin of Martin Luther King Jr. In my mind John Wilkes Booth and James Earl Ray were the same person. He had been an actor in life and played the role of many people. I was certain he could also do so in death. Since Ray had not yet been captured, my money was on Ray hiding in Booth's grave.

Convinced that not enough pennies had been left at Booth's headstone to keep the assassin in his grave, I literally wanted to put money on it. I planned on taking the coins out of my penny loafers to place on Booth's headstone to keep him entombed. Since the stores in my three-block area were still closed from the riot, I still had dare money left over from when the students had paid me to taunt the white soldiers. I approached the girl in my class who had been to Booth's grave and said I would pay her if she would take me there. She said, "No."

At times I thought I was bigger than I was, but I also knew when I needed help. I couldn't read and was afraid to go to the cemetery by myself. In the cafeteria I usually would sit with my classmates, but that day I needed courage and brain. Without hesitation I approached Jane's table, because she could read and probably knew where Booth's grave was. She seemed to know everything.

Ignoring everyone else at her table and without preamble, I told Jane I would give her ten cents if she would take me to Booth's grave. I had correctly assumed she knew where it was. In addition, she also knew what I wanted to do, but she wanted to know why.

Explaining my idea to someone else also clarified it for me. I wanted to make sure no one else was ever assassinated again. We were of the age when we dwelled in the land between education and superstition. Schools in East Baltimore were poor, but the stories we heard every day were rich. Neither Jane nor anyone else at the table ridiculed me. She was also decent enough to tell me my pennies probably would not be necessary, because this Easter Sunday was the anniversary of Lincoln being shot and there would be plenty of pennies on the grave. However, I had the innocent arrogance of a child and knew it would be my pennies that would keep the assassin forever in his grave. Had I known that Booth had been buried three times, my urgency would have been greater.

Jane would take my dime and Booth my pennies. She explained

to me that for some reason it would be easier for us to get into the cemetery the next day, which was Good Friday. Since we had the day off, we agreed to meet midmorning at the corner of E. Biddle and N Eden. One of her stipulations was that I had to fork over another dime to Robert, the boy I almost had a fight with at school. She wanted him along because there was a rough patch near my old school, Johnston Square Elementary, that could be a problem, and we had to walk by it.

On the morning of Good Friday, I rose with a purpose. It was easy enough to ditch my sisters and sneak out of the house wearing penny loafers. But somehow Willa had heard something was going on. She was sitting on our stoop when I opened the door. I didn't want her to come along or say anything. She refused my offer of a nickel to go away and keep her mouth shut, because today she was, 'I'm a tell'. She wanted to see what was happening in the cemetery and was going to report everything she saw. There was no getting rid of her. When I showed up with her unannounced, my unspoken thought was we had safety in numbers, against the living and the dead.

This was my first real adventure away from my three-block world unsupervised by an adult. Our group had everybody I thought we needed and then some. Jane had the brains, Robert the force, Willa was the unwanted, embedded journalist, and I had the venture capital. I thought my dimes and pennies were going to save the world.

There was a slight incident as we passed Johnston Square Elementary School, but Robert dealt with it with some severe facial expressions. No force was necessary. Soon after we came upon the entrance to Green Mount Cemetery.

Whoever designed the entrance to the cemetery must have been indecisive. The architectural features of the gate were equal portions fortress and church. Despite its resemblance to a church, the blend of Tudor and Gothic lent it an aura of foreboding. Built from dark granite from the bowels of the earth, the gate would be the perfect grand entrance for the second coming of Satan. The sight of it doubled the chill in the air.

A revelation occurred to me. This would be my first time going to a cemetery, and I could taste the misgivings roiling the contents of my stomach. I pulled an open hand down my face to squeegee away the fear openly displayed there.

My gesture had been too late. Jane had spotted my emotion and said something that greatly diminished my fear of cemeteries, "Don't be a fool. If you see someone come back from the dead, instead of running you better go up to them and ask how they came back. That's a secret you might want to hear."

A smile came to my face as I heard Mister Willy in my head. He was fond of saying, "I don't mind dying. I just don't want to stay dead."

In my head, his words were accompanied by a tinny piano, tambourines and a gospel choir. The refrain of the song in essence spelled out the desire of mankind. We don't want to stay dead. The appropriateness of having those words run through my head on Good Friday in front of a cemetery was lost to me at the time.

Robert interrupted the song in my head. "Well if you see someone rise from the dead you ask them for me. I'm staying here. I will walk you back home, but I am not going in there, not with all those dead white people in there."

Segregation applied to Americas' dead as well, a practice both sad and laughable, as if the color of one's skin mattered to the cold earth. Many of our prominent people were buried in The City of the Dead for Colored People. Now called Mount Auburn Cemetery, it is located just south of Pigtown. Green Mount Cemetery was the final resting place for many of Baltimore's prominent or notorious white citizens, including Booth and two of his co-conspirators, eight Confederate generals and hundreds of Confederate soldiers.

One of those Confederate soldiers had patented the Ouija Board. In 1968 Elijah J. Bond rested in an unmarked grave. He happened to have died in 1921, on the anniversary of the assassination of Lincoln. Later, at the turn of the next century, a marker with an image of the Ouija Board etched on its back was erected in his memory. Had the image of a tombstone in the shape of a Ouija Board greeted me at the cemetery, I don't think I would have had the fortitude to enter a graveyard containing the remains of a small portion of the Confederate Army and men who had plotted to kill Lincoln. It helped that the long dead Confederate Army, assassins, and Baltimore's prominent white citizens were now an island of dead white people surrounded by a sea of black life.

The dime I spent for Jane's help was well worth it. It had not occurred to me that children could not randomly roam one of Baltimore's finest treasures. She had provided an adult to escort us to Booth's grave. Jane introduced a rather nondescript man as her uncle. His name was Isley. The most distinguishing thing about him was his teeth, which were the color of the dingy, white walls in the home of a heavy smoker. I gathered that he worked for the cemetery in some capacity.

Robert overcame his fear at the sight of an adult escort and entered the cemetery. Instead of taking us directly to Booth's grave, Isley lead us up a slight hill to the Mortuary Chapel to partake in prayer or to enjoy the view of downtown Baltimore. He left the choice up to each individual.

While I had expected to feel fear, I was in awe. Not only did white people live well, they died well. Green Mount Cemetery was a grand outdoor museum. Up until that point I had not been in a place with so much art. For that was what the chapel and headstones were, true works of art. Chubby white children carved in stone, patina'd statues of angels, carved stone columns and vessels were in abundance. My pencil put to paper was not the equal to the stonecutter's chisel put to marble. Many partially unfurled marble scrolls had beautiful script forever carved into them. But most noticeable of all, the dead had manicured lawns, whereas we the living had only stoops.

Willa was taking notes with her eyes, which were bugged in awe from all they beheld. Robert was trying not to be impressed but he was. Jane had probably been here several times. Her awe was understated and focused on small details instead of the grand whole.

Green Mount Cemetery almost made death seem appealing. The grounds around the chapel were fit for royalty. Isley told us at one point the abdicated King Edward VIII and his wife, Wallis Simpson the Duchess of Windsor, had plans to be buried near the Duchess's father, who was interred not too far from the chapel. Eventually, they would be permitted to be buried in Royal Burial Ground, Frogmore near Windsor Castle. They certainly would not have been slumming it if they had been buried here.

Despite its grandeur I was not here for kings. I was here for assassins. Isley led us down the hill on a short walk to the Booth family plot. As we walked, he told us the story of a twist of fate, or rather entwined fates. Whereas one Booth brother had killed a Lincoln another brother, famous actor Edwin Thomas Booth, had saved one. A few years before the president's assassination, Edwin had saved Lincoln's son, Robert Todd Lincoln, from a fall onto train tracks in Jersey City.

Still absorbing this story, we came to an obelisk with a carved relief of the face of someone who I assumed to be the patriarch of the family, Junius Brutus Booth. He had been named after one of the assassins of Julius Caesar. Perhaps the characteristics of a namesake had skipped a generation and a son had become an assassin instead of the father.

Not far from the obelisk I saw a small stone with a few face-up pennies atop it and assumed I had reached my destination. Isley swiftly deflated my hopes and explained to us that most people mistook the footstone of Booth's sister to be his grave. He could be buried there but most likely was not. Supposedly, no one at the cemetery knew exactly where in the family plot John Wilkes Booth was buried.

Immediately my overzealous imagination seized on the ignorance of the general population as the reason the assassin did not stay in his grave. But just in case I still took a penny out of my left loafer and placed it face down on the footstone. I explained to everyone present how I thought it foolish that Lincoln would have his back to his assassin as he had that night at the Ford Theatre. Isley had no expression, but Jane, Willa and Robert were children of East Baltimore and enthusiastically nodded their heads in agreement.

I was not aware that there was a tradition of placing a penny face down to show support for Booth. Regardless, both traditions had started over forty years after Lincoln's assassination. As his image had not been placed on the penny until 1909, the embittered defeated and the victors had long memories. The Civil War was still being waged with pennies.

I pulled a penny from my other loafer, holding it in my hand as if it were a divining rod searching for Booth's real grave instead of water. Jane and Willa were whispering behind my back. The whispering ended with a gentle tap on my shoulder. I don't know which one of them came up with the idea, but Jane was the one who spoke.

She asked, "Why don't you put your penny on the main gravestone for the whole family?"

Pointing her finger to the back of the obelisk she continued, "See, his name is right there."

I didn't see, because I couldn't read. I knew my letters, but they had not yet married to form words. I saw letters only, not words. Taking her word for it I nodded my head in agreement.

Isley corrected his niece by stating the obelisk was a memorial to the family, not a gravestone. Undeterred, I placed my penny face down on a ledge at the base of the obelisk. As I believed John was the only member of the family to rise, I felt the gesture would not be an affront to the other members of the Booth family. My penny was solely to thwart him.

Isley nodded his head and said, "Well, I have never seen anyone put a coin there."

Jane's uncle looked at the ground just below where I had placed my penny. He spoke to the dead and the living. Later I would learn that he had paraphrased Oscar Wild. "A cause is not necessarily true or righteous because a man dies for it. Men equally forfeit their lives for lies as truths."

He ended his statement with a sweeping hand gesture that encompassed the entire cemetery. As I watched him, I hoped never to die from a pointy end of a lie. The truth in his statement proved more frightening than the rise of Booth. A penny doesn't buy much, not even in a cemetery. The dead did not rise to assassinate the living. Fear and lies had far too many recruits among the living to bother with enlisting the help of the dead. I had placed a penny on an empty Pandora's box.

CHAPTER 38   HANGING MISTLETOE IN MAY

What I had not confessed to those gathered at the cemetery was the second, more prominent reason for placing my talisman on Booth's grave. Two weeks before King's assassination there was a domestic violence incident in my home that changed how I saw my situation. I was a week away from being nine years old, and emotions were emerging faster than I could process or adapt to them. My body was always an emotion behind. I had hands when I needed wings. I had feet when I needed claws. I had tears when I needed dry eyes. Then, for one brief moment I had clarity and saw a narrow path to adulthood.

I was up before the airing of Saturday morning cartoons. My sisters were still asleep. I was sitting in the armchair in the living room contemplating nothing in particular. I don't remember how it started. Both my parents were in the dining room. Without warning my stepfather had both his hands around my mother's throat, choking her.

Violence in our home had a rhythm, and sunrise incidents were rare. Mornings were for making excuses and hinting at apologizing for last night's deeds. I was totally caught off guard. His slowly constricting fingers left her no air to scream. All the pleading for him to stop came from her eyes. But the rage in his eyes drowned out the pleading in hers.

Had I had any fear in me it would have been that he would break her back before he strangled her. The pose was that of a tango dancer dipping his partner in a most violent manner. He contorted her body to match his twisted mood. But for some reason, I was not afraid. In these situations, fear had been my companion for so long that its absence actually briefly concerned me. But another emotion pushed past fear to make its debut that day: contempt. I felt nothing but contempt for him.

Despite being a fledgling emotion, it took flight within moments of its appearance and flew straight toward my stepfather. I did not yell or whimper. I calmly asked with the voice of a child but the demeanor of an adult, "What the hell are you doing?"

I am fairly certain it was the first I time I had used a curse word. If not, it was definitely the first time I had spoken it to an adult. He heard me and dropped my mother as if she was a bale of less than nothing. Her quilted pink housecoat didn't dampen the sound of her hitting the floor. The violence of her fall disturbed a warren of dust bunnies dwelling beneath a cabinet. She lay among them gasping for breath.

Expecting a transfer of violence to me, I braced myself. But as he walked toward me, he had a concerned expression on his face. He sat on the arm of the chair and draped his hand over my shoulder as if I were his pal instead of a child and rested his hand on my bicep. It took all my emotional fortitude not to shrug off the hand that was still warm from choking my mother. But every moment it rested on my upper arm was one more my mother had to breathe.

He was confiding in me, and more disturbing than his actions was what he said. "Grant, you don't understand. Your mother is like you kids. When she misbehaves, she needs to be disciplined once in a while."

Normally a person who couldn't hide emotions very well, I willed my flesh not to crawl. I sported a friendly, inquisitive expression to hide my deep sense of revulsion. Behind a hastily, cheaply built smile I was fighting the urge to throw up, because I knew he believed what he had just said down to the bone.

With his next statement he was inviting me to be just like him. "You will understand when you get older and have a wife of your own. That or be a faggot."

Beat your wife or be a faggot? Despite all I knew about that word it was no contest, I would be choosing faggot. The Stonewall riots would erupt a year later, but it would take decades to wash people's mouths out with soap and replace that word with gay. But to me faggot was still better than wife-beater. Having given me my choice, he got up and strolled toward my mother.

Before he could start choking her again, I asked him, "Who disciplines you when you misbehave?"

Laughing as if I had made a joke he said, "In this family no one disciplines me."

He turned away from my silly question, stepped over my mother as if she was nothing more than a dirty spot on the floor and disappeared upstairs. She shortly followed him upstairs to dress for her day. Normally her fashion choices for domestic violence consisted of sunglasses, scarves and cake makeup. Today the finger marks on her neck would require a turtleneck sweater.

That was the moment I really knew what I was dealing with. My world was far more complicated than the vocabulary I had to describe it. I knew the meanings of words before I heard of them, but my personal experience would make the real definitions sound too polite for what was really happening.

Misogyny was not just the hatred of women. It seemed the word was borrowed from another language by men to take the sting out of it. Why not say it in plain English, a woman hater. A justifiably bitter woman is called a man hater, not a misandrist. There was inequality in defining the term for the problem. Men who hated women had the flu. Women who hated men had influenza. The clarity I experienced that day is still my definition. There is a type of man that despises a woman he claims to love, makes her despise herself as well, then makes it all her fault. Perhaps the people who wrote dictionaries needed an introduction to my stepfather.

That was the day I realized I lived in a dangerous, destructive household. I had been since 1964, and below the surface I had always known it. I could only acknowledge it fully when I thought there was a way out. The only escape route was to become a functional adult. But to reach that goal I had to walk a path that was as much gauntlet as road, with as many striking hands as supporting ones. Whether gauntlet or road, it would be a long, laborious journey with no promise of reaching the end a healthy, functioning adult. At least I had the hopes of arriving to a reasonably healthy functional world.

For a brief moment I hoped my life as an adult would be better than my current circumstance. I wanted to live in a world where I didn't dread the way the key turned in the door at night, or find myself the victim of someone's bad mood, or be lectured to by someone who was so full of himself that he was empty.

My mother and sometimes my sisters and I poured appeasement, kindness, support and accolades into a vessel that resembled a pitcher but was in reality a drain. I never, ever wanted to empty myself again to fill someone who could never be filled. But my far-off destination was looking very similar to my home. America was in a bad way in 1968; it too was so full of itself it was empty.

Out of desperation I had put pennies on a grave. I would have hung mistletoe in May, captured sunlight in jars to release at night, or painted the world grey so there would be no disagreement. I was years away from learning it was far easier to change yourself than a rigid world. First, I had to adapt to the world to learn its ways, then with the help of others, try to change it.

None of my talismans would have worked. The year would only get worse for the nation, the world and me. It was against the laws of nature, but my future was looking past tense before it even came into being. Eventually that future would appear brighter again but only by comparison, because life at home grew darker.

The day after my stepfather had choked my mother, I heard Uncle Reggie tell Mister Willy that my stepfather had gotten into a fight in a drinking establishment that didn't obey the liquor laws of the state of Maryland. The place served alcohol until sunrise. That is why he was already up when I went downstairs that morning. He must have just gotten home.

According to Uncle Reggie, my stepfather had gotten into a fight with a fellow patron and the man had pulled a switchblade on him. Twisting the man around and putting him in a headlock, he took the man's switchblade away from him and stabbed him in the back. Fortunately, the blade caught on one of the bones of the man's spinal column, broke and didn't penetrate any deeper. Before he could choke the man to death or stab him again with the broken blade, some bystanders pulled him off the man. So, he came home to finish the fight.

Hearing about the previous night's events only further clarified whom I was dealing with. After the assassination happened my front door no longer opened to the sanctuary of the world. My first clue that my talisman on Booth's grave was not working occurred a week after Easter.

That Saturday in Madison Square Park was a perfect spring day. The sun had the sky to itself, not a cloud to be seen, and the temperature was in the mid-seventies. I was on my knees watching ants excavate their nest. Gwen was gathering dandelions to make a bouquet and Peanut was twirling herself in the sun. Just a little north of us a small herd of horses from the stables were illegally grazing in the grass. Among them was Queen Pinky.

Had I been aware of such things I would have noticed how the bucolic scene drastically clashed with the wall of brick homes and parked cars that surrounded the park. Suddenly the urban landscape intruded. Either a car had backfired, or a gun had been fired. The horses were used to urban sounds, but being unyoked from their wagons, they must have reverted back to their natural tendencies.

I looked up from observing the ants and saw a herd of horses stampeding toward me. As I was already on the ground, I did a quick roll under a nearby park bench. I watched as hooves trampled the excavated entrance to the ant colony. Through the passing hooves I could see Peanut hugging the ground behind a hedge. I also saw Gwen's bouquet of dandelions trampled by one of the hooves. I blew a sigh of relief into the dirt when I saw Gwen had run to the street and ducked down between two parked cars.

The horses were running to the safest place they knew, which was their stable near our house. I was pulling myself from under the bench when I heard a crash and a thud, followed by a screeching neigh that reached the highest range of my hearing and beyond.

When I arrived at the corner of N. Eden and E. Eager Streets, I saw Queen Pinky lying in the gutter. There was a large gash on her left haunch. Her neighing became a constant high-pitched whistle that entered my soul pleading for help. Averting my eyes from her bloody haunch, I tried and failed to make contact with her darting eyes.

For a moment she raised her head and looked my direction. I saw in her gaze, "If I can only stand, I will be alright."

She commanded her left rear leg to move, but the searing pain pushed the command back to her brain. Perhaps I was anthropomorphizing, but pain and survival were not just human characteristics. Whether it was man or animal, I would come to recognize when a being was trying one last time to cling to life. Queen Pinky pushed with her good legs, but they merely thrashed about. Her thrashing soon diminished to trembles and twitches. Her neighs became quivering lips and frothing at the mouth.

I wondered where her owner, Sam, was. Suddenly he appeared at her side, assessing her injuries and patting her neck and head. His cooing and whispering were the only pain relief she would receive. He made his goodbye short and sweet. Unbeknownst to me at the time, a long goodbye would be cruel and only prolong her pain. With one swift motion he stood and pulled a gun seemingly from nowhere and shot Queen Pinky just below where her glitter antlers used to rest. A bullet was the only veterinarian Sam could afford.

I had a flashback to seeing the Vietcong shot on TV two months earlier. Both were disturbing, but Queen Pinky's death was more so because I knew her. Although I no longer believed in Santa Claus and knew she was not really a reindeer, it was hard to watch a childhood fantasy being shot in the head right before my eyes.

My sisters and I started to cry. We had seen death all around us, but never had seen something or someone killed. We had also seen bullet holes in people. From the size and shape of the bullet hole, I wondered if Sam had been the one who shot the holes into the refrigerator my sisters had been trapped in. Maybe the man who shot his horse had saved my sisters.

Gwen went back to retrieve her trampled bouquet of dandelions and dropped it near Queen Pinky's head, away from the blood. After a few minutes a man showed up with a wagon pulled by one of her stable mates. He pulled a tarp from the wagon, and some of the stronger men among the bystanders rolled her on a tarp and lifted her onto the wagon.

I assumed she would be taken to a cemetery until someone in the crowd asked, "Do they still take horses to the glue factory these days?"

No one answered. I don't know why it bothered me that the earth lost its claim for her remains to the glue factory, but it did. Maybe it was because although I had seen death, with the exception of watching Dr. King's funeral on TV, I had not actually been to a funeral. The closest I would come to Queen Pinky's was watching some of the neighbors bring buckets of water to wash her blood down the gutter. Two buckets turned the gutter pink. Three more turned it black again.

My innocence would not die of old age; it was swiftly being killed by the events around me.

CHAPTER 39 GOD'S MOTHER TONGUE

Over the Easter break the janitorial staff must have gone all out. Upon entering the school on Monday, we were greeted by floors that shined and reflected more than ever before. Usually the students could see only dark outlines of themselves on the floors, but now they were practically mirrors. The windows were so clean that for a moment I thought they had been broken out during the riots. All of this was done for the woman who would be bringing the ballet to our school this coming Wednesday.

I must say I remembered Robert's performance during intermission better, but I did enjoy the dancing as well and was grateful the white woman had brought the dancers. But I still wrestled with my new image of white people. None of them had treated me as badly as my stepfather, to be sure. But everyone I loved and trusted avoided dealing with them whenever possible. With the exception of my aunt and the soldier on the plane who taught me how to tie my shoes, my interactions were polite but brief. Additionally, nearly all the white people I'd encountered had been wearing uniforms.

Although I had confronted the white soldiers with the bayonets, I now was leery of white people. I had had good encounters as well, but the killers of Mister Willy's dog had become their standard bearers. Avoiding them was easier than avoiding my stepfather. It wasn't as if every day white people with bayonets and lorgnettes marched into my neighborhood. My next encounter would be one of reluctant choice.

The day after the ballet performance I was walking home through the park when I caught a glimpse of a young pigeon. It was hiding in the same hedge where Peanut had taken refuge during the horse stampede. Pigeons do not nest in trees, so it had to have fallen from the ledge of a nearby house. Miraculously the poor thing had crossed the street into the park, avoiding cars, dogs, cats and rats. Its easy capture and wet mangy state should have been my first clue the bird would not survive. But the bird was a living creature, and I had to try. Queen Pinky's death was still fresh in my mind, and it seemed as if no one had tried with her.

I ran the rest of the way home cradling the bird as if it was an infant. With the help of my sisters I wore down my mother until she allowed the bird to stay. She gave us a shoebox and put old rags in it, so the pigeon had a comfortable place to convalesce. Our mother's generosity ended at breaking bread with the pigeon. Bread was the only thing I knew to feed it. Instead she rummaged through her spices, pulled out a container of caraway seeds and sprinkled some in the box.

That night I punched holes in the box and brought the pigeon to bed with me to keep our cat, Ibo, from getting to it. The next morning before leaving for school my sisters and I argued over names for the pigeon. We were running late, so we postponed the decision until after school. My sisters could make suggestions, but the final decision would be mine. I spent most of my class time pondering names. Never having named a living thing before, I viewed the task as something very important.

Rarely did my sisters and I walk home together, but they were waiting for me at N. Caroline Street after school. On the way home I vetoed all their choices. Every name they chose would require the bird to wear pink frilly things. For some reason I had decided the pigeon was a male.

We raced single file upstairs to the only room in the house that had a closet, the front bedroom on the third floor. Ibo was fast behind us. She had not forgotten where we hid the pigeon. Peanut restrained the cat while I opened the closet door to check on the bird. We hoped to find that all the caraway seeds were gone. Instead, when I lifted the lid of the box, we found that the pigeon was still.

Gwen looked at the lifeless form, placed her finger to her lips and whispered "Shh, he's sleeping." I shook the shoebox in the same manner I would shake a cereal box to see how much was left. The caraway seeds and the body of the bird rattled around on the cardboard, but the shoebox was empty of life. At the bottom of the box were only the crumbs of what life once had been.

I shrieked and began to sob. Gwen followed suit an octave higher. There was no longer a need to hold the cat, so Peanut released Ibo. She didn't shriek, but tears pooled at the corners of her eyes.

Our mother burst into the room. Her eyes roamed swiftly up and down our bodies, searching for injuries.

We screamed in unison that the bird had died. Her sigh and the expression of relief on her face irritated me. How could she show relief when our bird had just died? But she was worried about us.

As a child I dealt only with emotions and motives that dwelled near the surface. Anything deeper remained undefined and nameless. I truly was upset that the bird had died. But as were my pennies on a grave, the pigeon in a shoebox was my attempt to change a world that wouldn't budge.

My mother reached for the box to dispose of it. But I held tight. Having witnessed a few days ago the callous funeral Queen Pinky had received, I was determined to provide better. The bird deserved more than a few buckets of water to wipe the memory of its existence away.

I would suffer any consequence, but the bird was going to have a proper burial. She acquiesced when she saw my grip on the box and the determination in my face.

She said, "I suppose you want a priest or minister too?"

It had not occurred to me, but now that she mentioned it, yes, I did. She was not mocking me but wanted to see how far I would go. I confirmed with her everything I knew about funerals. My sisters would gather the mourners, then cut some paper into the shape of a mourning wreath and color it black with crayon. When taped to the front door it looked like a tire or a black donut.

My mother left it up to me to find a minister or priest. I walked to the end of our block to the church on the corner but received no answer to my knock. Hopes dashed, I started back home when I encountered Willa and explained my plight.

She said she had an older cousin who was Catholic and went to Saint Francis Academy, which was located a block north of the Maryland State Penitentiary and two blocks west of my old elementary school. Originally, the school was established by the Oblate Sisters of Providence, the first Catholic order of black nuns in American. The order was associated with Saint Francis Xavier Church, and the parish could trace it roots back to 1791. Black refugees, free and enslaved, had fled the revolution in what would become Haiti. The revolution in Haiti was also a major reason why Napoleon Bonaparte sold America the Louisiana Purchase.

I still had no concept of history; therefore, I was not aware I lived in such a historical city. The church was a block away on the corner of N. Caroline and E. Eager Streets. It was just another red brick building I saw nearly every day but didn't take notice of. I was too busy building my own history.

Willa had heard from her cousin that Saint Francis Xavier Church had closed. The congregation had moved four blocks further north on N. Caroline Street into another church, which at one time had been a meeting hall and had held the Maryland convention to debate leaving the Union in 1861. But there was a priest still living in a home next to the old church. Three steps into my journey Willa informed me that the priest was white.

Though I had confronted the white soldiers with bayonets, I really didn't want to deal with another white person. Reluctantly, I approached the church instead of the house next to it. I spent several minutes nervously contemplating knocking on the door. Years later, none of my white friends would know how much I had to overcome and push past to become their friends. The first few months that I lived in an all-white neighborhood, I would feel as I did back then.

My small knuckles on the large door sounded like a whisper. I was summoning my courage to knock harder or run back home when the door opened. Unaware that I had hidden expectations, I was surprised to see a younger man open the door. He reminded me of a smaller version of the soldier who taught me to tie my shoes, dark hair and pale skin on a less sturdy frame. Both men resembled a man on TV who advertised a popular hair cream.

As was the case with nearly all the white people I interacted with, he too wore a uniform. From the neck down he looked stern in his cassock, Roman collar and sensible shiny black shoes. His broad, welcoming smile clashed drastically with his uniform. It briefly returned me to when I was five years old and didn't see color.

That smile invited me to ask anything, and I immediately launched into pleading for him to perform funeral services for my bird. My urgency came with tears and me pushing a nickel toward him. He said he would gladly do it and pushed my nickel back toward me. I begged him to keep the nickel. I hammed it up and said the nickel was the only kindness I had to offer right now. Although that was true, I wanted to make sure my bird got a real funeral, not a truncated, cheap, charitable one.

After he accepted my coin, I was emboldened to press for two more things. First, I asked if he could use some of that fancy language that Catholic priests use to talk to God. For some reason I thought that was God's native tongue. He informed me that the language was Latin and said he would throw in a few words.

Then I went from not wanting to deal with a white person at all to getting very personal. As he resembled the man in the hair cream commercial, I asked him, "Sir, may I touch your hair?"

His smile transformed into a robust laugh. Then he tilted his head down toward me. I touched his head and petted it as if he were a cat. It kind of felt similar to a longer version of Ibo's fur. When I pulled my hand away, whatever hair cream he was wearing came off as well.

Because of his kindness and remembering when I, too, was curious, in the future when asked by white children if they could touch my hair, I would let them. That is until I grew an Afro; then all hands were off. Unfortunately, one child caught me off guard and reached for my perfectly shaped Afro. Before I could catch myself, I exclaimed, "Don't touch my hair; black hair products are poisonous to white kids!"

He reacted as if my hair were a rabid dog; he snatched his hand back and tucked it safely under his armpit. In fact, without hair care products my hair was rather wild, and the child should have asked me if it bites before seeking to touch it.

That poor child didn't have the same positive experience I had with the priest. Fortunately, the priest could not be aware of my future transgressions and told me to come back in a half hour.

I ran home as fast as I could. The crayon colored wreath was already taped to the door. When I opened the door, I found all the mourners gathered in the living room. Willa had spread the word. In addition to Willa and my sisters there was Runny, the boy who was with me when I confronted the soldiers, his sister Cassy and my cousin Darla.

Peanut held a large stirring spoon in her right hand. She was thinking ahead. We needed a spade to dig a grave. Unfortunately, our mother chose that moment to enter the room and spotted the spoon. There was no way she would allow us to dig a grave, then bring it back to stir a pot of soup. Death soup would not be on the menu in our house today.

All the children grew excited when I told them I had a real priest to perform the services. Without any verbal communication we formed a funeral procession. The shoebox coffin only required one pallbearer. I led the procession, holding the shoebox in front of me as if it was a precious jewel.

The shoebox acted as a planchette on a Ouija board and chose its own gravesite. We reached the southwest corner of the park on the corner of E. Eager and N. Eden, just a few feet away from where Queen Pinky had been killed and not too far from where I found the bird. Without speaking to each other, we all stopped in that spot. I laid the shoebox in the grass, looked west toward the ledges atop the houses that lined N. Eden Street and saw a few pigeons that could possibly be my pigeon's parents. It was a good spot.

The hands on the clock in my head told me it had been a half an hour. I walked toward the church, but as I got to the bottom of the stairs the priest was already coming out. He had put more hair cream in his hair and parted it neatly on the left side. I was pleased that he made an effort for the pigeon.

As we walked back to the gravesite, he asked me my name and I told him. Then he told me his name, which very sadly I do not remember, which is even sadder because as we walked, he told me names were important. Then he asked me what the bird's name was. That's when it occurred to me that I had not named the pigeon yet.

Not to appear callous, I made up a name on the spot. "His name was Peter."

Nodding his head in approval he replied back, "That's a good name, but let's give him the same name in another language. How about Petrus? It's Peter in Latin."

I was ecstatic. With such a lofty name, Petrus was halfway to heaven, and surely his wings could carry him the rest of the way.

Returning to the group, I found that everyone had already dug a grave. Willa was putting the finishing touches on a cross, made from chewing gum and sticks. Runny and Gwen were sending out invitations for Petrus's family to attend the funeral. Runny had snuck a slice of bread from his home and was breaking it up and spreading it on the ground. Gwen had taken some caraway seeds from the shoebox and tossed them among the breadcrumbs. Petrus's family flocked to his funeral.

I realized I was not the only one feeling the increased stress around us. None of us came from abundance. We were all vulnerable. The surface of our world was a trampoline. Any movement by adults disturbed us as well. Early flight from such a surface would have been a gift. Maybe subconsciously we all feared we were Petrus, born to fly, yet our first attempt would become a fall.

Maybe someone would pick us up and nurse us back to health. Despite the violence around us, people were also very kind. I would live in places where people gave generously of their wallets. The world sorely needed those open wallets. But in East Baltimore, people had so little and could only give of themselves. Often that meant taking someone's place in a bad situation, going hungry so someone else didn't have to, taking a beating for a weaker person, being a mother or father to a child not their own and noticing and honoring the least among us. This was God's mother tongue.

The priest eulogized Petrus in a most beautiful manner. I could almost envision the angels donating their feathers to the flightless Petrus. Their long white feathers mixed in with his short black ones would look strange, but at least he would be able to fly. He ended the service by crossing himself and saying amen, which the priest told us was Latin for, "So be it."

Peanut and I went to our knees and pushed the dirt over the shoebox. Willa stuck her chewing gum and stick cross at the head the grave. Gwen threw the remainder of the caraways at its foot to encourage Petrus's parents to visit. This was our little mound of kindness in a cruel world.

I would see the priest one more time and only from a distance. But he would travel with me the rest of my life. He did not belittle a child who wanted a little bird to go to heaven. His kindness put a crack in the image of the white men who had killed Mister Willy's dog.

CHAPTER 40   GLASS THORNS

Oddly enough the first wage I had earned was from confronting white soldiers. Most of it had been spent on graves and trying to change the world. But spit, coins and dirt did not change the world.

Events at first seemed to slow down in May. Only one newsworthy event occurred in my vicinity, and all the adults were talking about it. A group of Catholic activists, priests, teachers, a nurse and an army veteran stormed the draft board office located in the Knights of Columbus building in Catonsville, about a mile from where my mother worked. They took hundreds of files, dumped them in a parking lot and used homemade napalm to set them on fire.

There was no footage of the event shown on TV. Real truth and justice were still too inconvenient and radical concepts for most Americans in 1968. Watching white middle class Americans practicing what they preached was deemed more shocking than watching them kill and die on TV.

By chance I would see footage of the event fifty years later. I was sure that I would recognize the priest who had performed the service for Petrus. Even decades later, I scanned all the priests' faces in the footage. But he was not among them. These were not hippies or draft dodgers. Most of them were over the eligible age to be drafted and two were women.

I watched as the activists crossed themselves and said the Lord's Prayer over the flames. They had held a mirror up to America's face, and she saw she was not the fairest one of them all. Therefore, the activists had to go to prison.

The group was known as the Catonsville Nine, and their protest would spark similar events at hundreds of draft boards across the country. But despite the protests and later perception, the vast majority of those who served in Vietnam were volunteers, whereas the vast majority of those who served in World War Two were drafted.

Then there were events that didn't make the news. May was coming to a close. My sister and I had Memorial Day off, which was a Thursday that year. The following month Congress passed the Uniform Monday Holiday Act, which moved five holidays to set Mondays and created the three-day weekend.

Our mother had to work, but our stepfather had the day off, which turned Wednesday night into a drinking evening. On Memorial Day morning his mood dominated everything; therefore, the entire house had a hangover. He was not violent, but he was unpleasant. To ensure that Memorial Day would not be memorable we left the house earlier than we would have if it had been a school day.

None of our playmates were on the street. It was still too early. So, we went into the alley next to our house with the intentions of sneaking into the abandoned house next door to ours. The windows on the back of our house faced directly into those windows. Yesterday, Gwen and I watched from our bathroom as a mother cat moved her litter of kittens underneath a clawfoot bathtub.

We also could see into the kitchen below the bathroom and had watched a man take off his shoes and socks. Then he put his foot on the windowsill and injected a needle in between his toes. His foot looked no better than the clawfoot tub above his head. We were not allowed to go in this house because it had become a heroin house. But we thought it preferable to a house where a drunk with a bad hangover and a mean disposition dwelled. The feral cat was moving her kittens as far away from the addict as she dared during the day. If only our mother could pick us up by the scruff of our necks and move us far from our addict.

Our concern for the kittens was heightened by the fact that we had gotten Ibo from that same house. We had recently moved into our house on Barnes Street. On the third or fourth day, we heard growling and barking emanating from the windows across the alley. Somehow stray dogs had gotten into the abandoned house and killed Ibo's mother and her littermates. An hour after the carnage we heard Ibo mewing, and our mother went over to fetch her. She was under the same tub where these new kittens were.

Perhaps some vague memory of the event had influenced her when it was time for Ibo to give birth a year later. Seeking a safe place, Ibo initially tried to do so on my mother's lap. Instead my mother gathered towels, and we watched Ibo give birth on our kitchen floor just a few yards from where her family had been massacred. Fortunately, all of Ibo's kittens would live.

It was merely an abandoned house then. Now it was a regular stop for junkies to inject. We could no longer shower in the rain, go barefoot, or wear sandals. There were too many needles in the alley.

The best point of entry into the house was through one of the kitchen windows. All the other windows were broken near the bottom, but the tops were all still intact. There was no easy access to the house. Although we had seen junkies enter through this kitchen window, it was not the main entrance for them. We didn't know where that was, but enough had passed this way for the bottom frame to be clear of any jagged glass. We hesitated for a moment. Now that we were paying attention, the window with its glass still intact at the top resembled a guillotine.

Upon entering the room, there was not much in it to clue a stranger that it had been a kitchen. But we were not strangers because the house was a mirror image of ours. At first the floor looked as if it was made of glitter, but closer inspection revealed that it was tiny bits of glass.

The glass reminded me of one of the reasons we were defying the restrictions about going into the abandoned house. Recently our stepfather, as part of his hangover, had taken to fabricating infractions we had committed and punishing us unjustly. Initially, we doubled our efforts to behave, but the enforcing of the rules had no structure and no justice to it. Eventually our attitude when he had a hangover became, "Why bother?" A couple of weeks ago we broke a drinking glass in our kitchen. Our first instinct was to sweep the glass up and hope it was not missed. We knew we were going to be punished regardless, so instead we picked up the larger visible pieces of glass, and with a broom we spread the invisible shards along the path our stepfather took to the kitchen sink.

We already had our shoes on, and our mother never came into the kitchen barefooted. Therefore, our trap was person specific. My shoulders sagged as our stepfather came downstairs and made it across our glass shard minefield unharmed. But as he retraced his steps, we heard an explosion of profanity coming from his mouth. One of the shards of glass had found its mark. Vigor returned to my shoulders, but I had to swallow my laugh. Unfortunately, it came back up as a giggle.

My sisters giggled too. But they had covered their mouths and turned their faces toward the wall. I had been too eager. I didn't want to miss a single grimace coming from our stepfather. So, I took the brunt of his wrath, but pain must have thrown off his aim. His slap just brushed off the side of my head without causing harm.

Since I was the one who laughed, I was the one who had to go upstairs and administer first aid. It was still early morning, so he was not flexible enough to remove the glass splinter himself. Once we reached the bathroom, I went to retrieve Band-Aids from our medicine cabinet but was scolded for being soft. He sat on the rim of the bathtub and rested his foot in my lap as I sat on the lid of the toilet.

Sunlight was beaming in through the eastern window, which caused the glass embedded in his foot to glimmer. There were tiny beads of blood around the glass, but it was still visible enough. It would be easy enough to remove, but I didn't want to make it easy for him. Instead of grabbing the tip of the shard, I grabbed as much flesh surrounding the shard as could fit between the pincher of the tweezers and pulled as hard as I could.

The tweezer had become a butcher knife and did more damage to his foot than the glass. This time when he slapped me, he connected full on. My face stung from the impact. Except for my head turning with the blow, I showed no reaction. I was expecting it and was prepared.

With an expressionless face I said, "I thought you said we were supposed to be tough."

He grunted an acknowledgment to his own words. No longer trusting me, he snatched the tweezers from my hands. The bloody shard fell to the bathroom floor, and briefly I hoped he would step on it again. But I had gotten my pound of feet meat, and from the additional skin attached to it, the shard was not hard to find.

An unexpected bonus from my botched attempt at first aid was that I had only removed the top portion of the shard. I watched him contort into a position to try to remove the rest of the glass. He had to dig deeper into the hole I had left in his foot, finally removing the rest of the glass. Apparently, my procedure had softened him up enough to now want the Band-Aid he disdained only moments ago.

In hindsight, I am amazed that he would trust his wound to someone he had mistreated. Some individuals want to think they are always in control, that is, until they are not. I never knew when I would summon the courage to rebel and retaliate. Therefore, he couldn't know either. Unexpectedly fear could become anger and enduring could become sick and tired. Many confuse brave with sick and tired. If they are prudent, the brave at least have the choice to retreat from a more powerful adversary. The sick and tired are no longer prudent and have no place to go but through their adversary.

At nine years old I was still terrified of him, but sick and tired had started to germinate. Under the right circumstances I could become dangerous. Those who have been hurt know how to hurt. But an unconscious part of me wanted to counter that skill. People had also been kind to me, so I knew how to be kind as well.

Thus, my sisters and I entered a heroin house to save some kittens and defy a tyrant. Briefly I considered scooping up some broken glass from this kitchen to scatter on the floor of our house. Even at that age I swiftly bored of repeating the same old cruelty. Besides, I needed to be kind more than I needed to be cruel.

Exiting the kitchen, we ascended the staircase to our left. One of the steps was completely gone. Our eyes had sufficiently adapted to the dim lighting to maneuver over the gaping hole.

The room leading into the bathroom had an old-fashioned wringer washer, except it wasn't old-fashioned to us. We still had one in the same room in our house. Each wet item of clothing had to be pulled through the top part of the machine, which contained two rolling pins that pressed most of the water out. There was actually a shirt still stuck between the rolling pins in this one.

Whoever had lived here had left suddenly and had returned to retrieve only some of the furnishings. The iron skeletal remains of a mattress were leaning against the wall. Most of the stuffing had been carted off by rats to make their nest. Tattered white curtains hung in the bathroom windows. They looked like something ghosts would wear. A mere touch from my finger would cause them to disintegrate and disappear. It was easy to imagine that ghosts had done their laundry in the old washer and hung it in the windows to dry.

Sunlight reflected off the windows from the house directly behind the heroin house. The light passing through the curtains barely made shadows on the floor. A blizzard of dust swirled in the beams of light. We could see the air we were breathing, and it was crowded with particles. Closer inspection revealed there were dozens of used needles on the floor. There were multiple hazards at play in the house.

We needed to get on our hands and knees to retrieve the kittens and used our shoes to brush aside the debris and needles in front of the bathtub. We could hear them but not see them. After multiple attempts we realized we could not reach the kittens. At that point it also dawned on us that we wouldn't be allowed to bring them all home. Instead we gathered debris from the second flood and built a wall around the base of the tub, leaving only enough room for the mother cat to get in. Hopefully this would be a deterrent for smaller dogs.

Curiosity motivated us to go further into the house. In our haste we had ignored the front two bedrooms. Heading towards the front of the second floor, we noticed three very dark shades covered the front bedroom windows. The rectangular coronas coming in from the edges of the shades were the only source of light for the entire room, yet it was sufficient to see rows of badly stained empty mattresses lying on the floor. The mattresses had human shaped indentations made from human misery. Some of those people had lain in snow in their youth and made snow angels, having no idea they would grow up to make fetal shaped dents in dirty mattresses. If cemeteries had a waiting room, this would be it.

I was nine, so I couldn't imagine any drug powerful enough to induce me to lie in such filth for hours. But I was only living my life. I had no clue what other's lives made people do, nor what vehicle I would choose when it was time to escape my situation. But I hoped this would not be my ticket out.

We didn't linger long. We tried to go to the third floor, but the staircase was blocked with debris. Having no other choice, we went back downstairs. After jumping over the hole in the stairs, we were back on the first floor. A combination of more sun rising above the horizon and our eyes fully adjusting to the dimness allowed us to see farther into the dining room. Areas that had been black now appeared gray, and gray areas were now anemic colors. Strips of wallpaper peeling from the wall had the pattern of lily of the valley printed on them. The floor was a sea of linoleum with islands of dark wood protruding through worn areas.

Except for a plate with a Christmas scene on it, there was nothing else interesting in the room. We almost avoided the living room, because we saw two rats scurry away from a pile of clothes. Despite the myth, cats rarely hunted rats. They generally avoided each other when possible but sometimes tolerated each other's presence, and they were not adversaries.

A piece of clothing moved. We thought it was another rat until we noticed it was a hand. The rats had not scurried far until my sisters and I entered the room full force. One more rat ran from the pile of clothes as we grew near. It followed its companion into the dark.

Once we came near the pile of clothes, we realized it was a pregnant woman. I didn't know how far along she was, but it was obvious enough to tell even in a poorly lit room. She was lying in as much of a fetal position as her belly would allow. Her position reminded me of the indentations in the mattresses upstairs. She was not really conscious. Her hand had been stirred by something in a heroin dream.

Apparently, she had not spent all her money on drugs, because she was dressed in reasonably fashionable maternity wear. Though her head rested in a pile of broken plaster that had fallen from the ceiling, she had a nicely styled Afro. I had heard rumors of rats biting some people in their sleep. Fortunately, the rats, normally nocturnal creatures, had been drawn to a bag of donuts that lay next to her. When heroin addicts chose to eat, for some reason they craved sweet things. There were no visible bite marks on her. The rats had only been attracted to the food.

My sisters and I didn't bother to try to revive her, nor did we report our discovery to our stepfather. No point in having a person with a hangover assisting someone who had come close to having an overdose. We went to the neighbors on the other side of our house for help. They were an elderly couple, and we only knew them as Mister and Mrs. Clark. We chose them because their nephew who was a heroin addict lived with them off and on. He reappeared about a year ago, and coincidentally things started turning up missing. His real name was Lester, but everyone I knew except his aunt and uncle called him Wiggy. Drug use gave him a different personality, so he got a new name to go with it, Wiggy, because he was so wigged out on drugs.

When we knocked and Wiggy answered the door we were not surprised. He was a really big man. I never thought about it until now, but I briefly wondered if he needed bigger needles and doses of heroin. Fortunately, we got the reasonable, responsive Wiggy instead of the wigged out one.

We told him there was a pregnant woman passed out and high on the floor in the house next to our house. He wasn't indignant that we had approached him, which told me we had made the right association. Wiggy knew the woman. He told us he would take care of it. The only acknowledgment of thanks we got was a look that said, "Scram."

Not wanting to go home to Hangover House nor back to Heroin House, we elected to sit on the stoop of the abandoned house diagonally across the street from us. It had been abandoned a week after the riots.

About five minutes later an old pickup truck pulled in front of the heroin house. Two nondescript men wearing leather jackets got out and carried the pregnant woman to their truck. They sat her in between them and made her drink a bottle of milk. The only resistance she offered was spitting the milk back up on their jackets. The entire time they were parked there, no signs of life appeared in her eyes. When they drove off, she was not moving. I wondered if she had died until a little over two weeks later the same men came back to pick up the same woman, minus the pregnancy.

Within eight weeks I watched three kittens emerge from the abandoned house to go start families of their own in other abandoned houses. But their mother was not addicted to heroin. I never found out what happened to the woman's baby.

Our stepfather never found out we had entered the heroin house. But as expected, he trumped up some false charges and sent us to bed without supper. He punished us just because he could. My stomach growled through the night at the injustice of it all. I wished I had brought home shards of glass and heroin needles from the house next door and scattered them on our kitchen floor. In my dream that night he came home drunk and barefoot.

CHAPTER 41 PREDICTING THE PAST

June 2nd, 1968, the Orioles were playing the Red Sox. The Orioles would go on to win the game. Mister Willy was not getting around as well as he used to, so Uncle Reggie had gone over to his house to listen to the game on the radio.

Miss Penny showed up a few minutes later with a copy of the Afro-American newspaper. It was and still is, the oldest family-owned black newspaper in the country. Once or twice a week, men would walk the streets of Baltimore chanting the name of the paper and sometimes the headlines.

The Afro-American was the only newspaper Mister Willy found credible. Miss Penny would read the titles of articles, and if any caught his interest, she would read the whole article. Despite being an election year, nothing really caught his interest. It was 1968, and it was very difficult for blind people to vote independently.

Mister Willy claimed that America put its democracy on the auction block every four years and sold it to the highest bidder, and he wanted to put his bid in. Uncle Reggie had very little interest in politics or voting, but he did agree to register and vote on Mister Willy's behalf. He became his seeing-eye voter.

Maryland did not have a primary that year. The state assembly had outlawed them the year before and joined the vast majority of states that didn't have presidential primaries. Only fourteen states held any that year. On May 10th, all of Maryland's delegates had been assigned to Hubert Humphrey.

Mister Willy briefly mentioned that if Robert F. Kennedy won the nomination, he wanted Uncle Reggie to vote for him because of his acts as Attorney General under his brother. He didn't need to hear anything else.

The game came on shortly after that. Miss Penny left and I soon followed. Before going home, I cut through the park and picked some dandelions to place on Petrus's grave. The rest of the day was uneventful.

Some things you remember only because they are bundled with events more relevant to your situation. This was the case with the shooting of Andy Warhol by Valerie Solanas. I knew very little about art, and my critiques were either a shrug of my shoulder to reflect no interest or declaring it was pretty.

There was one piece of art hanging in our house. It was a round, detailed puzzle of the moon. When we completed it, we glued it to some cardboard and hung it in the dining room next to the TV. Actually, it was never completed. One piece of the puzzle, a portion of the Sea of Tranquility, was missing. A year later, the first man on the moon would land on that missing piece. Because of the flawed puzzle and that landing, I can still look at a full moon and locate the Sea of Tranquility.

Andy Warhol was shot just before dinner that Monday, June 3rd. I vaguely remember hearing about it. My first thought was, "Why would anyone try to kill an artist?" I knew he was important because his shooting was hundreds of miles away, yet it was being reported locally. The next day, Jane brought it up on the playground, and probably she was the only one there who knew who he was. I was certain Jane didn't have any pictures of lenticular Jesus or puzzle art hanging on her wall.

Although her knowledge was greater than the rest of ours, it was limited to snippets she had overheard in her Bohemian household. I also remember the event because of erroneous information.

Robert asked Jane, "Is he the guy who painted *Whistler's Mama*?"

Jane neither laughed nor corrected him. Shrugging her shoulders, she said, "He could be."

Her shrug was authoritative enough for me to believe for a number of years that Andy Warhol had actually painted *Whistler's Mother*. The memory was reinforced many years later when I stood before the painting in a museum in Paris. By then, I knew the painting had not been painted by Andy Warhol. I was surprised to see the painting was nearly life size. But then I remembered Robert's name for the painting, *Whistler's Mama*. I giggled the whole time I stood in front the painting. The painting was originally known as *Arrangement in Grey and Black - Portrait of the Painter's Mother*. Then it became known simply as *Arrangement in Grey and Black No. 1*. The public dubbed it *Whistler's Mother*. But Robert's name of *Whistler's Mama* is still my favorite.

What also made Andy's shooting memorable was Jane's closing statement as we returned to our respective classroom: "I wonder who they are going to shoot next."

We didn't have to wait long. My knowledge of the world had

grown exponentially since the assassination of Martin Luther King Jr. It was about to increase again. I was vaguely aware this was election day in parts of the country. June 4th, 1968 was the Super Tuesday of its day.

The morning of June 5th, America found itself in a state of shock. Robert F. Kennedy was celebrating his victory in the California primary at the Ambassador Hotel in Los Angeles. He was shaking hands with seventeen-year-old Juan Romero when he was shot three times by Sirhan Sirhan.

America's collective cry was, "Please, not again!"

He did not die right away, so the nation held its breath and prayed for twenty-four hours. The TV news was full of hopeful, weeping young women. But by the early morning of June 6th our prayers had changed from pleading for his recovery to wishing well-being to his wife and their children, for he had died while most of America was asleep. For the next few days black and white Americans were on the same page.

When I saw Jane on the playground all she said was, "Now we know who was next."

School bells summoned us to our classes before she could say anything else. Our principal came over the intercom and gave us a moment of silence. Some students doodled, others stared blankly in front of them, but most prayed. Most of the teachers were sad but unlike with Martin Luther King Jr.'s assassination, none were angry.

Unbeknownst to us at the time, America's three most famous widows, Jacqueline, Coretta and Ethel accompanied the casket of Robert Kennedy on the flight to JFK International Airport in New York. They were part of an elite, if not desirable group, wives of slain American leaders. In the future I would wonder what they talked about on the flight and on the funeral train.

All of them had very young children at the time of their husband's assassinations. Ethel Kennedy was carrying a child who would never see its father, but at only three months pregnant she didn't show. It was a small blessing; the nation was already stressed and could not suffer to see a widow in a black veil wearing a mourning maternity dress.

From JFK, Robert Kennedy was taken to Saint Patrick's Cathedral for public viewing and a funeral. I don't remember his funeral at all. My memories of the event came from the archives of photojournalists. I saw none of it on TV. But I remember the funeral train as if it had just passed in front me moments ago.

Starting with Abraham Lincoln, nearly every presidential funeral train passed through Baltimore. Although not a president, Robert Kennedy had the cache of one. The train would journey over 200 miles to Washington DC and pass through the most densely populated region of the country and some of the poorest neighborhoods in the Northeast, including ours. I later heard estimates that one to two million people lined the route.

About an hour before the funeral train was leaving Penn Station in New York, I heard a man walking down N. Eden Street yelling that they had captured Martin Luther King Jr.'s assassin, James Earl Ray. We came inside to tell our mother, who soon turned on the radio, which confirmed what we had heard. He had been captured in London on the very same day Robert Kennedy was to be buried. In East Baltimore, his capture didn't lighten the mood. Within hours a train carrying the body of another slain leader would pass within less than a mile of our home.

At first, I wanted to go to the train tracks to watch the casket car come by, but our stepfather had made plans for us to visit Fort McHenry. It was a twenty-minute drive, and somehow, he had procured a car. Moments after confirming the arrest of James Earl Ray, we were heading to Locust Point where Fort McHenry was located.

It was the type of humid day that made loose fitting clothes skintight. The air glued your cotton clothes to your skin. The heat and humidity diminished somewhat the closer we got to Locust Point. I had not expected a fort to be beautiful. It had water on three sides and the grounds were lush and green. From the top of its walls you could see that the fort was in the shape of a star or, rather, a pentagon.

Despite not initially being interested, I was actually fascinated. Since April 4th I had experienced a burst of knowledge with regards to U.S. History. But the gaps in my knowledge were more like chasms. Briefly, I wondered if its star shape had inspired the title of our national anthem, Star-Spangled Banner. My stepfather soon corrected my wondering and explained to us the Battle of Baltimore and how the flag flying above Fort McHenry was the inspiration for the national anthem.

In 1968, the Star-Spangled Banner had been the national anthem for thirty-seven years, beating out "Hail, Columbia" and "My Country Tis of Thee" in 1931.

If I had paid attention, I would have noticed the flag was flying at half-staff for Robert Kennedy. But its sheer size caught me off guard. Although only a replica, it was as large as the garrison flag that flew above the fort in 1814. I believe at the time it was completed it was the largest flag in the world.

There were either four or five main buildings in the fort, and we went into all the ones open to the public. I could not read, so everything I learned I overheard. A man was telling his family and friends that the fort had been bombarded for twenty-five hours and suffered four fatalities. One of those casualties was a woman and the other was a runaway slave who had enlisted to fight. About eighty percent of those defending Fort McHenry were immigrants and blacks. Diversity was fighting for America's freedom long before it was acknowledged.

Most of this information I forgot, then rediscovered years later. But in one of the rooms was a display I would never forget. I don't remember if it was a re-creation or an authentic uniform of a soldier who had been shot in the heart. I don't even remember if the wearer had been a fatality from Fort McHenry or some other casualty from the Battle of Baltimore. The bloodstain on the chest of the uniform greatly disturbed me. My sisters and I had seen far worse. There had been so much death that year, yet my emotions had not built up any immunity to the violence. I was not becoming desensitized. If anything, I was more sensitive to it.

For some reason that uniform terrified me. Now I was glad we would miss the funeral train. I didn't want any more reminders of death. On the way home the radio announced that the funeral train had been delayed by several hours. Our stepfather said we could now go view the train as it passed through Baltimore. There was no option to voice my opposition; as a child you could not change your mind in his household. The rest of the ride home my stomach felt queasy.

We arrived home in time to have a quick dinner of fried bologna sandwiches, which was my favorite at the time. Putting pleasure on a queasy stomach seemed to help a little. I was still apprehensive about going. I was having flashbacks of the young man we had found dead in the junkyard when we lived on Forrest Street. The bloodstain on the uniform on display at Fort McHenry was in the same spot as the one on the boy in the junkyard.

The word no never exited my mouth, but my whole body unconsciously turned into dead weight. I still didn't want to go and plodded up the stairs to rewash my hands after dinner. Scrubbing them was not guilt-ridden and was only a delaying tactic. Yet I put Lady Macbeth to shame as I almost drew blood with my relentless scrubbing. Then I pretended to look for shoes I already knew the location of.

My mother caught on first, but it was my stepfather who asked, "I thought you wanted to go, why don't you want to go now?"

Up until that moment the answer had been eluding me as well. The real reason was trapped in a quagmire of emotions I couldn't possibly begin to explain. If I had tried to extricate the reason on my own, I would have failed miserably.

Without thinking I simply answered, "I am afraid the casket will be open when the train comes here."

Perhaps my answer reminded him of his own father's closed

casket funeral. My stepfather was nothing but sympathetic to me from that point on. He offered me all kinds of assurances the casket would be closed. The surprising thing was he didn't force me to go but took the time to explain why I should go. He was convincing, but I finally acquiesced because Mister Willy could not go and if he did, he could not see. I wanted to explain every detail to him, and now that one of those details wouldn't be an open casket, my desire returned.

I remember the day as much for my stepfather's sympathetic behavior as for its historical importance. He had been very nice all day. My sisters and I were allowed to set the pace. It was a twenty-minute walk to the 400 block of E. Preston Street, where there was a huge open space with unobstructed views of the train tracks.

A large crowd of whites and blacks tentatively approached the train tracks. We were wary of each other, but we were also just plain weary from our collective actions. An older white man gravitated towards us. He was on our side of the tracks, which was mostly black. The crowd on the other side of the tracks was smaller and mostly white.

My stepfather offered the white man a handshake, which he accepted. My stepfather said, "Let's look out for each other."

My concept of white people was still in its infancy. There were many bad experiences yet to come and good ones as well. I cherished the soldier who taught me to tie my shoes at 20,000 feet, the police officer who took Axel away, the soldier who told us food was coming into the city, the woman who brought the ballet dancers to our school and the priest who gave my bird a funeral. Their behavior was sometimes buried under cruel acts of racism by others, but I never forgot these people. I would never get over my dislike of white people, but I would grow to love many Caucasians. The latter is just a characteristic description of millions of people with varying personalities, while the former is a crippling, cruel mentality with a false sense of itself and others. I would come to realize I didn't dislike a skin color. I disliked a mentality.

The Caucasian man stood next to us the whole time and talked about life. He looked like he never hated a thing in his life and showed us a picture of his granddaughter who he said Gwen favored. This man was looking past race. Indeed, Gwen and his granddaughter did favor each other. Nearly everyone along the tracks that day was trying to look past race.

Since I wanted to describe the event in detail to Mister Willy, my senses were opened. I interrupted the adults' conversation to ask which way the train was coming. All of them pointed toward Green Mount Amtrak Rail Underpass, also known as Union Tunnel. I don't know if anyone came to the same conclusion that I did, but Robert

Kennedy would pass beneath not more than a hundred yards from John Wilkes Booth's grave. I was young and naive. It was easy for me to imagine a nefarious plot.

With some effort I pulled my mind from the imagined deeds of the dead and focused on the living. All walks of life lined the tracks. There were several nuns from the order of Oblate Sisters of Providence. Next to them was a white police officer. Across the track was an arabber atop his horse holding a large American flag. With the exception of the nuns and the police officer, neither whites nor blacks had to wear uniforms to stand next to each other.

Several people had portable radios, but I only heard static and muffled voices over the airways. They must have announced the train was close because heads began turning toward the tunnel. The crowd grew tense but reverent. Most craned their necks while trying to look dignified doing so. Some stumped out cigarettes while others lit new ones. Those with rumpled clothing from the heat used their hands to iron the wrinkles out.

We were gathered as one, yet I could see many were in their own private worlds. My imagination created a keyhole to peek into those private places. I need not have bothered; the emotions within were the same as those on public display: disorientation, shock, sadness and wondering. What would have happened if he had lived? Along with a man, the train was carrying a country's possible future to its grave.

I heard the train before I saw it. Trains are a symphony in motion. Before it exited the tunnel, squeaking brakes mimicked the sound of the string section and the roar of its engine acted as its percussion section. The sections competed with one another rather than harmonized. Then the brass section joined the symphony as the engine cleared the tunnel, and the engineer blew the horn. Finally, the mass of the train cutting through air imitated the sounds of the woodwind section. The engineer took control, blew the horn again and became a symphony conductor. For a brief moment he made the different sections shake hands and cooperate. Then the horn faded, the strings became intermittent, and the percussion grew distant as the engine drew farther away. All that was left was the light whistle of the wind as the air parted to make way for the train and the rhythm of the swaying cars.

Pulling twenty-one cars, the train must have been close to 1500 feet long. The engine had passed out of sight, yet cars were still pouring out of the tunnel. All I could see of the passengers were dark seated silhouettes. One of the silhouetted hands waved at the crowd and received hundreds of waves in return. By the time I raised my hand to wave, the car had moved on.

Each individual car passed by swiftly, but the totality of it seemed to suspend time. The passing train seemed as if it wouldn't end. It was not an impatient waiting. I felt as if I had been put in a trance. Seconds did not turn into minutes. They simply became irrelevant, ethereal, almost as if time had been assassinated as well as the senator. I only broke from my trance as the last car exited the tunnel.

I don't remember if I could actually see some of the taller monuments at Green Mount Cemetery from where I stood or that I imagined I could. Either way I knew it was there. So, when the last car, carrying the casket of Robert F. Kennedy, exited the tunnel under Green Mount Cemetery, it was a bit jarring. It would be the only time I would witness a casket leaving a cemetery.

Through the windows I could see the flag-draped casket. There was a father, a husband, a brother, a son, a senator and a possible future president beneath that American flag. The casket seemed too small to carry all of him, and it grew smaller the farther it pulled away from me. In reality I saw it only for a few seconds, but all the emotions surrounding the event and that brief glimpse would stay with me the rest of my life. The retreating train haunted the tracks as people stood still, and for some reason many began singing the "The Battle Hymn of the Republic." But only the ornate decorated balcony on the back of the train bore witness to the hymn.

Finally, the glare of the setting sun blocked the view of the last car as it retreated west, before it turned south. We could still hear it, but its retreat was covered in sunbeams and auras. The crowd continued singing to the sun. Although the temperatures had cooled a bit, the air was still humid and heavy from emotions. When we could no longer hear the train, we bid the Caucasian man goodbye. Other than that, we did not speak again until we were a respectable distance from the tracks.

We arrived home at sunset. Witnessing history had been tiring; my sisters and I went to bed early. Robert F. Kennedy's body arrived at Arlington National Cemetery around ten o'clock that night. He was buried not far from his brother's grave while we slept, his casket illuminated only by candles and floodlights. A short distance away, fire wept as the eternal flame of JFK witnessed another Kennedy laid to rest.

CHAPTER 42   JACK CAN'T FIT IN THE BOX

The next day I went over to Mister Willy's house. Since I had witnessed Robert Kennedy's funeral train passing through our city, I had his and Uncle Reggie's full attention. Though a talkative child, I was generally quiet around people I found credible and only interrupted their conversation with questions. They knew more than I did, and I knew it. But today I knew more than they did.

Having their attention was an honor, and I spared no detail. At one point I embellished a little and declared that the silhouetted hand that had waved at the crowd had been that of Ethel Kennedy. The hand had no gender, let alone an actual identity. I confused projection for perception. There was a slight chance it could have been her, but I had turned it into a certainty. Both took my comment at face value.

Not ready to relinquish the stage and feeling enough time had passed, I told them about the pennies I had placed at John Wilkes Booth's grave. Other than Jane's uncle, I had told no other adult. Robert Kennedy's assassination had dissuaded me of most of my little superstition, but I was interested in what Mister Willy thought.

In a broad sense I knew what he thought. Concepts had power if you lent it to them. That was one of the main reasons I had gone to the cemetery. But I had misinterpreted what Mister Willy had said. Concepts were not death defying. My two pennies were not powerful enough and never would be.

Further education would rid me of most of my superstitions. Though I would no longer believe in my own, I never would discount those of others. Beliefs could induce famines, economic collapse, wars and other calamities. Falsehoods dominate history and are a major contributor to human mortality. They may be foolish or impractical, but we dismiss them at our peril. I didn't have to believe what they believed, but I had to take them seriously. After all, my own beliefs made me waste money needlessly.

Though my trip to the cemetery bore no fruit, Mister Willy told me it had been a gallant effort on my part. He didn't ridicule me and went as far as saying he wished my coins had worked.

More importantly, he had guessed my real reason for placing pennies on Booth's grave, then asked and answered my unspoken question. "How do we stop all the killing? We can't, too many people benefit from it."

Uncle Reggie took a sip of his wine and said, "The Angel of Death will always take its tithe."

Mister Willy built on Uncle Reggie's statement, "I think his name is Azrael. The Angel of Death is more than he appears. He is also the angel of last moments, last thoughts, last wishes, recipient of the truest confession. We spill our soul when it is about to be taken from our bodies."

I asked him, "Is there an angel of life?"

He answered matter-of-factly, "We are the angels of life and bring it into the world by having children, or for those of us who choose not to have children, by living robustly."

As usual, Mister Willy had put no age restrictions on his answers and had raised additional questions. You didn't have to have children? I hadn't realized not having children was an option. I thought it was something that just happened to you when you got older or it didn't. Childless couples were apologetic or put parentheses of sadness around the statement, "We don't have children." Back then it was treated as an affliction, not a choice.

Perhaps this conversation would have faded from my memory, but the next day my mother brought home a used family physician book. A nurse at her job decided that since my mother had three children it would be handy for her to have. The book would be a fixture in our house for the remainder of my growing up years.

When Peanut learned to read, once a week she would gather Gwen, me and sometimes our mother, and with a solemn face she would announce that she had some illness. She would choose one she could barely pronounce which was usually fatal. The first couple of times we were concerned. Eventually our concerns turned into yawns or laughter, that is until she started making her illnesses contagious and began diagnosing the rest of us as well.

Peanut was very convincing. Within minutes she would have us believing we had most of the symptoms for any given illness, and the symptoms that hadn't manifested yet, soon would. After being assigned our illnesses, Gwen and I would race to the bathroom mirror to check for symptoms. Prominent features that had dominated my face since birth suddenly became suspect.

Riddled with paranoia I would question myself, "Where did that big nose come from? It wasn't there yesterday."

Any flaw on my face was a symptom. Crust at the corners of my eyes would be blindness in days. A blackhead was a symptom of Black Death. Bad breath was a sign I would soon draw my last one. Peanut planted a seed, but I reaped a field. For the sake of our sanity Gwen and I would hide the book from Peanut. But by then she had memorized so many diseases, she would give us reruns of old illnesses.

Fortunately, none of us could read yet, therefore, my mother guided us through its pages. Nearly all our attention was drawn to photos and illustrations. Appropriately, the book started with the beginning of life. Though somewhat suspect, I had been comfortable with the concept that mankind had domesticated storks to deliver babies. Initially the illustrations of human embryonic and fetal development were disturbing. I couldn't imagine that I had once been one of the little slugs with eyes in the illustrations. But the more our mother explained to us the process of birth, the more intrigued I became. My sisters' and my births had been more similar to Ibo having kittens than I realized.

This new source of information, coupled with a few dramatic but sanitized versions of births I had seen on TV, prepared me to combat death by bringing life into the world. All week I ran the scenario through my head and immediately discarded the idea of being the doctor or a midwife. I was going to be an unwed mother.

The rest of the week I spent scoping out the house, searching for my maternity wear. I also would have to bribe my sisters into being the doctor and nurse. They would pretend with me but would want to assign roles along gender lines. I needed money.

That Friday night, our drunk stepfather came home rumbling and grumbling but didn't erupt. Once again, I took advantage of his drunken stupor. The next morning, I threw away a half empty pack of cigarettes and hid his last full one. Of course, he sent me to the store to replace what, unbeknownst to him, he still had. I gave him back his own pack of cigarettes. With my nicotine funds I bought a pack of candy cigarettes and had enough left over to give Peanut and Gwen each a dime. The expectation was that their performance had to be as shiny as the coins.

Since our parents slept in late and TV was terrible on Sunday morning, I chose that as my due date. The night before, I snuck a pair of my mother's fancy mules out of her bedroom closet and placed them under my bed. The rest of my ensemble was scattered around our bedroom.

When my sisters and I awakened we went downstairs to have breakfast, which we hastily finished. While my sisters transformed our living room into a delivery room, I went upstairs to become pregnant. Sequestered in the bathroom with my garments, I stripped down to my underwear, held a pillow to my belly and wrapped my sisters' pink chenille bedspread around my body to make my maternity gown. Its rectangular shape forced me to go strapless, but fortunately there was enough fabric to allow me a little bit of a train at the bottom of the dress.

Then I fashioned a long sleeve shirt into a wig. It was big enough for me to have shoulder length plaid hair and bangs. I adjusted the pillow to the proper shape of a pregnancy. Not able to see my feet, my toes searched the bathroom floor for my mother's mules, and I slid into them.

Gazing in the bathroom mirror, even very lenient eyes would not have called me pretty or pregnant. The most generous of eyes would have seen a potbellied gnome. The only way I could have gotten pregnant was through pillow insemination. I salvaged as much pride as I could after looking in the mirror, grabbed the pack of candy cigarettes and headed toward the stairs.

When I reached the bottom of the stairs, Ibo had the nerve to give me a dirty look and hiss at me. I responded with a contemptuous stare to inform her that I was about to put her to shame. My gestation period was only going to be a few minutes long, and the birth would not be as messy as hers had been. Had it been a real birth I would have chosen to do so on the armchair covered in plastic and cigarette burn marks. Instead I had chosen to give birth on the couch.

I stepped into the dining room, placed the back of my right hand against my brow and announced dramatically, "I think it's time."

Peanut and Gwen were real gentlemen. Each took one of my hands, imitated the sound of sirens and escorted me the last few feet to the couch in the living room. They proved to be quite inventive. Two chairs from the dining room sat in front of the couch. They would serve as the stirrups to support my legs during labor. Our mother's meat loaf pan was at the foot of the couch. I thought it was a bit small for a bassinet, but they explained it was for the fictitious afterbirth. My sisters must have paid more attention to the book than I had and planned on more of a realistic birth than I was prepared to perform. I had not packed a placenta under my pink chenille maternity gown. It was not that type of pregnancy. Nor were my sisters that type of nurse or doctor.

They fell short in the execution of their costumes. Gwen had made herself a paper boat, which we pretended was a nurse's hat. Peanut had a saucer from a toy teacup set rubber banded to her forehead. I feared it would cut off the circulation to the upper part of her brain at a critical point in the procedure. Despite my minor concern, and no matter how hard I pretended, all I saw was a coal miner.

Before they helped me onto the couch, I pulled the pack of candy cigarettes from my nonexistent cleavage and handed them each one. It was 1968, and no one did anything important without having a cigarette before or after the event. As I was acting the part of the lady, I would have mine after giving birth.

Fortunately, when I had made the dress, I left a slit in the appropriate place. I had plenty of room to part the dress and easily sat on the couch. I gracefully rested my mules on the seats of the dining room chairs.

By this time my sisters each had a candy cigarette dangling from their lips. Gwen sat at the top of the couch. She blew powdered smoke toward the ceiling while using a damp sponge to cool my brow. She looked tender and caring. Peanut, on the other hand, was kneeling between my legs and blew her powdered smoke toward my cloth womb, almost as if she were trying to smoke out a nest of bees. With a cigarette dangling from her lip, she looked more akin to a mechanic under the hood of a car than a doctor. The expression on her face said, "Looks like everything needs to come out."

Gwen patted my forehead with the damp sponge several more times and said, "Push Mrs. Cole, push."

I let out a dainty, anemic little mew that was supposed to be a grunt. Peanut, not satisfied with my performance, pinched my thigh. There was not bit of testosterone in the scream that followed. I looked down between my legs and saw her give me the thumbs up.

She said, "That's more like it. You needed to put some soul into it."

Apparently, she wanted me to give birth and perform like James Brown. Although the dance would not come out for another year and was not by James Brown, I commenced the prone version of the Funky Chicken. My head made a pecking motion while my arms flapped with no destination in mind. I groaned and moaned loudly through gritted teeth. Giving the performance of my life, I twisted and convulsed to the point that one of my mules fell off my foot.

Both my sisters began chanting, "Push Mrs. Cole, push."

The wig I had made from a shirt was tight, hot and making me sweat. Gwen kept on patting my forehead with the damp sponge. But Peanut was rushing the birth. Push became pull as I gripped the top of the pillow to prevent Peanut from causing me to give birth prematurely. I grunted in earnest as my delivery had now become a tug-of-war. With gravity on her side, Peanut was gradually winning that war. I resorted to closing my legs, locking her head between my knees to get her attention. The sudden pressure was sufficient enough to pop the candy cigarette out of her mouth. I retrieved another cigarette and informed her I wanted to have a more laborious labor. Gwen stopped patting my forehead until I gave her another cigarette as well.

I gave an Academy Award performance, worthy of an Oscar. It would not have been a surprise if a replica of the gold man had emerged from my chenille gown instead of a pillow. But Peanut broke the mood with a final pull.

She retrieved a towel I had not noticed from under the chair, wrapped the pillow, then handed it to me and said, "Mrs. Cole, you have a lovely little girl."

Holding the pillow in my left hand, I retrieved a candy cigarette from my cleavage with my right. With a great sense of accomplishment, I blew powdered smoke into the air. All three of us had candy cigarettes dangling from our lips when we heard a sound coming from the door to the dining room.

We looked up and saw our mother standing in the doorway. From the look of consternation on her face, she must have witnessed quite a bit of my performance. Her eyes had been overwhelmed. Before her was a son who had just given birth dressed in a homemade chenille gown, wearing her mules. In addition, all three of her children were huffing on realistic candy cigarettes pulled from the box in her son's cleavage.

There were far too many issues to address in one day. My mother turned around and walked out of the room. I sensed we had done something untoward and said to my sisters, "I don't think we should play this game anymore."

My mother didn't mention the incident again until twelve years later when I told her I was gay and she responded, "Yes, I know you are."

I asked, "How did you know I was gay?"

She laughed and proceeded to describe in vivid detail the birth of her first grandchild all those years ago.

CHAPTER 43 PIN THE TAIL ON THE DONKEY

Not everyone could keep quiet for twelve years. Gwen couldn't wait to brag about her role in my giving birth. Although she exaggerated her patting of my forehead and diminished my labor pains, our stepfather got the picture.

Despite all his other traits, he was not particularly homophobic and only despised weakness. Faggot was not a sexual orientation to him. It was a term for weakness. The general sense I got from him was a man was entitled to anything he was man enough or strong enough to pull off, up to and including wearing a dress in public. He was enlightened from a Dark Ages point of view.

I was never told this story directly, but I overheard him tell it several times. Being straight, he left out the fashion details, but not far from our house he had witnessed a drag queen pummel this man who had more mouth than common sense. The homophobe, seeking higher status among his peers, thought a man in high heels was low hanging fruit. Initially the drag queen ignored the man's taunts, which only emboldened the homophobe. That was until the man reached out and tore his dress. Beneath the facade of femininity was a man who was more than a match for the homophobe. After brutally beating the man to the pavement, the drag queen relieved the man of his wallet as payment for the torn dress. It was also tuition for a well-learned lesson; a man in a dress is still man.

After hearing about my feminine exploits, my stepfather hinted that I was not like other boys. His sympathy was as roughly hewed as he was. He felt I needed to learn how to fight. I already knew how to take a punch, mainly from him. Generally, he pulled his punches somewhat because I was a child. But none of my peers hit as hard as he did. I didn't know what he had in mind, but I would have rather been back on the couch in my chenille gown giving birth.

The streets of Baltimore made no allowances for conscientious objectors or running from a fight. Retreat simply would embolden others. If destined to lose the fight, it was prudent to make the opponent's victory appear hard won. A strong showing by the vanquished left an exit route for their pride and discouraged further fights.

I had been in minor fights but preferred to make powerful friends and convert enemies into friends, or at least neutral acquaintances. After being abandoned by Darla in my almost-fight with Robert, I had devised a different strategy, one that ensured my tears would not be greeted with laughter. There had to be consequences for hurting or attempting to hurt me.

None of us had knowledge of, nor followed the Marquess of Queensberry Rules. Fighting was not a sport to me. It was a nuisance. We had our own societal restraints to be sure, but I did not subject myself to those either. They tended to diminish my advantage and accented that of others. If I let others set the terms, the battle was already lost.

Generally, fights didn't come out of nowhere; the person who thought they could win boasted in advance to ensure a large crowd. One such person was a boy named Alonzo, who everyone called Lonny. He enjoyed starting fights. Whether he had been wronged or not, it didn't matter. His victims were merely props in his emotional wasteland. In his soul ticked an emotional clock that announced it was time to boost his self-esteem at the expense of someone else.

Though he lived near the corner of E. Eager and N. Caroline Streets, we were not in the same circle of friends. We knew each other and interacted well together when we did play, but it was not often. There certainly wasn't any animosity between the two of us. But when low self-esteem is hungry, it will devour anything. Friends, family and acquaintances, it doesn't matter. Eventually he chose me as the morsel of the day. Proximity was my only offense.

Since he allotted me the time, I took advantage of his logistical mistake and set the time and place for the fight. I chose the alley behind my house an hour after school. His victory was assured, so his only concern was that there was room for an audience.

When I got home, I watched my afternoon cartoons. During a commercial break I went to our bathroom and looked out the window into the heroin house to ensure my weapon was still there. It was. Despite my impending fight, I enjoyed the rest of my cartoons and laughed as if I didn't have a care in the world.

A few minutes before four o'clock I climbed in the window of the heroin house and retrieved my weapon. It was stuck to the floor, so I used a piece of broken glass to scrape it loose from the floor. I approached Lonny in the alley with my hands dangling my weapon behind my back. He still didn't look particularly concerned; he was stronger than I was and no doubt thought he could take it from me, whatever it was.

Unbeknownst to him, he had brought fear to the fight, and I had the key to release it. As I passed one of the spectators, she saw my weapon and jumped back. Lonny showed some concern and backed into an indentation between two buildings. He had trapped himself. Before the girl could announce what I had in my hand, I pulled it from my back and cut off his escape.

Dangling in front of him was a dead rat. I knew he was terrified of them. As this one was dead, I squeaked and chirped to make the animal seem more animated. There was no need; he was just as scared of a dead one, if not more so. Death had given the rat a rictus smile that made its teeth appear more menacing. Lonny's face seesawed between fear and defiance, but fear was steadily gaining weight. Eventually defiance could no longer lift fear from his face.

I shook the rat in front of him to induce even more fear. His eyes began to dart, but he was surrounded by brick walls on three sides and one of his biggest fears guarded his exit. Before I could declare my demands, Lonny was already apologizing and making concessions. But I wanted to hear him swear on his mother that he wouldn't bother me again before I would relent. That was our code of truth. Despite his fears he remained reluctant to swear it. There was still a hint of revenge in his eye.

Until he swore that oath, I would not let him pass. I swung the rat a little closer to help persuade him. In desperation he tried to become part of the wall. Though I had not intended it, on the second swing towards Lonny, a piece of the rat came loose. I think it was an eye. To my benefit and his detriment, it landed on Lonny's right shoe.

He desperately shook his right foot. When he couldn't shake the rat's eye out of his shoestrings, he started crying. For sanity's sake he mentally amputated his right foot. He couldn't bear that there were rat bits clinging to his shoes. His eyes were now full of nothing but fear. He cried out his oath that he would not bother me ever again and pleaded with me to let him pass.

When I allowed him to escape, he ran home crying for his mother. Because he had cried, Lonny lost all his tough guy credentials. I knew he wouldn't bother me anymore, but to further ensure he wouldn't, I left the dead rat on his front stoop. Initially I had planned on taking pins from my mother's sewing box and sticking them in the rat. But fake Voodoo would have been overkill. Lonny didn't bother anyone after that.

Gossip of the nasty boy who had brought a dead rodent to a fight spread as swiftly as I had hoped. My stepfather found out about the incident, because my nickname for a time was Rat Eye. I shrugged off the moniker, but privately I was proud of it. I wanted the reputation of being unpredictable and cunning. Picking up a dead rat had disgusted me as well, but no one had to know that but me. A reputation was a preventive measure and as good a shield as any. Instigators thought twice before bothering me.

After hearing about me playing unwed mother, my stepfather wanted to turn my shield into a fist. Even before this incident he was growing annoyed with me because I had been avoiding this new boy who had been taunting me. I didn't run from him, I just walked away in search of more interesting company. He was annoying and petty, two behaviors I had disdained from an early age. We both were named Grant, and he wanted sole possession of our name.

Whenever I saw him, he would come up with a derogatory new name for me. They weren't even clever names. Very few of my playmates called me Rat Eye anymore. The petty Grant had not witnessed me sending Lonny scurrying home. I thought perhaps it was time for Rat Eye to make another appearance.

Gratefully, he didn't attend my school, and I generally encountered him only on weekends. His parents sent him to do chores and run errands for his grandmother who was convalescing from an illness. She lived around the corner from us, so he had to walk by our house. It being Sunday, I was bound to encounter him at some point during the day. But my stepfather was pushing me to confront the other Grant. When questioned about how I was going to deal with the petty Grant, I told my stepfather I was going to get another rat.

He challenged me and said, "You can't pull a rat out your pocket every time you get in a fight."

This was East Baltimore; there were plenty of rats. But I was forced to concede to his point. Confronting someone over something as silly as sharing a first name seemed pointless to me.

I pushed the conversation to the back of my mind and went outside to play. I was still experiencing a postnatal high from giving birth that morning. A few hours later, while playing not far from our front stoop, behind my back I heard the other Grant taunt me with a new nickname that sounded more like a speech impediment than an insult. Usually he was only passing through and rarely stopped to play. The other children tolerated him but didn't enthusiastically engage with him very much. He was easy to avoid.

Forgetting my earlier conversation with my stepfather, I walked toward our doorway. But he must have been periodically watching from the window, because he met me standing at the doorway, blocking my entrance. His stance and stare were more of a barrier than the wooden door would have been. I was not getting back into the house until I stood up for myself. Sighing, I turned to verbally challenge the annoying Grant.

My friends and sisters instantly formed up behind me, but my stepfather told them to back off because this was my fight. This emboldened the other Grant, which intensified his taunts. The huff and puff portion of the fight would be an easy victory for me. Grant couldn't put more than five words together in a sentence without mispronouncing two or three of them.

He swiftly lost the war of words, pushed me and said, "Do you want to fight about it?"

Honestly, I didn't want to fight. Goodness gracious, I had just given birth that morning, and preferred a maternity gown over boxing gloves. But if I wore one, I had to wear the other. Incentives are great fuel for fighting, but I felt I simply had none. If I were going to fight over the last piece of cake, he would have faced Gladiator Grant. But someone trying to erase the first name from my birth certificate with taunts just wasn't a worthwhile fight to me.

I glanced at my stepfather, who was now sitting on our stoop. Initially I hoped he was there for support, but I soon realized he was my incentive.

In front of everyone he said, "You fight him, or you fight me. You're not getting into the house until you do one or the other."

One had ten pounds over me, the other had at least a hundred. One had fists, the size of my mouth, the other had them the size of my face. One I saw occasionally, the other I lived with. It was a poor choice within a bad choice. I made my decision by forcefully pushing Grant back.

The fight escalated faster than I had anticipated. My opponent immediately started throwing punches, which were mostly ineffective because we were too young to be skilled fighters. Neither of us knew how to jab. Most of his punches were haymakers, which were easy to anticipate and defend against. But as we battled on, my forearms grew weary and sore from fending off blows.

Twice he threw roundhouse punches that left him open to counter strikes. But I didn't take advantage because I was fighting several battles: not getting hurt, not hurting him and making the fight look good so I didn't get beaten when I went home. Yet beneath my patience lurked a temper. I knew I had a dark side to my soul, but an individual had to dig deep to reach it. Unfortunately, there was no shortage of miners in this world and Grant was swiftly reaching the coal in my soul.

One of his wild swings threw him off balance, and he fell into me, taking us both to the pavement. He landed on top of me, which cushioned his fall. But my left shoulder hit the curb hard. The pain throbbing from it momentarily left me one handed. Grant recovered quickly and began punching down toward my face. He already had the advantage of strength over me, which was further enhanced by gravity. It became increasingly more difficult to fend off his blows with my right arm. To compensate for my disadvantage, I bucked my hips up to throw him off balance, but he soon moved his weight from my hips to my stomach. He was gradually inching his weight up my body, trying to pin my shoulders with his legs so he could throw unobstructed punches toward my face.

The throbbing from my left shoulder was diminishing, yet my left arm was still weak. My functioning arm was putting up a valiant defense. Grant's punches had a predictable rhythm. I swung my arms back-and-forth like an upside-down pendulum to deflect each blow as it came. Eventually the inevitable first punch connected. Fortunately for me it landed on my jaw, the sturdiest portion of my face. Grant pulled his hand away in pain, leaving my jaw unfazed.

My neck did not fare as well. It had been resting on the edge of the curb, so the force of the punch had traveled through my jaw, grinding my neck sharply into the cement edge of the pavement. The pain was intense but brief. Momentarily my pendulum stopped swinging, leaving my face vulnerable to Grant's one functioning fist. But instead, he was using that hand to rub the wrist of the hand that had connected with my jaw. Strong wrists are essential to throwing good punches. Apparently, he was a little more limped-wristed than I was.

His momentary pause gave my shoulder and arm time to recover. My jaw had saved the rest of my face. Grant's wrist wasn't recovering from its confrontation with my mandibles any time soon. He still held the high ground but had lost his momentum and half his offensive capabilities. To regain his edge, he went with his last resort, which should have been his first.

He was physically stronger than me. I could defend myself against his punches far longer than I could from his brute strength. Instead of punching he slowly started pushing his hands toward my face. Even with his injured wrist he was able to overpower my arms. With his good hand he grabbed my jaw and held it in place. Using both hands I still did not have the strength to break from his grip. But this left my face open to strike from the fist with the injured wrist.

When it came, the punch was more of a shock than painful. But he was the one who hissed in pain. His injured wrist was not up for the task, and he started slapping me instead of throwing punches. I still kept my two hands on his other arm, because the force he was using to hold my jaw in place was also painfully grinding my neck into the edge of the curb.

My opponent was so intent on hurting me, the concept that I could hurt him in return fled his consciousness. He continued to slap me, which was a fatal mistake for any fighter. Delivering blows that only enraged your opponent without inflicting substantial damage was a sure way to lose a fight. The burning pain in my neck and the sting on my cheeks awakened a rage within me.

Unlike other boys, and later in life, other men, I didn't roar. My rage announced its presence with body racking, stuttering sobs. On the surface it appeared as if I had completely caved to my opponent. It was a psychological reaction and an unintentional ruse that falsely emboldened my adversary. A smile swept across Grant's face as he felt the first sobs rack my body. Completely unaware that I was now transforming into something he should fear and retreat from, he again slapped my cheek, now wet and salty with tears.

A burst of adrenaline dampened my pain and temporarily boosted my strength. I was momentarily strong enough to push his hand away from my jaw. But it was too late for that; I now wanted to draw him in closer. From the very beginning my preferred option had been to disengage, but I was not permitted that option. Now that anger had overtaken me, I responded in kind and wouldn't allow Grant to disengage.

Instead of pushing him away, I guided his thumb to my mouth and bit down hard. It was not the defensive quick release bite of a frightened animal who bit in an attempt to escape. No, my bite was predatory. I locked my jaw and held my prey in place. Through blurry eyes I watched his triumphant smile arch into a scream of shock and pain. I didn't allow his incredulous expression to linger long before I rolled to the side, yanking him to the ground with my teeth. In the short term it was less painful for him to roll with me than to pull away.

Swiftly rolling on top of him, I reversed our roles. Except he now was at more of a disadvantage than I had been. He had an injured wrist and a portion of his hand was still locked between my teeth. My jaw had served me well, for it was the source of both his injuries.

Oddly, I was not a tough or skilled fighter, which made me more dangerous. Most neighborhood fights ended quickly, once one of the combatants had been subdued. But at home I was already at the mercy of my stepfather, who could beat me any time he chose. Being at the mercy of someone who showed none terrified me. I didn't want to hurt anyone, but even more so I didn't want to get hurt and couldn't allow myself to be beaten on the streets as well as at home. When my rage was aroused my opponents received not only their portion but in addition the pent-up rage I felt for my stepfather.

To me, nearly every fight felt like attempted murder. Inevitably I inferred more harm than my opponents intended. Those stronger than me were most at risk. I was afraid of what they might do to me, so I did worse to them: bite, punch, gouge, scratch, or choke.

Unaware and unafraid of blood-borne illness, I bit down harder on Grant's thumb as I began to choke him.

The metallic taste of someone else's blood was quite disturbing to the tongue. Repulsed, I released his thumb from my dental vice. His bloody hand immediately went to assist his other injured hand, but both were unable to keep me from choking him. Though my eyes were still cloudy from tears, I could see fear in his bulging eyes. He was looking up at me and saw his own blood hissing from my teeth. If I continued to choke him, I soon would have sole possession of our name. A part of me empathized with him because I could've been him, but I also couldn't stop myself.

My tormentor had unleashed a consequence he was unprepared to deal with. He couldn't speak with my hands coiled around his vocal cords, but his eyes were pleading for me to stop. I had to dig through layers of anger and fear to find a morsel of mercy. Slowly I let my grip slacken. He received just enough air to take the bulge out of his eyes, but I still was unable to completely release my grip.

Finally, my stepfather, who instigated the whole incident, grew concerned and pulled me from Grant's throat. He held my arm in the air, announcing my victory to the gathered crowd of neighborhood children. Still crying, I caught a glimpse of my deeds. Grant still lay in the gutter trying to take in enough air to get up and run. Despite my teeth marks on his thumb and my handprint around his throat, my tears were not for him. They were from the labor pains of giving birth to a darker, more primal Grant.

I disliked and feared the victorious Grant more than the vanquished one. The one in the gutter eventually caught enough breath to stand and run home. But the Grant I had given birth to was coming home with me.

Instead of chastising my tears, my stepfather had a puzzled expression on his face and asked, "Why are you crying? You won."

I lied and said they were tears of joy. How could I tell someone who let his demons prance freely around our house with no shame or reflection that I feared mine? He was proud of what I was ashamed of. Though I had won his fight, I didn't bask in his praise and felt nearly as helpless in victory as I would have in defeat. From an early age I knew every person contained both positive and negative attributes. But they were not equal portions; to nurse one causes the other to become the runt. I felt I had just nursed the wrong one.

Was my stepfather celebrating my win, or was he celebrating me taking one more step closer to being like him? I feared it was the latter. But this would be the last year I would tolerate being treated as an inanimate object. It felt as if I were the paper cutout in a game of Pin the Tail on the Donkey. I was in a room full of people wearing blindfolds, who were trying to pin a paper personality on me. Soon the donkey would bray and kick. It had already bitten once.

CHAPTER 44 WELL DRESSED JESUS

I resented that the world was full of those who searched for the worst in others. Rarely did I venture out of my way to hurt people's feelings, but there were many who went out of their way to have their feelings hurt. Without thought they ruthlessly pursued campaigns against others. Destroying big things to get little things, they ruined good relations for trinkets. Self-determination and resistance were perceived by them as attacks; retribution and consequences for their actions were viewed as unjust persecution by others.

The following week I encountered Grant one more time. He sheepishly walked by my house on the other side of the street, but he briefly summoned sufficient courage to show the wolf within and glared at me. I smiled and clacked my teeth at him twice. He swiftly averted his eyes and sped up his pace out of my life. Either his grandmother regained her health, or he traveled the long way to her house from that point on. I never saw him again.

Rumors that I had bitten a boy hadn't gathered traction as there were only a few days remaining to the school year. Our attention spans were reduced to near nothing as the scent of cut grass from Madison Square Park wafted into our classrooms. The aroma promised more of a summer than East Baltimore could provide for its children. By July it would be replaced by the smell of hot asphalt. Still, we daydreamed of those asphalt summers.

One of the last mornings of school, Robert, Jane and I fell into conversation about how we were going to spend those longer days and shorter nights. As I lived a few blocks away from the Chick Webb Recreation Center, on hot days I would be escorted by my mother to spend time cooling off in its pool. Although I could swim, I tended to stay in the shallow end. Very little swimming took place there, because we were like sardines packed in water.

Robert couldn't swim. Therefore, his only aquatic option was an adult illegally popping a fire hydrant for the neighborhood children. The water was similar to a high-powered sprinkler and fun as long as the main force of the water was avoided. It cooled the asphalt and gathered in low places in the street to form temporary kiddy pools.

Jane lived in a bigger world than Robert and I did. The Chesapeake Bay would be her swimming pool. She had a family member who lived in the exclusive community of Highland Beach. Located thirty-five miles south of Baltimore, it was founded by the son of abolitionist Frederick Douglass and was the first resort town in the country established for black people. But Jane didn't like going there because she was forced to wear a bathing cap on her Afro. She much preferred going to Hammerman Beach. Located where the Gun Powder River enters the Chesapeake Bay, it was much closer, only fifteen miles northeast of the city. There her tight curls could freely mingle with the river water and the bay.

Both Robert and I thought Jane was rather brave for wading in water full of creatures with claws and scales. I ate from the Chesapeake Bay but didn't swim in it. I had become so urban, the first time I entered God-made waters, full of life, I entered with some trepidation. In my mind, fictitious animals such as toe takers, chimp-gators and water snappers lurked beneath the surface. Eventually, I grew to love all forms of water. Though I would spend much of my life near the two biggest bays in America, San Francisco Bay and Chesapeake Bay, I never swam in either.

Jane promised to bring back seashells for me when we returned to school in autumn. I am sure she kept her promise, but I could not keep mine, as I would not be there when she returned. I would not be returning to that school and would never see Jane or Robert again. Completely unaware it was a summer of saying goodbye, I casually ended the conversations, believing I could resume them again at a later date.

Living in a violent household it was hard to form habits, make assumptions and have expectations. Yet I was able to create some. During the summer, at least once a week our mother would take us to Chick Webb to swim. But circumstances would change this.

Our parents had established boundaries we were not allowed to cross, N. Caroline Street to the east, N. Eden to the west, E. Biddle to the north and Ashland Avenue to the south. For the most part it kept us in but did nothing to keep others out. Some children had larger boundaries that overlapped ours. Somewhere to the east of us lived a boy who had taken a particular disliking to Peanut.

I never had to defend her. In all honesty, she was a more confident and better fighter than I was. Peanut viewed fights as annoying, so she tended to battle just enough to drive assailants away.

Continually losing to a girl must have been humiliating for the boy. Eventually he sunk deeper into cowardice and returned to attack her in front of our house with a beer bottle. Occupied at the time with something in our living room, I did not witness the attack. But apparently a beer bottle instilled no more fear in Peanut than his bare hands. She stood her ground.

A yelp of shock was the first indication I had of the confrontation. As her brother, I recognized every sound Peanut uttered and knew it was her. Then I heard the horrified screams of those who witnessed the attack. From their pitch I was expecting to find a dying sister on the street. I ran outside hoping to see any wound that was not fatal. With regards to injuries, I had absorbed enough of the ethos of stoicism from the men around me to view anything less than fatal as a mere scratch.

What should have been seen as horrific I viewed with relief. Flanked on both sides by an attentive Gwen and Willa, Peanut was standing there bleeding from a deep gash in her left tricep. In my peripheral vision I saw the boy slink away with a broken beer bottle in his hand. In retrospect, perhaps the saddest reality of the attack was that it was done by a nine-year old boy.

The wound was deep enough to see bone and needed the attention of an adult. Unfortunately, our mother was shopping, which left our stepfather as our only option. The severity of the wound dwarfed our hesitancy to present him with bad news. Peanut had not been crying much, but she swiftly dried up those few tears before facing our stepfather. He was as likely to add to her pain as to alleviate it.

As she walked into the house, she held her hand over the wound. I walked by her side and held the hem of her dress away from her body to catch any excess blood. She probably wouldn't be blamed for the blood on her dress, but any stains on the floor or furniture might set him off. As much as he had a favorite, Gwen was it, so she went upstairs to tell him what happened.

When he came downstairs, he saw Peanut and I casually examining the wound. Never having seen human bone before and despite the fact that it was her bone, we were fascinated that it really was white.

We caught him on a good day. Our stepfather didn't quite treat the wound as if it were a scratch, but there was no alarm in his voice either. The 911 emergency system was in its infancy. Only two or three small towns in the whole country had the service at the time. The first call had been made in February of that year. At the time, if there was a medical emergency, people called the operator, a taxi, or friends. I don't remember if he called a friend or a taxi, but he informed Peanut she was going to the hospital. Gwen and I were to stay home to wait for our mother to return so we could inform her about what happened.

Less than two minutes after they walked out the door, our mother returned toting two bags of groceries. Finally, Gwen felt safe enough to cry. Perhaps because she was the youngest, she elevated Peanut's wound to the appropriate level of severity. Before consoling Gwen, our mother called a taxi. While we waited, she began to nervously put some of the perishables away. As she told us everything was going to be alright, we watched her place a head of iceberg lettuce into the freezer. Before we could alert her to her mistake, we heard a knock at the door.

Our mother had made the call soon enough that the same taxi driver who had driven her home from the grocery store was now driving us to the hospital. We entered the hospital, stepping into a great hall that was bustling with people. Gwen and I were moved to a less traveled portion of the hall while our mother went to a window to inquire about Peanut.

We had only been to Johns Hopkins one other time, and that was when we had first arrived in Baltimore. That visit had been to the old section of the hospital. The reason for that visit had been banished from my memory by the sight of *The Divine Healer*. To my underexposed five-year-old eyes, the gray marble statue of Jesus towered toward a glass umbrella, which in actuality was the first glass dome I had ever seen. In reality, the statue was only ten and a half feet tall. But his strong outstretched stone arms looked as if they were reaching down to lift me up to the glass umbrella.

Our mother read out loud the inscription at its base. "COME unto ME All Ye That Are Weary And Heavy Laden And I Will Give You REST." I had accurately interpreted his outstretched arms. Though made of cold stone, they were welcoming.

Besides the message, the most striking aspect of the statue was the robe. Whereas most of the figure was clearly made of stone, the robe seemed as if it was made of moving water. The folds and drapes resembled gray waves that had no shore to break upon and appeared to travel the body in an endless loop. Jesus wore it well. For a brief sacrilegious moment, I wished the statue was a mannequin, and the water robe was for sale.

Most of the people milling around were dressed well, but none as well as Jesus. I saw men in wingtip shoes and women in felt hats. What I did not see at the age of five was color, but that colorblind memory would be painted over by a new one. Four years later I stood in a different section of the hospital with a different perspective. Here there was no stone Jesus, and most of the people were white. I was keenly aware that Johns Hopkins Hospital was a white iceberg in a sea of black. I now saw color first; then I saw wingtip shoes and felt hats.

Regardless, I was a people watcher, and color had not poisoned that joy. I saw a woman wearing a brooch that appeared to be more expensive than the garment it was pinned to. A man walked past us who had meticulously ironed a dingy white shirt. Most of the sick wore a mask of dignity. They draped their finest clothes over infirm and sick bodies, to dress their best when they felt their worst.

Then an orderly wheeled in a man on a gurney who didn't have the strength to wear his best. His attendant briefly left him alone in front of Gwen and me. Although a sheet covered him up to just below the shoulders, he was naked, or was wearing nothing but underwear. I could tell his skin burned scarlet from head to toe, almost as if his entire body was blushing. The weight of the sheet looked painful.

Whatever the illness, it had taken the fight out of him. He had awareness in his face and command of his eyes and lips but could move nothing else. Years later when I would be in a similar condition, I would know the feeling of lying in a hospital bed, whole paragraphs roaming my head, yet possessing sufficient strength to only convey them as a reassuring wink or a simple smile.

Then the man on the gurney winked and smiled at us. Those two simple gestures ignited recognition within me. The man on the gurney was Stevens the cop, who enjoyed jelly donuts and had arrested Axel.

Although he was a peripheral person in my life, my sympathy increased because I did at least know him. He was one of the few police officers, people in the neighborhood felt comfortable with. I tried to give him dignity and used my imagination to dress him as I was accustomed to seeing him, in good health and a blue uniform. But despite my best effort to keep him clothed and well, I could still see he was very ill.

Then I had an out-of-body experience, or rather an in-body experience. For a brief moment I felt as if I was inside Stevens' immobile form. Through his eyes I saw Gwen and me staring at him. We had concerned expressions on our faces that didn't look like makeup; they were real. Children rarely know how to apply emotional makeup.

Stevens was not thinking in whole paragraphs. I could feel coherent thoughts swirling in his head, but the thoughts of a feverish person weren't punctuated by periods, commas, or question marks. They blended together or backtracked and repeated, creating deep ruts. The more he tried to think new thoughts the deeper the old ones dug in. Then I left his feverish, itchy body and my sympathy turned to empathy, for I knew what it felt like to be trapped in a thought.

When the orderly returned, I asked him, "Could you take Mister Stevens to see, well dressed Jesus in the other building?"

The orderly gave me a confused expression and wheeled his patient away. I waved at Stevens until he was out of sight but never saw him again. He was among the growing number of people who would disappear from my life.

Our mother returned and took us to a waiting room. A nurse led her to a room. As soon as she entered our stepfather left the room to wait with us. We sat on hard chairs that magnified the minutes into hours and anesthetized our behinds. But finally, Peanut emerged from the room, proudly displaying seven stitches.

She had transformed her injury into a virtue, which caused Gwen and me to become envious. Upon returning home I drew stitches on my forehead. Gwen drew some around her wrist in the shape of a bracelet. Peanut scoffed at our ink stitches but begrudgingly allowed us into her club as lesser members. We looked like Frankenstein's children. The novelty of the club wore off by the next day and was replaced with a penalty.

Gwen's and my imaginary stitches had real consequences. Since Peanut's wound didn't allow her to go swimming for several weeks, neither could we. Several weeks turned into never. Not only was I saying goodbye to people and didn't know it, I also was unaware that I was bidding farewell to places. But the memories of places cling to you as well. To this day, when I smell an indoor chlorinated pool, my memories take me back half a century to the pool at Chick Webb Recreation Center.

Gwen and I were not happy that Peanut's after-care instruction became ours as well. But our first instinct was to circle the wagons around our injured sister rather than complain. We were not going to enjoy something at her expense, especially since the source of her situation was a hostile outsider.

My sisters and I generally shared everything, sometimes reluctantly, but it had been slowly ingrained in us to do so. We had learned this the hard way. Once Peanut and Gwen forgot that the rules of sharing were really to their benefit, because I was food aggressive. They had decided they would take the last piece of cake and lock themselves in the bathroom to eat it without sharing with me. I don't know what they were thinking, because I could smell cake and hear a fork clank against a plate a hundred paces away.

They mistakenly thought they were safe behind a locked door. Not one for physical force, instead of battering the door down I told them I would smoke them out. They scoffed at my threat, knowing full well I wouldn't start a fire in the house. Their scoffs soon turned to shrieks when a few moments later I returned with a can of roach spray and sprayed it through the keyhole and under the crack beneath the door. The insecticide added another layer to the layered cake. No one had cake that day, not even the roaches.

As the fight for cake had proven, battles could be wasteful and lead to diminishing returns. After that incident we were more likely to fight over plenty than scarcity. If there was one cookie, we graciously shared, but if there were a dozen we sometimes bickered. Disagreement was not a luxury we could always afford.

When all was well, we switched alliances constantly, the two youngest against the oldest, the two oldest against the youngest or the younger and older against the middle. But external threats or events would instantly end any squabbling, and we would form a united front. Despite our occasional infighting, we only truly felt safe in the presence of each other.

CHAPTER 45 DANCING IN THE SUN

Fears of more urban unrest and an act of crime brought music to the forefront of my life in the summer of 1968. Melodies and rhythms were such an integral component of life that they were taken for granted. Just as our hearts beat without conscious thought, so, too, did music drive our lives. The people of East Baltimore seemed to hear music even when it was not playing and walked as if each step at any moment could turn into dance. Mundane tasks looked as if they had been well choreographed, but their bodies just naturally swayed and undulated to the songs of life.

Watching the people around me stroll and strut their stuff was a free spectator's sport. I, along with the inanimate buildings that lined the streets, looked on with awe and envy. The buildings may have been envious of the graceful moves of the people around them but watching me walk made them grateful that they must remain still. I walked as if each step kept pace with a kazoo band that continuously played one note out of sync.

My dancing was not much better. A few days after school had closed for the summer, a band that reminded me of the Beatles gave a free concert on our playground. The band members were white, had long dark hair and played one Beatles song. I didn't have enough exposure to white people to question the resemblance beyond that.

Missing the point completely, as if the racial climate had been caused by weather, the news was broadcasting fears that the summer heat could reignite the riots of spring. The longhaired white men were as well-meaning as the white woman with the lorgnette who had brought ballet dancers to our school. At least they were trying to build a bridge to us.

A brief scan of the crowd revealed that Robert was not there, so this event was not going to be as entertaining as the ballet performance. Nor was Jane there, which meant the music was not cool.

The beats and sounds were more familiar than the ballet music, because the sounds the band played were derivatives of traditional black music. During this time period when white people copied our music, they usually put chains on it and made it stiff, but the white boy band was not bad.

The last time I had danced at the school I had been an ashy snowflake in the auditorium in the dead of winter. Now it was the beginning of summer, and along with many others, I danced in the sun. My dance could not be trapped and caged by choreography. In my head it was a river that overflowed its banks and flowed where it wanted. In reality, it was a flood that disrupted other dancers. Rhythm and I were not friends. Family and friends had grown accustomed to my form of dancing and gave me plenty of space, because my floundering often threw their rhythm off.

I couldn't see myself dance. But as we danced in the sun, occasionally I would catch glimpses of a shadow that was distinctive from all the others. I did a jazz leap toward the sun to confirm the shadow was mine. Now that I had singled it out, admittedly it did look as if it had fallen to the ground, twitching, convulsing and in need of medical attention. My shadow continued to flop around on the asphalt, so I did another jazz leap to revive it. I sincerely felt my dancing belonged in the sky, but no matter how high I leaped my dancing shadow returned to the ground twitching and convulsing.

My critics were hushed by my joy and enthusiasm, not my skill. As I danced, I moved about, sometimes close to the band and sometimes further away. On one of my orbits away from the band I saw a little boy standing near his mother. He was pointing at me.

Despite the music I could hear him say, "Mama, he's not dancing to the rhythm."

As if it was the most natural thing in the world, she said, "Oh baby, he's dancing to the lyrics."

At this point an intrusive cloud blocked the sun and deprived me of my shadow dance partner. But the mother had given me permission to never need a partner or rhythm ever again. I spun away with a smile on my face and a purpose in my soul and proceeded to glide on every word of the song. It was now the theme of my life. No matter what others played, I would always dance to my own lyrics.

About a week after that, James Brown gave a free summer concert. It was held on Gay Street, a little over a half mile from our house. But as desperately as I wanted to go, I was not permitted to attend. Instead I snuck into the kitchen of the heroin house next door and took a rickety chair to sit at the corner of N. Eden and Barnes Streets.

I was too far away to hear any lyrics clearly, but a muffled James Brown was better than no James Brown. The humid air was no deterrent to the rhythm and energy electrifying the air. As I watched the latecomers walk down N. Eden Street, they would start to feel the energy just after they crossed E. Eager Street. Walking literally turned into dance. The length of N. Eden Street became an asphalt and concrete ballroom floor.

The throng of people was also a parade that didn't know it was a parade. Vibrant new colors worn by the celebrants looked as if they had been freshly minted that day and competed aggressively with the sun to shine. There were some who could not afford new, but they could afford clean. None were dirty and no two people looked the same. It was a mild compliment to say someone looked good in an outfit. This was polite acknowledgement that they knew how to shop, but if someone said, "You make that outfit look good," that showed you knew how to wear it. They were definitely not the same compliment, because not everyone could wear what they bought.

Years later I was shopping with a white friend and had picked out a color that was rather conservative by my standards, when the person asked, "Why do black people wear such bright colors?"

I would return to the memory of people clad in bright colors marching and dancing down N. Eden Street to see James Brown and answered, "Because we can."

I spent much of the rest of the day watching the people of East Baltimore making the clothing they wore look good.

Another event gave me some control over the music I could listen to. It happened between the playground concert and James Brown's concert. A temporary loss would turn into a permanent gain.

Our parents had left us alone to go grocery shopping. Different standards applied back then. Parents generally didn't hire a baby-sitter for an hour to run errands. If they spotted a neighbor on the way out, they might ask them to keep an eye on us. But our safety instructions clearly stated, "Don't answer the door for anyone and if a burglar breaks in, hide until they're gone."

We never had to worry about burglary, because there was usually someone at home and this was an unlikely scenario. But heroin was changing that. Addicts would rather face an occupied house than veins empty of drugs and the withdrawals that followed.

My sisters and I were sitting at our kitchen table finishing up lunch when we saw our neighbor Wiggy climb out a window of the heroin house next door. This was not particularly unusual, except instead of disappearing down the alley he walked toward our dining room window.

Part of the window was covered in chicken wire, with just enough room for Ibo to climb in and out. We heard Wiggy pulling at the wire. Gwen immediately ran upstairs and hid. Peanut and I were more curious than scared. We stood at the base of the staircase and peeked around the corner, prepared to run if he came our way. He had to know we were there but didn't care. Also, he must have known what he wanted. He was so fixated on it that he ignored an unmarked envelope laying on the dining room table that contained a large portion of our parents' pay. He went straight for our color TV.

He was a big man. TVs were heavy in those days. Unplugging the power cord and wrapping it around his wrist, he carried it toward the front door as if it was merely a grocery bag of heavy canned goods. Peanut and I followed him. When he exited our house, he rudely left the door open, so we quietly closed it behind him and relocked it. There was nothing else we could do. The last thing we wanted was to have our stepfather blame us for letting him in.

When our parents came home, they were relieved that we were unharmed and that Wiggy had not noticed the envelope with the money in it. Faced with a few days of children with no TV, our stepfather allowed us to play our own records, after carefully instructing Peanut and me how to handle them with care.

We were not allowed to touch albums but could play any of the 45 singles we wanted. It took us a few tries to learn how to insert the yellow 45 rpm record adapter into the center of the record. Then a whole new world opened up.

There was a certain amount of anticipation in the pops and crackles as the spinning grooves of the record carried the needle closer to the song embedded in the vinyl. I soon developed the skill of dropping the needle as close to the song as possible to shorten the anticipation. But I rarely did this, as I preferred the pop and crackle intro to prepare myself for the emotions the songs would release.

I would eventually witness songs migrate from vinyl to tapes, then to discs, phones and into what seemed like thin air. In the future, with the command of my voice, I would be able to summon almost any song I wanted to hear. I would grow to love instantaneous but would remain madly in love with anticipation. Not all songs migrated from vinyl. I would keep one album, as much for the fond memories of the pops and crackles as for the songs.

When I hear pops and crackles, I remember learning to snap my fingers and singing along with female singers, which allowed the destination of my affection to be male. This was not questioned until my voice deepened and the sound of a baritone singing about loving a man disturbed some listeners. Around that age, it was strongly suggested that when singing, I should change my male pronouns to female. Instead I would emphasize the male pronoun by singing it louder. In some ways I camouflaged my gayness by throwing it directly in people's faces. I could be gay when I sang female parts and would be viewed as defiant more than gay.

As a child I wasn't obviously gay, but when it came out, I didn't hide it either. What I would hide was being a homosexual. A sexualized, black, gay man was America's boogeyman. We were limp-wristed yet dangerous. Once I hit puberty, it would take me several years to build the emotional infrastructure I needed to overpower this false narrative within myself and others.

Puberty is a challenging and confusing time for everyone. Before puberty, and despite not having the lips or hips for it, I pretended to be a female backup singer with my sisters. Unfortunately, my secondary sexual characteristics of armpit, chest and facial hair would manifest themselves so early and quickly it felt as if I had changed into a werewolf. This would give me the physical features to potentially be a backup singer for the Village People, except I couldn't sing or dance. I would have to be the sexy, hairy one that didn't dance and could only play the triangle.

Music would help me through all of this. I could make up an entire world from one song. In that world I slow danced with an imaginary male partner, picked flowers for him, did ordinary things that in the real world could get us killed. It would be music that would eventually lure me into a gay bar and then to a better world than I had created in my head.

At nine years old I had no idea that world could or did exist outside of my head. I was pleased with the unattended early gift I had received because Wiggy had stolen our TV. Snapping my fingers and playing 45 single records was all I was ready for at the time. Wiggy would commit one more crime against our family that would eventually change my meager path through life into a grand boulevard.

CHAPTER 46 MY SINCEREST APOLOGY

Snapping our fingers was not going to carry us through the summer. My sisters and I were given a choice. We could have a new TV by the end of the week, but we would have to cancel our upcoming trip to visit our grandparents in Connecticut, or we could wait until the end of summer for a new TV and go to Connecticut. There was no deliberation on our part. Our decision was unanimous; grandparents win over summer reruns every time.

The election was rigged. Our mother knew what our decision would be. We had just agreed to delay getting a TV we weren't going to have until the end of summer no matter our decision. Now it appeared as if it was our choice. She had just silenced half a summer of whining about not having a TV.

My suspicions were confirmed when our mother announced that in a few days Aunt Porch would drive us to Connecticut, except she showed up three hours after our mother had given us the choice. The drive from Bellefontaine to Baltimore took over seven hours, which meant the decision had been made long before Wiggy had stolen our TV.

If my memory serves me properly, my mother had been on the phone with Aunt Porch over a week and a half before that. They must have made the plans then, but I hadn't paid attention to the conversation because my food aggression once again resumed control of my actions.

While my mother was on the phone, I used it as an opportunity to beg for a snack before it was time. Gwen, Peanut and my stepfather were out somewhere so I had to wait until they returned home before any of us could have an oatmeal cookie. My stomach resented being on somebody else's schedule.

I was hoping after a few moments of whining and pleading she would send me away with an oatmeal cookie in my hand. She was focused on a million things and I on just one, getting that cookie. But that day my mother was particularly resistant to my tactics. So, I doubled down, becoming more annoying and obnoxious, reducing my mother's nerves down to her last. Then I jumped up and down on it as if it was a trampoline and I was wearing football cleats.

Finally, through gritted teeth I heard my mother say, "Let me call you back."

She hung up the phone and walked toward me. If I had had a tail, I would have been wagging it with glee. I was getting my treat early, and for a brief delusional moment I thought I had pushed her to the point that she might give me several cookies to be rid of me. Unfortunately, I had badly misread the situation and heard her words but not her tone.

When the last nerve snaps the energy released does not always break your way. As she leaned down in my face, for a brief moment I honestly thought she was going to ask me how many cookies I wanted. But her expression was one of a temper barely under control. It was finally dawning on me that my quest for cookies came with unintended consequences. The wage for my behavior was a lesson well learned and cherished. I now can never recount the event without seeing the humor in it.

With urgency in her voice she gently but firmly held both my hands and said, "Grant, listen to me carefully. When I release your hands, I want you to run upstairs to your room and lock yourself in. Please, no matter how hard I pound on the door or how loud I scream do not let me in, because your life depends on it. Run right now!"

She released my hands and I bounded up the stairs two at a time. Not only did I lock the door, I pushed my sisters' bed against it for added protection. Though generally not a guilt-ridden person, I felt remorse for my actions. My overactive imagination administered the remainder of my punishment. I wanted to apologize, but I also feared she was still angry.

After an hour and half had passed, I heard my mother ascending the stairs. I readied my apology, but as soon as she knocked it retreated back down my throat and was replaced by a knot instead. Her gentle knock was now suspect; she had said no matter how hard she pounded on the door. Was this a trick?

Then in a soft, sweet voice she said, "Baby, I'm sorry I overreacted. I want to apologize. I made you some rice pudding, and you can have as much as you want."

I did smell cinnamon in the air, but just as I had sprayed roach spray under the bathroom door to smoke out my sisters, I thought my mother had sprinkled cinnamon at the base of the bedroom door to lure me out. A suspicious mind creates ridiculous scenarios.

It was necessary to make sure my response was louder than my growling stomach. The task became more difficult because my mouth was smacking at the thought of having rice pudding, which was my favorite desert at the time. If my mother had thrown in the oatmeal cookie as well, I don't know if I would have had the strength to holdout.

I stopped smacking my lips long enough to answer; "Not now mommy, I want to take a nap. I'll have some later."

The next half hour I sat on my bed whittling down my soul with worry and regret. I felt bad that I was one of those people who destroyed big things to get little things and had driven my mother to the brink.

By today's standards my mother's reaction may seem cruel, but at the time I could still rely on her moral compass. She was generally fair to me and had sent me upstairs to give her time to return to a rational state. I was feeling remorse, something I never felt when my stepfather punished me. I had no such moral conflict with him. On a deep level, children know when a punishment is administered for their betterment and when it's just an outlet for their parents' rage.

My sisters and I usually received our spankings together from our stepfather. He would ask who wanted to go first. As afraid as I was, I offered to go first. I was taking my cues from our mother, who rarely spanked us. It was a time when the acceptable prescription for bad behavior in a child was a spanking. Time-outs were only relegated to sporting events and children's games. My mother's heart was not in it. Whoever went first got the worst of it. By the time our mother got to the last one, the belt in her tired, unwilling hand more fell on that child's behind than struck it. Our mother always looked worse than we did after our spankings.

Not so our stepfather. Unlike our mother, he didn't spank; he beat us and enjoyed it. Try as he might he could not take the predator out of his smile. The first couple of times we mistook this smile for mercy, but it was a Venus flytrap pretending to be mercy. Except he was worse than the carnivorous plant; he pulled the wings off the fly before devouring it. With him, going last could be horrendous. Going first sometimes was better. He was so eager to release his rage upon us that he would hurry on to the next one. When he realized this was the last one, he would linger over his victim like a stalled hurricane. Some days he realized he didn't have to stop and would start over again and beat us all a second time.

He never had any moral credibility with us. Nothing we did was bad enough to warrant what he unleashed upon us. My mother's actions at least taught me a valuable lesson without crushing my soul. Consequences are never pleasant, but they should never crush a child's soul.

Although I was in the third-floor bedroom, I could hear that my sisters and stepfather had returned. When I opened the door there was no cinnamon sprinkle at its threshold. My mother's apology had been sincere, and I felt I owed her one as well. I ran to the kitchen and gushed apologies all over her cinnamon stained apron.

My stepfather had a peculiar expression on his face. If I read it correctly it was a mixture of surprise and envy. He had never received a sincere apology from me. They all had been coerced from me by force. To him, my actions were uncharacteristic. He joked that I must have snuck into the heroin house next door and mockingly lifted my arms to check for track marks. There was not enough beatings or heroin in the world to make me give him a sincere apology.

If I was left alone with my transgressions, I eventually would emerge to engulf the person in a sincere apology. When I was sorry, I was truly sorry. But if someone attempted to extract an apology because of a perceived wrong or tried to make me do so because they thought they could, my reaction was never pleasant.

Later in life, not even a fake apology could be coerced from me. For a brief period in our early teens, Peanut and I didn't get along. Just the sight of each other gave us a rash. She and I had just recently taken up cussing but only when there were no adults around. One day she set me up for a fall. We lived in a house with halls at the time. I was standing in the hall outside my bedroom, but unbeknownst to me my mother was around the corner in the dining room. Peanut could see her, but I couldn't. At that point Peanut slapped me upside my head, knowing what my reaction would be.

Without hesitation I said, "You bitch!"

Before I knew what happened our mother rounded the corner fuming. Not only had I used a cuss word, it was one of the worst ones. She was in no mood to hear why I had called my sister out of her name and demanded that I apologize.

Making matters worse, Peanut stood next to our mother with a smug expression on her face, crossed her arms in a demanding gesture and said, "Yeah you apologize!"

Peanut knew I had no choice and was rubbing it in because our mother heard what I had said but hadn't seen what Peanut had done to provoke me. I weighed my options. Then I matched my sister's smug expression and said with all the sincerity I could muster, "I am sorry you're a bitch!"

Peanut and my mother were stunned by what I said. Not giving them time to recover, I walked away. Before entering my room, I heard our mother say to Peanut, "What did you do to your brother?" I closed my bedroom door on her explanation.

One thing my mother knew was that I was not stingy with my

sincere apologies. I felt no one should be, but there are some individuals who are. It annoyed me that someone could put a lot of thought and effort into hurting others yet would rush through their apology as if it was a burden or a necessary evil. Such individuals say they are sorry because they still consider you useful, not because they think they were wrong. Often, they demand or try to guilt you into accepting an apology that really isn't one. Or they compare their wrong to a greater wrong to justify their misdeed. By pointing to something worse they feel it makes things better. These apologies are punctuated at the end by exacerbated sighs or annoyed huffs.

If my stepfather bothered to apologize at all, he gave a, "This could be worse," apology, or a "You're a bad person if you don't forgive me," apology. These were generally reserved for our mother. He rarely bothered with us. Fortunately, Gwen, Peanut and I didn't have to endure these belittling apologies, nor pretend to accept them.

The nature of attraction, friendship or romantic, is that individuals collide, which can cause fissures and friction. Emotional mishaps are inevitable. Relationships are not an area to have deferred maintenance. My attitude is, if you break it, you fix it. Don't pretend to fix it. Nothing would end a relationship for me faster than discovering that someone damages a relationship with ease but is hesitant to make repairs. I am durable but not a punching bag. My stepfather saw to that.

During my early development my apologies did come with an ulterior motive. Not that I didn't feel sincere remorse, I did. But often my responses were fueled somewhat by my desire not to resemble my stepfather. If he lacked or discarded a desirable characteristic trait, I would retrieve it, not from the gutter but from within myself and bring it to the forefront.

I remembered that my Aunt Porch had been on the phone with my mother when I had misbehaved that day and wanted to apologize to her as well. But the excitement of her arrival had to dampen down before anyone could engage in serious conversation. Finally, she presented us with the coloring books she had brought us. Along with my thank you, I used this opportunity to apologize to her. I dusted off my prettiest words and used the newest, biggest word in my vocabulary, reprehensible. The word was a heavy lift for my tongue, but I was bound and determined to use this adult word to atone for my childish behavior.

From the expression on her face I could tell that Aunt Porch was struggling to remember the incident. As an adult I would experience that same expression on my face. Occasionally an individual would profusely and elegantly apologize for an incident that was so covered in cobwebs I could barely remember it. Normally I would be honest and admit as delicately as I could that I didn't remember the incident. But once in a while the apology would be particularly heartfelt and catch me so off guard that I would conjure up false hurt feelings worthy of their effort. Saying I didn't remember the incident somehow seemed disrespectful.

In retrospect I realize that Aunt Porch had performed for me. Although my big word tripped on my teeth and landed clumsily into my apology, she treated my unmemorable affront with respect.

Initially she stalled by saying, "Um um um," then her face displayed a stern forgiving expression and she continued, "Your behavior was very reprehensible, and I will have no more of it. Do you understand mister? Now come here and give your Aunt Porch a hug."

I ran to her, and she hugged the reprehensible behavior away. Wrapped in her hugs, I heard the phone ring. When the tone in my mother's voice changed, Aunt Porch released me. The concern in my mother's voice was for my Grandma Ruth, who had called.

On our end of the conversation, we heard my mother ask when, what and how, followed by long pauses of nervous listening on her part. When she hung up the phone, she seemed to be contemplating a dilemma more than feeling sad. She turned toward Aunt Porch and said, "That was David's mother. His brother Axel was stabbed to death in Chicago last night."

I am certain that, along with my sisters and me, this was the first time my mother knew someone personally who had been murdered. She was bereft of any feelings of sadness for Axel and seemed more concerned with how to inform her husband about his brother's death. Aunt Porch had never met Axel and didn't have the back-story, so she appeared to be the most upset of us all.

The last time we laid eyes on him was when we lived on Forrest Street. It was the day my mother and I thought I had trapped my sisters in a refrigerator in the junkyard. Fortunately, someone had the foresight to shoot bullet holes in it to keep the refrigerator from becoming a suffocation hazard, which saved my sisters' lives. But Axel had taken advantage of that situation and stolen money from us.

That had been the excuse my stepfather had used to unleash his rage against my mother. I was aware then and grew more so later, that Axel was not the reason, he was the cover story. Regardless, at some point my stepfather had planned on initiating my mother into the world of domestic violence. If Axel hadn't presented my stepfather with the opportunity, a single unwashed dish would have sufficed. Nonetheless, Axel was still attached to the memory and had left me with a memory of my own.

I had not forgotten that he had hung me upside down, threatened to bite me and told me I had sugar in my blood. But the memory was buried under a much larger pile of violence heaped on us by his brother. That first pain had been dulled by more recent pain. The fact that I felt nothing was confusing to me. No matter how deep I dug, I came up with nothing. I had more feelings for Petrus the pigeon than I had for Axel the person and didn't know how to fake the appropriate feelings for his death. All I could do was make certain I was not in the room when my mother told my stepfather.

Perhaps if I had been older, I would have seen the complexities of someone who most certainly had some type of undiagnosed mental illness. Axel became a demon in order to fight the demons that were tormenting him. But fighting fire with fire had created an inferno that ultimately consumed him. Twenty years later, I would exhume his memory to give him the sympathy he deserved. The dead can't change but the living can. I didn't feel I owed him an apology for misunderstanding his pain, for I was but a child myself, and he had hurt me. But I felt I owed his condition an adult's eyes and a new consideration.

If I owed him an apology, it was for feeling nothing at the time of his death. It wasn't exactly as if I had wronged him. But his death deserved more than a shrug of indifference, and I was sorry that was all I had to offer at the time.

Life being what it is, many apologies are made at the foot of graves or into thin air. But I preferred saying mine to a face not covered in dirt, to someone who could forgive you with a hug as my Aunt Porch had done.

CHAPTER 47   BIRDBATHS AND DOORBELLS

An unexpected benefit of Axel's death was that our stepfather would not join us in Connecticut for a few more days. Once again, we would be on the open road with my Aunt Porch and without him. The adults loaded our luggage into the trunk of our aunt's 1967 Lincoln Continental convertible. We skirted the edge of the Chesapeake Bay. Delaware was so small I blinked and then we were in New Jersey. I briefly remembered this was the state where Mister Willy's guide dog was born.

The New Jersey Turnpike was a wide ribbon of asphalt that cut a swath through the Garden State. As the name implied, it was a toll road. Most booths had toll takers, but many had metal baskets that drivers tossed coins into. Since I was sitting on the driver's side, Aunt Porch allowed me to toss nickels into several of the baskets along our route. I didn't miss once. I was far better at toll toss than I would ever be at free throws.

Despite the distraction of toll toss, New Jersey seemed to go on forever, until we reached the George Washington Bridge. Aunt Porch handed the toll taker paper money, but I didn't see her get any coins back. My seat had been an advantage on the turnpike but now crossing the George Washington Bridge, I was on the opposite side of a good view of the Manhattan skyline. Past my sisters' jutting jaw lines, I still could see its massive skyline, and it looked as if it had eaten ten cities the size of Baltimore, with room left over to consume more.

We continued through a sea of suburbs until we approached the toll gates of the Merritt Parkway at the Connecticut border. The toll station was constructed of wood and painted green to mimic the upcoming forest the parkway would pass through. There would be no coin tossing in Connecticut.

I didn't know a road could be so beautiful. Many of the bridges and overpasses were works of art. Though forested, this was part of Connecticut's Gold Coast, and the trees were natural curtains drawn to keep poor eyes from viewing the vast wealth beyond. Rest stops dare not mar its path. They were called service plazas and looked as if foresighted forefathers had built them in anticipation of the invention of the automobile. One looked as if modern gas pumps merely had been added to the front lawn of a colonial home.

We continued east and entered the Naugatuck Valley, birthplace of Naugahyde. The wealth faded away and became mill towns. Once industrial powerhouses of the nation, most towns were now past their heyday, yet still prosperous. In decades past, the valley was known as the "Switzerland of America." For over a century America could not tell time if not for the clock factories of this valley. Seth Thomas, Waterbury Clock Company and the William L. Gilbert Clock Company, along with many others, forged the hands of time for the nation. In fact, a trust set up by William L. Gilbert would help pay for a portion of my and my classmates', education. Later in life I would lovingly refer to the Naugatuck Valley as the Valley of Time.

Route 8 ran the length of the Naugatuck Valley, roughly following the path of the Naugatuck River. Steeples and smokestacks towered above deciduous trees. Industry and religion each preached a different gospel, but both announced the location of each town long before welcome signs did. We cruised past Waterbury and its most notable landmark, the clock tower of the Waterbury Union Station, a replica of the Torre del Mangia in Sienna, Italy. Fittingly, the clock tower was the tallest building in the Valley of Time.

North of Waterbury, near the banks of the Naugatuck River, we saw a movie screen towering over a lot full of hundreds of parking meters. This was my first impression of the Watertown Drive-in Theater. It was the first drive-in I remember seeing. I would spend many a summer parked next to those parking meters listening to and watching B rated movies. It was a B rated location. Lights from the passing cars from Route 8 often disturbed the ambiance of the experience. Cracking the windows to hear the speaker invited mosquitoes from the marshy area near the river. We ate popcorn while the mosquitoes ate us.

Once we passed Thomaston, there were nearly ten miles of nothing but trees. Then Aunt Porch took the exit for downtown Torrington. My sisters' and my excitement mounted. Our patience had been stretched across five states in over five hours and was about to snap. So much energy flowed through me that for a moment I thought I had more horsepower than my aunt's Lincoln Continental. Had I known the address of my grandparents I would have jumped from the seemingly slow-moving car and ran the remainder of the distance.

Our slow speed contradicted the fact that my first impression of Torrington was a blur. My enthusiasm had distorted my vision, and it didn't clear until we parked in front of a house on Benham Street. My grandparents stood on their porch looking like the couple in Grant Wood's *American Gothic*.

They stood close enough together that if I got out of the car first, I could hug both of them at once. But Peanut's door was closer, so she got her hugs first. Shortly after it turned into a hugging frenzy, and I accidentally hugged Gwen, who I had just spent over five hours with, in a car.

We all crowded into the bottom floor of the duplex my grandparents were renting. The space was much smaller than the home they had owned in Bellefontaine but was much nicer. As much as I cherished seeing my grandparents, during this trip I also realized how much safer I felt here than in our home in Baltimore. It was very noticeable, because I had never been to this home before and had no comforting memories here. It was safe because it was simply safe, and it felt good.

Before going to bed that night, our grandmother supervised us as we washed five states worth of dirt from our bodies. The long trip had caught up with us. We practically fell asleep with soap in our hands. After putting us to bed, the adults gathered at the kitchen table, reminiscing and painting the ceiling with puffs of smoke from their cigarettes. I drifted off to sleep too tired to eavesdrop.

Awakening the next morning, my sisters and I were eager to search for new playmates. First, we had to navigate a tower of buckwheat pancakes, a pile of bacon that we could snap in two and two eggs each that looked like yellow bulging eyes staring up at us from our plates. Gwen didn't like her eggs staring at her, so she covered them up with a pancake. Peanut asked for toast so she could stab the bulging eyes and soak up the yoke. I asked my grandmother to cook my eggs longer, until they didn't look like eyes.

After finishing breakfast, we had to wipe the excess cholesterol from our mouths and in Gwen's case her cheeks. Our grandmother made us memorize her address and repeat it back to her a dozen times. We were told not to cross N. Main Street, which was one block west of Benham Street. Other than that, we were not given any boundaries except time. She took us out on the porch just before eight o'clock and made us listen for the bells of Saint Maron and count the chimes. Located two blocks from her house and founded by immigrants from Lebanon, its bells could be heard over most of the North End of Torrington.

Thus, was born my desire for punctuality. The Valley of Time and my grandmother were exerting their influence over me. "Thou shall not be late," would become my eleventh commandment. As an adult, friends and family found it peculiar that I never used round numbers such as ten or twenty minutes to express my arrival time. When expressed as nine or nineteen minutes it got people's attention and let them know I took time seriously. People with the worst sense of timing wanted to set the schedule, and I wouldn't let them. More than for any other reason, I would end friendships with individuals who were habitually late.

My grandmother was not as strict as I would be. When she told us to listen for the chime eleven times, that meant she wanted us there at eleven thirty. She was giving us a grace period. The bells of Saint Maron would be the only watch I would have for years.

Once released into the neighborhood, what had been a blur on the way into town because of my excitement now came clearly into focus. With the exception of one brick house, all the others were made of wood. The few people I saw were all white but were cordial. Torrington didn't have a black section. The few black families who lived in town lived where they wanted to and could afford.

This was blue collar Connecticut, yet to me the wealth was impressive. Almost every house had a doorbell. In our neighborhood back in Baltimore only apartments had doorbells, very few row houses had them. Mister Willy railed against this modern convenience and wondered out loud why it was necessary to electrify a knock. Big doors were much easier to find than little buttons. But I had noticed the little buttons first.

Finally, I noticed all the lawns were neat and trim. Many of them had hedges instead of fences. But what struck me as extremely luxurious was that three of the yards contained birdbaths. Any place that could install outdoor plumbing for birds had to be wealthy. My favorite one was a large water basin atop a Grecian column, made of terracotta. The Greek key design circled both the base of the column and the rim of the basin. In addition, next to it was a shiny silver globe that sat on a pedestal. It looked like a scene from a cheap science fiction movie, and I loved it.

Another sign of wealth made it easy to locate the homes of the children who lived on the street. Hula hoops, balls and toys I'd never heard of were strewn on the front lawns of several houses. We were the wealthiest family on our block back in Baltimore, but we didn't have things in this abundance. Until recently we had a color TV but had lost it to crime. There seemed to be no worry of that here.

The house with the most toys happened to be next to the house with the nicest birdbath. Neat and tidy wealth contrasted with cluttered wealth, such great choices. My eyes couldn't focus until three children, one boy and two girls, all with bright red hair, came out the side door of the house and started playing with the toys. Initially they didn't notice Gwen, Peanut and me staring at them. I don't think any of us had seen people with red hair until that moment. If we had, it had been from a distance. I was fascinated with the color and found it beautiful. As it was summer, their freckles were on full display, and this added to my fascination.

Their last name was Baird. Since we only played with them that summer, I don't remember their first names. But I still remember them. The boy, who was about Peanut's age, noticed us first and invited us into their yard. Despite a yard full of toys, we ignored them and played the usual children's contact games such as tag and Red Rover. When we tired of those we sat on the grass and chatted about nothing.

I was still fascinated with their hair color, but familiarity had lessened it to some degree. My fascination was rekindled when their father came outside to retrieve something from the garage. His rugged body clashed with his pretty face, but I saw where his children had acquired their hair. He had a deeper shade of red than that of his children. I had only seen hair that red on a circus clown.

Though I was in a nearly all-white town, what I'd seen on TV or in entertainment still dominated my view of white people. I remembered seeing a live circus in Baltimore where a family of clowns piled out of a tiny car. The father clown was juggling bowling pins. Among the toys lying on the Bairds' lawn were plastic bowling pins. Because of their red hair and the plastic bowling pins, I was certain this was the family of clowns in that circus without their makeup. But I was confidently wrong.

Overcome with the thought I might potentially be rubbing elbows with stars, and despite child labor laws to the contrary, I asked them, "Does your whole family work for the circus?"

The boy looked confused and said, "No, why'd you think that?"

Before I could ignorantly point to their red hair and the bowling pins lying on the lawn as reasons, the boy's sister rescued me by answering, "Wouldn't that be fun? Let's pretend we all ran away and joined the circus."

Aptly, the role of clown was foisted on me by my fellow circus people. I kept tossing one bowling pin into the air and catching it and called that juggling. Not well received, I then moved on to pratfalls and funny faces. I didn't need red hair or bowling pins to be a clown. I could be a very amusing child when not under stress. When I felt safe, I could laugh at myself and invite others to laugh with me or even at me. People could laugh at me but only by invitation. I never sent invitations to individuals who could not laugh at themselves. Their laughter always seemed cruel.

Without my stepfather here, I felt very safe and did a few more pratfalls. Then we heard the bells of Saint Maron chime eleven times. I made a few more funny faces before my sisters and I returned to our grandparents' house.

We had a light lunch and said goodbye to Aunt Porch, who was driving to Pittsfield, Massachusetts to visit a friend. Then the rest of us piled into our grandparents' nondescript car for a propaganda tour specifically designed to entice our mother to move to Torrington. We drove through a pleasant, moderately busy and prosperous downtown. Though I noticed there were nothing but white people everywhere, I was not disturbed by this. With the exception of a statue in the center of town of a lone Union soldier with a bayonet hanging from his granite hip, none of the white people had bayonets. Nor did I see any with lorgnettes.

Driving south, we continued until we hit the town of Litchfield, which could have been a postcard model for a quaint historic New England town. It was home of the first proprietary law school in the country, and Aaron Burr was among its first students. Ethan Allen was also born here. Whereas Maryland had been cheek to cheek with the Confederate States, Connecticut had been near the heart of abolitionist country. Two giants of the movement were born in the area, Harriet Beecher Stowe in Litchfield and John Brown in Torrington. In addition, some of the recruits who formed the all black Connecticut Twenty-Ninth Regiment that fought in the Civil War came from the surrounding towns.

We made a left turn at the childhood home of Harriet Beecher Stowe on our way to meet the man who offered my grandfather the job that encouraged him to move to Connecticut. I was unaware of how fast my world was changing. A couple of months earlier, I had placed pennies on the grave of John Wilkes Booth in a cemetery full of Confederate soldiers. Then I found myself in abolitionist country passing the home of the author of *Uncle Tom's Cabin*. With some exaggeration, it could have been said that one started the Civil War, and the other ended it. The contrast was too complicated for my mind at the time.

Halfway down the road, a woman in a passing car waved my grandfather to stop. She apologized that a shipment of antiques had suddenly arrived, and his boss would not be able to meet us today. The delay would be worth the meeting; not only the man but the house would be impressive.

Both my grandparents thanked the woman. Our grandmother swiftly advanced to the next event of the day. She wanted to take us shopping, because she had a surprise for us. Gwen and Peanut shrieked and bounced on the seat, high on expectation. I knew better than to follow their example. Our grandmother tended to give you what you needed over what you wanted.

She tended to give time-release gifts, ones where the joy and appreciation followed you for years. Whereas other adults gave toys, she gave knowledge, hobbies and skills. But at nine years old I wanted meaningless plastic bobbles that eventually were destined for a landfill.

While the adults talked, I spent the rest of the journey plotting to separate my grandfather from my mother and grandmother. He was more likely to buy us the bobbles. But even with him we were not allowed to whine and beg while shopping. With him the best method was to stand next to a toy and look as pitiful as possible. Gwen and I were professionals at this. We would look at the toy, then back at our grandfather. Our expressions said we were in organ failure and this toy was an exact organ match. But if our grandmother was around, she would just pull the plug on our shenanigans, and miraculously we would recover.

We went back to Torrington, drove up E. Main Street and pulled into a modern shopping center. There was an A&P supermarket, Star's Department Store, one or two other nondescript businesses, and behind the building towered the movie screen of the Skyvue Drive-In. Gwen, Peanut and I never had been to such places before. Our parents tended to take us to mom and pop stores, the Belair Public Market and movie houses.

Collectively these Baltimore businesses had far more to offer than a shopping center in a small Connecticut town. But the businesses in the shopping center were streamlined and clean, and the department stores did not have the history of the ones in Baltimore. There were several grand department stores along Howard Street in Baltimore. Although around 1960 these stores started allowing black people to shop and try on clothes, we never shopped there. Our stepfather didn't have the desire to force money into a cash register that didn't want it, places where the sales tax was humiliation. Besides, there were closer, cheaper options.

My first department store shopping experience was Star's Department Store. The store's logo was a neon star. Fortune was with my sisters and me, because our grandfather parked closer to the A&P. Then our grandmother and mother went into the grocery store to purchase some nonperishable items, leaving us alone with our grandfather.

Entering Star's felt as if I was visiting the national park of stores. There were canyons and canyons of merchandise. Only the ceiling kept them from reaching the stars. Immediately I spotted the toy section at the center rear of the store, at which point all the other canyons of merchandise ceased to exist. There were two or three rows of toys. Belair Public Market probably had just as many if not more but scattered around at different booths, not concentrated.

I was practicing my pitiful facial expression as I neared the toy section. Glancing to my side I saw Gwen already had hers pasted on her face. I didn't bother with Peanut. She was useless in this case. Gwen and I relaxed when our grandfather said we could have any toy within reason. Our plotting turned into shopping.

Since that time, I have been to much larger and fancier stores, but my first impression of Star's dominates them all. Until that moment, I had never seen so many toys, but what happened next made it even more memorable and still brings a smile to my face and a chuckle to my chest.

While we were all standing in an aisle helping Gwen choose a toy, a little boy rounded the corner and stopped dead in his tracks.

He was no older than four and yelled excitedly for his mother. "Mommy, hurry! Come quick! Look! There's gingerbread people here!"

I turned around, looking for the gingerbread people. Not seeing anyone else I realized he was talking about us. He ran around the corner to retrieve his mother, pulling her hand to show us to her. The young boy was licking his lips. I remembered how I ate my Santa Claus cookies by biting the arms off first. Fortunately, I had not chosen a toy yet and folded my arms across my chest to look like a broken cookie. No child wanted a broken cookie when there were whole ones available such as my gingerbread sisters.

Then I realized the age of the child, and my momentary fear of cannibalistic white children faded. He was as curious about our skin color as I had been about the red-haired children that morning. The mother seemed relieved that we were laughing at the situation; it was merely embarrassing curiosity. Not all encounters would be so amusing.

We picked our toys and waited for our grandmother and mother. True to form, our grandmother bought us bamboo fishing poles. In addition, she had picked up some cornmeal and other ingredients to make dough balls as bait to catch catfish. This was a perfect introduction to fishing. It was fun to make the dough balls and was easier to bait the hook than with worms. The next day we went fishing in Bantam Lake in Litchfield. Everyone caught fish, except Gwen and me, and we used the remainder of the cornmeal to batter and fry the fish.

In two more days, our stepfather would join us in Connecticut. The day before his arrival we spent most of the day in the Bairds' yard. There was no friction between us. We got along well, and we were learning New England English from them. Garage sale was tag sale in New English, but we had no garage in East Baltimore, so both terms were alien to my sisters and me. Submarine sandwiches were called grinders. Although all of us were underage, we learned from them that a package store was a liquor store. We heard their father say he was going to the package store and they translated for us.

Sadly, we learned a local colloquialism from a small teenage boy who passed by the yard and taunted us with, "Look it's raggies playing with niggers."

Raggie was the local term for poor white trash, and nigger was known nationwide. This was the first time my sisters or I had been called that by a white person. In the back of my mind I was aware it could happen but was still caught off guard. I knew the word was offensive yet had been under the impression that its usage would be instigated by my poor behavior, not from merely existing. Then I remembered the story of the men who killed Mister Willy's dog for no reason.

Unfortunately, it sounded as if the Bairds were called raggies often. They seemed angrier on our behalf than about what had been said about them. The Bairds were as feral as we were. When the boy returned a few minutes later to torment us once again, the gingers and the gingerbreads were prepared for him and gave him a physical lesson in cultural sensitivity long before the term existed.

Being called a nigger in former abolitionist country, in the hometown of John Brown no less, is not something I would forget. Yet I also remember it was three red-haired children who came to our defense. To this day, I have a visceral reaction to anyone who insults a redhead. Some might say it's an overreaction, but if you are offensive, you don't get to measure my response. You get what you get.

For the remainder of our stay we grew closer to the Bairds. When we returned to Connecticut, despite not seeing toys in the yard, I rang their doorbell. Sadly, a woman answered the door and told me they had moved, but they never left my memory.

Aunt Porch returned from Pittsfield the same day my stepfather arrived from Baltimore. The house was too small for all of us, so she stayed at the historic Yankee Peddler Inn in downtown Torrington. Normally my stepfather's presence would set the mood of our house, but he had to contend with my grandparents in their house. My grandfather was no milquetoast, but my grandmother had a presence, which was further buttressed by Aunt Porch.

The remainder of our visit was pleasant. On the last day, my Uncle Vincent and Aunt Janet came over and we had a picnic at Burr Pond in Burrville, a place I would spend many a pleasant summer. My stepfather borrowed my fishing pole and looked as peaceful as I had ever seen him. He looked like a happy boy when he caught his first fish and a disappointed one when he had to throw it back because it was too small. It was a pleasant day to end our visit to Connecticut.

CHAPTER 48   FORGIVE ME FOR NOT FORGIVING YOU

Aunt Porch picked us up the next morning to return to Baltimore. For a brief moment our goodbyes became tense.

My stepfather, cloaking a chauvinistic attitude beneath a thin coating of chivalry, said, "Emma, I feel maybe that's a lot of driving for a woman. I can drive most of the way."

Aunt Porch was a very caring person and, despite having been a victim of emotional blackmail, was tuned into the feelings of others. Unbeknownst to anyone at the time, one of the reasons she came to Baltimore was to have breakup sex with Uncle Ike. This was the best way to break up with a man such as Ike. Their relationship had run its course, and she wanted one last good memory. I would overhear her comparing ending a relationship this way to having one last puff of a cigarette before quitting for good. She was a people pleaser, but she no longer did so at the expense of her own happiness. Emma Reeves knew how to put an end to things on her terms.

My stepfather was on unstable ground and was unwise to use emotions as a speed bump or a roadblock to slow or stop Aunt Porch. There are some who use their whines and cries as currency to obtain what they want. But some, such as my stepfather, use their emotions to bludgeon others to get what they want. Aunt Porch could spot a manipulative emotion a mile away. This simply gave her plenty of distance to speed up and send those emotions to intensive care or turn them into roadkill. Her attitude was, if someone used their emotions as a weapon, she would treat them as one.

With the frankness of a self-assured woman she responded to my stepfather, "Your emotions are my enemy. Have you driven a car right side up since New Year's Eve? I have money, but I am not made of it."

I could tell her retort stung him, but he recovered swiftly before his mask slipped. He had broken with decorum on several levels.

Sexism was normal background radiation for women of that time. She dismissed that out of hand. But he had mistaken my grandparents' forgiveness for wrecking their car on Year's Eve as a sign he was in good standing. Forgiveness in our family meant a second chance to be a better person, not a second chance at a repeat performance of the same bad behavior. Aunt Porch was particularly leery of those who thought sorry fixed everything and gave them permission to be continue being careless.

Aunt Porch continued and said, "What you can do for me is buy all of us lunch when we stop in New Jersey."

She had given him something manly to do, but this didn't appease him. The journey home seemed cordial and pleasant, but there was an undertone to my stepfather's demeanor that told me he had not completely forgotten Aunt Porch's slight. A woman had defied him. Someone had to suffer retribution. I was certain it would be me, because his usual punching bag would not be available. I was going to be left alone with him for a day or two. After dropping us off at home, everyone else was going to a girls-only event sponsored by the sorority of Aunt Porch's sister. It was being held at one of Maryland's black beaches, located about an hour or so south of the city.

Growing up in an abusive household, my sisters and I had developed a keenly accurate sense of our stepfather's mood. Gwen and Peanut validated my fears. For the past couple of days, they had been taunting me that they were going someplace I couldn't. But now they sensed the storm beneath our stepfather's cordial face and pleaded on my behalf that I should be allowed to come too. They really didn't want me to go with them but didn't want me to be left alone with him. Aunt Porch politely reiterated that it was a girls-only event. Gwen and Peanut gave me a pitying look and looked away. There was nothing more they could do.

For the remainder of the journey I tormented myself with images of what he would do to me. I would be his inflatable punching bag; he would fill me up with false accusations, then he would beat his lies out of me. At a young age, I knew the meaning of many horrible things before I had the words for them. My stepfather was a woman hater and beating a boy may not be enough to satisfy him. He needed the pain of a woman to extinguish his own pain. I had a silly, yet frightening fear he would make me dress in women's clothing to become a scapegoat in drag. He was broken inside, and instead of repairing himself, he broke others so that they matched him. He broke open pearls in search of sand.

My only hope was that Aunt Porch would be too weary to drive the last hour to the beach. Maybe an extra night would calm him down. But the event started early the next morning and Aunt Porch wanted to be in a nearby hotel, not an hour away. Our house was merely a pit stop, a bathroom break for the continuing travelers.

Back on his home turf, he became petulant and dropped all responsibility for me and instead chose to go drinking with some friends. Maybe he would get in a fight at the bar and take it out on somebody else there. He left saying he would be back around ten o'clock. He planned on using me as an anchor to keep my mother and sisters from leaving that night. He knew that since Wiggy had broken into our house our mother didn't feel comfortable leaving any of us alone in the house for too long. His intention was to ruin my mother's and Aunt Porch's plan. I had not misread his mood, just his reaction, and was relieved he had chosen pouting over punching.

Not to be deterred, my mother had two options, send me over to Grandma Ruth's house or call Runny's sister, Cassy. Grandma Ruth was not home, but my mother was able to reach Cassy. Cassy knew our TV had been stolen and only agreed after swiftly checking the TV guide to make sure there was nothing on that she would miss. We were in summer reruns, the time to watch episodes from shows missed during the fall and winter. In 1968, if you didn't view missed episodes during the summer they were gone. Cassy was all caught up on her reruns and said she would be over at five o'clock.

Cassy came over and made herself comfortable with our record player. I was relieved that she would be watching me. I was more afraid of my stepfather than of a burglar. We rarely had a babysitter but when we did, my mother usually chose Cassy. She was at that awkward age when you couldn't tell if her beauty would blossom into a pretty woman or a handsome one. Cassy was old enough to wear a skirt and had pressed hair, but her eyes didn't belong on such a young person. Two small pools of honey stared out at a world that she was indifferent to. Her eyes would look more at home on a face with crow's feet and deep lines, yet they retained a hint of her original sweetness. Witnessing life at its extremes had not changed her stare into something deep and unfathomable, nor into something shallow and vapid. Her eyes had a matter of fact look about them.

She and Runny lived with their older brother and aunt. I had learned not to question the absence of parents, not even that of my real father. Either death had taken them or something better or stronger had claimed them, leaving many abandoned children to ask what was better or stronger than them.

Cassy smiled when she was introduced to my Aunt Porch. I fully appreciated her smile, because I knew how much effort it took for her to make one. She had experienced enough that smiles were not natural to her face; each one was carefully constructed. It wouldn't be long before I had such a smile.

Now that Cassy had arrived, my sisters started making eye contact with me again. Averting our eyes was how we hid the shame of being able to do nothing on one another's behalf or gave each other privacy when we had been humiliated by our stepfather. I felt safe, because I saw relief in their eyes. Cassy's presence had made our home a public space, and for the most part our stepfather put on a good face in public. Who knew what would happen when Aunt Porch left in several more days? But I didn't borrow trouble or worry from that far away.

Before leaving, my mother instructed me to remind my stepfather to move our beds. Having lived here for two years, we still had more house than furniture. Although we had four bedrooms, my sisters and I always slept in the same room, they in one bed and I in another. Most of the year we slept in one of the bedrooms on the third flood. But in July and August, because of the heat, our beds were moved to the bedroom on the second floor outside our parent's room. After acknowledging my mother's request, I hugged them all goodbye.

Cassy played mostly dance songs and tried to teach me a few dance moves. Most of my steps caused the records to skip. Her words encouraged me, but her eyes told me I was hopeless. I finally grew tired. At some point I had cereal for dinner. The long drive and all the needless worrying, combined with dancing had caught up with me, and I went to bed an hour early.

I don't remember if I was awakened by being shaken or by the drunken eyes boring into my slumber. When my eyelashes parted I saw my stepfather towering above my bed. At first, I thought he was checking on me before going to bed himself. Before I could greet him, he punched me in my face. Fortunately, the blow glanced off my cheek into my pillow. Before I could react, he pulled his fist from the pillow and slapped me across the face. Then he forced the same hand over my mouth. It smelled of cigarette smoke, alcohol, sweat and rage.

He dug his fingers into my cheeks. He didn't yell but seethed into my face, "No matter what happens, it didn't happen. You're going to keep your damn mouth shut. If you yell or scream for help, I will kill you. Do you understand?"

He deprived me of all autonomy, dug his fingers harder into my cheeks and moved my head up and down, forcing me to nod in agreement. As a child, my sister threatened to kill me daily, but to hear it from someone who meant it and was capable of it terrified me. He walked away, leaving the stench of rage clinging to my face. I was literally paralyzed with fear. I could command nothing on my body to move except the tears pouring down my still burning cheeks and actually had no control of them either.

I was a rag doll limply lying in bed waiting for my stepfather to dress me in women's clothing. Not only would he have to dress me, he would have to hold me up to beat me. Rag dolls have no spine. He was misogynistic to his core, and his rage would not be denied. What I dreaded most was the lies he would tell to explain the marks and bruises he would leave. This was the emotional after-beating.

A crash from downstairs disrupted my thoughts. Then I heard a feminine voice scream, "Please!" I thought my stepfather had sent Cassy home, but he was dragging her upstairs. If he didn't have a woman to beat, a girl would do. He chose her instead of me. I knew something no nine-year-old child should know. My stepfather was going to rape a child in his wife's bed while her son listened. My ears turned every sound I heard into sight. I could see Cassy holding onto the banister as my stepfather tightened his grip around her waist and dragged her to the second floor. I knew she knew what was going to happen.

As he forced her through my sisters' and my summer bedroom, she screamed, "Please Mister Ketchum, don't do this!"

The sight of my parents' bed must have intensified her struggle. She dug her heels into the wood floor but to no avail.

I tried to get up, but my limbs would not budge. I surprised myself when I screamed out, "Leave her alone!"

Cassy must have forgotten I was there. In desperation she latched onto my voice. It was the worst thing I could have done. My voice gave her hope when there was none, but it was all she had, a boy purposely intimidated by a grown man into paralysis.

She screamed, "Grant please help me!" over and over again.

Every attempt to rise seemed to make me sink deeper into my bed. This brought back the nightmare on Forrest Street when my stepfather had raped my mother. I had pushed my fire truck across the windowsill to start its red light flashing as a signal for help, but no one came. The fire truck was long gone and had been an empty gesture. In the current situation, I didn't even have an empty gesture. Also, I didn't want to see any more than what I was already hearing. My stepfather could be very sadistic, and I feared he might force me to watch, or worse, make me join him. He certainly didn't care that I could hear him.

Cassy switched tactics and mustered enough strength to deliver one final plea and a threat. "Please don't do this. If my brother finds out, he will kill you."

Then I heard my stepfather say something for the first time. "If your brother finds out, I will be forced to kill him. Then where will you live and who will take care of your aunt and Runny?"

He was an expert at preying on the mind as well as the body.

If she wanted to protect her family, she now would be faced with the humiliating task of hiding her rape from them. He used the ties to her family as garrote to strangle her words. Except for some whimpering she grew silent and stopped resisting. I wanted the sun to rise and scold the night for its complicity and darkness, but I couldn't wait for the sun. All I could hear was the violent rocking of the bed that didn't lull me to sleep. Instead, I went to a dark place that eventually became sleep.

Cassy had agreed to come over to our house to babysit because she was caught up on her reruns. Unfortunately, she probably would experience the rerun of what happened to her in our house that night for the rest of her life.

The magnitude of what happened that night overwhelmed my childhood as nothing else had. My stepfather had raped a child and I had witnessed it. I remained in bed an hour after I had awakened, because I didn't have the strength to pretend the previous night didn't happen. We were supposed to move our beds to the second-floor bedroom, so at some point I had to wake him.

Summoning the courage to go downstairs, I was relieved that I could move my legs again. When I entered his room, he was in the fetal position sleeping the sleep of the righteous. How dare he look innocent? My nightmare didn't have nightmares, even in his most restless dreams he slept soundly. His conscience, if he had one, was anorexic and didn't weigh heavily on him. It no doubt was leery of him and kept its distance, leaving his soul a rusted, pitted derelict. His slumber should match his soul. But he lied even in his sleep.

Leaving the room without waking him, I went downstairs to pour myself a bowl of cereal, then poured it back into the box. I was ravenous but couldn't bring myself to eat. I decided whatever the consequences, I would let him sleep until noon. He couldn't do anything worse to me than he had done last night. Besides, I was in no hurry to move my bed closer to him. I would have rather suffered the heat of the third floor. Thinking of the heat made me realize all the windows in the house were shut. My stepfather had closed them in anticipation of assaulting Cassy. The rape had been premeditated.

After opening all the windows on the first floor, I sat in the plastic covered chair in the living room. I felt shattered and didn't know where many of the pieces had scattered. All the king's horses and all the king's men hadn't noticed my fall. In addition, there were invisible wounds all over my soul. Most bad behavior stems from poor repairs to a damaged soul. Yet unwittingly some put on a patch worse than the initial wound. How would I pull myself together and dress my wounds?

Unfortunately, the night had a hangover. I was to endure one more shameful incident. When my stepfather woke up, he sent me to the store to buy cigarettes. The task seemed almost perverse. He wanted me to buy his after-sex cigarettes. I knew too much.

My guilty conscience forced me to take the long way. I walked down N. Caroline Street to go to the store on the corner of N. Eden and Ashland Avenue. Passing Cassy's house, I held my head down, looking only far enough ahead to place my next step but no farther. I was both afraid and hoping that Cassy would pull me in off the street to be a witness for her to her brother and aunt. But my stepfather had done an unspeakable act which even a full-grown woman could not put words to. Cassy had to first unscramble the words, then gain the courage to speak them.

On the way back from the store I saw Cassy standing in front of her house with her arms folded. She must have seen me pass and waited for my return. I could have avoided her or walked swiftly by her house. Instead, I chose to walk slowly and absorb whatever she had to say. But she still didn't have the words for what happened to her and never said a word to me. Her eyes stared accusingly at me, asking "Why didn't you help?" I wanted to tell her that it was for the same reason she couldn't tell her family, but I couldn't. Nor could I say I feared he might make me join in. Cassy found no answers in my eyes and released me with a pitying stare that sent me back to my stepfather. I think she was angrier that I had witnessed her shame than at the fact that I had not helped her. Just as Cassy had her virginity brutally stolen from her, I also had my childhood stolen from me.

When I was older, the few times I recounted the incident to someone they would rip off my band aid, replace it with their own and claim this was what had made me gay. One male friend claimed this was the reason I didn't love women. I firmly let him know I loved women more than he did, because I wasn't physically attracted to them yet I still strongly desired women in my life. He was merely attracted to women and thought that was love. My stepfather made me realize that some men who claim to love women really don't.

For decades forgiveness was off the table. In time, I could forgive someone for a wrong done to me when I could imagine myself doing such a wrong in a similar circumstance. But in this case, I couldn't image the circumstance, so I couldn't imagine the forgiveness. Years later, I summoned the courage to finally tell someone who could help me with what happened that night, my Grandma Addy.

She surprised me when she said, "Do you remember the icicle wand you insisted on holding on to, despite the pain it caused?"

I nodded my head that I remembered.

She continued, "I had to convince you to drop it. Now I am reminding you again, drop it and let it melt away."

For twenty years I had been holding an icicle wand that had power only over me. I did as she said and dropped a wand again. It took a while for it to melt, but eventually it faded away. My grandmother taught me not to touch things that didn't belong to me. For years I thought it only meant physical or tangible things, until finally it dawned on me that it meant emotions too. Then I realized that horrible night belonged to my stepfather, not to me.

CHAPTER 49 ON THE FIRST DAY GOD CREATED CHANGE

When my family returned from the beach, I built a fake smile, hoping they would reciprocate with sincerer ones, signaling they were not suspicious of the slight bruise on my face.

Before suspicion could grow, my stepfather told my mother I was grounded for the day because I got in a fight with that other Grant again. If witnessing him raping my babysitter was not punishment enough, he trumped up charges to cover the bruise he had left on my face.

I was beyond livid and wanted to scream, "He punched me to keep me quiet while he raped Cassy in your bed."

How different would life have been if I had uttered the truth that day. I only considered it because Aunt Porch was there and would have tried to do something about it. I would never have been tempted if only my mother had been present. I hated to admit it to myself, but I wasn't sure who's side my mother would take.

Bringing my rage somewhat under control, I turned defiantly toward my stepfather and said, "The next time I get in a fight with that person, I'm not going to lose."

It was a veiled threat that only he picked up on. I was far from being capable of carrying out my promise, but he noticed the undertones of my words. One more stupid untrue word from him and I would run into the street screaming, "David Ketchum raped my babysitter Cassy in my mother's bed."

A part of me wanted him to push me too far, past my fear and any concerns of consequences. He backed off because he saw I could descend into an emotional frenzy he might not be able to control. Years later he pushed me too far. We were outside when he slapped Gwen for no reason. I completely lost it and threw an axe at him. It landed in the dirt between his feet although I was aiming for between his eyes. I wished I had played more baseball.

His lie didn't fool Gwen and Peanut; they knew the other Grant had not come through our neighborhood in weeks. When we were alone, my sisters tried to find out what happened, but I distracted them by asking them about their time at the beach. The distraction didn't work. Finally, I gave them a piece of the truth and told them our stepfather slapped me for looking at him the wrong way. I could have told them he slapped me for breathing and they would have believed me.

Two days later Aunt Porch came by to say goodbye. I would never see her in Baltimore again. I would see her once or twice on return trips to Ohio and another time when she visited us in Connecticut. Then she moved to Chicago. Over time, phone calls became Christmas and birthday cards, then postcards from her travels around the world, then finally a sympathy card from a friend of hers in Chicago that saddened me greatly. She was the first person I knew who lived life on her own terms, and she was the mother to many of the bold steps I would take in life.

The next few weeks were more routines than living. Life can herd you into routines with clocks, schedules and lists. Mine were miniaturized versions of adults' routines. For the sake of efficiency, many of our tasks run on autopilot. In the extreme we automate our hugs and later realize we really didn't feel them. In the few weeks following Aunt Porch's departure, I don't remember who I hugged or laughed with. My autopilot was more like training wheels that guided me through a difficult emotional time until I felt well enough to go random again.

Then one day, for some unexplained reason, just like Olivia, Willa moved away. 'I'm a tell' didn't live up to her nickname and didn't or couldn't tell us she was moving. I would never see her again. The one person I wanted gone from my life was a constant. I prayed nightly for my stepfather to go away. I didn't want him dead. I couldn't bring myself to ask God to become an assassin on my behalf. I just wanted him out of our lives.

My autopilot carried me past the middle of July, July 22nd to be exact. It was a Monday night, so my mother was working. Gwen, Peanut and I were now sleeping in the second-floor bedroom outside our parents' room. A loud bang startled us from a deep sleep. It was not the first time we had heard gunshots, but this one was really close. A portion of the incident my sisters and I witnessed ourselves. The initial incident, which we didn't witness, was recounted to us later.

Our stepfather and a friend of his were sitting on our front stoop. They were deep in conversation when a passerby became an assailant. He was not unknown to our stepfather. Wiggy pulled a gun from somewhere under his baggy clothes and with no pre-amble or hesitation put the gun to our stepfather's head and pulled the trigger. The gun misfired. Our stepfather turned to run into the house when Wiggy fired a second time, sending the bullet into his back.

A few moments after hearing the shot, we saw our stepfather trail blood as he stumbled through our bedroom into his. From my bed I could see him rummage around in a chest of drawers until he retrieved his own gun. He leaned out the bedroom window to try to shoot Wiggy. This was East Baltimore, if an ambulance wouldn't come for one maybe they would come for two. But Wiggy was long gone.

It wasn't that long ago when I lay in my bed paralyzed with fear. The night of the shooting I rolled toward the wall and, unmoved by concern for my stepfather, went back to sleep. My sisters did not stir to render aid either.

The next moment I remember was our mother waking us. She stepped over the dry blood on the floor, then gathered the girls onto my bed. She began hugging all of us and crying, reassuring us that our stepfather was going to be alright. I gave her my last autopilot hug of the summer and wished it was one I wouldn't remember. I pulled away from her as swiftly as I could. I stuck my sisters with the burden of giving my mother fake hugs. Peanut scowled at me for my betrayal.

Feeling a little guilty for abandoning them, I suggested to our mother that maybe she should let his job know he wouldn't be coming into work today. We went downstairs and she called our stepfather's job to inform them he had been shot and wouldn't be in today. She hung up after telling them she would keep them in-formed. To this day, it is hard to believe I lived in a place where it was not rare to call in shot instead of sick.

No one talked to us directly about his condition, but from over-heard phone conversations we determined that he indeed would live. The surgeon felt the risk of removing the bullet was too great and left it lodged in his body. Often bullets are left in gunshot vic-tims because the body doesn't react to lead and simply will wall it off, almost as if the bullet is an internal piercing. I was nine years old and couldn't read or write but knew about gunshot wound care.

The bullet was the last straw that broke all the resistance my mother had for moving to Connecticut. Before picking up the re-ceiver her hand hovered over the phone for a moment. Then her fingers whirled the numbers around the dial. On the third ring my grandmother answered. She told my grandmother we were mov-ing to Connecticut and asked for financial help. My grandmother was a hard sell when people asked her for money. She was a generous woman, but don't come to her asking to borrow when you really meant give. She was brutally honest when it came to lending money.

If they caught her in a pleasant mood the potential borrowers would be told, "So let me get this straight, you've mismanaged your money, so now you want to mismanage my money?"

If she was in a matter of fact mood, they might be told, "You're too minor a friend to ask for such a major favor."

I would learn from her to always make a written contract. When she had some work for me to do, that she was going to pay me for, she made me sign a contract.

I remember saying, "Grandma don't you trust me?"

She said "I trust who you are today, but I don't know who you will be tomorrow or two weeks from now. That's the person I am making the contract with."

My grandmother implicitly trusted me but had written a simple contract to establish the habit. Her lesson stayed with me the rest of my life. People change but sometimes not for the better. She was not going to allow someone to change their way out of a debt. My grandmother was very serious about money. I once heard her tell a flattering boss that she wanted all her compliments in cash. She was a pragmatist before all else.

She would teach me to stand up for myself. I remember an incident when a white veteran tried to bully her opinion by claiming he had fought for her rights, so she should listen to him.

Typical of her, she said, "If you fought for my rights I owe you more than I could ever pay you, but if you fought for the right to tell me what to do, I owe you less than nothing."

Her criticisms were constructive and didn't come from some lofty height but from a fellow traveler through life who was a little further up the road. She would give me discipline and stabilize my formative years, and I never received a surprise bill for her unconditional love. She would become my biggest champion.

When my mother told Gwen and Peanut, we were moving to Connecticut, they screamed for joy. The thought of living near my grandparents tremendously lightened my load. But despite or maybe because of all the things I had seen in Baltimore, I still had an attachment to the place. I would always feel both happy and solemn whenever I moved to a new place. I was not afraid of change but felt appreciative of where I had been. Where I was, became the way I was and made the next place possible. Connecticut would eventually do the same; every place would help shape me.

Before leaving Baltimore my sisters and I would suffer one more small indignity. When our stepfather returned from the hospital, there were some friends and family members waiting to greet him in our house. He played the wounded hero of the hearth well. Gwen, Peanut and I were less than enthused. The adults mistook our numb, blank expressions as lingering shock from hearing our stepfather was shot. I don't know if they would have felt that way if they had heard our unconcerned snores when we went back to sleep the night of the shooting.

Someone thought a snapshot of us with our stepfather would snap us out of our shock. The photo was a lie. He sat on the couch with me sitting on the floor between his legs and my sisters on either side with his arms draped around them. Nothing could get us to smile. I tried thinking of Cassy hearing that my stepfather had been shot. I smiled, but my sisters didn't. Our mother would have to perform the Heimlich maneuver to get a smile out of us. She chose bribery instead and promised to buy snowballs for us after she took the photo. The photo erroneously recorded our love of snowballs as love for our stepfather.

Our stepfather acted as if the idea to move to Connecticut was his, but our mother had told him she was moving with or without him. Out of fear of more violence, our borders and hours became more restrictive the last two and a half weeks we remained in Baltimore. We were no longer allowed to go to Madison Square Park or north of E. Eager Street. Since my goodbyes were not important to my parents, I defied the restrictions and crossed both E. Eager and N. Caroline Street to see Mister Willy one more time. He was aware we were moving to Connecticut.

He restated that moving up North had been an improvement for him and suggested that maybe moving further north might be better for us too, but only if we packed the good memories to bring to the new place. This was the reason I was here, to sit in the sun with him one more time and pack the moment away to carry with me.

He bought us a cantaloupe from a horse-drawn produce wagon, my last taste of fruit from an arabber, another memory to pack. It was sweet and tasted like the middle of summer. We talked of nothing important until it was time to say goodbye. Mister Willy didn't physically hug me, he hugged me with his interpretation of scripture that would forever encourage me to embrace change. Initially I thought he was misquoting the Bible, or maybe someone had misquoted it to him. That was until he joked that he was old enough to have been there personally to overhear God speak.

Then in all seriousness he said, "Remember Grant, on the first day God said, 'Let there be change.' Go into the world and enjoy those changes."

I thanked him and asked for a handshake. His rough hand shook my soft one and was symbolic of that change. Someday his hand would be gone and mine would be rough. I never saw Mister Willy again, but he drapes across my memory much as Spanish moss decorates the branches of oak and cypress trees.

Although all of our furniture was still in our house, it had been promised to or bought by neighbors and would be claimed when we left, including Ibo. The same coworker who took one of her kittens would take Ibo as well. With the exception of clothing, records and photos, we were taking nothing to Connecticut.

The goodbyes to our cousins, Grandma Ruth and Uncle Reggie were not final. We would see them regularly during the summers when we visited them, or they came to visit us. I had not seen Little Betty for a year and would never see her again. I had had only a couple of interactions with her, but my memory of some people is bigger than the amount of time I spent with them. Over the years, I have seen a few people who reminded me of her. My memory of her face is now a copy of a copy, fuzzy, but I still remember her.

There was one person I didn't get to say goodbye to, Miss Penny Pile. The empty lots and stables across from our house were still in our new borders. I played there every day until we left, but she never showed up.

Uncle Ike came by to take my mother, sisters and me to the train station. My stepfather would follow us in a couple of days, after closing down the house. We loaded the luggage into the trunk of the car. Unlike when we had left Bellefontaine, I had no desire to tie up the car to keep us from leaving. But as we drove off, I looked at the empty lots and stables one more time to see if Miss Penny would show up, to no avail.

As we drove to Baltimore's Pennsylvania Station, Uncle Ike lamented the present state of Baltimore. He praised my mother's decision to leave the city. When a criminal complains crime is getting worse, it is really time to leave. Bigger, more ruthless criminals were violently encroaching on his enterprises. By the time he went to jail, he was one of only several members of his gang still alive. I would see him one more time before he went to jail. Years later after he had gotten out, he admitted to my mother that he had Wiggy killed in prison for shooting his nephew.

I don't remember pulling up to Baltimore's Penn Station, but I do remember the inside of the train. It was so similar to the plane that had brought us to Baltimore that I looked out the window to check that it had not sprouted wings. I won whatever game my sisters and I played to get one of the window seats. We weren't dressed as well for the train as we had been for the plane, but we were still dressed up. It took a few more moments for our mother to get our behavior to match our attire.

Not long after settling down, I could feel the struggle of the engine as it pulled metal wheels across the metal tracks. The sensation was far different from that of the rubber wheels of a plane against a tarmac runway. The plane had said goodbye to the ground, while the train said hello and became intimate with it.

I looked out the window because I had won the privilege, but I wasn't enjoying the scenery that much. A bleak landscape slowly inched across the glass. It was still early morning and the train struggled to wake. Flying into Baltimore, I had searched the sky for angels and had found none. Not bothering to search from a train, I found one. They are not the lofty creatures I had imagined them to be. Angels don't fly above but walk among us and in East Baltimore may carry a gun.

The train was slowly picking up speed, when I saw Miss Penny Pile standing in a mound of weeds with a gun raised. I heard a muffled pop. I was wondering what she was shooting at. Then the train brought the target into view. It was an old refrigerator someone had discarded along the tracks. She was the one who had shot bullet holes into the refrigerator in the junkyard behind our house on Forrest Street, saving my sisters' lives. The last view I had of her was her putting the pistol back into her rag pouch. I never got to say goodbye to Miss Penny, but she had said goodbye to me.

Other events would bury Miss Penny Pile deep in my past. My memory of her was similar to an unattended grave in the cemetery of my mind. Future events such as the birth of each of my sisters' children would remind me to clear the weeds from the Miss Penny headstone in my head and thank her. Gwen would not remember her at all, and Peanut only has one or two memories of her.

I looked over to Gwen and Peanut, but they were focused on my mother rummaging through her purse for chewing gum and had not seen why they were still alive. Looking back on it now, I realize three people with guns altered the course of my life: an assassin, a heroin addict and a bag lady.

Before I knew it, the train passed the site where I had stood to watch Robert F. Kennedy's funeral train head south towards Arlington Cemetery. I was now on the opposite tracks heading north. Where I was, had become the way I was. Baltimore and Ohio had left their marks on my soul. Fittingly, I was traveling on the old tracks of the B&O Railroad, the first railroad in the country. Baltimore and Ohio were connected long before I was born. Within me, I would connect other places such as Connecticut and San Francisco and become them as well.

The maw of Union Tunnel loomed ahead of the train. I entered a black tunnel to enter a white world. With the exception of a few more tunnels, I traveled on the above ground railroad to leave de facto segregation behind forever. From my previous visit to Connecticut, I was aware I was coming from an inferior position but was not an inferior person. I had no intention of entering that world apology first, hat in hand, or explaining myself. What others thought of me was their property and did not belong to me.

Mister Willy's words sang in my head, "Don't explain yourself, just be yourself."

Yet beyond that world was a much larger one that I could not begin to imagine. The train from Baltimore was heading to a future where I would see the planting of six flags on the moon and computers on phones more powerful than the computer used to launch those rockets. I would move to San Francisco and within two years become HIV positive. My doctor informed me I would become sick within three years and would be dead in five. That was about thirty years ago. I would witness the election of the first black President of the United States of America. My grandmother missed the event by five years, so I sat in front of the TV on Inauguration Day with a photo of her in my lap. I would outlive the impossible.

There was still a winding rough road ahead of me. But as I look back over my shoulder, the road I had traveled now appears straight and smooth, almost as if my passage had transformed it. Our steps through life are a form of erosion, wearing our roads straighter and smoother for the next travelers.

Yet on August 9, 1968 I sat on a slow-moving train in a black tunnel, completely in the dark about my future. I lived in a nation that considered my every breath a vice, yet I would choose to breathe deeply. I would not hold my breath for anyone. Men were expected to keep their softer emotions malnourished to artificially boost other strengths. I would choose other ways to be strong. I was tasked with fighting for a seat at the table with all its bounty. But once I won that seat, what I thought was bounty soon seemed paltry. I had enjoyed the hunger more than the meal and would go elsewhere to set a new table and choose better company.

These guests were not yet known to me and were scattered all over the world. They were not prisoners of their cultures, passing on the ways of the long dead and continuing traditions unexamined. Nor did they consider hundreds of years of repetitive ignorance to be virtuous. For them, "Because we have always done it that way," was not sufficient justification to continue old ways in an ever-changing world.

All of them would come to know who they were and where they came from but would be open to other ways of being and try to have preferences without exclusions. My friends and I would dine at a bountiful table. For a brief moment, that unknown future came back in time to possess my mind and the train, melding us into one. The train strained to reach my future, and my breath became the huff and puff of the engine, unconsciously saying, "I'm coming to meet you."

My future friends were an orphan in Manila, a man driving a tractor in Iowa and another herding cattle in Switzerland. The engine and I huffed and puffed, saying, "I'm coming to meet you."

Many were in San Francisco, too young to have been flower children, but would start to bloom a decade later. One was making wigs for his paper dolls in Buenos Aires, and another was an armed guard on the eastern side of the Berlin Wall: "I'm coming to meet you."

One was playing in an arroyo in Albuquerque, New Mexico, another was a young boy putting lipstick on his lips for the first time in Melbourne, and one more had just had her bat mitzvah in Rockland County, New York: "I'm coming to meet you."

Today was another's birthday, but she sat at a table in a small Connecticut mill town with no cake or candles. "Come sit at my table with plenty of cake and candles, I'm coming to meet you."

Finally, there was a young boy being bullied in a small town in Southern Illinois. He would become my dream man that I would marry in my dream city. I was born in 1959 as a second-class citizen. But fifty-four years later, after saying, "I do" to the man I loved, I would become a first-class citizen of my country, at least on paper. The engine and I still had further to travel. But for now, the engine and I continued to huff and puff: "I'm coming to meet you. I'm coming to meet you. I'm coming."

ABOUT THE AUTHOR

Dwayne Ratleff

He was born in Belfountaine, Ohio but was raised in Baltimore, MD, Torrington and Winsted CT. A former happy resident of San Francisco for 40 years, he now lives in Palm Desert with his husband Michael and their dog Lizzy. Besides being an author, he is also an amateur photographer.

You can follow him on Twitter
https://twitter.com/a_ratleff

He can be reached via email at
sfratleff@gmail.com